The Fortunes of Nigel

The Fortunes of Nigel

Sir Walter Scott

The Fortunes of Nigel was first published in 1822.

This edition published by Mint Editions 2021.

ISBN 9781513280479 | E-ISBN 9781513285498

Published by Mint Editions®

 MINT
EDITIONS

minteditionbooks.com

Publishing Director: Jennifer Newens
Design & Production: Rachel Lopez Metzger
Project Manager: Micaela Clark
Typesetting: Westchester Publishing Services

Contents

I

Now Scot and English are agreed,
And Saunders hastes to cross the Tweed,
Where, such the splendours that attend him,
His very mother scarce had kend him.
His metamorphosis behold,
From Glasgow frieze to cloth of gold;
His back-sword, with the iron hilt,
To rapier, fairly hatch'd and gilt;
Was ever seen a gallant braver!
His very bonnet's grown a beaver.

—*The Reformation*

The long-continued hostilities which had for centuries separated the south and the north divisions of the Island of Britain, had been happily terminated by the succession of the pacific James I. to the English Crown. But although the united crown of England and Scotland was worn by the same individual, it required a long lapse of time, and the succession of more than one generation, ere the inveterate national prejudices which had so long existed betwixt the sister kingdoms were removed, and the subjects of either side of the Tweed brought to regard those upon the opposite bank as friends and as brethren.

These prejudices were, of course, most inveterate during the reign of King James. The English subjects accused him of partiality to those of his ancient kingdom; while the Scots, with equal injustice, charged him with having forgotten the land of his nativity, and with neglecting those early friends to whose allegiance he had been so much indebted.

The temper of the king, peaceable even to timidity, inclined him perpetually to interfere as mediator between the contending factions, whose brawls disturbed the Court. But, notwithstanding all his precautions, historians have recorded many instances, where the mutual hatred of two nations, who, after being enemies for a thousand years, had been so very recently united, broke forth with a fury which menaced a general convulsion; and, spreading from the highest to the lowest classes, as it occasioned debates in council and parliament, factions in the court, and duels among the gentry, was no less productive of riots and brawls amongst the lower orders.

While these heart-burnings were at the highest, there flourished in the city of London an ingenious but whimsical and self opinioned mechanic, much devoted to abstract studies, David Ramsay by name, who, whether recommended by his great skill in his profession, as the courtiers alleged, or, as was murmured among the neighbours, by his birthplace, in the good town of Dalkeith, near Edinburgh, held in James's household the post of maker of watches and horologes to his Majesty. He scorned not, however, to keep open shop within Temple Bar, a few yards to the eastward of Saint Dunstan's Church.

The shop of a London tradesman at that time, as it may be supposed, was something very different from those we now see in the same locality. The goods were exposed to sale in cases, only defended from the weather by a covering of canvass, and the whole resembled the stalls and booths now erected for the temporary accommodation of dealers at a country fair, rather than the established emporium of a respectable citizen. But most of the shopkeepers of note, and David Ramsay amongst others, had their booth connected with a small apartment which opened backward from it, and bore the same resemblance to the front shop that Robinson Crusoe's cavern did to the tent which he erected before it.

To this Master Ramsay was often accustomed to retreat to the labour of his abstruse calculations; for he aimed at improvements and discoveries in his own art, and sometimes pushed his researches, like Napier, and other mathematicians of the period, into abstract science. When thus engaged, he left the outer posts of his commercial establishment to be maintained by two stout-bodied and strong-voiced apprentices, who kept up the cry of, "What d'ye lack? what d'ye lack?" accompanied with the appropriate recommendations of the articles in which they dealt.

This direct and personal application for custom to those who chanced to pass by, is now, we believe, limited to Monmouth Street, (if it still exists even in that repository of ancient garments,) under the guardianship of the scattered remnant of Israel. But at the time we are speaking of, it was practised alike by Jew and Gentile, and served, instead of all our present newspaper puffs and advertisements, to solicit the attention of the public in general, and of friends in particular, to the unrivalled excellence of the goods, which they offered to sale upon such easy terms, that it might fairly appear that the venders had rather a view to the general service of the public, than to their own particular advantage.

The verbal proclaimers of the excellence of their commodities, had this advantage over those who, in the present day, use the public papers for the same purpose, that they could in many cases adapt their address to the peculiar appearance and apparent taste of the passengers.* This direct and personal mode of invitation to customers became, however, a dangerous temptation to the young wags who were employed in the task of solicitation during the absence of the principal person interested in the traffic; and, confiding in their numbers and civic union, the 'prentices of London were often seduced into taking liberties with the passengers, and exercising their wit at the expense of those whom they had no hopes of converting into customers by their eloquence. If this were resented by any act of violence, the inmates of each shop were ready to pour forth in succour; and in the words of an old song which Dr. Johnson was used to hum,—

> "Up then rose the 'prentices all,
> Living in London, both proper and tall."

Desperate riots often arose on such occasions, especially when the Templars, or other youths connected with the aristocracy, were insulted, or conceived themselves to be so. Upon such occasions, bare steel was frequently opposed to the clubs of the citizens, and death sometimes ensued on both sides. The tardy and inefficient police of the time had no other resource than by the Alderman of the ward calling out the householders, and putting a stop to the strife by overpowering numbers, as the Capulets and Montagues are separated upon the stage.

At the period when such was the universal custom of the most respectable, as well as the most inconsiderable, shopkeepers in London, David Ramsay, on the evening to which we solicit the attention of the reader, retiring to more abstruse and private labours, left the administration of his outer shop, or booth, to the aforesaid sharp-witted, active, able-bodied, and well-voiced apprentices, namely, Jenkin Vincent and Frank Tunstall.

---

* This, as we have said, was also the case in Monmouth Street in our remembrance. We have ourselves been reminded of the deficiencies of our femoral habiliments, and exhorted upon that score to fit ourselves more beseemingly; but this is a digression.

Vincent had been educated at the excellent foundation of Christ's Church Hospital, and was bred, therefore, as well as born, a Londoner, with all the acuteness, address, and audacity which belong peculiarly to the youth of a metropolis. He was now about twenty years old, short in stature, but remarkably strong made, eminent for his feats upon holidays at foot-ball, and other gymnastic exercises; scarce rivalled in the broad-sword play, though hitherto only exercised in the form of single-stick. He knew every lane, blind alley, and sequestered court of the ward, better than his catechism; was alike active in his master's affairs, and in his own adventures of fun and mischief; and so managed matters, that the credit he acquired by the former bore him out, or at least served for his apology, when the latter propensity led him into scrapes, of which, however, it is but fair to state, that they had hitherto inferred nothing mean or discreditable. Some aberrations there were, which David Ramsay, his master, endeavoured to reduce to regular order when he discovered them, and others which he winked at—supposing them to answer the purpose of the escapement of a watch, which disposes of a certain quantity of the extra power of that mechanical impulse which puts the whole in motion.

The physiognomy of Jin Vin—by which abbreviation he was familiarly known through the ward—corresponded with the sketch we have given of his character. His head, upon which his 'prentice's flat cap was generally flung in a careless and oblique fashion, was closely covered with thick hair of raven black, which curled naturally and closely, and would have grown to great length, but for the modest custom enjoined by his state in life and strictly enforced by his master, which compelled him to keep it short-cropped,—not unreluctantly, as he looked with envy on the flowing ringlets, in which the courtiers, and aristocratic students of the neighbouring Temple, began to indulge themselves, as marks of superiority and of gentility.

Vincent's eyes were deep set in his head, of a strong vivid black, full of fire, roguery, and intelligence, and conveying a humorous expression, even while he was uttering the usual small-talk of his trade, as if he ridiculed those who were disposed to give any weight to his commonplaces. He had address enough, however, to add little touches of his own, which gave a turn of drollery even to this ordinary routine of the booth; and the alacrity of his manner—his ready and obvious wish to oblige—his intelligence and civility, when he thought civility necessary, made him a universal favourite with his master's customers.

His features were far from regular, for his nose was flattish, his mouth tending to the larger size, and his complexion inclining to be more dark than was then thought consistent with masculine beauty. But, in despite of his having always breathed the air of a crowded city, his complexion had the ruddy and manly expression of redundant health; his turned-up nose gave an air of spirit and raillery to what he said, and seconded the laugh of his eyes; and his wide mouth was garnished with a pair of well-formed and well-coloured lips, which, when he laughed, disclosed a range of teeth strong and well set, and as white as the very pearl. Such was the elder apprentice of David Ramsay, Memory's Monitor, watchmaker, and constructor of horologes, to his Most Sacred Majesty James I.

Jenkin's companion was the younger apprentice, though, perhaps, he might be the elder of the two in years. At any rate, he was of a much more staid and composed temper. Francis Tunstall was of that ancient and proud descent who claimed the style of the "unstained;" because, amid the various chances of the long and bloody wars of the Roses, they had, with undeviating faith, followed the House of Lancaster, to which they had originally attached themselves. The meanest sprig of such a tree attached importance to the root from which it derived itself; and Tunstall was supposed to nourish in secret a proportion of that family pride, which had exhorted tears from his widowed and almost indigent mother, when she saw herself obliged to consign him to a line of life inferior, as her prejudices suggested, to the course held by his progenitors. Yet, with all this aristocratic prejudice, his master found the well-born youth more docile, regular, and strictly attentive to his duty, than his far more active and alert comrade. Tunstall also gratified his master by the particular attention which he seemed disposed to bestow on the abstract principles of science connected with the trade which he was bound to study, the limits of which were daily enlarged with the increase of mathematical science.

Vincent beat his companion beyond the distance-post, in every thing like the practical adaptation of thorough practice, in the dexterity of hand necessary to execute the mechanical branches of the art, and doubled-distanced him in all respecting the commercial affairs of the shop. Still David Ramsay was wont to say, that if Vincent knew how to do a thing the better of the two, Tunstall was much better acquainted with the principles on which it ought to be done; and he sometimes objected to the latter, that he knew critical excellence too well ever to be satisfied with practical mediocrity.

The disposition of Tunstall was shy, as well as studious; and, though perfectly civil and obliging, he never seemed to feel himself in his place while he went through the duties of the shop. He was tall and handsome, with fair hair, and well-formed limbs, good features, well-opened light-blue eyes, a straight Grecian nose, and a countenance which expressed both good-humour and intelligence, but qualified by a gravity unsuitable to his years, and which almost amounted to dejection. He lived on the best of terms with his companion, and readily stood by him whenever he was engaged in any of the frequent skirmishes, which, as we have already observed, often disturbed the city of London about this period. But though Tunstall was allowed to understand quarter-staff (the weapon of the North country) in a superior degree, and though he was naturally both strong and active, his interference in such affrays seemed always matter of necessity; and, as he never voluntarily joined either their brawls or their sports, he held a far lower place in the opinion of the youth of the ward than his hearty and active friend Jin Vin. Nay, had it not been for the interest made for his comrade, by the intercession of Vincent, Tunstall would have stood some chance of being altogether excluded from the society of his contemporaries of the same condition, who called him, in scorn, the Cavaliero Cuddy, and the Gentle Tunstall.

On the other hand, the lad himself, deprived of the fresh air in which he had been brought up, and foregoing the exercise to which he had formerly been accustomed, while the inhabitant of his native mansion, lost gradually the freshness of his complexion, and, without showing any formal symptoms of disease, grew more thin and pale as he grew older, and at length exhibited the appearance of indifferent health, without any thing of the habits and complaints of an invalid, excepting a disposition to avoid society, and to spend his leisure time in private study, rather than mingle in the sports of his companions, or even resort to the theatres, then the general rendezvous of his class; where, according to high authority, they fought for half-bitten apples, cracked nuts, and filled the upper gallery with their clamours.

Such were the two youths who called David Ramsay master; and with both of whom he used to fret from morning till night, as their peculiarities interfered with his own, or with the quiet and beneficial course of his traffic.

Upon the whole, however, the youths were attached to their master, and he, a good-natured, though an absent and whimsical man, was scarce less so to them; and when a little warmed with wine at an occasional junketing, he used to boast, in his northern dialect, of his "twa bonnie lads, and the looks that the court ladies threw at them, when visiting his shop in their caroches, when on a frolic into the city." But David Ramsay never failed, at the same time, to draw up his own tall, thin, lathy skeleton, extend his lean jaws into an alarming grin, and indicate, by a nod of his yard-long visage, and a twinkle of his little grey eye, that there might be more faces in Fleet Street worth looking at than those of Frank and Jenkin. His old neighbour, Widow Simmons, the sempstress, who had served, in her day, the very tip-top revellers of the Temple, with ruffs, cuffs, and bands, distinguished more deeply the sort of attention paid by the females of quality, who so regularly visited David Ramsay's shop, to its inmates. "The boy Frank," she admitted, "used to attract the attention of the young ladies, as having something gentle and downcast in his looks; but then he could not better himself, for the poor youth had not a word to throw at a dog. Now Jin Vin was so full of his jibes and jeers, and so willing, and so ready, and so serviceable, and so mannerly all the while, with a step that sprung like a buck's in Epping Forest, and his eye that twinkled as black as a gipsy's, that no woman who knew the world would make a comparison betwixt the lads. As for poor neighbour Ramsay himself, the man," she said, "was a civil neighbour, and a learned man, doubtless, and might be a rich man if he had common sense to back his learning; and doubtless, for a Scot, neighbour Ramsay was nothing of a bad man, but he was so constantly grimed with smoke, gilded with brass filings, and smeared with lamp-black and oil, that Dame Simmons judged it would require his whole shopful of watches to induce any feasible woman to touch the said neighbour Ramsay with any thing save a pair of tongs."

A still higher authority, Dame Ursula, wife to Benjamin Suddlechop, the barber, was of exactly the same opinion.

Such were, in natural qualities and public estimation, the two youths, who, in a fine April day, having first rendered their dutiful service and attendance on the table of their master and his daughter, at their dinner at one o'clock,—Such, O ye lads of London, was the severe discipline undergone by your predecessors!—and having regaled themselves upon the fragments, in company with two female domestics, one a cook, and maid of all work, the other called Mistress Margaret's maid, now relieved their master in the duty of the outward shop; and agreeably to the established custom, were soliciting, by their entreaties and recommendations of their master's manufacture, the attention and encouragement of the passengers.

In this species of service it may be easily supposed that Jenkin Vincent left his more reserved and bashful comrade far in the background. The latter could only articulate with difficulty, and as an act of duty which he was rather ashamed of discharging, the established words of form— "What d'ye lack?—What d'ye lack?—Clocks—watches—barnacles?— What d'ye lack?—Watches—clocks—barnacles?—What d'ye lack, sir? What d'ye lack, madam?—Barnacles—watches—clocks?"

But this dull and dry iteration, however varied by diversity of verbal arrangement, sounded flat when mingled with the rich and recommendatory oratory of the bold-faced, deep-mouthed, and ready-witted Jenkin Vincent.—"What d'ye lack, noble sir?—What d'ye lack, beauteous madam?" he said, in a tone at once bold and soothing, which often was so applied as both to gratify the persons addressed, and to excite a smile from other hearers.—"God bless your reverence," to a beneficed clergyman; "the Greek and Hebrew have harmed your reverence's eyes—Buy a pair of David Ramsay's barnacles. The King— God bless his Sacred Majesty!—never reads Hebrew or Greek without them."

"Are you well avised of that?" said a fat parson from the Vale of Evesham. "Nay, if the Head of the Church wears them,—God bless his Sacred Majesty!—I will try what they can do for me; for I have not been able to distinguish one Hebrew letter from another, since—I cannot remember the time—when I had a bad fever. Choose me a pair of his most Sacred Majesty's own wearing, my good youth."

"This is a pair, and please your reverence," said Jenkin, producing a pair of spectacles which he touched with an air of great deference and respect, "which his most blessed Majesty placed this day three weeks on his own blessed nose; and would have kept them for his own sacred use, but that the setting being, as your reverence sees, of the purest jet, was, as his Sacred Majesty was pleased to say, fitter for a bishop than for a secular prince."

"His Sacred Majesty the King," said the worthy divine, "was ever a very Daniel in his judgment. Give me the barnacles, my good youth, and who can say what nose they may bestride in two years hence?— our reverend brother of Gloucester waxes in years." He then pulled out his purse, paid for the spectacles, and left the shop with even a more important step than that which had paused to enter it.

"For shame," said Tunstall to his companion; "these glasses will never suit one of his years."

"You are a fool, Frank," said Vincent, in reply; "had the good doctor wished glasses to read with, he would have tried them before buying. He does not want to look through them himself, and these will serve the purpose of being looked at by other folks, as well as the best magnifiers in the shop.—What d'ye lack?" he cried, resuming his solicitations. "Mirrors for your toilette, my pretty madam; your head-gear is something awry—pity, since it is so well fancied." The woman stopped and bought a mirror.—"What d'ye lack?—a watch, Master Sergeant—a watch that will go as long as a lawsuit, as steady and true as your own eloquence?"

"Hold your peace, sir," answered the Knight of the Coif, who was disturbed by Vin's address whilst in deep consultation with an eminent attorney; "hold your peace! You are the loudest-tongued varlet betwixt the Devil's Tavern and Guildhall."

"A watch," reiterated the undaunted Jenkin, "that shall not lose thirteen minutes in a thirteen years' lawsuit.—He's out of hearing—A watch with four wheels and a bar-movement—a watch that shall tell you, Master Poet, how long the patience of the audience will endure your next piece at the Black Bull." The bard laughed, and fumbled in the pocket of his slops till he chased into a corner, and fairly caught, a small piece of coin.

"Here is a tester to cherish thy wit, good boy," he said.

"Gramercy," said Vin; "at the next play of yours I will bring down a set of roaring boys, that shall make all the critics in the pit, and the gallants on the stage, civil, or else the curtain shall smoke for it."

"Now, that I call mean," said Tunstall, "to take the poor rhymer's money, who has so little left behind."

"You are an owl, once again," said Vincent; "if he has nothing left to buy cheese and radishes, he will only dine a day the sooner with some patron or some player, for that is his fate five days out of the seven. It is unnatural that a poet should pay for his own pot of beer; I will drink his tester for him, to save him from such shame; and when his third night comes round, he shall have penniworths for his coin, I promise you.—But here comes another-guess customer. Look at that strange fellow—see how he gapes at every shop, as if he would swallow the wares.—O! Saint Dunstan has caught his eye; pray God he swallow not the images. See how he stands astonished, as old Adam and Eve ply their ding-dong! Come, Frank, thou art a scholar; construe me that same fellow, with his blue cap with a cock's feather in it, to show he's of gentle blood, God wot—his grey eyes, his yellow hair, his sword with a ton of iron in the handle—his grey thread-bare cloak—his step like a Frenchman—his look like a Spaniard—a book at his girdle, and a broad dudgeon-dagger on the other side, to show him half-pedant, half-bully. How call you that pageant, Frank?"

"A raw Scotsman," said Tunstall; "just come up, I suppose, to help the rest of his countrymen to gnaw old England's bones; a palmerworm, I reckon, to devour what the locust has spared."

"Even so, Frank," answered Vincent; "just as the poet sings sweetly,—

> *'In Scotland he was born and bred,*
> *And, though a beggar, must be fed.'"*

"Hush!" said Tunstall, "remember our master."

"Pshaw!" answered his mercurial companion; "he knows on which side his bread is buttered, and I warrant you has not lived so long among Englishmen, and by Englishmen, to quarrel with us for bearing an English mind. But see, our Scot has done gazing at St. Dunstan's, and comes our way. By this light, a proper lad and a sturdy, in spite of freckles and sun-burning.—He comes nearer still, I will have at him."

"And, if you do," said his comrade, "you may get a broken head—he looks not as if he would carry coals."

"A fig for your threat," said Vincent, and instantly addressed the stranger. "Buy a watch, most noble northern Thane—buy a watch, to count the hours of plenty since the blessed moment you left Berwick behind you.—Buy barnacles, to see the English gold lies ready for your gripe.—Buy what you will, you shall have credit for three days; for, were your pockets as bare as Father Fergus's, you are a Scot in London, and you will be stocked in that time." The stranger looked sternly at the waggish apprentice, and seemed to grasp his cudgel in rather a menacing fashion. "Buy physic," said the undaunted Vincent, "if you will buy neither time nor light—physic for a proud stomach, sir;—there is a 'pothecary's shop on the other side of the way."

Here the probationary disciple of Galen, who stood at his master's door in his flat cap and canvass sleeves, with a large wooden pestle in his hand, took up the ball which was flung to him by Jenkin, with,

"What d'ye lack, sir?—Buy a choice Caledonian salve, *Flos sulphur. cum butyro quant. suff.*"

"To be taken after a gentle rubbing-down with an English oaken towel," said Vincent.

The bonny Scot had given full scope to the play of this small artillery of city wit, by halting his stately pace, and viewing grimly, first the one assailant, and then the other, as if menacing either repartee or more violent revenge. But phlegm or prudence got the better of his indignation, and tossing his head as one who valued not the raillery to which he had been exposed, he walked down Fleet Street, pursued by the horse-laugh of his tormentors.

"The Scot will not fight till he see his own blood," said Tunstall, whom his north of England extraction had made familiar with all manner of proverbs against those who lay yet farther north than himself.

"Faith, I know not," said Jenkin; "he looks dangerous, that fellow—he will hit some one over the noddle before he goes far.—Hark!—hark!—they are rising."

Accordingly, the well-known cry of, "'Prentices—'prentices—Clubs—clubs!" now rang along Fleet Street; and Jenkin, snatching up his weapon, which lay beneath the counter ready at the slightest notice, and calling to Tunstall to take his bat and follow, leaped over the hatch-door which protected the outer-shop, and ran as fast as he could towards the affray, echoing the cry as he ran, and elbowing, or shoving aside, whoever stood in his way. His comrade, first calling to his master to give an eye to the shop, followed Jenkin's example, and ran after him as fast as he could, but with more attention to the safety and convenience of others; while old David Ramsay, with hands and eyes uplifted, a green apron before him, and a glass which he had been polishing thrust into his bosom, came forth to look after the safety of his goods and chattels, knowing, by old experience, that, when the cry of "Clubs" once arose, he would have little aid on the part of his apprentices.

II

This, sir, is one among the Seignory,
Has wealth at will, and will to use his wealth,
And wit to increase it. Marry, his worst folly
Lies in a thriftless sort of charity,
That goes a-gadding sometimes after objects,
Which wise men will not see when thrust upon them.

—*The Old Couple*

T he ancient gentleman bustled about his shop, in pettish displeasure at being summoned hither so hastily, to the interruption of his more abstract studies; and, unwilling to renounce the train of calculation which he had put in progress, he mingled whimsically with the fragments of the arithmetical operation, his oratory to the passengers, and angry reflections on his idle apprentices. "What d'ye lack, sir? Madam, what d'ye lack—clocks for hall or table—night-watches—day watches?— *Locking wheel being 48—the power of retort 8—the striking pins are 48—* What d'ye lack, honoured sir?—*The quotient—the multiplicand*—That the knaves should have gone out this blessed minute!—*the acceleration being at the rate of 5 minutes, 55 seconds, 53 thirds, 59 fourths*—I will switch them both when they come back—I will, by the bones of the immortal Napier!"

Here the vexed philosopher was interrupted by the entrance of a grave citizen of a most respectable appearance, who, saluting him familiarly by the name of "Davie, my old acquaintance," demanded what had put him so much out of sorts, and gave him at the same time a cordial grasp of his hand.

The stranger's dress was, though grave, rather richer than usual. His paned hose were of black velvet, lined with purple silk, which garniture appeared at the slashes. His doublet was of purple cloth, and his short cloak of black velvet, to correspond with his hose; and both were adorned with a great number of small silver buttons richly wrought in filigree. A triple chain of gold hung round his neck; and, in place of a sword or dagger, he wore at his belt an ordinary knife for the purpose of the table, with a small silver case, which appeared to contain writing materials. He might have seemed some secretary or clerk engaged in the service of the public, only that his low, flat, and unadorned cap, and his well-blacked, shining shoes, indicated that he belonged to the city. He was a well-made man, about the middle size, and seemed in firm health, though advanced in years. His looks expressed sagacity and good-humour: and the air of respectability which his dress announced, was well supported by his clear eye, ruddy cheek, and grey hair. He used the Scottish idiom in his first address, but in such a manner that it could hardly be distinguished whether he was passing upon his friend a sort of jocose mockery, or whether it was his own native dialect, for his ordinary discourse had little provincialism.

In answer to the queries of his respectable friend, Ramsay groaned heavily, answering by echoing back the question, "What ails me, Master George? Why, every thing ails me! I profess to you that a man may as well live in Fairyland as in the Ward of Farringdon-Without. My apprentices are turned into mere goblins—they appear and disappear like spunkies, and have no more regularity in them than a watch without a scapement. If there is a ball to be tossed up, or a bullock to be driven mad, or a quean to be ducked for scolding, or a head to be broken, Jenkin is sure to be at the one end or the other of it, and then away skips Francis Tunstall for company. I think the prize-fighters, bear-leaders, and mountebanks, are in a league against me, my dear friend, and that they pass my house ten times for any other in the city. Here's an Italian fellow come over, too, that they call Punchinello; and, altogether—"

"Well," interrupted Master George, "but what is all this to the present case?"

"Why," replied Ramsay, "here has been a cry of thieves or murder, (I hope that will prove the least of it amongst these English pock-pudding swine!) and I have been interrupted in the deepest calculation ever mortal man plunged into, Master George."

"What, man!" replied Master George, "you must take patience—You are a man that deals in time, and can make it go fast and slow at pleasure; you, of all the world, have least reason to complain, if a little of it be lost now and then.—But here come your boys, and bringing in a slain man betwixt them, I think—here has been serious mischief, I am afraid."

"The more mischief the better sport," said the crabbed old watchmaker. "I am blithe, though, that it's neither of the twa loons themselves.—What are ye bringing a corpse here for, ye fause villains?" he added, addressing the two apprentices, who, at the head of a considerable mob of their own class, some of whom bore evident marks of a recent fray, were carrying the body betwixt them.

"He is not dead yet, sir," answered Tunstall.

"Carry him into the apothecary's, then," replied his master. "D'ye think I can set a man's life in motion again, as if he were a clock or a timepiece?"

"For godsake, old friend," said his acquaintance, "let us have him here at the nearest—he seems only in a swoon."

"A swoon?" said Ramsay, "and what business had he to swoon in the streets? Only, if it will oblige my friend Master George, I would take in all the dead men in St. Dunstan's parish. Call Sam Porter to look after the shop." So saying, the stunned man, being the identical Scotsman who had passed a short time before amidst the jeers of the apprentices, was carried into the back shop of the artist, and there placed in an armed chair till the apothecary from over the way came to his assistance. This gentleman, as sometimes happens to those of the learned professions, had rather more lore than knowledge, and began to talk of the sinciput and occiput, and cerebrum and cerebellum, until he exhausted David Ramsay's brief stock of patience.

"Bell-um! bell-ell-um!" he repeated, with great indignation; "What signify all the bells in London, if you do not put a plaster on the child's crown?"

Master George, with better-directed zeal, asked the apothecary whether bleeding might not be useful; when, after humming and hawing for a moment, and being unable, upon the spur of the occasion, to suggest any thing else, the man of pharmacy observed, that it would, at all events, relieve the brain or cerebrum, in case there was a tendency to the deposition of any extravasated blood, to operate as a pressure upon that delicate organ.

Fortunately he was adequate to performing this operation; and, being powerfully aided by Jenkin Vincent (who was learned in all cases of broken heads) with plenty of cold water, and a little vinegar, applied according to the scientific method practised by the bottle-holders in a modern ring, the man began to raise himself on his chair, draw his cloak tightly around him, and look about like one who struggles to recover sense and recollection.

"He had better lie down on the bed in the little back closet," said Mr. Ramsay's visitor, who seemed perfectly familiar with the accommodations which the house afforded.

"He is welcome to my share of the truckle," said Jenkin,—for in the said back closet were the two apprentices accommodated in one truckle-bed,—"I can sleep under the counter."

"So can I," said Tunstall, "and the poor fellow can have the bed all night."

"Sleep," said the apothecary, "is, in the opinion of Galen, a restorative and febrifuge, and is most naturally taken in a truckle-bed."

"Where a better cannot be come by,"—said Master George; "but these are two honest lads, to give up their beds so willingly. Come, off with his cloak, and let us bear him to his couch—I will send for Dr. Irving, the king's chirurgeon—he does not live far off, and that shall be my share of the Samaritan's duty, neighbour Ramsay."

"Well, sir," said the apothecary, "it is at your pleasure to send for other advice, and I shall not object to consult with Dr. Irving or any other medical person of skill, neither to continue to furnish such drugs as may be needful from my pharmacopeia. However, whatever Dr. Irving, who, I think, hath had his degrees in Edinburgh, or Dr. Any-one-beside, be he Scottish or English, may say to the contrary, sleep, taken timeously, is a febrifuge, or sedative, and also a restorative."

He muttered a few more learned words, and concluded by informing Ramsay's friend in English far more intelligible than his Latin, that he would look to him as his paymaster, for medicines, care, and attendance, furnished, or to be furnished, to this party unknown.

Master George only replied by desiring him to send his bill for what he had already to charge, and to give himself no farther trouble unless he heard from him. The pharmacopolist, who, from discoveries made by the cloak falling a little aside, had no great opinion of the faculty of this chance patient to make reimbursement, had no sooner seen his case espoused by a substantial citizen, than he showed some reluctance to quit possession of it, and it needed a short and stern hint from Master George, which, with all his good-humour, he was capable of expressing when occasion required, to send to his own dwelling this Esculapius of Temple Bar.

When they were rid of Mr. Raredrench, the charitable efforts of Jenkin and Francis, to divest the patient of his long grey cloak, were firmly resisted on his own part.—"My life suner—my life suner," he muttered in indistinct murmurs. In these efforts to retain his upper garment, which was too tender to resist much handling, it gave way at length with a loud rent, which almost threw the patient into a second syncope, and he sat before them in his under garments, the looped and repaired wretchedness of which moved at once pity and laughter, and had certainly been the cause of his unwillingness to resign the mantle, which, like the virtue of charity, served to cover so many imperfections.

The man himself cast his eyes on his poverty-struck garb, and seemed so much ashamed of the disclosure, that, muttering between his teeth, that he would be too late for his appointment, he made an effort to rise and leave the shop, which was easily prevented by Jenkin Vincent and his comrade, who, at the nod of Master George, laid hold of and detained him in his chair.

The patient next looked round him for a moment, and then said faintly, in his broad northern language—"What sort of usage ca' ye this, gentlemen, to a stranger a sojourner in your town? Ye hae broken my head—ye hae riven my cloak, and now ye are for restraining my personal liberty! They were wiser than me," he said, after a moment's pause, "that counselled me to wear my warst claithing in the streets of London; and, if I could have got ony things warse than these mean garments,"—("which would have been very difficult," said Jin Vin, in a whisper to his companion,)—"they would have been e'en ower gude for the grips o' men sae little acquented with the laws of honest civility."

"To say the truth," said Jenkin, unable to forbear any longer, although the discipline of the times prescribed to those in his situation a degree of respectful distance and humility in the presence of parents, masters, or seniors, of which the present age has no idea—"to say the truth, the good gentleman's clothes look as if they would not brook much handling."

"Hold your peace, young man," said Master George, with a tone of authority; "never mock the stranger or the poor—the black ox has not trod on your foot yet—you know not what lands you may travel in, or what clothes you may wear, before you die."

Vincent held down his head and stood rebuked, but the stranger did not accept the apology which was made for him.

"I *am* a stranger, sir," said he, "that is certain; though methinks, that, being such, I have been somewhat familiarly treated in this town of yours; but, as for my being poor, I think I need not be charged with poverty, till I seek siller of somebody."

"The dear country all over," said Master George, in a whisper, to David Ramsay, "pride and poverty."

But David had taken out his tablets and silver pen, and, deeply immersed in calculations, in which he rambled over all the terms of arithmetic, from the simple unit to millions, billions, and trillions, neither heard nor answered the observation of his friend, who, seeing his abstraction, turned again to the Scot.

"I fancy now, Jockey, if a stranger were to offer you a noble, you would chuck it back at his head?"

"Not if I could do him honest service for it, sir," said the Scot; "I am willing to do what I may to be useful, though I come of an honourable house, and may be said to be in a sort indifferently weel provided for."

"Ay!" said the interrogator, "and what house may claim the honour of your descent?"

"An ancient coat belongs to it, as the play says," whispered Vincent to his companion.

"Come, Jockey, out with it," continued Master George, observing that the Scot, as usual with his countrymen, when asked a blunt, straightforward question, took a little time before answering it.

"I am no more Jockey, sir, than you are John," said the stranger, as if offended at being addressed by a name, which at that time was used, as Sawney now is, for a general appellative of the Scottish nation. "My name, if you must know it, is Richie Moniplies; and I come of the old and honourable house of Castle Collop, weel kend at the West-Port of Edinburgh."

"What is that you call the West-Port?" proceeded the interrogator.

"Why, an it like your honour," said Richie, who now, having recovered his senses sufficiently to observe the respectable exterior of Master George, threw more civility into his manner than at first, "the West-Port is a gate of our city, as yonder brick arches at Whitehall form the entrance of the king's palace here, only that the West-Port is of stonern work, and mair decorated with architecture and the policy of bigging."

"Nouns, man, the Whitehall gateways were planned by the great Holbein," answered Master George; "I suspect your accident has jumbled your brains, my good friend. I suppose you will tell me next, you have at Edinburgh as fine a navigable river as the Thames, with all its shipping?"

"The Thames!" exclaimed Richie, in a tone of ineffable contempt— "God bless your honour's judgment, we have at Edinburgh the Water-of-Leith and the Nor-loch!"

"And the Pow-Burn, and the Quarry-holes, and the Gusedub, ye fause loon!" answered Master George, speaking Scotch with a strong and natural emphasis; "it is such land-loupers as you, that, with your falset and fair fashions, bring reproach on our whole country."

"God forgie me, sir," said Richie, much surprised at finding the supposed southron converted into a native Scot, "I took your honour for an Englisher! But I hope there was naething wrang in standing up for ane's ain country's credit in a strange land, where all men cry her down?"

"Do you call it for your country's credit, to show that she has a lying, puffing rascal, for one of her children?" said Master George. "But come, man, never look grave on it,—as you have found a countryman, so you have found a friend, if you deserve one—and especially if you answer me truly."

"I see nae gude it wad do me to speak ought else but truth," said the worthy North Briton.

"Well, then—to begin," said Master George, "I suspect you are a son of old Mungo Moniplies, the flesher, at the West-Port."

"Your honour is a witch, I think," said Richie, grinning.

"And how dared you, sir, to uphold him for a noble?"

"I dinna ken, sir," said Richie, scratching his head; "I hear muckle of an Earl of Warwick in these southern parts,—Guy, I think his name was,—and he has great reputation here for slaying dun cows, and boars, and such like; and I am sure my father has killed more cows and boars, not to mention bulls, calves, sheep, ewes, lambs, and pigs, than the haill Baronage of England."

"Go to! you are a shrewd knave," said Master George; "charm your tongue, and take care of saucy answers. Your father was an honest burgher, and the deacon of his craft: I am sorry to see his son in so poor a coat."

"Indifferent, sir," said Richie Moniplies, looking down on his garments—"very indifferent; but it is the wonted livery of poor burghers' sons in our country—one of Luckie Want's bestowing upon us—rest us patient! The king's leaving Scotland has taken all custom frae Edinburgh; and there is hay made at the Cross, and a dainty crop of fouats in the Grass-market. There is as much grass grows where my father's stall stood, as might have been a good bite for the beasts he was used to kill."

"It is even too true," said Master George; "and while we make fortunes here, our old neighbours and their families are starving at home. This should be thought upon oftener.—And how came you by that broken head, Richie?—tell me honestly."

"Troth, sir, I'se no lee about the matter," answered Moniplies. "I was coming along the street here, and ilk ane was at me with their jests and roguery. So I thought to mysell, ye are ower mony for me to mell with; but let me catch ye in Barford's Park, or at the fit of the Vennel, I could gar some of ye sing another sang. Sae ae auld hirpling deevil of a potter behoved just to step in my way and offer me a pig, as he said, just to put my Scotch ointment in, and I gave him a push, as but natural, and the tottering deevil coupit ower amang his ain pigs, and damaged a score of them. And then the reird raise, and hadna these twa gentlemen helped me out of it, murdered I suld hae been, without remeid. And as it was, just when they got haud of my arm to have me out of the fray, I got the lick that donnerit me from a left-handed lighterman."

Master George looked to the apprentices as if to demand the truth of this story.

"It is just as he says, sir," replied Jenkin; "only I heard nothing about pigs.—The people said he had broke some crockery, and that—I beg pardon, sir—nobody could thrive within the kenning of a Scot."

"Well, no matter what they said, you were an honest fellow to help the weaker side.—And you, sirrah," continued Master George, addressing his countryman, "will call at my house to-morrow morning, agreeable to this direction."

"I will wait upon your honour," said the Scot, bowing very low; "that is, if my honourable master will permit me."

"Thy master?" said George,—"Hast thou any other master save Want, whose livery you say you wear?"

"Troth, in one sense, if it please your honour, I serve twa masters," said Richie; "for both my master and me are slaves to that same beldam, whom we thought to show our heels to by coming off from Scotland. So that you see, sir, I hold in a sort of black ward tenure, as we call it in our country, being the servant of a servant."

"And what is your master's name?" said Master George; and observing that Richie hesitated, he added, "Nay, do not tell me, if it is a secret."

"A secret that there is little use in keeping," said Richie; "only ye ken that our northern stomachs are ower proud to call in witnesses to our distress. No that my master is in mair than present pinch, sir," he added, looking towards the two English apprentices, "having a large sum in the Royal Treasury—that is," he continued, in a whisper to Master

George,—"the king is owing him a lot of siller; but it's ill getting at it, it's like.—My master is the young Lord Glenvarloch."

Master George testified surprise at the name.—" *You* one of the young Lord Glenvarloch's followers, and in such a condition?"

"Troth, and I am all the followers he has, for the present that is; and blithe wad I be if he were muckle better aff than I am, though I were to bide as I am."

"I have seen his father with four gentlemen and ten lackeys at his heels," said Master George, "rustling in their laces and velvets. Well, this is a changeful world, but there is a better beyond it.—The good old house of Glenvarloch, that stood by king and country five hundred years!"

"Your honour may say a thousand," said the follower.

"I will say what I know to be true, friend," said the citizen, "and not a word more.—You seem well recovered now—can you walk?"

"Bravely, sir," said Richie; "it was but a bit dover. I was bred at the West-Port, and my cantle will stand a clour wad bring a stot down."

"Where does your master lodge?"

"We pit up, an it like your honour," replied the Scot, "in a sma' house at the fit of ane of the wynds that gang down to the water-side, with a decent man, John Christie, a ship-chandler, as they ca't. His father came from Dundee. I wotna the name of the wynd, but it's right anent the mickle kirk yonder; and your honour will mind, that we pass only by our family-name of simple Mr. Nigel Olifaunt, as keeping ourselves retired for the present, though in Scotland we be called the Lord Nigel."

"It is wisely done of your master," said the citizen. "I will find out your lodgings, though your direction be none of the clearest." So saying, and slipping a piece of money at the same time into Richie Moniplies's hand, he bade him hasten home, and get into no more affrays.

"I will take care of that now, sir," said Richie, with a look of importance, "having a charge about me. And so, wussing ye a' weel, with special thanks to these twa young gentlemen—"

"I am no gentleman," said Jenkin, flinging his cap on his head; "I am a tight London 'prentice, and hope to be a freeman one day. Frank may write himself gentleman, if he will."

"I *was* a gentleman once," said Tunstall, "and I hope I have done nothing to lose the name of one."

"Weel, weel, as ye list," said Richie Moniplies; "but I am mickle beholden to ye baith—and I am not a hair the less like to bear it in mind that I say but little about it just now.—Gude-night to you, my kind countryman." So saying, he thrust out of the sleeve of his ragged doublet a long bony hand and arm, on which the muscles rose like whip-cord. Master George shook it heartily, while Jenkin and Frank exchanged sly looks with each other.

Richie Moniplies would next have addressed his thanks to the master of the shop, but seeing him, as he afterwards said, "scribbling on his bit bookie, as if he were demented," he contented his politeness with "giving him a hat," touching, that is, his bonnet, in token of salutation, and so left the shop.

"Now, there goes Scotch Jockey, with all his bad and good about him," said Master George to Master David, who suspended, though unwillingly, the calculations with which he was engaged, and keeping his pen within an inch of the tablets, gazed on his friend with great lack-lustre eyes, which expressed any thing rather than intelligence or interest in the discourse addressed to him.—"That fellow," proceeded Master George, without heeding his friend's state of abstraction, "shows, with great liveliness of colouring, how our Scotch pride and poverty make liars and braggarts of us; and yet the knave, whose every third word to an Englishman is a boastful lie, will, I warrant you, be a true and tender friend and follower to his master, and has perhaps parted with his mantle to him in the cold blast, although he himself walked *in cuerpo,* as the Don says.—Strange! that courage and fidelity—for I will warrant that the knave is stout—should have no better companion than this swaggering braggadocio humour.—But you mark me not, friend Davie."

"I do—I do, most heedfully," said Davie.—"For, as the sun goeth round the dial-plate in twenty-four hours, add, for the moon, fifty minutes and a half—"

"You are in the seventh heavens, man," said his companion.

"I crave your pardon," replied Davie.—"Let the wheel A go round in twenty-four hours—I have it—and the wheel B in twenty-four hours, fifty minutes and a half—fifty-seven being to fifty-four, as fifty-nine to twenty-four hours, fifty minutes and a half, or very nearly,—I crave your forgiveness, Master George, and heartily wish you good-even."

"Good-even?" said Master George; "why, you have not wished me good-day yet. Come, old friend, lay by these tablets, or you will crack the inner machinery of *your* skull, as our friend yonder has got the outer-case of his damaged.—Good-night, quotha! I mean not to part with you so easily. I came to get my four hours' nunchion from you, man, besides a tune on the lute from my god-daughter, Mrs. Marget."

"Good faith! I was abstracted, Master George—but you know me. Whenever I get amongst the wheels," said Mr. Ramsay, "why, 'tis—"

"Lucky that you deal in small ones," said his friend; as, awakened from his reveries and calculations, Ramsay led the way up a little back-stair to the first storey, occupied by his daughter and his little household.

The apprentices resumed their places in the front-shop, and relieved Sam Porter; when Jenkin said to Tunstall—"Didst see, Frank, how the old goldsmith cottoned in with his beggarly countryman? When would one of his wealth have shaken hands so courteously with a poor Englishman?—Well, I'll say that for the best of the Scots, that they will go over head and ears to serve a countryman, when they will not wet a nail of their finger to save a Southron, as they call us, from drowning. And yet Master George is but half-bred Scot neither in that respect; for I have known him do many a kind thing to the English too."

"But hark ye, Jenkin," said Tunstall, "I think you are but half-bred English yourself. How came you to strike on the Scotsman's side after all?"

"Why, you did so, too," answered Vincent.

"Ay, because I saw you begin; and, besides, it is no Cumberland fashion to fall fifty upon one," replied Tunstall.

"And no Christ Church fashion neither," said Jenkin. "Fair play and Old England for ever!—Besides, to tell you a secret, his voice had a twang in it—in the dialect I mean—reminded me of a little tongue, which I think sweeter—sweeter than the last toll of St. Dunstan's will sound, on the day that I am shot of my indentures—Ha!—you guess who I mean, Frank?"

"Not I, indeed," answered Tunstall.—"Scotch Janet, I suppose, the laundress."

"Off with Janet in her own bucking-basket!—No, no, no!—You blind buzzard,—do you not know I mean pretty Mrs. Marget?"

"Umph!" answered Tunstall, dryly.

A flash of anger, not unmingled with suspicion, shot from Jenkin's keen black eyes.

"Umph!—and what signifies umph? I am not the first 'prentice has married his master's daughter, I suppose?"

"They kept their own secret, I fancy," said Tunstall, "at least till they were out of their time."

"I tell you what it is, Frank," answered Jenkin, sharply, "that may be the fashion of you gentlefolks, that are taught from your biggin to carry two faces under the same hood, but it shall never be mine."

"There are the stairs, then," said Tunstall, coolly; "go up and ask Mrs. Marget of our master just now, and see what sort of a face he will wear under *his* hood."

"No, I wonnot," answered Jenkin; "I am not such a fool as that neither. But I will take my own time; and all the Counts in Cumberland shall not cut my comb, and this is that which you may depend upon."

Francis made no reply; and they resumed their usual attention to the business of the shop, and their usual solicitations to the passengers.

III

BOBADIL: *I pray you, possess no gallant of your acquaintance with a knowledge of my lodging.*
MASTER MATTHEW: *Who, I, sir?—Lord, sir!*

—Ben Jonson

The next morning found Nigel Olifaunt, the young Lord of Glenvarloch, seated, sad and solitary, in his little apartment, in the mansion of John Christie, the ship-chandler; which that honest tradesman, in gratitude perhaps to the profession from which he derived his chief support, appeared to have constructed as nearly as possible upon the plan of a ship's cabin.

It was situated near to Paul's Wharf, at the end of one of those intricate and narrow lanes, which, until that part of the city was swept away by the Great Fire in 1666, constituted an extraordinary labyrinth of small, dark, damp, and unwholesome streets and alleys, in one corner or other of which the plague was then as surely found lurking, as in the obscure corners of Constantinople in our own time. But John Christie's house looked out upon the river, and had the advantage, therefore, of free air, impregnated, however, with the odoriferous fumes of the articles in which the ship-chandler dealt, with the odour of pitch, and the natural scent of the ooze and sludge left by the reflux of the tide.

Upon the whole, except that his dwelling did not float with the flood-tide, and become stranded with the ebb, the young lord was nearly as comfortably accommodated as he was while on board the little trading brig from the long town of Kirkaldy, in Fife, by which he had come a passenger to London. He received, however, every attention which could be paid him by his honest landlord, John Christie; for Richie Moniplies had not thought it necessary to preserve his master's *incognito* so completely, but that the honest ship-chandler could form a guess that his guest's quality was superior to his appearance.

As for Dame Nelly, his wife, a round, buxom, laughter-loving dame, with black eyes, a tight well-laced bodice, a green apron, and a red petticoat edged with a slight silver lace, and judiciously shortened so as to show that a short heel, and a tight clean ankle, rested upon her well-burnished shoe,—she, of course, felt interest in a young man, who, besides being very handsome, good-humoured, and easily satisfied with the accommodations her house afforded, was evidently of a rank, as well as manners, highly superior to the skippers (or Captains, as they called themselves) of merchant vessels, who were the usual tenants of the apartments which she let to hire; and at whose departure she was sure to find her well-scrubbed floor soiled with the relics of tobacco, (which, spite of King James's Counterblast, was then forcing itself into use,) and her best curtains impregnated with the odour of Geneva and strong waters, to Dame Nelly's great indignation; for, as she truly said, the smell of the shop and warehouse was bad enough without these additions.

But all Mr. Olifaunt's habits were regular and cleanly, and his address, though frank and simple, showed so much of the courtier and gentleman, as formed a strong contrast with the loud halloo, coarse jests, and boisterous impatience of her maritime inmates. Dame Nelly saw that her guest was melancholy also, notwithstanding his efforts to seem contented and cheerful; and, in short, she took that sort of interest in him, without being herself aware of the extent, which an unscrupulous gallant might have been tempted to improve to the prejudice of honest John, who was at least a score of years older than his helpmate. Olifaunt, however, had not only other matters to think of, but would have regarded such an intrigue, had the idea ever occurred to him, as an abominable and ungrateful encroachment upon the laws of hospitality, his religion having been by his late father formed upon the strict principles of the national faith, and his morality upon those of the nicest honour. He had not escaped the predominant weakness of his country, an overweening sense of the pride of birth, and a disposition to value the worth and consequence of others according to the number and the fame of their deceased ancestors; but this pride of family was well subdued, and in general almost entirely concealed, by his good sense and general courtesy.

Such as we have described him, Nigel Olifaunt, or rather the young Lord Glenvarloch, was, when our narrative takes him up, under great perplexity respecting the fate of his trusty and only follower, Richard Moniplies, who had been dispatched by his young master, early the preceding morning, as far as the court at Westminster, but had not yet returned. His evening adventures the reader is already acquainted with, and so far knows more of Richie than did his master, who had not heard of him for twenty-four hours.

Dame Nelly Christie, in the meantime, regarded her guest with some anxiety, and a great desire to comfort him, if possible. She placed on the breakfast-table a noble piece of cold powdered beef, with its usual guards of turnip and carrot, recommended her mustard as coming direct from her cousin at Tewkesbury, and spiced the toast with her own hands—and with her own hands, also, drew a jug of stout and nappy ale, all of which were elements of the substantial breakfast of the period.

When she saw that her guest's anxiety prevented him from doing justice to the good cheer which she set before him, she commenced her career of verbal consolation with the usual volubility of those women in her station, who, conscious of good looks, good intentions, and good lungs, entertain no fear either of wearying themselves or of fatiguing their auditors.

"Now, what the good year! are we to send you down to Scotland as thin as you came up?—I am sure it would be contrary to the course of nature. There was my goodman's father, old Sandie Christie, I have heard he was an atomy when he came up from the North, and I am sure he died, Saint Barnaby was ten years, at twenty stone weight. I was a bare-headed girl at the time, and lived in the neighbourhood, though I had little thought of marrying John then, who had a score of years the better of me—but he is a thriving man and a kind husband—and his father, as I was saying, died as fat as a church-warden. Well, sir, but I hope I have not offended you for my little joke—and I hope the ale is to your honour's liking,—and the beef—and the mustard?"

"All excellent—all too good," answered Olifaunt; "you have every thing so clean and tidy, dame, that I shall not know how to live when I go back to my own country—if ever I go back there."

This was added as it seemed involuntarily, and with a deep sigh.

"I warrant your honour go back again if you like it," said the dame: "unless you think rather of taking a pretty well-dowered English lady, as some of your countryfolk have done. I assure you, some of the best of the city have married Scotsmen. There was Lady Trebleplumb, Sir Thomas Trebleplumb the great Turkey merchant's widow, married Sir Awley Macauley, whom your honour knows, doubtless; and pretty Mistress Doublefee, old Sergeant Doublefee's daughter, jumped out of window, and was married at May-fair to a Scotsman with a hard name; and old Pitchpost the timber merchant's daughters did little better, for they married two Irishmen; and when folks jeer me about having a

Scotsman for lodger, meaning your honour, I tell them they are afraid of their daughters and their mistresses; and sure I have a right to stand up for the Scots, since John Christie is half a Scotsman, and a thriving man, and a good husband, though there is a score of years between us; and so I would have your honour cast care away, and mend your breakfast with a morsel and a draught."

"At a word, my kind hostess, I cannot," said Olifaunt; "I am anxious about this knave of mine, who has been so long absent in this dangerous town of yours."

It may be noticed in passing that Dame Nelly's ordinary mode of consolation was to disprove the existence of any cause for distress; and she is said to have carried this so far as to comfort a neighbour, who had lost her husband, with the assurance that the dear defunct would be better to-morrow, which perhaps might not have proved an appropriate, even if it had been a possible, mode of relief.

On this occasion she denied stoutly that Richie had been absent altogether twenty hours; and as for people being killed in the streets of London, to be sure two men had been found in Tower-ditch last week, but that was far to the east, and the other poor man that had his throat cut in the fields, had met his mishap near by Islington; and he that was stabbed by the young Templar in a drunken frolic, by Saint Clement's in the Strand, was an Irishman. All which evidence she produced to show that none of these casualties had occurred in a case exactly parallel with that of Richie, a Scotsman, and on his return from Westminster.

"My better comfort is, my good dame," answered Olifaunt, "that the lad is no brawler or quarreller, unless strongly urged, and that he has nothing valuable about him to any one but me."

"Your honour speaks very well," retorted the inexhaustible hostess, who protracted her task of taking away, and putting to rights, in order that she might prolong her gossip. "I'll uphold Master Moniplies to be neither reveller nor brawler, for if he liked such things, he might be visiting and junketing with the young folks about here in the neighbourhood, and he never dreams of it; and when I asked the young man to go as far as my gossip's, Dame Drinkwater, to taste a glass of aniseed, and a bit of the groaning cheese,—for Dame Drinkwater has had twins, as I told your honour, sir,—and I meant it quite civilly to the young man, but he chose to sit and keep house with John Christie; and I dare say there is a score of years between them, for your honour's servant looks scarce much older than I am. I wonder what they could have to say to each other. I asked John Christie, but he bid me go to sleep."

"If he comes not soon," said his master, "I will thank you to tell me what magistrate I can address myself to; for besides my anxiety for the poor fellow's safety, he has papers of importance about him."

"O! your honour may be assured he will be back in a quarter of an hour," said Dame Nelly; "he is not the lad to stay out twenty-four hours at a stretch. And for the papers, I am sure your honour will pardon him for just giving me a peep at the corner, as I was giving him a small cup, not so large as my thimble, of distilled waters, to fortify his stomach against the damps, and it was directed to the King's Most Excellent Majesty; and so doubtless his Majesty has kept Richie out of civility to consider of your honour's letter, and send back a fitting reply."

Dame Nelly here hit by chance on a more available topic of consolation than those she had hitherto touched upon; for the youthful lord had himself some vague hopes that his messenger might have been delayed at Court until a fitting and favourable answer should be dispatched back to him. Inexperienced, however, in public affairs as he certainly was, it required only a moment's consideration to convince him of the improbability of an expectation so contrary to all he had heard of etiquette, as well as the dilatory proceedings in a court suit, and he answered the good-natured hostess with a sigh, that he doubted whether the king would even look on the paper addressed to him, far less take it into his immediate consideration.

"Now, out upon you for a faint-hearted gentleman!" said the good dame; "and why should he not do as much for us as our gracious Queen Elizabeth? Many people say this and that about a queen and a king, but I think a king comes more natural to us English folks; and this good gentleman goes as often down by water to Greenwich, and employs as many of the barge-men and water-men of all kinds; and maintains, in his royal grace, John Taylor, the water-poet, who keeps both a sculler and a pair of oars. And he has made a comely Court at Whitehall, just by the river; and since the king is so good a friend to the Thames, I cannot see, if it please your honour, why all his subjects, and your honour in specialty, should not have satisfaction by his hands."

"True, dame—true,—let us hope for the best; but I must take my cloak and rapier, and pray your husband in courtesy to teach me the way to a magistrate."

"Sure, sir," said the prompt dame, "I can do that as well as he, who has been a slow man of his tongue all his life, though I will give him his due for being a loving husband, and a man as well to pass in the world as any betwixt us and the top of the lane. And so there is the sitting alderman, that is always at the Guildhall, which is close by Paul's, and so I warrant you he puts all to rights in the city that wisdom can mend; and for the rest there is no help but patience. But I wish I were as sure of forty pounds as I am that the young man will come back safe and sound."

Olifaunt, in great and anxious doubt of what the good dame so strongly averred, flung his cloak on one shoulder, and was about to belt on his rapier, when first the voice of Richie Moniplies on the stair, and then that faithful emissary's appearance in the chamber, put the matter beyond question. Dame Nelly, after congratulating Moniplies on his return, and paying several compliments to her own sagacity for having foretold it, was at length pleased to leave the apartment. The truth was, that, besides some instinctive feelings of good breeding which combated her curiosity, she saw there was no chance of Richie's proceeding in his narrative while she was in the room, and she therefore retreated, trusting that her own address would get the secret out of one or other of the young men, when she should have either by himself.

"Now, in Heaven's name, what is the matter?" said Nigel Olifaunt.— "Where have you been, or what have you been about? You look as pale as death. There is blood on your hand, and your clothes are torn. What barns-breaking have you been at? You have been drunk, Richard, and fighting."

"Fighting I have been," said Richard, "in a small way; but for being drunk, that's a job ill to manage in this town, without money to come by liquor; and as for barns-breaking, the deil a thing's broken but my head. It's not made of iron, I wot, nor my claithes of chenzie-mail; so a club smashed the tane, and a claught damaged the tither. Some misleard rascals abused my country, but I think I cleared the causey of them. However, the haill hive was ower mony for me at last, and I got this eclipse on the crown, and then I was carried, beyond my kenning, to a sma' booth at the Temple Port, whare they sell the whirligigs and mony-go-rounds that measure out time as a man wad measure a tartan web; and then they bled me, wold I nold I, and were reasonably civil, especially an auld country-man of ours, of whom more hereafter."

"And at what o'clock might this be?" said Nigel.

"The twa iron carles yonder, at the kirk beside the Port, were just banging out sax o' the clock."

"And why came you not home as soon as you recovered?" said Nigel.

"In troth, my lord, every *why* has its *wherefore*, and this has a gude ane," answered his follower. "To come hame, I behoved to ken whare hame was; now, I had clean tint the name of the wynd, and the mair I asked, the mair the folk leugh, and the farther they sent me wrang; sae I gave it up till God should send daylight to help me; and as I saw mysell near a kirk at the lang run, I e'en crap in to take up my night's quarters in the kirkyard."

"In the churchyard?" said Nigel—"But I need not ask what drove you to such a pinch."

"It wasna sae much the want o' siller, my Lord Nigel," said Richie, with an air of mysterious importance, "for I was no sae absolute without means, of whilk mair anon; but I thought I wad never ware a saxpence sterling on ane of their saucy chamberlains at a hostelry, sae lang as I could sleep fresh and fine in a fair, dry, spring night. Mony a time, when I hae come hame ower late, and faund the West-Port steekit, and the waiter ill-willy, I have garr'd the sexton of Saint Cuthbert's calf-ward serve me for my quarters. But then there are dainty green graffs in Saint Cuthbert's kirkyard, whare ane may sleep as if they were in a down-bed, till they hear the lavrock singing up in the air as high as the Castle; whereas, and behold, these London kirkyards are causeyed with through-stanes, panged hard and fast thegither; and my cloak being something threadbare, made but a thin mattress, so I was fain to give up my bed before every limb about me was crippled. Dead folks may sleep yonder sound enow, but deil haet else."

"And what became of you next?" said his master.

"I just took to a canny bulkhead, as they ca' them here; that is, the boards on the tap of their bits of outshots of stalls and booths, and there I sleepit as sound as if I was in a castle. Not but I was disturbed with some of the night-walking queans and swaggering billies, but when they found there was nothing to be got by me but a slash of my Andrew Ferrara, they bid me good-night for a beggarly Scot; and I was e'en weel pleased to be sae cheap rid of them. And in the morning, I cam daikering here, but sad wark I had to find the way, for I had been east as far as the place they ca' Mile-End, though it is mair like sax-mile-end."

"Well, Richie," answered Nigel, "I am glad all this has ended so well—go get something to eat. I am sure you need it."

"In troth do I, sir," replied Moniplies; "but, with your lordship's leave—"

"Forget the lordship for the present, Richie, as I have often told you before."

"Faith," replied Richie, "I could weel forget that your honour was a lord, but then I behoved to forget that I am a lord's man, and that's not so easy. But, however," he added, assisting his description with the thumb and the two forefingers of his right hand, thrust out after the fashion of a bird's claw, while the little finger and ring-finger were closed upon the palm, "to the Court I went, and my friend that promised me a sight of his Majesty's most gracious presence, was as gude as his word, and carried me into the back offices, where I got the best breakfast I have had since we came here, and it did me gude for the rest of the day; for as to what I have eaten in this accursed town, it is aye sauced with the disquieting thought that it maun be paid for. After a', there was but beef banes and fat brose; but king's cauff, your honour kens, is better than ither folk's corn; at ony rate, it was a' in free awmous.—But I see," he added, stopping short, "that your honour waxes impatient."

"By no means, Richie," said the young nobleman, with an air of resignation, for he well knew his domestic would not mend his pace for goading; "you have suffered enough in the embassy to have a right to tell the story in your own way. Only let me pray for the name of the friend who was to introduce you into the king's presence. You were very mysterious on the subject, when you undertook, through his means, to have the Supplication put into his Majesty's own hands, since those sent heretofore, I have every reason to think, went no farther than his secretary's."

"Weel, my lord," said Richie, "I did not tell you his name and quality at first, because I thought you would be affronted at the like of him having to do in your lordship's affairs. But mony a man climbs up in Court by waur help. It was just Laurie Linklater, one of the yeomen of the kitchen, that was my father's apprentice lang syne."

"A yeoman in the kitchen—a scullion!" exclaimed Lord Nigel, pacing the room in displeasure.

"But consider, sir," said Richie, composedly, "that a' your great friends hung back, and shunned to own you, or to advocate your petition; and then, though I am sure I wish Laurie a higher office, for your lordship's sake and for mine, and specially for his ain sake, being a friendly lad, yet your lordship must consider, that a scullion, if a yeoman of the king's most royal kitchen may be called a scullion, may weel rank with a master-cook elsewhere; being that king's cauff, as I said before, is better than—"

"You are right, and I was wrong," said the young nobleman. "I have no choice of means of making my case known, so that they be honest."

"Laurie is as honest a lad as ever lifted a ladle," said Richie; "not but what I dare to say he can lick his fingers like other folk, and reason good. But, in fine, for I see your honour is waxing impatient, he brought me to the palace, where a' was astir for the king going out to hunt or hawk on Blackheath, I think they ca'd it. And there was a horse stood with all the quarries about it, a bonny grey as ever was foaled; and the saddle and the stirrups, and the curb and bit, o' burning gowd, or silver gilded at least; and down, sir, came the king, with all his nobles, dressed out in his hunting-suit of green, doubly laced, and laid down with gowd. I minded the very face o' him, though it was lang since I saw him. But my certie, lad, thought I, times are changed since ye came fleeing down the back stairs of auld Holyrood House, in grit fear, having your breeks in your hand without time to put them on, and Frank Stewart, the wild Earl of Bothwell, hard at your haunches; and if auld Lord Glenvarloch hadna cast his mantle about his arm, and taken bluidy wounds mair than ane in your behalf, you wald not have craw'd sae crouse this day; and so saying, I could not but think your lordship's Sifflication could not be less than most acceptable; and so I banged in among the crowd of lords. Laurie thought me mad, and held me by the cloak-lap till the cloth rave in his hand; and so I banged in right before the king just as he mounted, and crammed the Sifflication into his hand, and he opened it like in amaze; and just as he saw the first line, I was minded to make a reverence, and I had the ill luck to hit his jaud o' a beast on the nose with my hat, and scaur the creature, and she swarved aside, and the king, that sits na mickle better than a draff-pock on the saddle, was like to have gotten a clean coup, and that might have cost my craig a raxing—and he flung down the paper amang the beast's feet, and cried, 'Away wi' the fause loon that brought it!' And they grippit me, and cried treason; and I thought of the Ruthvens that were dirked in their ain house, for, it may be, as small a forfeit. However, they spak only of scourging me, and had me away to the porter's lodge to try the tawse on my back, and I was crying mercy as loud as I could; and the king, when he had righted himself on the saddle, and gathered his breath, cried to do me nae harm; for, said he, he is ane of our ain Norland stots, I ken by the rowt of him,—and they a' laughed and rowted loud eneugh. And then he said, 'Gie him a copy of the Proclamation, and let him go down to the North by the next light collier, before waur come o't.' So they let me go, and rode out, a sniggering, laughing, and rounding in ilk ither's lugs. A sair life I had wi' Laurie Linklater; for he said it wad be the ruin of him. And then, when I told him it was in your matter, he said if he had known before he would have risked a scauding for you, because he minded the brave old lord, your father. And then he showed how I suld have done,—and that I suld have held up my hand to my brow, as if the grandeur of the king and his horse-graith thegither had casten the glaiks in my een, and mair jackanape tricks I suld hae played, instead of offering the Sifflication, he said, as if I had been bringing guts to a bear."*

'For,' said he, 'Richie, the king is a weel-natured and just man of his ain kindly nature, but he has a wheen maggots that maun be cannily guided; and then, Richie,' says he, in a very laigh tone, 'I would tell it to nane but a wise man like yoursell, but the king has them about him wad corrupt an angel from heaven; but I could have gi'en you avisement how to have guided him, but now it's like after meat mustard.'—'Aweel, aweel, Laurie,' said I, 'it may be as you say', but since I am clear of the tawse and the porter's lodge, sifflicate wha like, deil hae Richie Moniplies if he come sifflicating here again.'—And so away I came, and I wasna far by the Temple Port, or Bar, or whatever they ca' it, when I met with the misadventure that I tauld you of before."

"Well, my honest Richie," said Lord Nigel, "your attempt was well meant, and not so ill conducted, I think, as to have deserved so bad an issue; but go to your beef and mustard, and we'll talk of the rest afterwards."

"There is nae mair to be spoken, sir," said his follower, "except that I met ane very honest, fair-spoken, weel-put-on gentleman, or rather burgher, as I think, that was in the whigmaleery man's back-shop; and when he learned wha I was, behold he was a kindly Scot himsell, and, what is more, a town's-bairn o' the gude town, and he behoved to compel me to take this Portugal piece, to drink, forsooth—my certie,

* I am certain this prudential advice is not original on Mr. Linklater's part, but I am not at present able to produce my authority. I think it amounted to this, that James flung down a petition presented by some supplicant who paid no compliments to his horse, and expressed no admiration at the splendour of his furniture, saying, "Shall a king cumber himself about the petition of a beggar, while the beggar disregards the king's splendour?" It is, I think, Sir John Harrington who recommends, as a sure mode to the king's favour, to praise the paces of the royal palfrey.

thought I, we ken better, for we will eat it—and he spoke of paying your lordship a visit."

"You did not tell him where I lived, you knave?" said the Lord Nigel, angrily. "'Sdeath! I shall have every clownish burgher from Edinburgh come to gaze on my distress, and pay a shilling for having seen the motion of the Poor Noble!"

"Tell him where you lived?" said Richie, evading the question; "How could I tell him what I kendna mysell? If I had minded the name of the wynd, I need not have slept in the kirkyard yestreen."

"See, then, that you give no one notice of our lodging," said the young nobleman; "those with whom I have business I can meet at Paul's, or in the Court of Requests."

"This is steeking the stable-door when the steed is stolen," thought Richie to himself; "but I must put him on another pin."

So thinking, he asked the young lord what was in the Proclamation which he still held folded in his hand; "for, having little time to spell at it," said he, "your lordship well knows I ken nought about it but the grand blazon at the tap—the lion has gotten a claught of our auld Scottish shield now, but it was as weel upheld when it had a unicorn on ilk side of it."

Lord Nigel read the Proclamation, and he coloured deep with shame and indignation as he read; for the purport was, to his injured feelings, like the pouring of ardent spirits upon a recent wound.

"What deil's in the paper, my lord?" said Richie, unable to suppress his curiosity as he observed his master change colour; "I wadna ask such a thing, only the Proclamation is not a private thing, but is meant for a' men's hearing."

"It is indeed meant for all men's hearing," replied Lord Nigel, "and it proclaims the shame of our country, and the ingratitude of our Prince."

"Now the Lord preserve us! and to publish it in London, too!" exclaimed Moniplies.

"Hark ye, Richard," said Nigel Olifaunt, "in this paper the Lords of the Council set forth, that, 'in consideration of the resort of idle persons of low condition forth from his Majesty's kingdom of Scotland to his English Court—filling the same with their suits and supplications, and dishonouring the royal presence with their base, poor, and beggarly persons, to the disgrace of their country in the estimation of the English; these are to prohibit the skippers, masters of vessels and others, in every part of Scotland, from bringing such miserable creatures up to Court under pain of fine and impisonment.'"

"I marle the skipper took us on board," said Richie.

"Then you need not marvel how you are to get back again," said Lord Nigel, "for here is a clause which says, that such idle suitors are to be transported back to Scotland at his Majesty's expense, and punished for their audacity with stripes, stocking, or incarceration, according to their demerits—that is to say, I suppose, according to the degree of their poverty, for I see no other demerit specified."

"This will scarcely," said Richie, "square with our old proverb—

A King's face
Should give grace—

But what says the paper farther, my lord?"

"O, only a small clause which especially concerns us, making some still heavier denunciations against those suitors who shall be so bold as to approach the Court, under pretext of seeking payment of old debts due to them by the king, which, the paper states, is, of all species of importunity, that which is most odious to his Majesty."

"The king has neighbours in that matter," said Richie; "but it is not every one that can shift off that sort of cattle so easily as he does."

Their conversation was here interrupted by a knocking at the door. Olifaunt looked out at the window, and saw an elderly respectable person whom he knew not. Richie also peeped, and recognised, but, recognising, chose not to acknowledge, his friend of the preceding evening. Afraid that his share in the visit might be detected, he made his escape out of the apartment under pretext of going to his breakfast; and left their landlady the task of ushering Master George into Lord Nigel's apartment, which she performed with much courtesy.

IV

Ay, sir, the clouted shoe hath oft times craft in't,
As says the rustic proverb; and your citizen,
In's grogram suit, gold chain, and well-black'd shoes,
Bears under his flat cap ofttimes a brain
Wiser than burns beneath the cap and feather,
Or seethes within the statesman's velvet nightcap.

—Read me my Riddle

The young Scottish nobleman received the citizen with distant politeness, expressing that sort of reserve by which those of the higher ranks are sometimes willing to make a plebeian sensible that he is an intruder. But Master George seemed neither displeased nor disconcerted. He assumed the chair, which, in deference to his respectable appearance, Lord Nigel offered to him, and said, after a moment's pause, during which he had looked attentively at the young man, with respect not unmingled with emotion—"You will forgive me for this rudeness, my lord; but I was endeavouring to trace in your youthful countenance the features of my good old lord, your excellent father."

There was a moment's pause ere young Glenvarloch replied, still with a reserved manner,—"I have been reckoned like my father, sir; and am happy to see any one that respects his memory. But the business which calls me to this city is of a hasty as well as a private nature, and—"

"I understand the hint, my lord," said Master George, "and would not be guilty of long detaining you from business, or more agreeable conversation. My errand is almost done when I have said that my name is George Heriot, warmly befriended, and introduced into the employment of the Royal Family of Scotland, more than twenty years since, by your excellent father; and that, learning from a follower of yours that your lordship was in this city in prosecution of some business of importance, it is my duty,—it is my pleasure,—to wait on the son of my respected patron; and, as I am somewhat known both at the Court, and in the city, to offer him such aid in the furthering of his affairs as my credit and experience may be able to afford."

"I have no doubt of either, Master Heriot," said Lord Nigel, "and I thank you heartily for the good-will with which you have placed them at a stranger's disposal; but my business at Court is done and ended, and I intend to leave London and, indeed, the island, for foreign travel and military service. I may add, that the suddenness of my departure occasions my having little time at my disposal."

Master Heriot did not take the hint, but sat fast, with an embarrassed countenance however, like one who had something to say that he knew not exactly how to make effectual. At length he said, with a dubious smile, "You are fortunate, my lord, in having so soon dispatched your business at Court. Your talking landlady informs me you have been but a fortnight in this city. It is usually months and years ere the Court and a suitor shake hands and part."

"My business," said Lord Nigel, with a brevity which was intended to stop further discussion, "was summarily dispatched."

Still Master Heriot remained seated, and there was a cordial good-humour added to the reverence of his appearance, which rendered it impossible for Lord Nigel to be more explicit in requesting his absence.

"Your lordship has not yet had time," said the citizen, still attempting to sustain the conversation, "to visit the places of amusement,—the playhouses, and other places to which youth resort. But I see in your lordship's hand one of the new-invented plots of the piece,* which they hand about of late—May I ask what play?"

"Oh! a well-known piece," said Lord Nigel, impatiently throwing down the Proclamation, which he had hitherto been twisting to and fro in his hand,—"an excellent and well-approved piece—*A New Way to Pay Old Debts.*"

Master Heriot stooped down, saying, "Ah! my old acquaintance, Philip Massinger;" but, having opened the paper and seen the purport, he looked at Lord Nigel with surprise, saying, "I trust your lordship does not think this prohibition can extend either to *your* person or your claims?"

"I should scarce have thought so myself," said the young nobleman; "but so it proves. His Majesty, to close this discourse at once, has been pleased to send me this Proclamation, in answer to a respectful Supplication for the repayment of large loans advanced by my father for the service of the State, in the king's utmost emergencies."

---

* Meaning, probably, playbills.

"It is impossible!" said the citizen—"it is absolutely impossible!—If the king could forget what was due to your father's memory, still he would not have wished—would not, I may say, have dared—to be so flagrantly unjust to the memory of such a man as your father, who, dead in the body, will long live in the memory of the Scottish people."

"I should have been of your opinion," answered Lord Nigel, in the same tone as before; "but there is no fighting with facts."

"What was the tenor of this Supplication?" said Heriot; "or by whom was it presented? Something strange there must have been in the contents, or else—"

"You may see my original draught," said the young lord, taking it out of a small travelling strong-box; "the technical part is by my lawyer in Scotland, a skilful and sensible man; the rest is my own, drawn, I hope, with due deference and modesty."

Master Heriot hastly cast his eye over the draught. "Nothing," he said, "can be more well-tempered and respectful. Is it possible the king can have treated this petition with contempt?"

"He threw it down on the pavement," said the Lord of Glenvarloch, "and sent me for answer that Proclamation, in which he classes me with the paupers and mendicants from Scotland, who disgrace his Court in the eyes of the proud English—that is all. Had not my father stood by him with heart, sword, and fortune, he might never have seen the Court of England himself."

"But by whom was this Supplication presented, my lord?" said Heriot; "for the distaste taken at the messenger will sometimes extend itself to the message."

"By my servant," said the Lord Nigel; "by the man you saw, and, I think, were kind to."

"By your servant, my lord?" said the citizen; "he seems a shrewd fellow, and doubtless a faithful; but surely—"

"You would say," said Lord Nigel, "he is no fit messenger to a king's presence?—Surely he is not; but what could I do? Every attempt I had made to lay my case before the king had miscarried, and my petitions got no farther than the budgets of clerks and secretaries; this fellow pretended he had a friend in the household that would bring him to the king's presence,—and so—"

"I understand," said Heriot; "but, my lord, why should you not, in right of your rank and birth, have appeared at Court, and required an audience, which could not have been denied to you?"

The young lord blushed a little, and looked at his dress, which was very plain; and, though in perfect good order, had the appearance of having seen service.

"I know not why I should be ashamed of speaking the truth," he said, after a momentary hesitation,—"I had no dress suitable for appearing at Court. I am determined to incur no expenses which I cannot discharge; and I think you, sir, would not advise me to stand at the palace-door, in person, and deliver my petition, along with those who are in very deed pleading their necessity, and begging an alms."

"That had been, indeed, unseemly," said the citizen; "but yet, my lord, my mind runs strangely that there must be some mistake.—Can I speak with your domestic?"

"I see little good it can do," answered the young lord, "but the interest you take in my misfortunes seems sincere, and therefore—" He stamped on the floor, and in a few seconds afterwards Moniplies appeared, wiping from his beard and mustaches the crumbs of bread, and the froth of the ale-pot, which plainly showed how he had been employed.—"Will your lordship grant permission," said Heriot, "that I ask your groom a few questions?"

"His lordship's page, Master George," answered Moniplies, with a nod of acknowledgment, "if you are minded to speak according to the letter."

"Hold your saucy tongue," said his master, "and reply distinctly to the questions you are to be asked."

"And *truly*, if it like your pageship," said the citizen, "for you may remember I have a gift to discover falset."

"Weel, weel, weel," replied the domestic, somewhat embarrassed, in spite of his effrontery—"though I think that the sort of truth that serves my master, may weel serve ony ane else."

"Pages lie to their masters by right of custom," said the citizen; "and you write yourself in that band, though I think you be among the oldest of such springalds; but to me you must speak truth, if you would not have it end in the whipping-post."

"And that's e'en a bad resting-place," said the well-grown page; "so come away with your questions, Master George."

"Well, then," demanded the citizen, "I am given to understand that you yesterday presented to his Majesty's hand a Supplication, or petition, from this honourable lord, your master."

"Troth, there's nae gainsaying that, sir," replied Moniplies; "there were enow to see it besides me."

"And you pretend that his Majesty flung it from him with contempt?" said the citizen. "Take heed, for I have means of knowing the truth; and you were better up to the neck in the Nor-Loch, which you like so well, than tell a leasing where his Majesty's name is concerned."

"There is nae occasion for leasing-making about the matter," answered Moniplies, firmly; "his Majesty e'en flung it frae him as if it had dirtied his fingers."

"You hear, sir," said Olifaunt, addressing Heriot.

"Hush!" said the sagacious citizen; "this fellow is not ill named— he has more plies than one in his cloak. Stay, fellow," for Moniplies, muttering somewhat about finishing his breakfast, was beginning to shamble towards the door, "answer me this farther question—When you gave your master's petition to his Majesty, gave you nothing with it?"

"Ou, what should I give wi' it, ye ken, Master George?"

"That is what I desire and insist to know," replied his interrogator.

"Weel, then—I am not free to say, that maybe I might not just slip into the king's hand a wee bit Sifflication of mine ain, along with my lord's—just to save his Majesty trouble—and that he might consider them baith at ance."

"A supplication of your own, you varlet!" said his master.

"Ou dear, ay, my lord," said Richie—"puir bodies hae their bits of sifflications as weel as their betters."

"And pray, what might your worshipful petition import?" said Master Heriot.—"Nay, for Heaven's sake, my lord, keep your patience, or we shall never learn the truth of this strange matter.—Speak out, sirrah, and I will stand your friend with my lord."

"It's a lang story to tell—but the upshot is, that it's a scrape of an auld accompt due to my father's yestate by her Majesty the king's maist gracious mother, when she lived in the Castle, and had sundry providings and furnishings forth of our booth, whilk nae doubt was an honour to my father to supply, and whilk, doubtless, it will be a credit to his Majesty to satisfy, as it will be grit convenience to me to receive the saam."

"What string of impertinence is this?" said his master.

"Every word as true as e'er John Knox spoke," said Richie; "here's the bit double of the Sifflication."

Master George took a crumpled paper from the fellow's hand, and said, muttering betwixt his teeth—"'Humbly showeth—um—um—

his Majesty's maist gracious mother—um—um—justly addebted and owing the sum of fifteen merks—the compt whereof followeth—Twelve nowte's feet for jellies—ane lamb, being Christmas—ane roasted capin in grease for the privy chalmer, when my Lord of Bothwell suppit with her Grace.'—I think, my lord, you can hardly be surprised that the king gave this petition a brisk reception; and I conclude, Master Page, that you took care to present your own Supplication before your master's?"

"Troth did I not," answered Moniplies. "I thought to have given my lord's first, as was reason gude; and besides that, it wad have redd the gate for my ain little bill. But what wi' the dirdum an' confusion, an' the loupin here and there of the skeigh brute of a horse, I believe I crammed them baith into his hand cheek-by-jowl, and maybe my ain was bunemost; and say there was aught wrang, I am sure I had a' the fright and a' the risk—"

"And shall have all the beating, you rascal knave," said Nigel; "am I to be insulted and dishonoured by your pragmatical insolence, in blending your base concerns with mine?"

"Nay, nay, nay, my lord," said the good-humoured citizen, interposing, "I have been the means of bringing the fellow's blunder to light—allow me interest enough with your lordship to be bail for his bones. You have cause to be angry, but still I think the knave mistook more out of conceit than of purpose; and I judge you will have the better service of him another time, if you overlook this fault—Get you gone, sirrah— I'll make your peace."

"Na, na," said Moniplies, keeping his ground firmly, "if he likes to strike a lad that has followed him for pure love, for I think there has been little servant's fee between us, a' the way frae Scotland, just let my lord be doing, and see the credit he will get by it—and I would rather (mony thanks to you though, Master George) stand by a lick of his baton, than it suld e'er be said a stranger came between us."

"Go, then," said his master, "and get out of my sight."

"Aweel I wot that is sune done," said Moniplies, retiring slowly; "I did not come without I had been ca'd for—and I wad have been away half an hour since with my gude will, only Maister George keepit me to answer his interrogation, forsooth, and that has made a' this stir."

And so he made his grumbling exit, with the tone much rather of one who has sustained an injury, than who has done wrong.

"There never was a man so plagued as I am with a malapert knave!— The fellow is shrewd, and I have found him faithful—I believe he loves me, too, and he has given proofs of it—but then he is so uplifted in his own conceit, so self-willed, and so self-opinioned, that he seems to become the master and I the man; and whatever blunder he commits, he is sure to make as loud complaints, as if the whole error lay with me, and in no degree with himself."

"Cherish him, and maintain him, nevertheless," said the citizen; "for believe my grey hairs, that affection and fidelity are now rarer qualities in a servitor, than when the world was younger. Yet, trust him, my good lord, with no commission above his birth or breeding, for you see yourself how it may chance to fall."

"It is but too evident, Master Heriot," said the young nobleman; "and I am sorry I have done injustice to my sovereign, and your master. But I am, like a true Scotsman, wise behind hand—the mistake has happened—my Supplication has been refused, and my only resource is to employ the rest of my means to carry Moniplies and myself to some counter-scarp, and die in the battle-front like my ancestors."

"It were better to live and serve your country like your noble father, my lord," replied Master George. "Nay, nay, never look down or shake your head—the king has not refused your Supplication, for he has not seen it—you ask but justice, and that his place obliges him to give to his subjects—ay, my lord, and I will say that his natural temper doth in this hold bias with his duty."

"I were well pleased to think so, and yet—" said Nigel Olifaunt,— "I speak not of my own wrongs, but my country hath many that are unredressed."

"My lord," said Master Heriot, "I speak of my royal master, not only with the respect due from a subject—the gratitude to be paid by a favoured servant, but also with the frankness of a free and loyal Scotsman. The king is himself well disposed to hold the scales of justice even; but there are those around him who can throw without detection their own selfish wishes and base interests into the scale. You are already a sufferer by this, and without your knowing it."

"I am surprised, Master Heriot," said the young lord, "to hear you, upon so short an acquaintance, talk as if you were familiarly acquainted with my affairs."

"My lord," replied the goldsmith, "the nature of my employment affords me direct access to the interior of the palace; I am well known to be no meddler in intrigues or party affairs, so that no favourite has as yet endeavoured to shut against me the door of the royal closet; on the contrary, I have stood well with each while he was in power, and I have not shared the fall of any. But I cannot be thus connected with the Court, without hearing, even against my will, what wheels are in motion, and how they are checked or forwarded. Of course, when I choose to seek such intelligence, I know the sources in which it is to be traced. I have told you why I was interested in your lordship's fortunes. It was last night only that I knew you were in this city, yet I have been able, in coming hither this morning, to gain for you some information respecting the impediments to your suit."

"Sir, I am obliged by your zeal, however little it may be merited," answered Nigel, still with some reserve; "yet I hardly know how I have deserved this interest."

"First let me satisfy you that it is real," said the citizen; "I blame you not for being unwilling to credit the fair professions of a stranger in my inferior class of society, when you have met so little friendship from relations, and those of your own rank, bound to have assisted you by so many ties. But mark the cause. There is a mortgage over your father's extensive estate, to the amount of 40,000 merks, due ostensibly to Peregrine Peterson, the Conservator of Scottish Privileges at Campvere."

"I know nothing of a mortgage," said the young lord; "but there is a wadset for such a sum, which, if unredeemed, will occasion the forfeiture of my whole paternal estate, for a sum not above a fourth of its value—and it is for that very reason that I press the king's government for a settlement of the debts due to my father, that I may be able to redeem my land from this rapacious creditor."

"A wadset in Scotland," said Heriot, "is the same with a mortgage on this side of the Tweed; but you are not acquainted with your real creditor. The Conservator Peterson only lends his name to shroud no less a man than the Lord Chancellor of Scotland, who hopes, under cover of this debt, to gain possession of the estate himself, or perhaps to gratify a yet more powerful third party. He will probably suffer his creature Peterson to take possession, and when the odium of the transaction shall be forgotten, the property and lordship of Glenvarloch will be conveyed to the great man by his obsequious instrument, under cover of a sale, or some similar device."

"Can this be possible?" said Lord Nigel; "the Chancellor wept when I took leave of him—called me his cousin—even his son—furnished me with letters, and, though I asked him for no pecuniary assistance, excused himself unnecessarily for not pressing it on me, alleging the expenses of his rank and his large family. No, I cannot believe a nobleman would carry deceit so far."

"I am not, it is true, of noble blood," said the citizen; "but once more I bid you look on my grey hairs, and think what can be my interest in dishonouring them with falsehood in affairs in which I have no interest, save as they regard the son of my benefactor. Reflect also, have you had any advantage from the Lord Chancellor's letters?"

"None," said Nigel Olifaunt, "except cold deeds and fair words. I have thought for some time, their only object was to get rid of me—one yesterday pressed money on me when I talked of going abroad, in order that I might not want the means of exiling myself."

"Right," said Heriot; "rather than you fled not, they would themselves furnish wings for you to fly withal."

"I will to him this instant," said the incensed youth, "and tell him my mind of his baseness."

"Under your favour," said Heriot, detaining him, "you shall not do so. By a quarrel you would become the ruin of me your informer; and though I would venture half my shop to do your lordship a service, I think you would hardly wish me to come by damage, when it can be of no service to you."

The word *shop* sounded harshly in the ear of the young nobleman, who replied hastily—"Damage, sir?—so far am I from wishing you to incur damage, that I would to Heaven you would cease your fruitless offers of serving one whom there is no chance of ultimately assisting!"

"Leave me alone for that," said the citizen: "you have now erred as far on the bow-hand. Permit me to take this Supplication—I will have it suitably engrossed, and take my own time (and it shall be an early one) for placing it, with more prudence, I trust, than that used by your follower, in the king's hand—I will almost answer for his taking up the matter as you would have him—but should he fail to do so, even then I will not give up the good cause."

"Sir," said the young nobleman, "your speech is so friendly, and my own state so helpless, that I know not how to refuse your kind proffer, even while I blush to accept it at the hands of a stranger."

"We are, I trust, no longer such," said the goldsmith; "and for my guerdon, when my mediation proves successful, and your fortunes are re-established, you shall order your first cupboard of plate from George Heriot."

"You would have a bad paymaster, Master Heriot," said Lord Nigel.

"I do not fear that," replied the goldsmith; "and I am glad to see you smile, my lord—methinks it makes you look still more like the good old lord your father; and it emboldens me, besides, to bring out a small request—that you would take a homely dinner with me to-morrow. I lodge hard by in Lombard Street. For the cheer, my lord, a mess of white broth, a fat capon well larded, a dish of beef collops for auld Scotland's sake, and it may be a cup of right old wine, that was barrelled before Scotland and England were one nation—Then for company, one or two of our own loving countrymen—and maybe my housewife may find out a bonny Scots lass or so."

"I would accept your courtesy, Master Heriot," said Nigel, "but I hear the city ladies of London like to see a man gallant—I would not like to let down a Scottish nobleman in their ideas, as doubtless you have said the best of our poor country, and I rather lack the means of bravery for the present."

"My lord, your frankness leads me a step farther," said Master George. "I—I owed your father some monies; and—nay, if your lordship looks at me so fixedly, I shall never tell my story—and, to speak plainly, for I never could carry a lie well through in my life—it is most fitting, that, to solicit this matter properly, your lordship should go to Court in a manner beseeming your quality. I am a goldsmith, and live by lending money as well as by selling plate. I am ambitious to put an hundred pounds to be at interest in your hands, till your affairs are settled."

"And if they are never favourably settled?" said Nigel.

"Then, my lord," returned the citizen, "the miscarriage of such a sum will be of little consequence to me, compared with other subjects of regret."

"Master Heriot," said the Lord Nigel, "your favour is generously offered, and shall be frankly accepted. I must presume that you see your way through this business, though I hardly do; for I think you would be grieved to add any fresh burden to me, by persuading me to incur debts which I am not likely to discharge. I will therefore take your money, under the hope and trust that you will enable me to repay you punctually."

"I will convince you, my lord," said the goldsmith, "that I mean to deal with you as a creditor from whom I expect payment; and therefore, you shall, with your own good pleasure, sign an acknowledgment for these monies, and an obligation to content and repay me."

He then took from his girdle his writing materials, and, writing a few lines to the purport he expressed, pulled out a small bag of gold from a side-pouch under his cloak, and, observing that it should contain an hundred pounds, proceeded to tell out the contents very methodically upon the table. Nigel Olifaunt could not help intimating that this was an unnecessary ceremonial, and that he would take the bag of gold on the word of his obliging creditor; but this was repugnant to the old man's forms of transacting business.

"Bear with me," he said, "my good lord,—we citizens are a wary and thrifty generation; and I should lose my good name for ever within the toll of Paul's, were I to grant quittance, or take acknowledgment, without bringing the money to actual tale. I think it be right now—and, body of me," he said, looking out at the window, "yonder come my boys with my mule; for I must Westward Hoe. Put your monies aside, my lord; it is not well to be seen with such goldfinches chirping about one in the lodgings of London. I think the lock of your casket be indifferent good; if not, I can serve you at an easy rate with one that has held thousands;—it was the good old Sir Faithful Frugal's;—his spendthrift son sold the shell when he had eaten the kernel—and there is the end of a city-fortune."

"I hope yours will make a better termination, Master Heriot," said the Lord Nigel.

"I hope it will, my lord," said the old man, with a smile; "but," to use honest John Bunyan's phrase—'therewithal the water stood in his eyes,' "it has pleased God to try me with the loss of two children; and for one adopted shild who lives—Ah! woe is me! and well-a-day!—But I am patient and thankful; and for the wealth God has sent me, it shall not want inheritors while there are orphan lads in Auld Reekie.—I wish you good-morrow, my lord."

"One orphan has cause to thank you already," said Nigel, as he attended him to the door of his chamber, where, resisting further escort, the old citizen made his escape.

As, in going downstairs, he passed the shop where Dame Christie stood becking, he made civil inquiries after her husband. The dame of course regretted his absence; but he was down, she said, at Deptford, to settle with a Dutch ship-master.

"Our way of business, sir," she said, "takes him much from home, and my husband must be the slave of every tarry jacket that wants but a pound of oakum."

"All business must be minded, dame," said the goldsmith. "Make my remembrances—George Heriot, of Lombard Street's remembrances—

to your goodman. I have dealt with him—he is just and punctual—true to time and engagements;—be kind to your noble guest, and see he wants nothing. Though it be his pleasure at present to lie private and retired, there be those that care for him, and I have a charge to see him supplied; so that you may let me know by your husband, my good dame, how my lord is, and whether he wants aught."

"And so he *is* a real lord after all?" said the good dame. "I am sure I always thought he looked like one. But why does he not go to Parliament, then?"

"He will, dame," answered Heriot, "to the Parliament of Scotland, which is his own country."

"Oh! he is but a Scots lord, then," said the good dame; "and that's the thing makes him ashamed to take the title, as they say."

"Let him not hear *you* say so, dame," replied the citizen.

"Who, I, sir?" answered she; "no such matter in my thought, sir. Scot or English, he is at any rate a likely man, and a civil man; and rather than he should want any thing, I would wait upon him myself, and come as far as Lombard Street to wait upon your worship too."

"Let your husband come to me, good dame," said the goldsmith, who, with all his experience and worth, was somewhat of a formalist and disciplinarian. "The proverb says, 'House goes mad when women gad;' and let his lordship's own man wait upon his master in his chamber—it is more seemly. God give ye good-morrow."

"Good-morrow to your worship," said the dame, somewhat coldly; and, so soon as the adviser was out of hearing, was ungracious enough to mutter, in contempt of his council, "Marry quep of your advice, for an old Scotch tinsmith, as you are! My husband is as wise, and very near as old, as yourself; and if I please him, it is well enough; and though he is not just so rich just now as some folks, yet I hope to see him ride upon his moyle, with a foot-cloth, and have his two blue-coats after him, as well as they do."

V

Wherefore come ye not to court? Certain 'tis the rarest sport; There are silks and jewels glistening, Prattling fools and wise men listening, Bullies among brave men justling, Beggars amongst nobles bustling; Low-breath'd talkers, minion lispers, Cutting honest throats by whispers; Wherefore come ye not to court? Skelton swears 'tis glorious sport.

—Skelton Skeltonizeth

It was not entirely out of parade that the benevolent citizen was mounted and attended in that manner, which, as the reader has been informed, excited a gentle degree of spleen on the part of Dame Christie, which, to do her justice, vanished in the little soliloquy which we have recorded. The good man, besides the natural desire to maintain the exterior of a man of worship, was at present bound to Whitehall in order to exhibit a piece of valuable workmanship to King James, which he deemed his Majesty might be pleased to view, or even to purchase. He himself was therefore mounted upon his caparisoned mule, that he might the better make his way through the narrow, dirty, and crowded streets; and while one of his attendants carried under his arm the piece of plate, wrapped up in red baize, the other two gave an eye to its safety; for such was then the state of the police of the metropolis, that men were often assaulted in the public street for the sake of revenge or of plunder; and those who apprehended being beset, usually endeavoured, if their estate admitted such expense, to secure themselves by the attendance of armed followers. And this custom, which was at first limited to the nobility and gentry, extended by degrees to those citizens of consideration, who, being understood to travel with a charge, as it was called, might otherwise have been selected as safe subjects of plunder by the street-robber.

As Master George Heriot paced forth westward with this gallant attendance, he paused at the shop door of his countryman and friend, the ancient horologer, and having caused Tunstall, who was in attendance, to adjust his watch by the real time, he desired to speak with his master; in consequence of which summons, the old Time-meter came forth from his den, his face like a bronze bust, darkened with dust, and glistening here and there with copper filings, and his senses so bemused in the intensity of calculation, that he gazed on his friend the goldsmith for a minute before he seemed perfectly to comprehend who he was, and heard him express his invitation to David Ramsay, and pretty Mistress Margaret, his daughter, to dine with him next day at noon, to meet with a noble young countrymen, without returning any answer.

"I'll make thee speak, with a murrain to thee," muttered Heriot to himself; and suddenly changing his tone, he said aloud,—"I pray you, neighbour David, when are you and I to have a settlement for the bullion wherewith I supplied you to mount yonder hall-clock at Theobald's, and that other whirligig that you made for the Duke of Buckingham? I have had the Spanish house to satisfy for the ingots, and I must needs put you in mind that you have been eight months behind-hand."

There is something so sharp and *aigre* in the demand of a peremptory dun, that no human tympanum, however inaccessible to other tones, can resist the application. David Ramsay started at once from his reverie, and answered in a pettish tone, "Wow, George, man, what needs aw this din about sax score o' pounds? Aw the world kens I can answer aw claims on me, and you proffered yourself fair time, till his maist gracious Majesty and the noble Duke suld make settled accompts wi' me; and ye may ken, by your ain experience, that I canna gang rowting like an unmannered Highland stot to their doors, as ye come to mine."

Heriot laughed, and replied, "Well, David, I see a demand of money is like a bucket of water about your ears, and makes you a man of the world at once. And now, friend, will you tell me, like a Christian man, if you will dine with me to-morrow at noon, and bring pretty Mistress Margaret, my god-daughter, with you, to meet with our noble young countryman, the Lord of Glenvarloch?"

"The young Lord of Glenvarloch!" said the old mechanist; "wi' aw my heart, and blithe I will be to see him again. We have not met these forty years—he was twa years before me at the humanity classes—he is a sweet youth."

"That was his father—his father—his father!—you old dotard Dot-and-carry-one that you are," answered the goldsmith. "A sweet youth he would have been by this time, had he lived, worthy nobleman! This is his son, the Lord Nigel."

"His son!" said Ramsay; "maybe he will want something of a chronometer, or watch—few gallants care to be without them now-a-days."

"He may buy half your stock-in-trade, if ever he comes to his own, for what I know," said his friend; "but, David, remember your bond, and use me not as you did when my housewife had the sheep's-head and the cock-a-leeky boiling for you as late as two of the clock afternoon."

"She had the more credit by her cookery," answered David, now fully awake; "a sheep's-head over-boiled, were poison, according to our saying."

"Well," answered Master George, "but as there will be no sheep's-head to-morrow, it may chance you to spoil a dinner which a proverb cannot mend. It may be you may forgather with your friend, Sir Mungo Malagrowther, for I purpose to ask his worship; so, be sure and bide tryste, Davie."

"That will I—I will be true as a chronometer," said Ramsay.

"I will not trust you, though," replied Heriot.—"Hear you, Jenkin boy, tell Scots Janet to tell pretty Mistress Margaret, my god-child, she must put her father in remembrance to put on his best doublet to-morrow, and to bring him to Lombard Street at noon. Tell her they are to meet a brave young Scots lord."

Jenkin coughed that sort of dry short cough uttered by those who are either charged with errands which they do not like, or hear opinions to which they must not enter a dissent.

"Umph!" repeated Master George—who, as we have already noticed, was something of a martinet in domestic discipline—"what does *umph* mean? Will you do mine errand or not, sirrah?"

"Sure, Master George Heriot," said the apprentice, touching his cap, "I only meant, that Mistress Margaret was not likely to forget such an invitation."

"Why, no," said Master George; "she is a dutiful girl to her god-father, though I sometimes call her a jill-flirt.—And, hark ye, Jenkin, you and your comrade had best come with your clubs, to see your master and her safely home; but first shut shop, and loose the bull-dog, and let the porter stay in the fore-shop till your return. I will send two of my knaves with you; for I hear these wild youngsters of the Temple are broken out worse and lighter than ever."

"We can keep their steel in order with good handbats," said Jenkin; "and never trouble your servants for the matter."

"Or, if need be," said Tunstall, "we have swords as well as the Templars."

"Fie upon it—fie upon it, young man," said the citizen;—"An apprentice with a sword!—Marry, heaven forefend! I would as soon see him in a hat and feather."

"Well, sir," said Jenkin—"we will find arms fitting to our station, and will defend our master and his daughter, if we should tear up the very stones of the pavement."

"There spoke a London 'prentice bold," said the citizen; "and, for your comfort, my lads, you shall crush a cup of wine to the health of the Fathers of the City. I have my eye on both of you—you are thriving lads, each in his own way.—God be wi' you, Davie. Forget not to-morrow at noon." And, so saying, he again turned his mule's head westward, and crossed Temple Bar, at that slow and decent amble, which at once became his rank and civic importance, and put his pedestrian followers to no inconvenience to keep up with him.

At the Temple gate he again paused, dismounted, and sought his way into one of the small booths occupied by scriveners in the neighbourhood. A young man, with lank smooth hair combed straight to his ears, and then cropped short, rose, with a cringing reverence, pulled off a slouched hat, which he would upon no signal replace on his head, and answered with much demonstration of reverence, to the goldsmith's question of, "How goes business, Andrew?"—"Aw the better for your worship's kind countenance and maintenance."

"Get a large sheet of paper, man, and make a new pen, with a sharp neb, and fine hair-stroke. Do not slit the quill up too high, it's a wastrife course in your trade, Andrew—they that do not mind corn-pickles, never come to forpits. I have known a learned man write a thousand pages with one quill."*

---

* A biblical commentary by Gill, which (if the author's memory serves him) occupies between five and six hundred printed quarto pages, and must therefore have filled more pages of manuscript than the number mentioned in the text, has this quatrain at the end of the volume—

> *"With one good pen I wrote this book,*
> *Made of a grey goose quill;*
> *A pen it was when it I took,*
> *And a pen I leave it still."*

"Ah! sir," said the lad, who listened to the goldsmith, though instructing him in his own trade, with an air of veneration and acquiescence, "how sune ony puir creature like mysell may rise in the world, wi' the instruction of such a man as your worship!"

"My instructions are few, Andrew, soon told, and not hard to practise. Be honest—be industrious—be frugal—and you will soon win wealth and worship.—Here, copy me this Supplication in your best and most formal hand. I will wait by you till it is done."

The youth lifted not his eye from the paper, and laid not the pen from his hand, until the task was finished to his employer's satisfaction. The citizen then gave the young scrivener an angel; and bidding him, on his life, be secret in all business intrusted to him, again mounted his mule, and rode on westward along the Strand.

It may be worth while to remind our readers, that the Temple Bar which Heriot passed, was not the arched screen, or gateway, of the present day; but an open railing, or palisade, which, at night, and in times of alarm, was closed with a barricade of posts and chains. The Strand also, along which he rode, was not, as now, a continued street, although it was beginning already to assume that character. It still might be considered as an open road, along the south side of which stood various houses and hotels belonging to the nobility, having gardens behind them down to the water-side, with stairs to the river, for the convenience of taking boat; which mansions have bequeathed the names of their lordly owners to many of the streets leading from the Strand to the Thames. The north side of the Strand was also a long line of houses, behind which, as in Saint Martin's Lane, and other points, buildings, were rapidly arising; but Covent Garden was still a garden, in the literal sense of the word, or at least but beginning to be studded with irregular buildings. All that was passing around, however, marked the rapid increase of a capital which had long enjoyed peace, wealth, and a regular government. Houses were rising in every direction; and the shrewd eye of our citizen already saw the period not distant, which should convert the nearly open highway on which he travelled, into a connected and regular street, uniting the Court and the town with the city of London.

He next passed Charing Cross, which was no longer the pleasant solitary village at which the judges were wont to breakfast on their way to Westminster Hall, but began to resemble the artery through which, to use Johnson's expression "pours the full tide of London population."

The buildings were rapidly increasing, yet certainly gave not even a faint idea of its present appearance.

At last Whitehall received our traveller, who passed under one of the beautiful gates designed by Holbein, and composed of tesselated brick-work, being the same to which Moniplies had profanely likened the West-Port of Edinburgh, and entered the ample precincts of the palace of Whitehall, now full of all the confusion attending improvement. It was just at the time when James,—little suspecting that he was employed in constructing a palace, from the window of which his only son was to pass in order that he might die upon a scaffold before it,—was busied in removing the ancient and ruinous buildings of De Burgh, Henry VIII, and Queen Elizabeth, to make way for the superb architecture on which Inigo Jones exerted all his genius. The king, ignorant of futurity, was now engaged in pressing on his work; and, for that purpose, still maintained his royal apartments at Whitehall, amidst the rubbish of old buildings, and the various confusion attending the erection of the new pile, which formed at present a labyrinth not easily traversed.

The goldsmith to the Royal Household, and who, if fame spoke true, oftentimes acted as their banker,—for these professions were not as yet separated from each other,—was a person of too much importance to receive the slightest interruption from sentinel or porter; and, leaving his mule and two of his followers in the outer-court, he gently knocked at a postern-gate of the building, and was presently admitted, while the most trusty of his attendants followed him closely, with the piece of plate under his arm. This man also he left behind him in an ante-room,—where three or four pages in the royal livery, but untrussed, unbuttoned, and dressed more carelessly than the place, and nearness to a king's person, seemed to admit, were playing at dice and draughts, or stretched upon benches, and slumbering with half-shut eyes. A corresponding gallery, which opened from the ante-room, was occupied by two gentlemen-ushers of the chamber, who gave each a smile of recognition as the wealthy goldsmith entered.

No word was spoken on either side; but one of the ushers looked first to Heriot, and then to a little door half-covered by the tapestry, which seemed to say, as plain as a look could, "Lies your business that way?" The citizen nodded; and the court-attendant, moving on tiptoe, and with as much caution as if the floor had been paved with eggs, advanced to the door, opened it gently, and spoke a few words in a low tone. The broad Scottish accent of King James was heard in reply,—"Admit him instanter, Maxwell. Have you hairboured sae lang at the Court, and not learned, that gold and silver are ever welcome?"

The usher signed to Heriot to advance, and the honest citizen was presently introduced into the cabinet of the Sovereign.

The scene of confusion amid which he found the king seated, was no bad picture of the state and quality of James's own mind. There was much that was rich and costly in cabinet pictures and valuable ornaments; but they were arranged in a slovenly manner, covered with dust, and lost half their value, or at least their effect, from the manner in which they were presented to the eye. The table was loaded with huge folios, amongst which lay light books of jest and ribaldry; and, amongst notes of unmercifully long orations, and essays on king-craft, were mingled miserable roundels and ballads by the Royal 'Prentice, as he styled himself, in the art of poetry, and schemes for the general pacification of Europe, with a list of the names of the king's hounds, and remedies against canine madness.

The king's dress was of green velvet, quilted so full as to be dagger-proof—which gave him the appearance of clumsy and ungainly protuberance; while its being buttoned awry, communicated to his figure an air of distortion. Over his green doublet he wore a sad-coloured nightgown, out of the pocket of which peeped his hunting-horn. His high-crowned grey hat lay on the floor, covered with dust, but encircled by a carcanet of large balas rubies; and he wore a blue velvet nightcap, in the front of which was placed the plume of a heron, which had been struck down by a favourite hawk in some critical moment of the flight, in remembrance of which the king wore this highly honoured feather.

But such inconsistencies in dress and appointments were mere outward types of those which existed in the royal character, rendering it a subject of doubt amongst his contemporaries, and bequeathing it as a problem to future historians. He was deeply learned, without possessing useful knowledge; sagacious in many individual cases, without having real wisdom; fond of his power, and desirous to maintain and augment it, yet willing to resign the direction of that, and of himself, to the most unworthy favourites; a big and bold asserter of his rights in words, yet one who tamely saw them trampled on in deeds; a lover of negotiations, in which he was always outwitted; and one who feared war, where conquest might have been easy. He was fond of his dignity, while he was perpetually degrading it by undue familiarity; capable of much public labour, yet often neglecting it for the meanest amusement; a wit, though a pedant; and a scholar, though fond of the conversation of the ignorant and uneducated. Even his timidity of temper was not uniform; and there were moments of his life, and those critical, in which he showed the spirit of his ancestors. He was laborious in trifles, and a trifler where serious labour was required; devout in his sentiments, and yet too often profane in his language; just and beneficent by nature, he yet gave way to the iniquities and oppression of others. He was penurious respecting money which he had to give from his own hand, yet inconsiderately and unboundedly profuse of that which he did not see. In a word, those good qualities which displayed themselves in particular cases and occasions, were not of a nature sufficiently firm and comprehensive to regulate his general conduct; and, showing themselves as they occasionally did, only entitled James to the character bestowed on him by Sully—that he was the wisest fool in Christendom.

That the fortunes of this monarch might be as little of apiece as his character, he, certainly the least able of the Stewarts, succeeded peaceably to that kingdom, against the power of which his predecessors had, with so much difficulty, defended his native throne; and, lastly, although his reign appeared calculated to ensure to Great Britain that lasting tranquillity and internal peace which so much suited the king's disposition, yet, during that very reign, were sown those seeds of dissension, which, like the teeth of the fabulous dragon, had their harvest in a bloody and universal civil war.

Such was the monarch, who, saluting Heriot by the name of Jingling Geordie, (for it was his well-known custom to give nicknames to all those with whom he was on terms of familiarity,) inquired what new clatter-traps he had brought with him, to cheat his lawful and native Prince out of his siller.

"God forbid, my liege," said the citizen, "that I should have any such disloyal purpose. I did but bring a piece of plate to show to your most gracious Majesty, which, both for the subject and for the workmanship, I were loath to put into the hands of any subject until I knew your Majesty's pleasure anent it."

"Body o' me, man, let's see it, Heriot; though, by my saul, Steenie's service o' plate was sae dear a bargain, I had 'maist pawned my word as a Royal King, to keep my ain gold and silver in future, and let you, Geordie, keep yours."

"Respecting the Duke of Buckingham's plate," said the goldsmith, "your Majesty was pleased to direct that no expense should be spared, and—"

"What signifies what I desired, man? when a wise man is with fules and bairns, he maun e'en play at the chucks. But you should have had mair sense and consideration than to gie Babie Charles and Steenie their ain gate; they wad hae floored the very rooms wi' silver, and I wonder they didna."

George Heriot bowed, and said no more. He knew his master too well to vindicate himself otherwise than by a distant allusion to his order; and James, with whom economy was only a transient and momentary twinge of conscience, became immediately afterwards desirous to see the piece of plate which the goldsmith proposed to exhibit, and dispatched Maxwell to bring it to his presence. In the meantime he demanded of the citizen whence he had procured it.

"From Italy, may it please your Majesty," replied Heriot.

"It has naething in it tending to papistrie?" said the king, looking graver than his wont.

"Surely not, please your Majesty," said Heriot; "I were not wise to bring any thing to your presence that had the mark of the beast."

"You would be the mair beast yourself to do so," said the king; "it is weel kend that I wrestled wi' Dagon in my youth, and smote him on the groundsill of his own temple; a gude evidence that I should be in time called, however unworthy, the Defender of the Faith.—But here comes Maxwell, bending under his burden, like the Golden Ass of Apuleius."

Heriot hastened to relieve the usher, and to place the embossed salver, for such it was, and of extraordinary dimensions, in a light favourable for his Majesty's viewing the sculpture.

"Saul of my body, man," said the king, "it is a curious piece, and, as I think, fit for a king's chalmer; and the subject, as you say, Master George, vera adequate and beseeming—being, as I see, the judgment of Solomon—a prince in whose paths it weel becomes a' leeving monarchs to walk with emulation."

"But whose footsteps," said Maxwell, "only one of them—if a subject may say so much—hath ever overtaken."

"Haud your tongue for a fause fleeching loon!" said the king, but with a smile on his face that showed the flattery had done its part. "Look at the bonny piece of workmanship, and haud your clavering tongue.— And whase handiwork may it be, Geordie?"

"It was wrought, sir," replied the goldsmith, "by the famous Florentine, Benvenuto Cellini, and designed for Francis the First of France; but I hope it will find a fitter master."

"Francis of France!" said the king; "send Solomon, King of the Jews, to Francis of France!—Body of me, man, it would have kythed Cellini mad, had he never done ony thing else out of the gate. Francis!—why, he was a fighting fule, man,—a mere fighting fule,—got himsell ta'en at Pavia, like our ain David at Durham lang syne;—if they could hae sent him Solomon's wit, and love of peace, and godliness, they wad hae dune him a better turn. But Solomon should sit in other gate company than Francis of France."

"I trust that such will be his good fortune," said Heriot.

"It is a curious and very artificial sculpture," said the king, in continuation; "but yet, methinks, the carnifex, or executioner there, is brandishing his gully ower near the king's face, seeing he is within reach of his weapon. I think less wisdom than Solomon's wad have taught him that there was danger in edge-tools, and that he wad have bidden the smaik either sheath his shabble, or stand farther back."

George Heriot endeavoured to alleviate this objection, by assuring the king that the vicinity betwixt Solomon and the executioner was nearer in appearance than in reality, and that the perspective should be allowed for.

"Gang to the deil wi' your prospective, man," said the king; "there canna be a waur prospective for a lawful king, wha wishes to reign in luve, and die in peace and honour, than to have naked swords flashing in his een. I am accounted as brave as maist folks; and yet I profess to ye I could never look on a bare blade without blinking and winking. But a'thegither it is a brave piece;—and what is the price of it, man?"

The goldsmith replied by observing, that it was not his own property, but that of a distressed countryman.

"Whilk you mean to mak your excuse for asking the double of its worth, I warrant?" answered the king. "I ken the tricks of you burrows-town merchants, man."

"I have no hopes of baffling your Majesty's sagacity," said Heriot; "the piece is really what I say, and the price a hundred and fifty pounds sterling, if it pleases your Majesty to make present payment."

"A hundred and fifty punds, man! and as mony witches and warlocks to raise them!" said the irritated Monarch. "My saul, Jingling Geordie, ye are minded that your purse shall jingle to a bonny tune!—How am I to tell you down a hundred and fifty punds for what will not weigh as many merks? and ye ken that my very household servitors, and the officers of my mouth, are sax months in arrear!"

The goldsmith stood his ground against all this objurgation, being what he was well accustomed to, and only answered, that, if his Majesty liked the piece, and desired to possess it, the price could be easily settled. It was true that the party required the money, but he, George Heriot, would advance it on his Majesty's account, if such were his pleasure, and wait his royal conveniency for payment, for that and other matters; the money, meanwhile, lying at the ordinary usage.

"By my honour," said James, "and that is speaking like an honest and reasonable tradesman. We maun get another subsidy frae the Commons, and that will make ae compting of it. Awa wi' it, Maxwell—awa wi' it, and let it be set where Steenie and Babie Charles shall see it as they return from Richmond.—And now that we are secret, my good auld friend Geordie, I do truly opine, that speaking of Solomon and ourselves, the haill wisdom in the country left Scotland, when we took our travels to the Southland here."

George Heriot was courtier enough to say, that "the wise naturally follow the wisest, as stags follow their leader."

"Troth, I think there is something in what thou sayest," said James; "for we ourselves, and those of our Court and household, as thou thyself, for example, are allowed by the English, for as self-opinioned as they are, to pass for reasonable good wits; but the brains of those we have left behind are all astir, and run clean hirdie-girdie, like sae mony warlocks and witches on the Devil's Sabbath e'en."

"I am sorry to hear this, my liege," said Heriot. "May it please your Grace to say what our countrymen have done to deserve such a character?"

"They are become frantic, man—clean brain-crazed," answered the king. "I cannot keep them out of the Court by all the proclamations that the heralds roar themselves hoarse with. Yesterday, nae farther gane, just as we were mounted, and about to ride forth, in rushed a thorough Edinburgh gutterblood—a ragged rascal, every dud upon whose back was bidding good-day to the other, with a coat and hat that would have served a pease-bogle, and without havings or reverence, thrusts into our hands, like a sturdy beggar, some Supplication about debts owing by our gracious mother, and siclike trash; whereat the horse spangs on end, and, but for our admirable sitting, wherein we have been thought to excel maist sovereign princes, as well as subjects, in Europe, I promise you we would have been laid endlang on the causeway."

"Your Majesty," said Heriot, "is their common father, and therefore they are the bolder to press into your gracious presence."

"I ken I am *pater patriae* well enough," said James; "but one would think they had a mind to squeeze my puddings out, that they may divide the inheritance, Ud's death, Geordie, there is not a loon among them can deliver a Supplication, as it suld be done in the face of majesty."

"I would I knew the most fitting and beseeming mode to do so," said Heriot, "were it but to instruct our poor countrymen in better fashions."

"By my halidome," said the king, "ye are a ceevileezed fellow, Geordie, and I carena if I fling awa as much time as may teach ye. And, first, see you, sir—ye shall approach the presence of majesty thus,—shadowing your eyes with your hand, to testify that you are in the presence of the Vice-gerent of Heaven.—Vera weel, George, that is done in a comely manner.—Then, sir, ye sail kneel, and make as if ye would kiss the hem of our garment, the latch of our shoe, or such like.—Very weel enacted—whilk we, as being willing to be debonair and pleasing towards our lieges, prevent thus,—and motion to you to rise;—whilk, having a boon to ask, as yet you obey not, but, gliding your hand into your pouch, bring forth your Supplication, and place it reverentially in our open palm." The goldsmith, who had complied with great accuracy with all the prescribed points of the ceremonial, here completed it, to James's no small astonishment, by placing in his hand the petition of the Lord of Glenvarloch. "What means this, ye fause loon?" said he, reddening and sputtering; "hae I been teaching you the manual exercise, that ye suld present your piece at our ain royal body?—Now, by this light, I had as lief that ye had bended a real pistolet against me, and yet this hae ye done in my very cabinet, where nought suld enter but at my ain pleasure."

"I trust your Majesty," said Heriot, as he continued to kneel, "will forgive my exercising the lesson you condescended to give me in the behalf of a friend?"

"Of a friend!" said the king; "so much the waur—so much the waur, I tell you. If it had been something to do *yoursell* good there would have been some sense in it, and some chance that you wad not have come back on me in a hurry; but a man may have a hundred friends, and petitions for every ane of them, ilk ane after other."

"Your Majesty, I trust," said Heriot, "will judge me by former experience, and will not suspect me of such presumption."

"I kenna," said the placable monarch; "the world goes daft, I think— *sed semel insanivimus omnes*—thou art my old and faithful servant, that is the truth; and, were't any thing for thy own behoof, man, thou shouldst not ask twice. But, troth, Steenie loves me so dearly, that he cares not that any one should ask favours of me but himself.—Maxwell," (for the usher had re-entered after having carried off the plate,) "get into the ante-chamber wi' your lang lugs.—In conscience, Geordie, I think as that thou hast been mine ain auld fiduciary, and wert my goldsmith when I might say with the Ethnic poet—*Non mea renidet in domo lacunar*—for, faith, they had pillaged my mither's auld house sae, that beechen bickers, and treen trenchers, and latten platters, were whiles the best at our board, and glad we were of something to put on them, without quarrelling with the metal of the dishes. D'ye mind, for thou wert in maist of our complots, how we were fain to send sax of the Blue-banders to harry the Lady of Loganhouse's dowcot and poultry-yard, and what an awfu' plaint the poor dame made against Jock of Milch, and the thieves of Annandale, wha were as sackless of the deed as I am of the sin of murder?"

"It was the better for Jock," said Heriot; "for, if I remember weel, it saved him from a strapping up at Dumfries, which he had weel deserved for other misdeeds."

"Ay, man, mind ye that?" said the king; "but he had other virtues, for he was a tight huntsman, moreover, that Jock of Milch, and could hollow to a hound till all the woods rang again. But he came to an Annandale end at the last, for Lord Torthorwald run his lance out through him.—Cocksnails, man, when I think of those wild passages, in my conscience, I am not sure but we lived merrier in auld Holyrood in those shifting days, than now when we are dwelling at heck and manger. *Cantabit vacuus*—we had but little to care for."

"And if your Majesty please to remember," said the goldsmith, "the awful task we had to gather silver-vessail and gold-work enough to make some show before the Spanish Ambassador."

"Vera true," said the king, now in a full tide of gossip, "and I mind not the name of the right leal lord that helped us with every unce he had in his house, that his native Prince might have some credit in the eyes of them that had the Indies at their beck."

"I think, if your Majesty," said the citizen, "will cast your eye on the paper in your hand, you will recollect his name."

"Ay!" said the king, "say ye sae, man?—Lord Glenvarloch, that was his name indeed—*Justus et tenax propositi*—A just man, but as obstinate as a baited bull. He stood whiles against us, that Lord Randal Olifaunt of Glenvarloch, but he was a loving and a leal subject in the main. But this supplicator maun be his son—Randal has been long gone where king and lord must go, Geordie, as weel as the like of you—and what does his son want with us?"

"The settlement," answered the citizen, "of a large debt due by your Majesty's treasury, for money advanced to your Majesty in great State emergency, about the time of the Raid of Ruthven."

"I mind the thing weel," said King James—"Od's death, man, I was just out of the clutches of the Master of Glamis and his complices, and there was never siller mair welcome to a born prince,—the mair the shame and pity that crowned king should need sic a petty sum. But what need he dun us for it, man, like a baxter at the breaking? We aught him the siller, and will pay him wi' our convenience, or make it otherwise up to him, whilk is enow between prince and subject—We are not *in meditatione fugae*, man, to be arrested thus peremptorily."

"Alas! an it please your Majesty," said the goldsmith, shaking his head, "it is the poor young nobleman's extreme necessity, and not his will, that makes him importunate; for he must have money, and that briefly, to discharge a debt due to Peregrine Peterson, Conservator of the Privileges at Campvere, or his haill hereditary barony and estate of Glenvarloch will be evicted in virtue of an unredeemed wadset."

"How say ye, man—how say ye?" exclaimed the king, impatiently; "the carle of a Conservator, the son of a Low-Dutch skipper, evict the auld estate and lordship of the house of Olifaunt?—God's bread, man, that maun not be—we maun suspend the diligence by writ of favour, or otherwise."

"I doubt that may hardly be," answered the citizen, "if it please your Majesty; your learned counsel in the law of Scotland advise, that there is no remeid but in paying the money."

"Ud's fish," said the king, "let him keep haud by the strong hand against the carle, until we can take some order about his affairs."

"Alas!" insisted the goldsmith, "if it like your Majesty, your own pacific government, and your doing of equal justice to all men, has made main force a kittle line to walk by, unless just within the bounds of the Highlands."

"Well—weel—weel, man," said the perplexed monarch, whose ideas of justice, expedience, and convenience, became on such occasions strangely embroiled; "just it is we should pay our debts, that the young man may pay his; and he must be paid, and *in verbo regis* he shall be paid—but how to come by the siller, man, is a difficult chapter—ye maun try the city, Geordie."

"To say the truth," answered Heriot, "please your gracious Majesty, what betwixt loans and benevolences, and subsidies, the city is at this present—"

"Donna tell me of what the city is," said King James; "our Exchequer is as dry as Dean Giles's discourses on the penitentiary psalms—*Ex nihilo nihil fit*—It's ill taking the breeks aff a wild Highlandman—they that come to me for siller, should tell me how to come by it—the city ye maun try, Heriot; and donna think to be called Jingling Geordie for nothing—and *in verbo regis* I will pay the lad if you get me the loan—I wonnot haggle on the terms; and, between you and me, Geordie, we will redeem the brave auld estate of Glenvarloch.—But wherefore comes not the young lord to Court, Heriot—is he comely—is he presentable in the presence?"

"No one can be more so," said George Heriot; "but—"

"Ay, I understand ye," said his Majesty—"I understand ye—*Res angusta domi*—puir lad-puir lad!—and his father a right true leal Scots heart, though stiff in some opinions. Hark ye, Heriot, let the lad have twa hundred pounds to fit him out. And, here—here"—(taking the carcanet of rubies from his old hat)—"ye have had these in pledge before for a larger sum, ye auld Levite that ye are. Keep them in gage, till I gie ye back the siller out of the next subsidy."

"If it please your Majesty to give me such directions in writing," said the cautious citizen.

"The deil is in your nicety, George," said the king; "ye are as preceese as a Puritan in form, and a mere Nullifidian in the marrow of the matter. May not a king's word serve ye for advancing your pitiful twa hundred pounds?"

"But not for detaining the crown jewels," said George Heriot.

And the king, who from long experience was inured to dealing with suspicious creditors, wrote an order upon George Heriot, his well-beloved goldsmith and jeweller, for the sum of two hundred pounds, to be paid presently to Nigel Olifaunt, Lord of Glenvarloch, to be imputed as so much debts due to him by the crown; and authorizing the retention of a carcanet of balas rubies, with a great diamond, as described in a Catalogue of his Majesty's Jewels, to remain in possession of the said George Heriot, advancer of the said sum, and so forth, until he was lawfully contented and paid thereof. By another rescript, his Majesty gave the said George Heriot directions to deal with some of the monied men, upon equitable terms, for a sum of money for his

Majesty's present use, not to be under 50,000 merks, but as much more as could conveniently be procured.

"And has he ony lair, this Lord Nigel of ours?" said the king.

George Heriot could not exactly answer this question; but believed "the young lord had studied abroad."

"He shall have our own advice," said the king, "how to carry on his studies to maist advantage; and it may be we will have him come to Court, and study with Steenie and Babie Charles. And, now we think on't, away—away, George—for the bairns will be coming hame presently, and we would not as yet they kend of this matter we have been treating anent. *Propera fedem*, O Geordie. Clap your mule between your boughs, and god-den with you."

Thus ended the conference betwixt the gentle King Jamie and his benevolent jeweller and goldsmith.

VI

O I do know him—tis the mouldy lemon
Which our court wits will wet their lips withal,
When they would sauce their honied conversation
With somewhat sharper flavour—Marry sir,
That virtue's wellnigh left him—all the juice
That was so sharp and poignant, is squeezed out,
While the poor rind, although as sour as ever,
Must season soon the draff we give our grunters,
For two legg'd things are weary on't.

—The Chamberlain—A Comedy

The good company invited by the hospitable citizen assembled at his house in Lombard Street at the "hollow and hungry hour" of noon, to partake of that meal which divides the day, being about the time when modern persons of fashion, turning themselves upon their pillow, begin to think, not without a great many doubts and much hesitation, that they will by and by commence it. Thither came the young Nigel, arrayed plainly, but in a dress, nevertheless, more suitable to his age and quality than he had formerly worn, accompanied by his servant Moniplies, whose outside also was considerably improved. His solemn and stern features glared forth from under a blue velvet bonnet, fantastically placed sideways on his head—he had a sound and tough coat of English blue broad-cloth, which, unlike his former vestment, would have stood the tug of all the apprentices in Fleet Street. The buckler and broadsword he wore as the arms of his condition, and a neat silver badge, bearing his lord's arms, announced that he was an appendage of aristocracy. He sat down in the good citizen's buttery, not a little pleased to find his attendance upon the table in the hall was likely to be rewarded with his share of a meal such as he had seldom partaken of.

Mr. David Ramsay, that profound and ingenious mechanic, was safely conducted to Lombard Street, according to promise, well washed, brushed, and cleaned, from the soot of the furnace and the forge. His daughter, who came with him, was about twenty years old, very pretty, very demure, yet with lively black eyes, that ever and anon contradicted the expression of sobriety, to which silence, reserve, a plain velvet hood, and a cambric ruff, had condemned Mistress Marget, as the daughter of a quiet citizen.

There were also two citizens and merchants of London, men ample in cloak, and many-linked golden chain, well to pass in the world, and experienced in their craft of merchandise, but who require no particular description. There was an elderly clergyman also, in his gown and cassock, a decent venerable man, partaking in his manners of the plainness of the citizens amongst whom he had his cure.

These may be dismissed with brief notice; but not so Sir Mungo Malagrowther, of Girnigo Castle, who claims a little more attention, as an original character of the time in which he flourished.

That good knight knocked at Master Heriot's door just as the clock began to strike twelve, and was seated in his chair ere the last stroke had chimed. This gave the knight an excellent opportunity of making sarcastic observations on all who came later than himself, not to mention a few rubs at the expense of those who had been so superfluous as to appear earlier.

Having little or no property save his bare designation, Sir Mungo had been early attached to Court in the capacity of whipping-boy, as the office was then called, to King James the Sixth, and, with his Majesty, trained to all polite learning by his celebrated preceptor, George Buchanan. The office of whipping-boy doomed its unfortunate occupant to undergo all the corporeal punishment which the Lord's Anointed, whose proper person was of course sacred, might chance to incur, in the course of travelling through his grammar and prosody. Under the stern rule, indeed, of George Buchanan, who did not approve of the vicarious mode of punishment, James bore the penance of his own faults, and Mungo Malagrowther enjoyed a sinecure; but James's other pedagogue, Master Patrick Young, went more ceremoniously to work, and appalled the very soul of the youthful king by the floggings which he bestowed on the whipping-boy, when the royal task was not suitably performed. And be it told to Sir Mungo's praise, that there were points about him in the highest respect suited to his official situation. He had even in youth a naturally irregular and grotesque set of features, which, when distorted by fear, pain, and anger, looked like one of the whimsical faces which present themselves in a Gothic cornice. His voice also was high-pitched and querulous, so that, when smarting under Master Peter Young's unsparing inflictions, the expression of his grotesque physiognomy, and the superhuman yells which he uttered, were well suited to produce all the effects on the Monarch who deserved the lash, that could possibly be produced by seeing another and an innocent individual suffering for his delict.

Sir Mungo Malagrowther, for such he became, thus got an early footing at Court, which another would have improved and maintained. But, when he grew too big to be whipped, he had no other means of rendering himself acceptable. A bitter, caustic, and backbiting humour, a malicious wit, and an envy of others more prosperous than the possessor of such amiable qualities, have not, indeed, always been found obstacles to a courtier's rise; but then they must be amalgamated with a degree of selfish cunning and prudence, of which Sir Mungo had no share. His satire ran riot, his envy could not conceal itself, and it was not long after his majority till he had as many quarrels upon his hands as would have required a cat's nine lives to answer. In one of these rencontres he received, perhaps we should say fortunately, a wound, which served him as an excuse for answering no invitations of the kind in future. Sir Rullion Rattray, of Ranagullion, cut off, in mortal combat, three of the fingers of his right hand, so that Sir Mungo never could hold sword again. At a later period, having written some satirical verses upon the Lady Cockpen, he received so severe a chastisement from some persons employed for the purpose, that he was found half dead on the spot where they had thus dealt with him, and one of his thighs having been broken, and ill set, gave him a hitch in his gait, with which he hobbled to his grave. The lameness of his leg and hand, besides that they added considerably to the grotesque appearance of this original, procured him in future a personal immunity from the more dangerous consequences of his own humour; and he gradually grew old in the service of the Court, in safety of life and limb, though without either making friends or attaining preferment. Sometimes, indeed, the king was amused with his caustic sallies, but he had never art enough to improve the favourable opportunity; and his enemies (who were, for that matter, the whole Court) always found means to throw him out of favour again. The celebrated Archie Armstrong offered Sir Mungo, in his generosity, a skirt of his own fool's coat, proposing thereby to communicate to him the privileges and immunities of a professed jester—"For," said the man of motley, "Sir Mungo, as he goes on just now, gets no more for a good jest than just the king's pardon for having made it."

Even in London, the golden shower which fell around him did

not moisten the blighted fortunes of Sir Mungo Malagrowther. He grew old, deaf, and peevish—lost even the spirit which had formerly animated his strictures—and was barely endured by James, who, though himself nearly as far stricken in years, retained, to an unusual and even an absurd degree, the desire to be surrounded by young people.

Sir Mungo, thus fallen into the yellow leaf of years and fortune, showed his emaciated form and faded embroidery at Court as seldom as his duty permitted; and spent his time in indulging his food for satire in the public walks, and in the aisles of Saint Paul's, which were then the general resort of newsmongers and characters of all descriptions, associating himself chiefly with such of his countrymen as he accounted of inferior birth and rank to himself. In this manner, hating and contemning commerce, and those who pursued it, he nevertheless lived a good deal among the Scottish artists and merchants, who had followed the Court to London. To these he could show his cynicism without much offence; for some submitted to his jeers and ill-humour in deference to his birth and knighthood, which in those days conferred high privileges—and others, of more sense, pitied and endured the old man, unhappy alike in his fortunes and his temper.

Amongst the latter was George Heriot, who, though his habits and education induced him to carry aristocratical feelings to a degree which would now be thought extravagant, had too much spirit and good sense to permit himself to be intruded upon to an unauthorized excess, or used with the slightest improper freedom, by such a person as Sir Mungo, to whom he was, nevertheless, not only respectfully civil, but essentially kind, and even generous.

Accordingly, this appeared from the manner in which Sir Mungo Malagrowther conducted himself upon entering the apartment. He paid his respects to Master Heriot, and a decent, elderly, somewhat severe-looking female, in a coif, who, by the name of Aunt Judith, did the honours of his house and table, with little or no portion of the supercilious acidity, which his singular physiognomy assumed when he made his bow successively to David Ramsay and the two sober citizens. He thrust himself into the conversation of the latter, to observe he had heard in Paul's, that the bankrupt concern of Pindivide, a great merchant,—who, as he expressed it, had given the crows a pudding, and on whom he knew, from the same authority, each of the honest citizens has some unsettled claim,—was like to prove a total loss—"stock and block, ship and cargo, keel and rigging, all lost, now and for ever."

The two citizens grinned at each other; but, too prudent to make their private affairs the subject of public discussion, drew their heads together, and evaded farther conversation by speaking in a whisper.

The old Scots knight next attacked the watchmaker with the same disrespectful familiarity.—"Davie," he said,—"Davie, ye donnard auld idiot, have ye no gane mad yet, with applying your mathematical science, as ye call it, to the book of Apocalypse? I expected to have heard ye make out the sign of the beast, as clear as a tout on a bawbee whistle."

"Why, Sir Mungo," said the mechanist, after making an effort to recall to his recollection what had been said to him, and by whom, "it may be, that ye are nearer the mark than ye are yoursell aware of; for, taking the ten horns o' the beast, ye may easily estimate by your digitals—"

"My digits! you d—d auld, rusty, good-for-nothing time-piece!" exclaimed Sir Mungo, while, betwixt jest and earnest, he laid on his hilt his hand, or rather his claw, (for Sir Rullion's broadsword has abridged it into that form,)—"D'ye mean to upbraid me with my mutilation?"

Master Heriot interfered. "I cannot persuade our friend David," he said, "that scriptural prophecies are intended to remain in obscurity, until their unexpected accomplishment shall make, as in former days, that fulfilled which was written. But you must not exert your knightly valour on him for all that."

"By my saul, and it would be throwing it away," said Sir Mungo, laughing. "I would as soon set out, with hound and horn, to hunt a sturdied sheep; for he is in a doze again, and up to the chin in numerals, quotients, and dividends.—Mistress Margaret, my pretty honey," for the beauty of the young citizen made even Sir Mungo Malagrowther's grim features relax themselves a little, "is your father always as entertaining as he seems just now?"

Mistress Margaret simpered, bridled, looked to either side, then straight before her; and, having assumed all the airs of bashful embarrassment and timidity which were necessary, as she thought, to cover a certain shrewd readiness which really belonged to her character, at length replied: "That indeed her father was very thoughtful, but she had heard that he took the habit of mind from her grandfather."

"Your grandfather!" said Sir Mungo,—after doubting if he had heard her aright,—"Said she her grandfather! The lassie is distraught!—I ken nae wench on this side of Temple Bar that is derived from so distant a relation."

"She has got a godfather, however, Sir Mungo," said George Heriot, again interfering; "and I hope you will allow him interest enough with you, to request you will not put his pretty godchild to so deep a blush."

"The better—the better," said Sir Mungo. "It is a credit to her, that, bred and born within the sound of Bow-bell, she can blush for any thing; and, by my saul, Master George," he continued, chucking the irritated and reluctant damsel under the chin, "she is bonny enough to make amends for her lack of ancestry—at least, in such a region as Cheapside, where, d'ye mind me, the kettle cannot call the porridge-pot—"

The damsel blushed, but not so angrily as before. Master George Heriot hastened to interrupt the conclusion of Sir Mungo's homely proverb, by introducing him personally to Lord Nigel.

Sir Mungo could not at first understand what his host said,—"Bread of Heaven, wha say ye, man?"

Upon the name of Nigel Olifaunt, Lord Glenvarloch, being again hollowed into his ear, he drew up, and, regarding his entertainer with some austerity, rebuked him for not making persons of quality acquainted with each other, that they might exchange courtesies before they mingled with other folks. He then made as handsome and courtly a congee to his new acquaintance as a man maimed in foot and hand could do; and, observing he had known my lord, his father, bid him welcome to London, and hoped he should see him at Court.

Nigel in an instant comprehended, as well from Sir Mungo's manner, as from a strict compression of their entertainer's lips, which intimated the suppression of a desire to laugh, that he was dealing with an original of no ordinary description, and accordingly, returned his courtesy with suitable punctiliousness. Sir Mungo, in the meanwhile, gazed on him with much earnestness; and, as the contemplation of natural advantages was as odious to him as that of wealth, or other adventitious benefits, he had no sooner completely perused the handsome form and good features of the young lord, than like one of the comforters of the man of Uz, he drew close up to him, to enlarge on the former grandeur of the Lords of Glenvarloch, and the regret with which he had heard, that their representative was not likely to possess the domains of his ancestry. Anon, he enlarged upon the beauties of the principal mansion of Glenvarloch—the commanding site of the old castle— the noble expanse of the lake, stocked with wildfowl for hawking— the commanding screen of forest, terminating in a mountain-ridge abounding with deer—and all the other advantages of that fine and ancient barony, till Nigel, in spite of every effort to the contrary, was unwillingly obliged to sigh.

Sir Mungo, skilful in discerning when the withers of those he conversed with were wrung, observed that his new acquaintance winced, and would willingly have pressed the discussion; but the cook's impatient knock upon the dresser with the haft of his dudgeon-knife, now gave a signal loud enough to be heard from the top of the house to the bottom, summoning, at the same time, the serving-men to place the dinner upon the table, and the guests to partake of it.

Sir Mungo, who was an admirer of good cheer,—a taste which, by the way, might have some weight in reconciling his dignity to these city visits,—was tolled off by the sound, and left Nigel and the other guests in peace, until his anxiety to arrange himself in his due place of pre-eminence at the genial board was duly gratified. Here, seated on the left hand of Aunt Judith, he beheld Nigel occupy the station of yet higher honour on the right, dividing that matron from pretty Mistress Margaret; but he saw this with the more patience, that there stood betwixt him and the young lord a superb larded capon.

The dinner proceeded according to the form of the times. All was excellent of the kind; and, besides the Scottish cheer promised, the board displayed beef and pudding, the statutory dainties of Old England. A small cupboard of plate, very choicely and beautifully wrought, did not escape the compliments of some of the company, and an oblique sneer from Sir Mungo, as intimating the owner's excellence in his own mechanical craft.

"I am not ashamed of the workmanship, Sir Mungo," said the honest citizen. "They say, a good cook knows how to lick his own fingers; and, methinks, it were unseemly that I, who have furnished half the cupboards in broad Britain, should have my own covered with paltry pewter."

The blessing of the clergyman now left the guests at liberty to attack what was placed before them; and the meal went forward with great decorum, until Aunt Judith, in farther recommendation of the capon, assured her company that it was of a celebrated breed of poultry, which she had herself brought from Scotland.

"Then, like some of his countrymen, madam," said the pitiless Sir Mungo, not without a glance towards his landlord, "he has been well larded in England."

"There are some others of his countrymen," answered Master Heriot, "to whom all the lard in England has not been able to render that good office."

Sir Mungo sneered and reddened, the rest of the company laughed; and the satirist, who had his reasons for not coming to extremity with Master George, was silent for the rest of the dinner.

The dishes were exchanged for confections, and wine of the highest quality and flavour; and Nigel saw the entertainments of the wealthiest burgomasters, which he had witnessed abroad, fairly outshone by the hospitality of a London citizen. Yet there was nothing ostentatious, or which seemed inconsistent with the degree of an opulent burgher.

While the collation proceeded, Nigel, according to the good-breeding of the time, addressed his discourse principally to Mrs. Judith, whom he found to be a woman of a strong Scottish understanding, more inclined towards the Puritans than was her brother George, (for in that relation she stood to him, though he always called her aunt,) attached to him in the strongest degree, and sedulously attentive to all his comforts. As the conversation of this good dame was neither lively nor fascinating, the young lord naturally addressed himself next to the old horologer's very pretty daughter, who sat upon his left hand. From her, however, there was no extracting any reply beyond the measure of a monosyllable; and when the young gallant had said the best and most complaisant things which his courtesy supplied, the smile that mantled upon her pretty mouth was so slight and evanescent, as scarce to be discernible.

Nigel was beginning to tire of his company, for the old citizens were speaking with his host of commercial matters in language to him totally unintelligible, when Sir Mungo Malagrowther suddenly summoned their attention.

That amiable personage had for some time withdrawn from the company into the recess of a projecting window, so formed and placed as to command a view of the door of the house, and of the street. This situation was probably preferred by Sir Mungo on account of the number of objects which the streets of a metropolis usually offer, of a kind congenial to the thoughts of a splenetic man. What he had hitherto seen passing there, was probably of little consequence; but now a trampling of horse was heard without, and the knight suddenly exclaimed,—"By my faith, Master George, you had better go look to shop; for here comes Knighton, the Duke of Buckingham's groom, and two fellows after him, as if he were my Lord Duke himself."

"My cash-keeper is below," said Heriot, without disturbing himself, "and he will let me know if his Grace's commands require my immediate attention."

"Umph!—cash-keeper?" muttered Sir Mungo to himself; "he would have had an easy office when I first kend ye.—But," said he, speaking aloud, "will you not come to the window, at least? for Knighton has trundled a piece of silver-plate into your house—ha! ha! ha!—trundled it upon its edge, as a callan' would drive a hoop. I cannot help laughing— ha! ha! ha!—at the fellow's impudence."

"I believe you could not help laughing," said George Heriot, rising up and leaving the room, "if your best friend lay dying."

"Bitter that, my lord—ha?" said Sir Mungo, addressing Nigel. "Our friend is not a goldsmith for nothing—he hath no leaden wit. But I will go down, and see what comes on't."

Heriot, as he descended the stairs, met his cash-keeper coming up, with some concern in his face.—"Why, how now, Roberts," said the goldsmith, "what means all this, man?"

"It is Knighton, Master Heriot, from the Court—Knighton, the Duke's man. He brought back the salver you carried to Whitehall, flung it into the entrance as if it had been an old pewter platter, and bade me tell you the king would have none of your trumpery."

"Ay, indeed," said George Heriot—"None of my trumpery!—Come hither into the compting-room, Roberts.—Sir Mungo," he added, bowing to the knight, who had joined, and was preparing to follow them, "I pray your forgiveness for an instant."

In virtue of this prohibition, Sir Mungo, who, as well as the rest of the company, had overheard what passed betwixt George Heriot and his cash-keeper, saw himself condemned to wait in the outer business-room, where he would have endeavoured to slake his eager curiosity by questioning Knighton; but that emissary of greatness, after having added to the uncivil message of his master some rudeness of his own, had again scampered westward, with his satellites at his heels.

In the meanwhile, the name of the Duke of Buckingham, the omnipotent favourite both of the king and the Prince of Wales, had struck some anxiety into the party which remained in the great parlour. He was more feared than beloved, and, if not absolutely of a tyrannical disposition, was accounted haughty, violent, and vindictive. It pressed on Nigel's heart, that he himself, though he could not conceive how, nor why, might be the original cause of the resentment of the Duke against his benefactor. The others made their comments in whispers, until the sounds reached Ramsay, who had not heard a word of what had previously passed, but, plunged in those studies with which he connected every other incident and event, took up only the catchword, and replied,—"The Duke—the Duke of Buckingham—George Villiers—ay—I have spoke with Lambe about him."

"Our Lord and our Lady! Now, how can you say so, father?" said his daughter, who had shrewdness enough to see that her father was touching upon dangerous ground.

"Why, ay, child," answered Ramsay; "the stars do but incline, they cannot compel. But well you wot, it is commonly said of his Grace, by those who have the skill to cast nativities, that there was a notable conjunction of Mars and Saturn—the apparent or true time of which, reducing the calculations of Eichstadius made for the latitude of Oranienburgh, to that of London, gives seven hours, fifty-five minutes, and forty-one seconds—"

"Hold your peace, old soothsayer," said Heriot, who at that instant entered the room with a calm and steady countenance; "your calculations are true and undeniable when they regard brass and wire, and mechanical force; but future events are at the pleasure of Him who bears the hearts of kings in his hands."

"Ay, but, George," answered the watchmaker, "there was a concurrence of signs at this gentleman's birth, which showed his course would be a strange one. Long has it been said of him, he was born at the very meeting of night and day, and under crossing and contending influences that may affect both us and him.

> 'Full moon and high sea,
> Great man shalt thou be;
> Red dawning, stormy sky,
> Bloody death shalt thou die.'"

"It is not good to speak of such things," said Heriot, "especially of the great; stone walls have ears, and a bird of the air shall carry the matter."

Several of the guests seemed to be of their host's opinion. The two merchants took brief leave, as if under consciousness that something was wrong. Mistress Margaret, her body-guard of 'prentices being in readiness, plucked her father by the sleeve, and, rescuing him from a brown study, (whether referring to the wheels of Time, or to that of

Fortune, is uncertain,) wished good-night to her friend Mrs. Judith, and received her godfather's blessing, who, at the same time, put upon her slender finger a ring of much taste and some value; for he seldom suffered her to leave him without some token of his affection. Thus honourably dismissed, and accompanied by her escort, she set forth on her return to Fleet Street.

Sir Mungo had bid adieu to Master Heriot as he came out from the back compting-room, but such was the interest which he took in the affairs of his friend, that, when Master George went upstairs, he could not help walking into that sanctum sanctorum, to see how Master Roberts was employed. The knight found the cash-keeper busy in making extracts from those huge brass-clasped leathern-bound manuscript folios, which are the pride and trust of dealers, and the dread of customers whose year of grace is out. The good knight leant his elbows on the desk, and said to the functionary in a condoling tone of voice,—"What! you have lost a good customer, I fear, Master Roberts, and are busied in making out his bill of charges?"

Now, it chanced that Roberts, like Sir Mungo himself, was a little deaf, and, like Sir Mungo, knew also how to make the most of it; so that he answered at cross purposes,—"I humbly crave your pardon, Sir Mungo, for not having sent in your bill of charge sooner, but my master bade me not disturb you. I will bring the items together in a moment." So saying, he began to turn over the leaves of his book of fate, murmuring, "Repairing ane silver seal-new clasp to his chain of office—ane over-gilt brooch to his hat, being a Saint Andrew's cross, with thistles—a copper gilt pair of spurs,—this to Daniel Driver, we not dealing in the article."

He would have proceeded; but Sir Mungo, not prepared to endure the recital of the catalogue of his own petty debts, and still less willing to satisfy them on the spot, wished the bookkeeper, cavalierly, good-night, and left the house without farther ceremony. The clerk looked after him with a civil city sneer, and immediately resumed the more serious labours which Sir Mungo's intrusion had interrupted.

VII

Things needful we have thought on; but the thing
Of all most needful—that which Scripture terms,
As if alone it merited regard,
The ONE thing needful—that's yet unconsider'd.

—*The Chamberlain*

When the rest of the company had taken their departure from Master Heriot's house, the young Lord of Glenvarloch also offered to take leave; but his host detained him for a few minutes, until all were gone excepting the clergyman.

"My lord," then said the worthy citizen, "we have had our permitted hour of honest and hospitable pastime, and now I would fain delay you for another and graver purpose, as it is our custom, when we have the benefit of good Mr. Windsor's company, that he reads the prayers of the church for the evening before we separate. Your excellent father, my lord, would not have departed before family worship—I hope the same from your lordship."

"With pleasure, sir," answered Nigel; "and you add in the invitation an additional obligation to those with which you have loaded me. When young men forget what is their duty, they owe deep thanks to the friend who will remind them of it."

While they talked together in this manner, the serving-men had removed the folding-tables, brought forward a portable reading-desk, and placed chairs and hassocks for their master, their mistress, and the noble stranger. Another low chair, or rather a sort of stool, was placed close beside that of Master Heriot; and though the circumstance was trivial, Nigel was induced to notice it, because, when about to occupy that seat, he was prevented by a sign from the old gentleman, and motioned to another of somewhat more elevation. The clergyman took his station behind the reading-desk. The domestics, a numerous family both of clerks and servants, including Moniplies, attended, with great gravity, and were accommodated with benches.

The household were all seated, and, externally at least, composed to devout attention, when a low knock was heard at the door of the apartment; Mrs. Judith looked anxiously at her brother, as if desiring to know his pleasure. He nodded his head gravely, and looked to the door. Mrs. Judith immediately crossed the chamber, opened the door, and led into the apartment a beautiful creature, whose sudden and singular appearance might have made her almost pass for an apparition. She was deadly pale-there was not the least shade of vital red to enliven features, which were exquisitely formed, and might, but for that circumstance, have been termed transcendently beautiful. Her long black hair fell down over her shoulders and down her back, combed smoothly and regularly, but without the least appearance of decoration or ornament, which looked very singular at a period when head-gear, as it was called, of one sort or other, was generally used by all ranks. Her dress was of white, of the simplest fashion, and hiding all her person excepting the throat, face, and hands. Her form was rather beneath than above the middle size, but so justly proportioned and elegantly made, that the spectator's attention was entirely withdrawn from her size. In contradiction of the extreme plainness of all the rest of her attire, she wore a necklace which a duchess might have envied, so large and lustrous were the brilliants of which it was composed; and around her waist a zone of rubies of scarce inferior value.

When this singular figure entered the apartment, she cast her eyes on Nigel, and paused, as if uncertain whether to advance or retreat. The glance which she took of him seemed to be one rather of uncertainty and hesitation, than of bashfulness or timidity. Aunt Judith took her by the hand, and led her slowly forward—her dark eyes, however, continued to be fixed on Nigel, with an expression of melancholy by which he felt strangely affected. Even when she was seated on the vacant stool, which was placed there probably for her accommodation, she again looked on him more than once with the same pensive, lingering, and anxious expression, but without either shyness or embarrassment, not even so much as to call the slightest degree of complexion into her cheek.

So soon as this singular female had taken up the prayer-book, which was laid upon her cushion, she seemed immersed in devotional duty; and although Nigel's attention to the service was so much disturbed by this extraordinary apparition, that he looked towards her repeatedly in the course of the service, he could never observe that her eyes or her thoughts strayed so much as a single moment from the task in which she was engaged. Nigel himself was less attentive, for the appearance of this lady seemed so extraordinary, that, strictly as he had been bred up by his father to pay the most reverential attention during performance of divine service, his thoughts in spite of himself were disturbed by her presence, and he earnestly wished the prayers were ended, that his curiosity might obtain some gratification. When the service was concluded, and each had remained, according to the decent and edifying practice of the church, concentrated in mental devotion for a short space, the mysterious visitant arose ere any other person stirred; and Nigel remarked that none of the domestics left their places, or even moved, until she had first kneeled on one knee to Heriot, who seemed to bless her with his hand laid on her head, and a melancholy solemnity of look and action. She then bended her body, but without kneeling, to Mrs. Judith, and having performed these two acts of reverence, she left the room; yet just in the act of her departure, she once more turned her penetrating eyes on Nigel with a fixed look, which compelled him to turn his own aside. When he looked towards her again, he saw only the skirt of her white mantle as she left the apartment.

The domestics then rose and dispersed themselves—wine, and fruit, and spices, were offered to Lord Nigel and to the clergyman, and the latter took his leave. The young lord would fain have accompanied him, in hope to get some explanation of the apparition which he had beheld, but he was stopped by his host, who requested to speak with him in his compting-room.

"I hope, my lord," said the citizen, "that your preparations for attending Court are in such forwardness that you can go thither the day after to-morrow. It is, perhaps, the last day, for some time, that his Majesty will hold open Court for all who have pretensions by birth, rank, or office to attend upon him. On the subsequent day he goes to Theobald's, where he is so much occupied with hunting and other pleasures, that he cares not to be intruded on."

"I shall be in all outward readiness to pay my duty," said the young nobleman, "yet I have little heart to do it. The friends from whom I ought to have found encouragement and protection, have proved cold and false—I certainly will not trouble *them* for their countenance on this occasion—and yet I must confess my childish unwillingness to enter quite alone upon so new a scene."

"It is bold of a mechanic like me to make such an offer to a nobleman," said Heriot; "but I must attend at Court to-morrow. I can accompany you as far as the presence-chamber, from my privilege as being of the household. I can facilitate your entrance, should you find difficulty, and I can point out the proper manner and time of approaching the king.

But I do not know," he added, smiling, "whether these little advantages will not be overbalanced by the incongruity of a nobleman receiving them from the hands of an old smith."

"From the hands rather of the only friend I have found in London," said Nigel, offering his hand.

"Nay, if you think of the matter in that way," replied the honest citizen, "there is no more to be said—I will come for you to-morrow, with a barge proper to the occasion.—But remember, my good young lord, that I do not, like some men of my degree, wish to take opportunity to step beyond it, and associate with my superiors in rank, and therefore do not fear to mortify my presumption, by suffering me to keep my distance in the presence, and where it is fitting for both of us to separate; and for what remains, most truly happy shall I be in proving of service to the son of my ancient patron."

The style of conversation led so far from the point which had interested the young nobleman's curiosity, that there was no returning to it that night. He therefore exchanged thanks and greetings with George Heriot, and took his leave, promising to be equipped and in readiness to embark with him on the second successive morning at ten o'clock.

The generation of linkboys, celebrated by Count Anthony Hamilton, as peculiar to London, had already, in the reign of James I., begun their functions, and the service of one of them with his smoky torch, had been secured to light the young Scottish lord and his follower to their lodgings, which, though better acquainted than formerly with the city, they might in the dark have run some danger of missing. This gave the ingenious Mr. Moniplies an opportunity of gathering close up to his master, after he had gone through the form of slipping his left arm into the handles of his buckler, and loosening his broadsword in the sheath, that he might be ready for whatever should befall.

"If it were not for the wine and the good cheer which we have had in yonder old man's house, my lord," said this sapient follower, "and that I ken him by report to be a just living man in many respects, and a real Edinburgh gutterblood, I should have been well pleased to have seen how his feet were shaped, and whether he had not a cloven cloot under the braw roses and cordovan shoon of his."

"Why, you rascal," answered Nigel, "you have been too kindly treated, and now that you have filled your ravenous stomach, you are railing on the good gentleman that relieved you."

"Under favour, no, my lord," said Moniplies,—"I would only like to see something mair about him. I have eaten his meat, it is true—more shame that the like of him should have meat to give, when your lordship and me could scarce have gotten, on our own account, brose and a bear bannock—I have drunk his wine, too."

"I see you have," replied his master, "a great deal more than you should have done."

"Under your patience, my lord," said Moniplies, "you are pleased to say that, because I crushed a quart with that jolly boy Jenkin, as they call the 'prentice boy, and that was out of mere acknowledgment for his former kindness—I own that I, moreover, sung the good old song of Elsie Marley, so as they never heard it chanted in their lives—"

And withal (as John Bunyan says) as they went on their way, he sung—

> "O, do ye ken Elsie Marley, honey—
> The wife that sells the barley, honey?
> For Elsie Marley's grown sae fine,
> She winna get up to feed the swine.—
> O, do ye ken—"

Here in mid career was the songster interrupted by the stern gripe of his master, who threatened to baton him to death if he brought the city-watch upon them by his ill-timed melody.

"I crave pardon, my lord—I humbly crave pardon—only when I think of that Jen Win, as they call him, I can hardly help humming—'O, do ye ken'—But I crave your honour's pardon, and will be totally dumb, if you command me so."

"No, sirrah!" said Nigel, "talk on, for I well know you would say and suffer more under pretence of holding your peace, than when you get an unbridled license. How is it, then? What have you to say against Master Heriot?"

It seems more than probable, that in permitting this license, the young lord hoped his attendant would stumble upon the subject of the young lady who had appeared at prayers in a manner so mysterious. But whether this was the case, or whether he merely desired that Moniplies should utter, in a subdued and under tone of voice, those spirits which might otherwise have vented themselves in obstreperous song, it is certain he permitted his attendant to proceed with his story in his own way.

"And therefore," said the orator, availing himself of his immunity, "I would like to ken what sort of carle this Maister Heriot is. He hath supplied your lordship with wealth of gold, as I can understand; and if he has, I make it for certain he hath had his ain end in it, according to the fashion of the world. Now, had your lordship your own good lands at your guiding, doubtless this person, with most of his craft—goldsmiths they call themselves—I say usurers—wad be glad to exchange so many pounds of African dust, by whilk I understand gold, against so many fair acres, and hundreds of acres, of broad Scottish land."

"But you know I have no land," said the young lord, "at least none that can be affected by any debt which I can at present become obliged for—I think you need not have reminded me of that."

"True, my lord, most true; and, as your lordship says, open to the meanest capacity, without any unnecessary expositions. Now, therefore, my lord, unless Maister George Heriot has something mair to allege as a motive for his liberality, vera different from the possession of your estate—and moreover, as he could gain little by the capture of your body, wherefore should it not be your soul that he is in pursuit of?"

"My soul, you rascal!" said the young lord; "what good should my soul do him?"

"What do I ken about that?" said Moniplies; "they go about roaring and seeking whom they may devour—doubtless, they like the food that they rage so much about—and, my lord, they say," added Moniplies, drawing up still closer to his master's side, "they say that Master Heriot has one spirit in his house already."

"How, or what do you mean?" said Nigel; "I will break your head, you drunken knave, if you palter with me any longer."

"Drunken?" answered his trusty adherent, "and is this the story?—why, how could I but drink your lordship's health on my bare knees, when Master Jenkin began it to me?—hang them that would not—I would have cut the impudent knave's hams with my broadsword, that should make scruple of it, and so have made him kneel when he should have found it difficult to rise again. But touching the spirit," he proceeded, finding that his master made no answer to his valorous tirade, "your lordship has seen her with your own eyes."

"I saw no spirit," said Glenvarloch, but yet breathing thick as one who expects some singular disclosure, "what mean you by a spirit?"

"You saw a young lady come in to prayers, that spoke not a word to any one, only made becks and bows to the old gentleman and lady of the house—ken ye wha she is?"

"No, indeed," answered Nigel; "some relation of the family, I suppose."

"Deil a bit—deil a bit," answered Moniplies, hastily, "not a blood-drop's kin to them, if she had a drop of blood in her body—I tell you but what all human beings allege to be truth, that swell within hue and cry of Lombard Street—that lady, or quean, or whatever you choose to call her, has been dead in the body these many a year, though she haunts them, as we have seen, even at their very devotions."

"You will allow her to be a good spirit at least," said Nigel Olifaunt, "since she chooses such a time to visit her friends?"

"For that I kenna, my lord," answered the superstitious follower; "I ken no spirit that would have faced the right down hammer-blow of Mess John Knox, whom my father stood by in his very warst days, bating a chance time when the Court, which my father supplied with butcher-meat, was against him. But yon divine has another airt from powerful Master Rollock, and Mess David Black, of North Leith, and sic like.—Alack-a-day! wha can ken, if it please your lordship, whether sic prayers as the Southron read out of their auld blethering black mess-book there, may not be as powerful to invite fiends, as a right red-het prayer warm fraw the heart, may be powerful to drive them away, even as the Evil Spirit was driven by he smell of the fish's liver from the bridal-chamber of Sara, the daughter of Raguel? As to whilk story, nevertheless, I make scruple to say whether it be truth or not, better men than I am having doubted on that matter."

"Well, well, well," said his master, impatiently, "we are now near home, and I have permitted you to speak of this matter for once, that we may have an end to your prying folly, and your idiotical superstitions, for ever. For whom do you, or your absurd authors or informers, take this lady?"

"I can sae naething preceesely as to that," answered Moniplies; "certain it is her body died and was laid in the grave many a day since, notwithstanding she still wanders on earth, and chiefly amongst Maister Heriot's family, though she hath been seen in other places by them that well knew her. But who she is, I will not warrant to say, or how she becomes attached, like a Highland Brownie, to some peculiar family. They say she has a row of apartments of her own, ante-room, parlour, and bedroom; but deil a bed she sleeps in but her own coffin, and the walls, doors, and windows are so chinked up, as to prevent the least blink of daylight from entering; and then she dwells by torchlight—"

"To what purpose, if she be a spirit?" said Nigel Olifaunt.

"How can I tell your lordship?" answered his attendant. "I thank God I know nothing of her likings, or mislikings—only her coffin is there; and I leave your lordship to guess what a live person has to do with a coffin. As little as a ghost with a lantern, I trow."

"What reason," repeated Nigel, "can a creature, so young and so beautiful, have already habitually to contemplate her bed of last-long rest?"

"In troth, I kenna, my lord," answered Moniplies; "but there is the coffin, as they told me who have seen it: it is made of heben-wood, with silver nails, and lined all through with three-piled damask, might serve a princess to rest in."

"Singular," said Nigel, whose brain, like that of most active young spirits, was easily caught by the singular and the romantic; "does she not eat with the family?"

"Who!—she!"—exclaimed Moniplies, as if surprised at the question; "they would need a lang spoon would sup with her, I trow. Always there is something put for her into the Tower, as they call it, whilk is a whigmaleery of a whirling-box, that turns round half on the tae side o' the wa', half on the tother."

"I have seen the contrivance in foreign nunneries," said the Lord of Glenvarloch. "And is it thus she receives her food?"

"They tell me something is put in ilka day, for fashion's sake," replied the attendant; "but it's no to be supposed she would consume it, ony mair than the images of Bel and the Dragon consumed the dainty vivers that were placed before them. There are stout yeomen and chamber-queans in the house, enow to play the part of Lick-it-up-a', as well as the threescore and ten priests of Bel, besides their wives and children."

"And she is never seen in the family but when the hour of prayer arrives?" said the master.

"Never, that I hear of," replied the servant.

"It is singular," said Nigel Olifaunt, musing. "Were it not for the ornaments which she wears, and still more for her attendance upon the service of the Protestant Church, I should know what to think, and should believe her either a Catholic votaress, who, for some cogent reason, was allowed to make her cell here in London, or some unhappy Popish devotee, who was in the course of undergoing a dreadful penance. As it is, I know not what to deem of it."

His reverie was interrupted by the linkboy knocking at the door of honest John Christie, whose wife came forth with "quips, and becks, and wreathed smiles," to welcome her honoured guest on his return to his apartment.

VIII

Ay! mark the matron well—and laugh not, Harry,
At her old steeple-hat and velvet guard—
I've call'd her like the ear of Dionysius;
I mean that ear-form'd vault, built o'er his dungeon,
To catch the groans and discontented murmurs
Of his poor bondsmen—Even so doth Martha
Drink up, for her own purpose, all that passes,
Or is supposed to pass, in this wide city—
She can retail it too, if that her profit
Shall call on her to do so; and retail it
For your advantage, so that you can make
Your profit jump with hers.

—The Conspiracy

W e must now introduce to the reader's acquaintance another character, busy and important far beyond her ostensible situation in society—in a word, Dame Ursula Suddlechop, wife of Benjamin Suddlechop, the most renowned barber in all Fleet Street. This dame had her own particular merits, the principal part of which was (if her own report could be trusted) an infinite desire to be of service to her fellow-creatures. Leaving to her thin half-starved partner the boast of having the most dexterous snap with his fingers of any shaver in London, and the care of a shop where starved apprentices flayed the faces of those who were boobies enough to trust them, the dame drove a separate and more lucrative trade, which yet had so many odd turns and windings, that it seemed in many respects to contradict itself.

Its highest and most important duties were of a very secret and confidential nature, and Dame Ursula Suddlechop was never known to betray any transaction intrusted to her, unless she had either been indifferently paid for her service, or that some one found it convenient to give her a double douceur to make her disgorge the secret; and these contingencies happened in so few cases, that her character for trustiness remained as unimpeached as that for honesty and benevolence.

In fact, she was a most admirable matron, and could be useful to the impassioned and the frail in the rise, progress, and consequences of their passion. She could contrive an interview for lovers who could show proper reasons for meeting privately; she could relieve the frail fair one of the burden of a guilty passion, and perhaps establish the hopeful offspring of unlicensed love as the heir of some family whose love was lawful, but where an heir had not followed the union. More than this she could do, and had been concerned in deeper and dearer secrets. She had been a pupil of Mrs. Turner, and learned from her the secret of making the yellow starch, and, it may be, two or three other secrets of more consequence, though perhaps none that went to the criminal extent of those whereof her mistress was accused. But all that was deep and dark in her real character was covered by the show of outward mirth and good-humour, the hearty laugh and buxom jest with which the dame knew well how to conciliate the elder part of her neighbours, and the many petty arts by which she could recommend herself to the younger, those especially of her own sex.

Dame Ursula was, in appearance, scarce past forty, and her full, but not overgrown form, and still comely features, although her person was plumped out, and her face somewhat coloured by good cheer, had a joyous expression of gaiety and good-humour, which set off the remains of beauty in the wane. Marriages, births, and christenings were seldom thought to be performed with sufficient ceremony, for a considerable distance round her abode, unless Dame Ursley, as they called her, was present. She could contrive all sorts of pastimes, games, and jests, which might amuse the large companies which the hospitality of our ancestors assembled together on such occasions, so that her presence was literally considered as indispensable in the families of all citizens of ordinary rank, at such joyous periods. So much also was she supposed to know of life and its labyrinths, that she was the willing confidant of half the loving couples in the vicinity, most of whom used to communicate their secrets to, and receive their counsel from, Dame Ursley. The rich rewarded her services with rings, owches, or gold pieces, which she liked still better; and she very generously gave her assistance to the poor, on the same mixed principles as young practitioners in medicine assist them, partly from compassion, and partly to keep her hand in use.

Dame Ursley's reputation in the city was the greater that her practice had extended beyond Temple Bar, and that she had acquaintances, nay, patrons and patronesses, among the quality, whose rank, as their members were much fewer, and the prospect of approaching the courtly sphere much more difficult, bore a degree of consequence unknown to the present day, when the toe of the citizen presses so close on the courtier's heel. Dame Ursley maintained her intercourse with this superior rank of customers, partly by driving a small trade in perfumes, essences, pomades, head-gears from France, dishes or ornaments from China, then already beginning to be fashionable; not to mention drugs of various descriptions, chiefly for the use of the ladies, and partly by other services, more or less connected with the esoteric branches of her profession heretofore alluded to.

Possessing such and so many various modes of thriving, Dame Ursley was nevertheless so poor, that she might probably have mended her own circumstances, as well as her husband's, if she had renounced them all, and set herself quietly down to the care of her own household, and to assist Benjamin in the concerns of his trade. But Ursula was luxurious and genial in her habits, and could no more have endured the stinted economy of Benjamin's board, than she could have reconciled herself to the bald chat of his conversation.

It was on the evening of the day on which Lord Nigel Olifaunt dined with the wealthy goldsmith, that we must introduce Ursula Suddlechop upon the stage. She had that morning made a long tour to Westminster, was fatigued, and had assumed a certain large elbow-chair, rendered smooth by frequent use, placed on one side of her chimney, in which there was lit a small but bright fire. Here she observed, betwixt sleeping and waking, the simmering of a pot of well-spiced ale, on the brown surface of which bobbed a small crab-apple, sufficiently roasted, while a little mulatto girl watched, still more attentively, the process of dressing a veal sweetbread, in a silver stewpan which occupied the other side of the chimney. With these viands, doubtless, Dame Ursula proposed concluding the well spent day, of which she reckoned the labour over, and the rest at her own command. She was deceived, however; for just as the ale, or, to speak technically, the lamb's-wool, was fitted for drinking, and the little dingy maiden intimated that the sweetbread was ready to be eaten, the thin cracked voice of Benjamin was heard from the bottom of the stairs.

"Why, Dame Ursley—why, wife, I say—why, dame—why, love, you are wanted more than a strop for a blunt razor—why, dame—"

"I would some one would draw a razor across thy windpipe, thou bawling ass!" said the dame to herself, in the first moment of irritation against her clamorous helpmate; and then called aloud,—"Why, what is the matter, Master Suddlechop? I am just going to slip into bed; I have been daggled to and fro the whole day."

"Nay, sweetheart, it is not me," said the patient Benjamin, "but the Scots laundry-maid from neighbour Ramsay's, who must speak with you incontinent."

At the word sweetheart, Dame Ursley cast a wistful look at the mess which was stewed to a second in the stewpan, and then replied, with a sigh,—"Bid Scots Jenny come up, Master Suddlechop. I shall be very happy to hear what she has to say;" then added in a lower tone, "and I hope she will go to the devil in the flame of a tar-barrel, like many a Scots witch before her!"

The Scots laundress entered accordingly, and having heard nothing of the last kind wish of Dame Suddlechop, made her reverence with considerable respect, and said, her young mistress had returned home unwell, and wished to see her neighbour, Dame Ursley, directly.

"And why will it not do to-morrow, Jenny, my good woman?" said Dame Ursley; "for I have been as far as Whitehall to-day already, and I am well-nigh worn off my feet, my good woman."

"Aweel!" answered Jenny, with great composure, "and if that sae be sae, I maun take the langer tramp mysell, and maun gae down the waterside for auld Mother Redcap, at the Hungerford Stairs, that deals in comforting young creatures, e'en as you do yoursell, hinny; for ane o' ye the bairn maun see before she sleeps, and that's a' that I ken on't."

So saying, the old emissary, without farther entreaty, turned on her heel, and was about to retreat, when Dame Ursley exclaimed,—"No, no—if the sweet child, your mistress, has any necessary occasion for good advice and kind tendance, you need not go to Mother Redcap, Janet. She may do very well for skippers' wives, chandlers' daughters, and such like; but nobody shall wait on pretty Mistress Margaret, the daughter of his most Sacred Majesty's horologer, excepting and saving myself. And so I will but take my chopins and my cloak, and put on my muffler, and cross the street to neighbour Ramsay's in an instant. But tell me yourself, good Jenny, are you not something tired of your young lady's frolics and change of mind twenty times a-day?"

"In troth, not I," said the patient drudge, "unless it may be when she is a wee fashious about washing her laces; but I have been her keeper since she was a bairn, neighbour Suddlechop, and that makes a difference."

"Ay," said Dame Ursley, still busied putting on additional defences against the night air; "and you know for certain that she has two hundred pounds a-year in good land, at her own free disposal?"

"Left by her grandmother, heaven rest her soul!" said the Scotswoman; "and to a daintier lassie she could not have bequeathed it."

"Very true, very true, mistress; for, with all her little whims, I have always said Mistress Margaret Ramsay was the prettiest girl in the ward; and, Jenny, I warrant the poor child has had no supper?"

Jenny could not say but it was the case, for, her master being out, the twa 'prentice lads had gone out after shutting shop, to fetch them home, and she and the other maid had gone out to Sandy MacGivan's, to see a friend frae Scotland.

"As was very natural, Mrs. Janet," said Dame Ursley, who found her interest in assenting to all sorts of propositions from all sorts of persons.

"And so the fire went out, too,"—said Jenny.

"Which was the most natural of the whole," said Dame Suddlechop; "and so, to cut the matter short, Jenny, I'll carry over the little bit of supper that I was going to eat. For dinner I have tasted none, and it may be my young pretty Mistress Marget will eat a morsel with me; for it is mere emptiness, Mistress Jenny, that often puts these fancies of illness into young folk's heads." So saying, she put the silver posset-cup with the ale into Jenny's hands and assuming her mantle with the alacrity of one determined to sacrifice inclination to duty, she hid the stewpan under its folds, and commanded Wilsa, the little mulatto girl, to light them across the street.

"Whither away, so late?" said the barber, whom they passed seated with his starveling boys round a mess of stockfish and parsnips, in the shop below.

"If I were to tell you, Gaffer," said the dame, with most contemptuous coolness, "I do not think you could do my errand, so I will e'en keep it to myself." Benjamin was too much accustomed to his wife's independent mode of conduct, to pursue his inquiry farther; nor did the dame tarry for farther question, but marched out at the door, telling the eldest of the boys "to sit up till her return, and look to the house the whilst."

The night was dark and rainy, and although the distance betwixt the two shops was short, it allowed Dame Ursley leisure enough, while she strode along with high-tucked petticoats, to embitter it by the following grumbling reflections—"I wonder what I have done, that I must needs trudge at every old beldam's bidding, and every young minx's maggot! I have been marched from Temple Bar to Whitechapel, on the matter of a pinmaker's wife having pricked her fingers—marry, her husband that made the weapon might have salved the wound.—And here is this fantastic ape, pretty Mistress Marget, forsooth—such a beauty as I could make of a Dutch doll, and as fantastic, and humorous, and conceited, as if she were a duchess. I have seen her in the same day as changeful as a marmozet and as stubborn as a mule. I should like to know whether her little conceited noddle, or her father's old crazy calculating jolter-pate, breeds most whimsies. But then there's that two hundred pounds a-year in dirty land, and the father is held a close chuff, though a fanciful—he is our landlord besides, and she has begged a late day from him for our rent; so, God help me, I must be comfortable—besides, the little capricious devil is my only key to get at Master George Heriot's secret, and it concerns my character to find that out; and so, ANDIAMOS, as the lingua franca hath it."

Thus pondering, she moved forward with hasty strides until she arrived at the watchmaker's habitation. The attendant admitted them by means of a pass-key. Onward glided Dame Ursula, now in glimmer and now in gloom, not like the lovely Lady Cristabelle through Gothic sculpture and ancient armour, but creeping and stumbling amongst relics of old machines, and models of new inventions in various branches of mechanics with which wrecks of useless ingenuity, either in a broken or half-finished shape, the apartment of the fanciful though ingenious mechanist was continually lumbered.

At length they attained, by a very narrow staircase, pretty Mistress Margaret's apartment, where she, the cynosure of the eyes of every bold young bachelor in Fleet Street, sat in a posture which hovered between the discontented and the disconsolate. For her pretty back and shoulders were rounded into a curve, her round and dimpled chin reposed in the hollow of her little palm, while the fingers were folded over her mouth; her elbow rested on a table, and her eyes seemed fixed upon the dying charcoal, which was expiring in a small grate. She scarce turned her head when Dame Ursula entered, and when the presence of that estimable matron was more precisely announced in words by the old Scotswoman, Mistress Margaret, without changing her posture, muttered some sort of answer that was wholly unintelligible.

"Go your ways down to the kitchen with Wilsa, good Mistress Jenny," said Dame Ursula, who was used to all sorts of freaks, on the part of her patients or clients, whichever they might be termed; "put the stewpan and the porringer by the fireside, and go down below—I must speak to my pretty love, Mistress Margaret, by myself—and there is not a bachelor betwixt this and Bow but will envy me the privilege."

The attendants retired as directed, and Dame Ursula, having availed herself of the embers of charcoal, to place her stewpan to the best advantage, drew herself as close as she could to her patient, and began in a low, soothing, and confidential tone of voice, to inquire what ailed her pretty flower of neighbours.

"Nothing, dame," said Margaret somewhat pettishly, and changing her posture so as rather to turn her back upon the kind inquirer.

"Nothing, lady-bird!" answered Dame Suddlechop; "and do you use to send for your friends out of bed at this hour for nothing?"

"It was not I who sent for you, dame," replied the malecontent maiden.

"And who was it, then?" said Ursula; "for if I had not been sent for, I had not been here at this time of night, I promise you!"

"It was the old Scotch fool Jenny, who did it out of her own head, I suppose," said Margaret; "for she has been stunning me these two hours about you and Mother Redcap."

"Me and Mother Redcap!" said Dame Ursula, "an old fool indeed, that couples folk up so.—But come, come, my sweet little neighbour, Jenny is no such fool after all; she knows young folks want more and better advice than her own, and she knows, too, where to find it for them; so you must take heart of grace, my pretty maiden, and tell me what you are moping about, and then let Dame Ursula alone for finding out a cure."

"Nay, an ye be so wise, Mother Ursula," replied the girl, "you may guess what I ail without my telling you."

"Ay, ay, child," answered the complaisant matron, "no one can play better than I at the good old game of What is my thought like? Now I'll warrant that little head of yours is running on a new head-tire, a foot higher than those our city dames wear—or you are all for a trip to Islington or Ware, and your father is cross and will not consent—or—"

"Or you are an old fool, Dame Suddlechop," said Margaret, peevishly, "and must needs trouble yourself about matters you know nothing of."

"Fool as much as you will, mistress," said Dame Ursula, offended in her turn, "but not so very many years older than yourself, mistress."

"Oh! we are angry, are we?" said the beauty; "and pray, Madam Ursula, how come you, that are not so many years older than me, to talk about such nonsense to me, who am so many years younger, and who yet have too much sense to care about head-gears and Islington?"

"Well, well, young mistress," said the sage counsellor, rising, "I perceive

I can be of no use here; and methinks, since you know your own matters so much better than other people do, you might dispense with disturbing folks at midnight to ask their advice."

"Why, now you are angry, mother," said Margaret, detaining her; "this comes of your coming out at eventide without eating your supper—I never heard you utter a cross word after you had finished your little morsel.—Here, Janet, a trencher and salt for Dame Ursula;—and what have you in that porringer, dame?—Filthy clammy ale, as I would live—Let Janet fling it out of the window, or keep it for my father's morning draught; and she shall bring you the pottle of sack that was set ready for him—good man, he will never find out the difference, for ale will wash down his dusty calculations quite as well as wine."

"Truly, sweetheart, I am of your opinion," said Dame Ursula, whose temporary displeasure vanished at once before these preparations for good cheer; and so, settling herself on the great easy-chair, with a three-legged table before her, she began to dispatch, with good appetite, the little delicate dish which she had prepared for herself. She did not, however, fail in the duties of civility, and earnestly, but in vain, pressed Mistress Margaret to partake her dainties. The damsel declined the invitation.

"At least pledge me in a glass of sack," said Dame Ursula; "I have heard my grandame say, that before the gospellers came in, the old Catholic father confessors and their penitents always had a cup of sack together before confession; and you are my penitent."

"I shall drink no sack, I am sure," said Margaret; "and I told you before, that if you cannot find out what ails me, I shall never have the heart to tell it."

So saying, she turned away from Dame Ursula once more, and resumed her musing posture, with her hand on her elbow, and her back, at least one shoulder, turned towards her confidant.

"Nay, then," said Dame Ursula, "I must exert my skill in good earnest.—You must give me this pretty hand, and I will tell you by palmistry, as well as any gipsy of them all, what foot it is you halt upon."

"As if I halted on any foot at all," said Margaret, something scornfully, but yielding her left hand to Ursula, and continuing at the same time her averted position.

"I see brave lines here," said Ursula, "and not ill to read neither—pleasure and wealth, and merry nights and late mornings to my Beauty, and such an equipage as shall shake Whitehall. O, have I touched you there?—and smile you now, my pretty one?—for why should not he be Lord Mayor, and go to Court in his gilded caroch, as others have done before him?"

"Lord Mayor? pshaw!" replied Margaret.

"And why pshaw at my Lord Mayor, sweetheart? or perhaps you pshaw at my prophecy; but there is a cross in every one's line of life as well as in yours, darling. And what though I see a 'prentice's flat cap in this pretty palm, yet there is a sparking black eye under it, hath not its match in the Ward of Farringdon-Without."

"Whom do you mean, dame?" said Margaret coldly.

"Whom should I mean," said Dame Ursula, "but the prince of 'prentices, and king of good company, Jenkin Vincent?"

"Out, woman—Jenkin Vincent?—a clown—a Cockney!" exclaimed the indignant damsel.

"Ay, sets the wind in that quarter, Beauty!" quoth the dame; "why, it has changed something since we spoke together last, for then I would have sworn it blew fairer for poor Jin Vin; and the poor lad dotes on you too, and would rather see your eyes than the first glimpse of the sun on the great holiday on May-day."

"I would my eyes had the power of the sun to blind his, then," said Margaret, "to teach the drudge his place."

"Nay," said Dame Ursula, "there be some who say that Frank Tunstall is as proper a lad as Jin Vin, and of surety he is third cousin to a knighthood, and come of a good house; and so mayhap you may be for northward ho!"

"Maybe I may"—answered Margaret, "but not with my father's 'prentice—I thank you, Dame Ursula."

"Nay, then, the devil may guess your thoughts for me," said Dame Ursula; "this comes of trying to shoe a filly that is eternally wincing and shifting ground!"

"Hear me, then," said Margaret, "and mind what I say.—This day I dined abroad—"

"I can tell you where," answered her counsellor,—"with your godfather the rich goldsmith—ay, you see I know something—nay, I could tell you, as I would, with whom, too."

"Indeed!" said Margaret, turning suddenly round with an accent of strong surprise, and colouring up to the eyes.

"With old Sir Mungo Malagrowther," said the oracular dame,—"he was trimmed in my Benjamin's shop in his way to the city."

"Pshaw! the frightful old mouldy skeleton!" said the damsel.

"Indeed you say true, my dear," replied the confidant,—"it is a shame to him to be out of Saint Pancras's charnel-house, for I know no other place he is fit for, the foul-mouthed old railer. He said to my husband—"

"Somewhat which signifies nothing to our purpose, I dare say," interrupted Margaret. "I must speak, then.—There dined with us a nobleman—"

"A nobleman! the maiden's mad!" said Dame Ursula.

"There dined with us, I say," continued Margaret, without regarding the interruption, "a nobleman—a Scottish nobleman."

"Now Our Lady keep her!" said the confidant, "she is quite frantic!— heard ever any one of a watchmaker's daughter falling in love with a nobleman—and a Scots nobleman, to make the matter complete, who are all as proud as Lucifer, and as poor as Job?—A Scots nobleman, quotha? I had lief you told me of a Jew pedlar. I would have you think how all this is to end, pretty one, before you jump in the dark."

"That is nothing to you, Ursula—it is your assistance," said Mistress Margaret, "and not your advice, that I am desirous to have, and you know I can make it worth your while."

"O, it is not for the sake of lucre, Mistress Margaret," answered the obliging dame; "but truly I would have you listen to some advice— bethink you of your own condition."

"My father's calling is mechanical," said Margaret, "but our blood is not so. I have heard my father say that we are descended, at a distance indeed, from the great Earls of Dalwolsey."*

"Ay, ay," said Dame Ursula; "even so—I never knew a Scot of you but was descended, as ye call it, from some great house or other; and a piteous descent it often is—and as for the distance you speak of, it is so great as to put you out of sight of each other. Yet do not toss your pretty head so scornfully, but tell me the name of this lordly northern gallant, and we will try what can be done in the matter."

"It is Lord Glenvarloch, whom they call Lord Nigel Olifaunt," said Margaret in a low voice, and turning away to hide her blushes.

---

* The head of the ancient and distinguished house of Ramsay, and to whom, as their chief, the individuals of that name look as their origin and source of gentry. Allan Ramsay, the pastoral poet, in the same manner, makes

> "Dalhousie of an auld descent,
> My chief, my stoup, my ornament."

"Marry, Heaven forefend!" exclaimed Dame Suddlechop; "this is the very devil, and something worse!"

"How mean you?" said the damsel, surprised at the vivacity of her exclamation.

"Why, know ye not," said the dame, "what powerful enemies he has at Court? know ye not—But blisters on my tongue, it runs too fast for my wit—enough to say, that you had better make your bridal-bed under a falling house, than think of young Glenvarloch."

"He Is unfortunate then?" said Margaret; "I knew it—I divined it—there was sorrow in his voice when he said even what was gay—there was a touch of misfortune in his melancholy smile—he had not thus clung to my thoughts had I seen him in all the mid-day glare of prosperity."

"Romances have cracked her brain!" said Dame Ursula; "she is a castaway girl—utterly distraught—loves a Scots lord—and likes him the better for being unfortunate! Well, mistress, I am sorry this is a matter I cannot aid you in—it goes against my conscience, and it is an affair above my condition, and beyond my management;—but I will keep your counsel."

"You will not be so base as to desert me, after having drawn my secret from me?" said Margaret, indignantly; "if you do, I know how to have my revenge; and if you do not, I will reward you well. Remember the house your husband dwells in is my father's property."

"I remember it but too well, Mistress Margaret," said Ursula, after a moment's reflection, "and I would serve you in any thing in my condition; but to meddle with such high matters—I shall never forget poor Mistress Turner, my honoured patroness, peace be with her!—she had the ill-luck to meddle in the matter of Somerset and Overbury, and so the great earl and his lady slipt their necks out of the collar, and left her and some half-dozen others to suffer in their stead. I shall never forget the sight of her standing on the scaffold with the ruff round her pretty neck, all done up with the yellow starch which I had so often helped her to make, and that was so soon to give place to a rough hempen cord. Such a sight, sweetheart, will make one loath to meddle with matters that are too hot or heavy for their handling."

"Out, you fool!" answered Mistress Margaret; "am I one to speak to you about such criminal practices as that wretch died for? All I desire of you is, to get me precise knowledge of what affair brings this young nobleman to Court."

"And when you have his secret," said Ursula, "what will it avail you, sweetheart?—and yet I would do your errand, if you could do as much for me."

"And what is it you would have of me?" said Mistress Margaret.

"What you have been angry with me for asking before," answered Dame Ursula. "I want to have some light about the story of your godfather's ghost, that is only seen at prayers."

"Not for the world," said Mistress Margaret, "will I be a spy on my kind godfather's secrets—No, Ursula—that I will never pry into, which he desires to keep hidden. But thou knowest that I have a fortune, of my own, which must at no distant day come under my own management—think of some other recompense."

"Ay, that I well know," said the counsellor—"it is that two hundred per year, with your father's indulgence, that makes you so wilful, sweetheart."

"It may be so,"—said Margaret Ramsay; "meanwhile, do you serve me truly, and here is a ring of value in pledge, that when my fortune is in my own hand, I will redeem the token with fifty broad pieces of gold."

"Fifty broad pieces of gold!" repeated the dame; "and this ring, which is a right fair one, in token you fail not of your word!—Well, sweetheart, if I must put my throat in peril, I am sure I cannot risk it for a friend more generous than you; and I would not think of more than the pleasure of serving you, only Benjamin gets more idle every day, and our family—"

"Say no more of it," said Margaret; "we understand each other. And now, tell me what you know of this young man's affairs, which made you so unwilling to meddle with them?"

"Of that I can say no great matter as yet," answered Dame Ursula; "only I know, the most powerful among his own countrymen are against him, and also the most powerful at the Court here. But I will learn more of it; for it will be a dim print that I will not read for your sake, pretty Mistress Margaret. Know you where this gallant dwells?"

"I heard by accident," said Margaret, as if ashamed of the minute particularity of her memory upon such an occasion,—"he lodges, I think—at one Christie's—if I mistake not—at Paul's Wharf—a ship-chandler's."

"A proper lodging for a young baron!—Well, but cheer you up, Mistress Margaret—If he has come up a caterpillar, like some of his countrymen, he may cast his slough like them, and come out a butterfly.— So I drink good-night, and sweet dreams to you, in another parting cup of sack; and you shall hear tidings of me within four-and-twenty hours.

And, once more, I commend you to your pillow, my pearl of pearls, and Marguerite of Marguerites!"

So saying, she kissed the reluctant cheek of her young friend, or patroness, and took her departure with the light and stealthy pace of one accustomed to accommodate her footsteps to the purposes of dispatch and secrecy.

Margaret Ramsay looked after her for some time, in anxious silence. "I did ill," she at length murmured, "to let her wring this out of me; but she is artful, bold and serviceable—and I think faithful—or, if not, she will be true at least to her interest, and that I can command. I would I had not spoken, however—I have begun a hopeless work. For what has he said to me, to warrant my meddling in his fortunes?—Nothing but words of the most ordinary import—mere table-talk, and terms of course. Yet who knows"—she said, and then broke off, looking at the glass the while, which, as it reflected back a face of great beauty, probably suggested to her mind a more favourable conclusion of the sentence than she cared to trust her tongue withal.

IX

So pitiful a thing is suitor's state!
Most miserable man, whom wicked fate
Hath brought to Court to sue, for had I wist,
That few have found, and many a one hath miss'd!
Full little knowest thou, that hast not tried,
What hell it is, in sueing long to bide:
To lose good days that might be better spent;
To waste long nights in pensive discontent;
To speed to-day, to be put back to-morrow;
To feed on hope, to pine with fear and sorrow;
To have thy Prince's grace, yet want her Peers';
To have thy asking, yet wait many years;
To fret thy soul with crosses and with cares—
To eat thy heart through comfortless despairs.
To fawn, to crouch, to wait, to ride, to run,
To spend, to give, to want, to be undone.

—Mother Hubbard's Tale

On the morning of the day on which George Heriot had prepared to escort the young Lord of Glenvarloch to the Court at Whitehall, it may be reasonably supposed, that the young man, whose fortunes were likely to depend on this cast, felt himself more than usually anxious. He rose early, made his toilette with uncommon care, and, being enabled, by the generosity of his more plebeian countryman, to set out a very handsome person to the best advantage, he obtained a momentary approbation from himself as he glanced at the mirror, and a loud and distinct plaudit from his landlady, who declared at once, that, in her judgment, he would take the wind out of the sail of every gallant in the presence—so much had she been able to enrich her discourse with the metaphors of those with whom her husband dealt.

At the appointed hour, the barge of Master George Heriot arrived, handsomely manned and appointed, having a tilt, with his own cipher, and the arms of his company, painted thereupon.

The young Lord of Glenvarloch received the friend, who had evinced such disinterested attachment, with the kind courtesy which well became him.

Master Heriot then made him acquainted with the bounty of his sovereign; which he paid over to his young friend, declining what he had himself formerly advanced to him. Nigel felt all the gratitude which the citizen's disinterested friendship had deserved, and was not wanting in expressing it suitably.

Yet, as the young and high-born nobleman embarked to go to the presence of his prince, under the patronage of one whose best, or most distinguished qualification, was his being an eminent member of the Goldsmiths' Incorporation, he felt a little surprised, if not abashed, at his own situation; and Richie Moniplies, as he stepped over the gangway to take his place forward in the boat, could not help muttering,—"It was a changed day betwixt Master Heriot and his honest father in the Kraemes;—but, doubtless, there was a difference between clinking on gold and silver, and clattering upon pewter."

On they glided, by the assistance of the oars of four stout watermen, along the Thames, which then served for the principal high-road betwixt London and Westminster; for few ventured on horseback through the narrow and crowded streets of the city, and coaches were then a luxury reserved only for the higher nobility, and to which no citizen, whatever was his wealth, presumed to aspire. The beauty of the banks, especially on the northern side, where the gardens of the nobility descended from their hotels, in many places, down to the water's edge, was pointed out to Nigel by his kind conductor, and was pointed out in vain. The mind of the young Lord of Glenvarloch was filled with anticipations, not the most pleasant, concerning the manner in which he was likely to be received by that monarch, in whose behalf his family had been nearly reduced to ruin; and he was, with the usual mental anxiety of those in such a situation, framing imaginary questions from the king, and over-toiling his spirit in devising answers to them.

His conductor saw the labour of Nigel's mind, and avoided increasing it by farther conversation; so that, when he had explained to him briefly the ceremonies observed at Court on such occasions of presentation, the rest of their voyage was performed in silence.

They landed at Whitehall Stairs, and entered the Palace after announcing their names,—the guards paying to Lord Glenvarloch the respect and honours due to his rank.

The young man's heart beat high and thick within him as he came into the royal apartments. His education abroad, conducted, as it had been, on a narrow and limited scale, had given him but imperfect ideas of the grandeur of a Court; and the philosophical reflections which taught him to set ceremonial and exterior splendour at defiance, proved, like other maxims of mere philosophy, ineffectual, at the moment they were weighed against the impression naturally made on the mind of an inexperienced youth, by the unusual magnificence of the scene. The splendid apartments through which they passed, the rich apparel of the grooms, guards, and apartments, had something in it, trifling and commonplace as it might appear to practised courtiers, embarrassing, and even alarming, to one, who went through these forms for the first time, and who was doubtful what sort of reception was to accompany his first appearance before his sovereign.

Heriot, in anxious attention to save his young friend from any momentary awkwardness, had taken care to give the necessary password to the warders, grooms of the chambers, ushers, or by whatever name they were designated; so they passed on without interruption.

In this manner they passed several ante-rooms, filled chiefly with guards, attendants of the Court, and their acquaintances, male and female, who, dressed in their best apparel, and with eyes rounded by eager curiosity to make the most of their opportunity, stood, with beseeming modesty, ranked against the wall, in a manner which indicated that they were spectators, not performers, in the courtly exhibition.

Through these exterior apartments Lord Glenvarloch and his city friend advanced into a large and splendid withdrawing-room, communicating with the presence-chamber, into which ante-room were admitted those only who, from birth, their posts in the state or household, or by the particular grant of the kings, had right to attend the Court, as men entitled to pay their respects to their sovereign.

Amid this favoured and selected company, Nigel observed Sir Mungo Malagrowther, who, avoided and discountenanced by those who knew how low he stood in Court interest and favour, was but too happy in the opportunity of hooking himself upon a person of Lord Glenvarloch's rank, who was, as yet, so inexperienced as to feel it difficult to shake off an intruder.

The knight forthwith framed his grim features to a ghastly smile, and, after a preliminary and patronising nod to George Heriot, accompanied with an aristocratic wave of the hand, which intimated at once superiority and protection, he laid aside altogether the honest citizen, to whom he owed many a dinner, to attach himself exclusively to the young lord, although he suspected he might be occasionally in the predicament of needing one as much as himself. And even the notice of this original, singular and unamiable as he was, was not entirely indifferent to Lord Glenvarloch, since the absolute and somewhat constrained silence of his good friend Heriot, which left him at liberty to retire painfully to his own agitating reflections, was now relieved; while, on the other hand, he could not help feeling interest in the sharp and sarcastic information poured upon him by an observant, though discontented courtier, to whom a patient auditor, and he a man of title and rank, was as much a prize, as his acute and communicative disposition rendered him an entertaining companion to Nigel Olifaunt. Heriot, in the meantime, neglected by Sir Mungo, and avoiding every attempt by which the grateful politeness of Lord Glenvarloch strove to bring him into the conversation, stood by, with a kind of half smile on his countenance; but whether excited by Sir Mungo's wit, or arising at his expense, did not exactly appear.

In the meantime, the trio occupied a nook of the ante-room, next to the door of the presence-chamber, which was not yet thrown open, when Maxwell, with his rod of office, came bustling into the apartment, where most men, excepting those of high rank, made way for him. He stopped beside the party in which we are interested, looked for a moment at the young Scots nobleman, then made a slight obeisance to Heriot, and lastly, addressing Sir Mungo Malagrowther, began a hurried complaint to him of the misbehaviour of the gentlemen-pensioners and warders, who suffered all sort of citizens, suitors, and scriveners, to sneak into the outer apartments, without either respect or decency.—"The English," he said, "were scandalised, for such a thing durst not be attempted in the queen's days. In her time, there was then the court-yard for the mobility, and the apartments for the nobility; and it reflects on your place, Sir Mungo," he added, "belonging to the household as you do, that such things should not be better ordered."

Here Sir Mungo, afflicted, as was frequently the case on such occasions, with one of his usual fits of deafness, answered, "It was no wonder the mobility used freedoms, when those whom they saw in office were so little better in blood and havings than themselves."

"You are right, sir—quite right," said Maxwell, putting his hand on the tarnished embroidery on the old knight's sleeve,—"when such fellows see men in office dressed in cast-off suits, like paltry stage-players, it is no wonder the Court is thronged with intruders."

"Were you lauding the taste of my embroidery, Maister Maxwell?" answered the knight, who apparently interpreted the deputy-chamberlain's meaning rather from his action than his words;—"it is of an ancient and liberal pattern, having been made by your mother's father, auld James Stitchell, a master-fashioner of honest repute, in Merlin's Wynd, whom I made a point to employ, as I am now happy to remember, seeing your father thought fit to intermarry with sic a person's daughter."

Maxwell looked stern; but, conscious there was nothing to be got of Sir Mungo in the way of amends, and that prosecuting the quarrel with such an adversary would only render him ridiculous, and make public a mis-alliance of which he had no reason to be proud, he covered his resentment with a sneer; and, expressing his regret that Sir Mungo was become too deaf to understand or attend to what was said to him, walked on, and planted himself beside the folding-doors of the presence-chamber, at which he was to perform the duty of deputy-chamberlain, or usher, so soon as they should be opened.

"The door of the presence is about to open," said the goldsmith, in a whisper, to his young friend; "my condition permits me to go no farther with you. Fail not to present yourself boldly, according to your birth, and offer your Supplication; which the king will not refuse to accept, and, as I hope, to consider favourably."

As he spoke, the door of the presence-chamber opened accordingly, and, as is usual on such occasions, the courtiers began to advance towards it, and to enter in a slow, but continuous and uninterrupted stream.

As Nigel presented himself in his turn at the entrance, and mentioned his name and title, Maxwell seemed to hesitate. "You are not known to any one," he said. "It is my duty to suffer no one to pass to the presence, my lord, whose face is unknown to me, unless upon the word of a responsible person."

"I came with Master George Heriot," said Nigel, in some embarrassment at this unexpected interruption.

"Master Heriot's name will pass current for much gold and silver, my lord," replied Maxwell, with a civil sneer, "but not for birth and rank. I am compelled by my office to be peremptory.—The entrance is impeded—I am much concerned to say it—your lordship must stand back."

"What is the matter?" said an old Scottish nobleman, who had been speaking with George Heriot, after he had separated from Nigel, and who now came forward, observing the altercation betwixt the latter and Maxwell.

"It is only Master Deputy-Chamberlain Maxwell," said Sir Mungo Malagrowther, "expressing his joy to see Lord Glenvarloch at Court, whose father gave him his office—at least I think he is speaking to that purport—for your lordship kens my imperfection." A subdued laugh, such as the situation permitted, passed round amongst those who heard this specimen of Sir Mungo's sarcastic temper. But the old nobleman stepped still more forward, saying,—"What!—the son of my gallant old opponent, Ochtred Olifaunt—I will introduce him to the presence myself."

So saying, he took Nigel by the arm, without farther ceremony, and was about to lead him forward, when Maxwell, still keeping his rod across the door, said, but with hesitation and embarrassment—"My lord, this gentleman is not known, and I have orders to be scrupulous."

"Tutti—taiti, man," said the old lord, "I will be answerable he is his father's son, from the cut of his eyebrow—and thou, Maxwell, knewest his father well enough to have spared thy scruples. Let us pass, man." So saying, he put aside the deputy-chamberlain's rod, and entered the presence-room, still holding the young nobleman by the arm.

"Why, I must know you, man," he said; "I must know you. I knew your father well, man, and I have broke a lance and crossed a blade with him; and it is to my credit that I am living to brag of it. He was king's-man and I was queen's-man during the Douglas wars—young fellows both, that feared neither fire nor steel; and we had some old feudal quarrels besides, that had come down from father to son, with our seal-rings, two-harided broad-swords, and plate-coats, and the crests on our burgonets."

"Too loud, my Lord of Huntinglen," whispered a gentleman of the chamber,—"The King!—the King!"

The old earl (for such he proved) took the hint, and was silent; and James, advancing from a side-door, received in succession the compliments of strangers, while a little group of favourite courtiers, or officers of the household, stood around him, to whom he addressed himself from time to time. Some more pains had been bestowed on his toilette than upon the occasion when we first presented the monarch to our readers; but there was a natural awkwardness about his figure which prevented his clothes from sitting handsomely, and the prudence or timidity of his disposition had made him adopt the custom already noticed, of wearing a dress so thickly quilted as might withstand the stroke of a dagger, which added an ungainly stiffness to his whole appearance, contrasting oddly with the frivolous, ungraceful, and fidgeting motions with which he accompanied his conversation. And yet, though the king's deportment was very undignified, he had a manner so kind, familiar, and good-humoured, was so little apt to veil over or conceal his own foibles, and had so much indulgence and sympathy for those of others, that his address, joined to his learning, and a certain proportion of shrewd mother-wit, failed not to make a favourable impression on those who approached his person.

When the Earl of Huntinglen had presented Nigel to his sovereign, a ceremony which the good peer took upon himself, the king received the young lord very graciously, and observed to his introducer, that he "was fain to see them twa stand side by side; for I trow, my Lord Huntinglen," continued he, "your ancestors, ay, and e'en your lordship's self and this lad's father, have stood front to front at the sword's point, and that is a worse posture."

"Until your Majesty," said Lord Huntinglen, "made Lord Ochtred and me cross palms, upon the memorable day when your Majesty feasted all the nobles that were at feud together, and made them join hands in your presence—"

"I mind it weel," said the king; "I mind it weel—it was a blessed day, being the nineteen of September, of all days in the year—and it was a blithe sport to see how some of the carles girned as they clapped loofs together. By my saul, I thought some of them, mair special the Hieland chiels, wad have broken out in our own presence; but we caused them to march hand in hand to the Cross, ourselves leading the way, and there drink a blithe cup of kindness with ilk other, to the stanching of feud, and perpetuation of amity. Auld John Anderson was Provost that year—the carle grat for joy, and the bailies and councillors danced bare-headed in our presence like five-year-auld colts, for very triumph."

"It was indeed a happy day," said Lord Huntinglen, "and will not be forgotten in the history of your Majesty's reign."

"I would not that it were, my lord," replied the monarch—"I would not that it were pretermitted in our annals. Ay, ay—BEATI PACIFICI. My English lieges here may weel make much of me, for I would have them to know, they have gotten the only peaceable man that ever came of my family. If James with the Fiery Face had come amongst you," he said, looking round him, "or my great grandsire, of Flodden memory!"

"We should have sent him back to the north again," whispered one English nobleman.

"At least," said another, in the same inaudible tone, "we should have had a MAN to our sovereign, though he were but a Scotsman."

"And now, my young springald," said the king to Lord Glenvarloch, "where have you been spending your calf-time?"

"At Leyden, of late, may it please your Majesty," answered Lord Nigel.

"Aha! a scholar," said the king; "and, by my saul, a modest and ingenuous youth, that hath not forgotten how to blush, like most of our travelled Monsieurs. We will treat him conformably."

Then drawing himself up, coughing slightly, and looking around him with the conscious importance of superior learning, while all the courtiers who understood, or understood not, Latin, pressed eagerly forward to listen, the sapient monarch prosecuted his inquiries as follows:—

"Hem! hem! *salve bis, quaterque salve, glenvarlochides noster! Nuperumne ab lugduno batavorum britanniam rediisti?*"

The young nobleman replied, bowing low—

"*Imo, rex augustissime—biennium fere apud lugdunenses Moratus sum.*" James proceeded—

"*Biennium dicis? Bene, bene, optume factum est—non uno Die, quod dicunt,—intelligisti, domine glenvarlochiensis?* Aha!"

Nigel replied by a reverent bow, and the king, turning to those behind him, said—

"*Adolescens quidem ingenui vultus ingenuique pudoris.*" Then resumed his learned queries. "*Et quid hodie lugdunenses loquuntur—vossius vester nihilne novi scripsit?—nihil certe, quod doleo, typis recenter editit.*"

"*Valet quidem vossius, rex benevole.*" replied Nigel, "*ast senex veneratissimus annum agit, ni fallor, septuagesimum.*"

"*Virum, mehercle, vix tam grandaevum crediderim,*" replied the monarch. "*et vorstius iste?—arminii improbi successor aeque ac sectator—herosne adhuc, ut cum homero loquar?*"

Nigel, by good fortune, remembered that Vorstius, the divine last mentioned in his Majesty's queries about the state of Dutch literature, had been engaged in a personal controversy with James, in which the king had taken so deep an interest, as at length to hint in his public correspondence with the United States, that they would do well to apply the secular arm to stop the progress of heresy by violent measures against the Professor's person—a demand which their Mighty Mightinesses' principles of universal toleration induced them to elude, though with some difficulty. Knowing all this, Lord Glenvarloch, though a courtier of only five minutes' standing, had address enough to reply—

"*Vivum quidem, haud diu est, hominem videbam—vigere autem quis dicat qui sub fulminibus eloquentiae tuae, rex magne, jamdudum pronus jacet, et prostratus?*"*

This last tribute to his polemical powers completed James's happiness, which the triumph of exhibiting his erudition had already raised to a considerable height.

He rubbed his hands, snapped his fingers, fidgeted, chuckled, exclaimed—"*Euge! Belle! Optime!*" and turning to the Bishops of Exeter and Oxford, who stood behind him, he said.—"Ye see, my lords, no bad specimen of our Scottish Latinity, with which language we would all our subjects of England were as well embued as this, and other youths of honourable birth, in our auld kingdom; also, we keep the genuine and Roman pronunciation, like other learned nations on the continent, sae that we hold communing with any scholar in the universe, who can but speak the Latin tongue; whereas ye, our learned subjects of England, have introduced into your universities, otherwise most learned, a fashion of pronouncing like unto the 'nippit foot and clippit foot' of the bride in the fairy tale, whilk manner of speech, (take it not amiss that I be round with you) can be understood by no nation on earth saving yourselves; whereby Latin, *quoad anglos*, ceaseth to be *communis lingua*, the general dragoman, or interpreter, between all the wise men of the earth."

The Bishop of Exeter bowed, as in acquiescence to the royal censure; but he of Oxford stood upright, as mindful over what subjects his see extended, and as being equally willing to become food for fagots in defence of the Latinity of the university, as for any article of his religious creed.

The king, without awaiting an answer from either prelate, proceeded to question Lord Nigel, but in the vernacular tongue,—"Weel, my likely Alumnus of the Muses, and what make you so far from the north?"

* Lest any lady or gentleman should suspect there is aught of mystery concealed under the sentences printed in Italics, they will be pleased to understand that they contain only a few commonplace Latin phrases, relating to the state of letters in Holland, which neither deserve, nor would endure, a literal translation.

"To pay my homage to your Majesty," said the young nobleman, kneeling on one knee, "and to lay before you," he added, "this my humble and dutiful Supplication."

The presenting of a pistol would certainly have startled King James more, but could (setting apart the fright) hardly have been more unpleasing to his indolent disposition.

"And is it even so, man?" said he; "and can no single man, were it but for the rarity of the case, ever come up frae Scotland, excepting Ex Proposito—on set purpose, to see what he can make out of his loving sovereign? It is but three days syne that we had weel nigh lost our life, and put three kingdoms into dule-weeds, from the over haste of a clumsy-handed peasant, to thrust a packet into our hand, and now we are beset by the like impediment in our very Court. To our Secretary with that gear, my lord—to our Secretary with that gear."

"I have already offered my humble Supplication to your Majesty's Secretary of State," said Lord Glenvarloch—"but it seems—"

"That he would not receive it, I warrant?" said the king, interrupting him; "bu my saul, our Secretary kens that point of king-craft, called refusing, better than we do, and will look at nothing but what he likes himsell—I think I wad make a better Secretary to him than he to me.— Weel, my lord, you are welcome to London; and, as ye seem an acute and learned youth, I advise ye to turn your neb northward as soon as ye like, and settle yoursell for a while at Saint Andrews, and we will be right glad to hear that you prosper in your studies.—*Incumbite Remis Fortiter.*"

While the king spoke thus, he held the petition of the young lord carelessly, like one who only delayed till the suppliant's back was turned, to throw it away, or at least lay it aside to be no more looked at. The petitioner, who read this in his cold and indifferent looks, and in the manner in which he twisted and crumpled together the paper, arose with a bitter sense of anger and disappointment, made a profound obeisance, and was about to retire hastily. But Lord Huntinglen, who stood by him, checked his intention by an almost imperceptible touch upon the skirt of his cloak, and Nigel, taking the hint, retreated only a few steps from the royal presence, and then made a pause. In the meantime, Lord Huntinglen kneeled before James, in his turn, and said—"May it please your Majesty to remember, that upon one certain occasion you did promise to grant me a boon every year of your sacred life?"

"I mind it weel, man," answered James, "I mind it weel, and good reason why—it was when you unclasped the fause traitor Ruthven's fangs from about our royal throat, and drove your dirk into him like a true subject. We did then, as you remind us, (whilk was unnecessary,) being partly beside ourselves with joy at our liberation, promise we would grant you a free boon every year; whilk promise, on our coming to menseful possession of our royal faculties, we did confirm, *restrictive* always and *conditionaliter*, that your lordship's demand should be such as we, in our royal discretion, should think reasonable."

"Even so, gracious sovereign," said the old earl, "and may I yet farther crave to know if I have ever exceeded the bounds of your royal benevolence?"

"By my word, man, no!'" said the king; "I cannot remember you have asked much for yourself, if it be not a dog or a hawk, or a buck out of our park at Theobald's, or such like. But to what serves this preface?"

"To the boon to which I am now to ask of your Grace," said Lord Huntinglen; "which is, that your Majesty would be pleased, on the instant, to look at the placet of Lord Glenvarloch, and do upon it what your own just and royal nature shall think meet and just, without reference to your Secretary or any other of your Council."

"By my saul, my lord, this is strange," said the king; "ye are pleading for the son of your enemy!"

"Of one who WAS my enemy till your Majesty made him my friend," answered Lord Huntinglen.

"Weel spoken, my lord!" said the king; "and with, a true Christian spirit. And, respecting the Supplication of this young man, I partly guess where the matter lies; and in plain troth I had promised to George Heriot to be good to the lad—But then, here the shoe pinches. Steenie and Babie Charles cannot abide him—neither can your own son, my lord; and so, methinks, he had better go down to Scotland before he comes toill luck by them."

"My son, an it please your Majesty, so far as he is concerned, shall not direct my doings," said the earl, "nor any wild-headed young man of them all."

"Why, neither shall they mine," replied the monarch; "by my father's saul, none of them all shall play Rex with me—I will do what I will, and what I ought, like a free king."

"Your Majesty will then grant me my boon?" said the Lord Huntinglen.

"Ay, marry will I—marry will I," said the king; "but follow me this way, man, where we may be more private."

He led Lord Huntinglen with rather a hurried step through the courtiers, all of whom gazed earnestly on this unwonted scene, as is the fashion of all Courts on similar occasions. The king passed into a little cabinet, and bade, in the first moment, Lord Huntinglen lock or bar the door; but countermanded his direction in the next, saying,— "No, no, no—bread o' life, man, I am a free king—will do what I will and what I should—I am *justus et tenax propositi*, man—nevertheless, keep by the door, Lord Huntinglen, in case Steenie should come in with his mad humour."

"O my poor master!" groaned the Earl of Huntinglen. "When you were in your own cold country, you had warmer blood in your veins."

The king hastily looked over the petition or memorial, every now and then glancing his eye towards the door, and then sinking it hastily on the paper, ashamed that Lord Huntinglen, whom he respected, should suspect him of timidity.

"To grant the truth," he said, after he had finished his hasty perusal, "this is a hard case; and harder than it was represented to me, though I had some inkling of it before. And so the lad only wants payment of the siller due from us, in order to reclaim his paternal estate? But then, Huntinglen, the lad will have other debts—and why burden himsell with sae mony acres of barren woodland? let the land gang, man, let the land gang; Steenie has the promise of it from our Scottish Chancellor—it is the best hunting-ground in Scotland—and Babie Charles and Steenie want to kill a buck there this next year—they maun hae the land—they maun hae the land; and our debt shall be paid to the young man plack and bawbee, and he may have the spending of it at our Court; or if he has such an eard hunger, wouns! man, we'll stuff his stomach with English land, which is worth twice as much, ay, ten times as much, as these accursed hills and heughs, and mosses and muirs, that he is sae keen after."

All this while the poor king ambled up and down the apartment in a piteous state of uncertainty, which was made more ridiculous by his shambling circular mode of managing his legs, and his ungainly fashion on such occasions of fiddling with the bunches of ribbons which fastened the lower part of his dress.

Lord Huntinglen listened with great composure, and answered, "An it please your Majesty, there was an answer yielded by Naboth when

Ahab coveted his vineyard—'The Lord forbid that I should give the inheritance of my fathers unto thee.'"

"Ey, my lord—ey, my lord!" exclaimed James, while all the colour mounted both to his cheek and nose; "I hope ye mean not to teach me divinity? Ye need not fear, my lord, that I will shun to do justice to every man; and, since your lordship will give me no help to take up this in a more peaceful manner—whilk, methinks, would be better for the young man, as I said before,—why—since it maun be so—'sdeath, I am a free king, man, and he shall have his money and redeem his land, and make a kirk and a miln of it, an he will." So saying, he hastily wrote an order on the Scottish Exchequer for the sum in question, and then added, "How they are to pay it, I see not; but I warrant he will find money on the order among the goldsmiths, who can find it for every one but me.—And now you see, my Lord of Huntinglen, that I am neither an untrue man, to deny you the boon whilk I became bound for, nor an Ahab, to covet Naboth's vineyard; nor a mere nose-of-wax, to be twisted this way and that, by favourites and counsellors at their pleasure. I think you will grant now that I am none of those?"

"You are my own native and noble prince," said Huntinglen, as he knelt to kiss the royal hand—"just and generous, whenever you listen to the workings of your own heart."

"Ay, ay," said the king, laughing good-naturedly, as he raised his faithful servant from the ground, "that is what ye all say when I do any thing to please ye. There—there, take the sign-manual, and away with you and this young fellow. I wonder Steenie and Babie Charles have not broken in on us before now."

Lord Huntinglen hastened from the cabinet, foreseeing a scene at which he was unwilling to be present, but which sometimes occurred when James roused himself so far as to exert his own free will, of which he boasted so much, in spite of that of his imperious favourite Steenie, as he called the Duke of Buckingham, from a supposed resemblance betwixt his very handsome countenance, and that with which the Italian artists represented the protomartyr Stephen. In fact, the haughty favourite, who had the unusual good fortune to stand as high in the opinion of the heir-apparent as of the existing monarch, had considerably diminished in his respect towards the latter; and it was apparent, to the more shrewd courtiers, that James endured his domination rather from habit, timidity, and a dread of encountering his stormy passions, than from any heartfelt continuation of regard towards him, whose greatness had been the work of his own hands. To save himself the pain of seeing what was likely to take place on the duke's return, and to preserve the king from the additional humiliation which the presence of such a witness must have occasioned, the earl left the cabinet as speedily as possible, having first carefully pocketed the important sign-manual.

No sooner had he entered the presence-room, than he hastily sought Lord Glenvarloch, who had withdrawn into the embrasure of one of the windows, from the general gaze of men who seemed disposed only to afford him the notice which arises from surprise and curiosity, and, taking him by the arm, without speaking, led him out of the presence-chamber into the first ante-room. Here they found the worthy goldsmith, who approached them with looks of curiosity, which were checked by the old lord, who said hastily, "All is well.—Is your barge in waiting?" Heriot answered in the affirmative. "Then," said Lord Huntinglen, "you shall give me a cast in it, as the watermen say; and I, in requital, will give you both your dinner; for we must have some conversation together."

They both followed the earl without speaking, and were in the second ante-room when the important annunciation of the ushers, and the hasty murmur with which all made ample way as the company repeated to each other,—"The Duke—the Duke!" made them aware of the approach of the omnipotent favourite.

He entered, that unhappy minion of Court favour, sumptuously dressed in the picturesque attire which will live for ever on the canvas of Vandyke, and which marks so well the proud age, when aristocracy, though undermined and nodding to its fall, still, by external show and profuse expense, endeavoured to assert its paramount superiority over the inferior orders. The handsome and commanding countenance, stately form, and graceful action and manners of the Duke of Buckingham, made him become that picturesque dress beyond any man of his time. At present, however, his countenance seemed discomposed, his dress a little more disordered than became the place, his step hasty, and his voice imperative.

All marked the angry spot upon his brow, and bore back so suddenly to make way for him, that the Earl of Huntinglen, who affected no extraordinary haste on the occasion, with his companions, who could not, if they would, have decently left him, remained as it were by themselves in the middle of the room, and in the very path of the angry favourite. He touched his cap sternly as he looked on Huntinglen, but unbonneted to Heriot, and sunk his beaver, with its shadowy plume, as low as the floor, with a profound air of mock respect. In returning his greeting, which he did simply and unaffectedly, the citizen only said,—"Too much courtesy, my lord duke, is often the reverse of kindness."

"I grieve you should think so, Master Heriot," answered the duke; "I only meant, by my homage, to claim your protection, sir—your patronage. You are become, I understand, a solicitor of suits—a promoter—an undertaker—a fautor of court suitors of merit and quality, who chance to be pennyless. I trust your bags will bear you out in your new boast."

"They will bear me the farther, my lord duke," answered the goldsmith, "that my boast is but small."

"O, you do yourself less than justice, my good Master Heriot," continued the duke, in the same tone of irony; "you have a marvellous court-faction, to be the son of an Edinburgh tinker. Have the goodness to prefer me to the knowledge of the high-born nobleman who is honoured and advantaged by your patronage."

"That shall be my task," said Lord Huntinglen, with emphasis. "My lord duke, I desire you to know Nigel Olifaunt, Lord Glenvarloch, representative of one of the most ancient and powerful baronial houses in Scotland.—Lord Glenvarloch, I present you to his Grace the Duke of Buckingham, representative of Sir George Villiers, Knight of Brookesby, in the county of Leicester."

The duke coloured still more high as he bowed to Lord Glenvarloch scornfully, a courtesy which the other returned haughtily, and with restrained indignation. "We know each other, then," said the duke, after a moment's pause; and as if he had seen something in the young nobleman which merited more serious notice than the bitter raillery with which he had commenced—"we know each other—and you know me, my lord, for your enemy."

"I thank you for your plainness, my lord duke," replied Nigel; "an open enemy is better than a hollow friend."

"For you, my Lord Huntinglen," said the duke, "methinks you have but now overstepped the limits of the indulgence permitted to you, as the father of the prince's friend, and my own."

"By my word, my lord duke," replied the earl, "it is easy for any one to outstep boundaries, of the existence of which he was not aware. It is neither to secure my protection nor approbation, that my son keeps such exalted company."

"O, my lord, we know you, and indulge you," said the duke; "you are one of those who presume for a life-long upon the merit of one good action."

"In faith, my lord, and if it be so," said the old earl, "I have at least the advantage of such as presume more than I do, without having done any action of merit whatever. But I mean not to quarrel with you, my lord—we can neither be friends nor enemies—you have your path, and I have mine."

Buckingham only replied by throwing on his bonnet, and shaking its lofty plume with a careless and scornful toss of the head. They parted thus; the duke walking onwards through the apartments, and the others leaving the Palace and repairing to Whitehall Stairs, where they embarked on board the barge of the citizen.

X

Bid not thy fortune troll upon the wheels
Of yonder dancing cubes of mottled bone;
And drown it not, like Egypt's royal harlot,
Dissolving her rich pearl in the brimm'd wine-cup.
These are the arts, Lothario, which shrink acres
Into brief yards—bring sterling pounds to farthings,
Credit to infamy; and the poor gull,
Who might have lived an honour'd, easy life,
To ruin, and an unregarded grave.

—*The Changes*

W hen they were fairly embarked on the Thames, the earl took from his pocket the Supplication, and, pointing out to George Heriot the royal warrant indorsed thereon, asked him, if it were in due and regular form? The worthy citizen hastily read it over, thrust forth his hand as if to congratulate the Lord Glenvarloch, then checked himself, pulled out his barnacles, (a present from old David Ramsay,) and again perused the warrant with the most business-like and critical attention. "It is strictly correct and formal," he said, looking to the Earl of Huntinglen; "and I sincerely rejoice at it."

"I doubt nothing of its formality," said the earl; "the king understands business well, and, if he does not practise it often, it is only because indolence obscures parts which are naturally well qualified for the discharge of affairs. But what is next to be done for our young friend, Master Heriot? You know how I am circumstanced. Scottish lords living at the English Court have seldom command of money; yet, unless a sum can be presently raised on this warrant, matters standing as you hastily hinted to me, the mortgage, wadset, or whatever it is called, will be foreclosed."

"It is true," said Heriot, in some embarrassment; "there is a large sum wanted in redemption—yet, if it is not raised, there will be an expiry of the legal, as our lawyers call it, and the estate will be evicted."

"My noble—my worthy friends, who have taken up my cause so undeservedly, so unexpectedly," said Nigel, "do not let me be a burden on your kindness. You have already done too much where nothing was merited."

"Peace, man, peace," said Lord Huntinglen, "and let old Heriot and I puzzle this scent out. He is about to open—hark to him!"

"My lord," said the citizen, "the Duke of Buckingham sneers at our city money-bags; yet they can sometimes open, to prop a falling and a noble house."

"We know they can," said Lord Huntinglen—"mind not Buckingham, he is a Peg-a-Ramsay—and now for the remedy."

"I partly hinted to Lord Glenvarloch already," said Heriot, "that the redemption money might be advanced upon such a warrant as the present, and I will engage my credit that it can. But then, in order to secure the lender, he must come in the shoes of the creditor to whom he advances payment."

"Come in his shoes!" replied the earl; "why, what have boots or shoes to do with this matter, my good friend?"

"It is a law phrase, my lord. My experience has made me pick up a few of them," said Heriot.

"Ay, and of better things along with them, Master George," replied Lord Huntinglen; "but what means it?"

"Simply this," resumed the citizen; "that the lender of this money will transact with the holder of the mortgage, or wadset, over the estate of Glenvarloch, and obtain from him such a conveyance to his right as shall leave the lands pledged for the debt, in case the warrant upon the Scottish Exchequer should prove unproductive. I fear, in this uncertainty of public credit, that without some such counter security, it will be very difficult to find so large a sum."

"Ho la!" said the Earl of Huntinglen, "halt there! a thought strikes me.—What if the new creditor should admire the estate as a hunting-field, as much as my Lord Grace of Buckingham seems to do, and should wish to kill a buck there in the summer season? It seems to me, that on your plan, Master George, our new friend will be as well entitled to block Lord Glenvarloch out of his inheritance as the present holder of the mortgage."

The citizen laughed. "I will engage," he said, "that the keenest sportsman to whom I may apply on this occasion, shall not have a thought beyond the Lord Mayor's Easter-Hunt, in Epping Forest. But your lordship's caution is reasonable. The creditor must be bound to allow Lord Glenvarloch sufficient time to redeem his estate by means of the royal warrant, and must wave in his favour the right of instant foreclosure, which may be, I should think, the more easily managed, as the right of redemption must be exercised in his own name."

"But where shall we find a person in London fit to draw the necessary writings?" said the earl. "If my old friend Sir John Skene of Halyards had lived, we should have had his advice; but time presses, and—"

"I know," said Heriot, "an orphan lad, a scrivener, that dwells by Temple Bar; he can draw deeds both after the English and Scottish fashion, and I have trusted him often in matters of weight and of importance. I will send one of my serving-men for him, and the mutual deeds may be executed in your lordship's presence; for, as things stand, there should be no delay." His lordship readily assented; and, as they now landed upon the private stairs leading down to the river from the gardens of the handsome hotel which he inhabited, the messenger was dispatched without loss of time.

Nigel, who had sat almost stupefied while these zealous friends volunteered for him in arranging the measures by which his fortune was to be disembarrassed, now made another eager attempt to force upon them his broken expressions of thanks and gratitude. But he was again silenced by Lord Huntinglen, who declared he would not hear a word on that topic, and proposed instead, that they should take a turn in the pleached alley, or sit upon the stone bench which overlooked the Thames, until his son's arrival should give the signal for dinner.

"I desire to introduce Dalgarno and Lord Glenvarloch to each other," he said, "as two who will be near neighbours, and I trust will be more kind ones than their fathers were formerly. There is but three Scots miles betwixt the castles, and the turrets of the one are visible from the battlements of the other."

The old earl was silent for a moment, and appeared to muse upon the recollections which the vicinity of the castles had summoned up.

"Does Lord Dalgarno follow the Court to Newmarket next week?" said Heriot, by way of removing the conversation.

"He proposes so, I think," answered Lord Huntinglen, relapsed into his reverie for a minute or two, and then addressed Nigel somewhat abruptly—

"My young friend, when you attain possession of your inheritance, as I hope you soon will, I trust you will not add one to the idle followers of the Court, but reside on your patrimonial estate, cherish your ancient tenants, relieve and assist your poor kinsmen, protect the poor against subaltern oppression, and do what our fathers used to do, with fewer lights and with less means than we have."

"And yet the advice to keep the country," said Heriot, "comes from an ancient and constant ornament of the Court."

"From an old courtier, indeed," said the earl, "and the first of my family that could so write himself—my grey beard falls on a cambric ruff and a silken doublet—my father's descended upon a buff coat and a breast-plate. I would not that those days of battle returned; but I should love well to make the oaks of my old forest of Dalgarno ring once more with halloo, and horn, and hound, and to have the old stone-arched hall return the hearty shout of my vassals and tenants, as the bicker and the quaigh walked their rounds amongst them. I should like to see the broad Tay once more before I die—not even the Thames can match it, in my mind."

"Surely, my lord," said the citizen, "all this might be easily done—it costs but a moment's resolution, and the journey of some brief days, and you will be where you desire to be—what is there to prevent you?"

"Habits, Master George, habits," replied the earl, "which to young men are like threads of silk, so lightly are they worn, so soon broken; but which hang on our old limbs as if time had stiffened them into gyves of iron. To go to Scotland for a brief space were but labour in vain; and when I think of abiding there, I cannot bring myself to leave my old master, to whom I fancy myself sometimes useful, and whose weal and woe I have shared for so many years. But Dalgarno shall be a Scottish noble."

"Has he visited the North?" said Heriot.

"He was there last year and made such a report of the country, that the prince has expressed a longing to see it."

"Lord Dalgarno is in high grace with his Highness and the Duke of Buckingham?" observed the goldsmith.

"He is so," answered the earl,—"I pray it may be for the advantage of them all. The prince is just and equitable in his sentiments, though cold and stately in his manners, and very obstinate in his most trifling purposes; and the duke, noble and gallant, and generous and open, is fiery, ambitious, and impetuous. Dalgarno has none of these faults, and such as he may have of his own, may perchance be corrected by the society in which he moves.—See, here he comes."

Lord Dalgarno accordingly advanced from the farther end of the alley to the bench on which his father and his guests were seated, so that Nigel had full leisure to peruse his countenance and figure. He was dressed point-device, and almost to extremity, in the splendid fashion of the time, which suited well with his age, probably about five-and-twenty, with a noble form and fine countenance, in which last could easily be traced the manly features of his father, but softened by a more habitual air of assiduous courtesy than the stubborn old earl had ever condescended to assume towards the world in general. In other respects, his address was gallant, free, and unencumbered either by pride or ceremony—far remote certainly from the charge either of haughty coldness or forward impetuosity; and so far his father had justly freed him from the marked faults which he ascribed to the manners of the prince and his favourite Buckingham.

While the old earl presented his young acquaintance Lord Glenvarloch to his son, as one whom he would have him love and honour, Nigel marked the countenance of Lord Dalgarno closely, to see if he could detect aught of that secret dislike which the king had, in one of his broken expostulations, seemed to intimate, as arising from a clashing of interests betwixt his new friend and the great Buckingham. But nothing of this was visible; on the contrary, Lord Dalgarno received his new acquaintance with the open frankness and courtesy which makes conquest at once, when addressed to the feelings of an ingenuous young man.

It need hardly be told that his open and friendly address met equally ready and cheerful acceptation from Nigel Olifaunt. For many months, and while a youth not much above two-and-twenty, he had been restrained by circumstances from the conversation of his equals. When, on his father's sudden death, he left the Low Countries for Scotland, he had found himself involved, to all appearance inextricably, with the details of the law, all of which threatened to end in the alienation of the patrimony which should support his hereditary rank. His term of sincere mourning, joined to injured pride, and the swelling of the heart under unexpected and undeserved misfortune, together with the uncertainty attending the issue of his affairs, had induced the young Lord of Glenvarloch to live, while in Scotland, in a very private and reserved manner. How he had passed his time in London, the reader is acquainted with. But this melancholy and secluded course of life was neither agreeable to his age nor to his temper, which was genial and sociable. He hailed, therefore, with sincere pleasure, the approaches which a young man of his own age and rank made towards him; and when he had exchanged with Lord Dalgarno some of those words and signals by which, as surely as by those of freemasonry, young people recognise a mutual wish to be agreeable to each other, it seemed as if the two noblemen had been acquainted for some time.

Just as this tacit intercourse had been established, one of Lord Huntinglen's attendants came down the alley, marshalling onwards a man dressed in black buckram, who followed him with tolerable speed, considering that, according to his sense of reverence and propriety, he kept his body bent and parallel to the horizon from the moment that he came in sight of the company to which he was about to be presented.

"Who is this, you cuckoldy knave," said the old lord, who had retained the keen appetite and impatience of a Scottish baron even during a long alienation from his native country; "and why does John Cook, with a murrain to him, keep back dinner?"

"I believe we are ourselves responsible for this person's intrusion," said George Heriot; "this is the scrivener whom we desired to see.— Look up, man, and see us in the face as an honest man should, instead of beating thy noddle charged against us thus, like a battering-ram."

The scrivener did look up accordingly, with the action of an automaton which suddenly obeys the impulse of a pressed spring. But, strange to tell, not even the haste he had made to attend his patron's mandate, a business, as Master Heriot's message expressed, of weight and importance—nay not even the state of depression in which, out of sheer humility, doubtless, he had his head stooped to the earth, from the moment he had trod the demesnes of the Earl of Huntinglen, had called any colour into his countenance. The drops stood on his brow from haste and toil, but his cheek was still pale and tallow-coloured as before; nay, what seemed stranger, his very hair, when he raised his head, hung down on either cheek as straight and sleek and undisturbed as it was when we first introduced him to our readers, seated at his quiet and humble desk.

Lord Dalgarno could not forbear a stifled laugh at the ridiculous and puritanical figure which presented itself like a starved anatomy to the company, and whispered at the same time into Lord Glenvarloch's ear—

"The devil damn thee black, thou cream-faced loon,
Where got'st thou that goose-look?"

Nigel was too little acquainted with the English stage to understand a quotation which had already grown matter of common allusion in London. Lord Dalgarno saw that he was not understood, and continued, "That fellow, by his visage, should either be a saint, or a most hypocritical rogue—and such is my excellent opinion of human nature, that I always suspect the worst. But they seem deep in business. Will you take a turn with me in the garden, my lord, or will you remain a member of the serious conclave?"

"With you, my lord, most willingly," said Nigel; and they were turning away accordingly, when George Heriot, with the formality belonging to his station, observed, that, "as their business concerned Lord Glenvarloch, he had better remain, to make himself master of it, and witness to it."

"My presence is utterly needless, my good lord;-and, my best friend, Master Heriot," said the young nobleman, "I shall understand nothing the better for cumbering you with my ignorance in these matters; and can only say at the end, as I now say at the beginning, that I dare not take the helm out of the hand of the kind pilots who have already guided my course within sight of a fair and unhoped-for haven. Whatever you recommend to me as fitting, I shall sign and seal; and the import of the deeds I shall better learn by a brief explanation from Master Heriot, if he will bestow so much trouble in my behalf, than by a thousand learned words and law terms from this person of skill."

"He is right," said Lord Huntinglen; "our young friend is right, in confiding these matters to you and me, Master George Heriot—he has not misplaced his confidence."

Master George Heriot cast a long look after the two young noblemen, who had now walked down the alley arm-in-arm, and at length said, "He hath not, indeed, misplaced his confidence, as your lordship well and truly says—but, nevertheless, he is not in the right path; for it behoves every man to become acquainted with his own affairs, so soon as he hath any that are worth attending to."

When he had made this observation, they applied themselves, with the scrivener, to look into various papers, and to direct in what manner writings should be drawn, which might at once afford sufficient security to those who were to advance the money, and at the same time preserve the right of the young nobleman to redeem the family estate, provided he should obtain the means of doing so, by the expected reimbursement from the Scottish Exchequer, or otherwise. It is needless to enter into those details. But it is not unimportant to mention, as an illustration of character, that Heriot went into the most minute legal details with a precision which showed that experience had made him master even of the intricacies of Scottish conveyancing; and that the Earl of Huntinglen, though far less acquainted with technical detail, suffered no step of the business to pass over, until he had attained a general but distinct idea of its import and its propriety.

They seemed to be admirably seconded in their benevolent intentions towards the young Lord Glenvarloch, by the skill and eager zeal of the scrivener, whom Heriot had introduced to this piece of business, the most important which Andrew had ever transacted in his life, and the particulars of which were moreover agitated in his presence between an actual earl, and one whose wealth and character might entitle him to be an alderman of his ward, if not to be lord mayor, in his turn.

While they were thus in eager conversation on business, the good earl even forgetting the calls of his appetite, and the delay of dinner, in his anxiety to see that the scrivener received proper instructions, and that all was rightly weighed and considered, before dismissing him to engross the necessary deeds, the two young men walked together on the terrace which overhung the river, and talked on the topics which Lord Dalgarno, the elder, and the more experienced, thought most likely to interest his new friend.

These naturally regarded the pleasures attending a Court life; and Lord Dalgarno expressed much surprise at understanding that Nigel proposed an instant return to Scotland.

"You are jesting with me," he said. "All the Court rings—it is needless to mince it—with the extraordinary success of your suit—against the highest interest, it is said, now influencing the horizon at Whitehall. Men think of you—talk of you—fix their eyes on you—ask each other, who is this young Scottish lord, who has stepped so far in a single day? They augur, in whispers to each other, how high and how far you may push your fortune—and all that you design to make of it, is, to return to Scotland, eat raw oatmeal cakes, baked upon a peat-fire, have your hand shaken by every loon of a blue-bonnet who chooses to dub you cousin, though your relationship comes by Noah; drink Scots twopenny ale, eat half-starved red-deer venison, when you can kill it, ride upon a galloway, and be called my right honourable and maist worthy lord!"

"There is no great gaiety in the prospect before me, I confess," said Lord Glenvarloch, "even if your father and good Master Heriot should succeed in putting my affairs on some footing of plausible hope. And yet I trust to do something for my vassals as my ancestors before me, and to teach my children, as I have myself been taught, to make some personal sacrifices, if they be necessary, in order to maintain with dignity the situation in which they are placed by Providence."

Lord Dalgarno, after having once or twice stifled his laughter during this speech, at length broke out into a fit of mirth, so hearty and so resistless, that, angry as he was, the call of sympathy swept Nigel along with him, and despite of himself, he could not forbear to join in a burst of laughter, which he thought not only causeless, but almost impertinent.

He soon recollected himself, however, and said, in a tone qualified to allay Lord Dalgarno's extreme mirth: "This is all well, my lord; but how am I to understand your merriment?" Lord Dalgarno only answered him with redoubled peals of laughter, and at length held by Lord Glenvarloch's cloak, as if to prevent his falling down on the ground, in the extremity of his convulsion.

At length, while Nigel stood half abashed, half angry, at becoming thus the subject of his new acquaintance's ridicule, and was only restrained from expressing his resentment against the son, by a sense of the obligations he owed the father, Lord Dalgarno recovered himself, and spoke in a half-broken voice, his eyes still running with tears: "I crave your pardon, my dear Lord Glenvarloch—ten thousand times do I crave your pardon. But that last picture of rural dignity, accompanied by your grave and angry surprise at my laughing at what would have made any court-bred hound laugh, that had but so much as bayed the moon once from the court-yard at Whitehall, totally overcame me. Why, my liefest and dearest lord, you, a young and handsome fellow, with high birth, a title, and the name of an estate, so well received by the king at your first starting, as makes your further progress scarce matter of doubt, if you know how to improve it—for the king has already said you are a 'braw lad, and well studied in the more humane letters'—you, too, whom all the women, and the very marked beauties of the Court, desire to see, because you came from Leyden, were born in Scotland, and have gained a hard-contested suit in England—you, I say, with a person like a prince, an eye of fire, and a wit as quick, to think of throwing your cards on the table when the game is in your very hand, running back to the frozen north, and marrying—let me see—a tall, stalking, blue-eyed, fair-skinned bony wench, with eighteen quarters in her scutcheon, a sort of Lot's wife, newly descended from her pedestal, and with her to shut yourself up in your tapestried chamber! Uh, gad!—Swouns, I shall never survive the idea!"

It is seldom that youth, however high-minded, is able, from mere strength of character and principle, to support itself against the force of ridicule. Half angry, half mortified, and, to say truth, half ashamed of his more manly and better purpose, Nigel was unable, and flattered himself it was unnecessary, to play the part of a rigid moral patriot, in presence of a young man whose current fluency of language, as well as his experience in the highest circles of society, gave him, in spite of Nigel's better and firmer thoughts, a temporary ascendency over him. He sought, therefore, to compromise the matter, and avoid farther debate, by frankly owning, that, if to return to his own country were not his choice, it was at least a matter of necessity. "His affairs," he said, "were unsettled, his income precarious."

"And where is he whose affairs are settled, or whose income is less than precarious, that is to be found in attendance on the Court?" said Lord Dalgarno; "all are either losing or winning. Those who have wealth, come hither to get rid of it, while the happy gallants, who, like you and I, dear Glenvarloch, have little or none, have every chance to be sharers in their spoils."

"I have no ambition of that sort," said Nigel, "and if I had, I must tell you plainly, Lord Dalgarno, I have not the means to do so. I can scarce as yet call the suit I wear my own; I owe it, and I do riot blush to say so, to the friendship of yonder good man."

"I will not laugh again, if I can help it," said Lord Dalgarno. "But, Lord! that you should have gone to a wealthy goldsmith for your habit— why, I could have brought you to an honest, confiding tailor, who should have furnished you with half-a-dozen, merely for love of the little word, 'lordship,' which you place before your name;—and then your goldsmith, if he be really a friendly goldsmith, should have equipped you with such a purse of fair rose-nobles as would have bought you thrice as many suits, or done better things for you."

"I do not understand these fashions, my lord," said Nigel, his displeasure mastering his shame; "were I to attend the Court of my sovereign, it should be when I could maintain, without shifting or borrowing, the dress and retinue which my rank requires."

"Which my rank requires!" said Lord Dalgarno, repeating his last words; "that, now, is as good as if my father had spoke it. I fancy you would love to move to Court with him, followed by a round score of old blue-bottles, with white heads and red noses, with bucklers and broadswords, which their hands, trembling betwixt age and strong waters, can make no use of—as many huge silver badges on their arms, to show whose fools they are, as would furnish forth a court cupboard of plate—rogues fit for nothing but to fill our ante-chambers with the flavour of onions and genievre—pah!"

"The poor knaves!" said Lord Glenvarloch; "they have served your father, it may be, in the wars. What would become of them were he to turn them off?"

"Why, let them go to the hospital," said Dalgarno, "or to the bridge-end, to sell switches. The king is a better man than my father, and you see those who have served in His wars do so every day; or, when their blue coats were well worn out, they would make rare scarecrows. Here is a fellow, now, comes down the walk; the stoutest raven dared not come within a yard of that copper nose. I tell you, there is more service, as you will soon see, in my valet of the chamber, and such a lither lad as my page Lutin, than there is in a score of these old memorials of the Douglas wars,* where they cut each other's throats for the chance of finding twelve pennies Scots on the person of the slain. Marry, my lord, to make amends, they will eat mouldy victuals, and drink stale ale, as if their bellies were puncheons.—But the dinner-bell is going to sound—hark, it is clearing its rusty throat, with a preliminary jowl. That is another clamorous relic of antiquity, that, were I master, should soon be at the bottom of the Thames. How the foul fiend can it interest the peasants and mechanics in the Strand, to know that the Earl of Huntinglen is sitting down to dinner? But my father looks our way— we must not be late for the grace, or we shall be in Dis-grace, if you will forgive a quibble which would have made his Majesty laugh. You will find us all of a piece, and, having been accustomed to eat in saucers abroad, I am ashamed you should witness our larded capons, our mountains of beef, and oceans of brewis, as large as Highland hills and lochs; but you shall see better cheer to-morrow. Where lodge you? I will call for you. I must be your guide through the peopled desert, to certain enchanted lands, which you will scarce discover without chart and pilot. Where lodge you?"

"I will meet you in Paul's," said Nigel, a good deal embarrassed, "at any hour you please to name."

---

* The cruel civil wars waged by the Scottish barons during the minority of James VI, had the name from the figure made in them by the celebrated James Douglas, Earl of Morton. Both sides executed their prisoners without mercy or favour.

"O, you would be private," said the young lord; "nay, fear not me—I will be no intruder. But we have attained this huge larder of flesh, fowl, and fish. I marvel the oaken boards groan not under it."

They had indeed arrived in the dining-parlour of the mansion, where the table was superabundantly loaded, and where the number of attendants, to a certain extent, vindicated the sarcasms of the young nobleman. The chaplain, and Sir Mungo Malagrowther, were of the party. The latter complimented Lord Glenvarloch upon the impression he had made at Court. "One would have thought ye had brought the apple of discord in your pouch, my lord, or that you were the very firebrand of whilk Althea was delivered, and that she had lain-in in a barrel of gunpowder, for the king, and the prince, and the duke, have been by the lugs about ye, and so have many more, that kendna before this blessed day that there was such a man living on the face of the earth."

"Mind your victuals, Sir Mungo," said the earl; "they get cold while you talk."

"Troth, and that needsna, my lord," said the knight; "your lordship's dinners seldom scald one's mouth—the serving-men are turning auld, like oursells, my lord, and it is far between the kitchen and the ha'."

With this little explosion of his spleen, Sir Mungo remained satisfied, until the dishes were removed, when, fixing his eyes on the brave new doublet of Lord Dalgarno, he complimented him on his economy, pretending to recognise it as the same which his father had worn in Edinburgh in the Spanish ambassador's time. Lord Dalgarno, too much a man of the world to be moved by any thing from such a quarter, proceeded to crack some nuts with great deliberation, as he replied, that the doublet was in some sort his father's, as it was likely to cost him fifty pounds some day soon. Sir Mungo forthwith proceeded in his own way to convey this agreeable intelligence to the earl, observing, that his son was a better maker of bargains than his lordship, for he had bought a doublet as rich as that his lordship wore when the Spanish ambassador was at Holyrood, and it had cost him but fifty pounds Scots;—"that was no fool's bargain, my lord."

"Pounds sterling, if you please, Sir Mungo," answered the earl, calmly; "and a fool's bargain it is, in all the tenses. Dalgarno Was a fool when he bought—I *will* be a fool when I pay—and you, Sir Mungo, craving your pardon, *are* a fool *in praesenti*, for speaking of what concerns you not."

So saying, the earl addressed himself to the serious business of the table and sent the wine around with a profusion which increased the hilarity, but rather threatened the temperance, of the company, until their joviality was interrupted by the annunciation that the scrivener had engrossed such deeds as required to be presently executed.

George Heriot rose from the table, observing, that wine-cups and legal documents were unseemly neighbours. The earl asked the scrivener if they had laid a trencher and set a cup for him in the buttery and received the respectful answer, that heaven forbid he should be such an ungracious beast as to eat or drink until his lordship's pleasure was performed.

"Thou shalt eat before thou goest," said Lord Huntinglen; "and I will have thee try, moreover, whether a cup of sack cannot bring some colour into these cheeks of thine. It were a shame to my household, thou shouldst glide out into the Strand after such a spectre-fashion as thou now wearest—Look to it, Dalgarno, for the honour of our roof is concerned."

Lord Dalgarno gave directions that the man should be attended to. Lord Glenvarloch and the citizen, in the meanwhile, signed and interchanged, and thus closed a transaction, of which the principal party concerned understood little, save that it was under the management of a zealous and faithful friend, who undertook that the money should be forthcoming, and the estate released from forfeiture, by payment of the stipulated sum for which it stood pledged, and that at the term of Lambmas, and at the hour of noon, and beside the tomb of the Regent Earl of Murray, in the High Kirk of Saint Giles, at Edinburgh, being the day and place assigned for such redemption.*

When this business was transacted, the old earl would fain have renewed his carouse; but the citizen, alleging the importance of the deeds he had about him, and the business he had to transact betimes the next morning, not only refused to return to table, but carried with him to his barge Lord Glenvarloch, who might, perhaps, have been otherwise found more tractable.

When they were seated in the boat, and fairly once more afloat on the river, George Heriot looked back seriously on the mansion they had

---

* As each covenant in those days of accuracy had a special place nominated for execution, the tomb of the Regent Earl of Murray in Saint Giles's Church was frequently assigned for the purpose.

left—"There live," he said, "the old fashion and the new. The father is like a noble old broadsword, but harmed with rust, from neglect and inactivity; the son is your modern rapier, well-mounted, fairly gilt, and fashioned to the taste of the time—and it is time must evince if the metal be as good as the show. God grant it prove so, says an old friend to the family."

Nothing of consequence passed betwixt them, until Lord Glenvarloch, landing at Paul's Wharf, took leave of his friend the citizen, and retired to his own apartment, where his attendant, Richie, not a little elevated with the events of the day, and with the hospitality of Lord Huntinglen's house-keeping, gave a most splendid account of them to the buxom Dame Nelly, who rejoiced to hear that the sun at length was shining upon what Richie called "the right side of the hedge."

XI

You are not for the manner nor the times,
They have their vices now most like to virtues;
You cannot know them apait by any difference,
They wear the same clothes, eat the same meat—
Sleep i' the self-same beds, ride in those coaches,
Or very like four horses in a coach,
As the best men and women.

—Ben Jonson

On the following morning, while Nigel, his breakfast finished, was thinking how he should employ the day, there was a little bustle upon the stairs which attracted his attention, and presently entered Dame Nelly, blushing like scarlet, and scarce able to bring out—"A young nobleman, sir—no one less," she added, drawing her hand slightly over her lips, "would be so saucy—a young nobleman, sir, to wait on you!"

And she was followed into the little cabin by Lord Dalgarno, gay, easy, disembarrassed, and apparently as much pleased to rejoin his new acquaintance as if he had found him in the apartments of a palace. Nigel, on the contrary, (for youth is slave to such circumstances,) was discountenanced and mortified at being surprised by so splendid a gallant in a chamber which, at the moment the elegant and high-dressed cavalier appeared in it, seemed to its inhabitant, yet lower, narrower, darker, and meaner than it had ever shown before. He would have made some apology for the situation, but Lord Dalgarno cut him short—

"Not a word of it," he said, "not a single word—I know why you ride at anchor here—but I can keep counsel—so pretty a hostess would recommend worse quarters."

"On my word—on my honour," said Lord Glenvarloch—

"Nay, nay, make no words of the matter," said Lord Dalgarno; "I am no tell-tale, nor shall I cross your walk; there is game enough in the forest, thank Heaven, and I can strike a doe for myself."

All this he said in so significant a manner, and the explanation which he had adopted seemed to put Lord Glenvarloch's gallantry on so respectable a footing, that Nigel ceased to try to undeceive him; and less ashamed, perhaps, (for such is human weakness,) of supposed vice than of real poverty, changed the discourse to something else, and left poor Dame Nelly's reputation and his own at the mercy of the young courtier's misconstruction.

He offered refreshments with some hesitation. Lord Dalgarno had long since breakfasted, but had just come from playing a set of tennis, he said, and would willingly taste a cup of the pretty hostess's single beer. This was easily procured, was drunk, was commended, and, as the hostess failed not to bring the cup herself, Lord Dalgarno profited by the opportunity to take a second and more attentive view of her, and then gravely drank to her husband's health, with an almost imperceptible nod to Lord Glenvarloch. Dame Nelly was much honoured, smoothed her apron down with her hands, and said

"Her John was greatly and truly honoured by their lordships—he was a kind painstaking man for his family, as was in the alley, or indeed, as far north as Paul's Chain."

She would have proceeded probably to state the difference betwixt their ages, as the only alloy to their nuptial happiness; but her lodger, who had no mind to be farther exposed to his gay friend's raillery, gave her, contrary to his wont, a signal to leave the room.

Lord Dalgarno looked after her, and then looked at Glenvarloch, shook his head, and repeated the well-known lines—

"'My lord, beware of jealousy—It is the green-eyed monster which doth make the meat it feeds on.'

"But come," he said, changing his tone, "I know not why I should worry you thus—I who have so many follies of my own, when I should rather make excuse for being here at all, and tell you wherefore I came."

So saying, he reached a seat, and, placing another for Lord Glenvarloch, in spite of his anxious haste to anticipate this act of courtesy, he proceeded in the same tone of easy familiarity:—

"We are neighbours, my lord, and are just made known to each other. Now, I know enough of the dear North, to be well aware that Scottish neighbours must be either dear friends or deadly enemies—must either walk hand-in-hand, or stand sword-point to sword-point; so I choose the hand-in-hand, unless you should reject my proffer."

"How were it possible, my lord," said Lord Glenvarloch, "to refuse what is offered so frankly, even if your father had not been a second father to me?"—And, as he took Lord Dalgarno's hand, he added—"I have, I think, lost no time, since, during one day's attendance at Court, I have made a kind friend and a powerful enemy."

"The friend thanks you," replied Lord Dalgarno, "for your just opinion; but, my dear Glenvarloch—or rather, for titles are too formal between us of the better file—what is your Christian name?"

"Nigel," replied Lord Glenvarloch.

"Then we will be Nigel and Malcolm to each other," said his visitor, "and my lord to the plebeian world around us. But I was about to ask you whom you suppose your enemy?"

"No less than the all-powerful favourite, the great Duke of Buckingham."

"You dream! What could possess you with such an opinion?" said Dalgarno.

"He told me so himself," replied Glenvarloch; "and, in so doing, dealt frankly and honourably with me."

"O, you know him not yet," said his companion; "the duke is moulded of an hundred noble and fiery qualities, that prompt him, like a generous horse, to spring aside in impatience at the least obstacle to his forward course. But he means not what he says in such passing heats—I can do more with him, I thank Heaven, than most who are around him; you shall go visit him with me, and you will see how you shall be received."

"I told you, my lord," said Glenvarloch firmly, and with some haughtiness, "the Duke of Buckingham, without the least offence, declared himself my enemy in the face of the Court; and he shall retract that aggression as publicly as it was given, ere I will make the slightest advance towards him."

"You would act becomingly in every other case," said Lord Dalgarno, "but here you are wrong. In the Court horizon Buckingham is Lord of the Ascendant, and as he is adverse or favouring, so sinks or rises the fortune of a suitor. The king would bid you remember your Phaedrus,

'Arripiens geminas, ripis cedentibus, ollas—'

and so forth. You are the vase of earth; beware of knocking yourself against the vase of iron."

"The vase of earth," said Glenvarloch, "will avoid the encounter, by getting ashore out of the current—I mean to go no more to Court."

"O, to Court you necessarily must go; you will find your Scottish suit move ill without it, for there is both patronage and favour necessary to enforce the sign-manual you have obtained. Of that we will speak more hereafter; but tell me in the meanwhile, my dear Nigel, whether you did not wonder to see me here so early?"

"I am surprised that you could find me out in this obscure corner," said Lord Glenvarloch.

"My page Lutin is a very devil for that sort of discovery," replied Lord Dalgarno; "I have but to say, 'Goblin, I would know where he or she dwells,' and he guides me thither as if by art magic."

"I hope he waits not now in the street, my lord," said Nigel; "I will send my servant to seek him."

"Do not concern yourself—he is by this time," said Lord Dalgarno, "playing at hustle-cap and chuck-farthing with the most blackguard imps upon the wharf, unless he hath foregone his old customs."

"Are you not afraid," said Lord Glenvarloch, "that in such company his morals may become depraved?"

"Let his company look to their own," answered Lord Dalgarno, cooly; "for it will be a company of real fiends in which Lutin cannot teach more mischief than he can learn: he is, I thank the gods, most thoroughly versed in evil for his years. I am spared the trouble of looking after his moralities, for nothing can make them either better or worse."

"I wonder you can answer this to his parents, my lord," said Nigel.

"I wonder where I should find his parents," replied his companion, "to render an account to them."

"He may be an orphan," said Lord Nigel; "but surely, being a page in your lordship's family, his parents must be of rank."

"Of as high rank as the gallows could exalt them to," replied Lord Dalgarno, with the same indifference; "they were both hanged, I believe—at least the gipsies, from whom I bought him five years ago, intimated as much to me.—You are surprised at this, now. But is it not better that, instead of a lazy, conceited, whey-faced slip of gentility, to whom, in your old-world idea of the matter, I was bound to stand Sir Pedagogue, and see that he washed his hands and face, said his prayers, learned his acddens, spoke no naughty words, brushed his hat, and wore his best doublet only on Sunday,—that, instead of such a Jacky Goodchild, I should have something like this?"

He whistled shrill and clear, and the page he spoke of darted into the room, almost with the effect of an actual apparition. From his height he seemed but fifteen, but, from his face, might be two or even three years older, very neatly made, and richly dressed; with a thin bronzed visage, which marked his gipsy descent, and a pair of sparkling black eyes, which seemed almost to pierce through those whom he looked at.

"There he is," said Lord Dalgarno, "fit for every element—prompt to execute every command, good, bad, or indifferent—unmatched in his tribe, as rogue, thief, and liar."

"All which qualities," said the undaunted page, "have each in turn stood your lordship in stead."

"Out, you imp of Satan!" said his master; "vanish-begone-or my conjuring rod goes about your ears." The boy turned, and disappeared as suddenly as he had entered. "You see," said Lord Dalgarno, "that, in choosing my household, the best regard I can pay to gentle blood is to exclude it from my service—that very gallows—bird were enough to corrupt a whole antechamber of pages, though they were descended from kings and kaisers."

"I can scarce think that a nobleman should need the offices of such an attendant as your goblin," said Nigel; "you are but jesting with my inexperience."

"Time will show whether I jest or not, my dear Nigel," replied Dalgarno; "in the meantime, I have to propose to you to take the advantage of the flood-tide, to run up the river for pastime; and at noon I trust you will dine with me."

Nigel acquiesced in a plan which promised so much amusement; and his new friend and he, attended by Lutin and Moniplies, who greatly resembled, when thus associated, the conjunction of a bear and a monkey, took possession of Lord Dalgarno's wherry, which, with its badged watermen, bearing his lordship's crest on their arms, lay in readiness to receive them. The air was delightful upon the river; and the lively conversation of Lord Dalgarno added zest to the pleasures of the little voyage. He could not only give an account of the various public buildings and noblemen's houses which they passed in ascending the Thames, but knew how to season his information with abundance of anecdote, political innuendo, and personal scandal; if he had not very much wit, he was at least completely master of the fashionable tone, which in that time, as in ours, more than amply supplies any deficiency of the kind.

It was a style of conversation entirely new to his companion, as was the world which Lord Dalgarno opened to his observation; and it is no wonder that Nigel, notwithstanding his natural good sense and high spirit, admitted, more readily than seemed consistent with either, the tone of authoritative instruction which his new friend assumed towards him. There would, indeed, have been some difficulty in making a stand. To attempt a high and stubborn tone of morality, in answer to the light strain of Lord Dalgarno's conversation, which kept on the frontiers between jest and earnest, would have seemed pedantic and ridiculous; and every attempt which Nigel made to combat his companion's propositions, by reasoning as jocose as his own, only showed his inferiority in that gay species of controversy. And it must be owned, besides, though internally disapproving much of what he heard, Lord Glenvarloch, young as he was in society, became less alarmed by the language and manners of his new associate, than in prudence he ought to have been.

Lord Dalgarno was unwilling to startle his proselyte, by insisting upon any topic which appeared particularly to jar with his habits or principles; and he blended his mirth and his earnest so dexterously, that it was impossible for Nigel to discover how far he was serious in his propositions, or how far they flowed from a wild and extravagant spirit of raillery. And, ever and anon, those flashes of spirit and honour crossed his conversation, which seemed to intimate, that, when stirred to action by some adequate motive, Lord Dalgarno would prove something very different from the court-haunting and ease-loving voluptuary, which he was pleased to represent as his chosen character.

As they returned down the river, Lord Glenvarloch remarked, that the boat passed the mansion of Lord Huntinglen, and noticed the circumstance to Lord Dalgarno, observing, that he thought they were to have dined there. "Surely no," said the young nobleman, "I have more mercy on you than to gorge you a second time with raw beef and canary wine. I propose something better for you, I promise you, than such a second Scythian festivity. And as for my father, he proposes to dine to-day with my grave, ancient Earl of Northampton, whilome that celebrated putter-down of pretended prophecies, Lord Henry Howard."

"And do you not go with him?" said his companion.

"To what purpose?" said Lord Dalgarno. "To hear his wise lordship speak musty politics in false Latin, which the old fox always uses, that he may give the learned Majesty of England an opportunity of correcting his slips in grammar? That were a rare employment!"

"Nay," said Lord Nigel, "but out of respect, to wait on my lord your father."

"My lord my father," replied Lord Dalgarno, "has blue-bottles enough to wait on him, and can well dispense with such a butterfly as myself. He can lift the cup of sack to his head without my assistance; and, should the said paternal head turn something giddy, there be men enough to guide his right honourable lordship to his lordship's right honourable couch.—Now, do not stare at me, Nigel, as if my words were to sink the boat with us. I love my father—I love him dearly—and I respect him, too, though I respect not many things; a trustier old Trojan never belted a broadsword by a loop of leather. But what then? He belongs to the old world, I to the new. He has his follies, I have mine; and the less either of us sees of the other's peccadilloes, the greater will be the honour and respect—that, I think, is the proper phrase—I say the *respect* in which we shall hold each other. Being apart, each of us is himself, such as nature and circumstances have made him; but, couple us up too closely together, you will be sure to have in your leash either an old hypocrite or a young one, or perhaps both the one and t'other."

As he spoke thus, the boat put into the landing-place at Blackfriars. Lord Dalgarno sprung ashore, and, flinging his cloak and rapier to his page, recommended to his companion to do the like. "We are coming among a press of gallants," he said; "and, if we walked thus muffled, we shall look like your tawny-visaged Don, who wraps him close in his cloak, to conceal the defects of his doublet."

"I have known many an honest man do that, if it please your lordship," said Richie Moniplies, who had been watching for an opportunity to intrude himself on the conversation, and probably remembered what had been his own condition, in respect to cloak and doublet, at a very recent period.

Lord Dalgarno stared at him, as if surprised at his assurance; but immediately answered, "You may have known many things, friend; but, in the meanwhile, you do not know what principally concerns your master, namely, how to carry his cloak, so as to show to advantage the gold-laced seams, and the lining of sables. See how Lutin holds the sword, with his cloak cast partly over it, yet so as to set off the embossed hilt, and the silver work of the mounting.—Give your familiar your sword, Nigel," he continued, addressing Lord Glenvarloch, "that he may practise a lesson in an art so necessary."

"Is it altogether prudent," said Nigel, unclasping his weapon, and giving it to Richie, "to walk entirely unarmed?"

"And wherefore not?" said his companion. "You are thinking now of Auld Reekie, as my father fondly calls your good Scottish capital, where there is such bandying of private feuds and public factions, that a man of any note shall not cross your High Street twice, without endangering his life thrice. Here, sir, no brawling in the street is permitted. Your bull-headed citizen takes up the case so soon as the sword is drawn, and clubs is the word."

"And a hard word it is," said Richie, "as my brain-pan kens at this blessed moment."

"Were I your master, sirrah," said Lord Dalgarno, "I would make your brain-pan, as you call it, boil over, were you to speak a word in my presence before you were spoken to."

Richie murmured some indistinct answer, but took the hint, and ranked himself behind his master along with Lutin, who failed not to expose his new companion to the ridicule of the passers-by, by mimicking, as often as he could do so unobserved by Richie, his stiff and upright stalking gait and discontented physiognomy.

"And tell me now, my dear Malcolm," said Nigel, "where we are bending our course, and whether we shall dine at an apartment of yours?"

"An apartment of mine—yes, surely," answered Lord Dalgarno, "you shall dine at an apartment of mine, and an apartment of yours, and of twenty gallants besides; and where the board shall present better cheer, better wine, and better attendance, than if our whole united exhibitions went to maintain it. We are going to the most noted ordinary of London."

"That is, in common language, an inn, or a tavern," said Nigel.

"An inn, or a tavern, my most green and simple friend!" exclaimed Lord Dalgarno. "No, no—these are places where greasy citizens take pipe and pot, where the knavish pettifoggers of the law spunge on their most unhappy victims—where Templars crack jests as empty as their nuts, and where small gentry imbibe such thin potations, that they get dropsies instead of getting drunk. An ordinary is a late-invented institution, sacred to Bacchus and Comus, where the choicest noble gallants of the time meet with the first and most ethereal wits of the age,—where the wine is the very soul of the choicest grape, refined as the genius of the poet, and ancient and generous as the blood of the nobles. And then the fare is something beyond your ordinary gross terrestrial food! Sea and land are ransacked to supply it; and the invention of six ingenious cooks kept eternally upon the rack to make their art hold pace with, and if possible enhance, the exquisite quality of the materials."

"By all which rhapsody," said Lord Glenvarloch, "I can only understand, as I did before, that we are going to a choice tavern, where we shall be handsomely entertained, on paying probably as handsome a reckoning."

"Reckoning!" exclaimed Lord Dalgarno in the same tone as before, "perish the peasantly phrase! What profanation! Monsieur le Chevalier de Beaujeu, pink of Paris and flower of Gascony—he who can tell the age of his wine by the bare smell, who distils his sauces in an alembic by the aid of Lully's philosophy—who carves with such exquisite precision, that he gives to noble, knight and squire, the portion of the pheasant which exactly accords with his rank—nay, he who shall divide a becafico into twelve parts with such scrupulous exactness, that of twelve guests not one shall have the advantage of the other in a hair's breadth, or the twentieth part of a drachm, yet you talk of him and of a reckoning in the same breath! Why, man, he is the well-known and general referee in all matters affecting the mysteries of Passage, Hazard, In and In, Penneeck, and Verquire, and what not—why, Beaujeu is King of the Card-pack, and Duke of the Dice-box—HE call a reckoning like a green-aproned, red-nosed son of the vulgar spigot! O, my dearest Nigel, what a word you have spoken, and of what a person! That you know him not, is your only apology for such blasphemy; and yet I scarce hold it adequate, for to have been a day in London and not to know Beaujeu, is a crime of its own kind. But you *shall* know him this blessed moment, and shall learn to hold yourself in horror for the enormities you have uttered."

"Well, but mark you," said Nigel, "this worthy chevalier keeps not all this good cheer at his own cost, does he?"

"No, no," answered Lord Dalgarno; "there is a sort of ceremony which my chevalier's friends and intimates understand, but with which you have no business at present. There is, as majesty might say, a *symbolum* to be disbursed—in other words, a mutual exchange of courtesies take place betwixt Beaujeu and his guests. He makes them a free present of the dinner and wine, as often as they choose to consult their own felicity by frequenting his house at the hour of noon, and they, in gratitude, make the chevalier a present of a Jacobus. Then you must know, that, besides Comus and Bacchus, that princess of sublunary affairs, the Diva Fortuna, is frequently worshipped at Beaujeu's, and he, as officiating high-priest, hath, as in reason he should, a considerable advantage from a share of the sacrifice."

"In other words," said Lord Glenvarloch, "this man keeps a gaming-house."

"A house in which you may certainly game," said Lord Dalgarno, "as you may in your own chamber if you have a mind; nay, I remember old Tom Tally played a hand at put for a wager with Quinze le Va, the Frenchman, during morning prayers in St. Paul's; the morning was misty, and the parson drowsy, and the whole audience consisted of themselves and a blind woman, and so they escaped detection."

"For all this, Malcolm," said the young lord, gravely, "I cannot dine with you to-day, at this same ordinary."

"And wherefore, in the name of heaven, should you draw back from your word?" said Lord Dalgarno.

"I do not retract my word, Malcolm; but I am bound, by an early promise to my father, never to enter the doors of a gaming-house."

"I tell you this is none," said Lord Dalgarno; "it is but, in plain terms, an eating-house, arranged on civiller terms, and frequented by better company, than others in this town; and if some of them do amuse themselves with cards and hazard, they are men of honour, and who play as such, and for no more than they can well afford to lose. It was not, and could not be, such houses that your father desired you to avoid. Besides, he might as well have made you swear you would never take accommodation of an inn, tavern, eating-house, or place of public reception of any kind; for there is no such place of public resort but where your eyes may be contaminated by the sight of a pack of pieces of painted pasteboard, and your ears profaned by the rattle of those little spotted cubes of ivory. The difference is, that where we go, we may happen to see persons of quality amusing themselves with a game; and in the ordinary houses you will meet bullies and sharpers, who will strive either to cheat or to swagger you out of your money."

"I am sure you would not willingly lead me to do what is wrong," said Nigel; "but my father had a horror for games of chance, religious I believe, as well as prudential. He judged from I know not what circumstance, a fallacious one I should hope, that I should have a propensity to such courses, and I have told you the promise which he exacted from me."

"Now, by my honour," said Dalgarno, "what you have said affords the strongest reason for my insisting that you go with me. A man who would shun any danger, should first become acquainted with its real bearing and extent, and that in the company of a confidential guide and guard. Do you think I myself game? Good faith, my father's oaks grow too far from London, and stand too fast rooted in the rocks of Perthshire, for me to troll them down with a die, though I have seen whole forests go down like nine-pins. No, no—these are sports for the wealthy Southron, not for the poor Scottish noble. The place is an eating-house, and as such you and I will use it. If others use it to game in, it is their fault, but neither that of the house nor ours."

Unsatisfied with this reasoning, Nigel still insisted upon the promise he had given to his father, until his companion appeared rather displeased, and disposed to impute to him injurious and unhandsome suspicions. Lord Glenvarloch could not stand this change of tone. He recollected that much was due from him to Lord Dalgarno, on account of his father's ready and efficient friendship, and something also on account of the frank manner in which the young man himself had offered him his intimacy. He had no reason to doubt his assurances, that the house where they were about to dine did not fall under the description of places which his father's prohibition referred; and finally, he was strong in his own resolution to resist every temptation to join in games of chance. He therefore pacified Lord Dalgarno, by intimating his willingness to go along with him; and, the good-humour of the young courtier instantaneously returning, he again ran on in a grotesque and rodomontade account of the host, Monsieur de Beaujeu, which he did not conclude until they had reached the temple of hospitality over which that eminent professor presided.

XII

—This is the very barn-yard,
Where muster daily the prime cocks o' the game,
Ruffle their pinions, crow till they are hoarse,
And spar about a barleycorn. Here too chickens,
The callow, unfledged brood of forward folly,
Learn first to rear the crest, and aim the spur,
And tune their note like full-plumed Chanticleer.

—The Bear-Garden

The Ordinary, now an ignoble sound, was in the days of James, a new institution, as fashionable among the youth of that age as the first-rate modern club-houses are amongst those of the present day. It differed chiefly, in being open to all whom good clothes and good assurance combined to introduce there. The company usually dined together at an hour fixed, and the manager of the establishment presided as master of the ceremonies.

Monsieur le Chevalier, (as he qualified himself,) Saint Priest de Beaujeu, was a sharp, thin Gascon, about sixty years old, banished from his own country, as he said, on account of an affair of honour, in which he had the misfortune to kill his antagonist, though the best swordsman in the south of France. His pretensions to quality were supported by a feathered hat, a long rapier, and a suit of embroidered taffeta, not much the worse for wear, in the extreme fashion of the Parisian court, and fluttering like a Maypole with many knots of ribbon, of which it was computed he bore at least five hundred yards about his person. But, notwithstanding this profusion of decoration, there were many who thought Monsieur le Chevalier so admirably calculated for his present situation, that nature could never have meant to place him an inch above it. It was, however, part of the amusement of the place, for Lord Dalgarno and other young men of quality to treat Monsieur de Beaujeu with a great deal of mock ceremony, which being observed by the herd of more ordinary and simple gulls, they paid him, in clumsy imitation, much real deference. The Gascon's natural forwardness being much enhanced by these circumstances, he was often guilty of presuming beyond the limits of his situation, and of course had sometimes the mortification to be disagreeably driven back into them.

When Nigel entered the mansion of this eminent person, which had been but of late the residence of a great Baron of Queen Elizabeth's court, who had retired to his manors in the country on the death of that princess, he was surprised at the extent of the accommodation which it afforded, and the number of guests who were already assembled. Feathers waved, spurs jingled, lace and embroidery glanced everywhere; and at first sight, at least, it certainly made good Lord Dalgarno's encomium, who represented the company as composed almost entirely of youth of the first quality. A more close review was not quite so favourable. Several individuals might be discovered who were not exactly at their ease in the splendid dresses which they wore, and who, therefore, might be supposed not habitually familiar with such finery. Again, there were others, whose dress, though on a general view it did not seem inferior to that of the rest of the company, displayed, on being observed more closely, some of these petty expedients, by which vanity endeavours to disguise poverty.

Nigel had very little time to make such observations, for the entrance of Lord Dalgarno created an immediate bustle and sensation among the company, as his name passed from one mouth to another. Some stood forward to gaze, others stood back to make way—those of his own rank hastened to welcome him—those of inferior degree endeavoured to catch some point of his gesture, or of his dress, to be worn and practised upon a future occasion, as the newest and most authentic fashion.

The *genius loci*, the Chevalier himself, was not the last to welcome this prime stay and ornament of his establishment. He came shuffling forward with a hundred apish *conges* and *chers milors*, to express his happiness at seeing Lord Dalgarno again.—"I hope you do bring back the sun with you, *Milor*—You did carry away the sun and moon from your pauvre Chevalier when you leave him for so long. Pardieu, I believe you take them away in your pockets."

"That must have been because you left me nothing else in them, Chevalier," answered Lord Dalgarno; "but Monsieur le Chevalier, I pray you to know my countryman and friend, Lord Glenvarloch!"

"Ah, ha! tres honore—Je m'en souviens,—oui. J'ai connu autrefois un Milor Kenfarloque en Ecosse. Yes, I have memory of him—le pere de milor apparemment-we were vera intimate when I was at Oly Root with Monsieur de la Motte—I did often play at tennis vit Milor

Kenfarloque at L'Abbaie d'Oly Root—il etoit meme plus fort que moi—Ah le beaucoup de revers qu'il avoit!—I have memory, too that he was among the pretty girls—ah, un vrai diable dechaine—Aha! I have memory—"

"Better have no more memory of the late Lord Glenvarloch," said Lord Dalgarno, interrupting the Chevalier without ceremony; who perceived that the encomium which he was about to pass on the deceased was likely to be as disagreeable to the son as it was totally undeserved by the father, who, far from being either a gamester or libertine, as the Chevalier's reminiscences falsely represented him, was, on the contrary, strict and severe in his course of life, almost to the extent of rigour.

"You have the reason, milor," answered the Chevalier, "you have the right—Qu'est ce que nous avons a faire avec le temps passe?—the time passed did belong to our fathers—our ancetres—very well—the time present is to us—they have their pretty tombs with their memories and armorials, all in brass and marbre—we have the petits plats exquis, and the soupe-a-Chevalier, which I will cause to mount up immediately."

So saying, he made a pirouette on his heel, and put his attendants in motion to place dinner on the table. Dalgarno laughed, and, observing his young friend looked grave, said to him, in a tone of reproach—"Why, what!—you are not gull enough to be angry with such an ass as that?"

"I keep my anger, I trust, for better purposes," said Lord Glenvarloch; "but I confess I was moved to hear such a fellow mention my father's name—and you, too, who told me this was no gaming-house, talked to him of having left it with emptied pockets."

"Pshaw, man!" said Lord Dalgarno, "I spoke but according to the trick of the time; besides, a man must set a piece or two sometimes, or he would be held a cullionly niggard. But here comes dinner, and we will see whether you like the Chevalier's good cheer better than his conversation."

Dinner was announced accordingly, and the two friends, being seated in the most honourable station at the board, were ceremoniously attended to by the Chevalier, who did the honours of his table to them and to the other guests, and seasoned the whole with his agreeable conversation. The dinner was really excellent, in that piquant style of cookery which the French had already introduced, and which the home-bred young men of England, when they aspired to the rank of connoisseurs and persons of taste, were under the necessity of admiring. The wine was also of the first quality, and circulated in great variety, and no less abundance. The conversation among so many young men was, of course, light, lively, and amusing; and Nigel, whose mind had been long depressed by anxiety and misfortune, naturally found himself at ease, and his spirits raised and animated.

Some of the company had real wit, and could use it both politely and to advantage; others were coxcombs, and were laughed at without discovering it; and, again, others were originals, who seemed to have no objection that the company should be amused with their folly instead of their wit. And almost all the rest who played any prominent part in the conversation had either the real tone of good society which belonged to the period, or the jargon which often passes current for it.

In short, the company and conversation was so agreeable, that Nigel's rigour was softened by it, even towards the master of ceremonies, and he listened with patience to various details which the Chevalier de Beaujeu, seeing, as he said, that Milor's taste lay for the "curieux and Futile," chose to address to him in particular, on the subject of cookery. To gratify, at the same time, the taste for antiquity, which he somehow supposed that his new guest possessed, he launched out in commendation of the great artists of former days, particularly one whom he had known in his youth, "Maitre de Cuisine to the Marechal Strozzi—tres bon gentilhomme pourtant;" who had maintained his master's table with twelve covers every day during the long and severe blockade of le petit Leyth, although he had nothing better to place on it than the quarter of a carrion-horse now and then, and the grass and weeds that grew on the ramparts. "Despardieux c'dtoit un homme superbe!" With one tistle-head, and a nettle or two, he could make a soupe for twenty guests—an haunch of a little puppy-dog made a roti des plus excellens; but his coupe de maitre was when the rendition— what you call the surrender, took place and appened; and then, dieu me damme, he made out of the hind quarter of one salted horse, forty-five couverts; that the English and Scottish officers and nobility, who had the honour to dine with Monseigneur upon the rendition, could not tell what the devil any of them were made upon at all.

The good wine had by this time gone so merrily round, and had such genial effect on the guests, that those of the lower end of the table, who had hitherto been listeners, began, not greatly to their own credit, or that of the ordinary, to make innovations.

"You speak of the siege of Leith," said a tall, raw-boned man, with thick mustaches turned up with a military twist, a broad buff belt, a long rapier, and other outward symbols of the honoured profession, which lives by killing other people—"you talk of the siege of Leith, and I have seen the place—a pretty kind of a hamlet it is, with a plain wall, or rampart, and a pigeon-house or so of a tower at every angle. Uds daggers and scabbards, if a leaguer of our days had been twenty-four hours, not to say so many months, before it, without carrying the place and all its cocklofts, one after another, by pure storm, they would have deserved no better grace than the Provost-Marshal gives when his noose is reeved."

"Saar," said the Chevalier, "Monsieur le Capitaine, I vas not at the siege of the petit Leyth, and I know not what you say about the cockloft; but I will say for Monseigneur de Strozzi, that he understood the grande guerre, and was grand capitaine—plus grand—that is more great, it may be, than some of the capitaines of Angleterre, who do speak very loud—tenez, Monsieur, car c'est a vous!"

"O Monsieur." answered the swordsman, "we know the Frenchman will fight well behind his barrier of stone, or when he is armed with back, breast, and pot."

"Pot!" exclaimed the Chevalier, "what do you mean by pot—do you mean to insult me among my noble guests? Saar, I have done my duty as a pauvre gentilhomme under the Grand Henri Quatre, both at Courtrai and Yvry, and, ventre saint gris! we had neither pot nor marmite, but did always charge in our shirt."

"Which refutes another base scandal," said Lord Dalgarno, laughing, "alleging that linen was scarce among the French gentlemen-at-arms."

"Gentlemen out at arms and elbows both, you mean, my lord," said the captain, from the bottom of the table. "Craving your lordship's pardon, I do know something of these same gens-d'armes."

"We will spare your knowledge at present, captain, and save your modesty at the same time the trouble of telling us how that knowledge was acquired," answered Lord Dalgarno, rather contemptuously.

"I need not speak of it, my lord," said the man of war; "the world knows it—all perhaps, but the men of mohair—the poor sneaking citizens of London, who would see a man of valour eat his very hilts for hunger, ere they would draw a farthing from their long purses to relieve them. O, if a band of the honest fellows I have seen were once to come near that cuckoo's nest of theirs!"

"A cuckoo's nest!-and that said of the city of London!" said a gallant who sat on the opposite side of the table, and who, wearing a splendid and fashionable dress, seemed yet scarce at home in it—"I will not brook to hear that repeated."

"What!" said the soldier, bending a most terrific frown from a pair of broad black eyebrows, handling the hilt of his weapon with one hand, and twirling with the other his huge mustaches; "will you quarrel for your city?"

"Ay, marry will I," replied the other. "I am a citizen, I care not who knows it; and he who shall speak a word in dispraise of the city, is an ass and a peremptory gull, and I will break his pate, to teach him sense and manners."

The company, who probably had their reasons for not valuing the captain's courage at the high rate which he himself put upon it, were much entertained at the manner in which the quarrel was taken up by the indignant citizen; and they exclaimed on all sides, "Well run, Bow-bell!"—"Well crowed, the cock of Saint Paul's!"—"Sound a charge there, or the soldier will mistake his signals, and retreat when he should advance."

"You mistake me, gentlemen," said the captain, looking round with an air of dignity. "I will but inquire whether this cavaliero citizen is of rank and degree fitted to measure swords with a man of action; (for, conceive me, gentlemen, it is not with every one that I can match myself without loss of reputation;) and in that case he shall soon hear from me honourably, by way of cartel."

"You shall feel me most dishonourably in the way of cudgel," said the citizen, starting up, and taking his sword, which he had laid in a corner. "Follow me."

"It is my right to name the place of combat, by all the rules of the sword," said the captain; "and I do nominate the Maze, in Tothill-Fields, for place—two gentlemen, who shall be indifferent judges, for witnesses;—and for time—let me say this day fortnight, at daybreak."

"And I," said the citizen, "do nominate the bowling-alley behind the house for place, the present good company for witnesses, and for time the present moment."

So saying, he cast on his beaver, struck the soldier across the shoulders with his sheathed sword, and ran down stairs. The captain showed no instant alacrity to follow him; yet, at last, roused by the laugh and sneer around him, he assured the company, that what he did he would do deliberately, and, assuming his hat, which he put on with the air of Ancient Pistol, he descended the stairs to the place of combat, where his more prompt adversary was already stationed, with his sword unsheathed. Of the company, all of whom seemed highly delighted with the approaching fray, some ran to the windows which overlooked the bowling-alley, and others followed the combatants down stairs. Nigel could not help asking Dalgarno whether he would not interfere to prevent mischief.

"It would be a crime against the public interest," answered his friend; "there can no mischief happen between two such originals, which will not be a positive benefit to society, and particularly to the Chevalier's establishment, as he calls it. I have been as sick of that captain's buff belt, and red doublet, for this month past, as e'er I was of aught; and now I hope this bold linendraper will cudgel the ass out of that filthy lion's hide. See, Nigel, see the gallant citizen has ta'en his ground about a bowl's-cast forward, in the midst of the alley—the very model of a hog in armour. Behold how he prances with his manly foot, and brandishes his blade, much as if he were about to measure forth cambric with it. See, they bring on the reluctant soldado, and plant him opposite to his fiery antagonist, twelve paces still dividing them—Lo, the captain draws his tool, but, like a good general, looks over his shoulder to secure his retreat, in case the worse come on't. Behold the valiant shop-keeper stoops his head, confident, doubtless, in the civic helmet with which his spouse has fortified his skull—Why, this is the rarest of sport. By Heaven, he will run a tilt at him, like a ram."

It was even as Lord Dalgarno had anticipated; for the citizen, who seemed quite serious in his zeal for combat, perceiving that the man of war did not advance towards him, rushed onwards with as much good fortune as courage, beat down the captain's guard, and, pressing on, thrust, as it seemed, his sword clear through the body of his antagonist, who, with a deep groan, measured his length on the ground. A score of voices cried to the conqueror, as he stood fixed in astonishment at his own feat, "Away, away with you!—fly, fly—fly by the back door!—get into the Whitefriars, or cross the water to the Bankside, while we keep off the mob and the constables." And the conqueror, leaving his vanquished foeman on the ground, fled accordingly, with all speed.

"By Heaven," said Lord Dalgarno, "I could never have believed that the fellow would have stood to receive a thrust—he has certainly been arrested by positive terror, and lost the use of his limbs. See, they are raising him."

Stiff and stark seemed the corpse of the swordsman, as one or two of the guests raised him from the ground; but, when they began to open his waistcoat to search for the wound which nowhere existed, the man of war collected, his scattered spirits; and, conscious that the ordinary was no longer a stage on which to display his valour, took to his heels as fast as he could run, pursued by the laughter and shouts of the company.

"By my honour," said Lord Dalgarno, "he takes the same course with his conqueror. I trust in heaven he will overtake him, and then the valiant citizen will suppose himself haunted by the ghost of him he has slain."

"Despardieux, milor," said the Chevalier, "if he had stayed one moment, he should have had a *torchon*—what you call a dishclout, pinned to him for a piece of shroud, to show he be de ghost of one grand fanfaron."

"In the meanwhile," said Lord Dalgarno, "you will oblige us, Monsieur le Chevalier, as well as maintain your own honoured reputation, by letting your drawers receive the man-at-arms with a cudgel, in case he should venture to come way again."

"Ventre saint gris, milor," said the Chevalier, "leave that to me.— Begar, the maid shall throw the wash-sud upon the grand poltron!"

When they had laughed sufficiently at this ludicrous occurrence, the party began to divide themselves into little knots—some took possession of the alley, late the scene of combat, and put the field to its proper use of a bowling-ground, and it soon resounded with all the terms of the game, as "run, run-rub, rub—hold bias, you infernal trundling timber!" thus making good the saying, that three things are thrown away in a bowling-green, namely, time, money, and oaths. In the house, many of the gentlemen betook themselves to cards or dice, and parties were formed at Ombre, at Basset, at Gleek, at Primero, and other games then in fashion; while the dice were used at various games, both with and without the tables, as Hazard, In-and-in, Passage, and so forth. The play, however, did not appear to be extravagantly deep; it was certainly conducted with great decorum and fairness; nor did there appear any thing to lead the young Scotsman in the least to doubt his companion's assurance, that the place was frequented by men of rank and quality, and that the recreations they adopted were conducted upon honourable principles.

Lord Dalgarno neither had proposed play to his friend, nor joined in the amusement himself, but sauntered from one table to another, remarking the luck of the different players, as well as their capacity to avail themselves of it, and exchanging conversation with the highest and most respectable of the guests. At length, as if tired of what in modern phrase would have been termed lounging, he suddenly remembered that Burbage was to act Shakespeare's King Richard, at the Fortune, that afternoon, and that he could not give a stranger in London, like Lord Glenvarloch, a higher entertainment than to carry him to that exhibition; "unless, indeed," he added, in a whisper, "there is paternal interdiction of the theatre as well as of the ordinary."

"I never heard my father speak of stage-plays," said Lord Glenvarloch, "for they are shows of a modern date, and unknown in Scotland. Yet, if what I have heard to their prejudice be true, I doubt much whether he would have approved of them."

"Approved of them!" exclaimed Lord Dalgarno—"why, George Buchanan wrote tragedies, and his pupil, learned and wise as himself, goes to see them, so it is next door to treason to abstain; and the cleverest men in England write for the stage, and the prettiest women in London resort to the playhouses, and I have a brace of nags at the door which will carry us along the streets like wild-fire, and the ride will digest our venison and ortolans, and dissipate the fumes of the wine, and so let's to horse—Godd'en to you, gentlemen—Godd'en, Chevalier de la Fortune."

Lord Dalgarno's grooms were in attendance with two horses, and the young men mounted, the proprietor upon a favourite barb, and Nigel upon a high-dressed jennet, scarce less beautiful. As they rode towards the theatre, Lord Dalgarno endeavoured to discover his friend's opinion of the company to which he had introduced him, and to combat the exceptions which he might suppose him to have taken. "And wherefore lookest thou sad," he said, "my pensive neophyte? Sage son of the Alma Mater of Low-Dutch learning, what aileth thee? Is the leaf of the living world which we have turned over in company, less fairly written than thou hadst been taught to expect? Be comforted, and pass over one little blot or two; thou wilt be doomed to read through many a page, as black as Infamy, with her sooty pinion, can make them. Remember, most immaculate Nigel, that we are in London, not Leyden—that we are studying life, not lore. Stand buff against the reproach of thine over-tender conscience, man, and when thou summest up, like a good arithmetician, the actions of the day, before you balance the account on your pillow, tell the accusing spirit, to his brimstone beard, that if thine ears have heard the clatter of the devil's bones, thy hand hath not trowled them—that if thine eye hath seen the brawling of two angry boys, thy blade hath not been bared in their fray."

"Now, all this may be wise and witty," replied Nigel; "yet I own I cannot think but that your lordship, and other men of good quality with whom we dined, might have chosen a place of meeting free from the intrusion of bullies, and a better master of your ceremonial than yonder foreign adventurer."

"All shall be amended, Sancte Nigelle, when thou shalt come forth a new Peter the Hermit, to preach a crusade against dicing, drabbing, and company-keeping. We will meet for dinner in Saint Sepulchre's Church; we will dine in the chancel, drink our flask in the vestry, the parson shall draw every cork, and the clerk say amen to every health. Come man, cheer up, and get rid of this sour and unsocial humour. Credit me, that the Puritans who object to us the follies and the frailties incident to human nature, have themselves the vices of absolute devils, privy malice and backbiting hypocrisy, and spiritual pride in all its presumption. There is much, too, in life which we must see, were it only to learn to shun it. Will Shakespeare, who lives after death, and who is presently to afford thee such pleasure as none but himself can confer, has described the gallant Falconbridge as calling that man

> ——' a bastard to the time,
> That doth not smack of observation;
> Which, though I will not practise to deceive,
> Yet, to avoid deceit, I mean to learn."

But here we are at the door of the Fortune, where we shall have matchless Will speaking for himself.—Goblin, and you other lout, leave the horses to the grooms, and make way for us through the press."

They dismounted, and the assiduous efforts of Lutin, elbowing, bullying, and proclaiming his master's name and title, made way through a crowd of murmuring citizens, and clamorous apprentices, to the door, where Lord Dalgarno speedily procured a brace of stools upon the stage for his companion and himself, where, seated among other gallants of the same class, they had an opportunity of displaying their fair dresses and fashionable manners, while they criticised the piece during its progress; thus forming, at the same time, a conspicuous part of the spectacle, and an important proportion of the audience.

Nigel Olifaunt was too eagerly and deeply absorbed in the interest of the scene, to be capable of playing his part as became the place where he was seated. He felt all the magic of that sorcerer, who had displayed, within the paltry circle of a wooden booth, the long wars of York and Lancaster, compelling the heroes of either line to stalk across the scene in language and fashion as they lived, as if the grave had given up the dead for the amusement and instruction of the living. Burbage, esteemed the best Richard until Garrick arose, played the tyrant and usurper with such truth and liveliness, that when the Battle of Bosworth seemed concluded by his death, the ideas of reality and deception were strongly contending in Lord Glenvarloch's imagination, and it required him to rouse himself from his reverie, so strange did the proposal at first sound when his companion declared King Richard should sup with them at the Mermaid.

They were joined, at the same time, by a small party of the gentlemen with whom they had dined, which they recruited by inviting two or three of the most accomplished wits and poets, who seldom failed to attend the Fortune Theatre, and were even but too ready to conclude a day of amusement with a night of pleasure. Thither the whole party adjourned, and betwixt fertile cups of sack, excited spirits, and the emulous wit of their lively companions, seemed to realise the joyous boast of one of Ben Jonson's contemporaries, when reminding the bard of

> *"Those lyric feasts,*
> *Where men such clusters had,*
> *As made them nobly wild, not mad;*
> *While yet each verse of thine*
> *Outdid the meat, outdid the frolic wine."*

XIII

Let the proud salmon gorge the feather'd hook,
Then strike, and then you have him—He will wince;
Spin out your line that it shall whistle from you
Some twenty yards or so, yet you shall have him—
Marry! you must have patience—the stout rock
Which is his trust, hath edges something sharp;
And the deep pool hath ooze and sludge enough
To mar your fishing—'less you are more careful.

—*Albion, or the Double Kings*

It is seldom that a day of pleasure, upon review, seems altogether so exquisite as the partaker of the festivity may have felt it while passing over him. Nigel Olifaunt, at least, did not feel it so, and it required a visit from his new acquaintance, Lord Dalgarno, to reconcile him entirely to himself. But this visit took place early after breakfast, and his friend's discourse was prefaced with a question, How he liked the company of the preceding evening?

"Why, excellently well," said Lord Glenvarloch; "only I should have liked the wit better had it appeared to flow more freely. Every man's invention seemed on the stretch, and each extravagant simile seemed to set one half of your men of wit into a brown study to produce something which should out-herod it."

"And wherefore not?" said Lord Dalgarno, "or what are these fellows fit for, but to play the intellectual gladiators before us? He of them who declares himself recreant, should, d—n him, be restricted to muddy ale, and the patronage of the Waterman's Company. I promise you, that many a pretty fellow has been mortally wounded with a quibble or a carwitchet at the Mermaid, and sent from thence, in a pitiable estate, to Wit's hospital in the Vintry, where they languish to this day amongst fools and aldermen."

"It may be so," said Lord Nigel; "yet I could swear by my honour, that last night I seemed to be in company with more than one man whose genius and learning ought either to have placed him higher in our company, or to have withdrawn him altogether from a scene, where, sooth to speak, his part seemed unworthily subordinate."

"Now, out upon your tender conscience," said Lord Dalgarno; "and the fico for such outcasts of Parnassus! Why, these are the very leavings of that noble banquet of pickled herrings and Rhenish, which lost London so many of her principal witmongers and bards of misrule. What would you have said had you seen Nash or Green, when you interest yourself about the poor mimes you supped with last night? Suffice it, they had their drench and their doze, and they drank and slept as much as may save them from any necessity of eating till evening, when, if they are industrious, they will find patrons or players to feed them.* For the rest of their wants, they can be at no loss for cold water while the New River head holds good; and your doublets of Parnassus are eternal in duration."

"Virgil and Horace had more efficient patronage," said Nigel.

"Ay," replied his countryman, "but these fellows are neither Virgil nor Horace; besides, we have other spirits of another sort, to whom I will introduce you on some early occasion. Our Swan of Avon hath sung his last; but we have stout old Ben, with as much learning and genius as ever prompted the treader of sock and buskin. It is not, however, of him I mean now to speak; but I come to pray you, of dear love, to row up with me as far as Richmond, where two or three of the gallants whom you saw yesterday, mean to give music and syllabubs to a set of beauties, with some curious bright eyes among them—such, I promise you, as might win an astrologer from his worship of the galaxy. My sister leads the bevy, to whom I desire to present you. She hath her admirers at Court; and is regarded, though I might dispense with sounding her praise, as one of the beauties of the time."

There was no refusing an engagement, where the presence of the party invited, late so low in his own regard, was demanded by a lady of quality, one of the choice beauties of the time. Lord Glenvarloch accepted, as was inevitable, and spent a lively day among the gay and the fair. He was the gallant in attendance, for the day, upon his friend's

---

* The condition of men of wit and talents was never more melancholy than about this period. Their lives were so irregular, and their means of living so precarious, that they were alternately rioting in debauchery, or encountering and struggling with the meanest necessities. Two or three lost their lives by a surfeit brought on by that fatal banquet of Rhenish wine and pickled herrings, which is familiar to those who study the lighter literature of that age. The whole history is a most melancholy picture of genius, degraded at once by its own debaucheries, and the patronage of heartless rakes and profligates.

sister, the beautiful Countess of Blackchester, who aimed at once at superiority in the realms of fashion, of power, and of wit.

She was, indeed, considerably older than her brother, and had probably completed her six lustres; but the deficiency in extreme youth was more than atoned for, in the most precise and curious accuracy in attire, an early acquaintance with every foreign mode, and a peculiar gift in adapting the knowledge which she acquired, to her own particular features and complexion. At Court, she knew as well as any lady in the circle, the precise tone, moral, political, learned, or jocose, in which it was proper to answer the monarch, according to his prevailing humour; and was supposed to have been very active, by her personal interest, in procuring her husband a high situation, which the gouty old viscount could never have deserved by any merit of his own commonplace conduct and understanding.

It was far more easy for this lady than for her brother, to reconcile so young a courtier as Lord Glenvarloch to the customs and habits of a sphere so new to him. In all civilised society, the females of distinguished rank and beauty give the tone to manners, and, through these, even to morals. Lady Blackchester had, besides, interest either in the Court, or over the Court, (for its source could not be well traced,) which created friends, and overawed those who might have been disposed to play the part of enemies.

At one time, she was understood to be closely leagued with the Buckingham family, with whom her brother still maintained a great intimacy; and, although some coldness had taken place betwixt the Countess and the Duchess of Buckingham, so that they were little seen together, and the former seemed considerably to have withdrawn herself into privacy, it was whispered that Lady Blackchester's interest with the great favourite was not diminished in consequence of her breach with his lady.

Our accounts of the private Court intrigues of that period, and of the persons to whom they were intrusted, are not full enough to enable us to pronounce upon the various reports which arose out of the circumstances we have detailed. It is enough to say, that Lady Blackchester possessed great influence on the circle around her, both from her beauty, her abilities, and her reputed talents for Court intrigue; and that Nigel Olifaunt was not long of experiencing its power, as he became a slave in some degree to that species of habit, which carries so many men into a certain society at a certain hour, without expecting or receiving any particular degree of gratification, or even amusement.

His life for several weeks may be thus described. The ordinary was no bad introduction to the business of the day; and the young lord quickly found, that if the society there was not always irreproachable, still it formed the most convenient and agreeable place of meeting with the fashionable parties, with whom he visited Hyde Park, the theatres, and other places of public resort, or joined the gay and glittering circle which Lady Blackchester had assembled around her. Neither did he entertain the same scrupulous horror which led him originally even to hesitate entering into a place where gaming was permitted; but, on the contrary, began to admit the idea, that as there could be no harm done in beholding such recreation when only indulged in to a moderate degree, so, from a parity of reasoning, there could be no objection to joining in it, always under the same restrictions. But the young lord was a Scotsman, habituated to early reflection, and totally unaccustomed to any habit which inferred a careless risk or profuse waste of money. Profusion was not his natural vice, or one likely to be acquired in the course of his education; and, in all probability, while his father anticipated with noble horror the idea of his son approaching the gaming-table, he was more startled at the idea of his becoming a gaining than a losing adventurer. The second, according to his principles, had a termination, a sad one indeed, in the loss of temporal fortune—the first quality went on increasing the evil which he dreaded, and perilled at once both body and soul.

However the old lord might ground his apprehension, it was so far verified by his son's conduct, that, from an observer of the various games of chance which he witnessed, he came, by degrees, by moderate hazards, and small bets or wagers, to take a certain interest in them. Nor could it be denied, that his rank and expectations entitled him to hazard a few pieces (for his game went no deeper) against persons, who, from the readiness with which they staked their money, might be supposed well able to afford to lose it.

It chanced, or, perhaps, according to the common belief, his evil genius had so decreed, that Nigel's adventures were remarkably successful. He was temperate, cautious, cool-headed, had a strong memory, and a ready power of calculation; was besides, of a daring and intrepid character, one upon whom no one that had looked even slightly, or spoken to though but hastily, would readily have ventured to practise any thing approaching to trick, or which required to be supported by intimidation. While Lord Glenvarloch chose to play, men played with him regularly, or, according to the phrase, upon the square; and, as he found his luck change, or wished to hazard his good fortune no farther, the more professed votaries of fortune, who frequented the house of Monsieur le Chevalier de Saint Priest Beaujeu, did not venture openly to express their displeasure at his rising a winner. But when this happened repeatedly, the gamesters murmured amongst themselves equally at the caution and the success of the young Scotsman; and he became far from being a popular character among their society.

It was no slight inducement to the continuance of this most evil habit, when it was once in some degree acquired, that it seemed to place Lord Glenvarloch, haughty as he naturally was, beyond the necessity of subjecting himself to farther pecuniary obligations, which his prolonged residence in London must otherwise have rendered necessary. He had to solicit from the ministers certain forms of office, which were to render his sign-manual effectually useful; and these, though they could not be denied, were delayed in such a manner, as to lead Nigel to believe there was some secret opposition, which occasioned the demur in his business. His own impulse was, to have appeared at Court a second time, with the king's sign-manual in his pocket, and to have appealed to his Majesty himself, whether the delay of the public officers ought to render his royal generosity unavailing. But the Lord Huntinglen, that good old peer, who had so frankly interfered in his behalf on a former occasion, and whom he occasionally visited, greatly dissuaded him from a similar adventure, and exhorted him quietly to await the deliverance of the ministers, which should set him free from dancing attendance in London.

Lord Dalgarno joined his father in deterring his young friend from a second attendance at Court, at least till he was reconciled with the Duke of Buckingham—"a matter in which," he said, addressing his father, "I have offered my poor assistance, without being able to prevail on Lord Nigel to make any—not even the least—submission to the Duke of Buckingham."

"By my faith, and I hold the laddie to be in the right on't, Malcom!" answered the stout old Scots lord.—"What right hath Buckingham, or, to speak plainly, the son of Sir George Villiers, to expect homage and fealty from one more noble than himself by eight quarters? I heard him myself, on no reason that I could perceive, term Lord Nigel his enemy;

and it will never be by my counsel that the lad speaks soft word to him, till he recalls the hard one."

"That is precisely my advice to Lord Glenvarloch," answered Lord Dalgarno; "but then you will admit, my dear father, that it would be the risk of extremity for our friend to return into the presence, the duke being his enemy—better to leave it with me to take off the heat of the distemperature, with which some pickthanks have persuaded the duke to regard our friend."

"If thou canst persuade Buckingham of his error, Malcolm," said his father, "for once I will say there hath been kindness and honesty in Court service. I have oft told your sister and yourself, that in the general I esteem it as lightly as may be."

"You need not doubt my doing my best in Nigel's case," answered Lord Dalgarno; "but you must think, my dear father, I must needs use slower and gentler means than those by which you became a favourite twenty years ago."

"By my faith, I am afraid thou wilt," answered his father.—"I tell thee, Malcolm, I would sooner wish myself in the grave, than doubt thine honesty or honour; yet somehow it hath chanced, that honest, ready service, hath not the same acceptance at Court which it has in my younger time—and yet you rise there."

"O, the time permits not your old-world service," said Lord Dalgarno; "we have now no daily insurrections, no nightly attempts at assassination, as were the fashion in the Scottish Court. Your prompt and uncourteous sword-in-hand attendance on the sovereign is no longer necessary, and would be as unbeseeming as your old-fashioned serving-men, with their badges, broadswords, and bucklers, would be at a court-mask. Besides, father, loyal haste hath its inconveniences. I have heard, and from royal lips too, that when you stuck your dagger into the traitor Ruthven, it was with such little consideration, that the point ran a quarter of an inch into the royal buttock. The king never talks of it but he rubs the injured part, and quotes his '*infandum— renovare dolorem.*' But this comes of old fashions, and of wearing a long Liddesdale whinger instead of a poniard of Parma. Yet this, my dear father, you call prompt and valiant service. The king, I am told, could not sit upright for a fortnight, though all the cushions in Falkland were placed in his chair of state, and the Provost of Dunfermline's borrowed to the boot of all."

"It is a lie," said the old earl, "a false lie, forge it who list!—It is true I wore a dagger of service by my side, and not a bodkin like yours, to pick one's teeth withal—and for prompt service—Odds nouns! it should be prompt to be useful when kings are crying treason and murder with the screech of a half-throttled hen. But you young courtiers know nought of these matters, and are little better than the green geese they bring over from the Indies, whose only merit to their masters is to repeat their own words after them—a pack of mouthers, and flatterers, and ear-wigs.—Well, I am old and unable to mend, else I would break all off, and hear the Tay once more flinging himself over the Campsie Linn."

"But there is your dinner-bell, father," said Lord Dalgarno, "which, if the venison I sent you prove seasonable, is at least as sweet a sound."

"Follow me, then, youngsters, if you list," said the old earl; and strode on from the alcove in which this conversation was held, towards the house, followed by the two young men.

In their private discourse, Lord Dalgarno had little trouble in dissuading Nigel from going immediately to Court; while, on the other hand, the offers he made him of a previous introduction to the Duke of Buckingham, were received by Lord Glenvarloch with a positive and contemptuous refusal. His friend shrugged his shoulders, as one who claims the merit of having given to an obstinate friend the best counsel, and desires to be held free of the consequences of his pertinacity.

As for the father, his table indeed, and his best liquor, of which he was more profuse than necessary, were at the command of his young friend, as well as his best advice and assistance in the prosecution of his affairs. But Lord Huntinglen's interest was more apparent than real; and the credit he had acquired by his gallant defence of the king's person, was so carelessly managed by himself, and so easily eluded by the favourites and ministers of the sovereign, that, except upon one or two occasions, when the king was in some measure taken by surprise, as in the case of Lord Glenvarloch, the royal bounty was never efficiently extended either to himself or to his friends.

"There never was a man," said Lord Dalgarno, whose shrewder knowledge of the English Court saw where his father's deficiency lay, "that had it so perfectly in his power to have made his way to the pinnacle of fortune as my poor father. He had acquired a right to build up a staircase, step by step, slowly and surely, letting every boon, which he begged year after year, become in its turn the resting-place for the next annual grant. But your fortunes shall not shipwreck upon the same coast, Nigel," he would conclude. "If I have fewer means of influence than my father has, or rather had, till he threw them away for butts of sack, hawks, hounds, and such carrion, I can, far better than he, improve that which I possess; and that, my dear Nigel, is all engaged in your behalf. Do not be surprised or offended that you now see me less than formerly. The stag-hunting is commenced, and the prince looks that I should attend him more frequently. I must also maintain my attendance on the duke, that I may have an opportunity of pleading your cause when occasion shall permit."

"I have no cause to plead before the duke," said Nigel, gravely; "I have said so repeatedly."

"Why, I meant the phrase no otherwise, thou churlish and suspicious disputant," answered Dalgarno, "than as I am now pleading the duke's cause with thee. Surely I only mean to claim a share in our royal master's favourite benediction, *Beati Pacifici.*"

Upon several occasions, Lord Glenvarloch's conversations, both with the old earl and his son, took a similar turn and had a like conclusion. He sometimes felt as if, betwixt the one and the other, not to mention the more unseen and unboasted, but scarce less certain influence of Lady Blackchester, his affair, simple as it had become, might have been somehow accelerated. But it was equally impossible to doubt the rough honesty of the father, and the eager and officious friendship of Lord Dalgarno; nor was it easy to suppose that the countenance of the lady, by whom he was received with such distinction, would be wanting, could it be effectual in his service.

Nigel was further sensible of the truth of what Lord Dalgarno often pointed out, that the favourite being supposed to be his enemy, every petty officer, through whose hands his affair must necessarily pass, would desire to make a merit of throwing obstacles in his way, which he could only surmount by steadiness and patience, unless he preferred closing the breach, or, as Lord Dalgarno called it, making his peace with the Duke of Buckingham.

Nigel might, and doubtless would, have had recourse to the advice of his friend George Heriot upon this occasion, having found it so advantageous formerly; but the only time he saw him after their visit to Court, he found the worthy citizen engaged in hasty preparations for a journey to Paris, upon business of great importance in the way of his profession, and by an especial commission from the Court and the Duke of Buckingham, which was likely to be attended with considerable profit. The good man smiled as he named the Duke of

Buckingham. He had been, he said, pretty sure that his disgrace in that quarter would not be of long duration. Lord Glenvarloch expressed himself rejoiced at that reconciliation, observing, that it had been a most painful reflection to him, that Master Heriot should, in his behalf, have incurred the dislike, and perhaps exposed himself to the ill offices, of so powerful a favourite.

"My lord," said Heriot, "for your father's son I would do much; and yet truly, if I know myself, I would do as much and risk as much, for the sake of justice, in the case of a much more insignificant person, as I have ventured for yours. But as we shall not meet for some time, I must commit to your own wisdom the farther prosecution of this matter."

And thus they took a kind and affectionate leave of each other.

There were other changes in Lord Glenvarloch's situation, which require to be noticed. His present occupations, and the habits of amusement which he had acquired, rendered his living so far in the city a considerable inconvenience. He may also have become a little ashamed of his cabin on Paul's Wharf, and desirous of being lodged somewhat more according to his quality. For this purpose, he had hired a small apartment near the Temple. He was, nevertheless, almost sorry for what he had done, when he observed that his removal appeared to give some pain to John Christie, and a great deal to his cordial and officious landlady. The former, who was grave and saturnine in every thing he did, only hoped that all had been to Lord Glenvarloch's mind, and that he had not left them on account of any unbeseeming negligence on their part. But the tear twinkled in Dame Nelly's eye, while she recounted the various improvements she had made in the apartment, of express purpose to render it more convenient to his lordship.

"There was a great sea-chest," she said, "had been taken upstairs to the shopman's garret, though it left the poor lad scarce eighteen inches of opening to creep betwixt it and his bed; and Heaven knew—she did not—whether it could ever be brought down that narrow stair again. Then the turning the closet into an alcove had cost a matter of twenty round shillings; and to be sure, to any other lodger but his lordship, the closet was more convenient. There was all the linen, too, which she had bought on purpose—But Heaven's will be done—she was resigned."

Everybody likes marks of personal attachment; and Nigel, whose heart really smote him, as if in his rising fortunes he were disdaining the lowly accommodations and the civilities of the humble friends which had been but lately actual favours, failed not by every assurance in his power, and by as liberal payment as they could be prevailed upon to accept, to alleviate the soreness of their feelings at his departure; and a parting kiss from the fair lips of his hostess sealed his forgiveness.

Richie Moniplies lingered behind his master, to ask whether, in case of need, John Christie could help a canny Scotsman to a passage back to his own country; and receiving assurance of John's interest to that effect, he said at parting, he would remind him of his promise soon.— "For," said he, "if my lord is not weary of this London life, I ken one that is, videlicet, mysell; and I am weel determined to see Arthur's Seat again ere I am many weeks older."

XIV

Bingo, why, Bingo! hey, boy—here, sir, here!—
He's gone and off, but he'll be home before us;—
'Tis the most wayward cur e'er mumbled bone,
Or dogg'd a master's footstep.—Bingo loves me
Better than ever beggar loved his alms;
Yet, when he takes such humour, you may coax
Sweet Mistress Fantasy, your worship's mistress,
Out of her sullen moods, as soon as Bingo.

—The Dominie and His Dog

Richie Moniplies was as good as his word. Two or three mornings after the young lord had possessed himself of his new lodgings, he appeared before Nigel, as he was preparing to dress, having left his pillow at an hour much later than had formerly been his custom.

As Nigel looked upon his attendant, he observed there was a gathering gloom upon his solemn features, which expressed either additional importance, or superadded discontent, or a portion of both.

"How now," he said, "what is the matter this morning, Richie, that you have made your face so like the grotesque mask on one of the spouts yonder?" pointing to the Temple Church, of which Gothic building they had a view from the window.

Richie swivelled his head a little to the right with as little alacrity as if he had the crick in his neck, and instantly resuming his posture, replied,—"Mask here, mask there—it were nae such matters that I have to speak anent."

"And what matters have you to speak anent, then?" said his master, whom circumstances had inured to tolerate a good deal of freedom from his attendant.

"My lord,"—said Richie, and then stopped to cough and hem, as if what he had to say stuck somewhat in his throat.

"I guess the mystery," said Nigel, "you want a little money, Richie; will five pieces serve the present turn?"

"My lord," said Richie, "I may, it is like, want a trifle of money; and I am glad at the same time, and sorry, that it is mair plenty with your lordship than formerly."

"Glad and sorry, man!" said Lord Nigel, "why, you are reading riddles to me, Richie."

"My riddle will be briefly read," said Richie; "I come to crave of your lordship your commands for Scotland."

"For Scotland!—why, art thou mad, man?" said Nigel; "canst thou not tarry to go down with me?"

"I could be of little service," said Richie, "since you purpose to hire another page and groom."

"Why, thou jealous ass," said the young lord, "will not thy load of duty lie the lighter?—Go, take thy breakfast, and drink thy ale double strong, to put such absurdities out of thy head—I could be angry with thee for thy folly, man—but I remember how thou hast stuck to me in adversity."

"Adversity, my lord, should never have parted us," said Richie; "methinks, had the warst come to warst, I could have starved as gallantly as your lordship, or more so, being in some sort used to it; for, though I was bred at a flasher's stall, I have not through my life had a constant intimacy with collops."

"Now, what is the meaning of all this trash?" said Nigel; "or has it no other end than to provoke my patience? You know well enough, that, had I twenty serving-men, I would hold the faithful follower that stood by me in my distress the most valued of them all. But it is totally out of reason to plague me with your solemn capriccios."

"My lord," said Richie, "in declaring your trust in me, you have done what is honourable to yourself, if I may with humility say so much, and in no way undeserved on my side. Nevertheless, we must part."

"Body of me, man, why?" said Lord Nigel; "what reason can there be for it, if we are mutually satisfied?"

"My lord," said Richie Moniplies, "your lordship's occupations are such as I cannot own or countenance by my presence."

"How now, sirrah!" said his master, angrily.

"Under favour, my lord," replied his domestic, "it is unequal dealing to be equally offended by my speech and by my silence. If you can hear with patience the grounds of my departure, it may be, for aught I know, the better for you here and hereafter—if not, let me have my license of departure in silence, and so no more about it."

"Go to, sir!" said Nigel; "speak out your mind—only remember to whom you speak it."

"Weel, weel, my lord—I speak it with humility;" (never did Richie look with more starched dignity than when he uttered the word;) "but do you think this dicing and card-shuffling, and haunting of taverns and playhouses, suits your lordship—for I am sure it does not suit me?"

"Why, you are not turned precisian or puritan, fool?" said Lord Glenvarloch, laughing, though, betwixt resentment and shame, it cost him some trouble to do so.

"My lord," replied the follower, "I ken the purport of your query. I am, it may be, a little of a precisian, and I wish to Heaven I was mair worthy of the name; but let that be a pass-over.—I have stretched the duties of a serving-man as far as my northern conscience will permit. I can give my gude word to my master, or to my native country, when I am in a foreign land, even though I should leave downright truth a wee bit behind me. Ay, and I will take or give a slash with ony man that speaks to the derogation of either. But this chambering, dicing, and play-haunting, is not my element—I cannot draw breath in it—and when I hear of your lordship winning the siller that some poor creature may full sairly miss—by my saul, if it wad serve your necessity, rather than you gained it from him, I wad take a jump over the hedge with your lordship, and cry 'Stand!' to the first grazier we met that was coming from Smithfield with the price of his Essex calves in his leathern pouch!"

"You are a simpleton," said Nigel, who felt, however, much conscience-struck; "I never play but for small sums."

"Ay, my lord," replied the unyielding domestic, "and—still with reverence—it is even sae much the waur. If you played with your equals, there might be like sin, but there wad be mair warldly honour in it. Your lordship kens, or may ken, by experience of your ain, whilk is not as yet mony weeks auld, that small sums can ill be missed by those that have nane larger; and I maun e'en be plain with you, that men notice it of your lordship, that ye play wi' nane but the misguided creatures that can but afford to lose bare stakes."

"No man dare say so!" replied Nigel, very angrily. "I play with whom I please, but I will only play for what stake I please."

"That is just what they say, my lord," said the unmerciful Richie, whose natural love of lecturing, as well as his bluntness of feeling, prevented him from having any idea of the pain which he was inflicting on his master; "these are even their own very words. It was but yesterday your lordship was pleased, at that same ordinary, to win from yonder young hafflins gentleman, with the crimson velvet doublet, and the cock's feather in his beaver—him, I mean, who fought with the ranting captain—a matter of five pounds, or thereby. I saw him come through the hall; and, if he was not cleaned out of cross and pile, I never saw a ruined man in my life."

"Impossible!" said Lord Glenvarloch—"Why, who is he? he looked like a man of substance."

"All is not gold that glistens, my lord," replied Richie; "'broidery and bullion buttons make bare pouches. And if you ask who he is—maybe I have a guess, and care not to tell."

"At least, if I have done any such fellow an injury," said the Lord Nigel, "let me know how I can repair it."

"Never fash your beard about that, my lord,—with reverence always," said Richie,—"he shall be suitably cared after. Think on him but as ane wha was running post to the devil, and got a shouldering from your lordship to help him on his journey. But I will stop him, if reason can; and so your lordship needs asks nae mair about it, for there is no use in your knowing it, but much the contrair."

"Hark you, sirrah," said his master, "I have borne with you thus far, for certain reasons; but abuse my good-nature no farther—and since you must needs go, why, go a God's name, and here is to pay your journey." So saying, he put gold into his hand, which Richie told over piece by piece, with the utmost accuracy.

"Is it all right—or are they wanting in weight—or what the devil keeps you, when your hurry was so great five minutes since?" said the young lord, now thoroughly nettled at the presumptuous precision with which Richie dealt forth his canons of morality.

"The tale of coin is complete," said Richie, with the most imperturbable gravity; "and, for the weight, though they are sae scrupulous in this town, as make mouths at a piece that is a wee bit light, or that has been cracked within the ring, my sooth, they will jump at them in Edinburgh like a cock at a grosart. Gold pieces are not so plenty there, the mair the pity!"

"The more is your folly, then," said Nigel, whose anger was only momentary, "that leave the land where there is enough of them."

"My lord," said Richie, "to be round with you, the grace of God is better than gold pieces. When Goblin, as you call yonder Monsieur Lutin,—and you might as well call him Gibbet, since that is what he is like to end in,—shall recommend a page to you, ye will hear little such doctrine as ye have heard from me.—And if they were my last words," he said, raising his voice, "I would say you are misled, and are forsaking the paths which your honourable father trode in; and, what is more, you are going—still under correction—to the devil with a dishclout, for ye are laughed at by them that lead you into these disordered bypaths."

"Laughed at!" said Nigel, who, like others of his age, was more sensible to ridicule than to reason—"Who dares laugh at me?"

"My lord, as sure as I live by bread—nay, more, as I am a true man—and, I think, your lordship never found Richie's tongue bearing aught but the truth—unless that your lordship's credit, my country's profit, or, it may be, some sma' occasion of my ain, made it unnecessary to promulgate the haill veritie,—I say then, as I am a true man, when I saw that puir creature come through the ha', at that ordinary, whilk is accurst (Heaven forgive me for swearing!) of God and man, with his teeth set, and his hands clenched, and his bonnet drawn over his brows like a desperate man, Goblin said to me, 'There goes a dunghill chicken, that your master has plucked clean enough; it will be long ere his lordship ruffle a feather with a cock of the game.' And so, my lord, to speak it out, the lackeys, and the gallants, and more especially your sworn brother, Lord Dalgarno, call you the sparrow-hawk.—I had some thought to have cracked Lutin's pate for the speech, but, after a', the controversy was not worth it."

"Do they use such terms of me?" said Lord Nigel. "Death and the devil!"

"And the devil's dam, my lord," answered Richie; "they are all three busy in London.—And, besides, Lutin and his master laughed at you, my lord, for letting it be thought that—I shame to speak it—that ye were over well with the wife of the decent honest man whose house you but now left, as not sufficient for your new bravery, whereas they said, the licentious scoffers, that you pretended to such favour when you had not courage enough for so fair a quarrel, and that the sparrow-hawk was too craven-crested to fly at the wife of a cheesemonger."—He stopped a moment, and looked fixedly in his master's face, which was inflamed with shame and anger, and then proceeded. "My lord, I did you justice in my thought, and myself too; for, thought I, he would have been as deep in that sort of profligacy as in others, if it hadna been Richie's four quarters."

"What new nonsense have you got to plague me with?" said Lord Nigel. "But go on, since it is the last time I am to be tormented with your impertinence,—go on, and make the most of your time."

"In troth," said Richie, "and so will I even do. And as Heaven has bestowed on me a tongue to speak and to advise—"

"Which talent you can by no means be accused of suffering to remain idle," said Lord Glenvarloch, interrupting him.

"True, my lord," said Richie, again waving his hand, as if to bespeak his master's silence and attention; "so, I trust, you will think some time hereafter. And, as I am about to leave your service, it is proper that ye suld know the truth, that ye may consider the snares to which your youth and innocence may be exposed, when aulder and doucer heads are withdrawn from beside you.—There has been a lusty, good-looking kimmer, of some forty, or bygane, making mony speerings about you, my lord."

"Well, sir, what did she want with me?" said Lord Nigel.

"At first, my lord," replied his sapient follower, "as she seemed to be a well-fashioned woman, and to take pleasure in sensible company, I was no way reluctant to admit her to my conversation."

"I dare say not," said Lord Nigel; "nor unwilling to tell her about my private affairs."

"Not I, truly, my lord," said the attendant;—"for, though she asked me mony questions about your fame, your fortune, your business here, and such like, I did not think it proper to tell her altogether the truth thereanent."

"I see no call on you whatever," said Lord Nigel, "to tell the woman either truth or lies upon what she had nothing to do with."

"I thought so, too, my lord," replied Richie, "and so I told her neither."

"And what *did* you tell her, then, you eternal babbler?" said his master, impatient of his prate, yet curious to know what it was all to end in.

"I told her," said Richie, "about your warldly fortune, and sae forth, something whilk is not truth just at this time; but which hath been truth formerly, suld be truth now, and will be truth again,—and that was, that you were in possession of your fair lands, whilk ye are but in right of as yet. Pleasant communing we had on that and other topics, until she showed the cloven foot, beginning to confer with me about some wench that she said had a good-will to your lordship, and fain she would have spoken with you in particular anent it; but when I heard of such inklings, I began to suspect she was little better than—whew! "—Here he concluded his narrative with a low, but very expressive whistle.

"And what did your wisdom do in these circumstances?" said Lord Nigel, who, notwithstanding his former resentment, could now scarcely forbear laughing.

"I put on a look, my lord," replied Richie, bending his solemn brows, "that suld give her a heartscald of walking on such errands. I laid her enormities clearly before her, and I threatened her, in sae mony words, that I would have her to the ducking-stool; and she, on the contrair part, miscawed me for a forward northern tyke—and so we parted never to meet again, as I hope and trust. And so I stood between your lordship and that temptation, which might have been worse than the ordinary, or the playhouse either; since you wot well what Solomon, King of the Jews, sayeth of the strange woman—for, said I to mysell, we have taken to dicing already, and if we take to drabbing next, the Lord kens what we may land in!"

"Your impertinence deserves correction, but it is the last which, for a time at least, I shall have to forgive—and I forgive it," said Lord Glenvarloch; "and, since we are to part, Richie, I will say no more respecting your precautions on my account, than that I think you might have left me to act according to my own judgment."

"Mickle better not," answered Richie—"mickle better not; we are a' frail creatures, and can judge better for ilk ither than in our ain cases. And for me, even myself, saving that case of the Sifflication, which might have happened to ony one, I have always observed myself to be much more prudential in what I have done in your lordship's behalf, than even in what I have been able to transact for my own interest— whilk last, I have, indeed, always postponed, as in duty I ought."

"I do believe thou hast," said Lord Nigel, "having ever found thee true and faithful. And since London pleases you so little, I will bid you a short farewell; and you may go down to Edinburgh until I come thither myself, when I trust you will re-enter into my service."

"Now, Heaven bless you, my lord," said Richie Moniplies, with uplifted eyes; "for that word sounds more like grace than ony has come out of your mouth this fortnight.—I give you godd'en, my lord."

So saying, he thrust forth his immense bony hand, seized on that of Lord Glenvarloch, raised it to his lips, then turned short on his heel, and left the room hastily, as if afraid of showing more emotion than was consistent with his ideas of decorum. Lord Nigel, rather surprised at his sudden exit, called after him to know whether he was sufficiently provided with money; but Richie, shaking his head, without making any other answer, ran hastily down stairs, shut the street-door heavily behind him, and was presently seen striding along the Strand.

His master almost involuntarily watched and distinguished the tall raw-boned figure of his late follower, from the window, for some time, until he was lost among the crowd of passengers. Nigel's reflections were not altogether those of self-approval. It was no good sign of his course of life, (he could not help acknowledging this much to himself,) that so faithful an adherent no longer seemed to feel the same pride in his service, or attachment to his person, which he had formerly manifested. Neither could he avoid experiencing some twinges of conscience, while he felt in some degree the charges which Richie had preferred against him, and experienced a sense of shame and mortification, arising from the colour given by others to that, which he himself would have called his caution and moderation in play. He had only the apology, that it had never occurred to himself in this light.

Then his pride and self-love suggested, that, on the other hand, Richie, with all his good intentions, was little better than a conceited, pragmatical domestic, who seemed disposed rather to play the tutor than the lackey, and who, out of sheer love, as he alleged, to his master's person, assumed the privilege of interfering with, and controlling, his actions, besides rendering him ridiculous in the gay world, from the antiquated formality, and intrusive presumption, of his manners.

Nigel's eyes were scarce turned from the window, when his new landlord entering, presented to him a slip of paper, carefully bound round with a string of flox-silk and sealed—it had been given in, he said, by a woman, who did not stop an instant. The contents harped upon the same string which Richie Moniplies had already jarred. The epistle was in the following words:

For the Right Honourable hands of Lord Glenvarloch, "These, from a friend unknown:—

MY LORD,

"You are trusting to an unhonest friend, and diminishing an honest reputation. An unknown but real friend of your lordship will speak in one word what you would not learn from flatterers in so many days, as should suffice for your utter ruin. He whom you think most true—I say your friend Lord Dalgarno—is utterly false to you, and doth but seek, under pretence of friendship, to mar your fortune, and diminish the good name by which you might mend it. The kind countenance which he shows to you, is more dangerous than the Prince's frown; even as to gain at Beaujeu's ordinary

is more discreditable than to lose. Beware of both.—And this
is all from your true but nameless friend,

IGNOTO

Lord Glenvarloch paused for an instant, and crushed the paper together—then again unfolded and read it with attention—bent his brows—mused for a moment, and then tearing it to fragments, exclaimed—"Begone for a vile calumny! But I will watch—I will observe—"

Thought after thought rushed on him; but, upon the whole, Lord Glenvarloch was so little satisfied with the result of his own reflections, that he resolved to dissipate them by a walk in the Park, and, taking his cloak and beaver, went thither accordingly.

XV

Twas when fleet Snowball's head was woxen grey,
A luckless lev'ret met him on his way.—
Who knows not Snowball—he, whose race renown'd
Is still victorious on each coursing ground?
Swaffhanm Newmarket, and the Roman Camp,
Have seen them victors o'er each meaner stamp—
In vain the youngling sought, with doubling wile,
The hedge, the hill, the thicket, or the stile.
Experience sage the lack of speed supplied,
And in the gap he sought, the victim died.
So was I once, in thy fair street, Saint James,
Through walking cavaliers, and car-borne dames,
Descried, pursued, turn'd o'er again, and o'er,
Coursed, coted, mouth'd by an unfeeling bore.

—&c. &c. &c

The Park of Saint James's, though enlarged, planted with verdant alleys, and otherwise decorated by Charles II, existed in the days of his grandfather, as a public and pleasant promenade; and, for the sake of exercise or pastime, was much frequented by the better classes.

Lord Glenvarloch repaired thither to dispel the unpleasant reflections which had been suggested by his parting with his trusty squire, Richie Moniplies, in a manner which was agreeable neither to his pride nor his feelings; and by the corroboration which the hints of his late attendant had received from the anonymous letter mentioned in the end of the last chapter.

There was a considerable number of company in the Park when he entered it, but, his present state of mind inducing him to avoid society, he kept aloof from the more frequented walks towards Westminster and Whitehall, and drew to the north, or, as we should now say, the Piccadilly verge of the enclosure, believing he might there enjoy, or rather combat, his own thoughts unmolested.

In this, however, Lord Glenvarloch was mistaken; for, as he strolled slowly along with his arms folded in his cloak, and his hat drawn over his eyes, he was suddenly pounced upon by Sir Mungo Malagrowther, who, either shunning or shunned, had retreated, or had been obliged to retreat, to the same less frequented corner of the Park.

Nigel started when he heard the high, sharp, and querulous tones of the knight's cracked voice, and was no less alarmed when he beheld his tall thin figure hobbling towards him, wrapped in a thread-bare cloak, on whose surface ten thousand varied stains eclipsed the original scarlet, and having his head surmounted with a well-worn beaver, bearing a black velvet band for a chain, and a capon's feather for an ostrich plume.

Lord Glenvarloch would fain have made his escape, but, as our motto intimates, a leveret had as little chance to free herself of an experienced greyhound. Sir Mungo, to continue the simile, had long ago learned to run cunning, and make sure of mouthing his game. So Nigel found himself compelled to stand and answer the hackneyed question—"What news to-day?"

"Nothing extraordinary, I believe," answered the young nobleman, attempting to pass on.

"O, ye are ganging to the French ordinary belive," replied the knight; "but it is early day yet—we will take a turn in the Park in the meanwhile—it will sharpen your appetite."

So saying, he quietly slipped his arm under Lord Glenvarloch's, in spite of all the decent reluctance which his victim could exhibit, by keeping his elbow close to his side; and having fairly grappled the prize, he proceeded to take it in tow.

Nigel was sullen and silent, in hopes to shake off his unpleasant companion; but Sir Mungo was determined, that if he did not speak, he should at least hear.

"Ye are bound for the ordinary, my lord?" said the cynic;—"weel, ye canna do better—there is choice company there, and peculiarly selected, as I am tauld, being, dootless, sic as it is desirable that young noblemen should herd withal—and your noble father wad have been blithe to see you keeping such worshipful society."

"I believe," said Lord Glenvarloch, thinking himself obliged to say something, "that the society is as good as generally can be found in such places, where the door can scarcely be shut against those who come to spend their money."

"Right, my lord—vera right," said his tormentor, bursting out into a chuckling, but most discordant laugh. "These citizen chuffs and clowns will press in amongst us, when there is but an inch of a door open. And what remedy?—Just e'en this, that as their cash gies them confidence, we should strip them of it. Flay them, my lord—singe them as the kitchen wench does the rats, and then they winna long to come back again.—Ay, ay—pluck them, plume them—and then the larded capons will not be for flying so high a wing, my lord, among the goss-hawks and sparrow-hawks, and the like."

And, therewithal, Sir Mungo fixed on Nigel his quick, sharp, grey eye, watching the effect of his sarcasm as keenly as the surgeon, in a delicate operation, remarks the progress of his anatomical scalpel.

Nigel, however willing to conceal his sensations, could not avoid gratifying his tormentor by wincing under the operation. He coloured with vexation and anger; but a quarrel with Sir Mungo Malagrowther would, he felt, be unutterably ridiculous; and he only muttered to himself the words, "Impertinent coxcomb!" which, on this occasion, Sir Mungo's imperfection of organ did not prevent him from hearing and replying to.

"Ay, ay—vera true," exclaimed the caustic old courtier—"Impertinent coxcombs they are, that thus intrude themselves on the society of their betters; but your lordship kens how to gar them as gude—ye have the trick on't.—They had a braw sport in the presence last Friday, how ye suld have routed a young shopkeeper, horse and foot, ta'en his *spolia ofima*, and a' the specie he had about him, down to the very silver buttons of his cloak, and sent him to graze with Nebuchadnezzar, King of Babylon. Muckle honour redounded to your lordship thereby.—We were tauld the loon threw himsell into the Thames in a fit of desperation. There's enow of them behind—there was mair tint on Flodden-edge."

"You have been told a budget of lies, so far as I am concerned, Sir Mungo," said Nigel, speaking loud and sternly.

"Vera likely—vera likely," said the unabashed and undismayed Sir Mungo; "naething but lies are current in the circle.—So the chield is not drowned, then?—the mair's the pity.—But I never believed that part of the story—a London dealer has mair wit in his anger. I dare swear the lad has a bonny broom-shank in his hand by this time, and is scrubbing the kennels in quest after rusty nails, to help him to begin his pack again.—He has three bairns, they say; they will help him bravely to grope in the gutters. Your good lordship may have the ruining of him again, my lord, if they have any luck in strand-scouring."

"This is more than intolerable," said Nigel, uncertain whether to make an angry vindication of his character, or to fling the old tormentor from his arm. But an instant's recollection convinced him, that, to do either, would only give an air of truth and consistency to the scandals which he began to see were affecting his character, both in the higher and lower circles. Hastily, therefore, he formed the wiser resolution, to endure Sir Mungo's studied impertinence, under the hope of ascertaining, if possible, from what source those reports arose which were so prejudicial to his reputation.

Sir Mungo, in the meanwhile, caught up, as usual, Nigel's last words, or rather the sound of them, and amplified and interpreted them in his own way. "Tolerable luck!" he repeated; "yes, truly, my lord, I am told that you have tolerable luck, and that ye ken weel how to use that jilting quean, Dame Fortune, like a canny douce lad, willing to warm yourself in her smiles, without exposing yourself to her frowns. And that is what I ca' having luck in a bag."

"Sir Mungo Malagrowther," said Lord Glenvarloch, turning towards him seriously, "have the goodness to hear me for a moment."

"As weel as I can, my lord—as weel as I can," said Sir Mungo, shaking his head, and pointing the finger of his left hand to his ear.

"I will try to speak very distinctly," said Nigel, arming himself with patience. "You take me for a noted gamester; I give you my word that you have not been rightly informed—I am none such. You owe me some explanation, at least, respecting the source from which you have derived such false information."

"I never heard ye were a *great* gamester, and never thought or said ye were such, my lord," said Sir Mungo, who found it impossible to avoid hearing what Nigel said with peculiarly deliberate and distinct pronunciation. "I repeat it—I never heard, said, or thought that you were a ruffling gamester,—such as they call those of the first head.— Look you, my lord, I call *him* a gamester, that plays with equal stakes and equal skill, and stands by the fortune of the game, good or bad; and I call *him* a ruffling gamester, or ane of the first head, who ventures frankly and deeply upon such a wager. But he, my lord, who has the patience and prudence never to venture beyond small game, such as, at most, might crack the Christmas-box of a grocer's 'prentice, who vies with those that have little to hazard, and who therefore, having the larger stock, can always rook them by waiting for his good fortune, and by rising from the game when luck leaves him—such a one as he, my lord, I do not call a *great* gamester, to whatever other name he may be entitled."

"And such a mean-spirited, sordid wretch, you would infer that I am," replied Lord Glenvarloch; "one who fears the skilful, and preys upon the ignorant—who avoids playing with his equals, that he may make sure of pillaging his inferiors?—Is this what I am to understand has been reported of me?"

"Nay, my lord, you will gain nought by speaking big with me," said Sir Mungo, who, besides that his sarcastic humour was really supported by a good fund of animal courage, had also full reliance on the immunities which he had derived from the broadsword of Sir Rullion Rattray, and the baton of the satellites employed by the Lady Cockpen. "And for the truth of the matter," he continued, "your lordship best knows whether you ever lost more than five pieces at a time since you frequented Beaujeu's—whether you have not most commonly risen a winner—and whether the brave young gallants who frequent the ordinary—I mean those of noble rank, and means conforming—are in use to play upon those terms?"

"My father was right," said Lord Glenvarloch, in the bitterness of his spirit; "and his curse justly followed me when I first entered that place. There is contamination in the air, and he whose fortune avoids ruin, shall be blighted in his honour and reputation."

Sir Mungo, who watched his victim with the delighted yet wary eye of an experienced angler, became now aware, that if he strained the line on him too tightly, there was every risk of his breaking hold. In order to give him room, therefore, to play, he protested that Lord Glenvarloch "should not take his free speech *in malam partem*. If you were a trifle ower sicker in your amusement, my lord, it canna be denied that it is the safest course to prevent farther endangerment of your somewhat dilapidated fortunes; and if ye play with your inferiors, ye are relieved of the pain of pouching the siller of your friends and equals; forby, that the plebeian knaves have had the advantage, *tecum certasse*, as Ajax Telamon sayeth, *apud Metamorphoseos*; and for the like of them to have played with ane Scottish nobleman is an honest and honourable consideration to compensate the loss of their stake, whilk, I dare say, moreover, maist of the churls can weel afford."

"Be that as it may, Sir Mungo," said Nigel, "I would fain know—"

"Ay, ay," interrupted Sir Mungo; "and, as you say, who cares whether the fat bulls of Bashan can spare it or no? gentlemen are not to limit their sport for the like of them."

"I wish to know, Sir Mungo," said Lord Glenvarloch, "in what company you have learned these offensive particulars respecting me?"

"Dootless—dootless, my lord," said Sir Mungo; "I have ever heard, and have ever reported, that your lordship kept the best of company in a private way.—There is the fine Countess of Blackchester, but I think she stirs not much abroad since her affair with his Grace of Buckingham; and there is the gude auld-fashioned Scottish nobleman, Lord Huntinglen, an undeniable man of quality—it is pity but he could keep caup and can frae his head, whilk now and then doth'minish his reputation. And there is the gay young Lord Dalgarno, that carries the craft of gray hairs under his curled love-locks—a fair race they are, father, daughter, and son, all of the same honourable family. I think we needna speak of George Heriot, honest man, when we have nobility in question. So that is the company I have heard of your keeping, my lord, out-taken those of the ordinary."

"My company has not, indeed, been much more extended than amongst those you mention," said Lord Glenvarloch; "but in short—"

"To Court?" said Sir Mungo, "that was just what I was going to say—Lord Dalgarno says he cannot prevail on ye to come to Court, and that does ye prejudice, my lord—the king hears of you by others, when he should see you in person—I speak in serious friendship, my lord. His Majesty, when you were named in the circle short while since, was heard to say, *Jacta est alea!*—Glenvarlochides is turned dicer and drinker.'—My Lord Dalgarno took your part, and he was e'en borne down by the popular voice of the courtiers, who spoke of you as one who had betaken yourself to living a town life, and risking your baron's coronet amongst the flatcaps of the city."

"And this was publicly spoken of me," said Nigel, "and in the king's presence?"

"Spoken openly?" repeated Sir Mungo Malagrowther; "ay, by my troth was it—that is to say, it was whispered privately—whilk is as open promulgation as the thing permitted; for ye may think the Court is not like a place where men are as sib as Simmie and his brother, and roar out their minds as if they were at an ordinary."

"A curse on the Court and the ordinary both!" cried Nigel, impatiently.

"With all my heart," said the knight; "I have got little by a knight's service in the Court; and the last time I was at the ordinary, I lost four angels."

"May I pray of you, Sir Mungo, to let me know," said Nigel, "the names of those who thus make free with the character of one who can be but little known to them, and who never injured any of them?"

"Have I not told you already," answered Sir Mungo, "that the king said something to that effect—so did the Prince too;—and such being the case, ye may take it on your corporal oath, that every man in the circle who was not silent, sung the same song as they did."

"You said but now," replied Glenvarloch, "that Lord Dalgarno interfered in my behalf."

"In good troth did he," answered Sir Mungo, with a sneer; "but the young nobleman was soon borne down—by token, he had something of a catarrh, and spoke as hoarse as a roopit raven. Poor gentleman, if he had had his full extent of voice, he would have been as well listened to, dootless, as in a cause of his ain, whilk no man kens better how to plead to purpose.—And let me ask you, by the way," continued Sir Mungo, "whether Lord Dalgarno has ever introduced your lordship to the Prince, or the Duke of Buckingham, either of whom might soon carry through your suit?"

"I have no claim on the favour of either the Prince or the Duke of Buckingham," said Lord Glenvarloch.—"As you seem to have made my affairs your study, Sir Mungo, although perhaps something unnecessarily, you may have heard that I have petitioned my Sovereign for payment of a debt due to my family. I cannot doubt the king's desire to do justice, nor can I in decency employ the solicitation of his Highness the Prince, or his Grace the Duke of Buckingham, to obtain from his Majesty what either should be granted me as a right, or refused altogether."

Sir Mungo twisted his whimsical features into one of his most grotesque sneers, as he replied—

"It is a vera clear and parspicuous position of the case, my lord; and in relying thereupon, you show an absolute and unimprovable acquaintance with the King, Court, and mankind in general.—But whom have we got here?—Stand up, my lord, and make way—by my word of honour, they are the very men we spoke of—talk of the devil, and—humph!"

It must be here premised, that, during the conversation, Lord Glenvarloch, perhaps in the hope of shaking himself free of Sir Mungo, had directed their walk towards the more frequented part of the Park; while the good knight had stuck to him, being totally indifferent which way they went, provided he could keep his talons clutched upon his companion. They were still, however, at some distance from the livelier part of the scene, when Sir Mungo's experienced eye noticed the appearances which occasioned the latter part of his speech to Lord Glenvarloch. A low respectful murmur arose among the numerous groups of persons which occupied the lower part of the Park. They first clustered together, with their faces turned towards Whitehall, then fell back on either hand to give place to a splendid party of gallants, who, advancing from the Palace, came onward through the Park; all the other company drawing off the pathway, and standing uncovered as they passed.

Most of these courtly gallants were dressed in the garb which the pencil of Vandyke has made familiar even at the distance of nearly two centuries; and which was just at this period beginning to supersede the more fluttering and frivolous dress which had been adopted from the French Court of Henri Quatre.

The whole train were uncovered excepting the Prince of Wales, afterwards the most unfortunate of British monarchs, who came onward, having his long curled auburn tresses, and his countenance, which, even in early youth, bore a shade of anticipated melancholy, shaded by the Spanish hat and the single ostrich feather which drooped from it. On his right hand was Buckingham, whose commanding, and at the same time graceful, deportment, threw almost into shade the personal demeanour and majesty of the Prince on whom he attended. The eye, movements, and gestures of the great courtier were so composed, so regularly observant of all etiquette belonging to his situation, as to form a marked and strong contrast with the forward gaiety and frivolity by which he recommended himself to the favour of his "dear dad and gossip," King James. A singular fate attended this accomplished courtier, in being at once the reigning favourite of a father and son so very opposite in manners, that, to ingratiate himself with the youthful Prince, he was obliged to compress within the strictest limits of respectful observance the frolicsome and free humour which captivated his aged father.

It is true, Buckingham well knew the different dispositions both of James and Charles, and had no difficulty in so conducting himself as to maintain the highest post in the favour of both. It has indeed been supposed, as we before hinted, that the duke, when he had completely possessed himself of the affections of Charles, retained his hold in those of the father only by the tyranny of custom; and that James, could he have brought himself to form a vigorous resolution, was, in the latter years of his life especially, not unlikely to have discarded Buckingham from his counsels and favour. But if ever the king indeed meditated such a change, he was too timid, and too much accustomed to the influence which the duke had long exercised over him, to summon up resolution enough for effecting such a purpose; and at all events it is certain, that Buckingham, though surviving the master by whom he was raised, had the rare chance to experience no wane of the most splendid court-favour during two reigns, until it was at once eclipsed in his blood by the dagger of his assassin Felton.

To return from this digression: The Prince, with his train, advanced, and were near the place where Lord Glenvarloch and Sir Mungo had stood aside, according to form, in order to give the Prince passage, and to pay the usual marks of respect. Nigel could now remark that Lord Dalgarno walked close behind the Duke of Buckingham, and, as he thought, whispered something in his ear as they came onward. At any rate, both the Prince's and Duke of Buckingham's attention seemed to be directed by such circumstance towards Nigel, for they turned their heads in that direction and looked at him attentively—the Prince with a countenance, the grave, melancholy expression of which was blended with severity; while Buckingham's looks evinced some degree of scornful triumph. Lord Dalgarno did not seem to observe his friend, perhaps because the sunbeams fell from the side of the walk on which Nigel stood, obliging Malcolm to hold up his hat to screen his eyes.

As the Prince passed, Lord Glenvarloch and Sir Mungo bowed, as respect required; and the Prince, returning their obeisance with that grave ceremony which paid to every rank its due, but not a tittle beyond it, signed to Sir Mungo to come forward. Commencing an apology for his lameness as he started, which he had just completed as his hobbling gait brought him up to the Prince, Sir Mungo lent an attentive, and, as it seemed, an intelligent ear, to questions, asked in a tone so low, that the knight would certainly have been deaf to them had they been put to him by any one under the rank of Prince of Wales. After about a minute's conversation, the Prince bestowed on Nigel the embarrassing notice of another fixed look, touched his hat slightly to Sir Mungo, and walked on.

"It is even as I suspected, my lord," said Sir Mungo, with an air which he designed to be melancholy and sympathetic, but which, in fact, resembled the grin of an ape when he has mouthed a scalding chestnut—"Ye have back-friends, my lord, that is, unfriends—or, to be plain, enemies—about the person of the Prince."

"I am sorry to hear it," said Nigel; "but I would I knew what they accuse me of."

"Ye shall hear, my lord," said Sir Mungo, "the Prince's vera words— 'Sir Mungo,' said he, 'I rejoice to see you, and am glad your rheumatic troubles permit you to come hither for exercise.'—I bowed, as in duty bound—ye might remark, my lord, that I did so, whilk formed the first branch of our conversation.—His Highness then demanded of me, 'if he with whom I stood, was the young Lord Glenvarloch.' I answered, 'that you were such, for his Highness's service;' whilk was the second branch.—Thirdly, his Highness, resuming the argument, said, that 'truly he had been told so,' (meaning that he had been told you were that personage,) 'but that he could not believe, that the heir of that noble and decayed house could be leading an idle, scandalous, and precarious life, in the eating-houses and taverns of London, while the king's drums were beating, and colours flying in Germany in the cause of the Palatine, his son-in-law.'—I could, your lordship is aware, do nothing but make an obeisance; and a gracious 'Give ye good-day, Sir Mungo Malagrowther,' licensed me to fall back to your lordship. And now, my lord, if your business or pleasure calls you to the ordinary, or anywhere in the direction of the city—why, have with you; for, dootless, ye will think ye have tarried lang enough in the Park, as they will likely turn at the head of the walk, and return this way—and you have a broad hint, I think, not to cross the Prince's presence in a hurry."

"*You* may stay or go as you please, Sir Mungo," said Nigel, with an expression of calm, but deep resentment; "but, for my own part, my resolution is taken. I will quit this public walk for pleasure of no man— still less will I quit it like one unworthy to be seen in places of public resort. I trust that the Prince and his retinue will return this way as you expect; for I will abide, Sir Mungo, and beard them."

"Beard them!" exclaimed Sir Mungo, in the extremity of surprise,— "Beard the Prince of Wales—the heir-apparent of the kingdoms!—By my saul, you shall beard him yourself then."

Accordingly, he was about to leave Nigel very hastily, when some unwonted touch of good-natured interest in his youth and experience, seemed suddenly to soften his habitual cynicism.

"The devil is in me for an auld fule!" said Sir Mungo; "but I must needs concern mysell—I that owe so little either to fortune or my fellow-creatures, must, I say, needs concern mysell—with this springald, whom I will warrant to be as obstinate as a pig possessed with a devil, for it's the cast of his family; and yet I maun e'en fling away some sound advice on him.—My dainty young Lord Glenvarloch, understand me distinctly, for this is no bairn's-play. When the Prince said sae much to me as I have repeated to you, it was equivalent to a command not to appear in his presence; wherefore take an auld man's advice that wishes you weel, and maybe a wee thing better than he has reason to wish ony body. Jouk, and let the jaw gae by, like a canny bairn—gang hame to your lodgings, keep your foot frae taverns, and your fingers frae the dice-box; compound your affairs quietly wi' some ane that has better favour than yours about Court, and you will get a round spell of money to carry you to Germany, or elsewhere, to push your fortune. It was a fortunate soldier that made your family four or five hundred years syne, and, if you are brave and fortunate, you may find the way to repair it. But, take my word for it, that in this Court you will never thrive."

When Sir Mungo had completed his exhortation, in which there was more of sincere sympathy with another's situation, than he had been heretofore known to express in behalf of any one, Lord Glenvarloch replied, "I am obliged to you, Sir Mungo—you have spoken, I think, with sincerity, and I thank you. But in return for your good advice, I heartily entreat you to leave me; I observe the Prince and his train are returning down the walk, and you may prejudice yourself, but cannot help me, by remaining with me."

"And that is true,"—said Sir Mungo; "yet, were I ten years younger, I would be tempted to stand by you, and gie them the meeting. But at threescore and upward, men's courage turns cauldrife; and they that canna win a living, must not endanger the small sustenance of their age. I wish you weel through, my lord, but it is an unequal fight." So saying, he turned and limped away; often looking back, however, as if his natural spirit, even in its present subdued state, aided by his love of contradiction and of debate, rendered him unwilling to adopt the course necessary for his own security.

Thus abandoned by his companion, whose departure he graced with better thoughts of him than those which he bestowed on his appearance, Nigel remained with his arms folded, and reclining against a solitary tree which overhung the path, making up his mind to encounter a moment which he expected to be critical of his fate. But he was mistaken in supposing that the Prince of Wales would either address him, or admit him to expostulation, in such a public place as the Park. He did not remain unnoticed, however, for, when he made a respectful but haughty obeisance, intimating in look and manner that he was possessed of, and undaunted by, the unfavourable opinion which the Prince had so lately expressed, Charles returned his reverence with such a frown, as is only given by those whose frown is authority and decision. The train passed on, the Duke of Buckingham not even appearing to see Lord Glenvarloch; while Lord Dalgarno, though no longer incommoded by the sunbeams, kept his eyes, which had perhaps been dazzled by their former splendour, bent upon the ground.

Lord Glenvarloch had difficulty to restrain an indignation, to which, in the circumstances, it would have been madness to have given vent. He started from his reclining posture, and followed the Prince's train so as to keep them distinctly in sight; which was very easy, as they walked slowly. Nigel observed them keep their road towards the Palace, where the Prince turned at the gate and bowed to the noblemen in attendance, in token of dismissing them, and entered the Palace, accompanied only by the Duke of Buckingham, and one or two of his equerries. The rest of the train, having returned in all dutiful humility the farewell of the Prince, began to disperse themselves through the Park.

All this was carefully noticed by Lord Glenvarloch, who, as he adjusted his cloak, and drew his sword-belt round so as to bring the hilt closer to his hand, muttered—"Dalgarno shall explain all this to me, for it is evident that he is in the secret!"

XVI

Give way—give way—I must and will have justice.
And tell me not of privilege and place;
Where I am injured, there I'll sue redress.
Look to it, every one who bars my access;
I have a heart to feel the injury,
A hand to night myself, and, by my honour,
That hand shall grasp what grey-beard Law denies me.

—*The Chamberlain*

It was not long ere Nigel discovered Lord Dalgarno advancing towards him in the company of another young man of quality of the Prince's train; and as they directed their course towards the south-eastern corner of the Park, he concluded they were about to go to Lord Huntinglen's. They stopped, however, and turned up another path leading to the north; and Lord Glenvarloch conceived that this change of direction was owing to their having seen him, and their desire to avoid him.

Nigel followed them without hesitation by a path which, winding around a thicket of shrubs and trees, once more conducted him to the less frequented part of the Park. He observed which side of the thicket was taken by Lord Dalgarno and his companion, and he himself, walking hastily round the other verge, was thus enabled to meet them face to face.

"Good-morrow, my Lord Dalgarno," said Lord Glenvarloch, sternly.

"Ha! my friend Nigel," answered Lord Dalgarno, in his usual careless and indifferent tone, "my friend Nigel, with business on his brow?—but you must wait till we meet at Beaujeu's at noon—Sir Ewes Haldimund and I are at present engaged in the Prince's service."

"If you were engaged in the king's, my lord," said Lord Glenvarloch, "you must stand and answer me."

"Hey-day!" said Lord Dalgarno, with an air of great astonishment, "what passion is this? Why, Nigel, this is King Cambyses' vein!—You have frequented the theatres too much lately—Away with this folly, man; go, dine upon soup and salad, drink succory-water to cool your blood, go to bed at sun-down, and defy those foul fiends, Wrath and Misconstruction."

"I have had misconstruction enough among you," said Glenvarloch, in the same tone of determined displeasure, "and from you, my Lord Dalgarno, in particular, and all under the mask of friendship."

"Here is a proper business!"—said Dalgarno, turning as if to appeal to Sir Ewes Haldimund; "do you see this angry ruffler, Sir Ewes? A month since, he dared not have looked one of yonder sheep in the face, and now he is a prince of roisterers, a plucker of pigeons, a controller of players and poets—and in gratitude for my having shown him the way to the eminent character which he holds upon town, he comes hither to quarrel with his best friend, if not his only one of decent station."

"I renounce such hollow friendship, my lord," said Lord Glenvarloch; "I disclaim the character which, even to my very face, you labour to fix upon me, and ere we part I will call you to a reckoning for it."

"My lords both," interrupted Sir Ewes Haldimund, "let me remind you that the Royal Park is no place to quarrel in."

"I will make my quarrel good," said Nigel, who did not know, or in his passion might not have recollected, the privileges of the place, "wherever I find my enemy."

"You shall find quarrelling enough," replied Lord Dalgarno, calmly, "so soon as you assign a sufficient cause for it. Sir Ewes Haldimund, who knows the Court, will warrant you that I am not backward on such occasions.—But of what is it that you now complain, after having experienced nothing save kindness from me and my family?"

"Of your family I complain not," replied Lord Glenvarloch; "they have done for me all they could, more, far more, than I could have expected; but you, my lord, have suffered me, while you called me your friend, to be traduced, where a word of your mouth would have placed my character in its true colours—and hence the injurious message which I just now received from the Prince of Wales. To permit the misrepresentation of a friend, my lord, is to share in the slander."

"You have been misinformed, my Lord Glenvarloch," said Sir Ewes Haldimund; "I have myself often heard Lord Dalgarno defend your character, and regret that your exclusive attachment to the pleasures of a London life prevented your paying your duty regularly to the King and Prince."

"While he himself," said Lord Glenvarloch, "dissuaded me from presenting myself at Court."

"I will cut this matter short," said Lord Dalgarno, with haughty coldness. "You seem to have conceived, my lord, that you and I were

Pylades and Orestes—a second edition of Damon and Pythias—Theseus and Pirithoüs at the least. You are mistaken, and have given the name of friendship to what, on my part, was mere good-nature and compassion for a raw and ignorant countryman, joined to the cumbersome charge which my father gave me respecting you. Your character, my lord, is of no one's drawing, but of your own making. I introduced you where, as in all such places, there was good and indifferent company to be met with—your habits, or taste, made you prefer the worse. Your holy horror at the sight of dice and cards degenerated into the cautious resolution to play only at those times, and with such persons, as might ensure your rising a winner—no man can long do so, and continue to be held a gentleman. Such is the reputation you have made for yourself, and you have no right to be angry that I do not contradict in society what yourself know to be true. Let us pass on, my lord; and if you want further explanation, seek some other time and fitter place."

"No time can be better than the present," said Lord Glenvarloch, whose resentment was now excited to the uttermost by the cold-blooded and insulting manner, in which Dalgarno vindicated himself,—"no place fitter than the place where we now stand. Those of my house have ever avenged insult, at the moment, and on the spot, where it was offered, were it at the foot of the throne.—Lord Dalgarno, you are a villain! draw and defend yourself." At the same moment he unsheathed his rapier.

"Are you mad?" said Lord Dalgarno, stepping back; "we are in the precincts of the Court."

"The better," answered Lord Glenvarloch; "I will cleanse them from a calumniator and a coward." He then pressed on Lord Dalgarno, and struck him with the flat of the sword.

The fray had now attracted attention, and the cry went round, "Keep the peace—keep the peace—swords drawn in the Park!—What, ho! guards!—keepers—yeomen—rangers!" and a number of people came rushing to the spot from all sides.

Lord Dalgarno, who had half drawn his sword on receiving the blow, returned it to his scabbard when he observed the crowd thicken, and, taking Sir Ewes Haldimund by the arm, walked hastily away, only saying to Lord Glenvarloch as they left him, "You shall dearly abye this insult—we will meet again."

A decent-looking elderly man, who observed that Lord Glenvarloch remained on the spot, taking compassion on his youthful appearance, said to him, "Are you aware that this is a Star-Chamber business, young gentleman, and that it may cost you your right hand?—Shift for yourself before the keepers or constables come up—Get into Whitefriars or somewhere, for sanctuary and concealment, till you can make friends or quit the city."

The advice was not to be neglected. Lord Glenvarloch made hastily towards the issue from the Park by Saint James's Palace, then Saint James's Hospital. The hubbub increased behind him; and several peace-officers of the Royal Household came up to apprehend the delinquent. Fortunately for Nigel, a popular edition of the cause of the affray had gone abroad. It was said that one of the Duke of Buckingham's companions had insulted a stranger gentleman from the country, and that the stranger had cudgelled him soundly. A favourite, or the companion of a favourite, is always odious to John Bull, who has, besides, a partiality to those disputants who proceed, as lawyers term it, *par wye du fait*, and both prejudices were in Nigel's favour. The officers, therefore, who came to apprehend him, could learn from the spectators no particulars of his appearance, or information concerning the road he had taken; so that, for the moment, he escaped being arrested.

What Lord Glenvarloch heard among the crowd as he passed along, was sufficient to satisfy him, that in his impatient passion he had placed himself in a predicament of considerable danger. He was no stranger to the severe and arbitrary proceedings of the Court of Star-Chamber, especially in cases of breach of privilege, which made it the terror of all men; and it was no farther back than the Queen's time that the punishment of mutilation had been actually awarded and executed, for some offence of the same kind which he had just committed. He had also the comfortable reflection, that, by his violent quarrel with Lord Dalgarno, he must now forfeit the friendship and good offices of that nobleman's father and sister, almost the only persons of consideration in whom he could claim any interest; while all the evil reports which had been put in circulation concerning his character, were certain to weigh heavily against him, in a case where much must necessarily depend on the reputation of the accused. To a youthful imagination, the idea of such a punishment as mutilation seems more ghastly than death itself; and every word which he overheard among the groups which he met, mingled with, or overtook and passed, announced this as the penalty of his offence. He dreaded to increase his pace for fear of attracting suspicion, and more than once saw the ranger's officers so near him, that his wrist tingled as if already under the blade of the dismembering knife. At length he got out of the Park, and had a little more leisure to consider what he was next to do.

Whitefriars, adjacent to the Temple, then well known by the cant name of Alsatia, had at this time, and for nearly a century afterwards, the privilege of a sanctuary, unless against the writ of the Lord Chief Justice, or of the Lords of the Privy-Council. Indeed, as the place abounded with desperadoes of every description,—bankrupt citizens, ruined gamesters, irreclaimable prodigals, desperate duellists, bravoes, homicides, and debauched profligates of every description, all leagued together to maintain the immunities of their asylum,—it was both difficult and unsafe for the officers of the law to execute warrants emanating even from the highest authority, amongst men whose safety was inconsistent with warrants or authority of any kind. This Lord Glenvarloch well knew; and odious as the place of refuge was, it seemed the only one where, for a space at least, he might be concealed and secure from the immediate grasp of the law, until he should have leisure to provide better for his safety, or to get this unpleasant matter in some shape accommodated.

Meanwhile, as Nigel walked hastily forward towards the place of sanctuary, he bitterly blamed himself for suffering Lord Dalgarno to lead him into the haunts of dissipation; and no less accused his intemperate heat of passion, which now had driven him for refuge into the purlieus of profane and avowed vice and debauchery.

"Dalgarno spoke but too truly in that," were his bitter reflections; "I have made myself an evil reputation by acting on his insidious counsels, and neglecting the wholesome admonitions which ought to have claimed implicit obedience from me, and which recommended abstinence even from the slightest approach of evil. But if I escape from the perilous labyrinth in which folly and inexperience, as well as violent passions, have involved me, I will find some noble way of redeeming the lustre of a name which was never sullied until I bore it."

As Lord Glenvarloch formed these prudent resolutions, he entered the Temple Walks, whence a gate at that time opened into Whitefriars, by which, as by the more private passage, he proposed to betake himself to the sanctuary. As he approached the entrance to that den of infamy, from which his mind recoiled even while in the act of taking shelter there, his pace slackened, while the steep and broken stairs reminded him of the *facilis* descensus Averni, and rendered him doubtful whether it were not better to brave the worst which could befall him in the public haunts of honourable men, than to evade punishment by secluding himself in those of avowed vice and profligacy.

As Nigel hesitated, a young gentleman of the Temple advanced towards him, whom he had often seen, and sometimes conversed with, at the ordinary, where he was a frequent and welcome guest, being a wild young gallant, indifferently well provided with money, who spent at the theatres and other gay places of public resort, the time which his father supposed he was employing in the study of the law. But Reginald Lowestoffe, such was the young Templar's name, was of opinion that little law was necessary to enable him to spend the revenues of the paternal acres which were to devolve upon him at his father's demose, and therefore gave himself no trouble to acquire more of that science than might be imbibed along with the learned air of the region in which he had his chambers. In other respects, he was one of the wits of the place, read Ovid and Martial, aimed at quick repartee and pun, (often very far fetched,) danced, fenced, played at tennis, and performed sundry tunes on the fiddle and French horn, to the great annoyance of old Counsellor Barratter, who lived in the chambers immediately below him. Such was Reginald Lowes-toffe, shrewd, alert, and well-acquainted with the town through all its recesses, but in a sort of disrespectable way. This gallant, now approaching the Lord Glenvarloch, saluted him by name and title, and asked if his lordship designed for the Chevalier's this day, observing it was near noon, and the woodcock would be on the board before they could reach the ordinary.

"I do not go there to-day," answered Lord Glenvarloch. "Which way, then, my lord?" said the young Templar, who was perhaps not undesirous to parade a part at least of the street in company with a lord, though but a Scottish one.

"I—I—" said Nigel, desiring to avail himself of this young man's local knowledge, yet unwilling and ashamed to acknowledge his intention to take refuge in so disreputable a quarter, or to describe the situation in which he stood—"I have some curiosity to see Whitefriars."

"What! your lordship is for a frolic into Alsatia?" said Lowestoffe— "—Have with you, my lord—you cannot have a better guide to the infernal regions than myself. I promise you there are bona-robas to be found there—good wine too, ay, and good fellows to drink it with, though somewhat suffering under the frowns of Fortune. But your lordship will pardon me—you are the last of our acquaintance to whom I would have proposed such a voyage of discovery."

"I am obliged to you, Master Lowestoffe, for the good opinion you have expressed in the observation," said Lord Glenvarloch; "but my present circumstances may render even a residence of a day or two in the sanctuary a matter of necessity."

"Indeed!" said Lowestoffe, in a tone of great surprise; "I thought your lordship had always taken care not to risk any considerable stake—I beg pardon, but if the bones have proved perfidious, I know just so much law as that a peer's person is sacred from arrest; and for mere impecuniosity, my lord, better shift can be made elsewhere than in Whitefriars, where all are devouring each other for very poverty."

"My misfortune has no connexion with want of money," said Nigel.

"Why, then, I suppose," said Lowestoffe, "you have been tilting, my lord, and have pinked your man; in which case, and with a purse reasonably furnished, you may lie perdu in Whitefriars for a twelvemonth—Marry, but you must be entered and received as a member of their worshipful society, my lord, and a frank burgher of Alsatia—so far you must condescend; there will be neither peace nor safety for you else."

"My fault is not in a degree so deadly, Master Lowestoffe," answered Lord Glenvarloch, "as you seem to conjecture—I have stricken a gentleman in the Park, that is all."

"By my hand, my lord, and you had better have struck your sword through him at Barns Elms," said the Templar. "Strike within the verge of the Court! You will find that a weighty dependence upon your hands, especially if your party be of rank and have favour."

"I will be plain with you, Master Lowestoffe," said Nigel, "since I have gone thus far. The person I struck was Lord Dalgarno, whom you have seen at Beaujeu's."

"A follower and favourite of the Duke of Buckingham!—It is a most unhappy chance, my lord; but my heart was formed in England, and cannot bear to see a young nobleman borne down, as you are like to be. We converse here greatly too open for your circumstances. The Templars would suffer no bailiff to execute a writ, and no gentleman to be arrested for a duel, within their precincts; but in such a matter between Lord Dalgarno and your lordship, there might be a party on either side. You must away with me instantly to my poor chambers here, hard by, and undergo some little change of dress, ere you take sanctuary; for else you will have the whole rascal rout of the Friars about you, like crows upon a falcon that strays into their rookery. We must have you arrayed something more like the natives of Alsatia, or there will be no life there for you."

While Lowestoffe spoke, he pulled Lord Glenvarloch along with him into his chambers, where he had a handsome library, filled with all the poems and play-books which were then in fashion. The Templar then dispatched a boy, who waited upon him, to procure a dish or two from the next cook's shop; "and this," he said, "must be your lordship's dinner, with a glass of old sack, of which my grandmother (the heavens requite her!) sent me a dozen bottles, with charge to use the liquor only with clarified whey, when I felt my breast ache with over study. Marry, we will drink the good lady's health in it, if it is your lordship's pleasure, and you shall see how we poor students eke out our mutton-commons in the hall."

The outward door of the chambers was barred so soon as the boy had re-entered with the food; the boy was ordered to keep close watch, and admit no one; and Lowestoffe, by example and precept, pressed his noble guest to partake of his hospitality. His frank and forward manners, though much differing from the courtly ease of Lord Dalgarno, were calculated to make a favourable impression; and Lord Glenvarloch, though his experience of Dalgarno's perfidy had taught him to be cautious of reposing faith in friendly professions, could not avoid testifying his gratitude to the young Templar, who seemed so anxious for his safety and accommodation.

"You may spare your gratitude any great sense of obligation, my lord," said the Templar. "No doubt I am willing to be of use to any gentleman that has cause to sing *Fortune my foe*, and particularly proud to serve your lordship's turn; but I have also an old grudge, to speak Heaven's truth, at your opposite, Lord Dalgarno."

"May I ask on what account, Master Lowestoffe?" said Lord Glenvarloch.

"O, my lord," replied the Templar, "it was for a hap that chanced after you left the ordinary, one evening about three weeks since—at least I think you were not by, as your lordship always left us before deep play began—I mean no offence, but such was your lordship's custom—when there were words between Lord Dalgarno and me concerning a certain game at gleek, and a certain mournival of aces held by his lordship, which went for eight—tib, which went for fifteen—twenty-three in all. Now I held king and queen, being three—a natural towser, making fifteen—and tiddy, nineteen. We vied the ruff, and revied, as your lordship may suppose, till the stake was equal to half my yearly exhibition, fifty as fair yellow canary birds as e'er chirped in the bottom of a green silk purse. Well, my lord, I gained the cards, and lo you! it pleases his lordship to say that we played without tiddy; and as the rest stood by and backed him, and especially the sharking Frenchman, why, I was obliged to lose more than I shall gain all the season.—So judge if I have not a crow to pluck with his lordship. Was it ever heard there was a game at gleek at the ordinary before, without counting tiddy?—marry quep upon his lordship!—Every man who comes there with his purse in his hand, is as free to make new laws as he, I hope, since touch pot touch penny makes every man equal."

As Master Lowestoffe ran over this jargon of the gaming-table, Lord Glenvarloch was both ashamed and mortified, and felt a severe pang of aristocratic pride, when he concluded in the sweeping clause that the dice, like the grave, levelled those distinguishing points of society, to which Nigel's early prejudices clung perhaps but too fondly. It was impossible, however, to object any thing to the learned reasoning of the young Templar, and therefore Nigel was contented to turn the conversation, by making some inquiries respecting the present state of White-friars. There also his host was at home.

"You know, my lord," said Master Lowestoffe, "that we Templars are a power and a dominion within ourselves, and I am proud to say that I hold some rank in our republic—was treasurer to the Lord of Misrule last year, and am at this present moment in nomination for that dignity myself. In such circumstances, we are under the necessity of maintaining an amicable intercourse with our neighbours of Alsatia, even as the Christian States find themselves often, in mere policy, obliged to make alliance with the Grand Turk, or the Barbary States."

"I should have imagined you gentlemen of the Temple more independent of your neighbours," said Lord Glenvarloch.

"You do us something too much honour, my lord," said the Templar; "the Alsatians and we have some common enemies, and we have, under the rose, some common friends. We are in the use of blocking all bailiffs out of our bounds, and we are powerfully aided by our neighbours, who tolerate not a rag belonging to them within theirs. Moreover the Alsatians have—I beg you to understand me—the power of protecting or distressing our friends, male or female, who may be obliged to seek sanctuary within their bounds. In short, the two communities serve each other, though the league is between states of unequal quality, and

I may myself say, that I have treated of sundry weighty affairs, and have been a negotiator well approved on both sides.—But hark—hark—what is that?"

The sound by which Master Lowestoffe was interrupted, was that of a distant horn, winded loud and keenly, and followed by a faint and remote huzza.

"There is something doing," said Lowestoffe, "in the Whitefriars at this moment. That is the signal when their privileges are invaded by tipstaff or bailiff; and at the blast of the horn they all swarm out to the rescue, as bees when their hive is disturbed.—Jump, Jim," he said, calling out to the attendant, "and see what they are doing in Alsatia.—That bastard of a boy," he continued, as the lad, accustomed to the precipitate haste of his master, tumbled rather than ran out of the apartment, and so down stairs, "is worth gold in this quarter—he serves six masters—four of them in distinct Numbers, and you would think him present like a fairy at the mere wish of him that for the time most needs his attendance. No scout in Oxford, no gip in Cambridge, ever matched him in speed and intelligence. He knows the step of a dun from that of a client, when it reaches the very bottom of the staircase; can tell the trip of a pretty wench from the step of a bencher, when at the upper end of the court; and is, take him all in all—But I see your lordship is anxious—May I press another cup of my kind grandmother's cordial, or will you allow me to show you my wardrobe, and act as your valet or groom of the chamber?"

Lord Glenvarloch hesitated not to acknowledge that he was painfully sensible of his present situation, and anxious to do what must needs be done for his extrication.

The good-natured and thoughtless young Templar readily acquiesced, and led the way into his little bedroom, where, from bandboxes, portmanteaus, mail-trunks, not forgetting an old walnut-tree wardrobe, he began to select the articles which he thought best suited effectually to disguise his guest in venturing into the lawless and turbulent society of Alsatia.

XVII

Come hither, young one,—Mark me! Thou art now
'Mongst men o' the sword, that live by reputation
More than by constant income—Single-suited
They are, I grant you; yet each single suit
Maintains, on the rough guess, a thousand followers—
And they be men, who, hazarding their all,
Needful apparel, necessary income,
And human body, and immortal soul,
Do in the very deed but hazard nothing—
So strictly is that ALL bound in reversion;
Clothes to the broker, income to the usurer,
And body to disease, and soul to the foul fiend;
Who laughs to see Soldadoes and Fooladoes,
Play better than himself his game on earth.

—*The Mohocks*

Y our lordship," said Reginald Lowestoffe, "must be content to exchange your decent and court-beseeming rapier, which I will retain in safe keeping, for this broadsword, with an hundredweight of rusty iron about the hilt, and to wear these huge-paned slops, instead of your civil and moderate hose. We allow no cloak, for your ruffian always walks in *cuerpo*; and the tarnished doublet of bald velvet, with its discoloured embroidery, and—I grieve to speak it—a few stains from the blood of the grape, will best suit the garb of a roaring boy. I will leave you to change your suit for an instant, till I can help to truss you."

Lowestoffe retired, while slowly, and with hesitation, Nigel obeyed his instructions. He felt displeasure and disgust at the scoundrelly disguise which he was under the necessity of assuming; but when he considered the bloody consequences which law attached to his rash act of violence, the easy and indifferent temper of James, the prejudices of his son, the overbearing influence of the Duke of Buckingham, which was sure to be thrown into the scale against him; and, above all, when he reflected that he must now look upon the active, assiduous, and insinuating Lord Dalgarno, as a bitter enemy, reason told him he was in a situation of peril which authorised all honest means, even the

SIR WALTER SCOTT

most unseemly in outward appearance, to extricate himself from so dangerous a predicament.

While he was changing his dress, and musing on these particulars, his friendly host re-entered the sleeping apartment—"Zounds!" he said, "my lord, it was well you went not straight into that same Alsatia of ours at the time you proposed, for the hawks have stooped upon it. Here is Jem come back with tidings, that he saw a pursuivant there with a privy-council warrant, and half a score of yeomen assistants, armed to the teeth, and the horn which we heard was sounded to call out the posse of the Friars. Indeed, when old Duke Hildebrod saw that the quest was after some one of whom he knew nothing, he permitted, out of courtesy, the man-catcher to search through his dominions, quite certain that they would take little by their motions; for Duke Hildebrod is a most judicious potentate.—Go back, you bastard, and bring us word when all is quiet."

"And who may Duke Hildebrod be?" said Lord Glenvarloch.

"Nouns! my lord," said the Templar, "have you lived so long on the town, and never heard of the valiant, and as wise and politic as valiant, Duke Hildebrod, grand protector of the liberties of Alsatia? I thought the man had never whirled a die but was familiar with his fame."

"Yet I have never heard of him, Master Lowestoffe," said Lord Glenvarloch; "or, what is the same thing, I have paid no attention to aught that may have passed in conversation respecting him."

"Why, then," said Lowestoffe—"but, first, let me have the honour of trussing you. Now, observe, I have left several of the points untied, of set purpose; and if it please you to let a small portion of your shirt be seen betwixt your doublet and the band of your upper stock, it will have so much the more rakish effect, and will attract you respect in Alsatia, where linen is something scarce. Now, I tie some of the points carefully asquint, for your ruffianly gallant never appears too accurately trussed—so."

"Arrange it as you will, sir," said Nigel; "but let me hear at least something of the conditions of the unhappy district into which, with other wretches, I am compelled to retreat."

"Why, my lord," replied the Templar, "our neighbouring state of Alsatia, which the law calls the Sanctuary of White-friars, has had its mutations and revolutions like greater kingdoms; and, being in some sort a lawless, arbitrary government, it follows, of course, that these have been more frequent than our own better regulated commonwealth of the Templars, that of Gray's Inn, and other similar associations, have had the fortune to witness. Our traditions and records speak of twenty revolutions within the last twelve years, in which the aforesaid state has repeatedly changed from absolute despotism to republicanism, not forgetting the intermediate stages of oligarchy, limited monarchy, and even gynocracy; for I myself remember Alsatia governed for nearly nine months by an old fish-woman. Then it fell under the dominion of a broken attorney, who was dethroned by a reformado captain, who, proving tyrannical, was deposed by a hedgeparson, who was succeeded, upon resignation of his power, by Duke Jacob Hildebrod, of that name the first, whom Heaven long preserve."

"And is this potentate's government," said Lord Glenvarloch, forcing himself to take some interest in the conversation, "of a despotic character?"

"Pardon me, my lord," said the Templar; "this said sovereign is too wise to incur, like many of his predecessors, the odium of wielding so important an authority by his own sole will. He has established a council of state, who regularly meet for their morning's draught at seven o'clock; convene a second time at eleven for their *ante-meridiem*, or whet; and, assembling in solemn conclave at the hour of two afternoon, for the purpose of consulting for the good of the commonwealth, are so prodigal of their labour in the service of the state, that they seldom separate before midnight. Into this worthy senate, composed partly of Duke Hildebrod's predecessors in his high office, whom he has associated with him to prevent the envy attending sovereign and sole authority, I must presently introduce your lordship, that they may admit you to the immunities of the Friars, and assign you a place of residence."

"Does their authority extend to such regulation?" said Lord Glenvarloch.

"The council account it a main point of their privileges, my lord," answered Lowestoffe; "and, in fact, it is one of the most powerful means by which they support their authority. For when Duke Ilildebrod and his senate find a topping householder in the Friars becomes discontented and factious, it is but assigning him, for a lodger, some fat bankrupt, or new lesidenter, whose circumstances require refuge, and whose purse can pay for it, and the malecontent becomes as tractable as a lamb. As for the poorer refugees, they let them shift as they can; but the registration of their names in the Duke's entry-book, and the payment of garnish conforming to their circumstances, is never dispensed with;

and the Friars would be a very unsafe residence for the stranger who should dispute these points of jurisdiction."

"Well, Master Lowestoffe," said Lord Glenvarloch, "I must be controlled by the circumstances which dictate to me this state of concealment—of course, I am desirous not to betray my name and rank."

"It will be highly advisable, my lord," said Lowestoffe; "and is a case thus provided for in the statutes of the republic, or monarchy, or whatsoever you call it.—He who desires that no questions shall be asked him concerning his name, cause of refuge, and the like, may escape the usual interrogations upon payment of double the garnish otherwise belonging to his condition. Complying with this essential stipulation, your lordship may register yourself as King of Bantam if you will, for not a question will be asked of you.—But here comes our scout, with news of peace and tranquillity. Now, I will go with your lordship myself, and present you to the council of Alsatia, with all the influence which I have over them as an office-bearer in the Temple, which is not slight; for they have come halting off upon all occasions when we have taken part against them, and that they well know. The time is propitious, for as the council is now met in Alsatia, so the Temple walks are quiet. Now, my lord, throw your cloak about you, to hide your present exterior. You shall give it to the boy at the foot of the stairs that go down to the Sanctuary; and as the ballad says that Queen Eleanor sunk at Charing Cross and rose at Queenhithe, so you shall sink a nobleman in the Temple Gardens, and rise an Alsatian at Whitefriars."

They went out accordingly, attended by the little scout, traversed the gardens, descended the stairs, and at the bottom the young Templar exclaimed,—"And now let us sing, with Ovid,

'In nova fert animus mutatas dicere formas—'

Off, off, ye lendings!" he continued, in the same vein. "Via, the curtain that shadowed Borgia!—But how now, my lord?" he continued, when he observed Lord Glenvarloch was really distressed at the degrading change in his situation, "I trust you are not offended at my rattling folly? I would but reconcile you to your present circumstances, and give you the tone of this strange place. Come, cheer up; I trust it will only be your residence for a very few days."

Nigel was only able to press his hand, and reply in a whisper, "I am sensible of your kindness. I know I must drink the cup which my own folly has filled for me. Pardon me, that, at the first taste, I feel its bitterness."

Reginald Lowestoffe was bustlingly officious and good-natured; but, used to live a scrambling, rakish course of life himself, he had not the least idea of the extent of Lord Glenvarloch's mental sufferings, and thought of his temporary concealment as if it were merely the trick of a wanton boy, who plays at hide-and-seek with his tutor. With the appearance of the place, too, he was familiar—but on his companion it produced a deep sensation.

The ancient Sanctuary at Whitefriars lay considerably lower than the elevated terraces and gardens of the Temple, and was therefore generally involved in the damps and fogs arising from the Thames. The brick buildings by which it was occupied, crowded closely on each other, for, in a place so rarely privileged, every foot of ground was valuable; but, erected in many cases by persons whose funds were inadequate to their speculations, the houses were generally insufficient, and exhibited the lamentable signs of having become ruinous while they were yet new. The wailing of children, the scolding of their mothers, the miserable exhibition of ragged linens hung from the windows to dry, spoke the wants and distresses of the wretched inhabitants; while the sounds of complaint were mocked and overwhelmed in the riotous shouts, oaths, profane songs, and boisterous laughter, that issued from the alehouses and taverns, which, as the signs indicated, were equal in number to all the other houses; and, that the full character of the place might be evident, several faded, tinselled and painted females, looked boldly at the strangers from their open lattices, or more modestly seemed busied with the cracked flower-pots, filled with mignonette and rosemary, which were disposed in front of the windows, to the great risk of the passengers.

"*Semi-reducta Venus*," said the Templar, pointing to one of these nymphs, who seemed afraid of observation, and partly concealed herself behind the casement, as she chirped to a miserable blackbird, the tenant of a wicker prison, which hung outside on the black brick wall.—"I know the face of yonder waistcoateer," continued the guide; "and I could wager a rose-noble, from the posture she stands in, that she has clean head-gear and a soiled night-rail.—But here come two of the male inhabitants, smoking like moving volcanoes! These are roaring blades, whom Nicotia and Trinidado serve, I dare swear, in lieu of beef and pudding; for be it known to you, my lord, that the king's counterblast against the Indian weed will no more pass current in Alsatia than will his writ of *capias*."

As he spoke, the two smokers approached; shaggy, uncombed ruffians, whose enormous mustaches were turned back over their ears, and mingled with the wild elf-locks of their hair, much of which was seen under the old beavers which they wore aside upon their heads, while some straggling portion escaped through the rents of the hats aforesaid. Their tarnished plush jerkins, large slops, or trunk-breeches, their broad greasy shoulder-belts, and discoloured scarfs, and, above all, the ostentatious manner in which the one wore a broad-sword and the other an extravagantly long rapier and poniard, marked the true Alsatian bully, then, and for a hundred years afterwards, a well-known character.

"Tour out," said the one ruffian to the other; "tour the bien mort twiring at the gentry cove!"*

"I smell a spy," replied the other, looking at Nigel. "Chalk him across the peepers with your cheery."**

"Bing avast, bing avast!" replied his companion; "yon other is rattling Reginald Lowestoffe of the Temple—I know him; he is a good boy, and free of the province."

So saying, and enveloping themselves in another thick cloud of smoke, they went on without farther greeting.

"*Grasso in aere!*" said the Templar. "You hear what a character the impudent knave gives me; but, so it serves your lordship's turn, I care not.—And, now, let me ask your lordship what name you will assume, for we are near the ducal palace of Duke Hildebrod."

"I will be called Grahame," said Nigel; "it was my mother's name."

"Grime," repeated the Templar, "will suit Alsatia well enough—both a grim and grimy place of refuge."

"I said Grahame, sir, not Grime," said Nigel, something shortly, and laying an emphasis on the vowel—for few Scotsmen understand raillery upon the subject of their names.

"I beg pardon, my lord," answered the undisconcerted punster; "but *Graam* will suit the circumstance, too—it signifies tribulation in the High Dutch, and your lordship must be considered as a man under trouble."

---

* Look sharp. See how the girl is coquetting with the strange gallants!
** Slash him over the eyes with your dagger.

Nigel laughed at the pertinacity of the Templar; who, proceeding to point out a sign representing, or believed to represent, a dog attacking a bull, and running at his head, in the true scientific style of onset,— "There," said he, "doth faithful Duke Hildebrod deal forth laws, as well as ale and strong waters, to his faithful Alsatians. Being a determined champion of Paris Garden, he has chosen a sign corresponding to his habits; and he deals in giving drink to the thirsty, that he himself may drink without paying, and receive pay for what is drunken by others.— Let us enter the ever-open gate of this second Axylus."

As they spoke, they entered the dilapidated tavern, which was, nevertheless, more ample in dimensions, and less ruinous, than many houses in the same evil neighbourhood. Two or three haggard, ragged drawers, ran to and fro, whose looks, like those of owls, seemed only adapted for midnight, when other creatures sleep, and who by day seemed bleared, stupid, and only half awake. Guided by one of these blinking Ganymedes, they entered a room, where the feeble rays of the sun were almost wholly eclipsed by volumes of tobacco-smoke, rolled from the tubes of the company, while out of the cloudy sanctuary arose the old chant of—

> "Old Sir Simon the King,
> And old Sir Simon the King,
> With his malmsey nose,
> And his ale-dropped hose,
> And sing hey ding-a-ding-ding."

Duke Hildebrod, who himself condescended to chant this ditty to his loving subjects, was a monstrously fat old man, with only one eye; and a nose which bore evidence to the frequency, strength, and depth of his potations. He wore a murrey-coloured plush jerkin, stained with the overflowings of the tankard, and much the worse for wear, and unbuttoned at bottom for the ease of his enormous paunch. Behind him lay a favourite bull-dog, whose round head and single black glancing eye, as well as the creature's great corpulence, gave it a burlesque resemblance to its master.

The well-beloved counsellors who surrounded the ducal throne, incensed it with tobacco, pledged its occupier in thick clammy ale, and echoed back his choral songs, were Satraps worthy of such a Soldan. The buff jerkin, broad belt, and long sword of one, showed him to be a

Low Country soldier, whose look of scowling importance, and drunken impudence, were designed to sustain his title to call himself a Roving Blade. It seemed to Nigel that he had seen this fellow somewhere or other. A hedge-parson, or buckle-beggar, as that order of priesthood has been irreverently termed, sat on the Duke's left, and was easily distinguished by his torn band, flapped hat, and the remnants of a rusty cassock. Beside the parson sat a most wretched and meagre-looking old man, with a threadbare hood of coarse kersey upon his head, and buttoned about his neck, while his pinched features, like those of old Daniel, were illuminated by

—*"an eye,*
Through the last look of dotage still cunning and sly."

On his left was placed a broken attorney, who, for some malpractices, had been struck from the roll of practitioners, and who had nothing left of his profession, except its roguery. One or two persons of less figure, amongst whom there was one face, which, like that of the soldier, seemed not unknown to Nigel, though he could not recollect where he had seen it, completed the council-board of Jacob Duke Hildebrod.

The strangers had full time to observe all this; for his grace the Duke, whether irresistibly carried on by the full tide of harmony, or whether to impress the strangers with a proper idea of his consequence, chose to sing his ditty to an end before addressing them, though, during the whole time, he closely scrutinized them with his single optic.

When Duke Hildebrod had ended his song, he informed his Peers that a worthy officer of the Temple attended them, and commanded the captain and parson to abandon their easy chairs in behalf of the two strangers, whom he placed on his right and left hand. The worthy representative of the army and the church of Alsatia went to place themselves on a crazy form at the bottom of the table, which, ill calculated to sustain men of such weight, gave way under them, and the man of the sword and man of the gown were rolled over each other on the floor, amidst the exulting shouts of the company. They arose in wrath, contending which should vent his displeasure in the loudest and deepest oaths, a strife in which the parson's superior acquaintance with theology enabled him greatly to excel the captain, and were at length with difficulty tranquillised by the arrival of the alarmed waiters with more stable chairs, and by a long draught of the cooling tankard.

When this commotion was appeased, and the strangers courteously accommodated with flagons, after the fashion of the others present, the Duke drank prosperity to the Temple in the most gracious manner, together with a cup of welcome to Master Reginald Lowestoffe; and, this courtesy having been thankfully accepted, the party honoured prayed permission to call for a gallon of Rhenish, over which he proposed to open his business.

The mention of a liquor so superior to their usual potations had an instant and most favourable effect upon the little senate; and its immediate appearance might be said to secure a favourable reception of Master Lowestoffe's proposition, which, after a round or two had circulated, he explained to be the admission of his friend Master Nigel Grahame to the benefit of the sanctuary and other immunities of Alsatia, in the character of a grand compounder; for so were those termed who paid a double fee at their matriculation, in order to avoid laying before the senate the peculiar circumstances which compelled them to take refuge there.

The worthy Duke heard the proposition with glee, which glittered in his single eye; and no wonder, as it was a rare occurrence, and of peculiar advantage to his private revenue. Accordingly, he commanded his ducal register to be brought him, a huge book, secured with brass clasps like a merchant's ledger, and whose leaves, stained with wine, and slabbered with tobacco juice, bore the names probably of as many rogues as are to be found in the Calendar of Newgate.

Nigel was then directed to lay down two nobles as his ransom, and to claim privilege by reciting the following doggerel verses, which were dictated to him by the Duke:—

> "Your suppliant, by name
> Nigel Grahame,
> In fear of mishap
> From a shoulder-tap;
> And dreading a claw
> From the talons of law,
> That are sharper than briers:
> His freedom to sue,
> And rescue by you—
> Thorugh weapon and wit,
> From warrant and writ,

From bailiff's hand,
From tipstaff's wand,
Is come hither to Whitefriars."

As Duke Hildebrod with a tremulous hand began to make the entry, and had already, with superfluous generosity, spelled Nigel with two g's instead of one, he was interrupted by the parson.* This reverend gentleman had been whispering for a minute or two, not with the captain, but with that other individual, who dwelt imperfectly, as we have already mentioned, in Nigel's memory, and being, perhaps, still something malecontent on account of the late accident, he now requested to be heard before the registration took place.

"The person," he said, "who hath now had the assurance to propose himself as a candidate for the privileges and immunities of this honourable society, is, in plain terms, a beggarly Scot, and we have enough of these locusts in London already—if we admit such palmer-worms and caterpillars to the Sanctuary, we shall soon have the whole nation."

"We are not entitled to inquire," said Duke Hildebrod, "whether he be Scot, or French, or English; seeing he has honourably laid down his garnish, he is entitled to our protection."

"Word of denial, most Sovereign Duke," replied the parson, "I ask him no questions—his speech betrayeth him—he is a Galilean—and his garnish is forfeited for his assurance in coming within this our realm; and I call on you, Sir Duke, to put the laws in force against him!"

The Templar here rose, and was about to interrupt the deliberations of the court, when the Duke gravely assured him that he should be heard in behalf of his friend, so soon as the council had finished their deliberations.

The attorney next rose, and, intimating that he was to speak to the point of law, said—"It was easy to be seen that this gentleman did not come here in any civil case, and that he believed it to be the story

---

* This curious register is still in existence, being in possession of that eminent antiquary, Dr. Dryasdust, who liberally offered the author permission to have the autograph of Duke Hildebrod engraved as an illustration of this passage. Unhappily, being rigorous as Ritson himself in adhering to the very letter of his copy, the worthy Doctor clogged his munificence with the condition that we should adopt the Duke's orthography, and entitle the work "The Fortunes of Niggle," with which stipulation we did not think it necessary to comply.

they had already heard of concerning a blow given within the verge of the Park—that the Sanctuary would not bear out the offender in such case—and that the queer old Chief would send down a broom which would sweep the streets of Alsatia from the Strand to the Stairs; and it was even policy to think what evil might come to their republic, by sheltering an alien in such circumstances."

The captain, who had sat impatiently while these opinions were expressed, now sprung on his feet with the vehemence of a cork bouncing from a bottle of brisk beer, and, turning up his mustaches with a martial air, cast a glance of contempt on the lawyer and churchman, while he thus expressed his opinion.

"Most noble Duke Hildebrod! When I hear such base, skeldering, coistril propositions come from the counsellors of your grace, and when I remember the Huffs, the Muns, and the Tityretu's by whom your grace's ancestors and predecessors were advised on such occasions, I begin to think the spirit of action is as dead in Alsatia as in my old grannam; and yet who thinks so thinks a lie, since I will find as many roaring boys in the Friars as shall keep the liberties against all the scavengers of Westminster. And, if we should be overborne for a turn, death and darkness! have we not time to send the gentleman off by water, either to Paris Garden or to the bankside? and, if he is a gallant of true breed, will he not make us full amends for all the trouble we have? Let other societies exist by the law, I say that we brisk boys of the Fleet live in spite of it; and thrive best when we are in right opposition to sign and seal, writ and warrant, sergeant and tipstaff, catchpoll, and bum-bailey."

This speech was followed by a murmur of approbation, and Lowestoffe, striking in before the favourable sound had subsided, reminded the Duke and his council how much the security of their state depended upon the amity of the Templars, who, by closing their gates, could at pleasure shut against the Alsatians the communication betwixt the Friars and the Temple, and that as they conducted themselves on this occasion, so would they secure or lose the benefit of his interest with his own body, which they knew not to be inconsiderable. "And, in respect of my friend being a Scotsman and alien, as has been observed by the reverend divine and learned lawyer, you are to consider," said Lowestoffe, "for what he is pursued hither—why, for giving the bastinado, not to an Englishman, but to one of his own countrymen. And for my own simple part," he continued, touching Lord Glenvarloch at the same time, to make him understand he spoke but in jest, "if all the Scots in London were to fight a Welsh main, and kill each other to a man, the survivor would, in my humble opinion, be entitled to our gratitude, as having done a most acceptable service to poor Old England."

A shout of laughter and applause followed this ingenious apology for the client's state of alienage; and the Templar followed up his plea with the following pithy proposition:—"I know well," said he, "it is the custom of the fathers of this old and honourable republic, ripely and well to consider all their proceedings over a proper allowance of liquor; and far be it from me to propose the breach of so laudable a custom, or to pretend that such an affair as the present can be well and constitutionally considered during the discussion of a pitiful gallon of Rhenish. But, as it is the same thing to this honourable conclave whether they drink first and determine afterwards, or whether they determine first and drink afterwards, I propose your grace, with the advice of your wise and potent senators, shall pass your edict, granting to mine honourable friend the immunities of the place, and assigning him a lodging, according to your wise forms, to which he will presently retire, being somewhat spent with this day's action; whereupon I will presently order you a rundlet of Rhenish, with a corresponding quantity of neats' tongues and pickled herrings, to make you all as glorious as George-a-Green."

This overture was received with a general shout of applause, which altogether drowned the voice of the dissidents, if any there were amongst the Alsatian senate who could have resisted a proposal so popular. The words of, kind heart! noble gentleman! generous gallant! flew from mouth to mouth; the inscription of the petitioner's name in the great book was hastily completed, and the oath administered to him by the worthy Doge. Like the Laws of the Twelve Tables, of the ancient Cambro-Britons, and other primitive nations, it was couched in poetry, and ran as follows:—

> "By spigot and barrel, By bilboe and buff;
> Thou art sworn to the quarrel
> Of the blades of the huff.
> For Whitefriars and its claims
> To be champion or martyr,
> And to fight for its dames
> Like a Knight of the Garter."

Nigel felt, and indeed exhibited, some disgust at this mummery; but, the Templar reminding him that he was too far advanced to draw back, he repeated the words, or rather assented as they were repeated by Duke Hildebrod, who concluded the ceremony by allowing him the privilege of sanctuary, in the following form of prescriptive doggerel:—

> *"From the touch of the tip,*
> *From the blight of the warrant,*
> *From the watchmen who skip*
> *On the Harman Beck's errand;*
> *From the bailiffs cramp speech,*
> *That makes man a thrall,*
> *I charm thee from each,*
> *And I charm thee from all.*
> *Thy freedom's complete*
> *As a Blade of the Huff,*
> *To be cheated and cheat,*
> *To be cuff'd and to cuff;*
> *To stride, swear, and swagger,*
> *To drink till you stagger,*
> *To stare and to stab,*
> *And to brandish your dagger*
> *In the cause of your drab;*
> *To walk wool-ward in winter,*
> *Drink brandy, and smoke,*
> *And go fresco in summer*
> *For want of a cloak;*
> *To eke out your living*
> *By the wag of your elbow,*
> *By fulham and gourd,*
> *And by baring of bilboe;*
> *To live by your shifts,*
> *And to swear by your honour,*
> *Are the freedom and gifts*
> *Of which I am the donor."**

---

* Of the cant words used in this inauguratory oration, some are obvious in their meaning, others, as Harman Beck (constable), and the like, derive their source from that ancient piece of lexicography, the Slang Dictionary.

This homily being performed, a dispute arose concerning the special residence to be assigned the new brother of the Sanctuary; for, as the Alsatians held it a maxim in their commonwealth, that ass's milk fattens, there was usually a competition among the inhabitants which should have the managing, as it was termed, of a new member of the society.

The Hector who had spoken so warmly and critically in Nigel's behalf, stood out now chivalrously in behalf of a certain Blowselinda, or Bonstrops, who had, it seems, a room to hire, once the occasional residence of Slicing Dick of Paddington, who lately suffered at Tyburn, and whose untimely exit had been hitherto mourned by the damsel in solitary widowhood, after the fashion of the turtle-dove.

The captain's interest was, however, overruled, in behalf of the old gentleman in the kersey hood, who was believed, even at his extreme age, to understand the plucking of a pigeon, as well, or better, than any man in Alsatia.

This venerable personage was an usurer of notoriety, called Trapbois, and had very lately done the state considerable service in advancing a subsidy necessary to secure a fresh importation of liquors to the Duke's cellars, the wine-merchant at the Vintry being scrupulous to deal with so great a man for any thing but ready money.

When, therefore, the old gentleman arose, and with much coughing, reminded the Duke that he had a poor apartment to let, the claims of all others were set aside, and Nigel was assigned to Trapbois as his guest.

No sooner was this arrangement made, than Lord Glenvarloch expressed to Lowestoffe his impatience to leave this discreditable assembly, and took his leave with a careless haste, which, but for the rundlet of Rhenish wine that entered just as he left the apartment, might have been taken in bad part. The young Templar accompanied his friend to the house of the old usurer, with the road to which he and some other youngsters about the Temple were even but too well acquainted. On the way, he assured Lord Glenvarloch that he was going to the only clean house in Whitefriars; a property which it owed solely to the exertions of the old man's only daughter, an elderly damsel, ugly enough to frighten sin, yet likely to be wealthy enough to tempt a puritan, so soon as the devil had got her old dad for his due. As Lowestoffe spoke thus, they knocked at the door of the house, and the sour stern countenance of the female by whom it was opened, fully confirmed all that the Templar had said of the hostess. She heard with an ungracious and discontented air the young Templar's information, that the gentleman, his companion, was to be her father's lodger, muttered something about the trouble it was likely to occasion, but ended by showing the stranger's apartment, which was better than could have been augured from the general appearance of the place, and much larger in extent than that which he occupied at Paul's Wharf, though inferior to it in neatness.

Lowestoffe, having thus seen his friend fairly installed in his new apartment, and having obtained for him a note of the rate at which he could be accommodated with victuals from a neighbouring cook's shop, now took his leave, offering, at the same time, to send the whole, or any part of Lord Glenvarloch's baggage, from his former place of residence to his new lodging. Nigel mentioned so few articles, that the Templar could not help observing, that his lordship, it would seem, did not intend to enjoy his new privileges long.

"They are too little suited to my habits and taste, that I should do so," replied Lord Glenvarloch.

"You may change your opinion to-morrow," said Lowestoffe; "and so I wish you a good even. To-morrow I will visit you betimes."

The morning came, but instead of the Templar, it brought only a letter from him. The epistle stated, that Lowestoffe's visit to Alsatia had drawn down the animadversions of some crabbed old pantaloons among the benchers, and that he judged it wise not to come hither at present, for fear of attracting too much attention to Lord Glenvarloch's place of residence. He stated, that he had taken measures for the safety of his baggage, and would send him, by a safe hand, his money-casket, and what articles he wanted. Then followed some sage advices, dictated by Lowestoffe's acquaintance with Alsatia and its manners. He advised him to keep the usurer in the most absolute uncertainty concerning the state of his funds-never to throw a main with the captain, who was in the habit of playing dry-fisted, and paying his losses with three vowels; and, finally, to beware of Duke Hildebrod, who was as sharp, he said, as a needle, though he had no more eyes than are possessed by that necessary implement of female industry.

XVIII

MOTHER: *What I dazzled by a flash from Cupid's mirror, With which the boy, as mortal urchins wont, Flings back the sunbeam in the eye of passengers—Then laughs to see them stumble!*
DAUGHTER: *Mother! no—It was a lightning-flash which dazzled me, And never shall these eyes see true again.*

—Beef and Pudding, An Old English Comedy

It is necessary that we should leave our hero Nigel for a time, although in a situation neither safe, comfortable, nor creditable, in order to detail some particulars which have immediate connexion with his fortunes.

It was but the third day after he had been forced to take refuge in the house of old Trapbois, the noted usurer of Whitefriars, commonly called Golden Trapbois, when the pretty daughter of old Ramsay, the watchmaker, after having piously seen her father finish his breakfast, (from the fear that he might, in an abstruse fit of thought, swallow the salt-cellar instead of a crust of the brown loaf,) set forth from the house as soon as he was again plunged into the depth of calculation, and, accompanied only by that faithful old drudge, Janet, the Scots laundress, to whom her whims were laws, made her way to Lombard Street, and disturbed, at the unusual hour of eight in the morning, Aunt Judith, the sister of her worthy godfather.

The venerable maiden received her young visitor with no great complacency; for, naturally enough, she had neither the same admiration of her very pretty countenance, nor allowance for her foolish and girlish impatience of temper, which Master George Heriot entertained. Still Mistress Margaret was a favourite of her brother's, whose will was to Aunt Judith a supreme law; and she contented herself with asking her untimely visitor, "what she made so early with her pale, chitty face, in the streets of London?"

"I would speak with the Lady Hermione," answered the almost breathless girl, while the blood ran so fast to her face as totally to remove the objection of paleness which Aunt Judith had made to her complexion.

"With the Lady Hermione?" said Aunt Judith—"with the Lady Hermione? and at this time in the morning, when she will scarce see any of the family, even at seasonable hours? You are crazy, you silly wench, or you abuse the indulgence which my brother and the lady have shown to you."

"Indeed, indeed I have not," repeated Margaret, struggling to retain the unbidden tear which seemed ready to burst out on the slightest occasion. "Do but say to the lady that your brother's god-daughter desires earnestly to speak to her, and I know she will not refuse to see me."

Aunt Judith bent an earnest, suspicious, and inquisitive glance on her young visitor, "You might make me your secretary, my lassie," she said, "as well as the Lady Hermione. I am older, and better skilled to advise. I live more in the world than one who shuts herself up within four rooms, and I have the better means to assist you."

"O! no—no—no," said Margaret, eagerly, and with more earnest sincerity than complaisance; "there are some things to which you cannot advise me, Aunt Judith. It is a case—pardon me, my dear aunt—a case beyond your counsel."

"I am glad on't, maiden," said Aunt Judith, somewhat angrily; "for I think the follies of the young people of this generation would drive mad an old brain like mine. Here you come on the viretot, through the whole streets of London, to talk some nonsense to a lady, who scarce sees God's sun, but when he shines on a brick wall. But I will tell her you are here."

She went away, and shortly returned with a dry—"Miss Marget, the lady will be glad to see you; and that's more, my young madam, than you had a right to count upon."

Mistress Margaret hung her head in silence, too much perplexed by the train of her own embarrassed thoughts, for attempting either to conciliate Aunt Judith's kindness, or, which on other occasions would have been as congenial to her own humour, to retaliate on her cross-tempered remarks and manner. She followed Aunt Judith, therefore, in silence and dejection, to the strong oaken door which divided the Lady Hermione's apartments from the rest of George Heriot's spacious house.

At the door of this sanctuary it is necessary to pause, in order to correct the reports with which Richie Moniplies had filled his master's ear, respecting the singular appearance of that lady's attendance at prayers, whom we now own to be by name the Lady Hermione. Some part of these exaggerations had been communicated to the worthy Scotsman by Jenkin Vincent, who was well experienced in the species of wit which has been long a favourite in the city, under the names of cross-biting, giving the dor, bamboozling, cramming, hoaxing, humbugging, and quizzing; for which sport Richie Moniplies, with his solemn gravity, totally unapprehensive of a joke, and his natural propensity to the marvellous, formed an admirable subject. Farther ornaments the tale had received from Richie himself, whose tongue, especially when oiled with good liquor, had a considerable tendency to amplification, and who failed not, while he retailed to his master all the wonderful circumstances narrated by Vincent, to add to them many conjectures of his own, which his imagination had over-hastily converted into facts.

Yet the life which the Lady Hermione had led for two years, during which she had been the inmate of George Heriot's house, was so singular, as almost to sanction many of the wild reports which went abroad. The house which the worthy goldsmith inhabited, had in former times belonged to a powerful and wealthy baronial family, which, during the reign of Henry VIII, terminated in a dowager lady, very wealthy, very devout, and most unalienably attached to the Catholic faith. The chosen friend of the Honourable Lady Foljambe was the Abbess of Saint Roque's Nunnery, like herself a conscientious, rigid, and devoted Papist. When the house of Saint Roque was despotically dissolved by the fiat of the impetuous monarch, the Lady Foljambe received her friend into her spacious mansion, together with two vestal sisters, who, like their Abbess, were determined to follow the tenor of their vows, instead of embracing the profane liberty which the Monarch's will had thrown in their choice. For their residence, the Lady Foljambe contrived, with all secrecy—for Henry might not have relished her interference— to set apart a suite of four rooms, with a little closet fitted up as an oratory, or chapel; the whole apartments fenced by a stout oaken door to exclude strangers, and accommodated with a turning wheel to receive necessaries, according to the practice of all nunneries. In this retreat, the Abbess of Saint Roque and her attendants passed many years, communicating only with the Lady Foljambe, who, in virtue of their prayers, and of the support she afforded them, accounted herself little less than a saint on earth. The Abbess, fortunately for herself, died before her munificent patroness, who lived deep in Queen Elizabeth's time, ere she was summoned by fate.

The Lady Foljambe was succeeded in this mansion by a sour fanatic knight, a distant and collateral relation, who claimed the same merit for expelling the priestess of Baal, which his predecessor had founded on maintaining the votaresses of Heaven. Of the two unhappy nuns, driven from their ancient refuge, one went beyond sea; the other, unable from old age to undertake such a journey, died under the roof of a faithful Catholic widow of low degree. Sir Paul Crambagge, having got rid of the nuns, spoiled the chapel of its ornaments, and had thoughts of altogether destroying the apartments, until checked by the reflection that the operation would be an unnecessary expense, since he only inhabited three rooms of the large mansion, and had not therefore the slightest occasion for any addition to its accommodations. His son proved a waster and a prodigal, and from him the house was bought by our friend George Heriot, who, finding, like Sir Paul, the house more than sufficiently ample for his accommodation, left the Foljambe apartments, or Saint Roque's rooms, as they were called, in the state in which he found them.

About two years and a half before our history opened, when Heriot was absent upon an expedition to the Continent, he sent special orders to his sister and his cash-keeper, directing that the Foljambe apartments should be fitted up handsomely, though plainly, for the reception of a lady, who would make them her residence for some time; and who would live more or less with his own family according to her pleasure. He also directed, that the necessary repairs should be made with secrecy, and that as little should be said as possible upon the subject of his letter.

When the time of his return came nigh, Aunt Judith and the household were on the tenter-hooks of impatience. Master George came, as he had intimated, accompanied by a lady, so eminently beautiful, that, had it not been for her extreme and uniform paleness, she might have been reckoned one of the loveliest creatures on earth. She had with her an attendant, or humble companion, whose business seemed only to wait upon her. This person, a reserved woman, and by her dialect a foreigner, aged about fifty, was called by the lady Monna Paula, and by Master Heriot, and others, Mademoiselle Pauline. She slept in the same room with her patroness at night, ate in her apartment, and was scarcely ever separated from her during the day.

These females took possession of the nunnery of the devout Abbess, and, without observing the same rigorous seclusion, according to the letter, seemed wellnigh to restore the apartments to the use to which they had been originally designed. The new inmates lived and took their meals apart from the rest of the family. With the domestics

Lady Hermione, for so she was termed, held no communication, and Mademoiselle Pauline only such as was indispensable, which she dispatched as briefly as possible. Frequent and liberal largesses reconciled the servants to this conduct; and they were in the habit of observing to each other, that to do a service for Mademoiselle Pauline, was like finding a fairy treasure.

To Aunt Judith the Lady Hermione was kind and civil, but their intercourse was rare; on which account the elder lady felt some pangs both of curiosity and injured dignity. But she knew her brother so well, and loved him so dearly, that his will, once expressed, might be truly said to become her own. The worthy citizen was not without a spice of the dogmatism which grows on the best disposition, when a word is a law to all around. Master George did not endure to be questioned by his family, and, when he had generally expressed his will, that the Lady Hermione should live in the way most agreeable to her, and that no inquiries should be made concerning their history, or her motives for observing such strict seclusion, his sister well knew that he would have been seriously displeased with any attempt to pry into the secret.

But, though Heriot's servants were bribed, and his sister awed into silent acquiescence in these arrangements, they were not of a nature to escape the critical observation of the neighbourhood. Some opined that the wealthy goldsmith was about to turn papist, and re-establish Lady Foljambe's nunnery—others that he was going mad—others that he was either going to marry, or to do worse. Master George's constant appearance at church, and the knowledge that the supposed votaress always attended when the prayers of the English ritual were read in the family, liberated him from the first of these suspicions; those who had to transact business with him upon 'Change, could not doubt the soundness of Master Heriot's mind; and, to confute the other rumours, it was credibly reported by such as made the matter their particular interest, that Master George Heriot never visited his guest but in presence of Mademoiselle Pauline, who sat with her work in a remote part of the same room in which they conversed. It was also ascertained that these visits scarcely ever exceeded an hour in length, and were usually only repeated once a week, an intercourse too brief and too long interrupted, to render it probable that love was the bond of their union.

The inquirers were, therefore, at fault, and compelled to relinquish the pursuit of Master Heriot's secret, while a thousand ridiculous tales were circulated amongst the ignorant and superstitious, with some specimens of which our friend Richie Moniplies had been *crammed*, as we have seen, by the malicious apprentice of worthy David Ramsay.

There was one person in the world who, it was thought, could (if she would) have said more of the Lady Hermione than any one in London, except George Heriot himself; and that was the said David Ramsay's only child, Margaret.

This girl was not much past the age of fifteen when the Lady Hermione first came to England, and was a very frequent visitor at her godfather's, who was much amused by her childish sallies, and by the wild and natural beauty with which she sung the airs of her native country. Spoilt she was on all hands; by the indulgence of her godfather, the absent habits and indifference of her father, and the deference of all around to her caprices, as a beauty and as an heiress. But though, from these circumstances, the city-beauty had become as wilful, as capricious, and as affected, as unlimited indulgence seldom fails to render those to whom it is extended; and although she exhibited upon many occasions that affectation of extreme shyness, silence, and reserve, which misses in their teens are apt to take for an amiable modesty; and, upon others, a considerable portion of that flippancy, which youth sometimes confounds with wit, Mistress Margaret had much real shrewdness and judgment, which wanted only opportunities of observation to refine it—a lively, good-humoured, playful disposition, and an excellent heart. Her acquired follies were much increased by reading plays and romances, to which she devoted a great deal of her time, and from which she adopted ideas as different as possible from those which she might have obtained from the invaluable and affectionate instructions of an excellent mother; and the freaks of which she was sometimes guilty, rendered her not unjustly liable to the charge of affectation and coquetry. But the little lass had sense and shrewdness enough to keep her failings out of sight of her godfather, to whom she was sincerely attached; and so high she stood in his favour, that, at his recommendation, she obtained permission to visit the recluse Lady Hermione.

The singular mode of life which that lady observed; her great beauty, rendered even more interesting by her extreme paleness; the conscious pride of being admitted farther than the rest of the world into the society of a person who was wrapped in so much mystery, made a deep impression on the mind of Margaret Ramsay; and though their conversations were at no time either long or confidential, yet, proud of the trust reposed in her, Margaret was as secret respecting their tenor as if every word repeated had been to cost her life. No inquiry, however artfully backed by flattery and insinuation, whether on the part of Dame Ursula, or any other person equally inquisitive, could wring from the little maiden one word of what she heard or saw, after she entered these mysterious and secluded apartments. The slightest question concerning Master Heriot's ghost, was sufficient, at her gayest moment, to check the current of her communicative prattle, and render her silent.

We mention this, chiefly to illustrate the early strength of Margaret's character—a strength concealed under a hundred freakish whims and humours, as an ancient and massive buttress is disguised by its fantastic covering of ivy and wildflowers. In truth, if the damsel had told all she heard or saw within the Foljambe apartments, she would have said but little to gratify the curiosity of inquirers.

At the earlier period of their acquaintance, the Lady Hermione was wont to reward the attentions of her little friend with small but elegant presents, and entertain her by a display of foreign rarities and curiosities, many of them of considerable value. Sometimes the time was passed in a way much less agreeable to Margaret, by her receiving lessons from Pauline in the use of the needle. But, although her preceptress practised these arts with a dexterity then only known in foreign convents, the pupil proved so incorrigibly idle and awkward, that the task of needlework was at length given up, and lessons of music substituted in their stead. Here also Pauline was excellently qualified as an instructress, and Margaret, more successful in a science for which Nature had gifted her, made proficiency both in vocal and instrumental music. These lessons passed in presence of the Lady Hermione, to whom they seemed to give pleasure. She sometimes added her own voice to the performance, in a pure, clear stream of liquid melody; but this was only when the music was of a devotional cast. As Margaret became older, her communications with the recluse assumed a different character. She was allowed, if not encouraged, to tell whatever she had remarked out of doors, and the Lady Hermione, while she remarked the quick, sharp, and retentive powers of observation possessed by her young friend, often found sufficient reason to caution her against rashness in forming opinions, and giddy petulance in expressing them.

The habitual awe with which she regarded this singular personage, induced Mistress Margaret, though by no means delighting in contradiction or reproof, to listen with patience to her admonitions, and to make full allowance for the good intentions of the patroness by whom they were bestowed; although in her heart she could hardly conceive how Madame Hermione, who never stirred from the Foljambe apartments, should think of teaching knowledge of the world to one who walked twice a-week between Temple Bar and Lombard Street, besides parading in the Park every Sunday that proved to be fair weather. Indeed, pretty Mistress Margaret was so little inclined to endure such remonstrances, that her intercourse with the inhabitants of the Foljambe apartments would have probably slackened as her circle of acquaintance increased in the external world, had she not, on the one hand, entertained an habitual reverence for her monitress, of which she could not divest herself, and been flattered, on the other, by being to a certain degree the depository of a confidence for which others thirsted in vain. Besides, although the conversation of Hermione was uniformly serious, it was not in general either formal or severe; nor was the lady offended by flights of levity which Mistress Margaret sometimes ventured on in her presence, even when they were such as made Monna Paula cast her eyes upwards, and sigh with that compassion which a devotee extends towards the votaries of a trivial and profane world. Thus, upon the whole, the little maiden was disposed to submit, though not without some wincing, to the grave admonitions of the Lady Hermione; and the rather that the mystery annexed to the person of her monitress was in her mind early associated with a vague idea of wealth and importance, which had been rather confirmed than lessened by many accidental circumstances which she had noticed since she was more capable of observation.

It frequently happens, that the counsel which we reckon intrusive when offered to us unasked, becomes precious in our eyes when the pressure of difficulties renders us more diffident of our own judgment than we are apt to find ourselves in the hours of ease and indifference; and this is more especially the case if we suppose that our adviser may also possess power and inclination to back his counsel with effectual assistance. Mistress Margaret was now in that situation. She was, or believed herself to be, in a condition where both advice and assistance might be necessary; and it was therefore, after an anxious and sleepless night, that she resolved to have recourse to the Lady Hermione, who she knew would readily afford her the one, and, as she hoped, might also possess means of giving her the other. The conversation between them will best explain the purport of the visit.

XIX

By this good light, a wench of matchless mettle!
This were a leaguer-lass to love a soldier,
To bind his wounds, and kiss his bloody brow,
And sing a roundel as she help'd to arm him,
Though the rough foeman's drums were beat so nigh,
They seem'd to bear the burden.

—Old Play

When Mistress Margaret entered the Foljambe apartment, she found the inmates employed in their usual manner; the lady in reading, and her attendant in embroidering a large piece of tapestry, which had occupied her ever since Margaret had been first admitted within these secluded chambers.

Hermione nodded kindly to her visitor, but did not speak; and Margaret, accustomed to this reception, and in the present case not sorry for it, as it gave her an interval to collect her thoughts, stooped over Monna Paula's frame and observed, in a half whisper, "You were just so far as that rose, Monna, when I first saw you—see, there is the mark where I had the bad luck to spoil the flower in trying to catch the stitch—I was little above fifteen then. These flowers make me an old woman, Monna Paula."

"I wish they could make you a wise one, my child," answered Monna Paula, in whose esteem pretty Mistress Margaret did not stand quite so high as in that of her patroness; partly owing to her natural austerity, which was something intolerant of youth and gaiety, and partly to the jealousy with which a favourite domestic regards any one whom she considers as a sort of rival in the affections of her mistress.

"What is it you say to Monna, little one?" asked the lady.

"Nothing, madam," replied Mistress Margaret, "but that I have seen the real flowers blossom three times over since I first saw Monna Paula working in her canvass garden, and her violets have not budded yet."

"True, lady-bird," replied Hermione; "but the buds that are longest in blossoming will last the longest in flower. You have seen them in the garden bloom thrice, but you have seen them fade thrice also; now,

Monna Paula's will remain in blow for ever—they will fear neither frost nor tempest."

"True, madam," answered Mistress Margaret; "but neither have they life or odour."

"That, little one," replied the recluse, "is to compare a life agitated by hope and fear, and chequered with success and disappointment, and fevered by the effects of love and hatred, a life of passion and of feeling, saddened and shortened by its exhausting alternations, to a calm and tranquil existence, animated but by a sense of duties, and only employed, during its smooth and quiet course, in the unwearied discharge of them. Is that the moral of your answer?"

"I do not know, madam," answered Mistress Margaret; "but, of all birds in the air, I would rather be the lark, that sings while he is drifting down the summer breeze, than the weathercock that sticks fast yonder upon his iron perch, and just moves so much as to discharge his duty, and tell us which way the wind blows."

"Metaphors are no arguments, my pretty maiden," said the Lady Hermione, smiling.

"I am sorry for that, madam," answered Margaret; "for they are such a pretty indirect way of telling one's mind when it differs from one's betters—besides, on this subject there is no end of them, and they are so civil and becoming withal."

"Indeed?" replied the lady; "let me hear some of them, I pray you."

"It would be, for example, very bold in me," said Margaret, "to say to your ladyship, that, rather than live a quiet life, I would like a little variety of hope and fear, and liking and disliking—and—and—and the other sort of feelings which your ladyship is pleased to speak of; but I may say freely, and without blame, that I like a butterfly better than a bettle, or a trembling aspen better than a grim Scots fir, that never wags a leaf—or that of all the wood, brass, and wire that ever my father's fingers put together, I do hate and detest a certain huge old clock of the German fashion, that rings hours and half hours, and quarters and half quarters, as if it were of such consequence that the world should know it was wound up and going. Now, dearest lady, I wish you would only compare that clumsy, clanging, Dutch-looking piece of lumber, with the beautiful timepiece that Master Heriot caused my father to make for your ladyship, which uses to play a hundred merry tunes, and turns out, when it strikes the hour, a whole band of morrice dancers, to trip the hays to the measure."

"And which of these timepieces goes the truest, Margaret?" said the lady.

"I must confess the old Dutchman has the advantage in that"—said Margaret. "I fancy you are right, madam, and that comparisons are no arguments; at least mine has not brought me through."

"Upon my word, maiden Margaret," said the lady, smiling, "you have been of late thinking very much of these matters."

"Perhaps too much, madam," said Margaret, so low as only to be heard by the lady, behind the back of whose chair she had now placed herself. The words were spoken very gravely, and accompanied by a half sigh, which did not escape the attention of her to whom they were addressed. The Lady Hermione turned immediately round, and looked earnestly at Margaret, then paused for a moment, and, finally, commanded Monna Paula to carry her frame and embroidery into the antechamber. When they were left alone, she desired her young friend to come from behind the chair on the back of which she still rested, and sit down beside her upon a stool.

"I will remain thus, madam, under your favour," answered Margaret, without changing her posture; "I would rather you heard me without seeing me."

"In God's name, maiden," returned her patroness, "what is it you can have to say, that may not be uttered face to face, to so true a friend as I am?"

Without making any direct answer, Margaret only replied, "You were right, dearest lady, when you said, I had suffered my feelings too much to engross me of late. I have done very wrong, and you will be angry with me—so will my godfather, but I cannot help it—he must be rescued."

"*He?*" repeated the lady, with emphasis; "that brief little word does, indeed, so far explain your mystery;—but come from behind the chair, you silly popinjay! I will wager you have suffered yonder gay young apprentice to sit too near your heart. I have not heard you mention young Vincent for many a day—perhaps he has not been out of mouth and out of mind both. Have you been so foolish as to let him speak to you seriously?—I am told he is a bold youth."

"Not bold enough to say any thing that could displease me, madam," said Margaret.

"Perhaps, then, you were *not* displeased," said the lady; "or perhaps he has not *spoken*, which would be wiser and better. Be open-hearted, my love—your godfather will soon return, and we will take him into our consultations. If the young man is industrious, and come of honest parentage, his poverty may be no such insurmountable obstacle. But you are both of you very young, Margaret—I know your godfather will expect, that the youth shall first serve out his apprenticeship."

Margaret had hitherto suffered the lady to proceed, under the mistaken impression which she had adopted, simply because she could not tell how to interrupt her; but pure despite at hearing her last words gave her boldness at length to say "I crave your pardon, madam; but neither the youth you mention, nor any apprentice or master within the city of London—"

"Margaret," said the lady, in reply, "the contemptuous tone with which you mention those of your own class, (many hundreds if not thousands of whom are in all respects better than yourself, and would greatly honour you by thinking of you,) is methinks, no warrant for the wisdom of your choice—for a choice, it seems, there is. Who is it, maiden, to whom you have thus rashly attached yourself?—rashly, I fear it must be."

"It is the young Scottish Lord Glenvarloch, madam," answered Margaret, in a low and modest tone, but sufficiently firm, considering the subject.

"The young Lord of Glenvarloch!" repeated the lady, in great surprise—"Maiden, you are distracted in your wits."

"I knew you would say so, madam," answered Margaret. "It is what another person has already told me—it is, perhaps, what all the world would tell me—it is what I am sometimes disposed to tell myself. But look at me, madam, for I will now come before you, and tell me if there is madness or distraction in my look and word, when I repeat to you again, that I have fixed my affections on this young nobleman."

"If there is not madness in your look or word, maiden, there is infinite folly in what you say," answered the Lady Hermione, sharply. "When did you ever hear that misplaced love brought any thing but wretchedness? Seek a match among your equals, Margaret, and escape the countless kinds of risk and misery that must attend an affection beyond your degree.—Why do you smile, maiden? Is there aught to cause scorn in what I say?"

"Surely no, madam," answered Margaret. "I only smiled to think how it should happen, that, while rank made such a wide difference between creatures formed from the same clay, the wit of the vulgar should, nevertheless, jump so exactly the same length with that of the accomplished and the exalted. It is but the variation of the phrase which divides them. Dame Ursley told me the very same thing which your ladyship has but now uttered; only you, madam, talk of countless misery, and Dame Ursley spoke of the gallows, and Mistress Turner, who was hanged upon it."

"Indeed?" answered the Lady Hermione; "and who may Dame Ursley be, that your wise choice has associated with me in the difficult task of advising a fool?"

"The barber's wife at next door, madam," answered Margaret, with feigned simplicity, but far from being sorry at heart, that she had found an indirect mode of mortifying her monitress. "She is the wisest woman that I know, next to your ladyship."

"A proper confidant," said the lady, "and chosen with the same delicate sense of what is due to yourself and others!—But what ails you, maiden—where are you going?"

"Only to ask Dame Ursley's advice," said Margaret, as if about to depart; "for I see your ladyship is too angry to give me any, and the emergency is pressing."

"What emergency, thou simple one?" said the lady, in a kinder tone.—"Sit down, maiden, and tell me your tale. It is true you are a fool, and a pettish fool to boot; but then you are a child—an amiable child, with all your self-willed folly, and we must help you, if we can.—Sit down, I say, as you are desired, and you will find me a safer and wiser counseller than the barber-woman. And tell me how you come to suppose, that you have fixed your heart unalterably upon a man whom you have seen, as I think, but once."

"I have seen him oftener," said the damsel, looking down; "but I have only spoken to him once. I should have been able to get that once out of my head, though the impression was so deep, that I could even now repeat every trifling word he said; but other things have since riveted it in my bosom for ever."

"Maiden," replied the lady, "*for ever* is the word which comes most lightly on the lips in such circumstances, but which, not the less, is almost the last that we should use. The fashion of this world, its passions, its joys, and its sorrows, pass away like the winged breeze—there is nought for ever but that which belongs to the world beyond the grave."

"You have corrected me justly, madam," said Margaret calmly; "I ought only to have spoken of my present state of mind, as what will last me for my lifetime, which unquestionably may be but short."

"And what is there in this Scottish lord that can rivet what concerns him so closely in your fancy?" said the lady. "I admit him a personable man, for I have seen him; and I will suppose him courteous and agreeable. But what are his accomplishments besides, for these surely are not uncommon attributes."

"He is unfortunate, madam—most unfortunate—and surrounded by snares of different kinds, ingeniously contrived to ruin his character, destroy his estate, and, perhaps, to reach even his life. These schemes have been devised by avarice originally, but they are now followed close by vindictive ambition, animated, I think, by the absolute and concentrated spirit of malice; for the Lord Dalgarno—"

"Here, Monna Paula—Monna Paula!" exclaimed the Lady Hermione, interrupting her young friend's narrative. "She hears me not," she answered, rising and going out, "I must seek her—I will return instantly." She returned accordingly very soon after. "You mentioned a name which I thought was familiar to me," she said; "but Monna Paula has put me right. I know nothing of your lord—how was it you named him?"

"Lord Dalgarno," said Margaret;—"the wickedest man who lives. Under pretence of friendship, he introduced the Lord Glenvarloch to a gambling-house with the purpose of engaging him in deep play; but he with whom the perfidious traitor had to deal, was too virtuous, moderate, and cautious, to be caught in a snare so open. What did they next, but turn his own moderation against him, and persuade others that—because he would not become the prey of wolves, he herded with them for a share of their booty! And, while this base Lord Dalgarno was thus undermining his unsuspecting countryman, he took every measure to keep him surrounded by creatures of his own, to prevent him from attending Court, and mixing with those of his proper rank. Since the Gunpowder Treason, there never was a conspiracy more deeply laid, more basely and more deliberately pursued."

The lady smiled sadly at Margaret's vehemence, but sighed the next moment, while she told her young friend how little she knew the world she was about to live in, since she testified so much surprise at finding it full of villainy.

"But by what means," she added, "could you, maiden, become possessed of the secret views of a man so cautious as Lord Dalgarno—as villains in general are?"

"Permit me to be silent on that subject," said the maiden; "I could not tell you without betraying others—let it suffice that my tidings are as certain as the means by which I acquired them are secret and sure. But I must not tell them even to you."

"You are too bold, Margaret," said the lady, "to traffic in such matters at your early age. It is not only dangerous, but even unbecoming and unmaidenly."

"I knew you would say that also," said Margaret, with more meekness and patience than she usually showed on receiving reproof; "but, God knows, my heart acquits me of every other feeling save that of the wish to assist this most innocent and betrayed man.—I contrived to send him warning of his friend's falsehood;—alas! my care has only hastened his utter ruin, unless speedy aid be found. He charged his false friend with treachery, and drew on him in the Park, and is now liable to the fatal penalty due for breach of privilege of the king's palace."

"This is indeed an extraordinary tale," said Hermione; "is Lord Glenvarloch then in prison?"

"No, madam, thank God, but in the Sanctuary at Whitefriars—it is matter of doubt whether it will protect him in such a case—they speak of a warrant from the Lord Chief Justice—A gentleman of the temple has been arrested, and is in trouble for having assisted him in his flight.—Even his taking temporary refuge in that base place, though from extreme necessity, will be used to the further defaming him. All this I know, and yet I cannot rescue him—cannot rescue him save by your means."

"By my means, maiden?" said the lady—"you are beside yourself!—What means can I possess in this secluded situation, of assisting this unfortunate nobleman?"

"You have means," said Margaret, eagerly; "you have those means, unless I mistake greatly, which can do anything—can do everything, in this city, in this world—you have wealth, and the command of a small portion of it will enable me to extricate him from his present danger. He will be enabled and directed how to make his escape—and I—" she paused.

"Will accompany him, doubtless, and reap the fruits of your sage exertions in his behalf?" said the Lady Hermione, ironically.

"May heaven forgive you the unjust thought, lady," answered Margaret. "I will never see him more—but I shall have saved him, and the thought will make me happy."

"A cold conclusion to so bold and warm a flame," said the lady, with a smile which seemed to intimate incredulity.

"It is, however, the only one which I expect, madam—I could almost say the only one which I wish—I am sure I will use no efforts to bring about any other; if I am bold in his cause, I am timorous enough in my own. During our only interview I was unable to speak a word to him. He knows not the sound of my voice—and all that I have risked, and must yet risk, I am doing for one, who, were he asked the question, would say he has long since forgotten that he ever saw, spoke to, or sat beside, a creature of so little signification as I am."

"This is a strange and unreasonable indulgence of a passion equally fanciful and dangerous," said Lady Hermione. "You will *not* assist me, then?" said Margaret; "have good-day, then, madam—my secret, I trust, is safe in such honourable keeping."

"Tarry yet a little," said the lady, "and tell me what resource you have to assist this youth, if you were supplied with money to put it in motion."

"It is superfluous to ask me the question, madam," answered Margaret, "unless you purpose to assist me; and, if you do so purpose, it is still superfluous. You could not understand the means I must use, and time is too brief to explain."

"But have you in reality such means?" said the lady.

"I have, with the command of a moderate sum," answered Margaret Ramsay, "the power of baffling all his enemies—of eluding the passion of the irritated king—the colder but more determined displeasure of the prince—the vindictive spirit of Buckingham, so hastily directed against whomsoever crosses the path of his ambition—the cold concentrated malice of Lord Dalgarno—all, I can baffle them all!"

"But is this to be done without your own personal risk, Margaret?" replied the lady; "for, be your purpose what it will, you are not to peril your own reputation or person, in the romantic attempt of serving another; and I, maiden, am answerable to your godfather,—to your benefactor, and my own,—not to aid you in any dangerous or unworthy enterprise."

"Depend upon my word,—my oath,—dearest lady," replied the supplicant, "that I will act by the agency of others, and do not myself design to mingle in any enterprise in which my appearance might be either perilous or unwomanly."

"I know not what to do," said the Lady Hermione; "it is perhaps incautious and inconsiderate in me to aid so wild a project; yet the end seems honourable, if the means be sure—what is the penalty if he fall into their power?"

"Alas, alas! the loss of his right hand!" replied Margaret, her voice almost stifled with sobs.

"Are the laws of England so cruel? Then there is mercy in heaven alone," said the lady, "since, even in this free land, men are wolves to each other.—Compose yourself, Margaret, and tell me what money is necessary to secure Lord Glenvarloch's escape."

"Two hundred pieces," replied Margaret; "I would speak to you of restoring them—and I must one day have the power—only that I know—that is, I think—your ladyship is indifferent on that score."

"Not a word more of it," said the lady; "call Monna Paula hither."

XX

Credit me, friend, it hath been ever thus,
Since the ark rested on Mount Ararat.
False man hath sworn, and woman hath believed—
Repented and reproach'd, and then believed once more.

—The New World

By the time that Margaret returned with Monna Paula, the Lady Hermione was rising from the table at which she had been engaged in writing something on a small slip of paper, which she gave to her attendant.

"Monna Paula," she said, "carry this paper to Roberts the cash-keeper; let them give you the money mentioned in the note, and bring it hither presently."

Monna Paula left the room, and her mistress proceeded.

"I do not know," she said, "Margaret, if I have done, and am doing, well in this affair. My life has been one of strange seclusion, and I am totally unacquainted with the practical ways of this world—an ignorance which I know cannot be remedied by mere reading.—I fear I am doing wrong to you, and perhaps to the laws of the country which affords me refuge, by thus indulging you; and yet there is something in my heart which cannot resist your entreaties."

"O, listen to it—listen to it, dear, generous lady!" said Margaret, throwing herself on her knees and grasping those of her benefactress and looking in that attitude like a beautiful mortal in the act of supplicating her tutelary angel; "the laws of men are but the injunctions of mortality, but what the heart prompts is the echo of the voice from heaven within us."

"Rise, rise, maiden," said Hermione; "you affect me more than I thought I could have been moved by aught that should approach me. Rise and tell me whence it comes, that, in so short a time, your thoughts, your looks, your speech, and even your slightest actions, are changed from those of a capricious and fanciful girl, to all this energy and impassioned eloquence of word and action?"

"I am sure I know not, dearest lady," said Margaret, looking down; "but I suppose that, when I was a trifler, I was only thinking of trifles.

What I now reflect is deep and serious, and I am thankful if my speech and manner bear reasonable proportion to my thoughts."

"It must be so," said the lady; "yet the change seems a rapid and strange one. It seems to be as if a childish girl had at once shot up into deep-thinking and impassioned woman, ready to make exertions alike, and sacrifices, with all that vain devotion to a favourite object of affection, which is often so basely rewarded."

The Lady Hermione sighed bitterly, and Monna Paula entered ere the conversation proceeded farther. She spoke to her mistress in the foreign language in which they frequently conversed, but which was unknown to Margaret.

"We must have patience for a time," said the lady to her visitor; "the cash-keeper is abroad on some business, but he is expected home in the course of half an hour."

Margaret wrung her hands in vexation and impatience.

"Minutes are precious," continued the lady; "that I am well aware of; and we will at least suffer none of them to escape us. Monna Paula shall remain below and transact our business, the very instant that Roberts returns home."

She spoke to her attendant accordingly, who again left the room.

"You are very kind, madam—very good," said the poor little Margaret, while the anxious trembling of her lip and of her hand showed all that sickening agitation of the heart which arises from hope deferred.

"Be patient, Margaret, and collect yourself," said the lady; "you may, you must, have much to do to carry through this your bold purpose—reserve your spirits, which you may need so much—be patient—it is the only remedy against the evils of life."

"Yes, madam," said Margaret, wiping her eyes, and endeavouring in vain to suppress the natural impatience of her temper,—"I have heard so—very often indeed; and I dare say I have myself, heaven forgive me, said so to people in perplexity and affliction; but it was before I had suffered perplexity and vexation myself, and I am sure I will never preach patience to any human being again, now that I know how much the medicine goes against the stomach."

"You will think better of it, maiden," said the Lady Hermione; "I also, when I first felt distress, thought they did me wrong who spoke to me of patience; but my sorrows have been repeated and continued till I have been taught to cling to it as the best, and—religious duties excepted, of which, indeed, patience forms a part—the only alleviation which life can afford them."

Margaret, who neither wanted sense nor feeling, wiped her tears hastily, and asked her patroness's forgiveness for her petulance.

"I might have thought"—she said, "I ought to have reflected, that even from the manner of your life, madam, it is plain you must have suffered sorrow; and yet, God knows, the patience which I have ever seen you display, well entitles you to recommend your own example to others."

The lady was silent for a moment, and then replied—

"Margaret, I am about to repose a high confidence in you. You are no longer a child, but a thinking and a feeling woman. You have told me as much of your secret as you dared—I will let you know as much of mine as I may venture to tell. You will ask me, perhaps, why, at a moment when your own mind is agitated, I should force upon you the consideration of my sorrows? and I answer, that I cannot withstand the impulse which now induces me to do so. Perhaps from having witnessed, for the first time these three years, the natural effects of human passion, my own sorrows have been awakened, and are for the moment too big for my own bosom—perhaps I may hope that you, who seem driving full sail on the very rock on which I was wrecked for ever, will take warning by the tale I have to tell. Enough, if you are willing to listen, I am willing to tell you who the melancholy inhabitant of the Foljambe apartments really is, and why she resides here. It will serve, at least, to while away the time until Monna Paula shall bring us the reply from Roberts."

At any other moment of her life, Margaret Ramsay would have heard with undivided interest a communication so flattering in itself, and referring to a subject upon which the general curiosity had been so strongly excited. And even at this agitating moment, although she ceased not to listen with an anxious ear and throbbing heart for the sound of Monna Paula's returning footsteps, she nevertheless, as gratitude and policy, as well as a portion of curiosity dictated, composed herself, in appearance at least, to the strictest attention to the Lady Hermione, and thanked her with humility for the high confidence she was pleased to repose in her. The Lady Hermione, with the same calmness which always attended her speech and actions, thus recounted her story to her young friend:

"My father," she said, "was a merchant, but he was of a city whose merchants are princes. I am the daughter of a noble house in Genoa, whose name stood as high in honour and in antiquity, as any inscribed in the Golden Register of that famous aristocracy.

"My mother was a noble Scottish woman. She was descended—do not start—and not remotely descended, of the house of Glenvarloch—no wonder that I was easily led to take concern in the misfortunes of this young lord. He is my near relation, and my mother, who was more than sufficiently proud of her descent, early taught me to take an interest in the name. My maternal grandfather, a cadet of that house of Glenvarloch, had followed the fortunes of an unhappy fugitive, Francis Earl of Bothwell, who, after showing his miseries in many a foreign court, at length settled in Spain upon a miserable pension, which he earned by conforming to the Catholic faith. Ralph Olifaunt, my grandfather, separated from him in disgust, and settled at Barcelona, where, by the friendship of the governor, his heresy, as it was termed, was connived at. My father, in the course of his commerce, resided more at Barcelona than in his native country, though at times he visited Genoa.

"It was at Barcelona that he became acquainted with my mother, loved her, and married her; they differed in faith, but they agreed in affection. I was their only child. In public I conformed to the docterins and ceremonial of the Church of Rome; but my mother, by whom these were regarded with horror, privately trained me up in those of the reformed religion; and my father, either indifferent in the matter, or unwilling to distress the woman whom he loved, overlooked or connived at my secretly joining in her devotions.

"But when, unhappily, my father was attacked, while yet in the prime of life, by a slow wasting disease, which he felt to be incurable, he foresaw the hazard to which his widow and orphan might be exposed, after he was no more, in a country so bigoted to Catholicism as Spain. He made it his business, during the two last years of his life, to realize and remit to England a large part of his fortune, which, by the faith and honour of his correspondent, the excellent man under whose roof I now reside, was employed to great advantage. Had my father lived to complete his purpose, by withdrawing his whole fortune from commerce, he himself would have accompanied us to England, and would have beheld us settled in peace and honour before his death. But heaven had ordained it otherwise. He died, leaving several sums engaged in the hands of his Spanish debtors; and, in particular, he had made a large and extensive consignment to a certain wealthy society of merchants at Madrid, who showed no willingness after his death to account for the proceeds. Would to God we had left these covetous and wicked men in possession of their booty, for such they seemed to hold the property of their deceased correspondent and friend! We had enough for comfort, and even splendour, already secured in England; but friends exclaimed upon the folly of permitting these unprincipled men to plunder us of our rightful property. The sum itself was large, and the claim having been made, my mother thought that my father's memory was interested in its being enforced, especially as the defences set up for the mercantile society went, in some degree, to impeach the fairness of his transactions.

"We went therefore to Madrid. I was then, my Margaret, about your age, young and thoughtless, as you have hitherto been—We went, I say, to Madrid, to solicit the protection of the Court and of the king, without which we were told it would be in vain to expect justice against an opulent and powerful association.

"Our residence at the Spanish metropolis drew on from weeks to months. For my part, my natural sorrow for a kind, though not a fond father, having abated, I cared not if the lawsuit had detained us at Madrid for ever. My mother permitted herself and me rather more liberty than we had been accustomed to. She found relations among the Scottish and Irish officers, many of whom held a high rank in the Spanish armies; their wives and daughters became our friends and companions, and I had perpetual occasion to exercise my mother's native language, which I had learned from my infancy. By degrees, as my mother's spirits were low, and her health indifferent, she was induced, by her partial fondness for me, to suffer me to mingle occasionally in society which she herself did not frequent, under the guardianship of such ladies as she imagined she could trust, and particularly under the care of the lady of a general officer, whose weakness or falsehood was the original cause of my misfortunes. I was as gay, Margaret, and thoughtless—I again repeat it—as you were but lately, and my attention, like yours, became suddenly riveted to one object, and to one set of feelings.

"The person by whom they were excited was young, noble, handsome, accomplished, a soldier, and a Briton. So far our cases are nearly parallel; but, may heaven forbid that the parallel should become complete! This man, so noble, so fairly formed, so gifted, and so brave—this villain, for that, Margaret, was his fittest name, spoke of love to me, and I listened—Could I suspect his sincerity? If he was wealthy, noble, and long-descended, I also was a noble and an opulent heiress. It is true, that he neither knew the extent of my father's wealth, nor did I communicate to him (I do not even remember if I myself knew it at the time) the important circumstance, that the greater part of that wealth was beyond the grasp of arbitrary power, and not subject to the precarious award of arbitrary judges. My lover might think, perhaps, as my mother was desirous the world at large should believe, that almost our whole fortune depended on the precarious suit which we had come to Madrid to prosecute—a belief which she had countenanced out of policy, being well aware that a knowledge of my father's having remitted such a large part of his fortune to England, would in no shape aid the recovery of further sums in the Spanish courts. Yet, with no more extensive views of my fortune than were possessed by the public, I believe that he, of whom I am speaking, was at first sincere in his pretensions. He had himself interest sufficient to have obtained a decision in our favour in the courts, and my fortune, reckoning only what was in Spain, would then have been no inconsiderable sum. To be brief, whatever might be his motives or temptation for so far committing himself, he applied to my mother for my hand, with my consent and approval. My mother's judgment had become weaker, but her passions had become more irritable, during her increasing illness.

"You have heard of the bitterness of the ancient Scottish feuds, of which it may be said, in the language of Scripture, that the fathers eat sour grapes, and the teeth of the children are set on edge. Unhappily—I should say *happily*, considering what this man has now shown himself to be—some such strain of bitterness had divided his house from my mother's, and she had succeeded to the inheritance of hatred. When he asked her for my hand, she was no longer able to command her passions—she raked up every injury which the rival families had inflicted upon each other during a bloody feud of two centuries—heaped him with epithets of scorn, and rejected his proposal of alliance, as if it had come from the basest of mankind.

"My lover retired in passion; and I remained to weep and murmur against fortune, and—I will confess my fault—against my affectionate parent. I had been educated with different feelings, and the traditions of the feuds and quarrels of my mother's family in Scotland, which we're to her monuments and chronicles, seemed to me as insignificant and unmeaning as the actions and fantasies of Don Quixote; and I blamed my mother bitterly for sacrificing my happiness to an empty dream of family dignity.

"While I was in this humour, my lover sought a renewal of our intercourse. We met repeatedly in the house of the lady whom I have mentioned, and who, in levity, or in the spirit of intrigue, countenanced our secret correspondence. At length we were secretly married—so far did my blinded passion hurry me. My lover had secured the assistance of a clergyman of the English church. Monna Paula, who had been my attendant from infancy, was one witness of our union. Let me do the faithful creature justice—She conjured me to suspend my purpose till my mother's death should permit us to celebrate our marriage openly; but the entreaties of my lover, and my own wayward passion, prevailed over her remonstrances. The lady I have spoken of was another witness, but whether she was in full possession of my bridegroom's secret, I had never the means to learn. But the shelter of her name and roof afforded us the means of frequently meeting, and the love of my husband seemed as sincere and as unbounded as my own.

"He was eager, he said, to gratify his pride, by introducing me to one or two of his noble English friends. This could not be done at Lady D—'s; but by his command, which I was now entitled to consider as my law, I contrived twice to visit him at his own hotel, accompanied only by Monna Paula. There was a very small party, of two ladies and two gentlemen. There was music, mirth, and dancing. I had heard of the frankness of the English nation, but I could not help thinking it bordered on license during these entertainments, and in the course of the collation which followed; but I imputed my scruples to my inexperience, and would not doubt the propriety of what was approved by my husband.

"I was soon summoned to other scenes: My poor mother's disease drew to a conclusion—Happy I am that it took place before she discovered what would have cut her to the soul.

"In Spain you may have heard how the Catholic priests, and particularly the monks, besiege the beds of the dying, to obtain bequests for the good of the church. I have said that my mother's temper was irritated by disease, and her judgment impaired in proportion. She gathered spirits and force from the resentment which the priests around her bed excited by their importunity, and the boldness of the stern sect of reformers, to which she had secretly adhered, seemed to animate her dying tongue. She avowed the religion she had so long concealed;

renounced all hope and aid which did not come by and through its dictates; rejected with contempt the ceremonial of the Romish church; loaded the astonished priests with reproaches for their greediness and hypocrisy, and commanded them to leave her house. They went in bitterness and rage, but it was to return with the inquisitorial power, its warrants, and its officers; and they found only the cold corpse left of her, on whom they had hoped to work their vengeance. As I was soon discovered to have shared my mother's heresy, I was dragged from her dead body, imprisoned in a solitary cloister, and treated with severity, which the Abbess assured me was due to the looseness of my life, as well as my spiritual errors. I avowed my marriage, to justify the situation in which I found myself—I implored the assistance of the Superior to communicate my situation to my husband. She smiled coldly at the proposal, and told me the church had provided a better spouse for me; advised me to secure myself of divine grace hereafter, and deserve milder treatment here, by presently taking the veil. In order to convince me that I had no other resource, she showed me a royal decree, by which all my estate was hypothecated to the convent of Saint Magdalen, and became their complete property upon my death, or my taking the vows. As I was, both from religious principle, and affectionate attachment to my husband, absolutely immovable in my rejection of the veil, I believe—may heaven forgive me if I wrong her—that the Abbess was desirous to make sure of my spoils, by hastening the former event.

"It was a small and a poor convent, and situated among the mountains of Guadarrama. Some of the sisters were the daughters of neighbouring Hidalgoes, as poor as they were proud and ignorant; others were women immured there on account of their vicious conduct. The Superior herself was of a high family, to which she owed her situation; but she was said to have disgraced her connexions by her conduct during youth, and now, in advanced age, covetousness and the love of power, a spirit too of severity and cruelty, had succeeded to the thirst after licentious pleasure. I suffered much under this woman—and still her dark, glassy eye, her tall, shrouded form, and her rigid features, haunt my slumbers.

"I was not destined to be a mother. I was very ill, and my recovery was long doubtful. The most violent remedies were applied, if remedies they indeed were. My health was restored at length, against my own expectation and that of all around me. But, when I first again beheld the reflection of my own face, I thought it was the visage of a ghost. I was wont to be flattered by all, but particularly by my husband, for the fineness of my complexion—it was now totally gone, and, what is more extraordinary, it has never returned. I have observed that the few who now see me, look upon me as a bloodless phantom—Such has been the abiding effect of the treatment to which I was subjected. May God forgive those who were the agents of it!—I thank Heaven I can say so with as sincere a wish, as that with which I pray for forgiveness of my own sins. They now relented somewhat towards me—moved perhaps to compassion by my singular appearance, which bore witness to my sufferings; or afraid that the matter might attract attention during a visitation of the bishop, which was approaching. One day, as I was walking in the convent-garden, to which I had been lately admitted, a miserable old Moorish slave, who was kept to cultivate the little spot, muttered as I passed him, but still keeping his wrinkled face and decrepit form in the same angle with the earth—'There is Heart's Ease near the postern.'

"I knew something of the symbolical language of flowers, once carried to such perfection among the Moriscoes of Spain; but if I had been ignorant of it, the captive would soon have caught at any hint which seemed to promise liberty. With all the haste consistent with the utmost circumspection—for I might be observed by the Abbess or some of the sisters from the window—I hastened to the postern. It was closely barred as usual, but when I coughed slightly, I was answered from the other side—and, O heaven! it was my husband's voice which said, 'Lose not a minute here at present, but be on this spot when the vesper bell has tolled.'

"I retired in an ecstasy of joy. I was not entitled or permitted to assist at vespers, but was accustomed to be confined to my cell while the nuns were in the choir. Since my recovery, they had discontinued locking the door; though the utmost severity was denounced against me if I left these precincts. But, let the penalty be what it would, I hastened to dare it.—No sooner had the last toll of the vesper bell ceased to sound, than I stole from my chamber, reached the garden unobserved, hurried to the postern, beheld it open with rapture, and in the next moment was in my husband's arms. He had with him another cavalier of noble mien—both were masked and armed. Their horses, with one saddled for my use, stood in a thicket hard by, with two other masked horsemen, who seemed to be servants. In less than two minutes we were mounted, and rode off as fast as we could through rough and devious roads, in which one of the domestics appeared to act as guide.

"The hurried pace at which we rode, and the anxiety of the moment, kept me silent, and prevented my expressing my surprise or my joy save in a few broken words. It also served as an apology for my husband's silence. At length we stopped at a solitary hut—the cavaliers dismounted, and I was assisted from my saddle, not by M——M——my husband, I would say, who seemed busied about his horse, but by the stranger.

"'Go into the hut,' said my husband, 'change your dress with the speed of lightning—you will find one to *assist* you—we must forward instantly when you have shifted your apparel.'

"I entered the hut, and was received in the arms of the faithful Monna Paula, who had waited my arrival for many hours, half distracted with fear and anxiety. With her assistance I speedily tore off the detested garments of the convent, and exchanged them for a travelling suit, made after the English fashion. I observed that Monna Paula was in a similar dress. I had but just huddled on my change of attire, when we were hastily summoned to mount. A horse, I found, was provided for Monna Paula, and we resumed our route. On the way, my convent-garb, which had been wrapped hastily together around a stone, was thrown into a lake, along the verge of which we were then passing. The two cavaliers rode together in front, my attendant and I followed, and the servants brought up the rear. Monna Paula, as we rode on, repeatedly entreated me to be silent upon the road, as our lives depended on it. I was easily reconciled to be passive, for, the first fever of spirits which attended the sense of liberation and of gratified affection having passed away, I felt as it were dizzy with the rapid motion; and my utmost exertion was necessary to keep my place on the saddle, until we suddenly (it was now very dark) saw a strong light before us.

"My husband reined up his horse, and gave a signal by a low whistle twice repeated, which was answered from a distance. The whole party then halted under the boughs of a large cork-tree, and my husband, drawing himself close to my side, said, in a voice which I then thought was only embarrassed by fear for my safety,—'We must now part. Those to whom I commit you are contrabandists, who only know you as English-women, but who, for a high bribe, have undertaken to escort you through the passes of the Pyrenees as far as Saint Jean de Luz.'

"'And do you not go with us?' I exclaimed with emphasis, though in a whisper.

"'It is impossible,' he said, 'and would ruin all—See that you speak in English in these people's hearing, and give not the least sign of understanding what they say in Spanish—your life depends on it; for, though they live in opposition to, and evasion of, the laws of Spain, they would tremble at the idea of violating those of the church—I see them coming—farewell—farewell.'

"The last words were hastily uttered-I endeavoured to detain him yet a moment by my feeble grasp on his cloak.

"'You will meet me, then, I trust, at Saint Jean de Luz?'

"'Yes, yes,' he answered hastily, 'at Saint Jean de Luz you will meet your protector.'

"He then extricated his cloak from my grasp, and was lost in the darkness. His companion approached—kissed my hand, which in the agony of the moment I was scarce sensible of, and followed my husband, attended by one of the domestics."

The tears of Hermione here flowed so fast as to threaten the interruption of her narrative. When she resumed it, it was with a kind of apology to Margaret.

"Every circumstance," she said, "occurring in those moments, when I still enjoyed a delusive idea of happiness, is deeply imprinted in my remembrance, which, respecting all that has since happened, is waste and unvaried as an Arabian desert. But I have no right to inflict on you, Margaret, agitated as you are with your own anxieties, the unavailing details of my useless recollections."

Margaret's eyes were full of tears—it was impossible it could be otherwise, considering that the tale was told by her suffering benefactress, and resembled, in some respects, her own situation; and yet she must not be severely blamed, if, while eagerly pressing her patroness to continue her narrative, her eye involuntarily sought the door, as if to chide the delay of Monna Paula.

The Lady Hermione saw and forgave these conflicting emotions; and she, too, must be pardoned, if, in her turn, the minute detail of her narrative showed, that, in the discharge of feelings so long locked in her own bosom, she rather forgot those which were personal to her auditor, and by which it must be supposed Margaret's mind was principally occupied, if not entirely engrossed.

"I told you, I think, that one domestic followed the gentlemen," thus the lady continued her story, "the other remained with us for the purpose, as it seemed, of introducing us to two persons whom M—, I say, whom my husband's signal had brought to the spot. A word or two of explanation passed between them and the servant, in a sort of *patois*, which I did not understand; and one of the strangers taking hold of my bridle, the other of Monna Paula's, they led us towards the light, which I have already said was the signal of our halting. I touched Monna Paula, and was sensible that she trembled very much, which surprised me, because I knew her character to be so strong and bold as to border upon the masculine.

"When we reached the fire, the gipsy figures of those who surrounded it, with their swarthy features, large Sombrero hats, girdles stuck full of pistols and poniards, and all the other apparatus of a roving and perilous life, would have terrified me at another moment. But then I only felt the agony of having parted from my husband almost in the very moment of my rescue. The females of the gang—for there were four or five women amongst these contraband traders—received us with a sort of rude courtesy. They were, in dress and manners, not extremely different from the men with whom they associated—were almost as hardy and adventurous, carried arms like them, and were, as we learned from passing circumstances, scarce less experienced in the use of them.

"It was impossible not to fear these wild people; yet they gave us no reason to complain of them, but used us on all occasions with a kind of clumsy courtesy, accommodating themselves to our wants and our weakness during the journey, even while we heard them grumbling to each other against our effeminacy,—like some rude carrier, who, in charge of a package of valuable and fragile ware, takes every precaution for its preservation, while he curses the unwonted trouble which it occasions him. Once or twice, when they were disappointed in their contraband traffic, lost some goods in a rencontre with the Spanish officers of the revenue, and were finally pursued by a military force, their murmurs assumed a more alarming tone, in the terrified ears of my attendant and myself, when, without daring to seem to understand them, we heard them curse the insular heretics, on whose account God, Saint James, and Our Lady of the Pillar, had blighted their hopes of profit. These are dreadful recollections, Margaret."

"Why, then, dearest lady," answered Margaret, "will you thus dwell on them?"

"It is only," said the Lady Hermione, "because I linger like a criminal on the scaffold, and would fain protract the time that must inevitably bring on the final catastrophe. Yes, dearest Margaret, I rest and dwell on the events of that journey, marked as it was by fatigue and danger, though the road lay through the wildest and most desolate deserts and mountains, and though our companions, both men and women, were fierce and lawless themselves, and exposed to the most merciless retaliation from those with whom they were constantly engaged—yet would I rather dwell on these hazardous events than tell that which awaited me at Saint Jean de Luz."

"But you arrived there in safety?" said Margaret.

"Yes, maiden," replied the Lady Hermione; "and were guided by the chief of our outlawed band to the house which had been assigned for reception, with the same punctilious accuracy with which he would have delivered a bale of uncustomed goods to a correspondent. I was told a gentleman had expected me for two days—I rushed into the apartment, and, when I expected to embrace my husband—I found myself in the arms of his friend!"

"The villain!" exclaimed Margaret, whose anxiety had, in spite of herself, been a moment suspended by the narrative of the lady.

"Yes," replied Hermione, calmly, though her voice somewhat faltered, "it is the name that best—that well befits him. He, Margaret, for whom I had sacrificed all—whose love and whose memory were dearer to me than my freedom, when I was in the convent—than my life, when I was on my perilous journey—had taken his measures to shake me off, and transfer me, as a privileged wanton, to the protection of his libertine friend. At first the stranger laughed at my tears and my agony, as the hysterical passion of a deluded and overreached wanton, or the wily affection of a courtezan. My claim of marriage he laughed at, assuring me he knew it was a mere farce required by me, and submitted to by his friend, to save some reserve of delicacy; and expressed his surprise that I should consider in any other light a ceremony which could be valid neither in Spain nor England, and insultingly offered to remove my scruples, by renewing such a union with me himself. My exclamations brought Monna Paula to my aid—she was not, indeed, far distant, for she had expected some such scene."

"Good heaven!" said Margaret, "was she a confidant of your base husband?"

"No," answered Hermione, "do her not that injustice. It was her persevering inquiries that discovered the place of my confinement—it was she who gave the information to my husband, and who remarked even then that the news was so much more interesting to his friend than to him, that she suspected, from an early period, it was the purpose of the villain to shake me off. On the journey, her suspicions were confirmed. She had heard him remark to his companion, with a cold sarcastic sneer, the total change which my prison and my illness had made on my complexion; and she had heard the other reply, that the defect might be cured by a touch of Spanish red. This, and other circumstances, having prepared her for such treachery, Monna Paula now entered, completely possessed of herself, and prepared to support me. Her calm representations went farther with the stranger than the expressions of my despair. If he did not entirely believe our tale, he at least acted the part of a man of honour, who would not intrude himself on defenceless females, whatever was their character; desisted from persecuting us with his presence; and not only directed Monna Paula how we should journey to Paris, but furnished her with money for the purpose of our journey. From the capital I wrote to Master Heriot, my father's most trusted correspondent; he came instantly to Paris on receiving the letter; and—But here comes Monna Paula, with more than the sum you desired. Take it, my dearest maiden—serve this youth if you will. But, O Margaret, look for no gratitude in return!"

The Lady Hermione took the bag of gold from her attendant, and gave it to her young friend, who threw herself into her arms, kissed her on both the pale cheeks, over which the sorrows so newly awakened by her narrative had drawn many tears, then sprung up, wiped her own overflowing eyes, and left the Foljambe apartments with a hasty and resolved step.

XXI

Rove not from pole to pole–the man lives here
Whose razor's only equall'd by his beer;
And where, in either sense, the cockney–put
May, if he pleases, get confounded cut.

—*On the sign of an Alehouse kept by a Barber*

W e are under the necessity of transporting our readers to the habitation of Benjamin Suddlechop, the husband of the active and efficient Dame Ursula, and who also, in his own person, discharged more offices than one. For, besides trimming locks and beards, and turning whiskers upward into the martial and swaggering curl, or downward into the drooping form which became mustaches of civil policy; besides also occasionally letting blood, either by cupping or by the lancet, extracting a stump, and performing other actions of petty pharmacy, very nearly as well as his neighbour Raredrench, the apothecary: he could, on occasion, draw a cup of beer as well as a tooth, tap a hogshead as well as a vein, and wash, with a draught of good ale, the mustaches which his art had just trimmed. But he carried on these trades apart from each other.

His barber's shop projected its long and mysterious pole into Fleet Street, painted party-coloured-wise, to represent the ribbons with which, in elder times, that ensign was garnished. In the window were seen rows of teeth displayed upon strings like rosaries—cups with a red rag at the bottom, to resemble blood, an intimation that patients might be bled, cupped, or blistered, with the assistance of "sufficient advice;" while the more profitable, but less honourable operations upon the hair of the head and beard, were briefly and gravely announced. Within was the well-worn leather chair for customers, the guitar, then called a ghittern or cittern, with which a customer might amuse himself till his predecessor was dismissed from under Benjamin's hands, and which, therefore, often flayed the ears of the patient metaphorically, while his chin sustained from the razor literal scarification. All, therefore, in this department, spoke the chirurgeon-barber, or the barber-chirurgeon.

But there was a little back-room, used as a private tap-room, which had a separate entrance by a dark and crooked alley, which communicated with Fleet Street, after a circuitous passage through several by-lanes and courts. This retired temple of Bacchus had also a connexion with Benjamin's more public shop by a long and narrow entrance, conducting to the secret premises in which a few old topers used to take their morning draught, and a few gill-sippers their modicum of strong waters, in a bashful way, after having entered the barber's shop under pretence of being shaved. Besides, this obscure tap-room gave a separate admission to the apartments of Dame Ursley, which she was believed to make use of in the course of her multifarious practice, both to let herself secretly out, and to admit clients and employers who cared not to be seen to visit her in public. Accordingly, after the hour of noon, by which time the modest and timid whetters, who were Benjamin's best customers, had each had his draught, or his thimbleful, the business of the tap was in a manner ended, and the charge of attending the back-door passed from one of the barber's apprentices to the little mulatto girl, the dingy Iris of Dame Suddlechop. Then came mystery thick upon mystery; muffled gallants, and masked females, in disguises of different fashions, were seen to glide through the intricate mazes of the alley; and even the low tap on the door, which frequently demanded the attention of the little Creole, had in it something that expressed secrecy and fear of discovery.

It was the evening of the same day when Margaret had held the long conference with the Lady Hermione, that Dame Suddlechop had directed her little portress to "keep the door fast as a miser's purse-strings; and, as she valued her saffron skin, to let in none but—" the name she added in a whisper, and accompanied it with a nod. The little domestic blinked intelligence, went to her post, and in brief time thereafter admitted and ushered into the presence of the dame, that very city-gallant whose clothes sat awkwardly upon him, and who had behaved so doughtily in the fray which befell at Nigel's first visit to Beaujeu's ordinary. The mulatto introduced him—"Missis, fine young gentleman, all over gold and velvet "—then muttered to herself as she shut the door, "fine young gentleman, he!—apprentice to him who makes the tick-tick."

It was indeed—we are sorry to say it, and trust our readers will sympathize with the interest we take in the matter—it was indeed honest Jin Vin, who had been so far left to his own devices, and abandoned by his better angel, as occasionally to travesty himself in this fashion, and to visit, in the dress of a gallant of the day, those places of pleasure and dissipation, in which it would have been everlasting discredit to him to have been seen in his real character and condition; that is, had it been possible for him in his proper shape to have gained admission. There was now a deep gloom on his brow, his rich habit was hastily put on, and buttoned awry; his belt buckled in a most disorderly fashion, so that his sword stuck outwards from his side, instead of hanging by it with graceful negligence; while his poniard, though fairly hatched and gilded, stuck in his girdle like a butcher's steel in the fold of his blue apron. Persons of fashion had, by the way, the advantage formerly of being better distinguished from the vulgar than at present; for, what the ancient farthingale and more modern hoop were to court ladies, the sword was to the gentleman; an article of dress, which only rendered those ridiculous who assumed it for the nonce, without being in the habit of wearing it. Vincent's rapier got between his legs, and, as he stumbled over it, he exclaimed—"Zounds! 'tis the second time it has served me thus—I believe the damned trinket knows I am no true gentleman, and does it of set purpose."

"Come, come, mine honest Jin Vin—come, my good boy," said the dame, in a soothing tone, "never mind these trankums—a frank and hearty London 'prentice is worth all the gallants of the inns of court."

"I was a frank and hearty London 'prentice before I knew you, Dame Suddlechop," said Vincent; "what your advice has made me, you may find a name for; since, fore George! I am ashamed to think about it myself."

"A-well-a-day," quoth the dame, "and is it even so with thee?—nay, then, I know but one cure;" and with that, going to a little corner cupboard of carved wainscoat, she opened it by the assistance of a key, which, with half-a-dozen besides, hung in a silver chain at her girdle, and produced a long flask of thin glass cased with wicker, bringing forth at the same time two Flemish rummer glasses, with long stalks and capacious wombs. She filled the one brimful for her guest, and the other more modestly to about two-thirds of its capacity, for her own use, repeating, as the rich cordial trickled forth in a smooth oily stream—"Right Rosa Solis, as ever washed mulligrubs out of a moody brain!"

But, though Jin Vin tossed off his glass without scruple, while the lady sippped hers more moderately, it did not appear to produce the expected amendment upon his humour. On the contrary, as he threw himself into the great leathern chair, in which Dame Ursley was wont to solace herself of an evening, he declared himself "the most miserable dog within the sound of Bow-bell."

"And why should you be so idle as to think yourself so, silly boy?" said Dame Suddlechop; "but 'tis always thus—fools and children never know when they are well. Why, there is not one that walks in St. Paul's, whether in flat cap, or hat and feather, that has so many kind glances from the wenches as you, when ye swagger along Fleet Street with your bat under your arm, and your cap set aside upon your head. Thou knowest well, that, from Mrs. Deputy's self down to the waist-coateers in the alley, all of them are twiring and peeping betwixt their fingers when you pass; and yet you call yourself a miserable dog! and I must tell you all this over and over again, as if I were whistling the chimes of London to a pettish child, in order to bring the pretty baby into good-humour!"

The flattery of Dame Ursula seemed to have the fate of her cordial—it was swallowed, indeed, by the party to whom she presented it, and that with some degree of relish, but it did not operate as a sedative on the disturbed state of the youth's mind. He laughed for an instant, half in scorn, and half in gratified vanity, but cast a sullen look on Dame Ursley as he replied to her last words,

"You do treat me like a child indeed, when you sing over and over to me a cuckoo song that I care not a copper-filing for."

"Aha!" said Dame Ursley; "that is to say, you care not if you please all, unless you please one—You are a true lover, I warrant, and care not for all the city, from here to Whitechapel, so you could write yourself first in your pretty Peg-a-Ramsay's good-will. Well, well, take patience, man, and be guided by me, for I will be the hoop will bind you together at last."

"It is time you were so," said Jenkin, "for hitherto you have rather been the wedge to separate us."

Dame Suddlechop had by this time finished her cordial—it was not the first she had taken that day; and, though a woman of strong brain, and cautious at least, if not abstemious, in her potations, it may nevertheless be supposed that her patience was not improved by the regimen which she observed.

"Why, thou ungracious and ingrate knave," said Dame Ursley, "have not I done every thing to put thee in thy mistress's good graces? She loves gentry, the proud Scottish minx, as a Welshman loves cheese, and has her father's descent from that Duke of Daldevil, or whatsoever she calls him, as close in her heart as gold in a miser's chest, though she as seldom shows it—and none she will think of, or have, but a gentleman—and a gentleman I have made of thee, Jin Vin, the devil cannot deny that."

"You have made a fool of me," said poor Jenkin, looking at the sleeve of his jacket.

"Never the worse gentleman for that," said Dame Ursley, laughing.

"And what is worse," said he, turning his back to her suddenly, and writhing in his chair, "you have made a rogue of me."

"Never the worse gentleman for that neither," said Dame Ursley, in the same tone; "let a man bear his folly gaily and his knavery stoutly, and let me see if gravity or honesty will look him in the face now-a-days. Tut, man, it was only in the time of King Arthur or King Lud, that a gentleman was held to blemish his scutcheon by a leap over the line of reason or honesty—It is the bold look, the ready hand, the fine clothes, the brisk oath, and the wild brain, that makes the gallant now-a-days."

"I know what you have made me," said Jin Vin; "since I have given up skittles and trap-ball for tennis and bowls, good English ale for thin Bordeaux and sour Rhenish, roast-beef and pudding for woodcocks and kickshaws—my bat for a sword, my cap for a beaver, my forsooth for a modish oath, my Christmas-box for a dice-box, my religion for the devil's matins, and mine honest name for—Woman, I could brain thee, when I think whose advice has guided me in all this!"

"Whose advice, then? whose advice, then? Speak out, thou poor, petty cloak-brusher, and say who advised thee!" retorted Dame Ursley, flushed and indignant—"Marry come up, my paltry companion—say by whose advice you have made a gamester of yourself, and a thief besides, as your words would bear—The Lord deliver us from evil!" And here Dame Ursley devoutly crossed herself.

"Hark ye, Dame Ursley Suddlechop," said Jenkin, starting up, his dark eyes flashing with anger; "remember I am none of your husband—and, if I were, you would do well not to forget whose threshold was swept when they last rode the Skimmington* upon such another scolding jade as yourself."

---

* A species of triumphal procession in honour of female supremacy, when it rose to such a height as to attract the attention of the neighbourhood. It is described at full length in Hudibras. (Part II. Canto II.) As the procession passed on, those who attended it in an official capacity were wont to sweep the threshold of the houses in which Fame affirmed the mistresses to exercise paramount authority, which was given and received as a hint that their inmates might, in their turn, be made the subject of a similar ovation. The Skimmington, which in some degree resembled the proceedings of Mumbo Jumbo in an

"I hope to see you ride up Holborn next," said Dame Ursley, provoked out of all her holiday and sugar-plum expressions, "with a nosegay at your breast, and a parson at your elbow!"

"That may well be," answered Jin Vin, bitterly, "if I walk by your counsels as I have begun by them; but, before that day comes, you shall know that Jin Vin has the brisk boys of Fleet Street still at his wink.— Yes, you jade, you shall be carted for bawd and conjurer, double-dyed in grain, and bing off to Bridewell, with every brass basin betwixt the Bar and Paul's beating before you, as if the devil were banging them with his beef-hook."

Dame Ursley coloured like scarlet, seized upon the half-emptied flask of cordial, and seemed, by her first gesture, about to hurl it at the head of her adversary; but suddenly, and as if by a strong internal effort, she checked her outrageous resentment, and, putting the bottle to its more legitimate use, filled, with wonderful composure, the two glasses, and, taking up one of them, said, with a smile, which better became her comely and jovial countenance than the fury by which it was animated the moment before—

"Here is to thee, Jin Vin, my lad, in all loving kindness, whatever spite thou bearest to me, that have always been a mother to thee."

Jenkin's English good-nature could not resist this forcible appeal; he took up the other glass, and lovingly pledged the dame in her cup of reconciliation, and proceeded to make a kind of grumbling apology for his own violence—

"For you know," he said, "it was you persuaded me to get these fine things, and go to that godless ordinary, and ruffle it with the best, and bring you home all the news; and you said, I, that was the cock of the ward, would soon be the cock of the ordinary, and would win ten times as much at gleek and primero, as I used to do at put and beggar-my-neighbour—and turn up doublets with the dice, as busily as I was wont to trowl down the ninepins in the skittle-ground—and then you said I should bring you such news out of the ordinary as should make us all, when used as you knew how to use it—and now you see what is to come of it all!"

"'Tis all true thou sayest, lad," said the dame; "but thou must have patience. Rome was not built in a day—you cannot become used to your

---

African village, has been long discontinued in England, apparently because female rule has become either milder or less frequent than among our ancestors.

court-suit in a month's time, any more than when you changed your long coat for a doublet and hose; and in gaming you must expect to lose as well as gain—'tis the sitting gamester sweeps the board."

"The board has swept me, I know," replied Jin Vin, "and that pretty clean out.—I would that were the worst; but I owe for all this finery, and settling-day is coming on, and my master will find my accompt worse than it should be by a score of pieces. My old father will be called in to make them good; and I—may save the hangman a labour and do the job myself, or go the Virginia voyage."

"Do not speak so loud, my dear boy," said Dame Ursley; "but tell me why you borrow not from a friend to make up your arrear. You could lend him as much when his settling-day came round."

"No, no—I have had enough of that work," said Vincent. "Tunstall would lend me the money, poor fellow, an he had it; but his gentle, beggarly kindred, plunder him of all, and keep him as bare as a birch at Christmas. No—my fortune may be spelt in four letters, and these read, RUIN."

"Now hush, you simple craven," said the dame; "did you never hear, that when the need is highest the help is nighest? We may find aid for you yet, and sooner than you are aware of. I am sure I would never have advised you to such a course, but only you had set heart and eye on pretty Mistress Marget, and less would not serve you—and what could I do but advise you to cast your city-slough, and try your luck where folks find fortune?"

"Ay, ay—I remember your counsel well," said Jenkin; "I was to be introduced to her by you when I was perfect in my gallantries, and as rich as the king; and then she was to be surprised to find I was poor Jin Vin, that used to watch, from matin to curfew, for one glance of her eye; and now, instead of that, she has set her soul on this Scottish sparrow-hawk of a lord that won my last tester, and be cursed to him; and so I am bankrupt in love, fortune, and character, before I am out of my time, and all along of you, Mother Midnight."

"Do not call me out of my own name, my dear boy, Jin Vin," answered Ursula, in a tone betwixt rage and coaxing,—"do not; because I am no saint, but a poor sinful woman, with no more patience than she needs, to carry her through a thousand crosses. And if I have done you wrong by evil counsel, I must mend it and put you right by good advice. And for the score of pieces that must be made up at settling-day, why, here is, in a good green purse, as much as will make that matter good; and we will get old Crosspatch, the tailor, to take a long day for your clothes; and—"

"Mother, are you serious?" said Jin Vin, unable to trust either his eyes or his ears.

"In troth am I," said the dame; "and will you call me Mother Midnight now, Jin Vin?"

"Mother Midnight!" exclaimed Jenkin, hugging the dame in his transport, and bestowing on her still comely cheek a hearty and not unacceptable smack, that sounded like the report of a pistol,—"Mother Midday, rather, that has risen to light me out of my troubles—a mother more dear than she who bore me; for she, poor soul, only brought me into a world of sin and sorrow, and your timely aid has helped me out of the one and the other." And the good-natured fellow threw himself back in his chair, and fairly drew his hand across his eyes.

"You would not have me be made to ride the Skimmington then," said the dame; "or parade me in a cart, with all the brass basins of the ward beating the march to Bridewell before me?"

"I would sooner be carted to Tyburn myself," replied the penitent.

"Why, then, sit up like a man, and wipe thine eyes; and, if thou art pleased with what I have done, I will show thee how thou mayst requite me in the highest degree."

"How?" said Jenkin Vincent, sitting straight up in his chair.—"You would have me, then, do you some service for this friendship of yours?"

"Ay, marry would I," said Dame Ursley; "for you are to know, that though I am right glad to stead you with it, this gold is not mine, but was placed in my hands in order to find a trusty agent, for a certain purpose; and so—But what's the matter with you?—are you fool enough to be angry because you cannot get a purse of gold for nothing? I would I knew where such were to come by. I never could find them lying in my road, I promise you."

"No, no, dame," said poor Jenkin, "it is not for that; for, look you, I would rather work these ten bones to the knuckles, and live by my labour; but—" (and here he paused.)

"But what, man?" said Dame Ursley. "You are willing to work for what you want; and yet, when I offer you gold for the winning, you look on me as the devil looks over Lincoln."

"It is ill talking of the devil, mother," said Jenkin. "I had him even now in my head—for, look you, I am at that pass, when they say he will appear to wretched ruined creatures, and proffer them gold for the fee-simple of their salvation. But I have been trying these two days to bring my mind strongly up to the thought, that I will rather sit down in shame, and sin, and sorrow, as I am like to do, than hold on in ill courses to get rid of my present straits; and so take care, Dame Ursula, how you tempt me to break such a good resolution."

"I tempt you to nothing, young man," answered Ursula; "and, as I perceive you are too wilful to be wise, I will e'en put my purse in my pocket, and look out for some one that will work my turn with better will, and more thankfulness. And you may go your own course,—break your indenture, ruin your father, lose your character, and bid pretty Mistress Margaret farewell, for ever and a day."

"Stay, stay," said Jenkin "the woman is in as great a hurry as a brown baker when his oven is overheated. First, let me hear that which you have to propose to me."

"Why, after all, it is but to get a gentleman of rank and fortune, who is in trouble, carried in secret down the river, as far as the Isle of Dogs, or somewhere thereabout, where he may lie concealed until he can escape aboard. I know thou knowest every place by the river's side as well as the devil knows an usurer, or the beggar knows his dish."

"A plague of your similes, dame," replied the apprentice; "for the devil gave me that knowledge, and beggary may be the end on't.—But what has this gentleman done, that he should need to be under hiding? No Papist, I hope—no Catesby and Piercy business—no Gunpowder Plot?"

"Fy, fy!—what do you take me for?" said Dame Ursula. "I am as good a churchwoman as the parson's wife, save that necessary business will not allow me to go there oftener than on Christmas-day, heaven help me!—No, no—this is no Popish matter. The gentleman hath but struck another in the Park—"

"Ha! what?" said Vincent, interrupting her with a start.

"Ay, ay, I see you guess whom I mean. It is even he we have spoken of so often—just Lord Glenvarloch, and no one else."

Vincent sprung from his seat, and traversed the room with rapid and disorderly steps.

"There, there it is now—you are always ice or gunpowder. You sit in the great leathern armchair, as quiet as a rocket hangs upon the frame in a rejoicing-night till the match be fired, and then, whizz! you are in the third heaven, beyond the reach of the human voice, eye, or brain.—

When you have wearied yourself with padding to and fro across the room, will you tell me your determination, for time presses? Will you aid me in this matter, or not?"

"No—no—no—a thousand times no," replied Jenkin. "Have you not confessed to me, that Margaret loves him?"

"Ay," answered the dame, "that she thinks she does; but that will not last long."

"And have I not told you but this instant," replied Jenkin, "that it was this same Glenvarloch that rooked me, at the ordinary, of every penny I had, and made a knave of me to boot, by gaining more than was my own?—O that cursed gold, which Shortyard, the mercer, paid me that morning on accompt, for mending the clock of Saint Stephen's! If I had not, by ill chance, had that about me, I could but have beggared my purse, without blemishing my honesty; and, after I had been rooked of all the rest amongst them, I must needs risk the last five pieces with that shark among the minnows!"

"Granted," said Dame Ursula. "All this I know; and I own, that as Lord Glenvarloch was the last you played with, you have a right to charge your ruin on his head. Moreover, I admit, as already said, that Margaret has made him your rival. Yet surely, now he is in danger to lose his hand, it is not a time to remember all this?"

"By my faith, but it is, though," said the young citizen. "Lose his hand, indeed? They may take his head, for what I care. Head and hand have made me a miserable wretch!"

"Now, were it not better, my prince of flat-caps," said Dame Ursula, "that matters were squared between you; and that, through means of the same Scottish lord, who has, as you say, deprived you of your money and your mistress, you should in a short time recover both?"

"And how can your wisdom come to that conclusion, dame?" said the apprentice. "My money, indeed, I can conceive—that is, if I comply with your proposal; but—my pretty Marget!—how serving this lord, whom she has set her nonsensical head upon, can do me good with her, is far beyond my conception."

"That is because, in simple phrase," said Dame Ursula, "thou knowest no more of a woman's heart than doth a Norfolk gosling. Look you, man. Were I to report to Mistress Margaret that the young lord has miscarried through thy lack of courtesy in refusing to help him, why, then, thou wert odious to her for ever. She will loathe thee as she will loathe the very cook who is to strike off Glenvarloch's hand with his cleaver—and then she will be yet more fixed in her affections towards this lord. London will hear of nothing but him—speak of nothing but him—think of nothing but him, for three weeks at least, and all that outcry will serve to keep him uppermost in her mind; for nothing pleases a girl so much as to bear relation to any one who is the talk of the whole world around her. Then, if he suffer this sentence of the law, it is a chance if she ever forgets him. I saw that handsome, proper young gentleman Babington, suffer in the Queen's time myself, and though I was then but a girl, he was in my head for a year after he was hanged. But, above all, pardoned or punished, Glenvarloch will probably remain in London, and his presence will keep up the silly girl's nonsensical fancy about him. Whereas, if he escapes—"

"Ay, show me how that is to avail me?" said Jenkin. "If he escapes," said the dame, resuming her argument, "he must resign the Court for years, if not for life; and you know the old saying, 'out of sight, and out of mind.'"

"True—most true," said Jenkin; "spoken like an oracle, most wise Ursula."

"Ay, ay, I knew you would hear reason at last," said the wily dame; "and then, when this same lord is off and away for once and for ever, who, I pray you, is to be pretty pet's confidential person, and who is to fill up the void in her affections?—why, who but thou, thou pearl of 'prentices! And then you will have overcome your own inclinations to comply with hers, and every woman is sensible of that—and you will have run some risk, too, in carrying her desires into effect—and what is it that woman likes better than bravery, and devotion to her will? Then you have her secret, and she must treat you with favour and observance, and repose confidence in you, and hold private intercourse with you, till she weeps with one eye for the absent lover whom she is never to see again, and blinks with the other blithely upon him who is in presence; and then if you know not how to improve the relation in which you stand with her, you are not the brisk lively lad that all the world takes you for—Said I well?"

"You have spoken like an empress, most mighty Ursula," said Jenkin Vincent; "and your will shall be obeyed."

"You know Alsatia well?" continued his tutoress.

"Well enough, well enough," replied he with a nod; "I have heard the dice rattle there in my day, before I must set up for gentleman, and go among the gallants at the Shavaleer Bojo's, as they call him,—the worse rookery of the two, though the feathers are the gayest."

"And they will have a respect for thee yonder, I warrant?"

"Ay, ay," replied Vin, "when I am got into my fustian doublet again, with my bit of a trunnion under my arm, I can walk Alsatia at midnight as I could do that there Fleet Street in midday—they will not one of them swagger with the prince of 'prentices, and the king of clubs—they know I could bring every tall boy in the ward down upon them."

"And you know all the watermen, and so forth?"

"Can converse with every sculler in his own language, from Richmond to Gravesend, and know all the water-cocks, from John Taylor the Poet to little Grigg the Grinner, who never pulls but he shows all his teeth from ear to ear, as if he were grimacing through a horse-collar."

"And you can take any dress or character upon you well, such as a waterman's, a butcher's, a foot-soldier's," continued Ursula, "or the like?"

"Not such a mummer as I am within the walls, and thou knowest that well enough, dame," replied the apprentice. "I can touch the players themselves, at the Ball and at the Fortune, for presenting any thing except a gentleman. Take but this d—d skin of frippery off me, which I think the devil stuck me into, and you shall put me into nothing else that I will not become as if I were born to it."

"Well, we will talk of your transmutation by and by," said the dame, "and find you clothes withal, and money besides; for it will take a good deal to carry the thing handsomely through."

"But where is that money to come from, dame?" said Jenkin; "there is a question I would fain have answered before I touch it."

"Why, what a fool art thou to ask such a question! Suppose I am content to advance it to please young madam, what is the harm then?"

"I will suppose no such thing," said Jenkin, hastily; "I know that you, dame, have no gold to spare, and maybe would not spare it if you had—so that cock will not crow. It must be from Margaret herself."

"Well, thou suspicious animal, and what if it were?" said Ursula.

"Only this," replied Jenkin, "that I will presently to her, and learn if she has come fairly by so much ready money; for sooner than connive at her getting it by any indirection, I would hang myself at once. It is enough what I have done myself, no need to engage poor Margaret in such villainy—I'll to her, and tell her of the danger—I will, by heaven!"

"You are mad to think of it," said Dame Suddlechop, considerably alarmed—"hear me but a moment. I know not precisely from whom she got the money; but sure I am that she obtained it at her godfather's."

"Why, Master George Heriot is not returned from France," said Jenkin.

"No," replied Ursula, "but Dame Judith is at home—and the strange lady, whom they call Master Heriot's ghost—she never goes abroad."

"It is very true, Dame Suddlechop," said Jenkin; "and I believe you have guessed right—they say that lady has coin at will; and if Marget can get a handful of fairy-gold, why, she is free to throw it away at will."

"Ah, Jin Vin," said the dame, reducing her voice almost to a whisper, "we should not want gold at will neither, could we but read the riddle of that lady!"

"They may read it that list," said Jenkin, "I'll never pry into what concerns me not—Master George Heriot is a worthy and brave citizen, and an honour to London, and has a right to manage his own household as he likes best.—There was once a talk of rabbling him the fifth of November before the last, because they said he kept a nunnery in his house, like old Lady Foljambe; but Master George is well loved among the 'prentices, and we got so many brisk boys of us together as should have rabbled the rabble, had they had but the heart to rise."

"Well, let that pass," said Ursula; "and now, tell me how you will manage to be absent from shop a day or two, for you must think that this matter will not be ended sooner."

"Why, as to that, I can say nothing," said Jenkin, "I have always served duly and truly; I have no heart to play truant, and cheat my master of his time as well as his money."

"Nay, but the point is to get back his money for him," said Ursula, "which he is not likely to see on other conditions. Could you not ask leave to go down to your uncle in Essex for two or three days? He may be ill, you know."

"Why, if I must, I must," said Jenkin, with a heavy sigh; "but I will not be lightly caught treading these dark and crooked paths again."

"Hush thee, then," said the dame, "and get leave for this very evening; and come back hither, and I will introduce you to another implement, who must be employed in the matter.—Stay, stay!—the lad is mazed—you would not go into your master's shop in that guise, surely? Your trunk is in the matted chamber, with your 'prentice things— go and put them on as fast as you can."

"I think I am bewitched," said Jenkin, giving a glance towards his dress, "or that these fool's trappings have made as great an ass of me as of many I have seen wear them; but let line once be rid of the harness, and if you catch me putting it on again, I will give you leave to sell me to a gipsy, to carry pots, pans, and beggar's bantlings, all the rest of my life." So saying, he retired to change his apparel.

XXII

Chance will not do the work—Chance sends the breeze;
But if the pilot slumber at the helm,
The very wind that wafts us towards the port
May dash us on the shelves.—The steersman's part is vigilance,
Blow it or rough or smooth.

—*Old Play*

We left Nigel, whose fortunes we are bound to trace by the engagement contracted in our title-page, sad and solitary in the mansion of Trapbois the usurer, having just received a letter instead of a visit from his friend the Templar, stating reasons why he could not at that time come to see him in Alsatia. So that it appeared that his intercourse with the better and more respectable class of society, was, for the present, entirely cut off. This was a melancholy, and, to a proud mind like that of Nigel, a degrading reflection.

He went to the window of his apartment, and found the street enveloped in one of those thick, dingy, yellow-coloured fogs, which often invest the lower part of London and Westminster. Amid the darkness, dense and palpable, were seen to wander like phantoms a reveller or two, whom the morning had surprised where the evening left them; and who now, with tottering steps, and by an instinct which intoxication could not wholly overcome, were groping the way to their own homes, to convert day into night, for the purpose of sleeping off the debauch which had turned night into day. Although it was broad day in the other parts of the city, it was scarce dawn yet in Alsatia; and none of the sounds of industry or occupation were there heard, which had long before aroused the slumberers in any other quarter. The prospect was too tiresome and disagreeable to detain Lord Glenvarloch at his station, so, turning from the window, he examined with more interest the furniture and appearance of the apartment which he tenanted.

Much of it had been in its time rich and curious—there was a huge four-post bed, with as much carved oak about it as would have made the head of a man-of-war, and tapestry hangings ample enough to have been her sails. There was a huge mirror with a massy frame of gilt brass-work, which was of Venetian manufacture, and must have been worth a considerable sum before it received the tremendous crack, which, traversing it from one corner to the other, bore the same proportion to the surface that the Nile bears to the map of Egypt. The chairs were of different forms and shapes, some had been carved, some gilded, some covered with damasked leather, some with embroidered work, but all were damaged and worm-eaten. There was a picture of Susanna and the Elders over the chimney-piece, which might have been accounted a choice piece, had not the rats made free with the chaste fair one's nose, and with the beard of one of her reverend admirers.

In a word, all that Lord Glenvarloch saw, seemed to have been articles carried off by appraisement or distress, or bought as pennyworths at some obscure broker's, and huddled together in the apartment, as in a sale-room, without regard to taste or congruity.

The place appeared to Nigel to resemble the houses near the sea-coast, which are too often furnished with the spoils of wrecked vessels, as this was probably fitted up with the relics of ruined profligates.—"My own skiff is among the breakers," thought Lord Glenvarloch, "though my wreck will add little to the profits of the spoiler."

He was chiefly interested in the state of the grate, a huge assemblage of rusted iron bars which stood in the chimney, unequally supported by three brazen feet, moulded into the form of lion's claws, while the fourth, which had been bent by an accident, seemed proudly uplifted as if to paw the ground; or as if the whole article had nourished the ambitious purpose of pacing forth into the middle of the apartment, and had one foot ready raised for the journey. A smile passed over Nigel's face as this fantastic idea presented itself to his fancy.—"I must stop its march, however," he thought; "for this morning is chill and raw enough to demand some fire."

He called accordingly from the top of a large staircase, with a heavy oaken balustrade, which gave access to his own and other apartments, for the house was old and of considerable size; but, receiving no answer to his repeated summons, he was compelled to go in search of some one who might accommodate him with what he wanted.

Nigel had, according to the fashion of the old world in Scotland, received an education which might, in most particulars, be termed simple, hardy, and unostentatious; but he had, nevertheless, been accustomed to much personal deference, and to the constant attendance and ministry of one or more domestics. This was the universal custom in Scotland, where wages were next to nothing, and where, indeed, a man of title or influence might have as many attendants as he pleased, for the mere expense of food, clothes, and countenance. Nigel was therefore mortified and displeased when he found himself without notice or attendance; and the more dissatisfied, because he was at the same time angry with himself for suffering such a trifle to trouble him at all, amongst matters of more deep concernment. "There must surely be some servants in so large a house as this," said he, as he wandered over the place, through which he was conducted by a passage which branched off from the gallery. As he went on, he tried the entrance to several apartments, some of which he found were locked and others unfurnished, all apparently unoccupied; so that at length he returned to the staircase, and resolved to make his way down to the lower part of the house, where he supposed he must at least find the old gentleman, and his ill-favoured daughter. With this purpose he first made his entrance into a little low, dark parlour, containing a well-worn leathern easy-chair, before which stood a pair of slippers, while on the left side rested a crutch-handled staff; an oaken table stood before it, and supported a huge desk clamped with iron, and a massive pewter inkstand. Around the apartment were shelves, cabinets, and other places convenient for depositing papers. A sword, musketoon, and a pair of pistols, hung over the chimney, in ostentatious display, as if to intimate that the proprietor would be prompt in the defence of his premises.

"This must be the usurer's den," thought Nigel; and he was about to call aloud, when the old man, awakened even by the slightest noise, for avarice seldom sleeps sound, soon was heard from the inner room, speaking in a voice of irritability, rendered more tremulous by his morning cough.

"Ugh, ugh, ugh—who is there? I say—ugh, ugh—who is there? Why, Martha!—ugh! ugh—Martha Trapbois—here be thieves in the house, and they will not speak to me—why, Martha!—thieves, thieves—ugh, ugh, ugh!"

Nigel endeavoured to explain, but the idea of thieves had taken possession of the old man's pineal gland, and he kept coughing and screaming, and screaming and coughing, until the gracious Martha entered the apartment; and, having first outscreamed her father, in order to convince him that there was no danger, and to assure him that the intruder was their new lodger, and having as often heard her sire exclaim—"Hold him fast—ugh, ugh—hold him fast till I come," she at length succeeded in silencing his fears and his clamour, and then coldly and dryly asked Lord Glenvarloch what he wanted in her father's apartment.

Her lodger had, in the meantime, leisure to contemplate her appearance, which did not by any means improve the idea he had formed of it by candlelight on the preceding evening. She was dressed in what was called a Queen Mary's ruff and farthingale; not the falling ruff with which the unfortunate Mary of Scotland is usually painted, but that which, with more than Spanish stiffness, surrounded the throat, and set off the morose head, of her fierce namesake, of Smithfield memory. This antiquated dress assorted well with the faded complexion, grey eyes, thin lips, and austere visage of the antiquated maiden, which was, moreover, enhanced by a black hood, worn as her head-gear, carefully disposed so as to prevent any of her hair from escaping to view, probably because the simplicity of the period knew no art of disguising the colour with which time had begun to grizzle her tresses. Her figure was tall, thin, and flat, with skinny arms and hands, and feet of the larger size, cased in huge high-heeled shoes, which added height to a stature already ungainly. Apparently some art had been used by the tailor, to conceal a slight defect of shape, occasioned by the accidental elevation of one shoulder above the other; but the praiseworthy efforts of the ingenious mechanic, had only succeeded in calling the attention of the observer to his benevolent purpose, without demonstrating that he had been able to achieve it.

Such was Mrs. Martha Trapbois, whose dry "What were you seeking here, sir?" fell again, and with reiterated sharpness, on the ear of Nigel, as he gazed upon her presence, and compared it internally to one of the faded and grim figures in the old tapestry which adorned his bedstead. It was, however, necessary to reply, and he answered, that he came in search of the servants, as he desired to have a fire kindled in his apartment on account of the rawness of the morning.

"The woman who does our char-work," answered Mistress Martha, "comes at eight o'clock-if you want fire sooner, there are fagots and a bucket of sea-coal in the stone-closet at the head of the stair—and there is a flint and steel on the upper shelf—you can light fire for yourself if you will."

"No—no—no, Martha," exclaimed her father, who, having donned his rustic tunic, with his hose all ungirt, and his feet slip-shod, hastily came out of the inner apartment, with his mind probably full of robbers, for he had a naked rapier in his hand, which still looked formidable, though rust had somewhat marred its shine.—What he had heard at entrance about lighting a fire, had changed, however, the current of his ideas. "No—no—no," he cried, and each negative was more emphatic than its predecessor-"The gentleman shall not have the trouble to put on a fire—ugh—ugh. I'll put it on myself, for a con-si-de-ra-ti-on."

This last word was a favourite expression with the old gentleman, which he pronounced in a peculiar manner, gasping it out syllable by syllable, and laying a strong emphasis upon the last. It was, indeed, a sort of protecting clause, by which he guarded himself against all inconveniences attendant on the rash habit of offering service or civility of any kind, the which, when hastily snapped at by those to whom they are uttered, give the profferer sometimes room to repent his promptitude.

"For shame, father," said Martha, "that must not be. Master Grahame will kindle his own fire, or wait till the char-woman comes to do it for him, just as likes him best."

"No, child—no, child. Child Martha, no," reiterated the old miser— "no char-woman shall ever touch a grate in my house; they put—ugh, ugh—the faggot uppermost, and so the coal kindles not, and the flame goes up the chimney, and wood and heat are both thrown away. Now, I will lay it properly for the gentleman, for a consideration, so that it shall last—ugh, ugh—last the whole day." Here his vehemence increased his cough so violently, that Nigel could only, from a scattered word here and there, comprehend that it was a recommendation to his daughter to remove the poker and tongs from the stranger's fireside, with an assurance, that, when necessary, his landlord would be in attendance to adjust it himself, "for a consideration."

Martha paid as little attention to the old man's injunctions as a predominant dame gives to those of a henpecked husband. She only repeated, in a deeper and more emphatic tone of censure,—"For shame, father—for shame!" then, turning to her guest, said, with her usual ungraciousness of manner—"Master Grahame—it is best to be plain with you at first. My father is an old, a very old man, and his wits, as you may see, are somewhat weakened—though I would not advise you to make a bargain with him, else you may find them too sharp for your own. For myself, I am a lone woman, and, to say truth, care little to see or converse with any one. If you can be satisfied with house-room, shelter, and safety, it will be your own fault if you have them not, and they are not always to be found in this unhappy quarter. But, if you seek deferential observance and attendance, I tell you at once you will not find them here."

"I am not wont either to thrust myself upon acquaintance, madam, or to give trouble," said the guest; "nevertheless, I shall need the assistance of a domestic to assist me to dress—Perhaps you can recommend me to such?"

"Yes, to twenty," answered Mistress Martha, "who will pick your purse while they tie your points, and cut your throat while they smooth your pillow."

"I will be his servant, myself," said the old man, whose intellect, for a moment distanced, had again, in some measure, got up with the conversation. "I will brush his cloak—ugh, ugh—and tie his points— ugh, ugh—and clean his shoes—ugh—and run on his errands with speed and safety—ugh, ugh, ugh, ugh—for a consideration."

"Good-morrow to you, sir," said Martha, to Nigel, in a tone of direct and positive dismissal. "It cannot be agreeable to a daughter that a stranger should hear her father speak thus. If you be really a gentleman, you will retire to your own apartment."

"I will not delay a moment," said Nigel, respectfully, for he was sensible that circumstances palliated the woman's rudeness. "I would but ask you, if seriously there can be danger in procuring the assistance of a serving-man in this place?"

"Young gentleman," said Martha, "you must know little of Whitefriars to ask the question. We live alone in this house, and seldom has a stranger entered it; nor should you, to be plain, had my will been consulted. Look at the door—see if that of a castle can be better secured; the windows of the first floor are grated on the outside, and within, look to these shutters."

She pulled one of them aside, and showed a ponderous apparatus of bolts and chains for securing the window-shutters, while her father, pressing to her side, seized her gown with a trembling hand, and said, in a low whisper, "Show not the trick of locking and undoing them. Show him not the trick on't, Martha—ugh, ugh—on *no* consideration." Martha went on, without paying him any attention.

"And yet, young gentleman, we have been more than once like to find all these defences too weak to protect our lives; such an evil effect on the wicked generation around us hath been made by the unhappy report of my poor father's wealth."

"Say nothing of that, housewife," said the miser, his irritability increased by the very supposition of his being wealthy—"Say nothing of that, or I will beat thee, housewife—beat thee with my staff, for fetching and carrying lies that will procure our throats to be cut at last—ugh, ugh.—I am but a poor man," he continued, turning to Nigel—"a very poor man, that am willing to do any honest turn upon earth, for a modest consideration."

"I therefore warn you of the life you must lead, young gentleman," said Martha; "the poor woman who does the char-work will assist you so far as in her power, but the wise man is his own best servant and assistant."

"It is a lesson you have taught me, madam, and I thank you for it—I will assuredly study it at leisure."

"You will do well," said Martha; "and as you seem thankful for advice, I, though I am no professed counsellor of others, will give you more. Make no intimacy with any one in Whitefriars—borrow no money, on any score, especially from my father, for, dotard as he seems, he will make an ass of you. Last, and best of all, stay here not an instant longer than you can help it. Farewell, sir."

"A gnarled tree may bear good fruit, and a harsh nature may give good counsel," thought the Lord of Glenvarloch, as he retreated to his own apartment, where the same reflection occurred to him again and again, while, unable as yet to reconcile himself to the thoughts of becoming his own fire-maker, he walked up and down his bedroom, to warm himself by exercise.

At length his meditations arranged themselves in the following soliloquy—by which expression I beg leave to observe once for all, that I do not mean that Nigel literally said aloud with his bodily organs, the words which follow in inverted commas, (while pacing the room by himself,) but that I myself choose to present to my dearest reader the picture of my hero's mind, his reflections and resolutions, in the form of a speech, rather than in that of a narrative. In other words, I have put his thoughts into language; and this I conceive to be the purpose of the soliloquy upon the stage as well as in the closet, being at once the most natural, and perhaps the only way of communicating to the spectator what is supposed to be passing in the bosom of the scenic personage. There are no such soliloquies in nature, it is true, but unless they were received as a conventional medium of communication betwixt the poet and the audience, we should reduce dramatic authors to the recipe of Master Puff, who makes Lord Burleigh intimate a long train of political reasoning to the audience, by one comprehensive shake of his noddle. In narrative, no doubt, the writer has the alternative of telling that his personages thought so and so, inferred thus and thus, and arrived at such and such a conclusion; but the soliloquy is a more concise and spirited mode of communicating the same information; and therefore thus communed, or thus might have communed, the Lord of Glenvarloch with his own mind.

"She is right, and has taught me a lesson I will profit by. I have been, through my whole life, one who leant upon others for that assistance, which it is more truly noble to derive from my own exertions. I am ashamed of feeling the paltry inconvenience which long habit had led me to annex to the want of a servant's assistance—I am ashamed of that; but far, far more am I ashamed to have suffered the same habit of throwing my own burden on others, to render me, since I came to this city, a mere victim of those events, which I have never even attempted to influence—a thing never acting, but perpetually acted upon—protected by one friend, deceived by another; but in the advantage which I received from the one, and the evil I have sustained from the other, as passive and helpless as a boat that drifts without oar or rudder at the mercy of the winds and waves. I became a courtier, because Heriot so advised it—a gamester, because Dalgarno so contrived it—an Alsatian, because Lowestoffe so willed it. Whatever of good or bad has befallen me, has arisen out of the agency of others, not from my own. My father's son must no longer hold this facile and puerile course. Live or die, sink or swim, Nigel Olifaunt, from this moment, shall owe his safety, success, and honour, to his own exertions, or shall fall with the credit of having at least exerted his own free agency. I will write it down in my tablets, in her very words,—'The wise man is his own best assistant.'"

He had just put his tablets in his pocket when the old charwoman, who, to add to her efficiency, was sadly crippled by rheumatism, hobbled into the room, to try if she could gain a small gratification by waiting on the stranger. She readily undertook to get Lord Glenvarloch's breakfast, and as there was an eating-house at the next door, she succeeded in a shorter time than Nigel had augured.

As his solitary meal was finished, one of the Temple porters, or inferior officers, was announced, as seeking Master Grahame, on the part of his friend, Master Lowestoffe; and, being admitted by the old woman to his apartment, he delivered to Nigel a small mail-trunk, with the clothes he had desired should be sent to him, and then, with more mystery, put into his hand a casket, or strong-boy, which he carefully concealed beneath his cloak. "I am glad to be rid on't," said the fellow, as he placed it on the table.

"Why, it is surely not so very heavy," answered Nigel, "and you are a stout young man."

"Ay, sir," replied the fellow; "but Samson himself would not have carried such a matter safely through Alsatia, had the lads of the Huff known what it was. Please to look into it, sir, and see all is right—I am an honest fellow, and it comes safe out of my hands. How long it may remain so afterwards, will depend on your own care. I would not my good name were to suffer by any after-clap."

To satisfy the scruples of the messenger, Lord Glenvarloch opened the casket in his presence, and saw that his small stock of money, with two or three valuable papers which it contained, and particularly the original sign-manual which the king had granted in his favour, were in the same order in which he had left them. At the man's further instance, he availed himself of the writing materials which were in the casket, in order to send a line to Master Lowestoffe, declaring that his property had reached him in safety. He added some grateful acknowledgments for Lowestoffe's services, and, just as he was sealing and delivering his billet to the messenger, his aged landlord entered the apartment. His threadbare suit of black clothes was now somewhat better arranged than they had been in the dishabille of his first appearance, and his nerves and intellects seemed to be less fluttered; for, without much coughing or hesitation, he invited Nigel to partake of a morning draught of wholesome single ale, which he brought in a large leathern tankard, or black-jack, carried in the one hand, while the other stirred it round with a sprig of rosemary, to give it, as the old man said, a flavour.

Nigel declined the courteous proffer, and intimated by his manner, while he did so, that he desired no intrusion on the privacy of his own apartment; which, indeed, he was the more entitled to maintain, considering the cold reception he had that morning met with when straying from its precincts into those of his landlord. But the open casket contained matter, or rather metal, so attractive to old Trapbois, that he remained fixed, like a setting-dog at a dead point, his nose advanced, and one hand expanded like the lifted forepaw, by which that sagacious quadruped sometimes indicates that it is a hare which he has in the wind. Nigel was about to break the charm which had thus arrested old Trapbois, by shutting the lid of the casket, when his attention was withdrawn from him by the question of the messenger, who, holding out the letter, asked whether he was to leave it at Mr. Lowestoffe's chambers in the Temple, or carry it to the Marshalsea?

"The Marshalsea?" repeated Lord Glenvarloch; "what of the Marshalsea?"

"Why, sir," said the man, "the poor gentleman is laid up there in lavender, because, they say, his own kind heart led him to scald his fingers with another man's broth."

Nigel hastily snatched back the letter, broke the seal, joined to the contents his earnest entreaty that he might be instantly acquainted with the cause of his confinement, and added, that, if it arose out of his own unhappy affair, it would be of a brief duration, since he had, even before hearing of a reason which so peremptorily demanded that he should surrender himself, adopted the resolution to do so, as the manliest and most proper course which his ill fortune and imprudence had left in his own power. He therefore conjured Mr. Lowestoffe to have no delicacy upon this score, but, since his surrender was what he had determined upon as a sacrifice due to his own character, that he would have the frankness to mention in what manner it could be best arranged, so as to extricate him, Lowestoffe, from the restraint to which the writer could not but fear his friend had been subjected, on account of the generous interest which he had taken in his concerns. The letter concluded, that the writer would suffer twenty-four hours to elapse in expectation of hearing from him, and, at the end of that period, was determined to put his purpose in execution. He delivered the billet to the messenger, and, enforcing his request with a piece of money, urged him, without a moment's delay, to convey it to the hands of Master Lowestoffe.

"I—I—I—will carry it to him myself," said the old usurer, "for half the consideration."

The man who heard this attempt to take his duty and perquisites over his head, lost no time in pocketing the money, and departed on his errand as fast as he could.

"Master Trapbois," said Nigel, addressing the old man somewhat impatiently, "had you any particular commands for me?"

"I—I—came to see if you rested well," answered the old man; "and—if I could do anything to serve you, on any consideration."

"Sir, I thank you," said Lord Glenvarloch—"I thank you;" and, ere he could say more, a heavy footstep was heard on the stair.

"My God!" exclaimed the old man, starting up—"Why, Dorothy—char-woman—why, daughter,—draw bolt, I say, housewives—the door hath been left a-latch!"

The door of the chamber opened wide, and in strutted the portly bulk of the military hero whom Nigel had on the preceding evening in vain endeavoured to recognise.

XXIII

SWASH-BUCKLER: *Bilboe's the word—*
PIERROT: *It hath been spoke too often, The spell hath lost its charm—*
  I tell thee, friend, The meanest cur that trots the street, will turn,
  And snarl against your proffer'd bastinado.
SWASH-BUCKLER: *'Tis art shall do it, then—I will dose the*
  mongrels—Or, in plain terms, I'll use the private knife 'Stead of
  the brandish'd falchion.

—*Old Play*

The noble Captain Colepepper or Peppercull, for he was known by both these names, and some others besides; had a martial and a swashing exterior, which, on the present occasion, was rendered yet more peculiar, by a patch covering his left eye and a part of the cheek. The sleeves of his thickset velvet jerkin were polished and shone with grease,—his buff gloves had huge tops, which reached almost to the elbow; his sword-belt of the same materials extended its breadth from his haunchbone to his small ribs, and supported on the one side his large black-hilted back-sword, on the other a dagger of like proportions He paid his compliments to Nigel with that air of predetermined effrontery, which announces that it will not be repelled by any coldness of reception, asked Trapbois how he did, by the familiar title of old Peter Pillory, and then, seizing upon the black-jack, emptied it off at a draught, to the health of the last and youngest freeman of Alsatia, the noble and loving master Nigel Grahame.

When he had set down the empty pitcher and drawn his breath, he began to criticise the liquor which it had lately contained.—"Sufficient single beer, old Pillory—and, as I take it, brewed at the rate of a nutshell of malt to a butt of Thames—as dead as a corpse, too, and yet it went hissing down my throat—bubbling, by Jove, like water upon hot iron.—You left us early, noble Master Grahame, but, good faith, we had a carouse to your honour—we heard *butt* ring hollow ere we parted; we were as loving as inkle-weavers—we fought, too, to finish off the gawdy. I bear some marks of the parson about me, you see—a note of the sermon or so, which should have been addressed to my ear, but missed its mark, and reached my left eye. The man of God bears my sign-manual too, but the Duke made us friends again, and it cost me more sack than I could carry, and all the Rhenish to boot, to pledge the seer in the way of love and reconciliation—But, Caracco! 'tis a vile old canting slave for all that, whom I will one day beat out of his devil's livery into all the colours of the rainbow.—Basta!—Said I well, old Trapbois? Where is thy daughter, man?—what says she to my suit?—'tis an honest one—wilt have a soldier for thy son-in-law, old Pillory, to mingle the soul of martial honour with thy thieving, miching, petty-larceny blood, as men put bold brandy into muddy ale?"

"My daughter receives not company so early, noble captain," said the usurer, and concluded his speech with a dry, emphatical "ugh, ugh."

"What, upon no con-si-de-ra-ti-on?" said the captain; "and wherefore not, old Truepenny? she has not much time to lose in driving her bargain, methinks."

"Captain," said Trapbois, "I was upon some little business with our noble friend here, Master Nigel Green—ugh, ugh, ugh—"

"And you would have me gone, I warrant you?" answered the bully; "but patience, old Pillory, thine hour is not yet come, man—You see," he said, pointing to the casket, "that noble Master Grahame, whom you call Green, has got the *decuses* and the *smelt*."

"Which you would willingly rid him of, ha! ha!—ugh, ugh," answered the usurer, "if you knew how—but, lack-a-day! thou art one of those that come out for wool, and art sure to go home shorn. Why now, but that I am sworn against laying of wagers, I would risk some consideration that this honest guest of mine sends thee home penniless, if thou darest venture with him—ugh, ugh—at any game which gentlemen play at."

"Marry, thou hast me on the hip there, thou old miserly cony-catcher!" answered the captain, taking a bale of dice from the sleeve of his coat; "I must always keep company with these damnable doctors, and they have made me every baby's cully, and purged my purse into an atrophy; but never mind, it passes the time as well as aught else—How say you, Master Grahame?"

The fellow paused; but even the extremity of his impudence could scarcely hardly withstand the cold look of utter contempt with which Nigel received his proposal, returning it with a simple, "I only play where I know my company, and never in the morning."

"Cards may be more agreeable," said Captain Colepepper; "and, for knowing your company, here is honest old Pillory will tell you Jack

Colepepper plays as truly on the square as e'er a man that trowled a die—Men talk of high and low dice, Fulhams and bristles, topping, knapping, slurring, stabbing, and a hundred ways of rooking besides; but broil me like a rasher of bacon, if I could ever learn the trick on 'em!"

"You have got the vocabulary perfect, sir, at the least," said Nigel, in the same cold tone.

"Yes, by mine honour have I," returned the Hector; "they are phrases that a gentleman learns about town.—But perhaps you would like a set at tennis, or a game at balloon—we have an indifferent good court hard by here, and a set of as gentleman-like blades as ever banged leather against brick and mortar."

"I beg to be excused at present," said Lord Glenvarloch; "and to be plain, among the valuable privileges your society has conferred on me, I hope I may reckon that of being private in my own apartment when I have a mind."

"Your humble servant, sir," said the captain; "and I thank you for your civility—Jack Colepepper can have enough of company, and thrusts himself on no one.—But perhaps you will like to make a match at skittles?"

"I am by no means that way disposed," replied the young nobleman,

"Or to leap a flea—run a snail—match a wherry, eh?"

"No—I will do none of these," answered Nigel.

Here the old man, who had been watching with his little peery eyes, pulled the bulky Hector by the skirt, and whispered, "Do not vapour him the huff, it will not pass—let the trout play, he will rise to the hook presently."

But the bully, confiding in his own strength, and probably mistaking for timidity the patient scorn with which Nigel received his proposals, incited also by the open casket, began to assume a louder and more threatening tone. He drew himself up, bent his brows, assumed a look of professional ferocity, and continued, "In Alsatia, look ye, a man must be neighbourly and companionable. Zouns! sir, we would slit any nose that was turned up at us honest fellows.—Ay, sir, we would slit it up to the gristle, though it had smelt nothing all its life but musk, ambergris, and court-scented water.—Rabbit me, I am a soldier, and care no more for a lord than a lamplighter!"

"Are you seeking a quarrel, sir?" said Nigel, calmly, having in truth no desire to engage himself in a discreditable broil in such a place, and with such a character.

"Quarrel, sir?" said the captain; "I am not seeking a quarrel, though I care not how soon I find one. Only I wish you to understand you must be neighbourly, that's all. What if we should go over the water to the garden, and see a bull hanked this fine morning—'sdeath, will you do nothing?"

"Something I am strangely tempted to do at this moment," said Nigel.

"Videlicet," said Colepepper, with a swaggering air, "let us hear the temptation."

"I am tempted to throw you headlong from the window, unless you presently make the best of your way down stairs."

"Throw me from the window?—hell and furies!" exclaimed the captain; "I have confronted twenty crooked sabres at Buda with my single rapier, and shall a chitty-faced, beggarly Scots lordling, speak of me and a window in the same breath?—Stand off, old Pillory, let me make Scotch collops of him—he dies the death!"

"For the love of Heaven, gentlemen," exclaimed the old miser, throwing himself between them, "do not break the peace on any consideration! Noble guest, forbear the captain—he is a very Hector of Troy—Trusty Hector, forbear my guest, he is like to prove a very Achilles-ugh-ugh—"

Here he was interrupted by his asthma, but, nevertheless, continued to interpose his person between Colepepper (who had unsheathed his whinyard, and was making vain passes at his antagonist) and Nigel, who had stepped back to take his sword, and now held it undrawn in his left hand.

"Make an end of this foolery, you scoundrel!" said Nigel—"Do you come hither to vent your noisy oaths and your bottled-up valour on me? You seem to know me, and I am half ashamed to say I have at length been able to recollect you—remember the garden behind the ordinary,—you dastardly ruffian, and the speed with which fifty men saw you run from a drawn sword.—Get you gone, sir, and do not put me to the vile labour of cudgelling such a cowardly rascal down stairs."

The bully's countenance grew dark as night at this unexpected recognition; for he had undoubtedly thought himself secure in his change of dress, and his black patch, from being discovered by a person who had seen him but once. He set his teeth, clenched his hands, and it seemed as if he was seeking for a moment's courage to fly upon his antagonist. But his heart failed, he sheathed his sword, turned his back in gloomy silence, and spoke not until he reached the door, when, turning round, he said, with a deep oath, "If I be not avenged of you for this insolence ere many days go by, I would the gallows had my body and the devil my spirit!"

So saying, and with a look where determined spite and malice made his features savagely fierce, though they could not overcome his fear, he turned and left the house. Nigel followed him as far as the gallery at the head of the staircase, with the purpose of seeing him depart, and ere he returned was met by Mistress Martha Trapbois, whom the noise of the quarrel had summoned from her own apartment. He could not resist saying to her in his natural displeasure—"I would, madam, you could teach your father and his friends the lesson which you had the goodness to bestow on me this morning, and prevail on them to leave me the unmolested privacy of my own apartment."

"If you came hither for quiet or retirement, young man," answered she, "you have been advised to an evil retreat. You might seek mercy in the Star-Chamber, or holiness in hell, with better success than quiet in Alsatia. But my father shall trouble you no longer."

So saying, she entered the apartment, and, fixing her eyes on the casket, she said with emphasis—"If you display such a loadstone, it will draw many a steel knife to your throat."

While Nigel hastily shut the casket, she addressed her father, upbraiding him, with small reverence, for keeping company with the cowardly, hectoring, murdering villain, John Colepepper.

"Ay, ay, child," said the old man, with the cunning leer which intimated perfect satisfaction with his own superior address—"I know—I know—ugh—but I'll crossbite him—I know them all, and I can manage them—ay, ay—I have the trick on't—ugh-ugh."

"*You* manage, father!" said the austere damsel; "you will manage to have your throat cut, and that ere long. You cannot hide from them your gains and your gold as formerly."

"My gains, wench? my gold?" said the usurer; "alack-a-day, few of these and hard got—few and hard got."

"This will not serve you, father, any longer," said she, "and had not served you thus long, but that Bully Colepepper had contrived a cheaper way of plundering your house, even by means of my miserable self.—But why do I speak to him of all this," she said, checking herself, and shrugging her shoulders with an expression of pity which did not fall much short of scorn. "He hears me not—he thinks not of me.—Is it not strange that the love of gathering gold should survive the care to preserve both property and life?"

"Your father," said Lord Glenvarloch, who could not help respecting the strong sense and feeling shown by this poor woman, even amidst all her rudeness and severity, "your father seems to have his faculties sufficiently alert when he is in the exercise of his ordinary pursuits and functions. I wonder he is not sensible of the weight of your arguments."

"Nature made him a man senseless of danger, and that insensibility is the best thing I have derived from him," said she; "age has left him shrewdness enough to tread his old beaten paths, but not to seek new courses. The old blind horse will long continue to go its rounds in the mill, when it would stumble in the open meadow."

"Daughter!—why, wench—why, housewife!" said the old man, awakening out of some dream, in which he had been sneering and chuckling in imagination, probably over a successful piece of roguery,— "go to chamber, wench—go to chamber—draw bolts and chain—look sharp to door—let none in or out but worshipful Master Grahame—I must take my cloak, and go to Duke Hildebrod—ay, ay, time has been, my own warrant was enough; but the lower we lie, the more are we under the wind."

And, with his wonted chorus of muttering and coughing, the old man left the apartment. His daughter stood for a moment looking after him, with her usual expression of discontent and sorrow.

"You ought to persuade your father," said Nigel, "to leave this evil neighbourhood, if you are in reality apprehensive for his safety."

"He would be safe in no other quarter," said the daughter; "I would rather the old man were dead than publicly dishonoured. In other quarters he would be pelted and pursued, like an owl which ventures into sunshine. Here he was safe, while his comrades could avail themselves of his talents; he is now squeezed and fleeced by them on every pretence. They consider him as a vessel on the strand, from which each may snatch a prey; and the very jealousy which they entertain respecting him as a common property, may perhaps induce them to guard him from more private and daring assaults."

"Still, methinks, you ought to leave this place," answered Nigel, "since you might find a safe retreat in some distant country."

"In Scotland, doubtless," said she, looking at him with a sharp and suspicious eye, "and enrich strangers with our rescued wealth—Ha! young man?"

"Madam, if you knew me," said Lord Glenvarloch, "you would spare the suspicion implied in your words."

"Who shall assure me of that?" said Martha, sharply. "They say you are a brawler and a gamester, and I know how far these are to be trusted by the unhappy."

"They do me wrong, by Heaven!" said Lord Glenvarloch.

"It may be so," said Martha; "I am little interested in the degree of your vice or your folly; but it is plain, that the one or the other has conducted you hither, and that your best hope of peace, safety, and happiness, is to be gone, with the least possible delay, from a place which is always a sty for swine, and often a shambles." So saying, she left the apartment.

There was something in the ungracious manner of this female, amounting almost to contempt of him she spoke to—an indignity to which Glenvarloch, notwithstanding his poverty, had not as yet been personally exposed, and which, therefore, gave him a transitory feeling of painful surprise. Neither did the dark hints which Martha threw out concerning the danger of his place of refuge, sound by any means agreeably to his ears. The bravest man, placed in a situation in which he is surrounded by suspicious persons, and removed from all counsel and assistance, except those afforded by a valiant heart and a strong arm, experiences a sinking of the spirit, a consciousness of abandonment, which for a moment chills his blood, and depresses his natural gallantry of disposition.

But, if sad reflections arose in Nigel's mind, he had not time to indulge them; and, if he saw little prospect of finding friends in Alsatia, he found that he was not likely to be solitary for lack of visitors.

He had scarcely paced his apartment for ten minutes, endeavouring to arrange his ideas on the course which he was to pursue on quitting Alsatia, when he was interrupted by the Sovereign of the quarter, the great Duke Hildebrod himself, before whose approach the bolts and chains of the miser's dwelling fell, or withdrew, as of their own accord; and both the folding leaves of the door were opened, that he might roll himself into the house like a huge butt of liquor, a vessel to which he bore a considerable outward resemblance, both in size, shape, complexion, and contents.

"Good-morrow to your lordship," said the greasy puncheon, cocking his single eye, and rolling it upon Nigel with a singular expression of familiar impudence; whilst his grim bull-dog, which was close at his heels, made a kind of gurgling in his throat, as if saluting, in similar fashion, a starved cat, the only living thing in Trapbois' house which we have not yet enumerated, and which had flown up to the top of the tester, where she stood clutching and grinning at the mastiff, whose greeting she accepted with as much good-will as Nigel bestowed on that of the dog's master.

"Peace, Belzie!—D—n thee, peace!" said Duke Hildebrod. "Beasts and fools will be meddling, my lord."

"I thought, sir," answered Nigel, with as much haughtiness as was consistent with the cool distance which he desired to preserve, "I thought I had told you, my name at present was Nigel Grahame."

His eminence of Whitefriars on this burst out into a loud, chuckling, impudent laugh, repeating the word, till his voice was almost inarticulate,—"Niggle Green—Niggle Green—Niggle Green!—why, my lord, you would be queered in the drinking of a penny pot of Malmsey, if you cry before you are touched. Why, you have told me the secret even now, had I not had a shrewd guess of it before. Why, Master Nigel, since that is the word, I only called you my lord, because we made you a peer of Alsatia last night, when the sack was predominant.—How you look now!—Ha! ha! ha!"

Nigel, indeed, conscious that he had unnecessarily betrayed himself, replied hastily,—"he was much obliged to him for the honours conferred, but did not propose to remain in the Sanctuary long enough to enjoy them."

"Why, that may be as you will, an you will walk by wise counsel," answered the ducal porpoise; and, although Nigel remained standing, in hopes to accelerate his guest's departure, he threw himself into one of the old tapestry-backed easy-chairs, which cracked under his weight, and began to call for old Trapbois.

The crone of all work appearing instead of her master, the Duke cursed her for a careless jade, to let a strange gentleman, and a brave guest, go without his morning's draught.

"I never take one, sir," said Glenvarloch.

"Time to begin—time to begin," answered the Duke.—"Here, you old refuse of Sathan, go to our palace, and fetch Lord Green's morning draught. Let us see—what shall it be, my lord?—a humming double pot of ale, with a roasted crab dancing in it like a wherry above bridge?—or, hum—ay, young men are sweet-toothed—a quart of burnt sack, with sugar and spice?—good against the fogs. Or, what say you to sipping a gill of right distilled waters? Come, we will have them all, and you shall take your choice.—Here, you Jezebel, let Tim send the ale, and the sack, and the nipperkin of double-distilled, with a bit of diet-loaf, or some such trinket, and score it to the new comer."

Glenvarloch, bethinking himself that it might be as well to endure this fellow's insolence for a brief season, as to get into farther discreditable quarrels, suffered him to take his own way, without interruption, only observing, "You make yourself at home, sir, in my apartment; but, for the time, you may use your pleasure. Meanwhile, I would fain know what has procured me the honour of this unexpected visit?"

"You shall know that when old Deb has brought the liquor—I never speak of business dry-lipped. Why, how she drumbles—I warrant she stops to take a sip on the road, and then you will think you have had unchristian measure.—In the meanwhile, look at that dog there—look Belzebub in the face, and tell me if you ever saw a sweeter beast—never flew but at head in his life."

And, after this congenial panegyric, he was proceeding with a tale of a dog and a bull, which threatened to be somewhat of the longest, when he was interrupted by the return of the old crone, and two of his own tapsters, bearing the various kinds of drinkables which he had demanded, and which probably was the only species of interruption he would have endured with equanimity.

When the cups and cans were duly arranged upon the table, and when Deborah, whom the ducal generosity honoured with a penny farthing in the way of gratuity, had withdrawn with her satellites, the worthy potentate, having first slightly invited Lord Glenvarloch to partake of the liquor which he was to pay for, and after having observed, that, excepting three poached eggs, a pint of bastard, and a cup of clary, he was fasting from every thing but sin, set himself seriously to reinforce the radical moisture. Glenvarloch had seen Scottish lairds and Dutch burgomasters at their potations; but their exploits (though each might be termed a thirsty generation) were nothing to those of Duke Hildebrod, who seemed an absolute sandbed, capable of absorbing any given quantity of liquid, without being either vivified or overflowed. He drank off the ale to quench a thirst which, as he said, kept him in a fever from morning to night, and night to morning; tippled off the sack to correct the crudity of the ale; sent the spirits after the sack to keep all quiet, and then declared that, probably, he should not taste liquor till *post meridiem*, unless it was in compliment to some especial friend.

Finally, he intimated that he was ready to proceed on the business which brought him from home so early, a proposition which Nigel readily received, though he could not help suspecting that the most important purpose of Duke Hildebrod's visit was already transacted.

In this, however, Lord Glenvarloch proved to be mistaken. Hildebrod, before opening what he had to say, made an accurate survey of the apartment, laying, from time to time, his finger on his nose, and winking on Nigel with his single eye, while he opened and shut the doors, lifted the tapestry, which concealed, in one or two places, the dilapidation of time upon the wainscoted walls, peeped into closets, and, finally, looked under the bed, to assure himself that the coast was clear of listeners and interlopers. He then resumed his seat, and beckoned confidentially to Nigel to draw his chair close to him.

"I am well as I am, Master Hildebrod," replied the young lord, little disposed to encourage the familiarity which the man endeavoured to fix on him; but the undismayed Duke proceeded as follows:

"You shall pardon me, my lord—and I now give you the title right seriously—if I remind you that our waters may be watched; for though old Trapbois be as deaf as Saint Paul's, yet his daughter has sharp ears, and sharp eyes enough, and it is of them that it is my business to speak."

"Say away, then, sir," said Nigel, edging his chair somewhat closer to the Quicksand, "although I cannot conceive what business I have either with mine host or his daughter."

"We will see that in the twinkling of a quart-pot," answered the gracious Duke; "and first, my lord, you must not think to dance in a net before old Jack Hildebrod, that has thrice your years o'er his head, and was born, like King Richard, with all his eye-teeth ready cut."

"Well, sir, go on," said Nigel.

"Why, then, my lord, I presume to say, that, if you are, as I believe you are, that Lord Glenvarloch whom all the world talk of—the Scotch gallant that has spent all, to a thin cloak and a light purse—be not moved, my lord, it is so noised of you—men call you the sparrow-hawk, who will fly at all—ay, were it in the very Park—Be not moved, my lord."

"I am ashamed, sirrah," replied Glenvarloch, "that you should have power to move me by your insolence—but beware—and, if you indeed guess who I am, consider how long I may be able to endure your tone of insolent familiarity."

"I crave pardon, my lord," said Hildebrod, with a sullen, yet apologetic look; "I meant no harm in speaking my poor mind. I know not what honour there may be in being familiar with your lordship, but I judge there is little safety, for Lowestoffe is laid up in lavender only for having shown you the way into Alsatia; and so, what is to come of those who maintain you when you are here, or whether they will get most honour or most trouble by doing so, I leave with your lordship's better judgment."

"I will bring no one into trouble on my account," said Lord Glenvarloch. "I will leave Whitefriars to-morrow. Nay, by Heaven, I will leave it this day."

"You will have more wit in your anger, I trust," said Duke Hildebrod; "listen first to what I have to say to you, and, if honest Jack Hildebrod puts you not in the way of nicking them all, may he never cast doublets, or dull a greenhorn again! And so, my lord, in plain words, you must wap and win."

"Your words must be still plainer before I can understand them," said Nigel.

"What the devil—a gamester, one who deals with the devil's bones and the doctors, and not understand Pedlar's French! Nay, then, I must speak plain English, and that's the simpleton's tongue."

"Speak, then, sir," said Nigel; "and I pray you be brief, for I have little more time to bestow on you."

"Well, then, my lord, to be brief, as you and the lawyers call it—I understand you have an estate in the north, which changes masters for want of the redeeming ready.—Ay, you start, but you cannot dance in a net before me, as I said before; and so the king runs the frowning humour on you, and the Court vapours you the go-by; and the Prince scowls at you from under his cap; and the favourite serves you out the puckered brow and the cold shoulder; and the favourite's favourite—"

"To go no further, sir," interrupted Nigel, "suppose all this true—and what follows?"

"What follows?" returned Duke Hildebrod. "Marry, this follows, that you will owe good deed, as well as good will, to him who shall put you in the way to walk with your beaver cocked in the presence, as an ye were Earl of Kildare; bully the courtiers; meet the Prince's blighting look with a bold brow; confront the favourite; baffle his deputy, and—"

"This is all well," said Nigel! "but how is it to be accomplished?"

"By making thee a Prince of Peru, my lord of the northern latitudes; propping thine old castle with ingots,—fertilizing thy failing fortunes with gold dust—it shall but cost thee to put thy baron's coronet for a day or so on the brows of an old Caduca here, the man's daughter of the house, and thou art master of a mass of treasure that shall do all I have said for thee, and—"

"What, you would have me marry this old gentlewoman here, the daughter of mine host?" said Nigel, surprised and angry, yet unable to suppress some desire to laugh.

"Nay, my lord, I would have you marry fifty thousand good sterling pounds; for that, and better, hath old Trapbois hoarded; and thou shall do a deed of mercy in it to the old man, who will lose his golden smelts in some worse way—for now that he is well-nigh past his day of work, his day of payment is like to follow."

"Truly, this is a most courteous offer," said Lord Glenvarloch; "but may I pray of your candour, most noble duke, to tell me why you dispose of a ward of so much wealth on a stranger like me, who may leave you to-morrow?"

"In sooth, my lord," said the Duke, "that question smacks more of the wit of Beaujeu's ordinary, than any word I have yet heard your lordship speak, and reason it is you should be answered. Touching my peers, it is but necessary to say, that Mistress Martha Trapbois will none of them, whether clerical or laic. The captain hath asked her, so hath the parson, but she will none of them—she looks higher than either, and is, to say truth, a woman of sense, and so forth, too profound, and of spirit something too high, to put up with greasy buff or rusty prunella. For ourselves, we need but hint that we have a consort in the land of the living, and, what is more to purpose, Mrs. Martha knows it. So, as she will not lace her kersey hood save with a quality binding, you, my lord, must be the man, and must carry off fifty thousand decuses, the spoils of five thousand bullies, cutters, and spendthrifts,—always deducting from the main sum some five thousand pounds for our princely advice and countenance, without which, as matters stand in Alsatia, you would find it hard to win the plate."

"But has your wisdom considered, sir," replied Glenvarloch, "how this wedlock can serve me in my present emergence?"

"As for that, my lord," said Duke Hildebrod, "if, with forty or fifty thousand pounds in your pouch, you cannot save yourself, you will deserve to lose your head for your folly, and your hand for being close-fisted."

"But, since your goodness has taken my matters into such serious consideration," continued Nigel, who conceived there was no prudence in breaking with a man, who, in his way, meant him favour rather than offence, "perhaps you may be able to tell me how my kindred will be likely to receive such a bride as you recommend to me?"

"Touching that matter, my lord, I have always heard your countrymen knew as well as other folks, on which side their bread was buttered. And, truly, speaking from report, I know no place where fifty thousand pounds—fifty thousand pounds, I say—will make a woman more welcome than it is likely to do in your ancient kingdom. And, truly, saving the slight twist in her shoulder, Mrs. Martha Trapbois is a person of very awful and majestic appearance, and may, for aught I know, be come of better blood than any one wots of; for old Trapbois looks not over like to be her father, and her mother was a generous, liberal sort of a woman."

"I am afraid," answered Nigel, "that chance is rather too vague to assure her a gracious reception into an honourable house."

"Why, then, my lord," replied Hildebrod, "I think it like she will be even with them; for I will venture to say, she has as much ill-nature as will make her a match for your whole clan."

"That may inconvenience me a little," replied Nigel.

"Not a whit—not a whit," said the Duke, fertile in expedients; "if she should become rather intolerable, which is not unlikely, your honourable house, which I presume to be a castle, hath, doubtless, both turrets and dungeons, and ye may bestow your bonny bride in either the one or the other, and then you know you will be out of hearing of her tongue, and she will be either above or below the contempt of your friends."

"It is sagely counselled, most equitable sir," replied Nigel, "and such restraint would be a fit meed for her folly that gave me any power over her."

"You entertain the project then, my lord?" said Duke Hildebrod.

"I must turn it in my mind for twenty-four hours," said Nigel; "and I will pray you so to order matters that I be not further interrupted by any visitors."

"We will utter an edict to secure your privacy," said the Duke; "and you do not think," he added, lowering his voice to a confidential whisper, "that ten thousand is too much to pay to the Sovereign, in name of wardship?"

"Ten thousand!" said Lord Glenvarloch; "why, you said five thousand but now."

"Aha! art avised of that?" said the Duke, touching the side of his nose with his finger; "nay, if you have marked me so closely, you are thinking on the case more nearly than I believed, till you trapped me. Well, well, we will not quarrel about the consideration, as old Trapbois would call it—do you win and wear the dame; it will be no hard matter with your face and figure, and I will take care that no one interrupts you. I will have an edict from the Senate as soon as they meet for their meridiem."

So saying, Duke Hildebrod took his leave.

XXIV

This is the time—Heaven's maiden sentinel
Hath quitted her high watch—the lesser spangles
Are paling one by one; give me the ladder
And the short lever—bid Anthony
Keep with his carabine the wicket-gate;
And do thou bare thy knife and follow me,
For we will in and do it—darkness like this
Is dawning of our fortunes.

—*Old Play*

When Duke Hildebrod had withdrawn, Nigel's first impulse was an irresistible feeling to laugh at the sage adviser, who would have thus connected him with age, ugliness, and ill-temper; but his next thought was pity for the unfortunate father and daughter, who, being the only persons possessed of wealth in this unhappy district, seemed like a wreck on the sea-shore of a barbarous country, only secured from plunder for the moment by the jealousy of the tribes among whom it had been cast. Neither could he help being conscious that his own residence here was upon conditions equally precarious, and that he was considered by the Alsatians in the same light of a godsend on the Cornish coast, or a sickly but wealthy caravan travelling through the wilds of Africa, and emphatically termed by the nations of despoilers through whose regions it passes *Dummalafong*, which signifies a thing given to be devoured—a common prey to all men.

Nigel had already formed his own plan to extricate himself, at whatever risk, from his perilous and degrading situation; and, in order that he might carry it into instant execution, he only awaited the return of Lowestoffe's messenger. He expected him, however, in vain, and could only amuse himself by looking through such parts of his baggage as had been sent to him from his former lodgings, in order to select a small packet of the most necessary articles to take with him, in the event of his quitting his lodgings secretly and suddenly, as speed and privacy would, he foresaw, be particularly necessary, if he meant to obtain an interview with the king, which was the course his spirit and his interest alike determined him to pursue.

While he was thus engaged, he found, greatly to his satisfaction, that Master Lowestoffe had transmitted not only his rapier and poniard, but a pair of pistols, which he had used in travelling; of a smaller and more convenient size than the large petronels, or horse pistols, which were then in common use, as being made for wearing at the girdle or in the pockets. Next to having stout and friendly comrades, a man is chiefly emboldened by finding himself well armed in case of need, and Nigel, who had thought with some anxiety on the hazard of trusting his life, if attacked, to the protection of the clumsy weapon with which Lowestoffe had equipped him, in order to complete his disguise, felt an emotion of confidence approaching to triumph, as, drawing his own good and well-tried rapier, he wiped it with his handkerchief, examined its point, bent it once or twice against the ground to prove its well-known metal, and finally replaced it in the scabbard, the more hastily, that he heard a tap at the door of his chamber, and had no mind to be found vapouring in the apartment with his sword drawn.

It was his old host who entered, to tell him with many cringes that the price of his apartment was to be a crown per diem; and that, according to the custom of Whitefriars, the rent was always payable per advance, although he never scrupled to let the money lie till a week or fortnight, or even a month, in the hands of any honourable guest like Master Grahame, always upon some reasonable consideration for the use. Nigel got rid of the old dotard's intrusion, by throwing down two pieces of gold, and requesting the accommodation of his present apartment for eight days, adding, however, he did not think he should tarry so long.

The miser, with a sparkling eye and a trembling hand, clutched fast the proffered coin, and, having balanced the pieces with exquisite pleasure on the extremity of his withered finger, began almost instantly to show that not even the possession of gold can gratify for more than an instant the very heart that is most eager in the pursuit of it. First, the pieces might be light—with hasty hand he drew a small pair of scales from his bosom, and weighed them, first together, then separately, and smiled with glee as he saw them attain the due depression in the balance—a circumstance which might add to his profits, if it were true, as was currently reported, that little of the gold coinage was current in Alsatia in a perfect state, and that none ever left the Sanctuary in that condition.

Another fear then occurred to trouble the old miser's pleasure. He had been just able to comprehend that Nigel intended to leave the Friars sooner than the arrival of the term for which he had deposited the rent. This might imply an expectation of refunding, which, as a Scotch wag said, of all species of funding, jumped least with the old gentleman's humour. He was beginning to enter a hypothetical caveat on this subject, and to quote several reasons why no part of the money once consigned as room-rent, could be repaid back on any pretence, without great hardship to the landlord, when Nigel, growing impatient, told him that the money was his absolutely, and without any intention on his part of resuming any of it—all he asked in return was the liberty of enjoying in private the apartment he had paid for. Old Trapbois, who had still at his tongue's end much of the smooth language, by which, in his time, he had hastened the ruin of many a young spendthrift, began to launch out upon the noble and generous disposition of his new guest, until Nigel, growing impatient, took the old gentleman by the hand, and gently, yet irresistibly, leading him to the door of the chamber, put him out, but with such decent and moderate exertion of his superior strength, as to render the action in no shape indecorous, and, fastening the door, began to do that for his pistols which he had done for his favourite sword, examining with care the flints and locks, and reviewing the state of his small provision of ammunition.

In this operation he was a second time interrupted by a knocking at the door—he called upon the person to enter, having no doubt that it was Lowestoffe's messenger at length arrived. It was, however, the ungracious daughter of old Trapbois, who, muttering something about her father's mistake, laid down upon the table one of the pieces of gold which Nigel had just given to him, saying, that what she retained was the full rent for the term he had specified. Nigel replied, he had paid the money, and had no desire to receive it again.

"Do as you will with it, then," replied his hostess, "for there it lies, and shall lie for me. If you are fool enough to pay more than is reason, my father shall not be knave enough to take it."

"But your father, mistress," said Nigel, "your father told me—"

"Oh, my father, my father," said she, interrupting him,—"my father managed these affairs while he was able—I manage them now, and that may in the long run be as well for both of us."

She then looked on the table, and observed the weapons.

"You have arms, I see," she said; "do you know how to use them?"

"I should do so mistress," replied Nigel, "for it has been my occupation."

"You are a soldier, then?" she demanded.

"No farther as yet, than as every gentleman of my country is a soldier."

"Ay, that is your point of honour—to cut the throats of the poor—a proper gentlemanlike occupation for those who should protect them!"

"I do not deal in cutting throats, mistress," replied Nigel; "but I carry arms to defend myself, and my country if it needs me."

"Ay," replied Martha, "it is fairly worded; but men say you are as prompt as others in petty brawls, where neither your safety nor your country is in hazard; and that had it not been so, you would not have been in the Sanctuary to-day."

"Mistress," returned Nigel, "I should labour in vain to make you understand that a man's honour, which is, or should be, dearer to him than his life, may often call on and compel us to hazard our own lives, or those of others, on what would otherwise seem trifling contingencies."

"God's law says nought of that," said the female; "I have only read there, that thou shall not kill. But I have neither time nor inclination to preach to you—you will find enough of fighting here if you like it, and well if it come not to seek you when you are least prepared. Farewell for the present—the char-woman will execute your commands for your meals."

She left the room, just as Nigel, provoked at her assuming a superior tone of judgment and of censure, was about to be so superfluous as to enter into a dispute with an old pawnbroker's daughter on the subject of the point of honour. He smiled at himself for the folly into which the spirit of self-vindication had so nearly hurried him.

Lord Glenvarloch then applied to old Deborah the char-woman, by whose intermediation he was provided with a tolerably decent dinner; and the only embarrassment which he experienced, was from the almost forcible entry of the old dotard his landlord, who insisted upon giving his assistance at laying the cloth. Nigel had some difficulty to prevent him from displacing his arms and some papers which were lying on a small table at which he had been sitting; and nothing short of a stern and positive injunction to the contrary could compel him to use another board (though there were two in the room) for the purpose of laying the cloth.

Having at length obliged him to relinquish his purpose, he could not help observing that the eyes of the old dotard seemed still anxiously fixed upon the small table on which lay his sword and pistols; and that, amidst all the little duties which he seemed officiously anxious to render to his guest, he took every opportunity of looking towards and approaching these objects of his attention. At length, when Trapbois thought he had completely avoided the notice of his guest, Nigel, through the observation of one of the cracked mirrors, oh which channel of communication the old man had not calculated, beheld him actually extend his hand towards the table in question. He thought it unnecessary to use further ceremony, but telling his landlord, in a stern voice, that he permitted no one to touch his arms, he commanded him to leave the apartment. The old usurer commenced a maundering sort of apology, in which all that Nigel distinctly apprehended, was a frequent repetition of the word *consideration*, and which did not seem to him to require any other answer than a reiteration of his command to him to leave the apartment, upon pain of worse consequences.

The ancient Hebe who acted as Lord Glenvarloch's cup-bearer, took his part against the intrusion of the still more antiquated Ganymede, and insisted on old Trapbois leaving the room instantly, menacing him at the same time with her mistress's displeasure if he remained there any longer. The old man seemed more under petticoat government than any other, for the threat of the char-woman produced greater effect upon him than the more formidable displeasure of Nigel. He withdrew grumbling and muttering, and Lord Glenvarloch heard him bar a large door at the nearer end of the gallery, which served as a division betwixt the other parts of the extensive mansion, and the apartment occupied by his guest, which, as the reader is aware, had its access from the landing-place at the head of the grand staircase.

Nigel accepted the careful sound of the bolts and bars as they were severally drawn by the trembling hand of old Trapbois, as an omen that the senior did not mean again to revisit him in the course of the evening, and heartily rejoiced that he was at length to be left to uninterrupted solitude.

The old woman asked if there was aught else to be done for his accommodation; and, indeed, it had hitherto seemed as if the pleasure of serving him, or more properly the reward which she expected, had renewed her youth and activity. Nigel desired to have candles, to have a fire lighted in his apartment, and a few fagots placed beside it, that he might feed it from time to time, as he began to feel the chilly effects of the damp and low situation of the house, close as it was to the Thames.

But while the old woman was absent upon his errand, he began to think in what way he should pass the long solitary evening with which he was threatened.

His own reflections promised to Nigel little amusement, and less applause. He had considered his own perilous situation in every light in which it could be viewed, and foresaw as little utility as comfort in resuming the survey. To divert the current of his ideas, books were, of course, the readiest resource; and although, like most of us, Nigel had, in his time, sauntered through large libraries, and even spent a long time there without greatly disturbing their learned contents, he was now in a situation where the possession of a volume, even of very inferior merit, becomes a real treasure. The old housewife returned shortly afterwards with fagots, and some pieces of half-burnt wax-candles, the perquisites, probably, real or usurped, of some experienced groom of the chambers, two of which she placed in large brass candlesticks, of different shapes and patterns, and laid the others on the table, that Nigel might renew them from time to time as they burnt to the socket. She heard with interest Lord Glenvarloch's request to have a book—any sort of book— to pass away the night withal, and returned for answer, that she knew of no other books in the house than her young mistress's (as she always denominated Mistress Martha Trapbois) Bible, which the owner would not lend; and her master's Whetstone of Witte, being the second part of Arithmetic, by Robert Record, with the Cossike Practice and Rule of Equation; which promising volume Nigel declined to borrow. She offered, however, to bring him some books from Duke Hildebrod— "who sometimes, good gentleman, gave a glance at a book when the State affairs of Alsatia left him as much leisure."

Nigel embraced the proposal, and his unwearied Iris scuttled away on this second embassy. She returned in a short time with a tattered quarto volume under her arm, and a bottle of sack in her hand; for the Duke, judging that mere reading was dry work, had sent the wine by way of sauce to help it down, not forgetting to add the price to the morning's score, which he had already run up against the stranger in the Sanctuary.

Nigel seized on the book, and did not refuse the wine, thinking that a glass or two, as it really proved to be of good quality, would be no bad interlude to his studies. He dismissed, with thanks and assurance of reward, the poor old drudge who had been so zealous in his service; trimmed his fire and candles, and placed the easiest of the old arm-chairs in a convenient posture betwixt the fire and the table at which he had dined, and which now supported the measure of sack and the lights; and thus accompanying his studies with such luxurious appliances as were in his power, he began to examine the only volume with which the ducal library of Alsatia had been able to supply him.

The contents, though of a kind generally interesting, were not well calculated to dispel the gloom by which he was surrounded. The book was entitled "God's Revenge against Murther;" not, as the bibliomaniacal reader may easily conjecture, the work which Reynolds published under that imposing name, but one of a much earlier date, printed and sold by old Wolfe; and which, could a copy now be found, would sell for much more than its weight in gold.* Nigel had soon enough of the doleful tales which the book contains, and attempted one or two other modes of killing the evening. He looked out at window, but the night was rainy, with gusts of wind; he tried to coax the fire, but the fagots were green, and smoked without burning; and as he was naturally temperate, he felt his blood somewhat heated by the canary sack which he had already drank, and had no farther inclination to that pastime. He next attempted to compose a memorial addressed to the king, in which he set forth his case and his grievances; but, speedily stung with the idea that his supplication would be treated with scorn, he flung the scroll into the fire, and, in a sort of desperation, resumed the book which he had laid aside.

Nigel became more interested in the volume at the second than at the first attempt which he made to peruse it. The narratives, strange and shocking as they were to human feeling, possessed yet the interest of sorcery or of fascination, which rivets the attention by its awakening horrors. Much was told of the strange and horrible acts of blood by which men, setting nature and humanity alike at defiance, had, for the thirst of revenge, the lust of gold, or the cravings of irregular ambition, broken into the tabernacle of life. Yet more surprising and mysterious tales were recounted of the mode in which such deeds of blood had come to be discovered and revenged. Animals, irrational animals, had told the secret, and birds of the air had carried the matter. The elements

---

* Only three copies are known to exist; one in the library at Kennaquhair, and two—one foxed and cropped, the other tall and in good condition—both in the possession of an eminent member of the Roxburghe Club.—*Note by* CAPTAIN CLUTTERBUCK.

had seemed to betray the deed which had polluted them—earth had ceased to support the murderer's steps, fire to warm his frozen limbs, water to refresh his parched lips, air to relieve his gasping lungs. All, in short, bore evidence to the homicide's guilt. In other circumstances, the criminal's own awakened conscience pursued and brought him to justice; and in some narratives the grave was said to have yawned, that the ghost of the sufferer might call for revenge.

It was now wearing late in the night, and the book was still in Nigel's hands, when the tapestry which hung behind him flapped against the wall, and the wind produced by its motion waved the flame of the candles by which he was reading. Nigel started and turned round, in that excited and irritated state of mind which arose from the nature of his studies, especially at a period when a certain degree of superstition was inculcated as a point of religious faith. It was not without emotion that he saw the bloodless countenance, meagre form, and ghastly aspect of old Trapbois, once more in the very act of extending his withered hand towards the table which supported his arms. Convinced by this untimely apparition that something evil was meditated towards him, Nigel sprung up, seized his sword, drew it, and placing it at the old man's breast, demanded of him what he did in his apartment at so untimely an hour. Trapbois showed neither fear nor surprise, and only answered by some imperfect expressions, intimating he would part with his life rather than with his property; and Lord Glenvarloch, strangely embarrassed, knew not what to think of the intruder's motives, and still less how to get rid of him. As he again tried the means of intimidation, he was surprised by a second apparition from behind the tapestry, in the person of the daughter of Trapbois, bearing a lamp in her hand. She also seemed to possess her father's insensibility to danger, for, coming close to Nigel, she pushed aside impetuously his naked sword, and even attempted to take it out of his hand.

"For shame," she said, "your sword on a man of eighty years and more!—this the honour of a Scottish gentleman!—give it to me to make a spindle of!"

"Stand back," said Nigel; "I mean your father no injury—but I *will* know what has caused him to prowl this whole day, and even at this late hour of night, around my arms."

"Your arms!" repeated she; "alas! young man, the whole arms in the Tower of London are of little value to him, in comparison of this miserable piece of gold which I left this morning on the table of a young spendthrift, too careless to put what belonged to him into his own purse."

So saying, she showed the piece of gold, which, still remaining on the table, where she left it, had been the bait that attracted old Trapbois so frequently to the spot; and which, even in the silence of the night, had so dwelt on his imagination, that he had made use of a private passage long disused, to enter his guest's apartment, in order to possess himself of the treasure during his slumbers. He now exclaimed, at the highest tones of his cracked and feeble voice—

"It is mine—it is mine!—he gave it to me for a consideration—I will die ere I part with my property!"

"It is indeed his own, mistress," said Nigel, "and I do entreat you to restore it to the person on whom I have bestowed it, and let me have my apartment in quiet."

"I will account with you for it, then,"—said the maiden, reluctantly giving to her father the morsel of Mammon, on which he darted as if his bony fingers had been the talons of a hawk seizing its prey; and then making a contented muttering and mumbling, like an old dog after he has been fed, and just when he is wheeling himself thrice round for the purpose of lying down, he followed his daughter behind the tapestry, through a little sliding-door, which was perceived when the hangings were drawn apart.

"This shall be properly fastened to-morrow," said the daughter to Nigel, speaking in such a tone that her father, deaf, and engrossed by his acquisition, could not hear her; "to-night I will continue to watch him closely.—I wish you good repose."

These few words, pronounced in a tone of more civility than she had yet made use of towards her lodger, contained a wish which was not to be accomplished, although her guest, presently after her departure, retired to bed.

There was a slight fever in Nigel's blood, occasioned by the various events of the evening, which put him, as the phrase is, beside his rest. Perplexing and painful thoughts rolled on his mind like a troubled stream, and the more he laboured to lull himself to slumber, the farther he seemed from attaining his object. He tried all the resources common in such cases; kept counting from one to a thousand, until his head was giddy—he watched the embers of the wood fire till his eyes were dazzled—he listened to the dull moaning of the wind, the swinging and creaking of signs which projected from the houses, and the baying of here and there a homeless dog, till his very ear was weary.

Suddenly, however, amid this monotony, came a sound which startled him at once. It was a female shriek. He sat up in his bed to listen, then remembered he was in Alsatia, where brawls of every sort were current among the unruly inhabitants. But another scream, and another, and another, succeeded so close, that he was certain, though the noise was remote and sounded stifled, it must be in the same house with himself.

Nigel jumped up hastily, put on a part of his clothes, seized his sword and pistols, and ran to the door of his chamber. Here he plainly heard the screams redoubled, and, as he thought, the sounds came from the usurer's apartment. All access to the gallery was effectually excluded by the intermediate door, which the brave young lord shook with eager, but vain impatience. But the secret passage occurred suddenly to his recollection. He hastened back to his room, and succeeded with some difficulty in lighting a candle, powerfully agitated by hearing the cries repeated, yet still more afraid lest they should sink into silence.

He rushed along the narrow and winding entrance, guided by the noise, which now burst more wildly on his ear; and, while he descended a narrow staircase which terminated the passage, he heard the stifled voices of men, encouraging, as it seemed, each other. "D—n her, strike her down—silence her—beat her brains out!"—while the voice of his hostess, though now almost exhausted, was repeating the cry of "murder," and "help." At the bottom of the staircase was a small door, which gave way before Nigel as he precipitated himself upon the scene of action,—a cocked pistol in one hand, a candle in the other, and his naked sword under his arm.

Two ruffians had, with great difficulty, overpowered, or, rather, were on the point of overpowering, the daughter of Trapbois, whose resistance appeared to have been most desperate, for the floor was covered with fragments of her clothes, and handfuls of her hair. It appeared that her life was about to be the price of her defence, for one villain had drawn a long clasp-knife, when they were surprised by the entrance of Nigel, who, as they turned towards him, shot the fellow with the knife dead on the spot, and when the other advanced to him, hurled the candlestick at his head, and then attacked him with his sword. It was dark, save some pale moonlight from the window; and the ruffian, after firing a pistol without effect, and fighting a traverse or two with his sword, lost heart, made for the window, leaped over it, and escaped. Nigel fired his remaining pistol after him at a venture, and then called for light.

"There is light in the kitchen," answered Martha Trapbois, with more presence of mind than could have been expected. "Stay, you know not the way; I will fetch it myself.—Oh! my father—my poor father!—I knew it would come to this—and all along of the accursed gold!—They have *murdered* him!"

XXV

Death finds us 'mid our playthings—snatches us,
As a cross nurse might do a wayward child,
From all our toys and baubles. His rough call
Unlooses all our favourite ties on earth;
And well if they are such as may be answer'd
In yonder world, where all is judged of truly.

—Old Play

It was a ghastly scene which opened, upon Martha Trapbois's return with a light. Her own haggard and austere features were exaggerated by all the desperation of grief, fear, and passion—but the latter was predominant. On the floor lay the body of the robber, who had expired without a groan, while his blood, flowing plentifully, had crimsoned all around. Another body lay also there, on which the unfortunate woman precipitated herself in agony, for it was that of her unhappy father. In the next moment she started up, and exclaiming—"There may be life yet!" strove to raise the body. Nigel went to her assistance, but not without a glance at the open window; which Martha, as acute as if undisturbed either by passion or terror, failed not to interpret justly.

"Fear not," she cried, "fear not; they are base cowards, to whom courage is as much unknown as mercy. If I had had weapons, I could have defended myself against them without assistance or protection.— Oh! my poor father! protection comes too late for this cold and stiff corpse.—He is dead—dead!"

While she spoke, they were attempting to raise the dead body of the old miser; but it was evident, even from the feeling of the inactive weight and rigid joints, that life had forsaken her station. Nigel looked for a wound, but saw none. The daughter of the deceased, with more presence of mind than a daughter could at the time have been supposed capable of exerting, discovered the instrument of his murder—a sort of scarf, which had been drawn so tight round his throat, as to stifle his cries for assistance, in the first instance, and afterwards to extinguish life.

She undid the fatal noose; and, laying the old man's body in the arms of Lord Glenvarloch, she ran for water, for spirits, for essences, in the vain hope that life might be only suspended. That hope proved indeed vain. She chafed his temples, raised his head, loosened his nightgown, (for it seemed as if he had arisen from bed upon hearing the entrance of the villains,) and, finally, opened, with difficulty, his fixed and closely-clenched hands, from one of which dropped a key, from the other the very piece of gold about which the unhappy man had been a little before so anxious, and which probably, in the impaired state of his mental faculties, he was disposed to defend with as desperate energy as if its amount had been necessary to his actual existence.

"It is in vain—it is in vain," said the daughter, desisting from her fruitless attempts to recall the spirit which had been effectually dislodged, for the neck had been twisted by the violence of the murderers; "It is in vain—he is murdered—I always knew it would be thus; and now I witness it!"

She then snatched up the key and the piece of money, but it was only to dash them again on the floor, as she exclaimed, "Accursed be ye both, for you are the causes of this deed!"

Nigel would have spoken—would have reminded her, that measures should be instantly taken for the pursuit of the murderer who had escaped, as well as for her own security against his return; but she interrupted him sharply.

"Be silent," she said, "be silent. Think you, the thoughts of my own heart are not enough to distract me, and with such a sight as this before me? I say, be silent," she said again, and in a yet sterner tone—"Can a daughter listen, and her father's murdered corpse lying on her knees?"

Lord Glenvarloch, however overpowered by the energy of her grief, felt not the less the embarrassment of his own situation. He had discharged both his pistols—the robber might return—he had probably other assistants besides the man who had fallen, and it seemed to him, indeed, as if he had heard a muttering beneath the windows. He explained hastily to his companion the necessity of procuring ammunition.

"You are right," she said, somewhat contemptuously, "and have ventured already more than ever I expected of man. Go, and shift for yourself, since that is your purpose—leave me to my fate."

Without stopping for needless expostulation, Nigel hastened to his own room through the secret passage, furnished himself with the ammunition he sought for, and returned with the same celerity; wondering himself at the accuracy with which he achieved, in the dark, all the meanderings of the passage which he had traversed only once, and that in a moment of such violent agitation.

He found, on his return, the unfortunate woman standing like a statue by the body of her father, which she had laid straight on the floor, having covered the face with the skirt of his gown. She testified neither surprise nor pleasure at Nigel's return, but said to him calmly—"My moan is made—my sorrow—all the sorrow at least that man shall ever have noting of, is gone past; but I will have justice, and the base villain who murdered this poor defenceless old man, when he had not, by the course of nature, a twelvemonth's life in him, shall not cumber the earth long after him. Stranger, whom heaven has sent to forward the revenge reserved for this action, go to Hildebrod's—there they are awake all night in their revels—bid him come hither—he is bound by his duty, and dare not, and shall not, refuse his assistance, which he knows well I can reward. Why do ye tarry?—go instantly."

"I would," said Nigel, "but I am fearful of leaving you alone; the villains may return, and—"

"True, most true," answered Martha, "he may return; and, though I care little for his murdering me, he may possess himself of what has most tempted him. Keep this key and this piece of gold; they are both of importance—defend your life if assailed, and if you kill the villain I will make you rich. I go myself to call for aid."

Nigel would have remonstrated with her, but she had departed, and in a moment he heard the house-door clank behind her. For an instant he thought of following her; but upon recollection that the distance was but short betwixt the tavern of Hildebrod and the house of Trapbois, he concluded that she knew it better than he—incurred little danger in passing it, and that he would do well in the meanwhile to remain on the watch as she recommended.

It was no pleasant situation for one unused to such scenes to remain in the apartment with two dead bodies, recently those of living and breathing men, who had both, within the space of less than half an hour, suffered violent death; one of them by the hand of the assassin, the other, whose blood still continued to flow from the wound in his throat, and to flood all around him, by the spectator's own deed of violence, though of justice. He turned his face from those wretched relics of mortality with a feeling of disgust, mingled with superstition; and he found, when he had done so, that the consciousness of the presence of these ghastly objects, though unseen by him, rendered him more uncomfortable than even when he had his eyes fixed upon, and reflected by, the cold, staring, lifeless eyeballs of the deceased. Fancy also played her usual sport with him. He now thought he heard the well-worn damask nightgown of the deceased usurer rustle; anon, that he heard the slaughtered bravo draw up his leg, the boot scratching the floor as if he was about to rise; and again he deemed he heard the footsteps and the whisper of the returned ruffian under the window from which he had lately escaped. To face the last and most real danger, and to parry the terrors which the other class of feelings were like to impress upon him, Nigel went to the window, and was much cheered to observe the light of several torches illuminating the street, and followed, as the murmur of voices denoted, by a number of persons, armed, it would seem, with firelocks and halberds, and attendant on Hildebrod, who (not in his fantastic office of duke, but in that which he really possessed of bailiff of the liberty and sanctuary of Whitefriars) was on his way to inquire into the crime and its circumstances.

It was a strange and melancholy contrast to see these debauchees, disturbed in the very depth of their midnight revel, on their arrival at such a scene as this. They stared on each other, and on the bloody work before them, with lack-lustre eyes; staggered with uncertain steps over boards slippery with blood; their noisy brawling voices sunk into stammering whispers; and, with spirits quelled by what they saw, while their brains were still stupefied by the liquor which they had drunk, they seemed like men walking in their sleep.

Old Hildebrod was an exception to the general condition. That seasoned cask, however full, was at all times capable of motion, when there occurred a motive sufficiently strong to set him a-rolling. He seemed much shocked at what he beheld, and his proceedings, in consequence, had more in them of regularity and propriety, than he might have been supposed capable of exhibiting upon any occasion whatever. The daughter was first examined, and stated, with wonderful accuracy and distinctness, the manner in which she had been alarmed with a noise of struggling and violence in her father's apartment, and that the more readily, because she was watching him on account of some alarm concerning his health. On her entrance, she had seen her father sinking under the strength of two men, upon whom she rushed with all the fury she was capable of. As their faces were blackened, and their figures disguised, she could not pretend, in the hurry of a moment so dreadfully agitating, to distinguish either of them as persons whom she had seen before. She remembered little more except the firing of shots, until she found herself alone with her guest, and saw that the ruffians had escaped. Lord Glenvarloch told his story as we have given it to the reader. The direct evidence thus received, Hildebrod examined the premises. He found that the villains had made their entrance by the window out of which the survivor had made his escape; yet it seemed singular that they should have done so, as it was secured with strong iron bars, which old Trapbois was in the habit of shutting with his own hand at nightfall. He minuted down with great accuracy, the state of every thing in the apartment, and examined carefully the features of the slain robber. He was dressed like a seaman of the lowest order, but his face was known to none present. Hildebrod next sent for an Alsatian surgeon, whose vices, undoing what his skill might have done for him, had consigned him to the wretched practice of this place. He made him examine the dead bodies, and make a proper declaration of the manner in which the sufferers seemed to have come by their end. The circumstances of the sash did not escape the learned judge, and having listened to all that could be heard or conjectured on the subject, and collected all particulars of evidence which appeared to bear on the bloody transaction, he commanded the door of the apartment to be locked until next morning; and carrying, the unfortunate daughter of the murdered man into the kitchen, where there was no one in presence but Lord Glenvarloch, he asked her gravely, whether she suspected no one in particular of having committed the deed.

"Do *you* suspect no one?" answered Martha, looking fixedly on him.

"Perhaps, I may, mistress; but it is my part to ask questions, yours to answer them. That's the rule of the game."

"Then I suspect him who wore yonder sash. Do not you know whom I mean?"

"Why, if you call on me for honours, I must needs say I have seen Captain Peppercull have one of such a fashion, and he was not a man to change his suits often."

"Send out, then," said Martha, "and have him apprehended."

"If it is he, he will be far by this time; but I will communicate with the higher powers," answered the judge.

"You would have him escape," resumed she, fixing her eyes on him sternly.

"By cock and pie," replied Hildebrod, "did it depend on me, the murdering cut-throat should hang as high as ever Haman did—but let me take my time. He has friends among us, *that* you wot well; and all that should assist me are as drunk as fiddlers."

"I will have revenge—I *will* have it," repeated she; "and take heed you trifle not with me."

"Trifle! I would sooner trifle with a she-bear the minute after they had baited her. I tell you, mistress, be but patient, and we will have him. I know all his haunts, and he cannot forbear them long; and I will have trap-doors open for him. You cannot want justice, mistress, for you have the means to get it."

"They who help me in my revenge," said Martha, "shall share those means."

"Enough said," replied Hildebrod; "and now I would have you go to my house, and get something hot—you will be but dreary here by yourself."

"I will send for the old char-woman," replied Martha, "and we have the stranger gentleman, besides."

"Umph, umph—the stranger gentleman!" said Hildebrod to Nigel, whom he drew a little apart. "I fancy the captain has made the stranger gentleman's fortune when he was making a bold dash for his own. I can tell your honour—I must not say lordship—that I think my having chanced to give the greasy buff-and-iron scoundrel some hint of what I recommended to you to-day, has put him on this rough game. The better for you—you will get the cash without the father-in-law.—You will keep conditions, I trust?"

"I wish you had said nothing to any one of a scheme so absurd," said Nigel.

"Absurd!—Why, think you she will not have thee? Take her with the tear in her eye, man—take her with the tear in her eye. Let me hear from you to-morrow. Good-night, good-night—a nod is as good as a wink. I must to my business of sealing and locking up. By the way, this horrid work has put all out of my head.—Here is a fellow from Mr. Lowestoffe has been asking to see you. As he said his business was express, the Senate only made him drink a couple of flagons, and he was just coming to beat up your quarters when this breeze blew up.— Ahey, friend! there is Master Nigel Grahame."

A young man, dressed in a green plush jerkin, with a badge on the sleeve, and having the appearance of a waterman, approached and took Nigel aside, while Duke Hildebrod went from place to place to exercise his authority, and to see the windows fastened, and the doors of the apartment locked up. The news communicated by Lowestoffe's messenger were not the most pleasant. They were intimated in a courteous whisper to Nigel, to the following effect:—That Master Lowestoffe prayed him to consult his safety by instantly leaving Whitefriars, for that a warrant from the Lord Chief-Justice had been issued out for apprehending him, and would be put in force to-morrow, by the assistance of a party of musketeers, a force which the Alsatians neither would nor dared to resist.

"And so, squire," said the aquatic emissary, "my wherry is to wait you at the Temple Stairs yonder, at five this morning, and, if you would give the blood-hounds the slip, why, you may."

"Why did not Master Lowestoffe write to me?" said Nigel.

"Alas! the good gentleman lies up in lavender for it himself, and has as little to do with pen and ink as if he were a parson."

"Did he send any token to me?" said Nigel.

"Token!—ay, marry did he—token enough, an I have not forgot it," said the fellow; then, giving a hoist to the waistband of his breeches, he said,—"Ay, I have it—you were to believe me, because your name was written with an O, for Grahame. Ay, that was it, I think.—Well, shall we meet in two hours, when tide turns, and go down the river like a twelve-oared barge?"

"Where is the king just now, knowest thou?" answered Lord Glenvarloch.

"The king! why, he went down to Greenwich yesterday by water, like a noble sovereign as he is, who will always float where he can. He was to have hunted this week, but that purpose is broken, they say; and the Prince, and the Duke, and all of them at Greenwich, are as merry as minnows."

"Well," replied Nigel, "I will be ready to go at five; do thou come hither to carry my baggage."

"Ay, ay, master," replied the fellow, and left the house mixing himself with the disorderly attendants of Duke Hildebrod, who were now retiring. That potentate entreated Nigel to make fast the doors behind him, and, pointing to the female who sat by the expiring fire with her limbs outstretched, like one whom the hand of Death had already arrested, he whispered, "Mind your hits, and mind your bargain, or I will cut your bow-string for you before you can draw it."

Feeling deeply the ineffable brutality which could recommend the prosecuting such views over a wretch in such a condition, Lord Glenvarloch yet commanded his temper so far as to receive the advice in silence, and attend to the former part of it, by barring the door carefully behind Duke Hildebrod and his suite, with the tacit hope that he should never again see or hear of them. He then returned to the kitchen, in which the unhappy woman remained, her hands still clenched, her eyes fixed, and her limbs extended, like those of a person in a trance. Much moved by her situation, and with the prospect which lay before her, he endeavoured to awaken her to existence by every means in his power, and at length apparently succeeded in dispelling her stupor, and attracting her attention. He then explained to her that he was in the act of leaving Whitefriars in a few hours—that his future destination was uncertain, but that he desired anxiously to know whether he could contribute to her protection by apprizing any friend of her situation, or otherwise. With some difficulty she seemed to comprehend his meaning, and thanked him with her usual short ungracious manner. "He might mean well," she said, "but he ought to know that the miserable had no friends."

Nigel said, "He would not willingly be importunate, but, as he was about to leave the Friars—" She interrupted him—

"You are about to leave the Friars? I will go with you."

"You go with me!" exclaimed Lord Glenvarloch.

"Yes," she said, "I will persuade my father to leave this murdering den." But, as she spoke, the more perfect recollection of what had passed crowded on her mind. She hid her face in her hands, and burst out into a dreadful fit of sobs, moans, and lamentations, which terminated in hysterics, violent in proportion to the uncommon strength of her body and mind.

Lord Glenvarloch, shocked, confused, and inexperienced, was about to leave the house in quest of medical, or at least female assistance; but the patient, when the paroxysm had somewhat spent its force, held him fast by the sleeve with one hand, covering her face with the other, while a copious flood of tears came to relieve the emotions of grief by which she had been so violently agitated.

"Do not leave me," she said—"do not leave me, and call no one. I have never been in this way before, and would not now," she said, sitting upright, and wiping her eyes with her apron,—"would not now—but that—but that he loved *me*. if he loved nothing else that was human— To die so, and by such hands!"

And again the unhappy woman gave way to a paroxysm of sorrow, mingling her tears with sobbing, wailing, and all the abandonment of female grief, when at its utmost height. At length, she gradually recovered the austerity of her natural composure, and maintained it as if by a forcible exertion of resolution, repelling, as she spoke, the repeated returns of the hysterical affection, by such an effort as that by which epileptic patients are known to suspend the recurrence of their fits. Yet her mind, however resolved, could not so absolutely overcome the affection of her nerves, but that she was agitated by strong fits of trembling, which, for a minute or two at a time, shook her whole frame in a manner frightful to witness. Nigel forgot his own situation, and, indeed, every thing else, in the interest inspired by the unhappy woman before him—an interest which affected a proud spirit the more deeply, that she herself, with correspondent highness of mind, seemed determined to owe as little as possible either to the humanity or the pity of others.

"I am not wont to be in this way," she said,—"but—but—Nature will have power over the frail beings it has made. Over you, sir, I have some right; for, without you, I had not survived this awful night. I wish your aid had been either earlier or later—but you have saved my life, and you are bound to assist in making it endurable to me."

"If you will show me how it is possible," answered Nigel.

"You are going hence, you say, instantly—carry me with you," said the unhappy woman. "By my own efforts, I shall never escape from this wilderness of guilt and misery."

"Alas! what can I do for you?" replied Nigel. "My own way, and I must not deviate from it, leads me, in all probability, to a dungeon. I might, indeed, transport you from hence with me, if you could afterwards bestow yourself with any friend."

"Friend!" she exclaimed—"I have no friend—they have long since discarded us. A spectre arising from the dead were more welcome than I should be at the doors of those who have disclaimed us; and, if they were willing to restore their friendship to me now, I would despise it, because they withdrew it from him—from him"—(here she underwent strong but suppressed agitation, and then added firmly)—"from *him* who lies yonder.—I have no friend." Here she paused; and then suddenly, as if recollecting herself, added, "I have no friend, but I have that will purchase many—I have that which will purchase both friends and avengers.—It is well thought of; I must not leave it for a prey to cheats and ruffians.—Stranger, you must return to yonder room. Pass through it boldly to his—that is, to the sleeping apartment; push the bedstead aside; beneath each of the posts is a brass plate, as if to support the weight, but it is that upon the left, nearest to the wall, which must serve your turn—press the corner of the plate, and it will spring up and show a keyhole, which this key will open. You will then lift a concealed trap-door, and in a cavity of the floor you will discover a small chest. Bring it hither; it shall accompany our journey, and it will be hard if the contents cannot purchase me a place of refuge."

"But the door communicating with the kitchen has been locked by these people," said Nigel.

"True, I had forgot; they had their reasons for that, doubtless," answered she. "But the secret passage from your apartment is open, and you may go that way."

Lord Glenvarloch took the key, and, as he lighted a lamp to show him the way, she read in his countenance some unwillingness to the task imposed.

"You fear?" said she—"there is no cause; the murderer and his victim are both at rest. Take courage, I will go with you myself—you cannot know the trick of the spring, and the chest will be too heavy for you."

"No fear, no fear," answered Lord Glenvarloch, ashamed of the construction she put upon a momentary hesitation, arising from a dislike to look upon what is horrible, often connected with those high-wrought minds which are the last to fear what is merely dangerous—"I will do your errand as you desire; but for you, you must not—cannot go yonder."

"I can—I will," she said. "I am composed. You shall see that I am so." She took from the table a piece of unfinished sewing-work, and, with steadiness and composure, passed a silken thread into the eye of a fine needle.—"Could I have done that," she said, with a smile yet more ghastly than her previous look of fixed despair, "had not my heart and hand been both steady?"

She then led the way rapidly up stairs to Nigel's chamber, and proceeded through the secret passage with the same haste, as if she had feared her resolution might have failed her ere her purpose was executed. At the bottom of the stairs she paused a moment, before entering the fatal apartment, then hurried through with a rapid step to the sleeping chamber beyond, followed closely by Lord Glenvarloch, whose reluctance to approach the scene of butchery was altogether lost in the anxiety which he felt on account of the survivor of the tragedy.

Her first action was to pull aside the curtains of her father's bed. The bed-clothes were thrown aside in confusion, doubtless in the action of his starting from sleep to oppose the entrance of the villains into the next apartment. The hard mattress scarcely showed the slight pressure where the emaciated body of the old miser had been deposited. His daughter sank beside the bed, clasped her hands, and prayed to heaven, in a short and affectionate manner, for support in her affliction, and for vengeance on the villains who had made her fatherless. A low-muttered and still more brief petition recommended to Heaven the soul of the sufferer, and invoked pardon for his sins, in virtue of the great Christian atonement.

This duty of piety performed, she signed to Nigel to aid her; and, having pushed aside the heavy bedstead, they saw the brass plate which Martha had described. She pressed the spring, and, at once, the plate starting up, showed the keyhole, and a large iron ring used in lifting the trap-door, which, when raised, displayed the strong box, or small chest, she had mentioned, and which proved indeed so very weighty, that it might perhaps have been scarcely possible for Nigel, though a very strong man, to have raised it without assistance.

Having replaced everything as they had found it, Nigel, with such help as his companion was able to afford, assumed his load, and made a shift to carry it into the next apartment, where lay the miserable owner, insensible to sounds and circumstances, which, if any thing could have broken his long last slumber, would certainly have done so. His unfortunate daughter went up to his body, and had even the courage to remove the sheet which had been decently disposed over it. She put her hand on the heart, but there was no throb—held a feather to the lips, but there was no motion—then kissed with deep reverence the starting veins of the pale forehead, and then the emaciated hand.

"I would you could hear me," she said,—"Father! I would you could hear me swear, that, if I now save what you most valued on earth, it is only to assist me in obtaining vengeance for your death."

She replaced the covering, and, without a tear, a sigh, or an additional word of any kind, renewed her efforts, until they conveyed the strong-box betwixt them into Lord Glenvarloch's sleeping apartment. "It must pass," she said, "as part of your baggage. I will be in readiness so soon as the waterman calls."

She retired; and Lord Glenvarloch, who saw the hour of their departure approach, tore down a part of the old hanging to make a covering, which he corded upon the trunk, lest the peculiarity of its shape, and the care with which it was banded and counterbanded with bars of steel, might afford suspicions respecting the treasure which it contained. Having taken this measure of precaution, he changed the rascally disguise, which he had assumed on entering Whitefriars, into a suit becoming his quality, and then, unable to sleep, though exhausted with the events of the night, he threw himself on his bed to await the summons of the waterman.

XXVI

Give us good voyage, gentle stream—we stun not
Thy sober ear with sounds of revelry;
Wake not the slumbering echoes of thy banks
With voice of flute and horn—we do but seek
On the broad pathway of thy swelling bosom
To glide in silent safety.

—*The Double Bridal*

G rey, or rather yellow light, was beginning to twinkle through the fogs of Whitefriars, when a low tap at the door of the unhappy miser announced to Lord Glenvarloch the summons of the boatman. He found at the door the man whom he had seen the night before, with a companion.

"Come, come, master, let us get afloat," said one of them, in a rough impressive whisper, "time and tide wait for no man."

"They shall not wait for me," said Lord Glenvarloch; "but I have some things to carry with me."

"Ay, ay—no man will take a pair of oars now, Jack, unless he means to load the wherry like a six-horse waggon. When they don't want to shift the whole kitt, they take a sculler, and be d—d to them. Come, come, where be your rattle-traps?"

One of the men was soon sufficiently loaded, in his own estimation at least, with Lord Glenvarloch's mail and its accompaniments, with which burden he began to trudge towards the Temple Stairs. His comrade, who seemed the principal, began to handle the trunk which contained the miser's treasure, but pitched it down again in an instant, declaring, with a great oath, that it was as reasonable to expect a man to carry Paul's on his back. The daughter of Trapbois, who had by this time joined them, muffled up in a long dark hood and mantle, exclaimed to Lord Glenvarloch—"Let them leave it if they will, let them leave it all; let us but escape from this horrible place."

We have mentioned elsewhere, that Nigel was a very athletic young man, and, impelled by a strong feeling of compassion and indignation, he showed his bodily strength singularly on this occasion, by seizing on the ponderous strong-box, and, by means of the rope he had cast around it, throwing it on his shoulders, and marching resolutely forward under a weight, which would have sunk to the earth three young gallants, at the least, of our degenerate day. The waterman followed him in amazement, calling out, "Why, master, master, you might as well gie me t'other end on't!" and anon offered his assistance to support it in some degree behind, which after the first minute or two Nigel was fain to accept. His strength was almost exhausted when he reached the wherry, which was lying at the Temple Stairs according to appointment; and, when he pitched the trunk into it, the weight sank the bow of the boat so low in the water as well-nigh to overset it.

"We shall have as hard a fare of it," said the waterman to his companion, "as if we were ferrying over an honest bankrupt with all his secreted goods—Ho, ho! good woman, what, are you stepping in for?—our gunwale lies deep enough in the water without live lumber to boot."

"This person comes with me," said Lord Glenvarloch; "she is for the present under my protection."

"Come, come, master," rejoined the fellow, "that is out of my commission. You must not double my freight on me—she may go by land—and, as for protection, her face will protect her from Berwick to the Land's End."

"You will not except at my doubling the loading, if I double the fare?" said Nigel, determined on no account to relinquish the protection of this unhappy woman, for which he had already devised some sort of plan, likely now to be baffled by the characteristic rudeness of the Thames watermen.

"Ay, by G——, but I will except, though," said the fellow with the green plush jacket: "I will overload my wherry neither for love nor money—I love my boat as well as my wife, and a thought better."

"Nay, nay, comrade," said his mate, "that is speaking no true water language. For double fare we are bound to row a witch in her eggshell if she bid us; and so pull away, Jack, and let us have no more prating."

They got into the stream-way accordingly, and, although heavily laden, began to move down the river with reasonable speed.

The lighter vessels which passed, overtook, or crossed them, in their course, failed not to assail them with their boisterous raillery, which was then called water-wit; for which the extreme plainness of Mistress Martha's features, contrasted with the youth, handsome figure, and good looks of Nigel, furnished the principal topics; while the circumstance of the boat being somewhat overloaded, did not escape their notice. They were hailed successively, as a grocer's wife upon a party of pleasure with her eldest apprentice—as an old woman carrying her grandson to school—and as a young strapping Irishman, conveying an ancient maiden to Dr. Rigmarole's, at Redriffe, who buckles beggars for a tester and a dram of Geneva. All this abuse was retorted in a similar strain of humour by Greenjacket and his companion, who maintained the war of wit with the same alacrity with which they were assailed.

Meanwhile, Lord Glenvarloch asked his desolate companion if she had thought on any place where she could remain in safety with her property. She confessed, in more detail than formerly, that her father's character had left her no friends; and that, from the time he had betaken himself to Whitefriars, to escape certain legal consequences of his eager pursuit of gain, she had lived a life of total seclusion; not associating with the society which the place afforded, and, by her residence there, as well as her father's parsimony, effectually cut off from all other company. What she now wished, was, in the first place, to obtain the shelter of a decent lodging, and the countenance of honest people, however low in life, until she should obtain legal advice as to the mode of obtaining justice on her father's murderer. She had no hesitation to charge the guilt upon Colepepper, (commonly called Peppercull,) whom she knew to be as capable of any act of treacherous cruelty, as he was cowardly, where actual manhood was required. He had been strongly suspected of two robberies before, one of which was coupled with an atrocious murder. He had, she intimated, made pretensions to her hand as the easiest and safest way of obtaining possession of her father's wealth; and, on her refusing his addresses, if they could be termed so, in the most positive terms, he had thrown out such obscure hints of vengeance, as, joined with some imperfect assaults upon the house, had kept her in frequent alarm, both on her father's account and her own.

Nigel, but that his feeling of respectful delicacy to the unfortunate woman forebade him to do so, could here have communicated a circumstance corroborative of her suspicions, which had already occurred to his own mind. He recollected the hint that old Hildebrod threw forth on the preceding night, that some communication betwixt himself and Colepepper had hastened the catastrophe. As this communication related to the plan which Hildebrod had been pleased to form, of promoting a marriage betwixt Nigel himself and the rich heiress of Trapbois, the fear of losing an opportunity not to be regained, together with the mean malignity of a low-bred ruffian, disappointed in a favourite scheme, was most likely to instigate the bravo to the deed of violence which had been committed. The reflection that his own name was in some degree implicated with the causes of this horrid tragedy, doubled Lord Glenvarloch's anxiety in behalf of the victim whom he had rescued, while at the same time he formed the tacit resolution, that, so soon as his own affairs were put upon some footing, he would contribute all in his power towards the investigation of this bloody affair.

After ascertaining from his companion that she could form no better plan of her own, he recommended to her to take up her lodging for the time, at the house of his old landlord, Christie the ship-chandler, at Paul's Wharf, describing the decency and honesty of that worthy couple, and expressing his hopes that they would receive her into their own house, or recommend her at least to that of some person for whom they would be responsible, until she should have time to enter upon other arrangements for herself.

The poor woman received advice so grateful to her in her desolate condition, with an expression of thanks, brief indeed, but deeper than any thing had yet extracted from the austerity of her natural disposition.

Lord Glenvarloch then proceeded to inform Martha, that certain reasons, connected with his personal safety, called him immediately to Greenwich, and, therefore, it would not be in his power to accompany her to Christie's house, which he would otherwise have done with pleasure: but, tearing a leaf from his tablet, he wrote on it a few lines, addressed to his landlord, as a man of honesty and humanity, in which he described the bearer as a person who stood in singular necessity of temporary protection and good advice, for which her circumstances enabled her to make ample acknowledgment. He therefore requested John Christie, as his old and good friend, to afford her the shelter of his roof for a short time; or, if that might not be consistent with his convenience, at least to direct her to a proper lodging-and, finally, he imposed on him the additional, and somewhat more difficult commission, to recommend her to the counsel and services of an honest, at least a reputable and skilful attorney, for the transacting some law business of importance. The note he subscribed with his real name, and, delivering it to his *protegee*, who received it with another deeply uttered "I thank you," which spoke the sterling feelings of her gratitude better than a thousand combined phrases, he commanded the watermen to pull in for Paul's Wharf, which they were now approaching.

"We have not time," said Green-jacket; "we cannot be stopping every instant."

But, upon Nigel insisting upon his commands being obeyed, and adding, that it was for the purpose of putting the lady ashore, the waterman declared that he would rather have her room than her company, and put the wherry alongside the wharf accordingly. Here two of the porters, who ply in such places, were easily induced to undertake the charge of the ponderous strong-box, and at the same time to guide the owner to the well-known mansion of John Christie, with whom all who lived in that neighbourhood were perfectly acquainted.

The boat, much lightened of its load, went down the Thames at a rate increased in proportion. But we must forbear to pursue her in her voyage for a few minutes, since we have previously to mention the issue of Lord Glenvarloch's recommendation.

Mistress Martha Trapbois reached the shop in perfect safety, and was about to enter it, when a sickening sense of the uncertainty of her situation, and of the singularly painful task of telling her story, came over her so strongly, that she paused a moment at the very threshold of her proposed place of refuge, to think in what manner she could best second the recommendation of the friend whom Providence had raised up to her. Had she possessed that knowledge of the world, from which her habits of life had completely excluded her, she might have known that the large sum of money which she brought along with her, might, judiciously managed, have been a passport to her into the mansions of nobles, and the palaces of princes. But, however conscious of its general power, which assumes so many forms and complexions, she was so inexperienced as to be most unnecessarily afraid that the means by which the wealth had been acquired, might exclude its inheretrix from shelter even in the house of a humble tradesman.

While she thus delayed, a more reasonable cause for hesitation arose, in a considerable noise and altercation within the house, which grew louder and louder as the disputants issued forth upon the street or lane before the door.

The first who entered upon the scene was a tall raw-boned hard-favoured man, who stalked out of the shop hastily, with a gait like that of a Spaniard in a passion, who, disdaining to add speed to his locomotion by running, only condescends, in the utmost extremity of his angry haste, to add length to his stride. He faced about, so soon as he was out of the house, upon his pursuer, a decent-looking, elderly, plain tradesman—no other than John Christie himself, the owner of the shop and tenement, by whom he seemed to be followed, and who was in a state of agitation more than is usually expressed by such a person.

"I'll hear no more on't," said the personage who first appeared on the scene.—"Sir, I will hear no more on it. Besides being a most false and impudent figment, as I can testify—it is *Scandaalum Magnaatum*, sir— *Scandaalum Magnaatum*" he reiterated with a broad accentuation of the first vowel, well known in the colleges of Edinburgh and Glasgow, which we can only express in print by doubling the said first of letters and of vowels, and which would have cheered the cockles of the reigning monarch had he been within hearing,—as he was a severer stickler for what he deemed the genuine pronunciation of the Roman tongue, than for any of the royal prerogatives, for which he was at times disposed to insist so strenuously in his speeches to Parliament.

"I care not an ounce of rotten cheese," said John Christie in reply, "what you call it—but it is TRUE; and I am a free Englishman, and have right to speak the truth in my own concerns; and your master is little better than a villain, and you no more than a swaggering coxcomb, whose head I will presently break, as I have known it well broken before on lighter occasion."

And, so saying, he flourished the paring-shovel which usually made clean the steps of his little shop, and which he had caught up as the readiest weapon of working his foeman damage, and advanced therewith upon him. The cautious Scot (for such our readers must have already pronounced him, from his language and pedantry) drew back as the enraged ship-chandler approached, but in a surly manner, and bearing his hand on his sword-hilt rather in the act of one who was losing habitual forbearance and caution of deportment, than as alarmed by the attack of an antagonist inferior to himself in youth, strength, and weapons.

"Bide back," he said, "Maister Christie—I say bide back, and consult your safety, man. I have evited striking you in your ain house under muckle provocation, because I am ignorant how the laws here may pronounce respecting burglary and hamesucken, and such matters; and, besides, I would not willingly hurt ye, man, e'en on the causeway, that is free to us baith, because I mind your kindness of lang syne, and partly consider ye as a poor deceived creature. But deil d—n me, sir, and I am not wont to swear, but if you touch my Scotch shouther with that shule of yours, I will make six inches of my Andrew Ferrara deevilish intimate with your guts, neighbour."

And therewithal, though still retreating from the brandished shovel, he made one-third of the basket-hilled broadsword which he wore, visible from the sheath. The wrath of John Christie was abated, either by his natural temperance of disposition, or perhaps in part by the glimmer of cold steel, which flashed on him from his adversary's last action.

"I would do well to cry clubs on thee, and have thee ducked at the wharf," he said, grounding his shovel, however, at the same time, "for a paltry swaggerer, that would draw thy bit of iron there on an honest citizen before his own door; but get thee gone, and reckon on a salt eel for thy supper, if thou shouldst ever come near my house again. I wish it had been at the bottom of the Thames when it first gave the use of its roof to smooth-faced, oily-tongued, double-minded Scots thieves!"

"It's an ill bird that fouls its own nest," replied his adversary, not perhaps the less bold that he saw matters were taking the turn of a pacific debate; "and a pity it is that a kindly Scot should ever have married in foreign parts, and given life to a purse-proud, pudding-headed, fat-gutted, lean-brained Southron, e'en such as you, Maister Christie. But fare ye weel—fare ye weel, for ever and a day; and, if you quarrel wi' a Scot again, man, say as mickle ill o' himsell as ye like, but say nane of his patron or of his countrymen, or it will scarce be your flat cap that will keep your lang lugs from the sharp abridgement of a Highland whinger, man."

"And, if you continue your insolence to me before my own door, were it but two minutes longer," retorted John Christie, "I will call the constable, and make your Scottish ankles acquainted with an English pair of stocks!"

So saying, he turned to retire into his shop with some show of victory; for his enemy, whatever might be his innate valour, manifested no desire to drive matters to extremity—conscious, perhaps, that whatever advantage he might gain in single combat with Jonn Christie, would be more than overbalanced by incurring an affair with the constituted authorities of Old England, not at that time apt to be particularly favourable to their new fellow-subjects, in the various successive broils which were then constantly taking place between the individuals of two proud nations, who still retained a stronger sense of their national animosity during centuries, than of their late union for a few years under the government of the same prince.

Mrs. Martha Trapbois had dwelt too long in Alsatia, to be either surprised or terrified at the altercation she had witnessed. Indeed, she only wondered that the debate did not end in some of those acts of violence by which they were usually terminated in the Sanctuary. As the disputants separated from each other, she, who had no idea that the cause of the quarrel was more deeply rooted than in the daily scenes of the same nature which she had heard of or witnessed, did not hesitate to stop Master Christie in his return to his shop, and present to him the letter which Lord Glenvarloch had given to her. Had she been better acquainted with life and its business, she would certainly have waited for a more temperate moment; and she had reason to repent of her precipitation, when, without saying a single word, or taking the trouble to gather more of the information contained in the letter than was expressed in the subscription, the incensed ship chandler threw it down on the ground, trampled it in high disdain, and, without addressing a single word to the bearer, except, indeed, something much more like a hearty curse than was perfectly consistent with his own grave appearance, he retired into his shop, and shut the hatch-door.

It was with the most inexpressible anguish that the desolate, friendless and unhappy female, thus beheld her sole hope of succour, countenance, and protection, vanish at once, without being able to conceive a reason; for, to do her justice, the idea that her friend, whom she knew by the name of Nigel Grahame, had imposed on her, a solution which might readily have occurred to many in her situation, never once entered her mind. Although it was not her temper easily to bend her mind to entreaty, she could not help exclaiming after the ireful and retreating ship-chandler,—"Good Master, hear me but a moment! for mercy's sake, for honesty's sake!"

"Mercy and honesty from him, mistress!" said the Scot, who, though he essayed not to interrupt the retreat of his antagonist, still kept stout possession of the field of action,—"ye might as weel expect brandy from bean-stalks, or milk from a craig of blue whunstane. The man is mad, bom mad, to boot."

"I must have mistaken the person to whom the letter was addressed, then;" and, as she spoke, Mistress Martha Trapbois was in the act of stooping to lift the paper which had been so uncourteously received. Her companion, with natural civility, anticipated her purpose; but, what was not quite so much in etiquette, he took a sly glance at it as he was about to hand it to her, and his eye having caught the subscription, he said, with surprise, "Glenvarloch—Nigel Olifaunt of Glenvarloch! Do you know the Lord Glenvarloch, mistress?"

"I know not of whom you speak," said Mrs. Martha, peevishly. "I had that paper from one Master Nigel Gram."

"Nigel Grahame!—umph.—O, ay, very true—I had forgot," said the Scotsman. "A tall, well-set young man, about my height; bright blue eyes like a hawk's; a pleasant speech, something leaning to the kindly north-country accentuation, but not much, in respect of his having been resident abroad?"

"All this is true—and what of it all?" said the daughter of the miser.

"Hair of my complexion?"

"Yours is red," replied she.

"I pray you peace," said the Scotsman. "I was going to say—of my complexion, but with a deeper shade of the chestnut. Weel, mistress, if I have guessed the man aright, he is one with whom I am, and have been, intimate and familiar,—nay,—I may truly say I have done him much service in my time, and may live to do him more. I had indeed a sincere good-will for him, and I doubt he has been much at a loss since we parted; but the fault is not mine. Wherefore, as this letter will not avail you with him to whom it is directed, you may believe that heaven hath sent it to me, who have a special regard for the writer—I have, besides, as much mercy and honesty within me as man can weel make his bread with, and am willing to aid any distressed creature, that is my friend's friend, with my counsel, and otherwise, so that I am not put to much charges, being in a strange country, like a poor lamb that has wandered from its ain native hirsel, and leaves a tait of its woo' in every d—d Southron bramble that comes across it." While he spoke thus, he read the contents of the letter, without waiting for permission, and then continued,—"And so this is all that you are wanting, my dove? nothing more than safe and honourable lodging, and sustenance, upon your own charges?"

"Nothing more," said she. "If you are a man and a Christian, you will help me to what I need so much."

"A man I am," replied the formal Caledonian, "e'en sic as ye see me; and a Christian I may call myself, though unworthy, and though I have heard little pure doctrine since I came hither—a' polluted with men's devices—ahem! Weel, and if ye be an honest woman," (here he peeped under her muffler,) "as an honest woman ye seem likely to be— though, let me tell you, they are a kind of cattle not so rife in the streets of this city as I would desire them—I was almost strangled with my own band by twa rampallians, wha wanted yestreen, nae farther gane, to harle me into a change-house—however, if ye be a decent honest woman," (here he took another peep at features certainly bearing no beauty which could infer suspicion,) "as decent and honest ye seem to be, why, I will advise you to a decent house, where you will get douce, quiet entertainment, on reasonable terms, and the occasional benefit of my own counsel and direction—that is, from time to time, as my other avocations may permit."

"May I venture to accept of such an offer from a stranger?" said Martha, with natural hesitation.

"Troth, I see nothing to hinder you, mistress," replied the bonny Scot; "ye can but see the place, and do after as ye think best. Besides, we are nae such strangers, neither; for I know your friend, and you, it's like, know mine, whilk knowledge, on either hand, is a medium of communication between us, even as the middle of the string connecteth its twa ends or extremities. But I will enlarge on this farther as we pass along, gin ye list to bid your twa lazy loons of porters there lift up your little kist between them, whilk ae true Scotsman might carry under his arm. Let me tell you, mistress, ye will soon make a toom pock-end of it in Lon'on, if you hire twa knaves to do the work of ane."

So saying, he led the way, followed by Mistress Martha Trapbois, whose singular destiny, though it had heaped her with wealth, had left her, for the moment, no wiser counsellor, or more distinguished protector, than honest Richie Moniplies, a discarded serving-man.

XXVII

This way lie safety and a sure retreat;
Yonder lie danger, shame, and punishment
Most welcome danger then—Nay, let me say,
Though spoke with swelling heart—welcome e'en shame
And welcome punishment—for, call me guilty,
I do but pay the tax that's due to justice;
And call me guiltless, then that punishment
Is shame to those alone who do inflict it,

—*The Tribunal*

We left Lord Glenvarloch, to whose fortunes our story chiefly attaches itself, gliding swiftly down the Thames. He was not, as the reader may have observed, very affable in his disposition, or apt to enter into conversation with those into whose company he was casually thrown. This was, indeed, an error in his conduct, arising less from pride, though of that feeling we do not pretend to exculpate him, than from a sort of bashful reluctance to mix in the conversation of those with whom he was not familiar. It is a fault only to be cured by experience and knowledge of the world, which soon teaches every sensible and acute person the important lesson, that amusement, and, what is of more consequence, that information and increase of knowledge, are to be derived from the conversation of every individual whatever, with whom he is thrown into a natural train of communication. For ourselves, we can assure the reader—and perhaps if we have ever been able to afford him amusement, it is owing in a great degree to this cause—that we never found ourselves in company with the stupidest of all possible companions in a post-chaise, or with the most arrant cumber-corner that ever occupied a place in the mail-coach, without finding, that, in the course of our conversation with him, we had some ideas suggested to us, either grave orgay, or some information communicated in the course of our journey, which we should have regretted not to have learned, and which we should be sorry to have immediately forgotten. But Nigel was somewhat immured within the Bastile of his rank, as some philosopher (Tom Paine, we think) has happily enough expressed that sort of shyness which men of dignified situations are apt to be beset with, rather from not exactly knowing how far, or with whom, they ought to be familiar, than from any real touch of aristocratic pride. Besides, the immediate pressure of our adventurer's own affairs was such as exclusively to engross his attention.

He sat, therefore, wrapt in his cloak, in the stern of the boat, with his mind entirely bent upon the probable issue of the interview with his Sovereign, which it was his purpose to seek; for which abstraction of mind he may be fully justified, although perhaps, by questioning the watermen who were transporting him down the river, he might have discovered matters of high concernment to him.

At any rate, Nigel remained silent till the wherry approached the town of Greenwich, when he commanded the men to put in for the nearest landing-place, as it was his purpose to go ashore there, and dismiss them from further attendance.

"That is not possible," said the fellow with the green jacket, who, as we have already said, seemed to take on himself the charge of pilotage. "We must go," he continued, "to Gravesend, where a Scottish vessel, which dropped down the river last tide for the very purpose, lies with her anchor a-peak, waiting to carry you to your own dear northern country. Your hammock is slung, and all is ready for you, and you talk of going ashore at Greenwich, as seriously as if such a thing were possible!"

"I see no impossibility," said Nigel, "in your landing me where I desire to be landed; but very little possibility of your carrying me anywhere I am not desirous of going."

"Why, whether do you manage the wherry, or we, master?" asked Green-jacket, in a tone betwixt jest and earnest; "I take it she will go the way we row her."

"Ay," retorted Nigel, "but I take it you will row her on the course I direct you, otherwise your chance of payment is but a poor one."

"Suppose we are content to risk that," said the undaunted waterman, "I wish to know how you, who talk so big—I mean no offence, master, but you do talk big—would help yourself in such a case?"

"Simply thus," answered Lord Glenvarloch—"You saw me, an hour since, bring down to the boat a trunk that neither of you could lift. If we are to contest the destination of our voyage, the same strength which tossed that chest into the wherry, will suffice to fling you out of it; wherefore, before we begin the scuffle, I pray you to remember, that, whither I would go, there I will oblige you to carry me."

"Gramercy for your kindness," said Green-jacket; "and now mark me in return. My comrade and I are two men—and you, were you as stout as George-a-Green, can pass but for one; and two, you will allow, are more than a match for one. You mistake in your reckoning, my friend."

"It is you who mistake," answered Nigel, who began to grow warm; "it is I who am three to two, sirrah—I carry two men's lives at my girdle."

So saying, he opened his cloak and showed the two pistols which he had disposed at his girdle. Green-jacket was unmoved at the display.

"I have got," said he, "a pair of barkers that will match yours," and he showed that he also was armed with pistols; "so you may begin as soon as you list."

"Then," said Lord Glenvarloch, drawing forth and cocking a pistol, "the sooner the better. Take notice, I hold you as a ruffian, who have declared you will put force on my person; and that I will shoot you through the head if you do not instantly put me ashore at Greenwich."

The other waterman, alarmed at Nigel's gesture, lay upon his oar; but Green-jacket replied coolly—"Look you, master, I should not care a tester to venture a life with you on this matter; but the truth is, I am employed to do you good, and not to do you harm."

"By whom are you employed?" said the Lord Glenvarloch; "or who dare concern themselves in me, or my affairs, without my authority?"

"As to that," answered the waterman, in the same tone of indifference, "I shall not show my commission. For myself, I care not, as I said, whether you land at Greenwich to get yourself hanged, or go down to get aboard the Royal Thistle, to make your escape to your own country; you will be equally out of my reach either way. But it is fair to put the choice before you."

"My choice is made," said Nigel. "I have told you thrice already it is my pleasure to be landed at Greenwich."

"Write it on a piece of paper," said the waterman, "that such is your positive will; I must have something to show to my employers, that the transgression of their orders lies with yourself, not with me."

"I choose to hold this trinket in my hand for the present," said Nigel, showing his pistol, "and will write you the acquittance when I go ashore."

"I would not go ashore with you for a hundred pieces," said the waterman. "Ill luck has ever attended you, except in small gaming; do me fair justice, and give me the testimony I desire. If you are afraid of foul play while you write it, you may hold my pistols, if you will." He offered the weapons to Nigel accordingly, who, while they were under his control, and all possibility of his being taken at disadvantage was excluded, no longer hesitated to give the waterman an acknowledgment, in the following terms:—

"Jack in the Green, with his mate, belonging to the wherry called the Jolly Raven, have done their duty faithfully by me, landing me at Greenwich by my express command; and being themselves willing and desirous to carry me on board the Royal Thistle, presently lying at Gravesend." Having finished this acknowledgment, which he signed with the letters, N. O. G. as indicating his name and title, he again requested to know of the waterman, to whom he delivered it, the name of his employers.

"Sir," replied Jack in the Green, "I have respected your secret, do not you seek to pry into mine. It would do you no good to know for whom I am taking this present trouble; and, to be brief, you shall not know it— and, if you will fight in the quarrel, as you said even now, the sooner we begin the better. Only this you may be cock-sure of, that we designed you no harm, and that, if you fall into any, it will be of your own wilful seeking." As he spoke, they approached the landing-place, where Nigel instantly jumped ashore. The waterman placed his small mail-trunk on the stairs, observing that there were plenty of spare hands about, to carry it where he would.

"We part friends, I hope, my lads," said the young nobleman, offering at the same time a piece of money more than double the usual fare, to the boatmen.

"We part as we met," answered Green-jacket; "and, for your money, I am paid sufficiently with this bit of paper. Only, if you owe me any love for the cast I have given you, I pray you not to dive so deep into the pockets of the next apprentice that you find fool enough to play the cavalier.—And you, you greedy swine," said he to his companion, who still had a longing eye fixed on the money which Nigel continued to offer, "push off, or, if I take a stretcher in hand, I'll break the knave's pate of thee." The fellow pushed off, as he was commanded, but still could not help muttering, "This was entirely out of waterman's rules."

Glenvarloch, though without the devotion of the "injured Thales" of the moralist, to the memory of that great princess, had now attained

> "The hallow'd soil which gave Eliza birth,"

whose halls were now less respectably occupied by her successor. It was not, as has been well shown by a late author, that James was void either of parts or of good intentions; and his predecessor was at least as arbitrary in effect as he was in theory. But, while Elizabeth possessed a sternness of masculine sense and determination which rendered even her weaknesses, some of which were in themselves sufficiently ridiculous, in a certain degree respectable, James, on the other hand, was so utterly devoid of "firm resolve," so well called by the Scottish bard,

"The stalk of carle-hemp in man,"

that even his virtues and his good meaning became laughable, from the whimsical uncertainty of his conduct; so that the wisest things he ever said, and the best actions he ever did, were often touched with a strain of the ludicrous and fidgety character of the man. Accordingly, though at different periods of his reign he contrived to acquire with his people a certain degree of temporary popularity, it never long outlived the occasion which produced it; so true it is, that the mass of mankind will respect a monarch stained with actual guilt, more than one whose foibles render him only ridiculous.

To return from this digression, Lord Glenvarloch soon received, as Green-jacket had assured him, the offer of an idle bargeman to transport his baggage where he listed; but that where was a question of momentary doubt. At length, recollecting the necessity that his hair and beard should be properly arranged before he attempted to enter the royal presence, and desirous, at the same time, of obtaining some information of the motions of the Sovereign and of the Court, he desired to be guided to the next barber's shop, which we have already mentioned as the place where news of every kind circled and centred. He was speedily shown the way to such an emporium of intelligence, and soon found he was likely to hear all he desired to know, and much more, while his head was subjected to the art of a nimble tonsor, the glibness of whose tongue kept pace with the nimbleness of his fingers while he ran on, without stint or stop, in the following excursive manner:—

"The Court here, master?—yes, master—much to the advantage of trade—good custom stirring. His Majesty loves Greenwich—hunts every morning in the Park—all decent persons admitted that have the entries of the Palace—no rabble—frightened the king's horse with their hallooing, the uncombed slaves.—Yes, sir, the beard more peaked? Yes, master, so it is worn. I know the last cut—dress several of the courtiers—one valet-of-the-chamber, two pages of the body, the clerk of the kitchen, three running footmen, two dog-boys, and an honourable Scottish knight, Sir Munko Malgrowler."

"Malagrowther, I suppose?" said Nigel, thrusting in his conjectural emendation, with infinite difficulty, betwixt two clauses of the barber's text.

"Yes, sir—Malcrowder, sir, as you say, sir—hard names the Scots have, sir, for an English mouth. Sir Munko is a handsome person, sir—perhaps you know him—bating the loss of his fingers, and the lameness of his leg, and the length of his chin. Sir, it takes me one minute, twelve seconds, more time to trim that chin of his, than any chin that I know in the town of Greenwich, sir. But he is a very comely gentleman, for all that; and a pleasant—a very pleasant gentleman, sir—and a good-humoured, saving that he is so deaf he can never hear good of any one, and so wise, that he can never believe it; but he is a very good-natured gentleman for all that, except when one speaks too low, or when a hair turns awry.— Did I graze you, sir? We shall put it to rights in a moment, with one drop of styptic—my styptic, or rather my wife's, sir—She makes the water herself. One drop of the styptic, sir, and a bit of black taffeta patch, just big enough to be the saddle to a flea, sir—Yes, sir, rather improves than otherwise. The Prince had a patch the other day, and so had the Duke: and, if you will believe me, there are seventeen yards three quarters of black taffeta already cut into patches for the courtiers."

"But Sir Mungo Malagrowther?" again interjected Nigel, with difficulty.

"Ay, ay, sir—Sir Munko, as you say; a pleasant, good-humoured gentleman as ever—To be spoken with, did you say? O ay, easily to be spoken withal, that is, as easily as his infirmity will permit. He will presently, unless some one hath asked him forth to breakfast, be taking his bone of broiled beef at my neighbour Ned Kilderkin's yonder, removed from over the way. Ned keeps an eating-house, sir, famous for pork-griskins; but Sir Munko cannot abide pork, no more than the King's most Sacred Majesty,[*] nor my Lord Duke of Lennox,

---

[*] The Scots, till within the last generation, disliked swine's flesh as an article of food as much as the Highlanders do at present. It was remarked as extraordinary rapacity, when the Border depredators condescended to make prey of the accursed race, whom the fiend

nor Lord Dalgarno,—nay, I am sure, sir, if I touched you this time, it was your fault, not mine.—But a single drop of the styptic, another little patch that would make a doublet for a flea, just under the left moustache; it will become you when you smile, sir, as well as a dimple; and if you would salute your fair mistress—but I beg pardon, you are a grave gentleman, very grave to be so young.—Hope I have given no offence; it is my duty to entertain customers—my duty, sir, and my pleasure—Sir Munko Malcrowther?—yes, sir, I dare say he is at this moment in Ned's eating-house, for few folks ask him out, now Lord Huntinglen is gone to London. You will get touched again—yes, sir—there you shall find him with his can of single ale, stirred with a sprig of rosemary, for he never drinks strong potations, sir, unless to oblige Lord Huntinglen—take heed, sir—or any other person who asks him forth to breakfast—but single beer he always drinks at Ned's, with his broiled bone of beef or mutton—or, it may be, lamb at the season—but not pork, though Ned is famous for his griskins. But the Scots never eat pork—strange that! some folk think they are a sort of Jews. There is a resemblance, sir,—Do you not think so? Then they call our most gracious Sovereign the Second Solomon, and Solomon, you know, was King of the Jews; so the thing bears a face, you see. I believe, sir, you will find yourself trimmed now to your content. I will be judged by the fair mistress of your affections. Crave pardon—no offence, I trust. Pray, consult the glass—one touch of the crisping tongs, to reduce this straggler.—Thank your munificence, sir—hope your custom while you stay in Greenwich. Would you have a tune on that ghittern, to put your temper in concord for the day?—Twang, twang—twang, twang, dillo. Something out of tune, sir—too many hands to touch it—we cannot keep these things like artists. Let me help you with your cloak, sir—yes, sir—You would not play yourself, sir, would you?—Way to Sir Munko's eating-house?—Yes, sir; but it is Ned's eating-house, not Sir Munko's.—The knight, to be sure, eats there, and makes it his eating-house in some sense, sir—ha, ha! Yonder it is, removed from over the way, new white-washed posts, and red lattice—fat man in his doublet at the door—Ned himself, sir—worth a thousand pounds, they say—better singeing pigs' faces than trimming courtiers—but ours is the less mechanical vocation.—Farewell, sir; hope your custom." So

---

made his habitation. Ben Jonson, in drawing James's character, says, he loved "no part of a swine."

saying, he at length permitted Nigel to depart, whose ears, so long tormented with continued babble, tingled when it had ceased, as if a bell had been rung close to them for the same space of time.

Upon his arrival at the eating-house, where he proposed to meet with Sir Mungo Malagrowther, from whom, in despair of better advice, he trusted to receive some information as to the best mode of introducing himself into the royal presence, Lord Glenvarloch found, in the host with whom he communed, the consequential taciturnity of an Englishman well to pass in the world. Ned Kilderkin spoke as a banker writes, only touching the needful. Being asked if Sir Mungo Malagrowther was there? he replied, No. Being interrogated whether he was expected? he said, Yes. And being again required to say when he was expected, he answered, Presently. As Lord Glenvarloch next inquired, whether he himself could have any breakfast? the landlord wasted not even a syllable in reply, but, ushering him into a neat room where there were several tables, he placed one of them before an armchair, and beckoning Lord Glenvarloch to take possession, he set before him, in a very few minutes, a substantial repast of roast-beef, together with a foaming tankard, to which refreshment the keen air of the river disposed him, notwithstanding his mental embarrassments, to do much honour.

While Nigel was thus engaged in discussing his commons, but raising his head at the same time whenever he heard the door of the apartment open, eagerly desiring the arrival of Sir Mungo Malagrowther, (an event which had seldom been expected by any one with so much anxious interest,) a personage, as it seemed, of at least equal importance with the knight, entered into the apartment, and began to hold earnest colloquy with the publican, who thought proper to carry on the conference on his side unbonneted. This important gentleman's occupation might be guessed from his dress. A milk-white jerkin, and hose of white kersey; a white apron twisted around his body in the manner of a sash, in which, instead of a war-like dagger, was stuck a long-bladed knife, hilted with buck's-horn; a white nightcap on his head, under which his hair was neatly tucked, sufficiently pourtrayed him as one of those priests of Comus whom the vulgar call cooks; and the air with which he rated the publican for having neglected to send some provisions to the Palace, showed that he ministered to royalty itself.

"This will never answer," he said, "Master Kilderkin—the king twice asked for sweetbreads, and fricasseed coxcombs, which are a favourite dish of his most Sacred Majesty, and they were not to be had, because Master Kilderkin had not supplied them to the clerk of the kitchen, as by bargain bound." Here Kilderkin made some apology, brief, according to his own nature, and muttered in a lowly tone after the fashion of all who find themselves in a scrape. His superior replied, in a lofty strain of voice, "Do not tell me of the carrier and his wain, and of the hen-coops coming from Norfolk with the poultry; a loyal man would have sent an express—he would have gone upon his stumps, like Widdrington. What if the king had lost his appetite, Master Kilderkin? What if his most Sacred Majesty had lost his dinner? O, Master Kilderkin, if you had but the just sense of the dignity of our profession, which is told of by the witty African slave, for so the king's most excellent Majesty designates him, Publius Terentius, *Tanguam in specula—in patinas inspicerejubeo.*"

"You are learned, Master Linklater," replied the English publican, compelling, as it were with difficulty, his mouth to utter three or four words consecutively.

"A poor smatterer," said Mr. Linklater; "but it would be a shame to us, who are his most excellent Majesty's countrymen, not in some sort to have cherished those arts wherewith he is so deeply embued— *Regis ad exemplar*, Master Kilderkin, *totus componitur orbis*—which is as much as to say, as the king quotes the cook learns. In brief, Master Kilderkin, having had the luck to be bred where humanities may be had at the matter of an English five groats by the quarter, I, like others, have acquired—ahem-hem!—" Here, the speaker's eye having fallen upon Lord Glenvarloch, he suddenly stopped in his learned harangue, with such symptoms of embarrassment as induced Ned Kilderkin to stretch his taciturnity so far as not only to ask him what he ailed, but whether he would take any thing.

"Ail nothing," replied the learned rival of the philosophical Syrus; "Nothing—and yet I do feel a little giddy. I could taste a glass of your dame's *aqua mirabilis.*"

"I will fetch it," said Ned, giving a nod; and his back was no sooner turned, than the cook walked near the table where Lord Glenvarloch was seated, and regarding him with a look of significance, where more was meant than met the ear, said,—"You are a stranger in Greenwich, sir. I advise you to take the opportunity to step into the Park—the western wicket was ajar when I came hither; I think it will be locked presently, so you had better make the best of your way—that is, if you have any curiosity. The venison are coming into season just now, sir, and there is a pleasure in looking at a hart of grease. I always think when they are bounding so blithely past, what a pleasure it would be, to broach their plump haunches on a spit, and to embattle their breasts in a noble fortification of puff-paste, with plenty of black pepper."

He said no more, as Kilderkin re-entered with the cordial, but edged off from Nigel without waiting any reply, only repeating the same look of intelligence with which he had accosted him.

Nothing makes men's wits so alert as personal danger. Nigel took the first opportunity which his host's attention to the yeoman of the royal kitchen permitted, to discharge his reckoning, and readily obtained a direction to the wicket in question. He found it upon the latch, as he had been taught to expect; and perceived that it admitted him to a narrow footpath, which traversed a close and tangled thicket, designed for the cover of the does and the young fawns. Here he conjectured it would be proper to wait; nor had he been stationary above five minutes, when the cook, scalded as much with heat of motion as ever he had been by his huge fire-place, arrived almost breathless, and with his pass-key hastily locked the wicket behind him.

Ere Lord Glenvarloch had time to speculate upon this action, the man approached with anxiety, and said—"Good lord, my Lord Glenvarloch!—why will you endanger yourself thus?"

"You know me then, my friend?" said Nigel.

"Not much of that, my lord—but I know your honour's noble house well.—My name is Laurie Linklater, my lord."

"Linklater!" repeated Nigel. "I should recollect—'

"Under your lordship's favour," he continued, "I was 'prentice, my lord, to old Mungo Moniplies, the flesher at the wanton West-Port of Edinburgh, which I wish I saw again before I died. And, your honour's noble father having taken Richie Moniplies into his house to wait on your lordship, there was a sort of connexion, your lordship sees."

"Ah!" said Lord Glenvarloch, "I had almost forgot your name, but not your kind purpose. You tried to put Richie in the way of presenting a supplication to his Majesty?"

"Most true, my lord," replied the king's cook. "I had like to have come by mischief in the job; for Richie, who was always wilful, 'wadna be guided by me,' as the sang says. But nobody amongst these brave English cooks can kittle up his Majesty's most sacred palate with our own gusty Scottish dishes. So I e'en betook myself to my craft, and concocted a mess of friar's chicken for the soup, and a savoury hachis, that made the whole cabal coup the crans; and, instead of disgrace, I came by preferment. I am one of the clerks of the kitchen now, make me thankful—with a finger in the purveyor's office, and may get my whole hand in by and by."

"I am truly glad," said Nigel, "to hear that you have not suffered on my account,—still more so at your good fortune."

"You bear a kind heart, my lord," said Linklater, "and do not forget poor people; and, troth, I see not why they should be forgotten, since the king's errand may sometimes fall in the cadger's gate. I have followed your lordship in the street, just to look at such a stately shoot of the old oak-tree; and my heart jumped into my throat, when I saw you sitting openly in the eating-house yonder, and knew there was such danger to your person."

"What! there are warrants against me, then?" said Nigel.

"It is even true, my lord; and there are those who are willing to blacken you as much as they can.—God forgive them, that would sacrifice an honourable house for their own base ends!"

"Amen," said Nigel.

"For, say your lordship may have been a little wild, like other young gentlemen—"

"We have little time to talk of it, my friend," said Nigel. "The point in question is, how am I to get speech of the king?"

"The king, my lord!" said Linklater in astonishment; "why, will not that be rushing wilfully into danger?—scalding yourself, as I may say, with your own ladle?"

"My good friend," answered Nigel, "my experience of the Court, and my knowledge of the circumstances in which I stand, tell me, that the manliest and most direct road is, in my case, the surest and the safest. The king has both a head to apprehend what is just, and a heart to do what is kind."

"It is e'en true, my lord, and so we, his old servants, know," added Linklater; "but, woe's me, if you knew how many folks make it their daily and nightly purpose to set his head against his heart, and his heart against his head—to make him do hard things because they are called just, and unjust things because they are represented as kind. Woe's me! it is with his Sacred Majesty, and the favourites who work upon him, even according to the homely proverb that men taunt my calling with,—'God sends good meat, but the devil sends cooks.'"

"It signifies not talking of it, my good friend," said Nigel, "I must take my risk, my honour peremptorily demands it. They may maim me, or beggar me, but they shall not say I fled from my accusers. My peers shall hear my vindication."

"Your peers?" exclaimed the cook—"Alack-a-day, my lord, we are not in Scotland, where the nobles can bang it out bravely, were it even with the king himself, now and then. This mess must be cooked in the Star-Chamber, and that is an oven seven times heated, my lord;—and yet, if you are determined to see the king, I will not say but you may find some favour, for he likes well any thing that is appealed directly to his own wisdom, and sometimes, in the like cases, I have known him stick by his own opinion, which is always a fair one. Only mind, if you will forgive me, my lord—mind to spice high with Latin; a curn or two of Greek would not be amiss; and, if you can bring in any thing about the judgment of Solomon, in the original Hebrew, and season with a merry jest or so, the dish will be the more palatable.—Truly, I think, that, besides my skill in art, I owe much to the stripes of the Rector of the High School, who imprinted on my mind that cooking scene in the Heautontimorumenos."

"Leaving that aside, my friend," said Lord Glenvarloch, "can you inform me which way I shall most readily get to the sight and speech of the king?"

"To the sight of him readily enough," said Linklater; "he is galloping about these alleys, to see them strike the hart, to get him an appetite for a nooning—and that reminds me I should be in the kitchen. To the speech of the king you will not come so easily, unless you could either meet him alone, which rarely chances, or wait for him among the crowd that go to see him alight. And now, farewell, my lord, and God speed!— if I could do more for you, I would offer it."

"You have done enough, perhaps, to endanger yourself," said Lord Glenvarloch. "I pray you to be gone, and leave me to my fate."

The honest cook lingered, but a nearer burst of the horns apprized him that there was no time to lose; and, acquainting Nigel that he would leave the postern-door on the latch to secure his retreat in that direction, he bade God bless him, and farewell.

In the kindness of this humble countryman, flowing partly from national partiality, partly from a sense of long-remembered benefits, which had been scarce thought on by those who had bestowed them, Lord Glenvarloch thought he saw the last touch of sympathy which he was to receive in this cold and courtly region, and felt that he must now be sufficient to himself, or be utterly lost.

He traversed more than one alley, guided by the sounds of the chase, and met several of the inferior attendants upon the king's sport, who regarded him only as one of the spectators who were sometimes permitted to enter the Park by the concurrence of the officers about the Court. Still there was no appearance of James, or any of his principal courtiers, and Nigel began to think whether, at the risk of incurring disgrace similar to that which had attended the rash exploit of Richie Moniplies, he should not repair to the Palace-gate, in order to address the king on his return, when Fortune presented him the opportunity of doing so, in her own way.

He was in one of those long walks by which the Park was traversed, when he heard, first a distant rustling, then the rapid approach of hoofs shaking the firm earth on which he stood; then a distant halloo, warned by which he stood up by the side of the avenue, leaving free room for the passage of the chase. The stag, reeling, covered with foam, and blackened with sweat, his nostrils extended as he gasped for breath, made a shift to come up as far as where Nigel stood, and, without turning to bay, was there pulled down by two tall greyhounds of the breed still used by the hardy deer-stalkers of the Scottish Highlands, but which has been long unknown in England. One dog struck at the buck's throat, another dashed his sharp nose and fangs, I might almost say, into the animal's bowels. It would have been natural for Lord Glenvarloch, himself persecuted as if by hunters, to have thought upon the occasion like the melancholy Jacques; but habit is a strange matter, and I fear that his feelings on the occasion were rather those of the practised huntsman than of the moralist. He had no time, however, to indulge them, for mark what befell.

A single horseman followed the chase, upon a steed so thoroughly subjected to the rein, that it obeyed the touch of the bridle as if it had been a mechanical impulse operating on the nicest piece of machinery; so that, seated deep in his demipique saddle, and so trussed up there as to make falling almost impossible, the rider, without either fear or hesitation, might increase or diminish the speed at which he rode, which, even on the most animating occasions of the chase, seldom exceeded three-fourths of a gallop, the horse keeping his haunches under him, and never stretching forward beyond the managed pace of the academy. The security with which he chose to prosecute even this

SIR WALTER SCOTT

favourite, and, in the ordinary case, somewhat dangerous amusement, as well as the rest of his equipage, marked King James. No attendant was within sight; indeed, it was often a nice strain of flattery to permit the Sovereign to suppose he had outridden and distanced all the rest of the chase.

"Weel dune, Bash—weel dune, Battie!" he exclaimed as he came up. "By the honour of a king, ye are a credit to the Braes of Balwhither!—Haud my horse, man," he called out to Nigel, without stopping to see to whom he had addressed himself—"Haud my naig, and help me doun out o' the saddle—deil ding your saul, sirrah, canna ye mak haste before these lazy smaiks come up?—haud the rein easy—dinna let him swerve—now, haud the stirrup—that will do, man, and now we are on terra firma." So saying, without casting an eye on his assistant, gentle King Jamie, unsheathing the short, sharp hanger, (*couteau de chasse,*) which was the only thing approaching to a sword that he could willingly endure the sight of, drew the blade with great satisfaction across the throat of the buck, and put an end at once to its struggles and its agonies.

Lord Glenvarloch, who knew well the silvan duty which the occasion demanded, hung the bridle of the king's palfrey on the branch of a tree, and, kneeling duteously down, turned the slaughtered deer upon its back, and kept the *quarree* in that position, while the king, too intent upon his sport to observe any thing else, drew his *couteau* down the breast of the animal, *secundum artem*; and, having made a cross cut, so as to ascertain the depth of the fat upon the chest, exclaimed, in a sort of rapture, "Three inches of white fat on the brisket!—prime—prime—as I am a crowned sinner—and deil ane o' the lazy loons in but mysell! Seven—aught—aught tines on the antlers. By G—d, a hart of aught tines, and the first of the season! Bash and Battie, blessings on the heart's-root of ye! Buss me, my bairns, buss me." The dogs accordingly fawned upon him, licked him with bloody jaws, and soon put him in such a state that it might have seemed treason had been doing its full work upon his anointed body. "Bide doun, with a mischief to ye—bide doun, with a wanion," cried the king, almost overturned by the obstreperous caresses of the large stag-hounds. "But ye are just like ither folks, gie ye an inch and ye take an ell.—And wha may ye be, friend?" he said, now finding leisure to take a nearer view of Nigel, and observing what in his first emotion of silvan delight had escaped him,—"Ye are nane of our train, man. In the name of God, what the devil are ye?"

"An unfortunate man, sire," replied Nigel.

"I dare say that," answered the king, snappishly, "or I wad have seen naething of you. My lieges keep a' their happiness to themselves; but let bowls row wrang wi' them, and I am sure to hear of it."

"And to whom else can we carry our complaints but to your Majesty, who is Heaven's vicegerent over us!" answered Nigel.

"Right, man, right—very weel spoken," said the king; "but you should leave Heaven's vicegerent some quiet on earth, too."

"If your Majesty will look on me," (for hitherto the king had been so busy, first with the dogs, and then with the mystic operation of *breaking*, in vulgar phrase, cutting up the deer, that he had scarce given his assistant above a transient glance,) "you will see whom necessity makes bold to avail himself of an opportunity which may never again occur."

King James looked; his blood left his cheek, though it continued stained with that of the animal which lay at his feet, he dropped the knife from his hand, cast behind him a faltering eye, as if he either meditated flight or looked out for assistance, and then exclaimed,— "Glenvarlochides! as sure as I was christened James Stewart. Here is a bonny spot of work, and me alone, and on foot too!" he added, bustling to get upon his horse.

"Forgive me that I interrupt you, my liege," said Nigel, placing himself between the king and his steed; "hear me but a moment!"

"I'll hear ye best on horseback," said the king. "I canna hear a word on foot, man, not a word; and it is not seemly to stand cheek-for-chowl confronting us that gate. Bide out of our gate, sir, we charge you on your allegiance.—The deil's in them a', what can they be doing?"

"By the crown that you wear, my liege," said Nigel, "and for which my ancestors have worthily fought, I conjure you to be composed, and to hear me but a moment!"

That which he asked was entirely out of the monarch's power to grant. The timidity which he showed was not the plain downright cowardice, which, like a natural impulse, compels a man to flight, and which can excite little but pity or contempt, but a much more ludicrous, as well as more mingled sensation. The poor king was frightened at once and angry, desirous of securing his safety, and at the same time ashamed to compromise his dignity; so that without attending to what Lord Glenvarloch endeavoured to explain, he kept making at his horse, and repeating, "We are a free king, man,—we are a free king—we will not be controlled by a subject.—In the name of God, what keeps

Steenie? And, praised be his name, they are coming—Hillo, ho—here, here—Steenie, Steenie!"

The Duke of Buckingham galloped up, followed by several courtiers and attendants of the royal chase, and commenced with his usual familiarity,—"I see Fortune has graced our dear dad, as usual.—But what's this?"

"What is it? It is treason for what I ken," said the king; "and a' your wyte, Steenie. Your dear dad and gossip might have been murdered, for what you care."

"Murdered? Secure the villain!" exclaimed the Duke. "By Heaven, it is Olifaunt himself!" A dozen of the hunters dismounted at once, letting their horses run wild through the park. Some seized roughly on Lord Glenvarloch, who thought it folly to offer resistance, while others busied themselves with the king. "Are you wounded, my liege—are you wounded?"

"Not that I ken of," said the king, in the paroxysm of his apprehension, (which, by the way, might be pardoned in one of so timorous a temper, and who, in his time, had been exposed to so many strange attempts)— "Not that I ken of—but search him—search him. I am sure I saw fire-arms under his cloak. I am sure I smelled powder—I am dooms sure of that."

Lord Glenvarloch's cloak being stripped off, and his pistols discovered, a shout of wonder and of execration on the supposed criminal purpose, arose from the crowd now thickening every moment. Not that celebrated pistol, which, though resting on a bosom as gallant and as loyal as Nigel's, spread such cause less alarm among knights and dames at a late high solemnity—not that very pistol caused more temporary consternation than was so groundlessly excited by the arms which were taken from Lord Glenvarloch's person; and not Mhic-Allastar-More himself could repel with greater scorn and indignation, the insinuations that they were worn for any sinister purposes.

"Away with the wretch—the parricide—the bloody-minded villain!" was echoed on all hands; and the king, who naturally enough set the same value on his own life, at which it was, or seemed to be, rated by others, cried out, louder than all the rest, "Ay, ay—away with him. I have had enough of him and so has the country. But do him no bodily harm—and, for God's sake, sirs, if ye are sure ye have thoroughly disarmed him, put up your swords, dirks, and skenes, for you will certainly do each other a mischief."

There was a speedy sheathing of weapons at the king's command; for those who had hitherto been brandishing them in loyal bravado, began thereby to call to mind the extreme dislike which his Majesty nourished against naked steel, a foible which seemed to be as constitutional as his timidity, and was usually ascribed to the brutal murder of Rizzio having been perpetrated in his unfortunate mother's presence before he yet saw the light.

At this moment, the Prince, who had been hunting in a different part of the then extensive Park, and had received some hasty and confused information of what was going forward, came rapidly up, with one or two noblemen in his train, and amongst others Lord Dalgarno. He sprung from his horse and asked eagerly if his father were wounded.

"Not that I am sensible of, Baby Charles—but a wee matter exhausted, with struggling single-handed with the assassin.—Steenie, fill up a cup of wine—the leathern bottle is hanging at our pommel.—Buss me, then, Baby Charles," continued the monarch, after he had taken this cup of comfort; "O man, the Commonwealth and you have had a fair escape from the heavy and bloody loss of a dear father; for we are *pater patriae*, as weel as *pater familias.—Quis desiderio sit pudor aut modus tarn cari capitis!*—Woe is me, black cloth would have been dear in England, and dry een scarce!"

And, at the very idea of the general grief which must have attended his death, the good-natured monarch cried heartily himself.

"Is this possible?" said Charles, sternly; for his pride was hurt at his father's demeanour on the one hand, while on the other, he felt the resentment of a son and a subject, at the supposed attempt on the king's life. "Let some one speak who has seen what happened—My Lord of Buckingham!"

"I cannot say my lord," replied the Duke, "that I saw any actual violence offered to his Majesty, else I should have avenged him on the spot."

"You would have done wrong, then, in your zeal, George," answered the Prince; "such offenders were better left to be dealt with by the laws. But was the villain not struggling with his Majesty?"

"I cannot term it so, my lord," said the Duke, who, with many faults, would have disdained an untruth; "he seemed to desire to detain his Majesty, who, on the contrary, appeared to wish to mount his horse; but they have found pistols on his person, contrary to the proclamation, and, as it proves to be by Nigel Olifaunt, of whose ungoverned disposition your Royal Highness has seen some samples, we seem to be justified in apprehending the worst."

"Nigel Olifaunt!" said the Prince; "can that unhappy man so soon have engaged in a new trespass? Let me see those pistols."

"Ye are not so unwise as to meddle with such snap-haunces, Baby Charles?" said James—"Do not give him them, Steenie—I command you on your allegiance! They may go off of their own accord, whilk often befalls.—You will do it, then?—Saw ever a man sic wilful bairns as we are cumbered with!—Havena we guardsmen and soldiers enow, but you must unload the weapons yoursell—you, the heir of our body and dignities, and sae mony men around that are paid for venturing life in our cause?"

But without regarding his father's exclamations, Prince Charles, with the obstinacy which characterised him in trifles, as well as matters of consequence, persisted in unloading the pistols with his own hand, of the double bullets with which each was charged. The hands of all around were held up in astonishment at the horror of the crime supposed to have been intended, and the escape which was presumed so narrow.

Nigel had not yet spoken a word—he now calmly desired to be heard.

"To what purpose?" answered the Prince coldly. "You knew yourself accused of a heavy offence, and, instead of rendering yourself up to justice, in terms of the proclamation, you are here found intruding yourself on his Majesty's presence, and armed with unlawful weapons."

"May it please you, sir," answered Nigel, "I wore these unhappy weapons for my own defence; and not very many hours since they were necessary to protect the lives of others."

"Doubtless, my lord," answered the Prince, still calm and unmoved,—"your late mode of life, and the associates with whom you have lived, have made you familiar with scenes and weapons of violence. But it is not to me you are to plead your cause."

"Hear me—hear me, noble Prince!" said Nigel, eagerly. "Hear me! You—even you yourself—may one day ask to be heard, and in vain."

"How, sir," said the Prince, haughtily—"how am I to construe that, my lord?"

"If not on earth, sir," replied the prisoner, "yet to Heaven we must all pray for patient and favourable audience."

"True, my lord," said the Prince, bending his head with haughty acquiescence; "nor would I now refuse such audience to you, could it avail you. But you shall suffer no wrong. We will ourselves look into your case."

"Ay, ay," answered the king, "he hath made *appellatio ad Casarem*—we will interrogate Glenvarlochides ourselves, time and place fitting; and, in the meanwhile, have him and his weapons away, for I am weary of the sight of them."

In consequence of directions hastily given, Nigel was accordingly removed from the presence, where, however, his words had not altogether fallen to the ground. "This is a most strange matter, George," said the Prince to the favourite; "this gentleman hath a good countenance, a happy presence, and much calm firmness in his look and speech. I cannot think he would attempt a crime so desperate and useless."

"I profess neither love nor favour to the young man," answered Buckingham, whose high-spirited ambition bore always an open character: "but I cannot but agree with your Highness, that our dear gossip hath been something hasty in apprehending personal danger from him."

"By my saul, Steenie, ye are not blate, to say so!" said the king. "Do I not ken the smell of pouther, think ye? Who else nosed out the Fifth of November, save our royal selves? Cecil, and Suffolk, and all of them, were at fault, like sae mony mongrel tikes, when I puzzled it out: and trow ye that I cannot smell pouther? Why, 'sblood, man, Joannes Barclaius thought my ingine was in some measure inspiration, and terms his history of the plot, Series patefacti divinitus parricidii; and Spondanus, in like manner, saith of us, Divinitus evasit."

"The land was happy in your Majesty's escape," said the Duke of Buckingham, "and not less in the quick wit which tracked that labyrinth of treason by so fine and almost invisible a clew."

"Saul, man, Steenie, ye are right! There are few youths have sic true judgment as you, respecting the wisdom of their elders; and, as for this fause, traitorous smaik, I doubt he is a hawk of the same nest. Saw ye not something papistical about him? Let them look that he bears not a crucifix, or some sic Roman trinket, about him."

"It would ill become me to attempt the exculpation of this unhappy man," said Lord Dalgarno, "considering the height of his present attempt, which has made all true men's blood curdle in their veins. Yet I cannot avoid intimating, with all due submission to his Majesty's infallible judgment, in justice to one who showed himself formerly only my enemy, though he now displays himself in much blacker colours, that this Olifaunt always appeared to me more as a Puritan than as a Papist."

"Ah, Dalgarno, art thou there, man?" said the king. "And ye behoved to keep back, too, and leave us to our own natural strength and the care of Providence, when we were in grips with the villain!"

"Providence, may it please your most Gracious Majesty, would not fail to aid, in such a strait, the care of three weeping kingdoms," said Lord Dalgarno.

"Surely, man—surely," replied the king—"but a sight of your father, with his long whinyard, would have been a blithe matter a short while syne; and in future we will aid the ends of Providence in our favour, by keeping near us two stout beef-eaters of the guard.—And so this Olifaunt is a Puritan?—not the less like to be a Papist, for all that—for extremities meet, as the scholiast proveth. There are, as I have proved in my book, Puritans of papistical principles—it is just a new tout on an old horn."

Here the king was reminded by the Prince, who dreaded perhaps that he was going to recite the whole Basilicon Doron, that it would be best to move towards the Palace, and consider what was to be done for satisfying the public mind, in whom the morning's adventure was likely to excite much speculation. As they entered the gate of the Palace, a female bowed and presented a paper, which the king received, and, with a sort of groan, thrust it into his side pocket. The Prince expressed some curiosity to know its contents. "The valet in waiting will tell you them," said the king, "when I strip off my cassock. D'ye think, Baby, that I can read all that is thrust into my hands? See to me, man"—(he pointed to the pockets of his great trunk breeches, which were stuffed with papers)—"We are like an ass—that we should so speak—stooping betwixt two burdens. Ay, ay, Asinus fortis accumbens inter terminos, as the Vulgate hath it—Ay, ay, Vidi terram quod esset optima, et supposui humerum ad portandum, et factus sum tributis serviens—I saw this land of England, and became an overburdened king thereof."

"You are indeed well loaded, my dear dad and gossip," said the Duke of Buckingham, receiving the papers which King James emptied out of his pockets.

"Ay, ay," continued the monarch; "take them to you per aversionem, bairns—the one pouch stuffed with petitions, t'other with pasquinadoes; a fine time we have on't. On my conscience, I believe the tale of Cadmus was hieroglyphical, and that the dragon's teeth whilk he sowed were the letters he invented. Ye are laughing, Baby Charles?—Mind what I say.—When I came here first frae our ain country, where the men are as rude as the weather, by my conscience, England was a bieldy bit; one would have thought the king had little to do but to walk by quiet waters, per aquam refectionis. But, I kenna how or why, the place is sair changed—read that libel upon us and on our regimen. The dragon's teeth are sown, Baby Charles; I pray God they bearna their armed harvest in your day, if I suld not live to see it. God forbid I should, for there will be an awful day's kemping at the shearing of them."

"I shall know how to stifle the crop in the blade,—ha, George?" said the Prince, turning to the favourite with a look expressive of some contempt for his father's apprehensions, and full of confidence in the superior firmness and decision of his own counsels.

While this discourse was passing, Nigel, in charge of a pursuivant-at-arms, was pushed and dragged through the small town, all the inhabitants of which, having been alarmed by the report of an attack on the king's life, now pressed forward to see the supposed traitor. Amid the confusion of the moment, he could descry the face of the victualler, arrested into a stare of stolid wonder, and that of the barber grinning betwixt horror and eager curiosity. He thought that he also had a glimpse of his waterman in the green jacket.

He had no time for remarks, being placed in a boat with the pursuivant and two yeomen of the guard, and rowed up the river as fast as the arms of six stout watermen could pull against the tide. They passed the groves of masts which even then astonished the stranger with the extended commerce of London, and now approached those low and blackened walls of curtain and bastion, which exhibit here and there a piece of ordnance, and here and there a solitary sentinel under arms, but have otherwise so little of the military terrors of a citadel. A projecting low-browed arch, which had loured over many an innocent, and many a guilty head, in similar circumstances, now spread its dark frowns over that of Nigel. The boat was put close up to the broad steps against which the tide was lapping its lazy wave. The warder on duty looked from the wicket, and spoke to the pursuivant in whispers. In a few minutes the Lieutenant of the Tower appeared, received, and granted an acknowledgment for the body of Nigel, Lord Glenvarloch.

XXVIII

Ye towers of Julius! London's lasting shame;
With many a foul and midnight murder fed!

—*Gray*

S uch is the exclamation of Gray. Bandello, long before him, has said
something like it; and the same sentiment must, in some shape or
other, have frequently occurred to those, who, remembering the fate of
other captives in that memorable state-prison, may have had but too
much reason to anticipate their own. The dark and low arch, which
seemed, like the entrance to Dante's Hell, to forbid hope of regress—
the muttered sounds of the warders, and petty formalities observed
in opening and shutting the grated wicket—the cold and constrained
salutation of the Lieutenant of the fortress, who showed his prisoner
that distant and measured respect which authority pays as a tax to
decorum, all struck upon Nigel's heart, impressing on him the cruel
consciousness of captivity.

"I am a prisoner," he said, the words escaping from him almost
unawares; "I am a prisoner, and in the Tower!"

The Lieutenant bowed—"And it is my duty," he said, "to show your
lordship your chamber, where, I am compelled to say, my orders are to
place you under some restraint. I will make it as easy as my duty permits."

Nigel only bowed in return to this compliment, and followed the
Lieutenant to the ancient buildings on the western side of the parade,
and adjoining to the chapel, used in those days as a state-prison, but
in ours as the mess-room of the officers of the guard upon duty at the
fortress. The double doors were unlocked, the prisoner ascended a few
steps, followed by the Lieutenant, and a warder of the higher class.
They entered a large, but irregular, low-roofed, and dark apartment,
exhibiting a very scanty proportion of furniture. The warder had orders
to light a fire, and attend to Lord Glenvarloch's commands in all things
consistent with his duty; and the Lieutenant, having made his reverence
with the customary compliment, that he trusted his lordship would not
long remain under his guardianship, took his leave.

Nigel would have asked some questions of the warder, who
remained to put the apartment into order, but the man had caught

the spirit of his office. He seemed not to hear some of the prisoner's questions, though of the most ordinary kind, did not reply to others, and when he did speak, it was in a short and sullen tone, which, though not positively disrespectful, was such as at least to encourage no farther communication.

Nigel left him, therefore, to do his work in silence, and proceeded to amuse himself with the melancholy task of deciphering the names, mottoes, verses, and hieroglyphics, with which his predecessors in captivity had covered the walls of their prison-house. There he saw the names of many a forgotten sufferer mingled with others which will continue in remembrance until English history shall perish. There were the pious effusions of the devout Catholic, poured forth on the eve of his sealing his profession at Tyburn, mingled with those of the firm Protestant, about to feed the fires of Smithfield. There the slender hand of the unfortunate Jane Grey, whose fate was to draw tears from future generations, might be contrasted with the bolder touch which impressed deep on the walls the Bear and Ragged Staff, the proud emblem of the proud Dudleys. It was like the roll of the prophet, a record of lamentation and mourning, and yet not unmixed with brief interjections of resignation, and sentences expressive of the firmest resolution.*

In the sad task of examining the miseries of his predecessors in captivity, Lord Glenvarloch was interrupted by the sudden opening of the door of his prison-room. It was the warder, who came to inform him, that, by order of the Lieutenant of the Tower, his lordship was to have the society and attendance of a fellow-prisoner in his place of confinement. Nigel replied hastily, that he wished no attendance, and would rather be left alone; but the warder gave him to understand, with a kind of grumbling civility, that the Lieutenant was the best judge how his prisoners should be accommodated, and that he would have no trouble with the boy, who was such a slip of a thing as was scarce worth turning a key upon.—"There, Giles," he said, "bring the child in."

Another warder put the "lad before him" into the room, and, both withdrawing, bolt crashed and chain clanged, as they replaced these

---

* These memorials of illustrious criminals, or of innocent persons who had the fate of such, are still preserved, though at one time, in the course of repairing the rooms, they were in some danger of being whitewashed. They are preserved at present with becoming respect, and have most of them been engraved.—See BAYLEY's *History and Antiquities of the Tower of London.*

ponderous obstacles to freedom. The boy was clad in a grey suit of the finest cloth, laid down with silver lace, with a buff-coloured cloak of the same pattern. His cap, which was a Montero of black velvet, was pulled over his brows, and, with the profusion of his long ringlets, almost concealed his face. He stood on the very spot where the warder had quitted his collar, about two steps from the door of the apartment, his eyes fixed on the ground, and every joint trembling with confusion and terror. Nigel could well have dispensed with his society, but it was not in his nature to behold distress, whether of body or mind, without endeavouring to relieve it.

"Cheer up," he said, "my pretty lad. We are to be companions, it seems, for a little time—at least I trust your confinement will be short, since you are too young to have done aught to deserve long restraint. Come, come—do not be discouraged. Your hand is cold and trembles? the air is warm too—but it may be the damp of this darksome room. Place you by the fire.—What! weeping-ripe, my little man? I pray you, do not be a child. You have no beard yet, to be dishonoured by your tears, but yet you should not cry like a girl. Think you are only shut up for playing truant, and you can pass a day without weeping, surely."

The boy suffered himself to be led and seated by the fire, but, after retaining for a long time the very posture which he assumed in sitting down, he suddenly changed it in order to wring his hands with an air of the bitterest distress, and then, spreading them before his face, wept so plentifully, that the tears found their way in floods through his slender fingers.

Nigel was in some degree rendered insensible to his own situation, by his feelings for the intense agony by which so young and beautiful a creature seemed to be utterly overwhelmed; and, sitting down close beside the boy, he applied the most soothing terms which occurred, to endeavour to alleviate his distress; and, with an action which the difference of their age rendered natural, drew his hand kindly along the long hair of the disconsolate child. The lad appeared so shy as even to shrink from this slight approach to familiarity—yet, when Lord Glenvarloch, perceiving and allowing for his timidity, sat down on the farther side of the fire, he appeared to be more at his ease, and to hearken with some apparent interest to the arguments which from time to time Nigel used, to induce him to moderate, at least, the violence of his grief. As the boy listened, his tears, though they continued to flow freely, seemed to escape from their source more easily, his sobs were less convulsive, and became gradually changed into low sighs, which succeeded each other, indicating as much sorrow, perhaps, but less alarm, than his first transports had shown.

"Tell me who and what you are, my pretty boy," said Nigel.—"Consider me, child, as a companion, who wishes to be kind to you, would you but teach him how he can be so."

"Sir—my lord, I mean," answered the boy, very timidly, and in a voice which could scarce be heard even across the brief distance which divided them, "you are very good—and I—am very unhappy—"

A second fit of tears interrupted what else he had intended to say, and it required a renewal of Lord Glenvarloch's good-natured expostulations and encouragements, to bring him once more to such composure as rendered the lad capable of expressing himself intelligibly. At length, however, he was able to say—"I am sensible of your goodness, my lord—and grateful for it—but I am a poor unhappy creature, and, what is worse, have myself only to thank for my misfortunes."

"We are seldom absolutely miserable, my young acquaintance," said Nigel, "without being ourselves more or less responsible for it—I may well say so, otherwise I had not been here to-day—but you are very young, and can have but little to answer for."

"O sir! I wish I could say so—I have been self-willed and obstinate—and rash and ungovernable—and now—now, how dearly do I pay the price of it!"

"Pshaw, my boy," replied Nigel; "this must be some childish frolic—some breaking out of bounds—some truant trick—And yet how should any of these have brought you to the Tower?—There is something mysterious about you, young man, which I must inquire into."

"Indeed, indeed, my lord, there is no harm about me," said the boy, more moved it would seem to confession by the last words, by which he seemed considerably alarmed, than by all the kind expostulations and arguments which Nigel had previously used. "I am innocent—that is, I have done wrong, but nothing to deserve being in this frightful place."

"Tell me the truth, then," said Nigel, in a tone in which command mingled with encouragement; "you have nothing to fear from me, and as little to hope, perhaps—yet, placed as I am, I would know with whom I speak."

"With an unhappy—boy, sir—and idle and truantly disposed, as your lordship said," answered the lad, looking up, and showing a countenance in which paleness and blushes succeeded each other, as fear and shamefacedness alternately had influence. "I left my father's house without leave, to see the king hunt in the Park at Greenwich; there came a cry of treason, and all the gates were shut—I was frightened, and hid myself in a thicket, and I was found by some of the rangers and examined—and they said I gave no good account of myself—and so I was sent hither."

"I am an unhappy, a most unhappy being," said Lord Glenvarloch, rising and walking through the apartment; "nothing approaches me but shares my own bad fate! Death and imprisonment dog my steps, and involve all who are found near me. Yet this boy's story sounds strangely.— You say you were examined, my young friend—Let me pray you to say whether you told your name, and your means of gaining admission into the Park—if so, they surely would not have detained you?"

"O, my lord," said the boy, "I took care not to tell them the name of the friend that let me in; and as to my father—I would not he knew where I now am for all the wealth in London!"

"But do you not expect," said Nigel, "that they will dismiss you till you let them know who and what you are?"

"What good will it do them to keep so useless a creature as myself?" said the boy; "they must let me go, were it but out of shame."

"Do not trust to that—tell me your name and station—I will communicate them to the Lieutenant—he is a man of quality and honour, and will not only be willing to procure your liberation, but also, I have no doubt, will intercede with your father. I am partly answerable for such poor aid as I can afford, to get you out of this embarrassment, since I occasioned the alarm owing to which you were arrested; so tell me your name, and your father's name."

"My name to you? O never, never!" answered the boy, in a tone of deep emotion, the cause of which Nigel could not comprehend.

"Are you so much afraid of me, young man," he replied, "because I am here accused and a prisoner? Consider, a man may be both, and deserve neither suspicion nor restraint. Why should you distrust me? You seem friendless, and I am myself so much in the same circumstances, that I cannot but pity your situation when I reflect on my own. Be wise; I have spoken kindly to you—I mean as kindly as I speak."

"O, I doubt it not, I doubt it not, my lord," said the boy, "and I could tell you all—that is, almost all."

"Tell me nothing, my young friend, excepting what may assist me in being useful to you," said Nigel.

"You are generous, my lord," said the boy; "and I am sure—O sure, I might safely trust to your honour—But yet—but yet—I am so sore beset—I have been so rash, so unguarded—I can never tell you of my folly. Besides, I have already told too much to one whose heart I thought I had moved—yet I find myself here."

"To whom did you make this disclosure?" said Nigel.

"I dare not tell," replied the youth.

"There is something singular about you, my young friend," said Lord Glenvarloch, withdrawing with a gentle degree of compulsion the hand with which the boy had again covered his eyes; "do not pain yourself with thinking on your situation just at present—your pulse is high, and your hand feverish—lay yourself on yonder pallet, and try to compose yourself to sleep. It is the readiest and best remedy for the fancies with which you are worrying yourself."

"I thank you for your considerate kindness, my lord," said the boy; "with your leave I will remain for a little space quiet in this chair—I am better thus than on the couch. I can think undisturbedly on what I have done, and have still to do; and if God sends slumber to a creature so exhausted, it shall be most welcome."

So saying, the boy drew his hand from Lord Nigel's, and, drawing around him and partly over his face the folds of his ample cloak, he resigned himself to sleep or meditation, while his companion, notwithstanding the exhausting scenes of this and the preceding day, continued his pensive walk up and down the apartment.

Every reader has experienced, that times occur, when far from being lord of external circumstances, man is unable to rule even the wayward realm of his own thoughts. It was Nigel's natural wish to consider his own situation coolly, and fix on the course which it became him as a man of sense and courage to adopt; and yet, in spite of himself, and notwithstanding the deep interest of the critical state in which he was placed, it did so happen that his fellow-prisoner's situation occupied more of his thoughts than did his own. There was no accounting for this wandering of the imagination, but also there was no striving with it. The pleading tones of one of the sweetest voices he had ever heard, still rung in his ear, though it seemed that sleep had now fettered the tongue of the speaker. He drew near on tiptoe to satisfy himself whether it were so. The folds of the cloak hid the lower part of his face entirely; but the bonnet, which had fallen a little aside, permitted him to see the forehead streaked with blue veins, the closed eyes, and the long silken eyelashes.

"Poor child," said Nigel to himself, as he looked on him, nestled up as it were in the folds of his mantle, "the dew is yet on thy eyelashes, and thou hast fairly wept thyself asleep. Sorrow is a rough nurse to one so young and delicate as thou art. Peace be to thy slumbers, I will not disturb them. My own misfortunes require my attention, and it is to their contemplation that I must resign myself."

He attempted to do so, but was crossed at every turn by conjectures which intruded themselves as before, and which all regarded the sleeper rather than himself. He was angry and vexed, and expostulated with himself concerning the overweening interest which he took in the concerns of one of whom he knew nothing, saving that the boy was forced into his company, perhaps as a spy, by those to whose custody he was committed—but the spell could not be broken, and the thoughts which he struggled to dismiss, continued to haunt him.

Thus passed half an hour, or more; at the conclusion of which, the harsh sound of the revolving bolts was again heard, and the voice of the warder announced that a man desired to speak with Lord Glenvarloch. "A man to speak with me, under my present circumstances!—Who can it be?" And John Christie, his landlord of Paul's Wharf, resolved his doubts, by entering the apartment. "Welcome—most welcome, mine honest landlord!" said Lord Glenvarloch. "How could I have dreamt of seeing you in my present close lodgings?" And at the same time, with the frankness of old kindness, he walked up to Christie and offered his hand; but John started back as from the look of a basilisk.

"Keep your courtesies to yourself, my lord," said he, gruffly; "I have had as many of them already as may serve me for my life."

"Why, Master Christie," said Nigel, "what means this? I trust I have not offended you?"

"Ask me no questions, my lord," said Christie, bluntly. "I am a man of peace—I came not hither to wrangle with you at this place and season. Just suppose that I am well informed of all the obligements from your honour's nobleness, and then acquaint me, in as few words as may be, where is the unhappy woman—What have you done with her?"

"What have I done with her!" said Lord Glenvarloch—"Done with whom? I know not what you are speaking of."

"Oh, yes, my lord," said Christie; "play surprise as well as you will, you must have some guess that I am speaking of the poor fool that was my wife, till she became your lordship's light-o'-love."

"Your wife! Has your wife left you? and, if she has, do you come to ask her of me?"

"Yes, my lord, singular as it may seem," returned Christie, in a tone of bitter irony, and with a sort of grin widely discording from the discomposure of his features, the gleam of his eye, and the froth which stood on his lip, "I do come to make that demand of your lordship. Doubtless, you are surprised I should take the trouble; but, I cannot tell, great men and little men think differently. She has lain in my bosom, and drunk of my cup; and, such as she is, I cannot forget that— though I will never see her again—she must not starve, my lord, or do worse, to gain bread, though I reckon your lordship may think I am robbing the public in trying to change her courses."

"By my faith as a Christian, by my honour as a gentleman," said Lord Glenvarloch, "if aught amiss has chanced with your wife, I know nothing of it. I trust in Heaven you are as much mistaken in imputing guilt to her, as in supposing me her partner in it."

"Fie! fie! my lord," said Christie, "why will you make it so tough? She is but the wife of a clod-pated old chandler, who was idiot enough to marry a wench twenty years younger than himself. Your lordship cannot have more glory by it than you have had already; and, as for advantage and solace, I take it Dame Nelly is now unnecessary to your gratification. I should be sorry to interrupt the course of your pleasure; an old wittol should have more consideration of his condition. But, your precious lordship being mewed up here among other choice jewels of the kingdom, Dame Nelly cannot, I take it, be admitted to share the hours of dalliance which"—Here the incensed husband stammered, broke off his tone of irony, and proceeded, striking his staff against the ground—"O that these false limbs of yours, which I wish had been hamstrung when they first crossed my honest threshold, were free from the fetters they have well deserved! I would give you the odds of your youth, and your weapon, and would bequeath my soul to the foul fiend if I, with this piece of oak, did not make you such an example to all ungrateful, pick-thank courtiers, that it should be a proverb to the end of time, how John Christie swaddled his wife's fine leman!"

"I understand not your insolence," said Nigel, "but I forgive it, because you labour under some strange delusion. In so far as I can comprehend your vehement charge, it is entirely undeserved on my part. You seem to impute to me the seduction of your wife—I trust she is innocent. For me, at least, she is as innocent as an angel in bliss.

I never thought of her—never touched her hand or cheek, save in honourable courtesy."

"O, ay—courtesy!—that is the very word. She always praised your lordship's honourable courtesy. Ye have cozened me between ye, with your courtesy. My lord—my lord, you came to us no very wealthy man—you know it. It was for no lucre of gain I took you and your swash-buckler, your Don Diego yonder, under my poor roof. I never cared if the little room were let or no; I could live without it. If you could not have paid for it, you should never have been asked. All the wharf knows John Christie has the means and spirit to do a kindness. When you first darkened my honest doorway, I was as happy as a man need to be, who is no youngster, and has the rheumatism. Nelly was the kindest and best-humoured wench—we might have a word now and then about a gown or a ribbon, but a kinder soul on the whole, and a more careful, considering her years, till you come—and what is she now!—But I will not be a fool to cry, if I can help it. *What* she is, is not the question, but where she is; and that I must learn, sir, of you."

"How can you, when I tell you," replied Nigel, "that I am as ignorant as yourself, or rather much more so? Till this moment, I never heard of any disagreement betwixt your dame and you."

"That is a lie," said John Christie, bluntly.

"How, you base villain!" said Lord Glenvarloch—"do you presume on my situation? If it were not that I hold you mad, and perhaps made so by some wrong sustained, you should find my being weaponless were no protection, I would beat your brains out against the wall."

"Ay, ay," answered Christie, "bully as ye list. Ye have been at the ordinaries, and in Alsatia, and learned the ruffian's rant, I doubt not. But I repeat, you have spoken an untruth, when you said you knew not of my wife's falsehood; for, when you were twitted with it among your gay mates, it was a common jest among you, and your lordship took all the credit they would give you for your gallantry and gratitude."

There was a mixture of truth in this part of the charge which disconcerted Lord Glenvarloch exceedingly; for he could not, as a man of honour, deny that Lord Dalgarno, and others, had occasionally jested with him on the subject of Dame Nelly, and that, though he had not played exactly *le fanfaron des vices qu'il n'avoit pas*, he had not at least been sufficiently anxious to clear himself of the suspicion of such a crime to men who considered it as a merit. It was therefore with some hesitation, and in a sort of qualifying tone, that he admitted that some idle jests had passed upon such a supposition, although without the least foundation in truth. John Christie would not listen to his vindication any longer. "By your own account," he said, "you permitted lies to be told of you injest. How do I know you are speaking truth, now you are serious? You thought it, I suppose, a fine thing to wear the reputation of having dishonoured an honest family,—who will not think that you had real grounds for your base bravado to rest upon? I will not believe otherwise for one, and therefore, my lord, mark what I have to say. You are now yourself in trouble—As you hope to come through it safely, and without loss of life and property, tell me where this unhappy woman is. Tell me, if you hope for heaven—tell me, if you fear hell—tell me, as you would not have the curse of an utterly ruined woman, and a broken-hearted man, attend you through life, and bear witness against you at the Great Day, which shall come after death. You are moved, my lord, I see it. I cannot forget the wrong you have done me. I cannot even promise to forgive it—but—tell me, and you shall never see me again, or hear more of my reproaches."

"Unfortunate man," said Lord Glenvarloch, "you have said more, far more than enough, to move me deeply. Were I at liberty, I would lend you my best aid to search out him who has wronged you, the rather that I do suspect my having been your lodger has been in some degree the remote cause of bringing the spoiler into the sheepfold."

"I am glad your lordship grants me so much," said John Christie, resuming the tone of embittered irony with which he had opened the singular conversation; "I will spare you farther reproach and remonstrance—your mind is made up, and so is mine.—So, ho, warder!" The warder entered, and John went on,—"I want to get out, brother. Look well to your charge—it were better that half the wild beasts in their dens yonder were turned loose upon Tower Hill, than that this same smooth-faced, civil-spoken gentleman, were again returned to honest men's company!"

So saying, he hastily left the apartment; and Nigel had full leisure to lament the waywardness of his fate, which seemed never to tire of persecuting him for crimes of which he was innocent, and investing him with the appearances of guilt which his mind abhorred. He could not, however, help acknowledging to himself, that all the pain which he might sustain from the present accusation of John Christie, was so far deserved, from his having suffered himself, out of vanity, or rather an unwillingness to encounter ridicule, to be supposed capable of a base inhospitable crime, merely because fools called it an affair of gallantry; and it was no balsam to the wound, when he recollected what Richie had told him of his having been ridiculed behind his back by the gallants of the ordinary, for affecting the reputation of an intrigue which he had not in reality spirit enough to have carried on. His simulation had, in a word, placed him in the unlucky predicament of being rallied as a braggart amongst the dissipated youths, with whom the reality of the amour would have given him credit; whilst, on the other hand, he was branded as an inhospitable seducer by the injured husband, who was obstinately persuaded of his guilt.

XXIX

How fares the man on whom good men would look
With eyes where scorn and censure combated,
But that kind Christian love hath taught the lesson—
That they who merit most contempt and hate,
Do most deserve our pity.—

—Old Play

I t might have seemed natural that the visit of John Christie should have entirely diverted Nigel's attention from his slumbering companion, and, for a time, such was the immediate effect of the chain of new ideas which the incident introduced; yet, soon after the injured man had departed, Lord Glenvarloch began to think it extraordinary that the boy should have slept so soundly, while they talked loudly in his vicinity. Yet he certainly did not appear to have stirred. Was he well—was he only feigning sleep? He went close to him to make his observations, and perceived that he had wept, and was still weeping, though his eyes were closed. He touched him gently on the shoulder—the boy shrunk from his touch, but did not awake. He pulled him harder, and asked him if he was sleeping.

"Do they waken folk in your country to know whether they are asleep or no?" said the boy, in a peevish tone.

"No, my young sir," answered Nigel; "but when they weep in the manner you do in your sleep, they awaken them to see what ails them."

"It signifies little to any one what ails me," said the boy.

"True," replied Lord Glenvarloch; "but you knew before you went to sleep how little I could assist you in your difficulties, and you seemed disposed, notwithstanding, to put some confidence in me."

"If I did, I have changed my mind," said the lad.

"And what may have occasioned this change of mind, I trow?" said Lord Glenvarloch. "Some men speak through their sleep—perhaps you have the gift of hearing in it?"

"No, but the Patriarch Joseph never dreamt truer dreams than I do."

"Indeed!" said Lord Glenvarloch. "And, pray, what dream have you had that has deprived me of your good opinion; for that, I think, seems the moral of the matter?"

"You shall judge yourself," answered the boy. "I dreamed I was in a wild forest, where there was a cry of hounds, and winding of horns, exactly as I heard in Greenwich Park."

"That was because you were in the Park this morning, you simple child," said Nigel.

"Stay, my lord," said the youth. "I went on in my dream, till, at the top of a broad green alley, I saw a noble stag which had fallen into the toils; and methought I knew that he was the very stag which the whole party were hunting, and that if the chase came up, the dogs would tear him to pieces, or the hunters would cut his throat; and I had pity on the gallant stag, and though I was of a different kind from him, and though I was somewhat afraid of him, I thought I would venture something to free so stately a creature; and I pulled out my knife, and just as I was beginning to cut the meshes of the net, the animal started up in my face in the likeness of a tiger, much larger and fiercer than any you may have seen in the ward of the wild beasts yonder, and was just about to tear me limb from limb, when you awaked me."

"Methinks," said Nigel, "I deserve more thanks than I have got, for rescuing you from such a danger by waking you. But, my pretty master, methinks all this tale of a tiger and a stag has little to do with your change of temper towards me."

"I know not whether it has or no," said the lad; "but I will not tell you who I am."

"You will keep your secret to yourself then, peevish boy," said Nigel, turning from him, and resuming his walk through the room; then stopping suddenly, he said—"And yet you shall not escape from me without knowing that I penetrate your mystery."

"My mystery!" said the youth, at once alarmed and irritated—"what mean you, my lord?"

"Only that I can read your dream without the assistance of a Chaldean interpreter, and my exposition is—that my fair companion does not wear the dress of her sex."

"And if I do not, my lord," said his companion, hastily starting up, and folding her cloak tight around her, "my dress, such as it is, covers one who will not disgrace it."

"Many would call that speech a fair challenge," said Lord Glenvarloch, looking on her fixedly; "women do not masquerade in men's clothes, to make use of men's weapons."

"I have no such purpose," said the seeming boy; "I have other means of protection, and powerful—but I would first know what is *your* purpose."

"An honourable and a most respectful one," said Lord Glenvarloch; "whatever you are—whatever motive may have brought you into this ambiguous situation, I am sensible—every look, word, and action of yours, makes me sensible, that you are no proper subject of importunity, far less of ill usage. What circumstances can have forced you into so doubtful a situation, I know not; but I feel assured there is, and can be, nothing in them of premeditated wrong, which should expose you to cold-blooded insult. From me you have nothing to dread."

"I expected nothing less from your nobleness, my lord," answered the female; "my adventure, though I feel it was both desperate and foolish, is not so very foolish, nor my safety here so utterly unprotected, as at first sight—and in this strange dress, it may appear to be. I have suffered enough, and more than enough, by the degradation of having been seen in this unfeminine attire, and the comments you must necessarily have made on my conduct—but I thank God that I am so far protected, that I could not have been subjected to insult unavenged." When this extraordinary explanation had proceeded thus far, the warder appeared, to place before Lord Glenvarloch a meal, which, for his present situation, might be called comfortable, and which, if not equal to the cookery of the celebrated Chevalier Beaujeu, was much superior in neatness and cleanliness to that of Alsatia. A warder attended to do the honours of the table, and made a sign to the disguised female to rise and assist him in his functions. But Nigel, declaring that he knew the youth's parents, interfered, and caused his companion to eat along with him. She consented with a sort of embarrassment, which rendered her pretty features yet more interesting. Yet she maintained with a natural grace that sort of good-breeding which belongs to the table; and it seemed to Nigel, whether already prejudiced in her favour by the extraordinary circumstances of their meeting, or whether really judging from what was actually the fact, that he had seldom seen a young person comport herself with more decorous propriety, mixed with ingenuous simplicity; while the consciousness of the peculiarity of her situation threw a singular colouring over her whole demeanour, which could be neither said to be formal, nor easy, nor embarrassed, but was compounded of, and shaded with, an interchange of all these three characteristics. Wine was placed on the table, of which she could not be prevailed on to taste a glass. Their conversation was, of course, limited by the presence of the warder to the business of the table: but Nigel had, long ere the cloth was removed, formed the resolution, if possible, of making himself master of this young person's history, the more especially as he now began to think that the tones of her voice and her features were not so strange to him as he had originally supposed. This, however, was a conviction which he adopted slowly, and only as it dawned upon him from particular circumstances during the course of the repast.

At length the prison-meal was finished, and Lord Glenvarloch began to think how he might most easily enter upon the topic he meditated, when the warder announced a visitor.

"Soh!" said Nigel, something displeased, "I find even a prison does not save one from importunate visitations."

He prepared to receive his guest, however, while his alarmed companion flew to the large cradle-shaped chair, which had first served her as a place of refuge, drew her cloak around her, and disposed herself as much as she could to avoid observation. She had scarce made her arrangements for that purpose when the door opened, and the worthy citizen, George Heriot, entered the prison-chamber.

He cast around the apartment his usual sharp, quick glance of observation, and, advancing to Nigel, said—"My lord, I wish I could say I was happy to see you."

"The sight of those who are unhappy themselves, Master Heriot, seldom produces happiness to their friends—I, however, am glad to see you."

He extended his hand, but Heriot bowed with much formal complaisance, instead of accepting the courtesy, which in those times, when the distinction of ranks was much guarded by etiquette and ceremony, was considered as a distinguished favour.

"You are displeased with me, Master Heriot," said Lord Glenvarloch, reddening, for he was not deceived by the worthy citizen's affectation of extreme reverence and respect.

"By no means, my lord," replied Heriot; "but I have been in France, and have thought it is well to import, along with other more substantial articles, a small sample of that good-breeding which the French are so renowned for."

"It is not kind of you," said Nigel, "to bestow the first use of it on an old and obliged friend."

Heriot only answered to this observation with a short dry cough, and then proceeded.

"Hem! hem! I say, ahem! My lord, as my French politeness may not carry me far, I would willingly know whether I am to speak as a friend, since your lordship is pleased to term me such; or whether I am, as befits my condition, to confine myself to the needful business which must be treated of between us."

"Speak as a friend by all means, Master Heriot," said Nigel; "I perceive you have adopted some of the numerous prejudices against me, if not all of them. Speak out, and frankly—what I cannot deny I will at least confess."

"And I trust, my lord, redress," said Heriot.

"So far as in my power, certainly," answered Nigel.

"Ah I my lord," continued Heriot, "that is a melancholy though a necessary restriction; for how lightly may any one do an hundred times more than the degree of evil which it may be within his power to repair to the sufferers and to society! But we are not alone here," he said, stopping, and darting his shrewd eye towards the muffled figure of the disguised maiden, whose utmost efforts had not enabled her so to adjust her position as altogether to escape observation. More anxious to prevent her being discovered than to keep his own affairs private, Nigel hastily answered—"'Tis a page of mine; you may speak freely before him. He is of France, and knows no English."

"I am then to speak freely," said Heriot, after a second glance at the chair; "perhaps my words may be more free than welcome."

"Go on, sir," said Nigel, "I have told you I can bear reproof."

"In one word, then, my lord—why do I find you in this place, and whelmed with charges which must blacken a name rendered famous by ages of virtue?"

"Simply, then, you find me here," said Nigel, "because, to begin from my original error, I would be wiser than my father."

"It was a difficult task, my lord," replied Heriot; "your father was voiced generally as the wisest and one of the bravest men of Scotland."

"He commanded me," continued Nigel, "to avoid all gambling; and I took upon me to modify this injunction into regulating my play according to my skill, means, and the course of my luck."

"Ay, self opinion, acting on a desire of acquisition, my lord—you hoped to touch pitch and not to be defiled," answered Heriot. "Well, my lord, you need not say, for I have heard with much regret, how far this conduct diminished your reputation. Your next error I may without scruple remind you of—My lord, my lord, in whatever degree Lord

Dalgarno may have failed towards you, the son of his father should have been sacred from your violence."

"You speak in cold blood, Master Heriot, and I was smarting under a thousand wrongs inflicted on me under the mask of friendship."

"That is, he gave your lordship bad advice, and you," said Heriot—

"Was fool enough to follow his counsel," answered Nigel—"But we will pass this, Master Heriot, if you please. Old men and young men, men of the sword and men of peaceful occupation, always have thought, always will think, differently on such subjects."

"I grant," answered Heriot, "the distinction between the old goldsmith and the young nobleman—still you should have had patience for Lord Huntinglen's sake, and prudence for your own. Supposing your quarrel just—"

"I pray you to pass on to some other charge," said Lord Glenvarloch.

"I am not your accuser, my lord; but I trust in heaven, that your own heart has already accused you bitterly on the inhospitable wrong which your late landlord has sustained at your hand."

"Had I been guilty of what you allude to," said Lord Glenvarloch,— "had a moment of temptation hurried me away, I had long ere now most bitterly repented it. But whoever may have wronged the unhappy woman, it was not I—I never heard of her folly until within this hour."

"Come, my lord," said Heriot, with some severity, "this sounds too much like affectation. I know there is among our modern youth a new creed respecting adultery as well as homicide—I would rather hear you speak of a revision of the Decalogue, with mitigated penalties in favour of the privileged orders—I would rather hear you do this than deny a fact in which you have been known to glory."

"Glory!—I never did, never would have taken honour to myself from such a cause," said Lord Glenvarloch. "I could not prevent other idle tongues, and idle brains, from making false inferences."

"You would have known well enough how to stop their mouths, my lord," replied Heriot, "had they spoke of you what was unpleasing to your ears, and what the truth did not warrant.—Come, my lord, remember your promise to confess; and, indeed, to confess is, in this case, in some slight sort to redress. I will grant you are young—the woman handsome—and, as I myself have observed, light-headed enough. Let me know where she is. Her foolish husband has still some compassion for her—will save her from infamy—perhaps, in time, receive her back; for we are a good-natured generation we traders. Do not, my lord, emulate those who work mischief merely for the pleasure of doing so—it is the very devil's worst quality."

"Your grave remonstrances will drive me mad," said Nigel. "There is a show of sense and reason in what you say; and yet, it is positively insisting on my telling the retreat of a fugitive of whom I know nothing earthly."

"It is well, my lord," answered Heriot, coldly. "You have a right, such as it is, to keep your own secrets; but, since my discourse on these points seems so totally unavailing, we had better proceed to business. Yet your father's image rises before me, and seems to plead that I should go on."

"Be it as you will, sir," said Glenvarloch; "he who doubts my word shall have no additional security for it."

"Well, my lord.—In the Sanctuary at Whitefriars—a place of refuge so unsuitable to a young man of quality and character—I am told a murder was committed."

"And you believe that I did the deed, I suppose?"

"God forbid, my lord!" said Heriot. "The coroner's inquest hath sat, and it appeared that your lordship, under your assumed name of Grahame, behaved with the utmost bravery."

"No compliment, I pray you," said Nigel; "I am only too happy to find, that I did not murder, or am not believed to have murdered, the old man."

"True, my lord," said Heriot; "but even in this affair there lacks explanation. Your lordship embarked this morning in a wherry with a female, and, it is said, an immense sum of money, in specie and other valuables—but the woman has not since been heard of."

"I parted with her at Paul's Wharf," said Nigel, "where she went ashore with her charge. I gave her a letter to that very man, John Christie."

"Ay, that is the waterman's story; but John Christie denies that he remembers anything of the matter."

"I am sorry to hear this," said the young nobleman; "I hope in Heaven she has not been trepanned, for the treasure she had with her."

"I hope not, my lord," replied Heriot; "but men's minds are much disturbed about it. Our national character suffers on all hands. Men remember the fatal case of Lord Sanquhar, hanged for the murder of a fencing-master; and exclaim, they will not have their wives whored, and their property stolen, by the nobility of Scotland."

"And all this is laid to my door!" said Nigel; "my exculpation is easy."

"I trust so, my lord," said Heriot;—"nay, in this particular, I do not doubt it.—But why did you leave Whitefriars under such circumstances?"

"Master Reginald Lowestoffe sent a boat for me, with intimation to provide for my safety."

"I am sorry to say," replied Heriot, "that he denies all knowledge of your lordship's motions, after having dispatched a messenger to you with some baggage."

"The watermen told me they were employed by him."

"Watermen!" said Heriot; "one of these proves to be an idle apprentice, an old acquaintance of mine—the other has escaped; but the fellow who is in custody persists in saying he was employed by your lordship, and you only."

"He lies!" said Lord Glenvarloch, hastily;—"He told me Master Lowestoffe had sent him.—I hope that kind-hearted gentleman is at liberty?"

"He is," answered Heriot; "and has escaped with a rebuke from the benchers, for interfering in such a matter as your lordship's. The Court desire to keep well with the young Templars in these times of commotion, or he had not come off so well."

"That is the only word of comfort I have heard from you," replied Nigel. "But this poor woman,—she and her trunk were committed to the charge of two porters."

"So said the pretended waterman; but none of the fellows who ply at the wharf will acknowledge the employment.—I see the idea makes you uneasy, my lord; but every effort is made to discover the poor woman's place of retreat—if, indeed, she yet lives.—And now, my lord, my errand is spoken, so far as it relates exclusively to your lordship; what remains, is matter of business of a more formal kind."

"Let us proceed to it without delay," said Lord Glenvarloch. "I would hear of the affairs of any one rather than of my own."

"You cannot have forgotten, my lord," said Heriot, "the transaction which took place some weeks since at Lord Huntinglen's—by which a large sum of money was advanced for the redemption of your lordship's estate?"

"I remember it perfectly," said Nigel; "and your present austerity cannot make me forget your kindness on the occasion."

Heriot bowed gravely, and went on.—"That money was advanced under the expectation and hope that it might be replaced by the contents of a grant to your lordship, under the royal sign-manual, in payment of certain monies due by the crown to your father.—I trust your lordship understood the transaction at the time—I trust you now understand my resumption of its import, and hold it to be correct?"

"Undeniably correct," answered Lord Glenvarloch. "If the sums contained in the warrant cannot be recovered, my lands become the property of those who paid off the original holders of the mortgage, and now stand in their right."

"Even so, my lord," said Heriot. "And your lordship's unhappy circumstances having, it would seem, alarmed these creditors, they are now, I am sorry to say, pressing for one or other of these alternatives—possession of the land, or payment of their debt."

"They have a right to one or other," answered Lord Glenvarloch; "and as I cannot do the last in my present condition, I suppose they must enter on possession."

"Stay, my lord," replied Heriot; "if you have ceased to call me a friend to your person, at least you shall see I am willing to be such to your father's house, were it but for the sake of your father's memory. If you will trust me with the warrant under the sign-manual, I believe circumstances do now so stand at Court, that I may be able to recover the money for you."

"I would do so gladly," said Lord Glenvarloch, "but the casket which contains it is not in my possession. It was seized when I was arrested at Greenwich."

"It will be no longer withheld from you," said Heriot; "for, I understand, my Master's natural good sense, and some information which he has procured, I know not how, has induced him to contradict the whole charge of the attempt on his person. It is entirely hushed up; and you will only be proceeded against for your violence on Lord Dalgarno, committed within the verge of the Palace—and that you will find heavy enough to answer."

"I will not shrink under the weight," said Lord Glenvarloch. "But that is not the present point.—If I had that casket—"

"Your baggage stood in the little ante-room, as I passed," said the citizen; "the casket caught my eye. I think you had it of me. It was my old friend Sir Faithful Frugal's. Ay; he, too, had a son—"

Here he stopped short.

"A son who, like Lord Glenvarloch's, did no credit to his father.—Was it not so you would have ended the sentence, Master Heriot?" asked the young nobleman.

"My lord, it was a word spoken rashly," answered Heriot. "God may mend all in his own good time. This, however, I will say, that I have sometimes envied my friends their fair and flourishing families; and yet have I seen such changes when death has removed the head, so many rich men's sons penniless, the heirs of so many knights and nobles acreless, that I think mine own estate and memory, as I shall order it, has a fair chance of outliving those of greater men, though God has given me no heir of my name. But this is from the purpose.—Ho! warder, bring in Lord Glenvarloch's baggage." The officer obeyed. Seals had been placed upon the trunk and casket, but were now removed, the warder said, in consequence of the subsequent orders from Court, and the whole was placed at the prisoner's free disposal.

Desirous to bring this painful visit to a conclusion, Lord Glenvarloch opened the casket, and looked through the papers which it contained, first hastily, and then more slowly and accurately; but it was all in vain. The Sovereign's signed warrant had disappeared.

"I thought and expected nothing better," said George Heriot, bitterly. "The beginning of evil is the letting out of water. Here is a fair heritage lost, I dare say, on a foul cast at dice, or a conjuring trick at cards!—My lord, your surprise is well played. I give you full joy of your accomplishments. I have seen many as young brawlers and spendthrifts, but never as young and accomplished a dissembler.—Nay, man, never bend your angry brows on me. I speak in bitterness of heart, from what I remember of your worthy father; and if his son hears of his degeneracy from no one else, he shall hear it from the old goldsmith."

This new suspicion drove Nigel to the very extremity of his patience; yet the motives and zeal of the good old man, as well as the circumstances of suspicion which created his displeasure, were so excellent an excuse for it, that they formed an absolute curb on the resentment of Lord Glenvarloch, and constrained him, after two or three hasty exclamations, to observe a proud and sullen silence. At length, Master Heriot resumed his lecture.

"Hark you, my lord," he said, "it is scarce possible that this most important paper can be absolutely assigned away. Let me know in what obscure corner, and for what petty sum, it lies pledged—something may yet be done."

"Your efforts in my favour are the more generous," said Lord Glenvarloch, "as you offer them to one whom you believe you have cause to think hardly of—but they are altogether unavailing. Fortune has taken the field against me at every point. Even let her win the battle."

"Zouns!" exclaimed Heriot, impatiently,—"you would make a saint swear! Why, I tell you, if this paper, the loss of which seems to sit so light on you, be not found, farewell to the fair lordship of Glenvarloch—firth and forest—lea and furrow—lake and stream—all that has been in the house of Olifaunt since the days of William the Lion!"

"Farewell to them, then," said Nigel,—"and that moan is soon made."

"'Sdeath! my lord, you will make more moan for it ere you die," said Heriot, in the same tone of angry impatience.

"Not I, my old friend," said Nigel. "If I mourn, Master Heriot, it will be for having lost the good opinion of a worthy man, and lost it, as I must say, most undeservedly."

"Ay, ay, young man," said Heriot, shaking his head, "make me believe that if you can.—To sum the matter up," he said, rising from his seat, and walking towards that occupied by the disguised female, "for our matters are now drawn into small compass, you shall as soon make me believe that this masquerading mummer, on whom I now lay the hand of paternal authority, is a French page, who understands no English."

So saying, he took hold of the supposed page's cloak, and, not without some gentle degree of violence, led into the middle of the apartment the disguised fair one, who in vain attempted to cover her face, first with her mantle, and afterwards with her hands; both which impediments Master Heriot removed something unceremoniously, and gave to view the detected daughter of the old chronologist, his own fair god-daughter, Margaret Ramsay.

"Here is goodly gear!" he said; and, as he spoke, he could not prevent himself from giving her a slight shake, for we have elsewhere noticed that he was a severe disciplinarian.—"How comes it, minion, that I find you in so shameless a dress, and so unworthy a situation? Nay, your modesty is now mistimed—it should have come sooner. Speak, or I will—"

"Master Heriot," said Lord Glenvarloch, "whatever right you may have over this maiden elsewhere, while in my apartment she is under my protection."

"Your protection, my lord!—a proper protector!—and how long, mistress, have you been under my lord's protection? Speak out forsooth!"

"For the matter of two hours, godfather," answered the maiden, with a countenance bent to the ground, and covered with blushes, "but it was against my will."

"Two hours!" repeated Heriot,—"space enough for mischief.—My lord, this is, I suppose, another victim offered to your character of gallantry—another adventure to be boasted of at Beaujeu's ordinary? Methinks the roof under which you first met this silly maiden should have secured *her*, at least, from such a fate."

"On my honour, Master Heriot," said Lord Glenvarloch, "you remind me now, for the first time, that I saw this young lady in your family. Her features are not easily forgotten, and yet I was trying in vain to recollect where I had last looked on them. For your suspicions, they are as false as they are injurious both to her and me. I had but discovered her disguise as you entered. I am satisfied, from her whole behaviour, that her presence here in this dress was involuntary; and God forbid that I have been capable of taking advantage of it to her prejudice."

"It is well mouthed, my lord," said Master Heriot; "but a cunning clerk can read the Apocrypha as loud as the Scripture. Frankly, my lord, you are come to that pass, where your words will not be received without a warrant."

"I should not speak, perhaps," said Margaret, the natural vivacity of whose temper could never be long suppressed by any situation, however disadvantageous, "but I cannot be silent. Godfather, you do me wrong—and no less wrong to this young nobleman. You say his words want a warrant. I know where to find a warrant for some of them, and the rest I deeply and devoutly believe without one."

"And I thank you, maiden," replied Nigel, "for the good opinion you have expressed. I am at that point, it seems, though how I have been driven to it I know not, where every fair construction of my actions and motives is refused me. I am the more obliged to her who grants me that right which the world denies me. For you, lady, were I at liberty, I have a sword and arm should know how to guard your reputation."

"Upon my word, a perfect Amadis and Oriana!" said George Heriot. "I should soon get my throat cut betwixt the knight and the princess, I suppose, but that the beef-eaters are happily within halloo.—Come, come, Lady Light-o'-Love—if you mean to make your way with me, it must be by plain facts, not by speeches from romaunts and play-books. How, in Heaven's name, came you here?"

"Sir," answered Margaret, "since I must speak, I went to Greenwich this morning with Monna Paula, to present a petition to the king on the part of the Lady Hermione."

"Mercy-a-gad!" exclaimed Heriot, "is she in the dance, too? Could she not have waited my return to stir in her affairs? But I suppose the intelligence I sent her had rendered her restless. Ah! woman, woman— he that goes partner with you, had need of a double share of patience, for you will bring none into the common stock.—Well, but what on earth had this embassy of Monna Paula's to do with your absurd disguise? Speak out."

"Monna Paula was frightened," answered Margaret, "and did not know how to set about the errand, for you know she scarce ever goes out of doors—and so—and so—I agreed to go with her to give her courage; and, for the dress, I am sure you remember I wore it at a Christmas mumming, and you thought it not unbeseeming."

"Yes, for a Christmas parlour," said Heriot, "but not to go a-masking through the country in. I do remember it, minion, and I knew it even now; that and your little shoe there, linked with a hint I had in the morning from a friend, or one who called himself such, led to your detection."—Here Lord Glenvarloch could not help giving a glance at the pretty foot, which even the staid citizen thought worth recollection—it was but a glance, for he saw how much the least degree of observation added to Margaret's distress and confusion. "And tell me, maiden," continued Master Heriot, for what we have observed was by-play,—"did the Lady Hermione know of this fair work?"

"I dared not have told her for the world," said Margaret—"she thought one of our apprentices went with Monna Paula."

It may be here noticed, that the words, "our apprentices," seemed to have in them something of a charm to break the fascination with which Lord Glenvarloch had hitherto listened to the broken, yet interesting details of Margaret's history.

"And wherefore went he not?—he had been a fitter companion for Monna Paula than you, I wot," said the citizen.

"He was otherwise employed," said Margaret, in a voice scarce audible.

Master George darted a hasty glance at Nigel, and when he saw his features betoken no consciousness, he muttered to himself,—"It must be better than I feared.—And so this cursed Spaniard, with her head full, as they all have, of disguises, trap-doors, rope-ladders, and masks, was jade and fool enough to take you with her on this wild goose errand?—And how sped you, I pray?"

"Just as we reached the gate of the Park," replied Margaret, "the cry of treason was raised. I know not what became of Monna, but I ran till I fell into the arms of a very decent serving-man, called Linklater; and I was fain to tell him I was your god-daughter, and so he kept the rest of them from me, and got me to speech of his Majesty, as I entreated him to do."

"It is the only sign you showed in the whole matter that common sense had not utterly deserted your little skull," said Heriot.

"His Majesty," continued the damsel, "was so gracious as to receive me alone, though the courtiers cried out against the danger to his person, and would have searched me for arms, God help me, but the king forbade it. I fancy he had a hint from Linklater how the truth stood with me."

"Well, maiden, I ask not what passed," said Heriot; "it becomes not me to pry into my Master's secrets. Had you been closeted with his grandfather the Red Tod of Saint Andrews, as Davie Lindsay used to call him, by my faith, I should have had my own thoughts of the matter; but our Master, God bless him, is douce and temperate, and Solomon in every thing, save in the chapter of wives and concubines."

"I know not what you mean, sir," answered Margaret. "His Majesty was most kind and compassionate, but said I must be sent hither, and that the Lieutenant's lady, the Lady Mansel, would have a charge of me, and see that I sustained no wrong; and the king promised to send me in a tilted barge, and under conduct of a person well known to you; and thus I come to be in the Tower."

"But how, or why, in this apartment, nymph?" said George Heriot—"Expound that to me, for I think the riddle needs reading."

"I cannot explain it, sir, further, than that the Lady Mansel sent me here, in spite of my earnest prayers, tears, and entreaties. I was not afraid of any thing, for I knew I should be protected. But I could have died then—could die now—for very shame and confusion!"

"Well, well, if your tears are genuine," said Heriot, "they may the sooner wash out the memory of your fault—Knows your father aught of this escape of yours?"

"I would not for the world he did," replied she; "he believes me with the Lady Hermione."

"Ay, honest Davy can regulate his horologes better than his family.—Come, damsel, now I will escort you back to the Lady Mansel, and pray her, of her kindness, that when she is again trusted with a goose, she will not give it to the fox to keep.—The warders will let us pass to my lady's lodgings, I trust."

"Stay but one moment," said Lord Glenvarloch. "Whatever hard opinion you may have formed of me, I forgive you, for time will show that you do me wrong; and you yourself, I think, will be the first to regret the injustice you have done me. But involve not in your suspicions this young person, for whose purity of thought angels themselves should be vouchers. I have marked every look, every gesture; and whilst I can draw breath, I shall ever think of her with—"

"Think not at all of her, my lord," answered George Heriot, interrupting him; "it is, I have a notion, the best favour you can do her;—or think of her as the daughter of Davy Ramsay, the clockmaker, no proper subject for fine speeches, romantic adventures, or high-flown Arcadian compliments. I give you god-den, my lord. I think not altogether so harshly as my speech may have spoken. If I can help—that is, if I saw my way clearly through this labyrinth—but it avails not talking now. I give your lordship god-den.—Here, warder! Permit us to pass to the Lady Hansel's apartment." The warder said he must have orders from the Lieutenant; and as he retired to procure them, the parties remained standing near each other, but without speaking, and scarce looking at each other save by stealth, a situation which, in two of the party at least, was sufficiently embarrassing. The difference of rank, though in that age a consideration so serious, could not prevent Lord Glenvarloch from seeing that Margaret Ramsay was one of the prettiest young women he had ever beheld—from suspecting, he could scarce tell why, that he himself was not indifferent to her—from feeling assured that he had been the cause of much of her present distress—admiration, self-love, and generosity, acting in favour of the same object; and when the yeoman returned with permission to his guests to withdraw, Nigel's obeisance to the beautiful daughter of the mechanic was marked with an expression, which called up in her cheeks as much colour as any incident of the eventful day had hitherto excited. She returned the courtesy timidly and irresolutely—clung to her godfather's arm, and left the apartment, which, dark as it was, had never yet appeared so obscure to Nigel, as when the door closed behind her.

XXX

Yet though thou shouldst be dragg'd in scorn
To yonder ignominious tree,
Thou shall not want one faithful friend
To share the cruel fates' decree.

—*Ballad of Jemmy Dawson*

Master George Heriot and his ward, as she might justly be termed, for his affection to Margaret imposed on him all the cares of a guardian, were ushered by the yeoman of the guard to the lodging of the Lieutenant, where they found him seated with his lady. They were received by both with that decorous civility which Master Heriot's character and supposed influence demanded, even at the hand of a punctilious old soldier and courtier like Sir Edward Mansel. Lady Mansel received Margaret with like courtesy, and informed Master George that she was now only her guest, and no longer her prisoner.

"She is at liberty," she said, "to return to her friends under your charge—such is his Majesty's pleasure."

"I am glad of it, madam," answered Heriot, "but only I could have wished her freedom had taken place before her foolish interview with that singular young man; and I marvel your ladyship permitted it."

"My good Master Heriot," said Sir Edward, "we act according to the commands of one better and wiser than ourselves—our orders from his Majesty must be strictly and literally obeyed; and I need not say that the wisdom of his Majesty doth more than ensure—"

"I know his Majesty's wisdom well," said Heriot; "yet there is an old proverb about fire and flax—well, let it pass."

"I see Sir Mungo Malagrowther stalking towards the door of the lodging," said the Lady Mansel, "with the gait of a lame crane—it is his second visit this morning."

"He brought the warrant for discharging Lord Glenvarloch of the charge of treason," said Sir Edward.

"And from him," said Heriot, "I heard much of what had befallen; for I came from France only late last evening, and somewhat unexpectedly."

As they spoke, Sir Mungo entered the apartment—saluted the Lieutenant of the Tower and his lady with ceremonious civility—honoured

George Heriot with a patronising nod of acknowledgment, and accosted Margaret with—"Hey! my young charge, you have not doffed your masculine attire yet?"

"She does not mean to lay it aside, Sir Mungo," said Heriot, speaking loud, "until she has had satisfaction from you, for betraying her disguise to me, like a false knight—and in very deed, Sir Mungo, I think when you told me she was rambling about in so strange a dress, you might have said also that she was under Lady Mansel's protection."

"That was the king's secret, Master Heriot," said Sir Mungo, throwing himself into a chair with an air of atrabilarious importance; "the other was a well-meaning hint to yourself, as the girl's friend."

"Yes," replied Heriot, "it was done like yourself—enough told to make me unhappy about her—not a word which could relieve my uneasiness."

"Sir Mungo will not hear that remark," said the lady; "we must change the subject.—Is there any news from Court, Sir Mungo? you have been to Greenwich?"

"You might as well ask me, madam," answered the Knight, "whether there is any news from hell."

"How, Sir Mungo, how!" said Sir Edward, "measure your words something better—You speak of the Court of King James."

"Sir Edward, if I spoke of the court of the twelve Kaisers, I would say it is as confused for the present as the infernal regions. Courtiers of forty years' standing, and such I may write myself, are as far to seek in the matter as a minnow in the Maelstrom. Some folk say the king has frowned on the Prince—some that the Prince has looked grave on the duke—some that Lord Glenvarloch will be hanged for high treason—and some that there is matter against Lord Dalgarno that may cost him as much as his head's worth."

"And what do you, that are a courtier of forty years' standing, think of it all?" said Sir Edward Mansel.

"Nay, nay, do not ask him, Sir Edward," said the lady, with an expressive look to her husband.

"Sir Mungo is too witty," added Master Heriot, "to remember that he who says aught that may be repeated to his own prejudice, does but load a piece for any of the company to shoot him dead with, at their pleasure and convenience."

"What!" said the bold Knight, "you think I am afraid of the trepan? Why now, what if I should say that Dalgarno has more wit than honesty,—the duke more sail than ballast,—the Prince more pride than prudence,—and that the king—" The Lady Mansel held up her finger in a warning manner—"that the king is my very good master, who has given me, for forty years and more, dog's wages, videlicet, bones and beating.—Why now, all this is said, and Archie Armstrong* says worse than this of the best of them every day."

"The more fool he," said George Heriot; "yet he is not so utterly wrong, for folly is his best wisdom. But do not you, Sir Mungo, set your wit against a fool's, though he be a court fool."

"A fool, said you?" replied Sir Mungo, not having fully heard what Master Heriot said, or not choosing to have it thought so,—"I have been a fool indeed, to hang on at a close-fisted Court here, when men of understanding and men of action have been making fortunes in every other place of Europe. But here a man comes indifferently off unless he gets a great key to turn," (looking at Sir Edward,) "or can beat tattoo with a hammer on a pewter plate.—Well, sirs, I must make as much haste back on mine errand as if I were a fee'd messenger.—Sir Edward and my lady, I leave my commendations with you—and my good-will with you, Master Heriot—and for this breaker of bounds, if you will act by my counsel, some maceration by fasting, and a gentle use of the rod, is the best cure for her giddy fits."

"If you propose for Greenwich, Sir Mungo," said the Lieutenant, "I can spare you the labour—the king comes immediately to Whitehall."

"And that must be the reason the council are summoned to meet in such hurry," said Sir Mungo. "Well—I will, with your permission, go to the poor lad Glenvarloch, and bestow some comfort on him."

The Lieutenant seemed to look up, and pause for a moment as if in doubt.

"The lad will want a pleasant companion, who can tell him the nature of the punishment which he is to suffer, and other matters of concernment. I will not leave him until I show him how absolutely he hath ruined himself from feather to spur, how deplorable is his present state, and how small his chance of mending it."

"Well, Sir Mungo," replied the Lieutenant, "if you really think all this likely to be very consolatory to the party concerned, I will send a warder to conduct you."

---

* The celebrated Court jester.

"And I," said George Heriot, "will humbly pray of Lady Mansel, that she will lend some of her handmaiden's apparel to this giddy-brained girl; for I shall forfeit my reputation if I walk up Tower Hill with her in that mad guise—and yet the silly lassie looks not so ill in it neither."

"I will send my coach with you instantly," said the obliging lady.

"Faith, madam, and if you will honour us by such courtesy, I will gladly accept it at your hands," said the citizen, "for business presses hard on me, and the forenoon is already lost, to little purpose."

The coach being ordered accordingly, transported the worthy citizen and his charge to his mansion in Lombard Street. There he found his presence was anxiously expected by the Lady Hermione, who had just received an order to be in readiness to attend upon the Royal Privy Council in the course of an hour; and upon whom, in her inexperience of business, and long retirement from society and the world, the intimation had made as deep an impression as if it had not been the necessary consequence of the petition which she had presented to the king by Monna Paula. George Heriot gently blamed her for taking any steps in an affair so important until his return from France, especially as he had requested her to remain quiet, in a letter which accompanied the evidence he had transmitted to her from Paris. She could only plead in answer the influence which her immediately stirring in the matter was likely to have on the affair of her kinsman Lord Glenvarloch, for she was ashamed to acknowledge how much she had been gained on by the eager importunity of her youthful companion. The motive of Margaret's eagerness was, of course, the safety of Nigel; but we must leave it to time to show in what particulars that came to be connected with the petition of the Lady Hermione. Meanwhile, we return to the visit with which Sir Mungo Malagrowther favoured the afflicted young nobleman in his place of captivity.

The Knight, after the usual salutations, and having prefaced his discourse with a great deal of professed regret for Nigel's situation, sat down beside him, and composing his grotesque features into the most lugubrious despondence, began his raven song as follows:—

"I bless God, my lord, that I was the person who had the pleasure to bring his Majesty's mild message to the Lieutenant, discharging the higher prosecution against ye, for any thing meditated against his Majesty's sacred person; for, admit you be prosecuted on the lesser offence, or breach of privilege of the Palace and its precincts, *usque ad mutilationem*, even to dismemberment, as it is most likely you will, yet the loss of a member is nothing to being hanged and drawn quick, after the fashion of a traitor."

"I should feel the shame of having deserved such a punishment," answered Nigel, "more than the pain of undergoing it."

"Doubtless, my lord, the having, as you say, deserved it, must be an excruciation to your own mind," replied his tormentor; "a kind of mental and metaphysical hanging, drawing, and quartering, which may be in some measure equipollent with the external application of hemp, iron, fire, and the like, to the outer man."

"I say, Sir Mungo," repeated Nigel, "and beg you to understand my words, that I am unconscious of any error, save that of having arms on my person when I chanced to approach that of my Sovereign."

"Ye are right, my lord, to acknowledge nothing," said Sir Mungo. "We have an old proverb,—Confess, and—so forth. And indeed, as to the weapons, his Majesty has a special ill-will at all arms whatsoever, and more especially pistols; but, as I said, there is an end of that matter.[*] I wish you as well through the next, which is altogether unlikely."

"Surely, Sir Mungo," answered Nigel, "you yourself might say something in my favour concerning the affair in the Park. None knows better than you that I was at that moment urged by wrongs of the most heinous nature, offered to me by Lord Dalgarno, many of which were reported to me by yourself, much to the inflammation of my passion."

"Alack-a-day!-Alack-a-day!" replied Sir Mungo, "I remember but too well how much your choler was inflamed, in spite of the various remonstrances which I made to you respecting the sacred nature of the place. Alas! alas! you cannot say you leaped into the mire for want of warning."

"I see, Sir Mungo, you are determined to remember nothing which can do me service," said Nigel.

"Blithely would I do ye service," said the Knight; "and the best whilk I can think of is, to tell you the process of the punishment to the

---

[*] Wilson informs us that when Colonel Grey, a Scotsman who affected the buff dress even in the time of peace, appeared in that military garb at Court, the king, seeing him with a case of pistols at his girdle, which he never greatly liked, told him, merrily, "he was now so fortified, that, if he were but well victualled, he would be impregnable."— Wilson's *Life and Reign of James VI*, apud Kennet's *History of England*, vol. ii. p. 389. In 1612, the tenth year of James's reign, there was a rumour abroad that a shipload of pocket-pistols had been exported from Spain, with a view to a general massacre of the Protestants. Proclamations were of consequence sent forth, prohibiting all persons from carrying pistols under a foot long in the barrel. *Ibid*. p. 690.

whilk you will be indubitably subjected, I having had the good fortune to behold it performed in the Queen's time, on a chield that had written a pasquinado. I was then in my Lord Gray's train, who lay leaguer here, and being always covetous of pleasing and profitable sights, I could not dispense with being present on the occasion."

"I should be surprised, indeed," said Lord Glenvarloch, "if you had so far put restraint upon your benevolence, as to stay away from such an exhibition."

"Hey! was your lordship praying me to be present at your own execution?" answered the Knight. "Troth, my lord, it will be a painful sight to a friend, but I will rather punish myself than baulk you. It is a pretty pageant, in the main—a very pretty pageant. The fallow came on with such a bold face, it was a pleasure to look on him. He was dressed all in white, to signify harmlessness and innocence. The thing was done on a scaffold at Westminster—most likely yours will be at the Charing. There were the Sheriffs and the Marshal's men, and what not—the executioner, with his cleaver and mallet, and his man, with a pan of hot charcoal, and the irons for cautery. He was a dexterous fallow that Derrick. This man Gregory is not fit to jipper a joint with him; it might be worth your lordship's while to have the loon sent to a barber-surgeon's, to learn some needful scantling of anatomy—it may be for the benefit of yourself and other unhappy sufferers, and also a kindness to Gregory."

"I will not take the trouble," said Nigel.—"If the laws will demand my hand, the executioner may get it off as he best can. If the king leaves it where it is, it may chance to do him better service."

"Vera noble—vera grand, indeed, my lord," said Sir Mungo; "it is pleasant to see a brave man suffer. This fallow whom I spoke of—This Tubbs, or Stubbs, or whatever the plebeian was called, came forward as bold as an emperor, and said to the people, 'Good friends, I come to leave here the hand of a true Englishman,' and clapped it on the dressing-block with as much ease as if he had laid it on his sweetheart's shoulder; whereupon Derrick the hangman, adjusting, d'ye mind me, the edge of his cleaver on the very joint, hit it with the mallet with such force, that the hand flew off as far from the owner as a gauntlet which the challenger casts down in the tilt-yard. Well, sir, Stubbs, or Tubbs, lost no whit of countenance, until the fallow clapped the hissing-hot iron on his raw stump. My lord, it fizzed like a rasher of bacon, and the fallow set up an elritch screech, which made some think his courage was abated; but not a whit, for he plucked off his hat with his left hand, and waved it, crying, 'God save the Queen, and confound all evil counsellors!' The people gave him three cheers, which he deserved for his stout heart; and, truly, I hope to see your lordship suffer with the same magnanimity."

"I thank you, Sir Mungo," said Nigel, who had not been able to forbear some natural feelings of an unpleasant nature during this lively detail,—"I have no doubt the exhibition will be a very engaging one to you and the other spectators, whatever it may prove to the party principally concerned."

"Vera engaging," answered Sir Mungo, "vera interesting—vera interesting indeed, though not altogether so much so as an execution for high treason. I saw Digby, the Winters, Fawkes, and the rest of the gunpowder gang, suffer for that treason, whilk was a vera grand spectacle, as well in regard to their sufferings, as to their constancy in enduring."

"I am the more obliged to your goodness, Sir Mungo," replied Nigel, "that has induced you, although you have lost the sight, to congratulate me on my escape from the hazard of making the same edifying appearance."

"As you say, my lord," answered Sir Mungo, "the loss is chiefly in appearance. Nature has been very bountiful to us, and has given duplicates of some organs, that we may endure the loss of one of them, should some such circumstance chance in our pilgrimage. See my poor dexter, abridged to one thumb, one finger, and a stump,—by the blow of my adversary's weapon, however, and not by any carnificial knife. Weel, sir, this poor maimed hand doth me, in some sort, as much service as ever; and, admit yours to be taken off by the wrist, you have still your left hand for your service, and are better off than the little Dutch dwarf here about town, who threads a needle, limns, writes, and tosses a pike, merely by means of his feet, without ever a hand to help him."

"Well, Sir Mungo," said Lord Glenvarloch, "this is all no doubt very consolatory; but I hope the king will spare my hand to fight for him in battle, where, notwithstanding all your kind encouragement, I could spend my blood much more cheerfully than on a scaffold."

"It is even a sad truth," replied Sir Mungo, "that your lordship was but too like to have died on a scaffold—not a soul to speak for you but that deluded lassie Maggie Ramsay."

"Whom mean you?" said Nigel, with more interest than he had hitherto shown in the Knight's communications.

"Nay, who should I mean, but that travestied lassie whom we dined with when we honoured Heriot the goldsmith? Ye ken best how you have made interest with her, but I saw her on her knees to the king for you. She was committed to my charge, to bring her up hither in honour and safety. Had I had my own will, I would have had her to Bridewell, to flog the wild blood out of her—a cutty quean, to think of wearing the breeches, and not so much as married yet!"

"Hark ye, Sir Mungo Malagrowther," answered Nigel, "I would have you talk of that young person with fitting respect."

"With all the respect that befits your lordship's paramour, and Davy Ramsay's daughter, I shall certainly speak of her, my lord," said Sir Mungo, assuming a dry tone of irony.

Nigel was greatly disposed to have made a serious quarrel of it, but with Sir Mungo such an affair would have been ridiculous; he smothered his resentment, therefore, and conjured him to tell what he had heard and seen respecting this young person.

"Simply, that I was in the ante-room when she had audience, and heard the king say, to my great perplexity, '*Pulchra sane puella;*' and Maxwell, who hath but indifferent Latin ears, thought that his Majesty called on him by his own name of Sawney, and thrust into the presence, and there I saw our Sovereign James, with his own hand, raising up the lassie, who, as I said heretofore, was travestied in man's attire. I should have had my own thoughts of it, but our gracious Master is auld, and was nae great gillravager amang the queans even in his youth; and he was comforting her in his own way and saying,—'Ye needna greet about it, my bonnie woman, Glenvarlochides shall have fair play; and, indeed, when the hurry was off our spirits, we could not believe that he had any design on our person. And touching his other offences, we will look wisely and closely into the matter.' So I got charge to take the young fence-louper to the Tower here, and deliver her to the charge of Lady Mansel; and his Majesty charged me to say not a word to her about your offences, for, said he, the poor thing is breaking her heart for him."

"And on this you have charitably founded the opinion to the prejudice of this young lady, which you have now thought proper to express?" said Lord Glenvarloch.

"In honest truth, my lord," replied Sir Mungo, "what opinion would you have me form of a wench who gets into male habiliments, and goes on her knees to the king for a wild young nobleman? I wot not what the fashionable word may be, for the phrase changes, though the custom abides. But truly I must needs think this young leddy—if you call Watchie Ramsay's daughter a young leddy—demeans herself more like a leddy of pleasure than a leddy of honour."

"You do her egregious wrong, Sir Mungo," said Nigel; "or rather you have been misled by appearances."

"So will all the world be misled, my lord," replied the satirist, "unless you were doing that to disabuse them which your father's son will hardly judge it fit to do."

"And what may that be, I pray you?"

"E'en marry the lass—make her Leddy Glenvarloch.—Ay, ay, ye may start—but it's the course you are driving on. Rather marry than do worse, if the worst be not done already."

"Sir Mungo," said Nigel, "I pray you to forbear this subject, and rather return to that of the mutilation, upon which it pleased you to enlarge a short while since."

"I have not time at present," said Sir Mungo, hearing the clock strike four; "but so soon as you shall have received sentence, my lord, you may rely on my giving you the fullest detail of the whole solemnity; and I give you my word, as a knight and a gentleman, that I will myself attend you on the scaffold, whoever may cast sour looks on me for doing so. I bear a heart, to stand by a friend in the worst of times."

So saying, he wished Lord Glenvarloch farewell; who felt as heartily rejoiced at his departure, though it may be a bold word, as any person who had ever undergone his society.

But, when left to his own reflections, Nigel could not help feeling solitude nearly as irksome as the company of Sir Mungo Malagrowther. The total wreck of his fortune,—which seemed now to be rendered unavoidable by the loss of the royal warrant, that had afforded him the means of redeeming his paternal estate,—was an unexpected and additional blow. When he had seen the warrant he could not precisely remember; but was inclined to think, it was in the casket when he took out money to pay the miser for his lodgings at Whitefriars. Since then, the casket had been almost constantly under his own eye, except during the short time he was separated from his baggage by the arrest in Greenwich Park. It might, indeed, have been taken out at that time, for he had no reason to think either his person or his property was in the hands of those who wished him well; but, on the other hand, the locks of the strong-box had sustained no violence that he could observe, and, being of a particular and complicated construction, he thought they could scarce be opened without an instrument made on purpose, adapted to their peculiarities, and for this there had been no time. But, speculate as he would on the matter, it was clear that this important document was gone, and probable that it had passed into no friendly hands. "Let it be so," said Nigel to himself; "I am scarcely worse off respecting my prospects of fortune, than when I first reached this accursed city. But to be hampered with cruel accusations, and stained with foul suspicions-to be the object of pity of the most degrading kind to yonder honest citizen, and of the malignity of that envious and atrabilarious courtier, who can endure the good fortune and good qualities of another no more than the mole can brook sunshine—this is indeed a deplorable reflection; and the consequences must stick to my future life, and impede whatever my head, or my hand, if it is left me, might be able to execute in my favour."

The feeling, that he is the object of general dislike and dereliction, seems to be one of the most unendurably painful to which a human being can be subjected. The most atrocious criminals, whose nerves have not shrunk from perpetrating the most horrid cruelty, endure more from the consciousness that no man will sympathise with their sufferings, than from apprehension of the personal agony of their impending punishment; and are known often to attempt to palliate their enormities, and sometimes altogether to deny what is established by the clearest proof, rather than to leave life under the general ban of humanity. It was no wonder that Nigel, labouring under the sense of general, though unjust suspicion, should, while pondering on so painful a theme, recollect that one, at least, had not only believed him innocent, but hazarded herself, with all her feeble power, to interpose in his behalf.

"Poor girl!" he repeated; "poor, rash, but generous maiden! your fate is that of her in Scottish story, who thrust her arm into the staple of the door, to oppose it as a bar against the assassins who threatened the murder of her sovereign. The deed of devotion was useless; save to give an immortal name to her by whom it was done, and whose blood flows, it is said, in the veins of my house."

I cannot explain to the reader, whether the recollection of this historical deed of devotion, and the lively effect which the comparison, a little overstrained perhaps, was likely to produce in favour of Margaret Ramsay, was not qualified by the concomitant ideas of ancestry and ancient descent with which that recollection was mingled. But the contending feelings suggested a new train of ideas.—"Ancestry," he thought, "and ancient descent, what are they to me?—My patrimony alienated—my title become a reproach—for what can be so absurd as titled beggary?—my character subjected to suspicion,—I will not remain in this country; and should I, at leaving it, procure the society of one so lovely, so brave, and so faithful, who should say that I derogated from the rank which I am virtually renouncing?"

There was something romantic and pleasing, as he pursued this picture of an attached and faithful pair, becoming all the world to each other, and stemming the tide of fate arm in arm; and to be linked thus with a creature so beautiful, and who had taken such devoted and disinterested concern in his fortunes, formed itself into such a vision as romantic youth loves best to dwell upon.

Suddenly his dream was painfully dispelled, by the recollection, that its very basis rested upon the most selfish ingratitude on his own part. Lord of his castle and his towers, his forests and fields, his fair patrimony and noble name, his mind would have rejected, as a sort of impossibility, the idea of elevating to his rank the daughter of a mechanic; but, when degraded from his nobility, and plunged into poverty and difficulties, he was ashamed to feel himself not unwilling, that this poor girl, in the blindness of her affection, should abandon all the better prospects of her own settled condition, to embrace the precarious and doubtful course which he himself was condemned to. The generosity of Nigel's mind recoiled from the selfishness of the plan of happiness which he projected; and he made a strong effort to expel from his thoughts for the rest of the evening this fascinating female, or, at least, not to permit them to dwell upon the perilous circumstance, that she was at present the only creature living who seemed to consider him as an object of kindness.

He could not, however, succeed in banishing her from his slumbers, when, after having spent a weary day, he betook himself to a perturbed couch. The form of Margaret mingled with the wild mass of dreams which his late adventures had suggested; and even when, copying the lively narrative of Sir Mungo, fancy presented to him the blood bubbling and hissing on the heated iron, Margaret stood behind him like a spirit of light, to breathe healing on the wound. At length nature was exhausted by these fantastic creations, and Nigel slept, and slept soundly, until awakened in the morning by the sound of a well-known voice, which had often broken his slumbers about the same hour.

XXXI

Many, come up, sir, with your gentle blood!
Here's a red stream beneath this coarse blue doublet,
That warms the heart as kindly as if drawn
From the far source of old Assyrian kings.
Who first made mankind subject to their sway.

—*Old Play*

The sounds to which we alluded in our last, were no other than the grumbling tones of Richie Moniplies's voice.

This worthy, like some other persons who rank high in their own opinion, was very apt, when he could have no other auditor, to hold conversation with one who was sure to be a willing listener—I mean with himself. He was now brushing and arranging Lord Glenvarloch's clothes, with as much composure and quiet assiduity as if he had never been out of his service, and grumbling betwixt whiles to the following purpose:—"Hump—ay, time cloak and jerkin were through my hands—I question if horsehair has been passed over them since they and I last parted. The embroidery finely frayed too—and the gold buttons of the cloak—By my conscience, and as I am an honest man, there is a round dozen of them gane! This comes of Alsatian frolics—God keep us with his grace, and not give us over to our own devices!—I see no sword—but that will be in respect of present circumstances."

Nigel for some time could not help believing that he was still in a dream, so improbable did it seem that his domestic, whom he supposed to be in Scotland, should have found him out, and obtained access to him, in his present circumstances. Looking through the curtains, however, he became well assured of the fact, when he beheld the stiff and bony length of Richie, with a visage charged with nearly double its ordinary degree of importance, employed sedulously in brushing his master's cloak, and refreshing himself with whistling or humming, from interval to interval, some snatch of an old melancholy Scottish ballad-tune. Although sufficiently convinced of the identity of the party, Lord Glenvarloch could not help expressing his surprise in the superfluous question—"In the name of Heaven, Richie, is this you?"

"And wha else suld it be, my lord?" answered Richie; "I dreamna that your lordship's levee in this place is like to be attended by ony that are not bounded thereto by duty."

"I am rather surprised," answered Nigel, "that it should be attended by any one at all—especially by you, Richie; for you know that we parted, and I thought you had reached Scotland long since."

"I crave your lordship's pardon, but we have not parted yet, nor are soon likely so to do; for there gang twa folk's votes to the unmaking of a bargain, as to the making of ane. Though it was your lordship's pleasure so to conduct yourself that we were like to have parted, yet it was not, on reflection, my will to be gone. To be plain, if your lordship does not ken when you have a good servant, I ken when I have a kind master; and to say truth, you will be easier served now than ever, for there is not much chance of your getting out of bounds."

"I am indeed bound over to good behaviour," said Lord Glenvarloch, with a smile; "but I hope you will not take advantage of my situation to be too severe on my follies, Richie?"

"God forbid, my lord—God forbid!" replied Richie, with an expression betwixt a conceited consciousness of superior wisdom and real feeling—"especially in consideration of your lordship's having a due sense of them. I did indeed remonstrate, as was my humble duty, but I scorn to cast that up to your lordship now—Na, na, I am myself an erring creature—very conscious of some small weaknesses—there is no perfection in man."

"But, Richie," said Lord Glenvarloch, "although I am much obliged to you for your proffered service, it can be of little use to me here, and may be of prejudice to yourself."

"Your lordship shall pardon me again," said Richie, whom the relative situation of the parties had invested with ten times his ordinary dogmatism; "but as I will manage the matter, your lordship shall be greatly benefited by my service, and I myself no whit prejudiced."

"I see not how that can be, my friend," said Lord Glenvarloch, "since even as to your pecuniary affairs—"

"Touching my pecuniars, my lord," replied Richie, "I am indifferently weel provided; and, as it chances, my living here will be no burden to your lordship, or distress to myself. Only I crave permission to annex certain conditions to my servitude with your lordship."

"Annex what you will," said Lord Glenvarloch, "for you are pretty sure to take your own way, whether you make any conditions or not. Since you will not leave me, which were, I think, your wisest course, you must, and I suppose will, serve me only on such terms as you like yourself."

"All that I ask, my lord," said Richie, gravely, and with a tone of great moderation, "is to have the uninterrupted command of my own motions, for certain important purposes which I have now in hand, always giving your lordship the solace of my company and attendance, at such times as may be at once convenient for me, and necessary for your service."

"Of which, I suppose, you constitute yourself sole judge," replied Nigel, smiling.

"Unquestionably, my lord," answered Richie, gravely; "for your lordship can only know what yourself want; whereas I, who see both sides of the picture, ken both what is the best for your affairs, and what is the most needful for my own."

"Richie, my good friend," said Nigel, "I fear this arrangement, which places the master much under the disposal of the servant, would scarce suit us if we were both at large; but a prisoner as I am, I may be as well at your disposal as I am at that of so many other persons; and so you may come and go as you list, for I suppose you will not take my advice, to return to your own country, and leave me to my fate."

"The deil be in my feet if I do," said Moniplies,—"I am not the lad to leave your lordship in foul weather, when I followed you and fed upon you through the whole summer day, And besides, there may be brave days behind, for a' that has come and gane yet; for

"It's hame, and it's hame, and it's hame we fain would be, Though the cloud is in the lift, and the wind is on the lea; For the sun through the mirk blinks blithe on mine ee, Says,—'I'll shine on ye yet in our ain country!"

Having sung this stanza in the manner of a ballad-singer, whose voice has been cracked by matching his windpipe against the bugle of the north blast, Richie Moniplies aided Lord Glenvarloch to rise, attended his toilet with every possible mark of the most solemn and deferential respect, then waited upon him at breakfast, and finally withdrew, pleading that he had business of importance, which would detain him for some hours.

Although Lord Glenvarloch necessarily expected to be occasionally annoyed by the self-conceit and dogmatism of Richie Moniplies's character, yet he could not but feel the greatest pleasure from the firm and devoted attachment which this faithful follower had displayed in the present instance, and indeed promised himself an alleviation of the ennui of his imprisonment, in having the advantage of his services. It was, therefore, with pleasure that he learned from the warder, that his servant's attendance would be allowed at all times when the general rules of the fortress permitted the entrance of strangers.

In the meanwhile, the magnanimous Richie Moniplies had already reached Tower Wharf. Here, after looking with contempt on several scullers by whom he was plied, and whose services he rejected with a wave of his hand, he called with dignity, "First oars!" and stirred into activity several lounging Tritons of the higher order, who had not, on his first appearance, thought it worth while to accost him with proffers of service. He now took possession of a wherry, folded his arms within his ample cloak, and sitting down in the stern with an air of importance, commanded them to row to Whitehall Stairs. Having reached the Palace in safety, he demanded to see Master Linklater, the under-clerk of his Majesty's kitchen. The reply was, that he was not to be spoken withal, being then employed in cooking a mess of cock-a-leekie for the king's own mouth.

"Tell him," said Moniplies, "that it is a dear countryman of his, who seeks to converse with him on matter of high import."

"A dear countryman?" said Linklater, when this pressing message was delivered to him. "Well, let him come in and be d—d, that I should say sae! This now is some red-headed, long-legged, gillie-white-foot frae the West Port, that, hearing of my promotion, is come up to be a turn-broche, or deputy scullion, through my interest. It is a great hinderance to any man who would rise in the world, to have such friends to hang by his skirts, in hope of being towed up along with him.—Ha! Richie Moniplies, man, is it thou? And what has brought ye here? If they should ken thee for the loon that scared the horse the other day!—"

"No more o' that, neighbour," said Richie,—"I am just here on the auld errand—I maun speak with the king."

"The king? Ye are red wud," said Linklater; then shouted to his assistant in the kitchen, "Look to the broches, ye knaves—*pisces purga—Salsamenta fac macerentur pulchre*—I will make you understand Latin, ye knaves, as becomes the scullions of King James." Then in a cautious tone, to Richie's private ear, he continued, "Know ye not how ill your master came off the other day?—I can tell you that job made some folk shake for their office."

"Weel, but, Laurie, ye maun befriend me this time, and get this wee bit sifflication slipped into his Majesty's ain most gracious hand. I promise you the contents will be most grateful to him."

"Richie," answered Linklater, "you have certainly sworn to say your prayers in the porter's lodge, with your back bare; and twa grooms, with dog-whips, to cry amen to you."

"Na, na, Laurie, lad," said Richie, "I ken better what belangs to sifflications than I did yon day; and ye will say that yoursell, if ye will but get that bit note to the king's hand."

"I will have neither hand nor foot in the matter," said the cautious Clerk of the Kitchen; "but there is his Majesty's mess of cock-a-leekie just going to be served to him in his closet—I cannot prevent you from putting the letter between the gilt bowl and the platter; his sacred Majesty will see it when he lifts the bowl, for he aye drinks out the broth."

"Enough said," replied Richie, and deposited the paper accordingly, just before a page entered to carry away the mess to his Majesty.

"Aweel, aweel, neighbour," said Laurence, when the mess was taken away, "if ye have done ony thing to bring yoursell to the withy, or the scourging post, it is your ain wilful deed."

"I will blame no other for it," said Richie; and with that undismayed pertinacity of conceit, which made a fundamental part of his character, he abode the issue, which was not long of arriving.

In a few minutes Maxwell himself arrived in the apartment, and demanded hastily who had placed a writing on the king's trencher, Linklater denied all knowledge of it; but Richie Moniplies, stepping boldly forth, pronounced the emphatical confession, "I am the man."

"Follow me, then," said Maxwell, after regarding him with a look of great curiosity.

They went up a private staircase,—even that private staircase, the privilege of which at Court is accounted a nearer road to power than the *grandes entrees* themselves. Arriving in what Richie described as an "ill redd-up" ante-room, the usher made a sign to him to stop, while he went into the king's closet. Their conference was short, and as Maxwell opened the door to retire, Richie heard the conclusion of it.

"Ye are sure he is not dangerous?—I was caught once.—Bide within call, but not nearer the door than within three geometrical cubits. If I speak loud, start to me like a falcon—If I speak loun, keep your lang lugs out of ear-shot—and now let him come in."

SIR WALTER SCOTT

Richie passed forward at Maxwell's mute signal, and in a moment found himself in the presence of the king. Most men of Richie's birth and breeding, and many others, would have been abashed at finding themselves alone with their Sovereign. But Richie Moniplies had an opinion of himself too high to be controlled by any such ideas; and having made his stiff reverence, he arose once more into his perpendicular height, and stood before James as stiff as a hedge-stake.

"Have ye gotten them, man? have ye gotten them?" said the king, in a fluttered state, betwixt hope and eagerness, and some touch of suspicious fear. "Gie me them—gie me them—before ye speak a word, I charge you, on your allegiance."

Richie took a box from his bosom, and, stooping on one knee, presented it to his Majesty, who hastily opened it, and having ascertained that it contained a certain carcanet of rubies, with which the reader was formerly made acquainted, he could not resist falling into a sort of rapture, kissing the gems, as if they had been capable of feeling, and repeating again and again with childish delight, "*Onyx cum prole, silexque—Onyx cum prole!* Ah, my bright and bonny sparklers, my heart loups light to see you again." He then turned to Richie, upon whose stoical countenance his Majesty's demeanour had excited something like a grim smile, which James interrupted his rejoicing to reprehend, saying, "Take heed, sir, you are not to laugh at us—we are your anointed Sovereign."

"God forbid that I should laugh!" said Richie, composing his countenance into its natural rigidity. "I did but smile, to bring my visage into coincidence and conformity with your Majesty's physiognomy."

"Ye speak as a dutiful subject, and an honest man," said the king; "but what deil's your name, man?"

"Even Richie Moniplies, the son of auld Mungo Moniplies, at the West Port of Edinburgh, who had the honour to supply your Majesty's mother's royal table, as weel as your Majesty's, with flesh and other vivers, when time was."

"Aha!" said the king, laughing,—for he possessed, as a useful attribute of his situation, a tenacious memory, which recollected every one with whom he was brought into casual contact,—"Ye are the self-same traitor who had weelnigh coupit us endlang on the causey of our ain courtyard? but we stuck by our mare. *Equam memento rebus in arduis servare.* Weel, be not dismayed, Richie; for, as many men have turned traitors, it is but fair that a traitor, now and then, suld prove to be, contra expectanda, a true man. How cam ye by our jewels, man?—cam ye on the part of George Heriot?"

"In no sort," said Richie. "May it please your Majesty, I come as Harry Wynd fought, utterly for my own hand, and on no man's errand; as, indeed, I call no one master, save Him that made me, your most gracious Majesty who governs me, and the noble Nigel Olifaunt, Lord of Glenvarloch, who maintained me as lang as he could maintain himself, poor nobleman!"

"Glenvarlochides again!" exclaimed the king; "by my honour, he lies in ambush for us at every corner!—Maxwell knocks at the door. It is George Heriot come to tell us he cannot find these jewels.—Get thee behind the arras, Richie—stand close, man—sneeze not—cough not—breathe not!—Jingling Geordie is so damnably ready with his gold-ends of wisdom, and sae accursedly backward with his gold-ends of siller, that, by our royal saul, we are glad to get a hair in his neck."

Richie got behind the arras, in obedience to the commands of the good-natured king, while the Monarch, who never allowed his dignity to stand in the way of a frolic, having adjusted, with his own hand, the tapestry, so as to complete the ambush, commanded Maxwell to tell him what was the matter without. Maxwell's reply was so low as to be lost by Richie Moniplies, the peculiarity of whose situation by no means abated his curiosity and desire to gratify it to the uttermost.

"Let Geordie Heriot come in," said the king; and, as Richie could observe through a slit in the tapestry, the honest citizen, if not actually agitated, was at least discomposed. The king, whose talent for wit, or humour, was precisely of a kind to be gratified by such a scene as ensued, received his homage with coldness, and began to talk to him with an air of serious dignity, very different from the usual indecorous levity of his behaviour. "Master Heriot," he said, "if we aright remember, we opignorated in your hands certain jewels of the Crown, for a certain sum of money—Did we, or did we not?"

"My most gracious Sovereign," said Heriot, "indisputably your Majesty was pleased to do so."

"The property of which jewels and *cimelia* remained with us," continued the king, in the same solemn tone, "subject only to your claim of advance thereupon; which advance being repaid, gives us right to repossession of the thing opignorated, or pledged, or laid in wad. Voetius, Vinnius, Groenwigeneus, Pagenstecherus,—all who have treated *de Contractu Opignerationis, consentiunt in eundem,*—gree on the same point. The Roman law, the English common law, and the municipal law of our ain ancient kingdom of Scotland, though they split in mair particulars than I could desire, unite as strictly in this as the three strands of a twisted rope."

"May it please your Majesty," replied Heriot, "it requires not so many learned authorities to prove to any honest man, that his interest in a pledge is determined when the money lent is restored."

"Weel, sir, I proffer restoration of the sum lent, and I demand to be repossessed of the jewels pledged with you. I gave ye a hint, brief while since, that this would be essential to my service, for, as approaching events are like to call us into public, it would seem strange if we did not appear with those ornaments, which are heirlooms of the Crown, and the absence whereof is like to place us in contempt and suspicion with our liege subjects."

Master George Heriot seemed much moved by this address of his Sovereign, and replied with emotion, "I call Heaven to witness, that I am totally harmless in this matter, and that I would willingly lose the sum advanced, so that I could restore those jewels, the absence of which your Majesty so justly laments. Had the jewels remained with me, the account of them would be easily rendered; but your Majesty will do me the justice to remember, that, by your express order, I transferred them to another person, who advanced a large sum, just about the time of my departure for Paris. The money was pressingly wanted, and no other means to come by it occurred to me. I told your Majesty, when I brought the needful supply, that the man from whom the monies were obtained, was of no good repute; and your most princely answer was, smelling to the gold—*Non olet*, it smells not of the means that have gotten it."

"Weel, man," said the king, "but what needs a' this din? If ye gave my jewels in pledge to such a one, suld ye not, as a liege subject, have taken care that the redemption was in our power? And are we to suffer the loss of our *cimelia* by your neglect, besides being exposed to the scorn and censure of our lieges, and of the foreign ambassadors?"

"My lord and liege king," said Heriot, "God knows, if my bearing blame or shame in this matter would keep it from your Majesty, it were my duty to endure both, as a servant grateful for many benefits; but when your Majesty considers the violent death of the man himself, the disappearance of his daughter, and of his wealth, I trust you will remember that I warned your Majesty, in humble duty, of the possibility of such casualties, and prayed you not to urge me to deal with him on your behalf."

"But you brought me nae better means," said the king—"Geordie, ye brought me nae better means. I was like a deserted man; what could I do but grip to the first siller that offered, as a drowning man grasps to the willow-wand that comes readiest?—And now, man, what for have ye not brought back the jewels? they are surely above ground, if ye wad make strict search."

"All strict search has been made, may it please your Majesty," replied the citizen; "hue and cry has been sent out everywhere, and it has been found impossible to recover them."

"Difficult, ye mean, Geordie, not impossible," replied the king; "for that whilk is impossible, is either naturally so, *exempli gratia*, to make two into three; or morally so, as to make what is truth falsehood; but what is only difficult may come to pass, with assistance of wisdom and patience; as, for example, Jingling Geordie, look here!" And he displayed the recovered treasure to the eyes of the astonished jeweller, exclaiming, with great triumph, "What say ye to that, Jingler?—By my sceptre and crown, the man stares as if he took his native prince for a warlock! us that are the very *malleus maleficarum*, the contunding and contriturating hammer of all witches, sorcerers, magicians, and the like; he thinks we are taking a touch of the black art outsells!—But gang thy way, honest Geordie; thou art a good plain man, but nane of the seven sages of Greece; gang thy way, and mind the soothfast word which you spoke, small time syne, that there is one in this land that comes near to Solomon, King of Israel, in all his gifts, except in his love to strange women, forby the daughter of Pharaoh."

If Heriot was surprised at seeing the jewels so unexpectedly produced at the moment the king was upbraiding him for the loss of them, this allusion to the reflection which had escaped him while conversing with Lord Glenvarloch, altogether completed his astonishment; and the king was so delighted with the superiority which it gave him at the moment, that he rubbed his hands, chuckled, and finally, his sense of dignity giving way to the full feeling of triumph, he threw himself into his easy-chair, and laughed with unconstrained violence till he lost his breath, and the tears ran plentifully down his cheeks as he strove to recover it. Meanwhile, the royal cachinnation was echoed out by a discordant and portentous laugh from behind the arras, like that of one who, little accustomed to give way to such emotions, feels himself at some particular impulse unable either to control or to modify his obstreperous mirth. Heriot turned his head with new surprise towards the place, from which sounds so unfitting the presence of a monarch seemed to burst with such emphatic clamour.

The king, too, somewhat sensible of the indecorum, rose up, wiped his eyes, and calling,—"Todlowrie, come out o' your den," he produced from behind the arras the length of Richie Moniplies, still laughing with as unrestrained mirth as ever did gossip at a country christening. "Whisht, man, whisht, man," said the king; "ye needna nicher that gait, like a cusser at a caup o' corn, e'en though it was a pleasing jest, and our ain framing. And yet to see Jingling Geordie, that bauds himself so much the wiser than other folk—to see him, ha! ha! ha!—in the vein of Euclio apud Plautum, distressing himself to recover what was lying at his elbow—'Peril, interii, occidi—quo curram? quo non curram?— Tene, tene—quem? quis? nescio—nihil video."

"Ah! Geordie, your een are sharp enough to look after gowd and silver, gems, rubies, and the like of that, and yet ye kenna how to come by them when they are lost.—Ay, ay—look at them, man—look at them—they are a' right and tight, sound and round, not a doublet crept in amongst them."

George Heriot, when his first surprise was over, was too old a courtier to interrupt the king's imaginary triumph, although he darted a look of some displeasure at honest Richie, who still continued on what is usually termed the broad grin. He quietly examined the stones, and finding them all perfect, he honestly and sincerely congratulated his Majesty on the recovery of a treasure which could not have been lost without some dishonour to the crown; and asked to whom he himself was to pay the sums for which they had been pledged, observing, that he had the money by him in readiness.

"Ye are in a deevil of a hurry, when there is paying in the case, Geordie," said the king.—"What's a' the haste, man? The jewels were restored by an honest, kindly countryman of ours. There he stands, and wha kens if he wants the money on the nail, or if he might not be as weel pleased wi' a bit rescript on our treasury some six months hence? Ye ken that our Exchequer is even at a low ebb just now, and ye cry pay, pay, pay, as if we had all the mines of Ophir."

"Please your Majesty," said Heriot, "if this man has the real right to these monies, it is doubtless at his will to grant forbearance, if he will. But when I remember the guise in which I first saw him, with a tattered cloak and a broken head, I can hardly conceive it.—Are not you Richie Moniplies, with the king's favour?"

"Even sae, Master Heriot—of the ancient and honourable house of Castle Collop, near to the West Port of Edinburgh," answered Richie.

"Why, please your Majesty, he is a poor serving-man," said Heriot. "This money can never be honestly at his disposal."

"What for no?" said the king. "Wad ye have naebody spraickle up the brae but yoursell, Geordie? Your ain cloak was thin enough when ye cam here, though ye have lined it gay and weel. And for serving-men, there has mony a red-shank cam over the Tweed wi' his master's wallet on his shoulders, that now rustles it wi' his six followers behind him. There stands the man himsell; speer at him, Geordie."

"His may not be the best authority in the case," answered the cautious citizen.

"Tut, tut, man," said the king, "ye are over scrupulous. The knave deer-stealers have an apt phrase, *Non est inquirendum unde venit* VENISON. He that brings the gudes hath surely a right to dispose of the gear.—Hark ye, friend, speak the truth and shame the deil. Have ye plenary powers to dispose on the redemption-money as to delay of payments, or the like, ay or no?"

"Full power, an it like your gracious Majesty," answered Richie Moniplies; "and I am maist willing to subscrive to whatsoever may in ony wise accommodate your Majesty anent the redemption-money, trusting your Majesty's grace will be kind to me in one sma' favour."

"Ey, man," said the king, "come ye to me there? I thought ye wad e'en be like the rest of them.—One would think our subjects' lives and goods were all our ain, and holden of us at our free will; but when we stand in need of ony matter of siller from them, which chances more frequently than we would it did, deil a boddle is to be had, save on the auld terms of giff-gaff. It is just niffer for niffer.—Aweel, neighbour, what is it that ye want—some monopoly, I reckon? Or it may be a grant of kirk-lands and teinds, or a knighthood, or the like? Ye maun be reasonable, unless ye propose to advance more money for our present occasions."

"My liege," answered Richie Moniplies, "the owner of these monies places them at your Majesty's command, free of all pledge or usage as long as it is your royal pleasure, providing your Majesty will condescend to show some favour to the noble Lord Glenvarloch, presently prisoner in your royal Tower of London."

"How, man—how,—man—how, man!" exclaimed the king, reddening

and stammering, but with emotions more noble than those by which he was sometimes agitated—"What is that you dare to say to us?—Sell our justice!—sell our mercy!—and we a crowned king, sworn to do justice to our subjects in the gate, and responsible for our stewardship to Him that is over all kings?"—Here he reverently looked up, touched his bonnet, and continued, with some sharpness,—"We dare not traffic in such commodities, sir; and, but that ye are a poor ignorant creature, that have done us this day some not unpleasant service, we wad have a red iron driven through your tongue, *in terrorem* of others.—Awa with him, Geordie,—pay him, plack and bawbee, out of our monies in your hands, and let them care that come ahint."

Richie, who had counted with the utmost certainty upon the success of this master-stroke of policy, was like an architect whose whole scaffolding at once gives way under him. He caught, however, at what he thought might break his fall. "Not only the sum for which the jewels were pledged," he said, "but the double of it, if required, should be placed at his Majesty's command, and even without hope or condition of repayment, if only—"

But the king did not allow him to complete the sentence, crying out with greater vehemence than before, as if he dreaded the stability of his own good resolutions,—"Awa wi' him—swith awa wi' him! It is time he were gane, if he doubles his bode that gate. And, for your life, letna Steenie, or ony of them, hear a word from his mouth; for wha kens what trouble that might bring me into! *Ne inducas in tentationem—Vade retro, Sathanas!—Amen.*"

In obedience to the royal mandate, George Heriot hurried the abashed petitioner out of the presence and out of the Palace; and, when they were in the Palace-yard, the citizen, remembering with some resentment the airs of equality which Richie had assumed towards him in the commencement of the scene which had just taken place, could not forbear to retaliate, by congratulating him with an ironical smile on his favour at Court, and his improved grace in presenting a supplication.

"Never fash your beard about that, Master George Heriot," said Richie, totally undismayed; "but tell me when and where I am to sifflicate you for eight hundred pounds sterling, for which these jewels stood engaged?"

"The instant that you bring with you the real owner of the money," replied Heriot; "whom it is important that I should see on more accounts than one."

"Then will I back to his Majesty," said Richie Moniplies, stoutly, "and get either the money or the pledge back again. I am fully commissionate to act in that matter."

"It may be so, Richie," said the citizen, "and perchance it may *not* be so neither, for your tales are not all gospel; and, therefore, be assured I will see that it *is* so, ere I pay you that large sum of money. I shall give you an acknowledgment for it, and I will keep it prestable at a moment's warning. But, my good Richard Moniplies, of Castle Collop, near the West Port of Edinburgh, in the meantime I am bound to return to his Majesty on matters of weight." So speaking, and mounting the stair to re-enter the Palace, he added, by way of summing up the whole,— "George Heriot is over old a cock to be caught with chaff."

Richie stood petrified when he beheld him re-enter the Palace, and found himself, as he supposed, left in the lurch.—"Now, plague on ye," he muttered, "for a cunning auld skinflint! that, because ye are an honest man yoursell, forsooth, must needs deal with all the world as if they were knaves. But deil be in me if ye beat me yet!—Gude guide us! yonder comes Laurie Linklater next, and he will be on me about the sifflication.—I winna stand him, by Saint Andrew!"

So saying, and changing the haughty stride with which he had that morning entered the precincts of the Palace, into a skulking shamble, he retreated for his wherry, which was in attendance, with speed which, to use the approved phrase on such occasions, greatly resembled a flight.

XXXII

BENEDICT: *This looks not like a nuptial.*

—*Much Ado About Nothing*

Master George Heriot had no sooner returned to the king's apartment, than James inquired of Maxwell if the Earl of Huntinglen was in attendance, and, receiving an answer in the affirmative, desired that he should be admitted. The old Scottish Lord having made his reverence in the usual manner, the king extended his hand to be kissed, and then began to address him in a tone of great sympathy.

"We told your lordship in our secret epistle of this morning, written with our ain hand, in testimony we have neither pretermitted nor forgotten your faithful service, that we had that to communicate to you that would require both patience and fortitude to endure, and therefore exhorted you to peruse some of the most pithy passages of Seneca, and of Boethius *de Consolatione*, that the back may be, as we say, fitted for the burden—This we commend to you from our ain experience.

'Non ignara mail, miseris succurrere disco,'

sayeth Dido, and I might say in my own person, *non ignarus*; but to change the gender would affect the prosody, whereof our southern subjects are tenacious. So, my Lord of Huntinglen, I trust you have acted by our advice, and studied patience before ye need it—*venienti occurrite morbo*—mix the medicament when the disease is coming on."

"May it please your Majesty," answered Lord Huntinglen, "I am more of an old soldier than a scholar—and if my own rough nature will not bear me out in any calamity, I hope I shall have grace to try a text of Scripture to boot."

"Ay, man, are you there with your bears?" said the king; "The Bible, man," (touching his cap,) "is indeed *principium et fons*—but it is pity your lordship cannot peruse it in the original. For although we did ourselves promote that work of translation,—since ye may read, at the beginning of every Bible, that when some palpable clouds of darkness were thought like to have overshadowed the land, after the setting of that bright occidental star, Queen Elizabeth; yet our appearance, like that of the sun in his strength, instantly dispelled these surmised mists,—I say, that although, as therein mentioned, we countenanced the preaching of the gospel, and especially the translation of the Scriptures out of the original sacred tongues; yet nevertheless, we ourselves confess to have found a comfort in consulting them in the original Hebrew, whilk we do not perceive even in the Latin version of the Septuagint, much less in the English traduction."

"Please your Majesty," said Lord Huntinglen, "if your Majesty delays communicating the bad news with which your honoured letter threatens me, until I am capable to read Hebrew like your Majesty, I fear I shall die in ignorance of the misfortune which hath befallen, or is about to befall, my house."

"You will learn it but too soon, my lord," replied the king. "I grieve to say it, but your son Dalgarno, whom I thought a very saint, as he was so much with Steenie and Baby Charles, hath turned out a very villain."

"Villain!" repeated Lord Huntinglen; and though he instantly checked himself, and added, "but it is your Majesty speaks the word," the effect of his first tone made the king step back as if he had received a blow. He also recovered himself again, and said in the pettish way which usually indicated his displeasure—"Yes, my lord, it was we that said it—*non surdo canis*—we are not deaf—we pray you not to raise your voice in speech with us—there is the bonny memorial—read, and judge for yourself."

The king then thrust into the old nobleman's hand a paper, containing the story of the Lady Hermione, with the evidence by which it was supported, detailed so briefly and clearly, that the infamy of Lord Dalgarno, the lover by whom she had been so shamefully deceived, seemed undeniable. But a father yields not up so easily the cause of his son.

"May it please your Majesty," he said, "why was this tale not sooner told? This woman hath been here for years—wherefore was the claim on my son not made the instant she touched English ground?"

"Tell him how that came about, Geordie," said the king, dressing Heriot.

"I grieve to distress my Lord Huntinglen," said Heriot; "but I must speak the truth. For a long time the Lady Hermione could not brook the idea of making her situation public; and when her mind became changed in that particular, it was necessary to recover the evidence of the false marriage, and letters and papers connected with it, which, when she came to Paris, and just before I saw her, she had deposited with a correspondent of her father in that city. He became afterwards bankrupt, and in consequence of that misfortune the lady's papers passed into other hands, and it was only a few days since I traced and recovered them. Without these documents of evidence, it would have been imprudent for her to have preferred her complaint, favoured as Lord Dalgarno is by powerful friends."

"Ye are saucy to say sae," said the king; "I ken what ye mean weel eneugh—ye think Steenie wad hae putten the weight of his foot into the scales of justice, and garr'd them whomle the bucket—ye forget, Geordie, wha it is whose hand uphaulds them. And ye do poor Steenie the mair wrang, for he confessed it ance before us and our privy council, that Dalgarno would have put the quean aff on him, the puir simple bairn, making him trow that she was a light-o'-love; in whilk mind he remained assured even when he parted from her, albeit Steenie might hae weel thought ane of thae cattle wadna hae resisted the like of him."

"The Lady Hermione," said George Heriot, "has always done the utmost justice to the conduct of the duke, who, although strongly possessed with prejudice against her character, yet scorned to avail himself of her distress, and on the contrary supplied her with the means of extricating herself from her difficulties."

"It was e'en like himsell—blessings on his bonny face!" said the king; "and I believed this lady's tale the mair readily, my Lord Huntinglen, that she spake nae ill of Steenie—and to make a lang tale short, my lord, it is the opinion of our council and ourself, as weel as of Baby Charles and Steenie, that your son maun amend his wrong by wedding this lady, or undergo such disgrace and discountenance as we can bestow."

The person to whom he spoke was incapable of answering him. He stood before the king motionless, and glaring with eyes of which even the lids seemed immovable, as if suddenly converted into an ancient statue of the times of chivalry, so instantly had his hard features and strong limbs been arrested into rigidity by the blow he had received—And in a second afterwards, like the same statue when the lightning breaks upon it, he sunk at once to the ground with a heavy groan. The king was in the utmost alarm, called upon Heriot and Maxwell for help, and, presence of mind not being his *forte*, ran to and fro in his cabinet, exclaiming—"My ancient and beloved servant—who saved our anointed self! *vae atque dolor!* My Lord of Huntinglen, look up—look up, man, and your son may marry the Queen of Sheba if he will."

By this time Maxwell and Heriot had raised the old nobleman, and placed him on a chair; while the king, observing that he began to recover himself, continued his consolations more methodically.

"Haud up your head—haud up your head, and listen to your ain kind native Prince. If there is shame, man, it comesna empty-handed—there is siller to gild it—a gude tocher, and no that bad a pedigree;—if she has been a loon, it was your son made her sae, and he can make her an honest woman again."

These suggestions, however reasonable in the common case, gave no comfort to Lord Huntinglen, if indeed he fully comprehended them; but the blubbering of his good-natured old master, which began to accompany and interrupt his royal speech, produced more rapid effect. The large tear gushed reluctantly from his eye, as he kissed the withered hands, which the king, weeping with less dignity and restraint, abandoned to him, first alternately and then both together, until the feelings of the man getting entirely the better of the Sovereign's sense of dignity, he grasped and shook Lord Huntinglen's hands with the sympathy of an equal and a familiar friend.

"*Compone lachrymas*," said the Monarch; "be patient, man, be patient; the council, and Baby Charles, and Steenie, may a' gang to the deevil— he shall not marry her since it moves you so deeply."

"He *shall* marry her, by God!" answered the earl, drawing himself up, dashing the tear from his eyes, and endeavouring to recover his composure. "I pray your Majesty's pardon, but he shall marry her, with her dishonour for her dowry, were she the veriest courtezan in all Spain—If he gave his word, he shall make his word good, were it to the meanest creature that haunts the streets—he shall do it, or my own dagger shall take the life that I gave him. If he could stoop to use so base a fraud, though to deceive infamy, let him wed infamy."

"No, no!" the Monarch continued to insinuate, "things are not so bad as that—Steenie himself never thought of her being a streetwalker, even when he thought the worst of her."

"If it can at all console my Lord of Huntinglen," said the citizen, "I can assure him of this lady's good birth, and most fair and unspotted fame."

"I am sorry for it," said Lord Huntinglen—then interrupting himself, he said—"Heaven forgive me for being ungrateful for such comfort!— but I am well-nigh sorry she should be as you represent her, so much better than the villain deserves. To be condemned to wed beauty and innocence and honest birth—"

"Ay, and wealth, my lord—wealth," insinuated the king, "is a better sentence than his perfidy has deserved."

"It is long," said the embittered father, "since I saw he was selfish and hardhearted; but to be a perjured liar—I never dreaded that such a blot would have fallen on my race! I will never look on him again."

"Hoot ay, my lord, hoot ay," said the king; "ye maun tak him to task roundly. I grant you should speak more in the vein of Demea than Mitio, *vi nempe et via pervulgata patrum*; but as for not seeing him again, and he your only son, that is altogether out of reason. I tell ye, man, (but I would not for a boddle that Baby Charles heard me,) that he might gie the glaiks to half the lasses of Lonnun, ere I could find in my heart speak such harsh words as you have said of this deil of a Dalgarno of yours."

"May it please your Majesty to permit me to retire," said Lord Huntinglen, "and dispose of the case according to your own royal sense of justice, for I desire no favour for him."

"Aweel, my lord, so be it; and if your lordship can think," added the Monarch, "of any thing in our power which might comfort you—"

"Your Majesty's gracious sympathy," said Lord Huntinglen, "has already comforted me as far as earth can; the rest must be from the King of kings."

"To Him I commend you, my auld and faithful servant," said James with emotion, as the earl withdrew from his presence. The king remained fixed in thought for some time, and then said to Heriot, "Jingling Geordie, ye ken all the privy doings of our Court, and have dune so these thirty years, though, like a wise man, ye hear, and see, and say nothing. Now, there is a thing I fain wad ken, in the way of philosophical inquiry—Did you ever hear of the umquhile Lady Huntinglen, the departed Countess of this noble earl, ganging a wee bit gleed in her walk through the world; I mean in the way of slipping a foot, casting a leglin-girth, or the like, ye understand me?"*

"On my word as an honest man," said George Heriot, somewhat surprised at the question, "I never heard her wronged by the slightest breath of suspicion. She was a worthy lady, very circumspect in her

---

* A leglin-girth is the lowest hoop upon a *leglin*, or milk-pail. Allan Ramsay applies the phrase in the same metaphorical sense.

"*Or bairns can read, they first maun spell, I learn'd this frae my mammy, And cast a leglin-girth mysell,*
    Lang ere I married Tammy."

—*Christ's Kirk on the Green*

walk, and lived in great concord with her husband, save that the good Countess was something of a puritan, and kept more company with ministers than was altogether agreeable to Lord Huntinglen, who is, as your Majesty well knows, a man of the old rough world, that will drink and swear."

"O Geordie!" exclaimed the king, "these are auld-warld frailties, of whilk we dare not pronounce even ourselves absolutely free. But the warld grows worse from day to day, Geordie. The juveniles of this age may weel say with the poet—

'Aetas parentum, pejor avis, tulit Nos nequiores—'

This Dalgarno does not drink so much, or swear so much, as his father; but he wenches, Geordie, and he breaks his word and oath baith. As to what you say of the leddy, and the ministers, we are a' fallible creatures, Geordie, priests and kings, as weel as others; and wha kens but what that may account for the difference between this Dalgarno and his father? The earl is the vera soul of honour, and cares nae mair for warld's gear than a noble hound for the quest of a foulmart; but as for his son, he was like to brazen us a' out—ourselves, Steenie, Baby Charles, and our council—till he heard of the tocher, and then, by my kingly crown, he lap like a cock at a grossart! These are discrepancies betwixt parent and son not to be accounted for naturally, according to Baptista Porta, Michael Scott *de secretis*, and others.—Ah, Jingling Geordie, if your clouting the caldron, and jingling on pots, pans, and veshels of all manner of metal, hadna jingled a' your grammar out of your head, I could have touched on that matter to you at mair length."

Heriot was too plain-spoken to express much concern for the loss of his grammar learning on this occasion; but after modestly hinting that he had seen many men who could not fill their father's bonnet, though no one had been suspected of wearing their father's nightcap, he inquired "whether Lord Dalgarno had consented to do the Lady Hermione justice."

"Troth, man, I have small doubt that he will," quoth the king; "I gave him the schedule of her worldly substance, which you delivered to us in the council, and we allowed him half-an-hour to chew the cud upon that. It is rare reading for bringing him to reason. I left Baby Charles and Steenie laying his duty before him; and if he can resist doing what *they* desire him—why, I wish he would teach *me* the gate of it. O Geordie, Jingling Geordie, it was grand to hear Baby Charles laying down the guilt of dissimulation, and Steenie lecturing on the turpitude of incontinence!"

"I am afraid," said George Heriot, more hastily than prudently, "I might have thought of the old proverb of Satan reproving sin."

"Deil hae our saul, neighbour," said the king, reddening, "but ye are not blate! I gie ye license to speak freely, and, by our saul, ye do not let the privilege become lost *non utendo*—it will suffer no negative prescription in your hands. Is it fit, think ye, that Baby Charles should let his thoughts be publicly seen?—No—no—princes' thoughts are *arcana imperii—Qui nescit dissimulare nescit regnare*. Every liege subject is bound to speak the whole truth to the king, but there is nae reciprocity of obligation—and for Steenie having been whiles a dike-louper at a time, is it for you, who are his goldsmith, and to whom, I doubt, he awes an uncomatable sum, to cast that up to him?"

Heriot did not feel himself called on to play the part of Zeno and sacrifice himself for upholding the cause of moral truth; he did not desert it, however, by disavowing his words, but simply expressed sorrow for having offended his Majesty, with which the placable king was sufficiently satisfied.

"And now, Geordie, man," quoth he, "we will to this culprit, and hear what he has to say for himself, for I will see the job cleared this blessed day. Ye maun come wi' me, for your evidence may be wanted."

The king led the way, accordingly, into a larger apartment, where the Prince, the Duke of Buckingham, and one or two privy counsellors were seated at a table, before which stood Lord Dalgarno, in an attitude of as much elegant ease and indifference as could be expressed, considering the stiff dress and manners of the times.

All rose and bowed reverently, while the king, to use a north country word, expressive of his mode of locomotion, *toddled* to his chair or throne, making a sign to Heriot to stand behind him.

"We hope," said his Majesty, "that Lord Dalgarno stands prepared to do justice to this unfortunate lady, and to his own character and honour?"

"May I humbly inquire the penalty," said Lord Dalgarno, "in case I should unhappily find compliance with your Majesty's demands impossible?"

"Banishment frae our Court, my lord," said the king; "frae our Court and our countenance."

"Unhappy exile that I may be!" said Lord Dalgarno, in a tone of subdued irony—"I will at least carry your Majesty's picture with me, for I shall never see such another king."

"And banishment, my lord," said the Prince, sternly, "from these our dominions."

"That must be by form of law, please your Royal Highness," said Dalgarno, with an affectation of deep respect; "and I have not heard that there is a statute, compelling us, under such penalty, to marry every woman we may play the fool with. Perhaps his Grace of Buckingham can tell me?"

"You are a villain, Dalgarno," said the haughty and vehement favourite.

"Fie, my lord, fie!—to a prisoner, and in presence of your royal and paternal gossip!" said Lord Dalgarno. "But I will cut this deliberation short. I have looked over this schedule of the goods and effects of Erminia Pauletti, daughter of the late noble—yes, he is called the noble, or I read wrong, Giovanni Pauletti, of the Houee of Sansovino, in Genoa, and of the no less noble Lady Maud Olifaunt, of the House of Glenvarloch— Well, I declare that I was pre-contracted in Spain to this noble lady, and there has passed betwixt us some certain *proelibatio matrimonii*; and now, what more does this grave assembly require of me?"

"That you should repair the gross and infamous wrong you have done the lady, by marrying her within this hour," said the Prince.

"O, may it please your Royal Highness," answered Dalgarno, "I have a trifling relationship with an old Earl, who calls himself my father, who may claim some vote in the matter. Alas! every son is not blessed with an obedient parent!" He hazarded a slight glance towards the throne, to give meaning to his last words.

"We have spoken ourselves with Lord Huntinglen," said the king, "and are authorised to consent in his name."

"I could never have expected this intervention of a *proxaneta*, which the vulgar translate blackfoot, of such eminent dignity," said Dalgarno, scarce concealing a sneer. "And my father hath consented? He was wont to say, ere we left Scotland, that the blood of Huntinglen and of Glenvarloch would not mingle, were they poured into the same basin. Perhaps he has a mind to try the experiment?"

"My lord," said James, "we will not be longer trifled with—Will you instantly, and *sine mora*, take this lady to your wife, in our chapel?"

"*Statim atque instanter*," answered Lord Dalgarno; "for I perceive by doing so, I shall obtain power to render great services to the commonwealth—I shall have acquired wealth to supply the wants of your Majesty, and a fair wife to be at the command of his Grace of Buckingham."

The Duke rose, passed to the end of the table where Lord Dalgarno was standing, and whispered in his ear, "You have placed a fair sister at my command ere now."

This taunt cut deep through Lord Dalgarno's assumed composure. He started as if an adder had stung him, but instantly composed himself, and, fixing on the Duke's still smiling countenance an eye which spoke unutterable hatred, he pointed the forefinger of his left hand to the hilt of his sword, but in a manner which could scarce be observed by any one save Buckingham. The Duke gave him another smile of bitter scorn, and returned to his seat, in obedience to the commands of the king, who continued calling out, "Sit down, Steenie, sit down, I command ye—we will hae nae harnsbreaking here."

"Your Majesty needs not fear my patience," said Lord Dalgarno; "and that I may keep it the better, I will not utter another word in this presence, save those enjoined to me in that happy portion of the Prayer-Book, which begins with *Dearly Beloved*, and ends with *amazement*."

"You are a hardened villain, Dalgarno," said the king; "and were I the lass, by my father's saul, I would rather brook the stain of having been your concubine, than run the risk of becoming your wife. But she shall be under our special protection.—Come, my lords, we will ourselves see this blithesome bridal." He gave the signal by rising, and moved towards the door, followed by the train. Lord Dalgarno attended, speaking to none, and spoken to by no one, yet seeming as easy and unembarrassed in his gait and manner as if in reality a happy bridegroom.

They reached the Chapel by a private entrance, which communicated from the royal apartment. The Bishop of Winchester, in his pontifical dress, stood beside the altar; on the other side, supported by Monna Paula, the colourless, faded, half-lifeless form of the Lady Hermione, or Erminia Pauletti. Lord Dalgarno bowed profoundly to her, and the Prince, observing the horror with which she regarded him, walked up, and said to her, with much dignity,—"Madam, ere you put yourself under the authority of this man, let me inform you, he hath in the fullest degree vindicated your honour, so far as concerns your former intercourse. It is for you to consider whether you will put your fortune and happiness into the hands of one, who has shown himself unworthy of all trust."

The lady, with much difficulty, found words to make reply. "I owe to his Majesty's goodness," she said, "the care of providing me some reservation out of my own fortune, for my decent sustenance. The rest cannot be better disposed than in buying back the fair fame of which I am deprived, and the liberty of ending my life in peace and seclusion."

"The contract has been drawn up," said the king, "under our own eye, specially discharging the *potestas maritalis*, and agreeing they shall live separate. So buckle them, my Lord Bishop, as fast as you can, that they may sunder again the sooner."

The Bishop accordingly opened his book and commenced the marriage ceremony, under circumstances so novel and so inauspicious. The responses of the bride were only expressed by inclinations of the head and body; while those of the bridegroom were spoken boldly and distinctly, with a tone resembling levity, if not scorn. When it was concluded, Lord Dalgarno advanced as if to salute the bride, but seeing that she drew back in fear and abhorrence, he contented himself with making her a low bow. He then drew up his form to its height, and stretched himself as if examining the power of his limbs, but elegantly, and without any forcible change of attitude. "I could caper yet," he said "though I am in fetters—but they are of gold, and lightly worn.—Well, I see all eyes look cold on me, and it is time I should withdraw. The sun shines elsewhere than in England! But first I must ask how this fair Lady Dalgarno is to be bestowed. Methinks it is but decent I should know. Is she to be sent to the harem of my Lord Duke? Or is this worthy citizen, as before—"

"Hold thy base ribald tongue!" said his father, Lord Huntinglen, who had kept in the background during the ceremony, and now stepping suddenly forward, caught the lady by the arm, and confronted her unworthy husband.—"The Lady Dalgarno," he continued, "shall remain as a widow in my house. A widow I esteem her, as much as if the grave had closed over her dishonoured husband."

Lord Dalgarno exhibited momentary symptoms of extreme confusion, and said, in a submissive tone, "If you, my lord, can wish me dead, I cannot, though your heir, return the compliment. Few of the first-born of Israel," he added, recovering himself from the single touch of emotion he had displayed, "can say so much with truth. But I will convince you ere I go, that I am a true descendant of a house famed for its memory of injuries."

SIR WALTER SCOTT

"I marvel your Majesty will listen to him longer," said Prince Charles. "Methinks we have heard enough of his daring insolence."

But James, who took the interest of a true gossip in such a scene as was now passing, could not bear to cut the controversy short, but imposed silence on his son, with "Whisht, Baby Charles—there is a good bairn, whisht!—I want to hear what the frontless loon can say."

"Only, sir," said Dalgarno, "that but for one single line in this schedule, all else that it contains could not have bribed me to take that woman's hand into mine."

"That line maun have been the SUMMA TOTALIS," said the king.

"Not so, sire," replied Dalgarno. "The sum total might indeed have been an object for consideration even to a Scottish king, at no very distant period; but it would have had little charms for me, save that I see here an entry which gives me the power of vengeance over the family of Glenvarloch; and learn from it that yonder pale bride, when she put the wedding-torch into my hand, gave me the power of burning her mother's house to ashes!"

"How is that?" said the king. "What is he speaking about, Jingling Geordie?"

"This friendly citizen, my liege," said Lord Dalgarno, "hath expended a sum belonging to my lady, and now, I thank heaven, to me, in acquiring a certain mortgage, or wanset, over the estate of Glenvarloch, which, if it be not redeemed before to-morrow at noon, will put me in possession of the fair demesnes of those who once called themselves our house's rivals."

"Can this be true?" said the king.

"It is even but too true, please your Majesty," answered the citizen. "The Lady Hermione having advanced the money for the original creditor, I was obliged, in honour and honesty, to take the rights to her; and doubtless, they pass to her husband."

"But the warrant, man," said the king—"the warrant on our Exchequer—Couldna that supply the lad wi' the means of redemption?"

"Unhappily, my liege, he has lost it, or disposed of it—It is not to be found. He is the most unlucky youth!"

"This is a proper spot of work!" said the king, beginning to amble about and play with the points of his doublet and hose, in expression of dismay. "We cannot aid him without paying our debts twice over, and we have, in the present state of our Exchequer, scarce the means of paying them once."

"You have told me news," said Lord Dalgarno, "but I will take no advantage."

"Do not," said his father, "be a bold villain, since thou must be one, and seek revenge with arms, and not with the usurer's weapons."

"Pardon me, my lord," said Lord Dalgarno. "Pen and ink are now my surest means of vengeance; and more land is won by the lawyer with the ram-skin, than by the Andrea Ferrara with his sheepshead handle. But, as I said before, I will take no advantages. I will await in town to-morrow, near Covent Garden; if any one will pay the redemption-money to my scrivener, with whom the deeds lie, the better for Lord Glenvarloch; if not, I will go forward on the next day, and travel with all dispatch to the north, to take possession."

"Take a father's malison with you, unhappy wretch!" said Lord Huntinglen.

"And a king's, who is *pater patriae*," said James.

"I trust to bear both lightly," said Lord Dalgarno; and bowing around him, he withdrew; while all present, oppressed, and, as it were, overawed, by his determined effrontery, found they could draw breath more freely, when he at length relieved them of his society. Lord Huntinglen, applying himself to comfort his new daughter-in-law, withdrew with her also; and the king, with his privy-council, whom he had not dismissed, again returned to his council-chamber, though the hour was unusually late. Heriot's attendance was still commanded, but for what reason was not explained to him.

XXXIII

—I'll play the eavesdropper.

—Richard III, Act V, Scene 3

James had no sooner resumed his seat at the council-board than he began to hitch in his chair, cough, use his handkerchief, and make other intimations that he meditated a long speech. The council composed themselves to the beseeming degree of attention. Charles, as strict in his notions of decorum, as his father was indifferent to it, fixed himself in an attitude of rigid and respectful attention, while the haughty favourite, conscious of his power over both father and son, stretched himself more easily on his seat, and, in assuming an appearance of listening, seemed to pay a debt to ceremonial rather than to duty.

"I doubt not, my lords," said the Monarch, "that some of you may be thinking the hour of refection is past, and that it is time to ask with the slave in the comedy—*Quid de symbolo?*—Nevertheless, to do justice and exercise judgment is our meat and drink; and now we are to pray your wisdom to consider the case of this unhappy youth, Lord Glenvarloch, and see whether, consistently with our honour, any thing can be done in his favour."

"I am surprised at your Majesty's wisdom making the inquiry," said the Duke; "it is plain this Dalgarno hath proved one of the most insolent villains on earth, and it must therefore be clear, that if Lord Glenvarloch had run him through the body, there would but have been out of the world a knave who had lived in it too long. I think Lord Glenvarloch hath had much wrong; and I regret that, by the persuasions of this false fellow, I have myself had some hand in it."

"Ye speak like a child, Steenie—I mean my Lord of Buckingham," answered the king, "and as one that does not understand the logic of the schools; for an action may be inconsequential or even meritorious, *quoad hominem*, that is, as touching him upon *whom* it is acted; and yet most criminal, *quoad locum*, or considering the place *wherein* it is done; as a man may lawfully dance Chrighty Beardie or any other dance in a tavern, but not *inter parietes ecclesiae*. So that, though it may have been a good deed to have sticked Lord Dalgarno, being such as he has shown himself, anywhere else, yet it fell under the plain statute, when violence was offered within the verge of the Court. For, let me tell you, my lords, the statute against striking would be of no small use in our Court, if it could be eluded by justifying the person stricken to be a knave. It is much to be lamented that I ken nae Court in Christendom where knaves are not to be found; and if men are to break the peace under pretence of beating them, why, it will rain Jeddart staves* in our very ante-chamber."

"What your Majesty says," replied Prince Charles, "is marked with your usual wisdom—the precincts of palaces must be sacred as well as the persons of kings, which are respected even in the most barbarous nations, as being one step only beneath their divinities. But your Majesty's will can control the severity of this and every other law, and it is in your power, on consideration of his case, to grant the rash young man a free pardon."

"*Rem acu tetigisti, Carole, mi puerule,*" answered the king; "and know, my lords, that we have, by a shrewd device and gift of our own, already sounded the very depth of this Lord Glenvarloch's disposition. I trow there be among you some that remember my handling in the curious case of my Lady Lake, and how I trimmed them about the story of hearkening behind the arras. Now this put me to cogitation, and I remembered me of having read that Dionysius, King of Syracuse, whom historians call Tyrannos, which signifieth not in the Greek tongue, as in ours, a truculent usurper, but a royal king who governs, it may be, something more strictly than we and other lawful monarchs, whom the ancients termed Basileis—Now this Dionysius of Syracuse caused cunning workmen to build for himself a *lugg*—D'ye ken what that is, my Lord Bishop?"

"A cathedral, I presume to guess," answered the Bishop.

"What the deil, man—I crave your lordship's pardon for swearing—but it was no cathedral—only a lurking-place called the king's *lugg*, or *ear*, where he could sit undescried, and hear the converse of his prisoners. Now, sirs, in imitation of this Dionysius, whom I took for my pattern, the rather that he was a great linguist and grammarian, and taught a school with good applause after his abdication, (either he or

---

* The old-fashioned weapon called the Jeddart staff was a species of battle-axe. Of a very great tempest, it is said, in the south of Scotland, that it rains Jeddart staffs, as in England the common people talk of its raining cats and dogs.

his successor of the same name, it matters not whilk)—I have caused them to make a *lugg* up at the state-prison of the Tower yonder, more like a pulpit than a cathedral, my Lord Bishop—and communicating with the arras behind the Lieutenant's chamber, where we may sit and privily hear the discourse of such prisoners as are pent up there for state-offences, and so creep into the very secrets of our enemies."

The Prince cast a glance towards the Duke, expressive of great vexation and disgust. Buckingham shrugged his shoulders, but the motion was so slight as to be almost imperceptible.

"Weel, my lords, ye ken the fray at the hunting this morning—I shall not get out of the trembling exies until I have a sound night's sleep—just after that, they bring ye in a pretty page that had been found in the Park. We were warned against examining him ourselves by the anxious care of those around us; nevertheless, holding our life ever at the service of these kingdoms, we commanded all to avoid the room, the rather that we suspected this boy to be a girl. What think ye, my lords?—few of you would have thought I had a hawk's eye for sic gear; but we thank God, that though we are old, we know so much of such toys as may beseem a man of decent gravity. Weel, my lords, we questioned this maiden in male attire ourselves, and I profess it was a very pretty interrogatory, and well followed. For, though she at first professed that she assumed this disguise in order to countenance the woman who should present us with the Lady Hermione's petition, for whom she professed entire affection; yet when we, suspecting *anguis in herba*, did put her to the very question, she was compelled to own a virtuous attachment for Glenvarlochides, in such a pretty passion of shame and fear, that we had much ado to keep our own eyes from keeping company with hers in weeping. Also, she laid before us the false practices of this Dalgarno towards Glenvarlochides, inveigling him into houses of ill resort, and giving him evil counsel under pretext of sincere friendship, whereby the inexperienced lad was led to do what was prejudicial to himself, and offensive to us. But, however prettily she told her tale, we determined not altogether to trust to her narration, but rather to try the experiment whilk we had devised for such occasions. And having ourselves speedily passed from Greenwich to the Tower, we constituted ourselves eavesdropper, as it is called, to observe what should pass between Glenvarlochides and his page, whom we caused to be admitted to his apartment, well judging that if they were of counsel together to deceive us, it could not be but something of it would spunk out—And what think ye we saw, my lords?—Naething for you to sniggle and laugh at, Steenie—for I question if you could have played the temperate and Christian-like part of this poor lad Glenvarloch. He might be a Father of the Church in comparison of you, man.—And then, to try his patience yet farther, we loosed on him a courtier and a citizen, that is Sir Mungo Malagrowther and our servant George Heriot here, wha dang the poor lad about, and didna greatly spare our royal selves.—You mind, Geordie, what you said about the wives and concubines? but I forgie ye, man—nae need of kneeling, I forgie ye—the readier, that it regards a certain particular, whilk, as it added not much to Solomon's credit, the lack of it cannot be said to impinge on ours. Aweel, my lords, for all temptation of sore distress and evil ensample, this poor lad never loosed his tongue on us to say one unbecoming word—which inclines us the rather, acting always by your wise advice, to treat this affair of the Park as a thing done in the heat of blood, and under strong provocation, and therefore to confer our free pardon on Lord Glenvarloch."

"I am happy your gracious Majesty," said the Duke of Buckingham, "has arrived at that conclusion, though I could never have guessed at the road by which you attained it."

"I trust," said Prince Charles, "that it is not a path which your Majesty will think it consistent with your high dignity to tread frequently."

"Never while I live again, Baby Charles, that I give you my royal word on. They say that hearkeners hear ill tales of themselves—by my saul, my very ears are tingling wi' that auld sorrow Sir Mungo's sarcasms. He called us close-fisted, Steenie—I am sure you can contradict that. But it is mere envy in the auld mutilated sinner, because he himself has neither a noble to hold in his loof, nor fingers to close on it if he had." Here the king lost recollection of Sir Mungo's irreverence in chuckling over his own wit, and only farther alluded to it by saying—"We must give the old maunderer *bos in linguam*—something to stop his mouth, or he will rail at us from Dan to Beersheba.—And now, my lords, let our warrant of mercy to Lord Glenvarloch be presently expedited, and he put to his freedom; and as his estate is likely to go so sleaveless a gate, we will consider what means of favour we can show him.—My lords, I wish you an appetite to an early supper—for our labours have approached that term.—Baby Charles and Steenie, you will remain till our couchee.—My Lord Bishop, you will be pleased to stay to bless our meat.—Geordie Heriot, a word with you apart."

His Majesty then drew the citizen into a corner, while the counsellors, those excepted who had been commanded to remain, made their obeisance, and withdrew. "Geordie," said the king, "my good and trusty servant"—Here he busied his fingers much with the points and ribbons of his dress,—"Ye see that we have granted, from our own natural sense of right and justice, that which yon long-backed fallow, Moniplies I think they ca' him, proffered to purchase from us with a mighty bribe; whilk we refused, as being a crowned king, who wad neither sell our justice nor our mercy for pecuniar consideration. Now, what think ye should be the upshot of this?"

"My Lord Glenvarloch's freedom, and his restoration to your Majesty's favour," said Heriot.

"I ken that," said the king, peevishly. "Ye are very dull to-day. I mean, what do you think this fallow Moniplies should think about the matter?"

"Surely that your Majesty is a most good and gracious sovereign," answered Heriot.

"We had need to be gude and gracious baith," said the king, still more pettishly, "that have idiots about us that cannot understand what we mint at, unless we speak it out in braid Lowlands. See this chield Moniplies, sir, and tell him what we have done for Lord Glenvarloch, in whom he takes such part, out of our own gracious motion, though we refused to do it on ony proffer of private advantage. Now, you may put it till him, as if of your own mind, whether it will be a gracious or a dutiful part in him, to press us for present payment of the two or three hundred miserable pounds for whilk we were obliged to opignorate our jewels? Indeed, mony men may think ye wad do the part of a good citizen, if you took it on yourself to refuse him payment, seeing he hath had what he professed to esteem full satisfaction, and considering, moreover, that it is evident he hath no pressing need of the money, whereof we have much necessity."

George Heriot sighed internally. "O my Master," thought he—"my dear Master, is it then fated you are never to indulge any kingly or noble sentiment, without its being sullied by some afterthought of interested selfishness!"

The king troubled himself not about what he thought, but taking him by the collar, said,—"Ye ken my meaning now, Jingler—awa wi' ye. You are a wise man—manage it your ain gate—but forget not our present straits." The citizen made his obeisance, and withdrew.

"And now, bairns," said the king, "what do you look upon each other for—and what have you got to ask of your dear dad and gossip?"

"Only," said the Prince, "that it would please your Majesty to command the lurking-place at the prison to be presently built up—the groans of a captive should not be brought in evidence against him."

"What! build up my lugg, Baby Charles? And yet, better deaf than hear ill tales of oneself. So let them build it up, hard and fast, without delay, the rather that my back is sair with sitting in it for a whole hour.—And now let us see what the cooks have been doing for us, bonny bairns."

XXXIV

To this brave man the knight repairs
For counsel in his law affairs;
And found him mounted in his pew.
With books and money placed for show,
Like nest-eggs to make clients lay,
And for his false opinion pay.

—Hudibras

O ur readers may recollect a certain smooth-tongued, lank-haired, buckram-suited, Scottish scrivener, who, in the earlier part of this history, appeared in the character of a protege of George Heriot. It is to his house we are about to remove, but times have changed with him. The petty booth hath become a chamber of importance—the buckram suit is changed into black velvet; and although the wearer retains his puritanical humility and politeness to clients of consequence, he can now look others broad in the face, and treat them with a full allowance of superior opulence, and the insolence arising from it. It was but a short period that had achieved these alterations, nor was the party himself as yet entirely accustomed to them, but the change was becoming less embarrassing to him with every day's practice. Among other acquisitions of wealth, you may see one of Davy Ramsay's best timepieces on the table, and his eye is frequently observing its revolutions, while a boy, whom he employs as a scribe, is occasionally sent out to compare its progress with the clock of Saint Dunstan.

The scrivener himself seemed considerably agitated. He took from a strong-box a bundle of parchments, and read passages of them with great attention; then began to soliloquize—"There is no outlet which law can suggest—no back-door of evasion—none—if the lands of Glenvarloch are not redeemed before it rings noon, Lord Dalgarno has them a cheap pennyworth. Strange, that he should have been at last able to set his patron at defiance, and achieve for himself the fair estate, with the prospect of which he so long flattered the powerful Buckingham.—Might not Andrew Skurliewhitter nick him as neatly? He hath been my patron—true—not more than Buckingham was his; and he can be so no more, for he departs presently for Scotland. I am glad of it—I hate him, and

I fear him. He knows too many of my secrets—I know too many of his. But, no—no—no—I need never attempt it, there are no means of over-reaching him.—Well, Willie, what o'clock?"

"Ele'en hours just chappit, sir."

"Go to your desk without, child," said the scrivener. "What to do next—I shall lose the old Earl's fair business, and, what is worse, his son's foul practice. Old Heriot looks too close into business to permit me more than the paltry and ordinary dues. The Whitefriars business was profitable, but it has become unsafe ever since—pah!—what brought that in my head just now? I can hardly hold my pen—if men should see me in this way!—Willie," (calling aloud to the boy,) "a cup of distilled waters—Soh!—now I could face the devil."

He spoke the last words aloud, and close by the door of the apartment, which was suddenly opened by Richie Moniplies, followed by two gentlemen, and attended by two porters bearing money-bags. "If ye can face the devil, Maister Skurliewhitter," said Richie, "ye will be the less likely to turn your back on a sack or twa o' siller, which I have ta'en the freedom to bring you. Sathanas and Mammon are near akin." The porters, at the same time, ranged their load on the floor.

"I—I,"—stammered the surprised scrivener—"I cannot guess what you mean, sir."

"Only that I have brought you the redemption-money on the part of Lord Glenvarloch, in discharge of a certain mortgage over his family inheritance. And here, in good time, comes Master Reginald Lowestoffe, and another honourable gentleman of the Temple, to be witnesses to the transaction."

"I—I incline to think," said the scrivener, "that the term is expired."

"You will pardon us, Master Scrivener," said Lowestoffe. "You will not baffle us—it wants three-quarters of noon by every clock in the city."

"I must have time, gentlemen," said Andrew, "to examine the gold by tale and weight."

"Do so at your leisure, Master Scrivener," replied Lowestoffe again. "We have already seen the contents of each sack told and weighed, and we have put our seals on them. There they stand in a row, twenty in number, each containing three hundred yellow-hammers—we are witnesses to the lawful tender."

"Gentlemen," said the scrivener, "this security now belongs to a mighty lord. I pray you, abate your haste, and let me send for Lord Dalgarno,—or rather I will run for him myself."

So saying, he took up his hat; but Lowestoffe called out,—"Friend Moniplies, keep the door fast, an thou be'st a man! he seeks but to put off the time.—In plain terms, Andrew, you may send for the devil, if you will, who is the mightiest lord of my acquaintance, but from hence you stir not till you have answered our proposition, by rejecting or accepting the redemption-money fairly tendered—there it lies—take it, or leave it, as you will. I have skill enough to know that the law is mightier than any lord in Britain—I have learned so much at the Temple, if I have learned nothing else. And see that you trifle not with it, lest it make your long ears an inch shorter, Master Skurliewhitter."

"Nay, gentlemen, if you threaten me," said the scrivener, "I cannot resist compulsion."

"No threats—no threats at all, my little Andrew," said Lowestoffe; "a little friendly advice only—forget not, honest Andrew, I have seen you in Alsatia."

Without answering a single word, the scrivener sat down, and drew in proper form a full receipt for the money proffered.

"I take it on your report, Master Lowestoffe," he said; "I hope you will remember I have insisted neither upon weight nor tale—I have been civil—if there is deficiency I shall come to loss."

"Fillip his nose with a gold-piece, Richie," quoth the Templar. "Take up the papers, and now wend we merrily to dine thou wot'st where."

"If I might choose," said Richie, "it should not be at yonder roguish ordinary; but as it is your pleasure, gentlemen, the treat shall be given wheresoever you will have it."

"At the ordinary," said the one Templar.

"At Beaujeu's," said the other; "it is the only house in London for neat wines, nimble drawers, choice dishes, and—"

"And high charges," quoth Richie Moniplies. "But, as I said before, gentlemen, ye have a right to command me in this thing, having so frankly rendered me your service in this small matter of business, without other stipulation than that of a slight banquet."

The latter part of this discourse passed in the street, where, immediately afterwards, they met Lord Dalgarno. He appeared in haste, touched his hat slightly to Master Lowestoffe, who returned his reverence with the same negligence, and walked slowly on with his companion, while Lord Dalgarno stopped Richie Moniplies with a commanding sign, which the instinct of education compelled Moniplies, though indignant, to obey.

"Whom do you now follow, sirrah?" demanded the noble.

"Whomsoever goeth before me, my lord," answered Moniplies.

"No sauciness, you knave—I desire to know if you still serve Nigel Olifaunt?" said Dalgarno.

"I am friend to the noble Lord Glenvarloch," answered Moniplies, with dignity.

"True," replied Lord Dalgarno, "that noble lord has sunk to seek friends among lackeys—Nevertheless,—hark thee hither,—nevertheless, if he be of the same mind as when we last met, thou mayst show him, that, on to-morrow, at four afternoon, I shall pass northward by Enfield Chase—I will be slenderly attended, as I design to send my train through Barnet. It is my purpose to ride an easy pace through the forest, and to linger a while by Camlet Moat—he knows the place; and, if he be aught but an Alsatian bully, will think it fitter for some purposes than the Park. He is, I understand, at liberty, or shortly to be so. If he fail me at the place nominated, he must seek me in Scotland, where he will find me possessed of his father's estate and lands."

"Humph!" muttered Richie; "there go twa words to that bargain."

He even meditated a joke on the means which he was conscious he possessed of baffling Lord Dalgarno's expectations; but there was something of keen and dangerous excitement in the eyes of the young nobleman, which prompted his discretion for once to rule his vit, and he only answered—

"God grant your lordship may well brook your new conquest—when you get it. I shall do your errand to my lord—whilk is to say," he added internally, "he shall never hear a word of it from Richie. I am not the lad to put him in such hazard."

Lord Dalgarno looked at him sharply for a moment, as if to penetrate the meaning of the dry ironical tone, which, in spite of Richie's awe, mingled with his answer, and then waved his hand, in signal he should pass on. He himself walked slowly till the trio were out of sight, then turned back with hasty steps to the door of the scrivener, which he had passed in his progress, knocked, and was admitted.

Lord Dalgarno found the man of law with the money-bags still standing before him; and it escaped not his penetrating glance, that Skurliewhitter was disconcerted and alarmed at his approach.

"How now, man," he said; "what! hast thou not a word of oily compliment to me on my happy marriage?—not a word of most philosophical consolation on my disgrace at Court?—Or has my mien, as a wittol and discarded favourite, the properties of the Gorgon's head, the *turbatae Palladis arma*, as Majesty might say?"

"My lord, I am glad—my lord, I am sorry,"—answered the trembling scrivener, who, aware of the vivacity of Lord Dalgarno's temper, dreaded the consequence of the communication he had to make to him.

"Glad and sorry!" answered Lord Dalgarno. "That is blowing hot and cold, with a witness. Hark ye, you picture of petty-larceny personified— if you are sorry I am a cuckold, remember I am only mine own, you knave—there is too little blood in her cheeks to have sent her astray elsewhere. Well, I will bear mine antler'd honours as I may—gold shall gild them; and for my disgrace, revenge shall sweeten it. Ay, revenge— and there strikes the happy hour!"

The hour of noon was accordingly heard to peal from Saint Dunstan's. "Well banged, brave hammers!" said Lord Dalgarno, in triumph.—"The estate and lands of Glenvarloch are crushed beneath these clanging blows. If my steel to-morrow prove but as true as your iron maces to-day, the poor landless lord will little miss what your peal hath cut him out from.—The papers—the papers, thou varlet! I am to-morrow Northward, ho! At four, afternoon, I am bound to be at Camlet Moat, in the Enfield Chase. To-night most of my retinue set forward. The papers!—Come, dispatch."

"My lord, the—the papers of the Glenvarloch mortgage—I—I have them not."

"Have them not!" echoed Lord Dalgarno,—"Hast thou sent them to my lodgings, thou varlet? Did I not say I was coming hither?—What mean you by pointing to that money? What villainy have you done for it? It is too large to be come honestly by."

"Your lordship knows best," answered the scrivener, in great perturbation. "The gold is your own. It is—it is—"

"Not the redemption-money of the Glenvarloch estate!" said Dalgarno. "Dare not say it is, or I will, upon the spot, divorce your pettifogging soul from your carrion carcass!" So saying, he seized the scrivener by the collar, and shook him so vehemently, that he tore it from the cassock.

"My lord, I must call for help," said the trembling caitiff, who felt at that moment all the bitterness of the mortal agony—"It was the law's act, not mine. What could I do?"

"Dost ask?—why, thou snivelling dribblet of damnation, were all thy oaths, tricks, and lies spent? or do you hold yourself too good to utter them in my service? Thou shouldst have lied, cozened, out-sworn truth itself, rather than stood betwixt me and my revenge! But mark me," he continued; "I know more of your pranks than would hang thee. A line from me to the Attorney-General, and thou art sped."

"What would you have me to do, my lord?" said the scrivener. "All that art and law can accomplish, I will try."

"Ah, are you converted? do so, or pity of your life!" said the lord; "and remember I never fail my word.—Then keep that accursed gold," he continued. "Or, stay, I will not trust you—send me this gold home presently to my lodging. I will still forward to Scotland, and it shall go hard but that I hold out Glenvarloch Castle against the owner, by means of the ammunition he has himself furnished. Thou art ready to serve me?" The scrivener professed the most implicit obedience.

"Then remember, the hour was past ere payment was tendered—and see thou hast witnesses of trusty memory to prove that point."

"Tush, my lord, I will do more," said Andrew, reviving—"I will prove that Lord Glenvarloch's friends threatened, swaggered, and drew swords on me.—Did your lordship think I was ungrateful enough to have suffered them to prejudice your lordship, save that they had bare swords at my throat?"

"Enough said," replied Dalgarno; "you are perfect—mind that you continue so, as you would avoid my fury. I leave my page below—get porters, and let them follow me instantly with the gold."

So saying, Lord Dalgarno left the scrivener's habitation.

Skurliewhitter, having dispatched his boy to get porters of trust for transporting the money, remained alone and in dismay, meditating by what means he could shake himself free of the vindictive and ferocious nobleman, who possessed at once a dangerous knowledge of his character, and the power of exposing him, where exposure would be ruin. He had indeed acquiesced in the plan, rapidly sketched, for obtaining possession of the ransomed estate, but his experience foresaw that this would be impossible; while, on the other hand, he could not anticipate the various consequences of Lord Dalgarno's resentment, without fears, from which his sordid soul recoiled. To be in the power, and subject both to the humours and the extortions of a spendthrift young lord, just when his industry had shaped out the means of fortune,—it was the most cruel trick which fate could have played the incipient usurer.

While the scrivener was in this fit of anxious anticipation, one knocked at the door of the apartment; and, being desired to enter, appeared in the coarse riding-cloak of uncut Wiltshire cloth, fastened by a broad leather belt and brass buckle, which was then generally worn by graziers and countrymen. Skurliewhitter, believing he saw in his visitor a country client who might prove profitable, had opened his mouth to request him to be seated, when the stranger, throwing back his frieze hood which he had drawn over his face, showed the scrivener features well imprinted in his recollection, but which he never saw without a disposition to swoon.

"Is it you?" he said, faintly, as the stranger replaced the hood which concealed his features.

"Who else should it be?" said his visitor.

"Thou son of parchment, got betwixt the inkhorn And the stuff'd process-bag—that mayest call The pen thy father, and the ink thy mother,

> *The wax thy brother, and the sand thy sister*
> *And the good pillory thy cousin allied—*
> *Rise, and do reverence unto me, thy better!"*

"Not yet down to the country," said the scrivener, "after every warning? Do not think your grazier's cloak will bear you out, captain— no, nor your scraps of stage-plays."

"Why, what would you have me to do?" said the captain—"Would you have me starve? If I am to fly, you must eke my wings with a few feathers. You can spare them, I think."

"You had means already—you have had ten pieces—What is become of them?"

"Gone," answered Captain Colepepper—"Gone, no matter where—I had a mind to bite, and I was bitten, that's all—I think my hand shook at the thought of t'other night's work, for I trowled the doctors like a very baby."

"And you have lost all, then?—Well, take this and be gone," said the scrivener.

"What, two poor smelts! Marry, plague of your bounty!—But remember, you are as deep in as I."

"Not so, by Heaven!" answered the scrivener; "I only thought of easing the old man of some papers and a trifle of his gold, and you took his life."

"Were he living," answered Colepepper, "he would rather have lost it than his money.—But that is not the question, Master Skurliewhitter— you undid the private bolts of the window when you visited him about some affairs on the day ere he died—so satisfy yourself, that, if I am taken, I will not swing alone. Pity Jack Hempsfield is dead, it spoils the old catch,

> *'And three merry men, and three merry men,*
> *And three merry men are we,*
> *As ever did sing three parts in a string,*
> *All under the triple tree.'"*

"For God's sake, speak lower," said the scrivener; "is this a place or time to make your midnight catches heard?—But how much will serve your turn? I tell you I am but ill provided."

"You tell me a lie, then," said the bully—"a most palpable and gross lie.—How much, d'ye say, will serve my turn? Why, one of these bags will do for the present."

"I swear to you that these bags of money are not at my disposal."

"Not honestly, perhaps," said the captain, "but that makes little difference betwixt us."

"I swear to you," continued the scrivener "they are in no way at my disposal—they have been delivered to me by tale—I am to pay them over to Lord Dalgarno, whose boy waits for them, and I could not skelder one piece out of them, without risk of hue and cry."

"Can you not put off the delivery?" said the bravo, his huge hand still fumbling with one of the bags, as if his fingers longed to close on it.

"Impossible," said the scrivener, "he sets forward to Scotland to-morrow."

"Ay!" said the bully, after a moment's thought—"Travels he the north road with such a charge?"

"He is well accompanied," added the scrivener; "but yet—"

"But yet—but what?" said the bravo.

"Nay, I meant nothing," said the scrivener.

"Thou didst—thou hadst the wind of some good thing," replied Colepepper; "I saw thee pause like a setting dog. Thou wilt say as little, and make as sure a sign, as a well-bred spaniel."

"All I meant to say, captain, was, that his servants go by Barnet, and he himself, with his page, pass through Enfield Chase; and he spoke to me yesterday of riding a soft pace."

"Aha!—Comest thou to me there, my boy?"

"And of resting"—continued the scrivener,—"resting a space at Camlet Moat."

"Why, this is better than cock-fighting!" said the captain.

"I see not how it can advantage you, captain," said the scrivener. "But, however, they cannot ride fast, for his page rides the sumpter-horse, which carries all that weight," pointing to the money on the table. "Lord Dalgarno looks sharp to the world's gear."

"That horse will be obliged to those who may ease him of his burden," said the bravo; "and egad, he may be met with.—He hath still that page—that same Lutin—that goblin? Well, the boy hath set game for me ere now. I will be revenged, too, for I owe him a grudge for an old score at the ordinary. Let me see—Black Feltham, and Dick Shakebag— we shall want a fourth—I love to make sure, and the booty will stand parting, besides what I can bucket them out of. Well, scrivener, lend me two pieces.—Bravely done—nobly imparted! Give ye good-den." And wrapping his disguise closer around him, away he went.

When he had left the room, the scrivener wrung his hands, and exclaimed, "More blood—more blood! I thought to have had done with it, but this time there was no fault with me—none—and then I shall have all the advantage. If this ruffian falls, there is truce with his tugs at my purse-strings; and if Lord Dalgarno dies—as is most likely, for though as much afraid of cold steel as a debtor of a dun, this fellow is a deadly shot from behind a bush,—then am I in a thousand ways safe—safe—safe."

We willingly drop the curtain over him and his reflections.

XXXV

We are not worst at once—the course of evil
Begins so slowly, and from such slight source,
An infant's hand might stem its breach with clay;
But let the stream get deeper, and philosophy—
Ay, and religion too—shall strive in vain
To turn the headlong torrent.

—Old Play

T he Templars had been regaled by our friend Richie Moniplies in
a private chamber at Beaujeu's, where he might be considered as
good company; for he had exchanged his serving-man's cloak and jerkin
for a grave yet handsome suit of clothes, in the fashion of the times,
but such as might have befitted an older man than himself. He had
positively declined presenting himself at the ordinary, a point to which
his companions were very desirous to have brought him, for it will
be easily believed that such wags as Lowestoffe and his companion
were not indisposed to a little merriment at the expense of the raw and
pedantic Scotsman; besides the chance of easing him of a few pieces,
of which he appeared to have acquired considerable command. But
not even a succession of measures of sparkling sack, in which the little
brilliant atoms circulated like motes in the sun's rays, had the least effect
on Richie's sense of decorum. He retained the gravity of a judge, even
while he drank like a fish, partly from his own natural inclination to
good liquor, partly in the way of good fellowship towards his guests.
When the wine began to make some innovation on their heads, Master
Lowestoffe, tired, perhaps, of the humours of Richie, who began to
become yet more stoically contradictory and dogmatical than even in
the earlier part of the entertainment, proposed to his friend to break up
their debauch and join the gamesters.

The drawer was called accordingly, and Richie discharged the
reckoning of the party, with a generous remuneration to the attendants,
which was received with cap and knee, and many assurances of—
"Kindly welcome, gentlemen."

"I grieve we should part so soon, gentlemen," said Richie to his
companions,—"and I would you had cracked another quart ere you

went, or stayed to take some slight matter of supper, and a glass of Rhenish. I thank you, however, for having graced my poor collation thus far; and I commend you to fortune, in your own courses, for the ordinary neither was, is, nor shall be, an element of mine."

"Fare thee well, then," said Lowestoffe, "most sapient and sententious Master Moniplies. May you soon have another mortgage to redeem, and may I be there to witness it; and may you play the good fellow, as heartily as you have done this day."

"Nay, gentlemen, it is merely of your grace to say so—but, if you would but hear me speak a few words of admonition respecting this wicked ordinary—"

"Reserve the lesson, most honourable Richie," said Lowestoffe, "until I have lost all my money," showing, at the same time, a purse indifferently well provided, "and then the lecture is likely to have some weight."

"And keep my share of it, Richie," said the other Templar, showing an almost empty purse, in his turn, "till this be full again, and then I will promise to hear you with some patience."

"Ay, ay, gallants," said Richie, "the full and the empty gang a' ae gate, and that is a grey one—but the time will come."

"Nay, it is come already," said Lowestoffe; "they have set out the hazard table. Since you will peremptorily not go with us, why, farewell, Richie."

"And farewell, gentlemen," said Richie, and left the house, into which they had returned.

Moniplies was not many steps from the door, when a person, whom, lost in his reflections on gaming, ordinaries, and the manners of the age, he had not observed, and who had been as negligent on his part, ran full against him; and, when Richie desired to know whether he meant "ony incivility," replied by a curse on Scotland, and all that belonged to it. A less round reflection on his country would, at any time, have provoked Richie, but more especially when he had a double quart of Canary and better in his pate. He was about to give a very rough answer, and to second his word by action, when a closer view of his antagonist changed his purpose.

"You are the vera lad in the warld," said Richie, "whom I most wished to meet."

"And you," answered the stranger, "or any of your beggarly countrymen, are the last sight I should ever wish to see. You Scots are ever fair and false, and an honest man cannot thrive within eyeshot of you."

"As to our poverty, friend," replied Richie, "that is as Heaven pleases; but touching our falset, I'll prove to you that a Scotsman bears as leal and true a heart to his friend as ever beat in English doublet."

"I care not whether he does or not," said the gallant. "Let me go—why keep you hold of my cloak? Let me go, or I will thrust you into the kennel."

"I believe I could forgie ye, for you did me a good turn once, in plucking me out of it," said the Scot.

"Beshrew my fingers, then, if they did so," replied the stranger. "I would your whole country lay there, along with you; and Heaven's curse blight the hand that helped to raise them!—Why do you stop my way?" he added, fiercely.

"Because it is a bad one, Master Jenkin," said Richie. "Nay, never start about it, man—you see you are known. Alack-a-day! that an honest man's son should live to start at hearing himself called by his own name!" Jenkin struck his brow violently with his clenched fist.

"Come, come," said Richie, "this passion availeth nothing. Tell me what gate go you?"

"To the devil!" answered Jin Vin.

"That is a black gate, if you speak according to the letter," answered Richie; "but if metaphorically, there are worse places in this great city than the Devil Tavern; and I care not if I go thither with you, and bestow a pottle of burnt sack on you—it will correct the crudities of my stomach, and form a gentle preparative for the leg of a cold pullet."

"I pray you, in good fashion, to let me go," said Jenkin. "You may mean me kindly, and I wish you to have no wrong at my hand; but I am in the humour to be dangerous to myself, or any one."

"I will abide the risk," said the Scot, "if you will but come with me; and here is a place convenient, a howff nearer than the Devil, whilk is but an ill-omened drouthy name for a tavern. This other of the Saint Andrew is a quiet place, where I have ta'en my whetter now and then, when I lodged in the neighbourhood of the Temple with Lord Glenvarloch.—What the deil's the matter wi' the man, garr'd him gie sic a spang as that, and almaist brought himself and me on the causeway?"

"Do not name that false Scot's name to me," said Jin Vin, "if you would not have me go mad!—I was happy before I saw him—he has been the cause of all the ill that has befallen me—he has made a knave and a madman of me!"

"If you are a knave," said Richie, "you have met an officer—if you are daft, you have met a keeper; but a gentle officer and a kind keeper. Look you, my gude friend, there has been twenty things said about this same lord, in which there is no more truth than in the leasings of Mahound. The warst they can say of him is, that he is not always so amenable to good advice as I would pray him, you, and every young man to be. Come wi' me—just come ye wi' me; and, if a little spell of siller and a great deal of excellent counsel can relieve your occasions, all I can say is, you have had the luck to meet one capable of giving you both, and maist willing to bestow them."

The pertinacity of the Scot prevailed over the sullenness of Vincent, who was indeed in a state of agitation and incapacity to think for himself, which led him to yield the more readily to the suggestions of another. He suffered himself to be dragged into the small tavern which Richie recommended, and where they soon found themselves seated in a snug niche, with a reeking pottle of burnt sack, and a paper of sugar betwixt them. Pipes and tobacco were also provided, but were only used by Richie, who had adopted the custom of late, as adding considerably to the gravity and importance of his manner, and affording, as it were, a bland and pleasant accompaniment to the words of wisdom which flowed from his tongue. After they had filled their glasses and drank them in silence, Richie repeated the question, whither his guest was going when they met so fortunately.

"I told you," said Jenkin, "I was going to destruction—I mean to the gaming-house. I am resolved to hazard these two or three pieces, to get as much as will pay for a passage with Captain Sharker, whose ship lies at Gravesend, bound for America—and so Eastward, ho!—I met one devil in the way already, who would have tempted me from my purpose, but I spurned him from me—you may be another for what I know.—What degree of damnation do you propose for me," he added wildly, "and what is the price of it?"

"I would have you to know," answered Richie, "that I deal in no such commodities, whether as buyer or seller. But if you will tell me honestly the cause of your distress, I will do what is in my power to help you out of it,—not being, however, prodigal of promises, until I know the case; as a learned physician only gives advice when he has observed the diagnostics."

"No one has any thing to do with my affairs," said the poor lad; and folding his arms on the table, he laid his head upon them, with the sullen dejection of the overburdened lama, when it throws itself down to die in desperation.

Richard Moniplies, like most folk who have a good opinion of themselves, was fond of the task of consolation, which at once displayed his superiority, (for the consoler is necessarily, for the time at least, superior to the afflicted person,) and indulged his love of talking. He inflicted on the poor penitent a harangue of pitiless length, stuffed full of the usual topics of the mutability of human affairs—the eminent advantages of patience under affliction—the folly of grieving for what hath no remedy—the necessity of taking more care for the future, and some gentle rebukes on account of the past, which acid he threw in to assist in subduing the patient's obstinacy, as Hannibal used vinegar in cutting his way through rocks. It was not in human nature to endure this flood of commonplace eloquence in silence; and Jin Vin, whether desirous of stopping the flow of words—crammed thus into his ear, "against the stomach of his sense," or whether confiding in Richie's protestations of friendship, which the wretched, says Fielding, are ever so ready to believe, or whether merely to give his sorrows vent in words, raised his head, and turning his red and swollen eyes to Richie—

"Cocksbones, man, only hold thy tongue, and thou shall know all about it,—and then all I ask of thee is to shake hands and part.—This Margaret Ramsay,—you have seen her, man?"

"Once," said Richie, "once, at Master George Heriot's in Lombard Street—I was in the room when they dined."

"Ay, you helped to shift their trenchers, I remember," said Jin Vin. "Well, that same pretty girl—and I will uphold her the prettiest betwixt Paul's and the Bar—she is to be wedded to your Lord Glenvarloch, with a pestilence on him!"

"That is impossible," said Richie; "it is raving nonsense, man—they make April gouks of you cockneys every month in the year—The Lord Glenvarloch marry the daughter of a Lonnon mechanic! I would as soon believe the great Prester John would marry the daughter of a Jew packman."

"Hark ye, brother," said Jin Vin, "I will allow no one to speak disregardfully of the city, for all I am in trouble."

"I crave your pardon, man—I meant no offence," said Richie; "but as to the marriage, it is a thing simply impossible."

"It is a thing that will take place, though, for the Duke and the Prince, and all of them, have a finger in it; and especially the old fool of a king, that makes her out to be some great woman in her own country, as all the Scots pretend to be, you know."

"Master Vincent, but that you are under affliction," said the consoler, offended on his part, "I would hear no national reflections."

The afflicted youth apologised in his turns, but asserted, "it was true that the king said Peg-a-Ramsay was some far-off sort of noblewoman; and that he had taken a great interest in the match, and had run about like an old gander, cackling about Peggie ever since he had seen her in hose and doublet—and no wonder," added poor Vin, with a deep sigh.

"This may be all true," said Richie, "though it sounds strange in my ears; but, man, you should not speak evil of dignities—Curse not the king, Jenkin; not even in thy bed-chamber—stone walls have ears—no one has a right to know better than I."

"I do not curse the foolish old man," said Jenkin; "but I would have them carry things a peg lower.—If they were to see on a plain field thirty thousand such pikes as I have seen in the artillery gardens, it would not be their long-haired courtiers would help them, I trow."*

"Hout tout, man," said Richie, "mind where the Stewarts come frae, and never think they would want spears or claymores either; but leaving sic matters, whilk are perilous to speak on, I say once more, what is your concern in all this matter?"

"What is it?" said Jenkin; "why, have I not fixed on Peg-a-Ramsay to be my true love, from the day I came to her old father's shop? and have I not carried her pattens and her chopines for three years, and borne her prayer-book to church, and brushed the cushion for her to kneel down upon, and did she ever say me nay?"

"I see no cause she had," said Richie, "if the like of such small services were all that ye proffered. Ah, man! there are few—very few, either of fools or of wise men, ken how to guide a woman."

"Why, did I not serve her at the risk of my freedom, and very nigh at the risk of my neck? Did she not—no, it was not her neither, but that accursed beldam whom she caused to work upon me—persuade me like a fool to turn myself into a waterman to help my lord, and a plague to him, down to Scotland? and instead of going peaceably down to the ship at Gravesend, did not he rant and bully, and show his pistols, and

---

* Clarendon remarks, that the importance of the military exercise of the citizens was severely felt by the cavaliers during the civil war, notwithstanding the ridicule that had been showered upon it by the dramatic poets of the day. Nothing less than habitual practice could, at the battle of Newbury and elsewhere, have enabled the Londoners to keep their ranks as pikemen, in spite of the repeated charge of the fiery Prince Rupert and his gallant cavaliers.

make me land him at Greenwich, where he played some swaggering pranks, that helped both him and me into the Tower?"

"Aha!" said Richie, throwing more than his usual wisdom into his looks, "so you were the green-jacketed waterman that rowed Lord Glenvarloch down the river?"

"The more fool I, that did not souse him in the Thames," said Jenkin; "and I was the lad who would not confess one word of who and what I was, though they threatened to make me hug the Duke of Exeter's daughter."*

"Wha is she, man?" said Richie; "she must be an ill-fashioned piece, if you're so much afraid of her, and she come of such high kin."

"I mean the rack—the rack, man," said Jenkin. "Where were you bred that never heard of the Duke of Exeter's daughter? But all the dukes and duchesses in England could have got nothing out of me—so the truth came out some other way, and I was set free.—Home I ran, thinking myself one of the cleverest and happiest fellows in the ward. And she—she—she wanted to pay me with *money* for all my true service! and she spoke so sweetly and so coldly at the same time, I wished myself in the deepest dungeon of the Tower—I wish they had racked me to death before I heard this Scottishman was to chouse me out of my sweetheart!"

"But are ye sure ye have lost her?" said Richie; "it sounds strange in my ears that my Lord Glenvarloch should marry the daughter of a dealer,—though there are uncouth marriages made in London, I'll allow that."

"Why, I tell you this lord was no sooner clear of the Tower, than he and Master George Heriot comes to make proposals for her, with the king's assent, and what not; and fine fair-day prospects of Court favour for this lord, for he hath not an acre of land."

"Well, and what said the auld watch-maker?" said Richie; "was he not, as might weel beseem him, ready to loop out of his skin-case for very joy?"

"He multiplied six figures progressively, and reported the product—then gave his consent."

"And what did you do?"

"I rushed into the streets," said the poor lad, "with a burning heart and a blood-shot eye—and where did I first find myself, but with that

---

* A particular species of rack, used at the Tower of London, was so called.

　　　　　　　　　　　　　SIR WALTER SCOTT

beldam, Mother Suddlechop—and what did she propose to me, but to take the road?"

"Take the road, man? in what sense?" said Richie.

"Even as a clerk to Saint Nicholas—as a highwayman, like Poins and Peto, and the good fellows in the play—and who think you was to be my captain?—for she had the whole out ere I could speak to her—I fancy she took silence for consent, and thought me damned too unutterably to have one thought left that savoured of redemption—who was to be my captain, but the knave that you saw me cudgel at the ordinary when you waited on Lord Glenvarloch, a cowardly, sharking, thievish bully about town here, whom they call Colepepper."

"Colepepper—umph—I know somewhat of that smaik," said Richie; "ken ye by ony chance where he may be heard of, Master Jenkin?—ye wad do me a sincere service to tell me."

"Why, he lives something obscurely," answered the apprentice, "on account of suspicion of some villainy—I believe that horrid murder in Whitefriars, or some such matter. But I might have heard all about him from Dame Suddlechop, for she spoke of my meeting him at Enfield Chase, with some other good fellows, to do a robbery on one that goes northward with a store of treasure."

"And you did not agree to this fine project?" said Moniplies.

"I cursed her for a hag, and came away about my business," answered Jenkin.

"Ay, and what said she to that, man? That would startle her," said Richie.

"Not a whit. She laughed, and said she was in jest," answered Jenkin; "but I know the she-devil's jest from her earnest too well to be taken in that way. But she knows I would never betray her.'

"Betray her! No," replied Richie; "but are ye in any shape bound to this birkie Peppercull, or Colepepper, or whatever they call him, that ye suld let him do a robbery on the honest gentleman that is travelling to the north, and may be a kindly Scot, for what we know?"

"Ay—going home with a load of English money," said Jenkin. "But be he who he will, they may rob the whole world an they list, for I am robbed and ruined."

Richie filled his friend's cup up to the brim, and insisted that he should drink what he called "clean caup out." "This love," he said, "is but a bairnly matter for a brisk young fellow like yourself, Master Jenkin. And if ye must needs have a whimsy, though I think it would be safer to venture on a staid womanly body, why, here be as bonny lasses in London as this Peg-a-Ramsay. You need not sigh sae deeply, for it is very true—there is as good fish in the sea as ever came out of it. Now wherefore should you, who are as brisk and trig a young fellow of your inches as the sun needs to shine on—wherefore need you sit moping this way, and not try some bold way to better your fortune?"

"I tell you, Master Moniplies," said Jenkin, "I am as poor as any Scot among you—I have broke my indenture, and I think of running my country."

"A-well-a-day!" said Richie; "but that maunna be, man—I ken weel, by sad experience, that poortith takes away pith, and the man sits full still that has a rent in his breeks.*

But courage, man; you have served me heretofore, and I will serve you now. If you will but bring me to speech of this same captain, it will be the best day's work you ever did."

"I guess where you are, Master Richard—you would save your countryman's long purse," said Jenkin. "I cannot see how that should advantage me, but I reck not if I should bear a hand. I hate that braggart, that bloody-minded, cowardly bully. If you can get me mounted I care not if I show you where the dame told me I should meet him—but you must stand to the risk, for though he is a coward himself, I know he will have more than one stout fellow with him."

"We'll have a warrant, man," said Richie, "and the hue and cry, to boot."

"We will have no such thing," said Jenkin, "if I am to go with you. I am not the lad to betray any one to the harmanbeck. You must do it by manhood if I am to go with you. I am sworn to cutter's law, and will sell no man's blood."

"Aweel," said Richie, "a wilful man must have his way; ye must think that I was born and bred where cracked crowns were plentier than whole ones. Besides, I have two noble friends here, Master Lowestoffe of the Temple, and his cousin Master Ringwood, that will blithely be of so gallant a party."

---

* This elegant speech was made by the Earl of Douglas, called Tineman after being wounded and made prisoner at the battle of Shrewsbury, where

> *His well labouring sword*
> *Had three times slain the semblance of the king,"*

"Lowestoffe and Ringwood!" said Jenkin; "they are both brave gallants—they will be sure company. Know you where they are to be found?"

"Ay, marry do I," replied Richie. "They are fast at the cards and dice, till the sma' hours, I warrant them."

"They are gentlemen of trust and honour," said Jenkin, "and, if they advise it, I will try the adventure. Go, try if you can bring them hither, since you have so much to say with, them. We must not be seen abroad together.—I know not how it is, Master Moniplies," continued he, as his countenance brightened up, and while, in his turn, he filled the cups, "but I feel my heart something lighter since I have thought of this matter."

"Thus it is to have counsellors, Master Jenkin," said Richie; "and truly I hope to hear you say that your heart is as light as a lavrock's, and that before you are many days aulder. Never smile and shake your head, but mind what I tell you—and bide here in the meanwhile, till I go to seek these gallants. I warrant you, cart-ropes would not hold them back from such a ploy as I shall propose to them."

XXXVI

The thieves have bound the true men—
Now, could thou and I rob the thieves, and go
merrily to London.

—Henry IV, Part I

The sun was high upon the glades of Enfield Chase, and the deer, with which it then abounded, were seen sporting in picturesque groups among the ancient oaks of the forest, when a cavalier and a lady, on foot, although in riding apparel, sauntered slowly up one of the long alleys which were cut through the park for the convenience of the hunters. Their only attendant was a page, who, riding a Spanish jennet, which seemed to bear a heavy cloak-bag, followed them at a respectful distance. The female, attired in all the fantastic finery of the period, with more than the usual quantity of bugles, flounces, and trimmings, and holding her fan of ostrich feathers in one hand, and her riding-mask of black velvet in the other, seemed anxious, by all the little coquetry practised on such occasions, to secure the notice of her companion, who sometimes heard her prattle without seeming to attend to it, and at other times interrupted his train of graver reflections, to reply to her.

"Nay, but, my lord—my lord, you walk so fast, you will leave me behind you.—Nay, I will have hold of your arm, but how to manage with my mask and my fan? Why would you not let me bring my waiting-gentlewoman to follow us, and hold my things? But see, I will put my fan in my girdle, soh!—and now that I have a hand to hold you with, you shall not run away from me."

"Come on, then," answered the gallant, "and let us walk apace, since you would not be persuaded to stay with your gentlewoman, as you call her, and with the rest of the baggage.—You may perhaps see *that*, though, you will not like to see."

She took hold of his arm accordingly; but as he continued to walk at the same pace, she shortly let go her hold, exclaiming that he had hurt her hand. The cavalier stopped, and looked at the pretty hand and arm which she showed him, with exclamations against his cruelty. "I dare say," she said, baring her wrist and a part of her arm, "it is all black and blue to the very elbow."

"I dare say you are a silly little fool," said the cavalier, carelessly kissing the aggrieved arm; "it is only a pretty incarnate which sets off the blue veins."

"Nay, my lord, now it is you are silly," answered the dame; "but I am glad I can make you speak and laugh on any terms this morning. I am sure, if I did insist on following you into the forest, it was all for the sake of diverting you. I am better company than your page, I trow.—And now, tell me, these pretty things with horns, be they not deer?"

"Even such they be, Nelly," answered her neglectful attendant.

"And what can the great folk do with so many of them, forsooth?"

"They send them to the city, Nell, where wise men make venison pasties of their flesh, and wear their horns for trophies," answered Lord Dalgarno, whom our reader has already recognised.

"Nay, now you laugh at me, my lord," answered his companion; "but I know all about venison, whatever you may think. I always tasted it once a year when we dined with Mr. Deputy," she continued, sadly, as a sense of her degradation stole across a mind bewildered with vanity and folly, "though he would not speak to me now, if we met together in the narrowest lane in the Ward!"

"I warrant he would not," said Lord Dalgarno, "because thou, Nell, wouldst dash him with a single look; for I trust thou hast more spirit than to throw away words on such a fellow as he?"

"Who, I!" said Dame Nelly. "Nay, I scorn the proud princox too much for that. Do you know, he made all the folk in the Ward stand cap in hand to him, my poor old John Christie and all?" Here her recollection began to overflow at her eyes.

"A plague on your whimpering," said Dalgarno, somewhat harshly,—"Nay, never look pale for the matter, Nell. I am not angry with you, you simple fool. But what would you have me think, when you are eternally looking back upon your dungeon yonder by the river, which smelt of pitch and old cheese worse than a Welshman does of onions, and all this when I am taking you down to a castle as fine as is in Fairy Land!"

"Shall we be there to-night, my lord?" said Nelly, drying her tears.

"To-night, Nelly?—no, nor this night fortnight."

"Now, the Lord be with us, and keep us!—But shall we not go by sea, my lord?—I thought everybody came from Scotland by sea. I am sure Lord Glenvarloch and Richie Moniplies came up by sea."

"There is a wide difference between coming up and going down, Nelly," answered Lord Dalgarno.

"And so there is, for certain," said his simple companion. "But yet I think I heard people speaking of going down to Scotland by sea, as well as coming up. Are you well advised of the way?—Do you think it possible we can go by land, my sweet lord?"

"It is but trying, my sweet lady," said Lord Dalgarno. "Men say England and Scotland are in the same island, so one would hope there may be some road betwixt them by land."

"I shall never be able to ride so far," said the lady.

"We will have your saddle stuffed softer," said the lord. "I tell you that you shall mew your city slough, and change from the caterpillar of a paltry lane into the butterfly of a prince's garden. You shall have as many tires as there are hours in the day—as many handmaidens as there are days in the week—as many menials as there are weeks in the year—and you shall ride a hunting and hawking with a lord, instead of waiting upon an old ship-chandler, who could do nothing but hawk and spit."

"Ay, but will you make me your lady?" said Dame Nelly.

"Ay, surely—what else?" replied the lord—"My lady-love."

"Ay, but I mean your lady-wife," said Nelly.

"Truly, Nell, in that I cannot promise to oblige you. A lady-wife," continued Dalgarno, "is a very different thing from a lady-love."

"I heard from Mrs. Suddlechop, whom you lodged me with since I left poor old John Christie, that Lord Glenvarloch is to marry David Ramsay the clockmaker's daughter?"

"There is much betwixt the cup and the lip, Nelly. I wear something about me may break the bans of that hopeful alliance, before the day is much older," answered Lord Dalgarno.

"Well, but my father was as good a man as old Davy Ramsay, and as well to pass in the world, my lord; and, therefore, why should you not marry me? You have done me harm enough, I trow—wherefore should you not do me this justice?"

"For two good reasons, Nelly. Fate put a husband on you, and the king passed a wife upon me," answered Lord Dalgarno.

"Ay, my lord," said Nelly, "but they remain in England, and we go to Scotland."

"Thy argument is better than thou art aware of," said Lord Dalgarno. "I have heard Scottish lawyers say the matrimonial tie may be unclasped in our happy country by the gentle hand of the ordinary course of law, whereas in England it can only be burst by an act of Parliament. Well,

Nelly, we will look into that matter; and whether we get married again or no, we will at least do our best to get unmarried."

"Shall we indeed, my honey-sweet lord? and then I will think less about John Christie, for he will marry again, I warrant you, for he is well to pass; and I would be glad to think he had somebody to take care of him, as I used to do, poor loving old man! He was a kind man, though he was a score of years older than I; and I hope and pray he will never let a young lord cross his honest threshold again!"

Here the dame was once more much inclined to give way to a passion of tears; but Lord Dalgarno conjured down the emotion, by saying with some asperity—"I am weary of these April passions, my pretty mistress, and I think you will do well to preserve your tears for some more pressing occasion. Who knows what turn of fortune may in a few minutes call for more of them than you can render?"

"Goodness, my lord! what mean you by such expressions? John Christie (the kind heart!) used to keep no secrets from me, and I hope your lordship will not hide your counsel from me?"

"Sit down beside me on this bank," said the nobleman; "I am bound to remain here for a short space, and if you can be but silent, I should like to spend a part of it in considering how far I can, on the present occasion, follow the respectable example which you recommend to me."

The place at which he stopped was at that time little more than a mound, partly surrounded by a ditch, from which it derived the name of Camlet Moat. A few hewn stones there were, which had escaped the fate of many others that had been used in building different lodges in the forest for the royal keepers. These vestiges, just sufficient to show that "herein former times the hand of man had been," marked the ruins of the abode of a once illustrious but long-forgotten family, the Mandevilles, Earls of Essex, to whom Enfield Chase and the extensive domains adjacent had belonged in elder days. A wild woodland prospect led the eye at various points through broad and seemingly interminable alleys, which, meeting at this point as at a common centre, diverged from each other as they receded, and had, therefore, been selected by Lord Dalgarno as the rendezvous for the combat, which, through the medium of Richie Moniplies, he had offered to his injured friend, Lord Glenvarloch.

"He will surely come?" he said to himself; "cowardice was not wont to be his fault—at least he was bold enough in the Park.—Perhaps yonder churl may not have carried my message? But no—he is a sturdy knave—one of those would prize their master's honour above their life.—Look to the palfrey, Lutin, and see thou let him not loose, and cast thy falcon glance down every avenue to mark if any one comes.— Buckingham has undergone my challenge, but the proud minion pleads the king's paltry commands for refusing to answer me. If I can baffle this Glenvarloch, or slay him—If I can spoil him of his honour or his life, I shall go down to Scotland with credit sufficient to gild over past mischances. I know my dear countrymen—they never quarrel with any one who brings them home either gold or martial glory, much more if he has both gold and laurels."

As he thus reflected, and called to mind the disgrace which he had suffered, as well as the causes he imagined for hating Lord Glenvarloch, his countenance altered under the influence of his contending emotions, to the terror of Nelly, who, sitting unnoticed at his feet, and looking anxiously in his face, beheld the cheek kindle, the mouth become compressed, the eye dilated, and the whole countenance express the desperate and deadly resolution of one who awaits an instant and decisive encounter with a mortal enemy. The loneliness of the place, the scenery so different from that to which alone she had been accustomed, the dark and sombre air which crept so suddenly over the countenance of her seducer, his command imposing silence upon her, and the apparent strangeness of his conduct in idling away so much time without any obvious cause, when a journey of such length lay before them, brought strange thoughts into her weak brain. She had read of women, seduced from their matrimonial duties by sorcerers allied to the hellish powers, nay, by the Father of Evil himself, who, after conveying his victim into some desert remote from human kind, exchanged the pleasing shape in which he gained her affections, for all his natural horrors. She chased this wild idea away as it crowded itself upon her weak and bewildered imagination; yet she might have lived to see it realised allegorically, if not literally, but for the accident which presently followed.

The page, whose eyes were remarkably acute, at length called out to his master, pointing with his finger at the same time down one of the alleys, that horsemen were advancing in that direction. Lord Dalgarno started up, and shading his eyes with his hand, gazed eagerly down the alley; when, at the same instant, he received a shot, which, grazing his hand, passed right through his brain, and laid him a lifeless corpse at the feet, or rather across the lap, of the unfortunate victim of his profligacy. The countenance, whose varied expression she had been watching for the last five minutes, was convulsed for an instant, and then stiffened into rigidity for ever. Three ruffians rushed from the brake from which the shot had been fired, ere the smoke was dispersed. One, with many imprecations seized on the page; another on the female, upon whose cries he strove by the most violent threats to impose silence; whilst the third began to undo the burden from the page's horse. But an instant rescue prevented their availing themselves of the advantage they had obtained.

It may easily be supposed that Richie Moniplies, having secured the assistance of the two Templars, ready enough to join in any thing which promised a fray, with Jin Vin to act as their guide, had set off, gallantly mounted and well armed, under the belief that they would reach Camlet Moat before the robbers, and apprehend them in the fact. They had not calculated that, according to the custom of robbers in other countries, but contrary to that of the English highwayman of those days, they meant to ensure robbery by previous murder. An accident also happened to delay them a little while on the road. In riding through one of the glades of the forest, they found a man dismounted and sitting under a tree, groaning with such bitterness of spirit, that Lowestoffe could not forbear asking if he was hurt. In answer, he said he was an unhappy man in pursuit of his wife, who had been carried off by a villain; and as he raised his countenance, the eyes of Richie, to his great astonishment, encountered the visage of John Christie.

"For the Almighty's sake, help me, Master Moniplies!" he said; "I have learned my wife is but a short mile before, with that black villain Lord Dalgarno."

"Have him forward by all means," said Lowestoffe; "a second Orpheus seeking his Eurydice!—Have him forward—we will save Lord Dalgarno's purse, and ease him of his mistress—Have him with us, were it but for the variety of the adventure. I owe his lordship a grudge for rooking me. We have ten minutes good."

But it is dangerous to calculate closely in matters of life and death. In all probability the minute or two which was lost in mounting John Christie behind one of their party, might have saved Lord Dalgarno from his fate. Thus his criminal amour became the indirect cause of his losing his life; and thus "our pleasant vices are made the whips to scourge us."

The riders arrived on the field at full gallop the moment after the shot was fired; and Richie, who had his own reasons for attaching himself to

Colepepper, who was bustling to untie the portmanteau from the page's saddle, pushed against him with such violence as to overthrow him, his own horse at the same time stumbling and dismounting his rider, who was none of the first equestrians. The undaunted Richie immediately arose, however, and grappled with the ruffian with such good-will, that, though a strong fellow, and though a coward now rendered desperate, Moniplies got him under, wrenched a long knife from his hand, dealt him a desperate stab with his own weapon, and leaped on his feet; and, as the wounded man struggled to follow his example, he struck him upon the head with the butt-end of a musketoon, which last blow proved fatal.

"Bravo, Richie!" cried Lowestoffe, who had himself engaged at sword-point with one of the ruffians, and soon put him to flight,— "Bravo! why, man, there lies Sin, struck down like an ox, and Iniquity's throat cut like a calf."

"I know not why you should upbraid me with my upbringing, Master Lowestoffe," answered Richie, with great composure; "but I can tell you, the shambles is not a bad place for training one to this work."

The other Templar now shouted loudly to them,—"If ye be men, come hither—here lies Lord Dalgarno, murdered!"

Lowestoffe and Richie ran to the spot, and the page took the opportunity, finding himself now neglected on all hands, to ride off in a different direction; and neither he, nor the considerable sum with which his horse was burdened, were ever heard of from that moment.

The third ruffian had not waited the attack of the Templar and Jin Vin, the latter of whom had put down old Christie from behind him that he might ride the lighter; and the whole five now stood gazing with horror on the bloody corpse of the young nobleman, and the wild sorrow of the female, who tore her hair and shrieked in the most disconsolate manner, until her agony was at once checked, or rather received a new direction, by the sudden and unexpected appearance of her husband, who, fixing on her a cold and severe look, said, in a tone suited to his manner—"Ay, woman! thou takest on sadly for the loss of thy paramour."—Then, looking on the bloody corpse of him from whom he had received so deep an injury, he repeated the solemn words of Scripture,—"'Vengeance is mine, saith the Lord, and I will repay it.'—I, whom thou hast injured, will be first to render thee the decent offices due to the dead."

So saying, he covered the dead body with his cloak, and then looking on it for a moment, seemed to reflect on what he had next to perform. As the eye of the injured man slowly passed from the body of the seducer to the partner and victim of his crime, who had sunk down to his feet, which she clasped without venturing to look up, his features, naturally coarse and saturnine, assumed a dignity of expression which overawed the young Templars, and repulsed the officious forwardness of Richie Moniplies, who was at first eager to have thrust in his advice and opinion. "Kneel not to me, woman," he said, "but kneel to the God thou hast offended, more than thou couldst offend such another worm as thyself. How often have I told thee, when thou wert at the gayest and the lightest, that pride goeth before destruction, and a haughty spirit before a fall? Vanity brought folly, and folly brought sin, and sin hath brought death, his original companion. Thou must needs leave duty, and decency, and domestic love, to revel it gaily with the wild and with the wicked; and there thou liest like a crushed worm, writhing beside the lifeless body of thy paramour. Thou hast done me much wrong—dishonoured me among friends—driven credit from my house, and peace from my fireside—But thou wert my first and only love, and I will not see thee an utter castaway, if it lies with me to prevent it.—Gentlemen, I render ye such thanks as a broken-hearted man can give.—Richard, commend me to your honourable master. I added gall to the bitterness of his affliction, but I was deluded.—Rise up, woman, and follow me."

He raised her up by the arm, while, with streaming eyes, and bitter sobs, she endeavoured to express her penitence. She kept her hands spread over her face, yet suffered him to lead her away; and it was only as they turned around a brake which concealed the scene they had left, that she turned back, and casting one wild and hurried glance towards the corpse of Dalgarno, uttered a shriek, and clinging to her husband's arm, exclaimed wildly,—"Save me—save me! They have murdered him!"

Lowestoffe was much moved by what he had witnessed; but he was ashamed, as a town-gallant, of his own unfashionable emotion, and did a force to his feelings when he exclaimed,—"Ay, let them go—the kind-hearted, believing, forgiving husband—the liberal, accommodating spouse. O what a generous creature is your true London husband!— Horns hath he, but, tame as a fatted ox, he goeth not. I should like to see her when she hath exchanged her mask and riding-beaver for her peaked hat and muffler. We will visit them at Paul's Wharf, coz—it will be a convenient acquaintance."

"You had better think of catching the gipsy thief, Lutin," said Richie Moniplies; "for, by my faith, he is off with his master's baggage and the siller."

A keeper, with his assistants, and several other persons, had now come to the spot, and made hue and cry after Lutin, but in vain. To their custody the Templars surrendered the dead bodies, and after going through some formal investigation, they returned, with Richard and Vincent, to London, where they received great applause for their gallantry.—Vincent's errors were easily expiated, in consideration of his having been the means of breaking up this band of villains; and there is some reason to think, that what would have diminished the credit of the action in other instances, rather added to it in the actual circumstances, namely, that they came too late to save Lord Dalgarno.

George Heriot, who suspected how matters stood with Vincent, requested and obtained permission from his master to send the poor young fellow on an important piece of business to Paris. We are unable to trace his fate farther, but believe it was prosperous, and that he entered into an advantageous partnership with his fellow-apprentice, upon old Davy Ramsay retiring from business, in consequence of his daughter's marriage. That eminent antiquary, Dr. Dryasdust, is possessed of an antique watch, with a silver dial-plate, the mainspring being a piece of catgut instead of a chain, which bears the names of Vincent and Tunstall, Memory-Monitors.

Master Lowestoffe failed not to vindicate his character as a man of gaiety, by inquiring after John Christie and Dame Nelly; but greatly to his surprise, (indeed to his loss, for he had wagered ten pieces that he would domesticate himself in the family,) he found the good-will, as it was called, of the shop, was sold, the stock auctioned, and the late proprietor and his wife gone, no one knew whither. The prevailing belief was, that they had emigrated to one of the new settlements in America.

Lady Dalgarno received the news of her unworthy husband's death with a variety of emotions, among which, horror that he should have been cut off in the middle career of his profligacy, was the most prominent. The incident greatly deepened her melancholy, and injured her health, already shaken by previous circumstances. Repossessed of her own fortune by her husband's death, she was anxious to do justice to Lord Glenvarloch, by treating for the recovery of the mortgage.

But the scrivener, having taken fright at the late events, had left the city and absconded, so that it was impossible to discover into whose hands the papers had now passed. Richard Moniplies was silent, for his own reasons; the Templars, who had witnessed the transaction, kept the secret at his request, and it was universally believed that the scrivener had carried off the writings along with him. We may here observe, that fears similar to those of Skurliewhitter freed London for ever from the presence of Dame Suddlechop, who ended her career in the *Rasp-haus*, (viz. Bridewell,) of Amsterdam.

The stout old Lord Huntinglen, with a haughty carriage and unmoistened eye, accompanied the funeral procession of his only son to its last abode; and perhaps the single tear which fell at length upon the coffin, was given less to the fate of the individual, than to the extinction of the last male of his ancient race.

XXXVII

JACQUES: *There is, suie, another flood toward, and these couples are coming to the ark!—Here comes a pair of very strange beasts.*

—*As You Like It*

The fashion of such narratives as the present, changes like other earthly things. Time was that the tale-teller was obliged to wind up his story by a circumstantial description of the wedding, bedding, and throwing the stocking, as the grand catastrophe to which, through so many circumstances of doubt and difficulty, he had at length happily conducted his hero and heroine. Not a circumstance was then omitted, from the manly ardour of the bridegroom, and the modest blushes of the bride, to the parson's new surplice, and the silk tabinet mantua of the bridesmaid. But such descriptions are now discarded, for the same reason, I suppose, that public marriages are no longer fashionable, and that, instead of calling together their friends to a feast and a dance, the happy couple elope in a solitary post-chaise, as secretly as if they meant to go to Gretna-Green, or to do worse. I am not ungrateful for a change which saves an author the trouble of attempting in vain to give a new colour to the commonplace description of such matters; but, notwithstanding, I find myself forced upon it in the present instance, as circumstances sometimes compel a stranger to make use of an old road which has been for some time shut up. The experienced reader may have already remarked, that the last chapter was employed in sweeping out of the way all the unnecessary and less interesting characters, that I might clear the floor for a blithe bridal.

In truth, it would be unpardonable to pass over slightly what so deeply interested our principal personage, King James. That learned and good-humoured monarch made no great figure in the politics of Europe; but then, to make amends, he was prodigiously busy, when he could find a fair opportunity of intermeddling with the private affairs of his loving subjects, and the approaching marriage of Lord Glenvarloch was matter of great interest to him. He had been much struck (that is, for him, who was not very accessible to such emotions) with the beauty and embarrassment of the pretty Peg-a-Ramsay, as he called her, when he first saw her, and he glorified himself greatly on the acuteness which he had displayed in detecting her disguise, and in carrying through the whole inquiry which took place in consequence of it.

He laboured for several weeks, while the courtship was in progress, with his own royal eyes, so as wellnigh to wear out, he declared, a pair of her father's best barnacles, in searching through old books and documents, for the purpose of establishing the bride's pretensions to a noble, though remote descent, and thereby remove the only objection which envy might conceive against the match. In his own opinion, at least, he was eminently successful; for, when Sir Mungo Malagrowther one day, in the presence-chamber, took upon him to grieve bitterly for the bride's lack of pedigree, the monarch cut him short with, "Ye may save your grief for your ain next occasions, Sir Mungo; for, by our royal saul, we will uphauld her father, Davy Ramsay, to be a gentleman of nine descents, whase great gudesire came of the auld martial stock of the House of Dalwolsey, than whom better men never did, and better never will, draw sword for king and country. Heard ye never of Sir William Ramsay of Dalwolsey, man, of whom John Fordoun saith,—'He was *bellicosissimus, nobilissimus?'*—His castle stands to witness for itsell, not three miles from Dalkeith, man, and within a mile of Bannockrig. Davy Ramsay came of that auld and honoured stock, and I trust he hath not derogated from his ancestors by his present craft. They all wrought wi' steel, man; only the auld knights drilled holes wi' their swords in their enemies' corslets, and he saws nicks in his brass wheels. And I hope it is as honourable to give eyes to the blind as to slash them out of the head of those that see, and to show us how to value our time as it passes, as to fling it away in drinking, brawling, spear-splintering, and such-like unchristian doings. And you maun understand, that Davy Ramsay is no mechanic, but follows a liberal art, which approacheth almost to the act of creating a living being, seeing it may be said of a watch, as Claudius saith of the sphere of Archimedes, the Syracusan—

"Inclusus variis famulatur spiritus astris, Et vivum certis motibus urget opus.'"

"Your Majesty had best give auld Davy a coat-of-arms, as well as a pedigree," said Sir Mungo.

"It's done, or ye bade, Sir Mungo," said the king; "and I trust we, who are the fountain of all earthly honour, are free to spirit a few drops of it on one so near our person, without offence to the Knight of Castle Girnigo. We have already spoken with the learned men of the Herald's College, and we propose to grant him an augmented coat-of-arms, being his paternal coat, charged with the crown-wheel of a watch in chief, for a difference; and we purpose to add Time and Eternity, for supporters, as soon as the Garter King-at-Arms shall be able to devise how Eternity is to be represented."

"I would make him twice as muckle as Time,"* said Archie Armstrong, the Court fool, who chanced to be present when the king stated this dilemma. "Peace, man—ye shall be whippet," said the king, in return for this hint; "and you, my liege subjects of England, may weel take a hint from what we have said, and not be in such a hurry to laugh at our Scottish pedigrees, though they be somewhat long derived, and difficult to be deduced. Ye see that a man of right gentle blood may, for a season, lay by his gentry, and yet ken whare to find it, when he has occasion for it. It would be as unseemly for a packman, or pedlar, as ye call a travelling merchant, whilk is a trade to which our native subjects of Scotland are specially addicted, to be blazing his genealogy in the faces of those to whom he sells a bawbee's worth of ribbon, as it would be to him to have a beaver on his head, and a rapier by his side, when the pack was on his shoulders. Na, na—he hings his sword on the cleek, lays his beaver on the shelf, puts his pedigree into his pocket, and gangs as doucely and cannily about his peddling craft as if his blood was nae better than ditch-water; but let our pedlar be transformed, as I have kend it happen mair than ance, into a bein thriving merchant, then ye shall have a transformation, my lords.

'In nova fert animus mutatas dicere formas—'

Out he pulls his pedigree, on he buckles his sword, gives his beaver a brush, and cocks it in the face of all creation. We mention these things at the mair length, because we would have you all to know, that it is not without due consideration of the circumstances of all parties, that we design, in a small and private way, to honour with our own royal presence the marriage of Lord Glenvarloch with Margaret Ramsay, daughter and heiress of David Ramsay, our horologer, and a cadet only thrice removed from the ancient house of Dalwolsey. We are grieved we cannot have the presence of the noble Chief of that House at

---

* Chaucer says, there is nothing new but what it has been old. The reader has here the original of an anecdote which has since been fathered on a Scottish Chief of our own time.

the ceremony; but where there is honour to be won abroad the Lord Dalwolsey is seldom to be found at home. *Sic fuit, est, et erit.*—Jingling Geordie, as ye stand to the cost of the marriage feast, we look for good cheer."

Heriot bowed, as in duty bound. In fact, the king, who was a great politician about trifles, had manoeuvred greatly on this occasion, and had contrived to get the Prince and Buckingham dispatched on an expedition to Newmarket, in order that he might find an opportunity in their absence of indulging himself in his own gossiping, *coshering* habits, which were distasteful to Charles, whose temper inclined to formality, and with which even the favourite, of late, had not thought it worth while to seem to sympathise. When the levee was dismissed, Sir Mungo Malagrowther seized upon the worthy citizen in the court-yard of the Palace, and detained him, in spite of all his efforts, for the purpose of subjecting him to the following scrutiny:—

"This is a sair job on you, Master George—the king must have had little consideration—this will cost you a bonny penny, this wedding dinner?"

"It will not break me, Sir Mungo," answered Heriot; "the king hath a right to see the table which his bounty hath supplied for years, well covered for a single day."

"Vera true, vera true—we'll have a' to pay, I doubt, less or mair—a sort of penny-wedding it will prove, where all men contribute to the young folk's maintenance, that they may not have just four bare legs in a bed together. What do you propose to give, Master George?—we begin with the city when money is in question."*

"Only a trifle, Sir Mungo—I give my god-daughter the marriage ring; it is a curious jewel—I bought it in Italy; it belonged to Cosmo de Medici. The bride will not need my help—she has an estate which belonged to her maternal grandfather."

"The auld soap-boiler," said Sir Mungo; "it will need some of his suds to scour the blot out of the Glenvarloch shield—I have heard that estate was no great things."

"It is as good as some posts at Court, Sir Mungo, which are coveted by persons of high quality," replied George Heriot.

---

* The penny-wedding of the Scots, now disused even among the lowest ranks, was a peculiar species of merry-making, at which, if the wedded pair were popular, the guests who convened, contributed considerable sums under pretence of paying for the bridal festivity, but in reality to set the married folk afloat in the world.

"Court favour, said ye? Court favour, Master Heriot?" replied Sir Mungo, choosing then to use his malady of misapprehension; "Moonshine in water, poor thing, if that is all she is to be tochered with—I am truly solicitous about them."

"I will let you into a secret," said the citizen, "which will relieve your tender anxiety. The dowager Lady Dalgarno gives a competent fortune to the bride, and settles the rest of her estate upon her nephew the bridegroom."

"Ay, say ye sae?" said Sir Mungo, "just to show her regard to her husband that is in the tomb—lucky that her nephew did not send him there; it was a strange story that death of poor Lord Dalgarno—some folk think the poor gentleman had much wrong. Little good comes of marrying the daughter of the house you are at feud with; indeed, it was less poor Dalgarno's fault, than theirs that forced the match on him; but I am glad the young folk are to have something to live on, come how it like, whether by charity or inheritance. But if the Lady Dalgarno were to sell all she has, even to her very wylie-coat, she canna gie them back the fair Castle of Glenvarloch—that is lost and gane—lost and gane."

"It is but too true," said George Heriot; "we cannot discover what has become of the villain Andrew Skurliewhitter, or what Lord Dalgarno has done with the mortgage."

"Assigned it away to some one, that his wife might not get it after he was gane; it would have disturbed him in his grave, to think Glenvarloch should get that land back again," said Sir Mungo; "depend on it, he will have ta'en sure measures to keep that noble lordship out of her grips or her nevoy's either."

"Indeed it is but too probable, Sir Mungo," said Master Heriot; "but as I am obliged to go and look after many things in consequence of this ceremony, I must leave you to comfort yourself with the reflection."

"The bride-day, you say, is to be on the thirtieth of the instant month?" said Sir Mungo, holloing after the citizen; "I will be with you in the hour of cause."

"The king invites the guests," said George Heriot, without turning back.

"The base-born, ill-bred mechanic!" soliloquised Sir Mungo, "if it were not the odd score of pounds he lent me last week, I would teach him how to bear himself to a man of quality! But I will be at the bridal banquet in spite of him."

Sir Mungo contrived to get invited, or commanded, to attend on the bridal accordingly, at which there were but few persons present; for James, on such occasions, preferred a snug privacy, which gave him liberty to lay aside the encumbrance, as he felt it to be, of his regal dignity. The company was very small, and indeed there were at least two persons absent whose presence might have been expected. The first of these was the Lady Dalgarno, the state of whose health, as well as the recent death of her husband, precluded her attendance on the ceremony. The other absentee was Richie Moniplies, whose conduct for some time past had been extremely mysterious. Regulating his attendance on Lord Glenvarloch entirely according to his own will and pleasure, he had, ever since the rencounter in Enfield Chase, appeared regularly at his bedside in the morning, to assist him to dress, and at his wardrobe in the evening. The rest of the day he disposed of at his own pleasure, without control from his lord, who had now a complete establishment of attendants. Yet he was somewhat curious to know how the fellow disposed of so much of his time; but on this subject Richie showed no desire to be communicative.

On the morning of the bridal-day, Richie was particularly attentive in doing all a valet-de-chambre could, so as to set off to advantage the very handsome figure of his master; and when he had arranged his dress to the utmost exactness, and put to his long curled locks what he called "the finishing touch of the redding-kaim," he gravely kneeled down, kissed his hand, and bade him farewell, saying that he humbly craved leave to discharge himself of his lordship's service.

"Why, what humour is this?" said Lord Glenvarloch; "if you mean to discharge yourself of my service, Richie, I suppose you intend to enter my wife's?"

"I wish her good ladyship that shall soon be, and your good lordship, the blessings of as good a servant as myself, in heaven's good time," said Richie; "but fate hath so ordained it, that I can henceforth only be your servant in the way of friendly courtesy."

"Well, Richie," said the young lord, "if you are tired of service, we will seek some better provision for you; but you will wait on me to the church, and partake of the bridal dinner?"

"Under favour, my lord," answered Richie; "I must remind you of our covenant, having presently some pressing business of mine own, whilk will detain me during the ceremony; but I will not fail to prie Master George's good cheer, in respect he has made very costly fare, whilk it would be unthankful not to partake of."

"Do as you list," answered Lord Glenvarloch; and having bestowed a passing thought on the whimsical and pragmatical disposition of his follower, he dismissed the subject for others better suited to the day.

The reader must fancy the scattered flowers which strewed the path of the happy couple to church—the loud music which accompanied the procession—the marriage service performed by a bishop—the king, who met them at Saint Paul's, giving away the bride,—to the great relief of her father, who had thus time, during the ceremony, to calculate the just quotient to be laid on the pinion of report in a timepiece which he was then putting together.

When the ceremony was finished, the company were transported in the royal carriages to George Heriot's, where a splendid collation was provided for the marriage-guests in the Foljambe apartments. The king no sooner found himself in this snug retreat, than, casting from him his sword and belt with such haste as if they burnt his fingers, and flinging his plumed hat on the table, as who should say, Lie there, authority! he swallowed a hearty cup of wine to the happiness of the married couple, and began to amble about the room, mumping, laughing, and cracking jests, neither the wittiest nor the most delicate, but accompanied and applauded by shouts of his own mirth, in order to encourage that of the company. Whilst his Majesty was in the midst of this gay humour, and a call to the banquet was anxiously expected, a servant whispered Master Heriot forth of the apartment. When he re-entered, he walked up to the king, and, in his turn whispered something, at which James started.

"He is not wanting his siller?" said the king, shortly and sharply.

"By no means, my liege," answered Heriot. "It is a subject he states himself as quite indifferent about, so long as it can pleasure your Majesty."

"Body of us, man!" said the king, "it is the speech of a true man and a loving subject, and we will grace him accordingly—what though he be but a carle—a twopenny cat may look at a king. Swith, man! have him—*pundite fores.*—Moniplies?—They should have called the chield Monypennies, though I sall warrant you English think we have not such a name in Scotland."

"It is an ancient and honourable stock, the Monypennies," said Sir Mungo Malagrowther; "the only loss is, there are sae few of the name."

"The family seems to increase among your countrymen, Sir Mungo," said Master Lowestoffe, whom Lord Glenvarloch had invited to be present, "since his Majesty's happy accession brought so many of you here."

"Right, sir—right," said Sir Mungo, nodding and looking at George Heriot; "there have some of ourselves been the better of that great blessing to the English nation."

As he spoke, the door flew open, and in entered, to the astonishment of Lord Glenvarloch, his late serving-man Richie Moniplies, now sumptuously, nay, gorgeously, attired in a superb brocaded suit, and leading in his hand the tall, thin, withered, somewhat distorted form of Martha Trapbois, arrayed in a complete dress of black velvet, which suited so strangely with the pallid and severe melancholy of her countenance, that the king himself exclaimed, in some perturbation, "What the deil has the fallow brought us here? Body of our regal selves! it is a corpse that has run off with the mort-cloth!"

"May I sifflicate your Majesty to be gracious unto her?" said Richie; "being that she is, in respect of this morning's wark, my ain wedded wife, Mrs. Martha Moniplies by name."

"Saul of our body, man! but she looks wondrous grim," answered King James. "Art thou sure she has not been in her time maid of honour to Queen Mary, our kinswoman, of redhot memory?"

"I am sure, an it like your Majesty, that she has brought me fifty thousand pounds of good siller, and better; and that has enabled me to pleasure your Majesty, and other folk."

"Ye need have said naething about that, man," said the king; "we ken our obligations in that sma' matter, and we are glad this rudas spouse of thine hath bestowed her treasure on ane wha kens to put it to the profit of his king and country.—But how the deil did ye come by her, man?"

"In the auld Scottish fashion, my liege. She is the captive of my bow and my spear," answered Moniplies. "There was a convention that she should wed me when I avenged her father's death—so I slew, and took possession."

"It is the daughter of Old Trapbois, who has been missed so long," said Lowestoffe.—"Where the devil could you mew her up so closely, friend Richie?"

"Master Richard, if it be your will," answered Richie; "or Master Richard Moniplies, if you like it better. For mewing of her up, I found her a shelter, in all honour and safety, under the roof of an honest countryman of my own—and for secrecy, it was a point of prudence, when wantons like you were abroad, Master Lowestoffe."

There was a laugh at Richie's magnanimous reply, on the part of every one but his bride, who made to him a signal of impatience, and said, with her usual brevity and sternness,—"Peace—peace, I pray you, peace. Let us do that which we came for." So saying, she took out a bundle of parchments, and delivering them to Lord Glenvarloch, she said aloud,—"I take this royal presence, and all here, to witness, that I restore the ransomed lordship of Glenvarloch to the right owner, as free as ever it was held by any of his ancestors."

"I witnessed the redemption of the mortgage," said Lowestoffe; "but I little dreamt by whom it had been redeemed."

"No need ye should," said Richie; "there would have been small wisdom in crying roast-meat."

"Peace," said his bride, "once more.—This paper," she continued, delivering another to Lord Glenvarloch, "is also your property—take it, but spare me the question how it came into my custody."

The king had bustled forward beside Lord Glenvarloch, and fixing an eager eye on the writing, exclaimed—"Body of ourselves, it is our royal sign-manual for the money which was so long out of sight!—How came you by it, Mistress Bride?"

"It is a secret," said Martha, dryly.

"A secret which my tongue shall never utter," said Richie, resolutely,— "unless the king commands me on my allegiance."

"I do—I do command you," said James, trembling and stammering with the impatient curiosity of a gossip; while Sir Mungo, with more malicious anxiety to get at the bottom of the mystery, stooped his long thin form forward like a bent fishing-rod, raised his thin grey locks from his ear, and curved his hand behind it to collect every vibration of the expected intelligence. Martha in the meantime frowned most ominously on Richie, who went on undauntedly to inform the king, "that his deceased father-in-law, a good careful man in the main, had a' touch of worldly wisdom about him, that at times marred the uprightness of his walk; he liked to dabble among his neighbour's gear, and some of it would at times stick to his fingers in the handling."

"For shame, man, for shame!" said Martha; "since the infamy of the deed must be told, be it at least briefly.—Yes, my lord," she added, addressing Glenvarloch, "the piece of gold was not the sole bait which brought the miserable old man to your chamber that dreadful night— his object, and he accomplished it, was to purloin this paper. The wretched scrivener was with him that morning, and, I doubt not, urged the doting old man to this villainy, to offer another bar to the ransom of your estate. If there was a yet more powerful agent at the bottom of this conspiracy, God forgive it to him at this moment, for he is now where the crime must be answered!"

"Amen!" said Lord Glenvarloch, and it was echoed by all present.

"For my father," continued she, with her stern features twitched by an involuntary and convulsive movement, "his guilt and folly cost him his life; and my belief is constant, that the wretch, who counselled him that morning to purloin the paper, left open the window for the entrance of the murderers."

Every body was silent for an instant; the king was first to speak, commanding search instantly to be made for the guilty scrivener. "*I, lictor,*" he concluded, "*colliga manus—caput obnubito-infelici suspendite arbori.*"

Lowestoffe answered with due respect, that the scrivener had absconded at the time of Lord Dalgarno's murder, and had not been heard of since.

"Let him be sought for," said the king. "And now let us change the discourse—these stories make one's very blood grew, and are altogether unfit for bridal festivity. Hymen, O Hymenee!" added he, snapping his fingers, "Lord Glenvarloch, what say you to Mistress Moniplies, this bonny bride, that has brought you back your father's estate on your bridal day?"

"Let him say nothing, my liege," said Martha; "that will best suit his feelings and mine."

"There is redemption-money, at the least, to be repaid," said Lord Glenvarloch; "in that I cannot remain debtor."

"We will speak of it hereafter," said Martha; "*my* debtor *you* cannot be." And she shut her mouth as if determined to say nothing more on the subject.

Sir Mungo, however, resolved not to part with the topic, and availing himself of the freedom of the moment, said to Richie—"A queer story that of your father-in-law, honest man; methinks your bride thanked you little for ripping it up."

"I make it a rule, Sir Mungo," replied Richie, "always to speak any evil I know about my family myself, having observed, that if I do not, it is sure to be told by ither folks."

"But, Richie," said Sir Mungo, "it seems to me that this bride of yours is like to be master and mair in the conjugal state."

"If she abides by words, Sir Mungo," answered Richie, "I thank heaven I can be as deaf as any one; and if she comes to dunts, I have twa hands to paik her with."

"Weel said, Richie, again," said the king; "you have gotten it on baith haffits, Sir Mungo.—Troth, Mistress Bride, for a fule, your gudeman has a pretty turn of wit."

"There are fools, sire," replied she, "who have wit, and fools who have courage—aye, and fools who have learning, and are great fools notwithstanding.—I chose this man because he was my protector when I was desolate, and neither for his wit nor his wisdom. He is truly honest, and has a heart and hand that make amends for some folly. Since I was condemned to seek a protector through the world, which is to me a wilderness, I may thank God that I have come by no worse."

"And that is sae sensibly said," replied the king, "that, by my saul, I'll try whether I canna make him better. Kneel down, Richie—somebody lend me a rapier—yours, Mr. Langstaff, (that's a brave name for a lawyer,)—ye need not flash it out that gate, Templar fashion, as if ye were about to pink a bailiff!"

He took the drawn sword, and with averted eyes, for it was a sight he loved not to look on, endeavoured to lay it on Richie's shoulder, but nearly stuck it into his eye. Richie, starting back, attempted to rise, but was held down by Lowestoffe, while Sir Mungo, guiding the royal weapon, the honour-bestowing blow was given and received: "*Surge, carnifex*—Rise up, Sir Richard Moniplies, of Castle-Collop!—And, my lords and lieges, let us all to our dinner, for the cock-a-leekie is cooling."

A Note About the Author

Sir Walter Scott (1771–1832) was a Scottish novelist, poet, playwright, and historian who also worked as a judge and legal administrator. Scott's extensive knowledge of history and his exemplary literary technique earned him a role as a prominent author of the romantic movement and innovator of the historical fiction genre. After rising to fame as a poet, Scott started to venture into prose fiction as well, which solidified his place as a popular and widely-read literary figure, especially in the 19th century. Scott left behind a legacy of innovation, and is praised for his contributions to Scottish culture.

A Note from the Publisher

Spanning many genres, from non-fiction essays to literature classics to children's books and lyric poetry, Mint Edition books showcase the master works of our time in a modern new package. The text is freshly typeset, is clean and easy to read, and features a new note about the author in each volume. Many books also include exclusive new introductory material. Every book boasts a striking new cover, which makes it as appropriate for collecting as it is for gift giving. Mint Edition books are only printed when a reader orders them, so natural resources are not wasted. We're proud that our books are never manufactured in excess and exist only in the exact quantity they need to be read and enjoyed.

Discover more of your favorite classics with Bookfinity™.

- Track your reading with custom book lists.
- Get great book recommendations for your personalized Reader Type.
- Add reviews for your favorite books.
- AND MUCH MORE!

Visit **bookfinity.com** and take the fun Reader Type quiz to get started.

Enjoy our classic and modern companion pairings!